to Shean

The great thing
in life is to survive it

D Skerta

Dec 23/2014

About D. F. Skertchly

Almost an orphan, world famous as
an unpublished author of many
books though now on Kindle and
hereby in hard back, long time Fleet
Street (that's London) sub-editor,
long time Army officer, noted
gardener and very married with
buckets of kids all over the world. As
you see, a dull life !

Also by D.F. Skertchly

Charlie Priest's Telegram

Baker & Son

From The East End to Korea via D-Day,

A Soldier's Life and Loves

By

D. F. Skertchly

From The East End to Korea via D-Day, A Soldier's Life and Loves

By D. F. Skertchly

For my Cousin Rick Green

Who faced life, as he did death, bravely.

Chapter One

The Empty Quarter, January 27, 1959

MAJOR Robert Beard was freezing, and he thought how bloody silly this was, here in Arabia's Empty Quarter, the hottest place on earth. He knew that in a few short hours the temperature could get up to 140 F, but right now it was cold; bloody cold. His fingers were numb, and that too was ridiculous. Even the sand was cold.

It was so still and quiet it was as though the whole earth was asleep, but it wasn't. It was 4am. The SAS had begun its assault on the Jebel Akhdar – known as the Green Mountain because it was like a fertile garden on top – in the Oman the previous evening, and must be near the top by now; possibly already there. He'd felt the ground tremble and was almost certain he'd heard the sound of gunfire in the stillness of the night. That was before midnight. Nothing since, only the perfect peace of a desert night. But, now, it was time for him to act.

Shivering beneath his camel blanket, he glanced about him. They were probably still inside Saudi, but the mountain above them stretched its protective wings well into Oman, and shielded the bridge still some distance ahead. The moon had slipped below the horizon but the myriad stars shone so brightly in the black sky that he could see quite clearly. Ruth would love this, he mused; and for an instant, the time it took one of those stars to wink, he longed to feel her warmth against him. And then reality returned.

He looked at the misshapen bundles of his four men and the two Arabs and knew that they were all wide awake, waiting for his signal. They had left their camels hobbled a couple of miles farther back in a wadi soon after midnight, and moved stealthily forward as far as was practical. It had been slow progress for they were all laden down with the impedimenta necessary for a short, sharp war.

Beard gave the nod, and they began moving slowly forward in a low crouch, ready to drop flat on the ground at the first hint of danger. The nearer they got to the enemy, the slower they moved. Presently, they were inching their way on their bellies towards the first machine-gun post. They had to crawl for some distance for they knew that sound, any sound, carried in the desert, and never more so than in the hours of darkness.

It was slow going, made especially more so for Beard and his men as, in addition to all the weaponry and explosives they had to hump, they were further handicapped by having to wear Arab clothing over their uniforms; this comprised a long white tunic and a sleeveless cloak, as well as the headpiece – the *kufiyya*. The two Arabs, of course, slid as easily and silently as snakes over the gritty ground.

Fifty yards from the sand-bagged machine-gun emplacement, Salim bin Khalid, the older of their two Arabs, who was in the lead, suddenly stopped, and sniffed the air. Beard, who was immediately behind him, and knew the others were close on either side, could just about identify the smell of the camel dung camp fire. But Salim, whose nose was longer and far more experienced in such things, could easily distinguish something more potent. Someone up ahead was smoking opium, which meant at least one man would be in no fit state to react to any sudden emergency. They shed their cumbersome back-packs, and moved forward.

As it happened, the luckless smoker was the nearest guard, and he was the first to die. Salim came up behind the happy man without a whisper of sound, clapped one hand over his mouth and plunged his huge curved dagger through the man's heart – holding the blade there while Sgt Piper held the man's legs till they stopped kicking out convulsively. Even before the death throes were complete, Beard had crawled into a low-standing grey tent alongside and shot dead two sleeping men with a revolver fitted with a silencer, and Blossom had accounted for another who had been dozing beside the machine-gun in the shallow sand-bagged pit. The man had suddenly sat bolt upright just as his throat was being cut. Blossom scowled as the man's blood sprayed over him: he hastily rolled the body over on its front.

Walid Imbarak, the second of Beard's Arabs, who had been scouting around in case there were other guards sleeping among the rocks, crept back wiping his blood-stained knife. He said he'd found two more keeping company with their camels; no, he grinned, he hadn't disturbed the camels: they were still farting and snoring blissfully.

So far, so good. Six of the enemy accounted for, and one side of the bridge secured. Of course, there might be more wide-awake sentries on the actual bridge. But, there wasn't, not a single one, as far as Beard could see. This was very poor soldiery, he thought as he wriggled to a point from which he was able to view the entire length of the bridge. Nor was there any sound from the far side to suggest that those there were aware of anything wrong. Beard supposed that there would be at least a similar number of the rebels on the other side; the trouble was they had to cross the bridge to get at them and they could hardly do that without them becoming aware of it – it was too much to expect that everyone was asleep.

Beard, looking and smelling like an Arab camel dealer, took a moment to reflect on the circumstances that had led him to this barren spot on the border of Saudi and Oman. Three days ago he and his men – his team, as he called them, had been pursuing gun-running Radfan tribesmen in the Yemen mountains. An urgent signal had whisked them at a moment's notice to the Oman and a camp near Bahlah, to the west of Nazwa. Here, he'd been directed to the SAS HQ – a local sheikh's palace which had been taken over, where he was greeted by Colonel Eugene Oldroyds, who looked up from a map-strewn trestle-table at the dusty, dishevelled, bearded Arab figure, and said jokingly: "Mr Beard, I presume?"

"I'm sorry, sir," responded Beard, straightening his back and shoulders in a most un-Arab-like manner. "I was being an Arab inside Saudi when I received a signal to come here post-haste. I've just this minute arrived. I'll be only too happy to get out of this dress-thing and have bath and a shave ..."

"Nonsense, you look absolutely perfect for our job, Mr Beard," grinned Oldroyds, shaking hands and offering him sweet black coffee and a bowl of dates. "Don't change a thing. We need you to look like an Arab a little longer."

"Sir," said Beard very correctly, almost holding his breath in his impatience to hear what was expected of him.

"I'm aware that you belong more to the Foreign Office than the War Office, but the GOC has authorized us to call on you for assistance." Beard, juggling with the coffee and a fistful of sticky dates, stared back at the colonel, his sweaty face blank. "I know your work is classified, Mr Beard, so I won't ask you what you were up to in Saudi," Col Oldroyds continued, his pale blue eyes examining Beard with renewed intensity. "I was informed of your presence in that area and – well, we need someone of your ... er, talents, shall we say, to blow up a bridge for us."

Beard nodded. "Be happy to oblige, sir," he said, very correctly; very suspiciously. He knew the SAS were active in the area: any one of them possessed as much knowledge of blowing up bridges as he did, probably a damn sight more.

"You've heard of the Green Mountain, I expect?" demanded Col Oldroyds, breaking in on Beard's thoughts with a quite startling suddenness.

"Yes, sir," answered Beard automatically. "It's about 10,000 feet, and said to be impregnable."

"I've been told that, too. We're going to take it," said the colonel in a matter-of-fact tone.

"I thought we might be, sir," said Beard, who had had no such thought.

"You won't be concerned in that affair," declared the colonel. He then spent half an hour explaining to Beard what his role was to be, and together they poured over the maps. The colonel pointed to a spot on one of the maps. The word "bridge" had been printed on it with an arrow pointing vaguely towards Saudi Arabia. Like most things in the Oman, the bridge appeared to be in the middle of nowhere, being neither part of the mountains nor the desert, and yet manifestly connected to them both. The bridge, according to the aerial photos available, spanned what looked like a crack in the ground – perhaps some ancient dry wadi – with hundreds of miles of desert one side and, on the other, the farthest from the Green Mountain, more desert and the protection of an umbrella-like overhang of another mountain. Beard instinctively wondered if the bridge was anywhere near the spot indicated on the maps, but, of course, the coordinates were provided by the maps. It still looked an awkward spot to reach undetected.

"The rebels on the Green Mountain are extraordinarily well supplied with food and ammunition and everything else they need," said Oldroyds, deciding that Beard had had long enough to study the map," and this bridge is their supply route. It's almost invisible at ground level because of sand dunes, some several hundred feet high, and it can't be seen from the air because of this massive rock overlap. The RAF can't bomb the thing without infringing Saudi air space, the same goes for artillery, and besides it's protected by mountains all round. The bridge is approximately 14 miles from the Green Mountain but constant heat hazes make it quite impossible to spot anything on the move – although whenever our boys are on the desert floor they tend to get hammered. It is assumed that there is some track or secret tunnel leading to the top, but we haven't found it as yet. Needless to say, what few tracks there are have been mined and the whole area is covered by all the most sophisticated weapons for which the rebels seem to have an unlimited amount of ammunition."

"You can thank Egypt for supplying the goods, and the Saudis for providing access," said Beard, who had spent much of the past year watching these routes on both sides of the border. "The weapons and ammo are transported by sea from Saudi to places like Sharjah, thence overland to somewhere along the Al-Batinah coast, from where they're ferried in lorries to, say, Rustaq and then humped on foot to any convenient point in Oman."

"You're remarkably well informed, major," commented Oldroyds, somewhat wryly.

"It's what I do, sir," responded Beard.

"Of course," nodded the other.

There was a brief silence, then the colonel asked quietly, "What do you know about camels, Mr Beard?" The question came in much the same tone as though asking the cricket score.

"I know one when I see one, sir," replied Beard with a grin. "I expect I've eaten a few in my time." Then, deciding this was not the time for flippancy, said "We all ride camels, if that's what's in your mind, sir."

"Excellent," exclaimed Oldroyds, "because I don't see any other way for you to get to the bridge except as masquerading as an Arab – and from the Saudi side."

"Do we have a date for this mission of yours, colonel?"

Oldroyds suddenly looked very serious; he looked all round them to make sure they were alone, and said in a slightly lower voice, "For the moment, major, this is for your ears only. Our D Squadron will begin their ascent at 21.00 hours on January 26. I'm afraid that doesn't allow you much time to get organized."

"We'll go tonight," said Beard decisively. "Where are these camels of yours?"

And that had been all the briefing Beard had got. A rendezvous point with the camels and their handlers was fixed. The plan entailed Beard and his team parachuting in, making contact with the Arabs and the camels, and then riding them for all of two days. A Major Everett produced the latest photographs of the bridge. It was a single-span British-made bridge, 80-90 ft across, with a steel frame embedded in concrete buttresses. It didn't look very wide, perhaps enough for two lanes of traffic, and concrete blocks interspersed with steel rods for the edges; the drop below looked a mile deep – but was probably only about 120 feet. Another officer proved most helpful with explosives and suggestions, and between them they agreed that the charges should be detonated non-electrically.

"There's always the chance you may be under fire at the crucial moment," the officer said concernedly, "so you don't want to be tripping over wires in the dark – and toppling over the edge."

Beard agreed.

And he agreed again now, up to a point, as his thoughts returned to the present. He'd use timing devices to set off his charges : there'd still be cables involved. So far everything had gone smoothly. He should be worried; but he wasn't. Beard was careful, but he was no worrier. He couldn't afford to be. Besides, it never helped.

He glanced up at the sky: it didn't seem quite so black as before. Dawn would soon be upon them, and there was a desert legend that said the first hour after dawn was borrowed from paradise. Beard knew the myth referred only to the wakening of the sun as it lit up the vast landscape, turning the sand quite rosy for a while. But that first hour of cool paradise was the prelude to the hellish heat to come, and then the beauty vanished and everything in sight returned to an endless straw-colour, and men like him shrivelled beneath the baking sun.

Beard shook himself. That was still to come. His thoughts turned to the SAS men who had been climbing the Green Mountain during the night. He wondered how they were faring, and wished them – and himself – good luck. There was not a breath of sound in the air; no flashes in the sky from explosions. All was well, and it was time for him to cross that bridge.

The darkness had been their ally, and now there were the faintest fingers of light stretching up over the horizon to the east; orangey finger tips, already glowing warmly. Another hour, even less, and it would be light enough to see – and they would be discovered. He went into a huddle with his men to discuss their options. Obviously they had to cross the bridge straight away, certainly while the light favoured them, but how to do so without rousing suspicion? Perhaps they were already being watched? Salim doubted this. Arabs, he declared, would have raised the alarm and opened fire at the first hint of danger. After a few minutes a plan was agreed.

Salim, Walid and Sgt Piper, with as much stealth as was possible, brought the rebels' camels up to the bridge; and despite having their sleep disturbed, the beasts did not object too loudly – not enough to raise the alarm, though the noise they did make seemed sufficient to wake the dead. The camels had been Salim's idea; he'd said they would add a touch of naturalness to their presence, apart from affording them a degree of cover. Now, all was ready for the bridge crossing.

Trooper Blake, the marksman, was left to man the Arab machine-gun, training it on the opposite bank but with orders not to open fire unless it was necessary. Trooper Jones, the R/T man, was positioned so that he had an uninterrupted field of fire of the entire length of the bridge. The remainder moved openly across the bridge, Salim and Walid leading the way. Beard thought it sensible that the two Arabs should be in the front since they would be able to answer any challenge and so gain them all a few precious seconds. Sgt Piper, whose many forms of marriages included one to a lady from Aden and so was fairly fluent in Arabic by now, came next, and Beard and Cpl Blossom brought up the rear. Every one of them had his hand on a weapon, either gun or knife.

They were half way across the bridge when a shout assailed them. Who were they? Who'd sent them? What did they want? Was anything wrong? Salim shouted back the age-old greeting of travellers, *Salam alaikum*, which required an obligatory response, and so gave them a moment's breathing space. "Keep bloody moving," whispered Beard urgently. Salim, volubly aided by Walid, maintained a meaningless volley of words about a dried-up well, about the price of coffee, about the perfection of his camel, about the perfidy of women, about the manliness of his seven sons ... and suddenly they were all safely on the other side.

By now other guards had gathered to see what was going on and to add their voices to the discussion over worldly affairs, and the two groups moved towards each other, slowly but surely. Beard unconsciously counted five guards coming towards them; he was more concerned about who might still be inside the two small tents some thirty yards from the bridge and about the two men who had remained where they were – with the machine-gun. Neither was standing by the gun – they seemed more interested in looking across the chasm towards their colleagues in the opposite gun pit. Trooper Blake obligingly waved back, and that was the moment Beard chose to spring into action.

The two groups were now almost together and, whispering to Blossom to "sort 'em out," Beard stepped aside and shot the two men by the gun while they were still waving to Blake. His action, and especially his silenced weapon, seemed to mesmerize the remaining guards. They were still gaping at Beard when Blossom and the rest fell upon them. They did not stand a chance. In a moment all five were dead: all stabbed to death. Beard raced to one of the tents just as an Arab emerged clutching a rifle. He shot the man the second he saw him. Unfortunately the man squeezed the trigger of his rifle in the instant of dying. No one was hurt, the bullet disappearing somewhere in the heavens, but the sound of the shot reverberated across the desert for moments on end, shattering the utter quiet. Blossom emerged from the second tent wiping the blade of his knife, looking hastily around as if following the sounds of the shot. It was a startling conclusion to the killings which, in themselves, had been something of an anti-climax. Beard checked his tent, made sure it was empty, and then walked quickly towards the gun pit to make sure the two men he'd shot were dead; one was not quite dead, and he put him out of his misery.

"If there's anybody for miles around that shot will have told them something's up," said Beard grimly, as he hurried back to his men who were examining the bodies of their victims – or perhaps they were more interested in collecting souvenirs. "The sooner we blow this bridge sky high and get the hell out of here, the better."

It was now quite light, and both Salim and Walid scanned the desert in all directions. Beard knew that they were able to see twice the distance he could, and when they reported that they could see nothing, he felt relieved. Even so, it seemed right and proper not to take anything for granted, and he prepared for an immediate departure once the bridge was blown. Beard waved Trooper Blake to cross over and take up position on this side of the bridge, and likewise told Trooper Jones to find a safe hole and to be ready to send a signal back to HQ the instant the bridge was destroyed. Salim, Walid and Sgt Piper went off on the rebels' camels to retrieve their own beasts, and there really wasn't any need to tell them to hurry. Even as they galloped away, Beard and Blossom busied themselves carrying the explosives on to the bridge.

Beard, who now decided the bridge was no longer than 90ft, had decided on a double explosion, one at either end, so that the middle of the bridge would simply drop into valley below. Simple and effective, and quick. The three men returned with the camels and clattered across the bridge almost at the moment Beard finished laying the charges at one end. He shouted to them to get well back from the bridge, which they didn't need any second telling, trotting well out of sight behind one of the immense sand dunes. Blossom then called out that his charges were in place, and after they had joined the charges, Beard sent Blossom off to take cover and then, after a last look round, he inserted the timers. He'd decided on two minutes. He didn't want to hang about. There was plenty of time for him to join Blossom in safety and keep his head down.

He started walking off the bridge – remembering the oft-repeated exhortation of Captain "Fingers" Horton, his explosives mentor: Never run from a lighted fuse! Well, this wasn't quite the same, but the timers would already be at work. Beard continued walking at a regular pace, but he knew his stride was lengthening all the time.

It was over: it was done. This was very likely his last field mission. He was heading home for some quiet job at the Foreign Office; perhaps some embassy job as military attaché, some safe place where a man might raise a family. Oh, Ruth, my darling, his thoughts whispered, I'm on my way home and this time we will be married.

Sultan bin Muhammad had been asleep in a rocky hollow some 400 yards from the bridge when that one and only shot had been fired. He'd woken with a start, commended his soul to Allah, recited a few prayers from the Koran, cautiously unwrapped himself from his blanket and reached out for the comforting feel of his rifle. Sultan waited for the sound of more shots, and thought it strange that there were none. After several minutes, he raised his head fractionally to peer over the boulder behind which he'd been sleeping. He could see nothing, only the empty sands and the dark mass of the Green Mountain far in the distance. Nothing seemed to be happening over there. He couldn't see the bridge from where he lay and, after some thought, he began crawling along a crack in the rocks to a point from which he knew it would be visible.

The sun was in Sultan's eyes but it wasn't strong enough to affect his vision. He was shocked to see all the bodies lying around. What had happened? Were they ill? They couldn't have been shot, could they, else he'd have heard the shots? But there'd only been the one – the one that had wakened him. Ah, there were some men moving around. Actually, they weren't moving at all. They all seemed to be crouching, hiding, behind rocks. All except one, who was standing on the bridge. Sultan was about to rise to his feet and shout to him, and ask what was happening, but froze instead. He took a tiny telescope from a bag he carried, and examined the lone figure intently. There was something wrong, and it took him a moment or two to discover what it was that had sounded a warning bell.

It was the boots! The man was wearing boots! Arabs never wore boots: they wore sandals, or nothing at all. This man was not an Arab. He studied those that he could see crouching behind rocks with a fresh concentration. They were too big, their faces were wrong, their skins too light. And finally the penny dropped. They were infidels!

The one on the bridge must be their leader: he was waving to the others to shelter behind some rocks. Sultan watched the tall man on the bridge; watched him stoop a couple of times to do something, he couldn't make out what: watched him start to walk away. And it was then that the second penny dropped.

"He's going to blow up the bridge!" he exclaimed to himself, and even as the realisation took root in his brain, he was reaching for his rifle. It was a very old rifle, even older than himself; it was a 1907-pattern breech-loading Lee-Enfield, Mark 111. Sultan had only seven bullets for the weapon, and all looked rusty and the worse for wear. He took up two of his precious cartridges and, seeing that the figure was moving slowly, as if to leave the bridge, he pushed one of the cartridges into the breech and lined up on the man who had started to move. A scorpion scuttled across the boulder a scant few inches in front of his great hooked nose, and he paused an instant to spit at it and send it scampering away. He then returned to his target, took aim and, very slowly, squeezed the trigger. At the moment of firing a smile that was pure venom lit his dark face.

The man on the bridge fell, and Sultan inserted a second cartridge, and fired almost casually – but the bullet must have struck its mark again for the man, who had started to haul himself along the bridge, suddenly came to a dead stop and lay there immobile.

Seconds later, the bridge blew up.

The explosion seemed to last for ever, and even when it had subsided clouds of dust prevented Sultan from seeing what had happened. But, finally, the dust settled and he saw the gaping hole in the centre of the bridge. The body of the man he'd shot had been tossed up in the air and now lay in a crumpled heap just short of the edge of the cliff. A foot or so more and it would have finished up on the floor of the wadi 120 feet below with the rubble of the bridge.

Sultan's exultation was such that, without thinking, he leapt to his feet with screams of praise to Allah, to his camel, and to himself ... and that was the moment Trooper Blake, the marksman, shot him dead with a single bullet.

The first of Sultan's bullets had hit Beard's left leg. It passed straight through the fleshy part of the thigh, quite high up, scorched across the bottom of his scrotum and dug a furrow along the soft part of his right thigh before spending itself on the floor of the bridge. He did not know whether it was the impact of the bullet, or the shock of it, that caused him to fall down. He simply knew he couldn't help himself; his leg seemed to crumple beneath him, disappear in fact, and he fell for want of support. He wasn't conscious of any great pain. There was some pain, of course, but it felt no worse than a burning sting; it was as though he had been skewered by a red hot needle. After the initial sensation, it didn't seem half so bad. He tried to put all thoughts of his wounds aside, for he was conscious of a greater urgency: the need to get off the bridge. Even as he endeavoured to use his hands to drag himself forward, he could feel the blood trickling from his wounds.

The second bullet struck less than two inches above the first almost immediately after. It smashed like a hammer against a bone, turned sharply at right angles and passed through his left buttock. For about 15 cms it travelled in a straight line, then it began to roll and turn, it even about-turned, and then it fragmented and there were several tracks as the various shards ploughed on creating carnage as they went. But Beard knew nothing of this, he was not even aware of any pain – not after the impact of the second bullet: that had felt rather like his leg being crushed, and the pain in that fleeting instant had been unbearable. He'd shrieked in agony. But now, there was no pain at all. When the bullet disintegrated, the largest fragment had come to an abrupt stop at the base of his spine, paralysing him instantly.

For the space of, perhaps, three seconds, Beard lay there wondering what on earth had happened. He couldn't move, he couldn't feel anything, though when that second bullet had first struck him, the pain had been so excruciatingly awful he'd been unable to stop himself screaming, or even to control it. Now, a sort of numbness was creeping over him; and now, even that was fading. He could feel nothing. He couldn't move. Only his brain seemed to be alive, and it reminded him that the bridge he was lying on was about to blow up. For possibly the first time in his life, Beard was frightened. He was terrified ... he was helpless, and the worst of it was that he knew it.

The bridge blew up at this moment, and for the merest fraction of a second, he was conscious of being thrown up in the air, conscious of terrible pain again – and then the agony ended, and he entered a black world of nothingness.

Cpl Blossom and Sgt Piper raced towards Beard's body. Blossom stooped to pick up a boot: it oozed blood and two toes and a bit of foot fell out. "Oh, fuck!" he exclaimed. He called out to Piper: "How is he?" The sergeant shook his head without looking up. "I think Mr Beard's gone, mate. I can't find any pulse," said Sgt Piper. "Oh God!" muttered Cpl Blossom.

Col Oldroyds chanced to be in the radio room back at Bahlah when Trooper Jones came through with the news. "The bridge is blown, sir. But the major went up with it."

"Beard? Major Beard?" cried Col Oldroyds, staring blankly into the mouth-piece.

"Yes, sir."

"Is he badly hurt?"

"Sgt Piper says he's dead, sir. Said he's been blown up," said Jones. "The sarge says he can't find any sign of life, no pulse – though he says the major's still bleeding heavily, which he can't understand. Says it must be an artery draining away."

"What happened, Jones? Was there a premature explosion?" demanded the colonel.

"No, sir," answered Jones immediately. "Mr Beard was shot before the bridge went up, sir. Twice, I think. Bloody sniper in the mountains. Blake shot him. The major went down, and the bridge went up – almost at the same time."

Oldroyds sighed tiredly, and said that a helicopter would come and collect them all directly. Then, he remembered the batch of letters for Major Beard that had arrived at the base only the day before. Capt Richard Starling, the officer who'd handed them to him, had commented: "They seem to have been following him round the world for years." And now that same officer commented, "I reckon a whole batch of post bags must have got misplaced somewhere.

"Well, he won't be reading them now, will he?" sighed the colonel. "I'm not sure if his body will be brought back here. He wasn't actually on our strength, just doing us a favour. He's a Foreign Office chap, really."

"It's her fault," said Starling, staring at one of the envelopes and speaking with some feeling. "You'd think a girl could remember the name of her boyfriend – at least, the one she's writing to. I can understand her getting the post code wrong, but not his name."

"Let's have another look, Dick," said Oldroyds, stretching out his hand. It was an unusually fat envelope, obviously containing many pages; it was also a much-travelled letter having been there and back to England at least twice, and been delivered to at least half a dozen camps in as many different countries. It wasn't entirely the fault of the Army Post Office: in fact, not theirs at all. Ruth had addressed the envelope first to a Jarvis Brook and then, when it had been returned, changed it to Robert Beard; and somewhere along the line all sorts of Army post codes had been added. It was a wonder it wasn't still on its travels: it was his Army number which saved it.

"Have them sent to the Foreign Office, Dick. He was their man," Oldroyds decided, tossing the envelope back. "As for Jarvis Brook," he added thoughtfully, "I suspect in his line of work, Mr Beard has many names, and this is one of them. Might even be his real one." He gave a sigh and muttered softly, "Poor little lady."

Chapter Two

Vermont, U.S., January, 1959

On the matter of names, if Col Oldroyds had studied the envelopes more intently, he would have discovered a mountain of information. A Sherlock Holmes would have noticed at a glance that Beard was not the only one with more than one name; he would have observed at once that the sender, Ruth, herself appeared to have several surnames; and further, that her title had changed to indicate her status as a married woman. But the colonel was no Holmes.

A close study of the envelopes would have traced Ruth's surnames from Miss Hoggins to Miss Trotter, then Miss Fennell and finally (one supposes) to Mrs Henry O. K. Marchant. There, that name alone should have been enough to raise the colonel's curiosity. But clearly his eyes did not see what there was to read, else he would have said to himself, "Wow! This is some lady chasing Mr Beard."

And there was so much more to be garnered from the well-travelled, grimy, dog-eared envelopes. For a start, there were the several different return addresses given. In date sequence, the first, which had been severely underscored, was The Seven Dials, central London, clearly a public house; the next was a house in Battersea, still in London; then came a cottage in Essex; and lastly, and one definitely to catch the eye, was one in Vermont, United States of America, belonging to Mrs Ruth Marchant – 2405 Circle Road, East York, near Bennington. At least the gorgeous stamps on these should have attracted the attention of the colonel; but, they didn't.

He could be excused, perhaps, being a mere man, for not sniffing at the envelopes for surely some perfume would have lingered over the years leaving further messages of love, for these were clearly love-letters: only lovers wrote at such length to tell one another what they both knew, but wanted to read … over and over again. Words that Beard had never received.

Oh yes, Mr Holmes would have had a field-day with these envelopes and thorough, and a thorough scoundrel to boot, as he was, he would indubitably have steamed them open to read over a pipe or two, and perhaps ejaculate an occasional "Wow!" with a dark smile. And he would think deeply amid the clouds of smoke from his pipe as to the character and even the appearance of the lady herself.

Elementary!

He would deduce, in his exasperatingly logical manner, that she was obviously British, five feet seven tall, dark-haired with eyes to match, was right-handed and at one time had been employed as a secretary in an office associated with the manufacture of soap ; good-class soap, with a strong perfume ; but lately had been concerned in similar secretarial work, though in a far more up-market atmosphere. Yes, he'd insist, the lady had known hard times but recently her fortunes had improved. It was all there on the envelopes, which he sniffed between puffs, and he would point them out, methodically ticking off the clues.

And, being Holmes, he would not be far wrong.

Around the time Beard was blown up in Oman, Ruth was coming to terms with being a widow at the age of "nearly 28" in a foreign country. Although she had lived and worked in the United States for more than ten years now and was an accredited American Citizen with a Permanent Resident Card, passport, social security card and driver's licence – the "whole kit and caboodle" as she was wont to refer to them – and loved everything about the country, like millions of others who were born elsewhere, she still regarded herself as a foreigner while fiercely proud of her new allegiance.

Ruth, whose home now was close to the Green Mountain National Forest in Vermont,   had been born in London, England, and had family living there. Ruth had been introduced to America in the late forties by an earlier fiancé who was an accountant in New York. When that broke up, for no better reason than that he married another woman, she remained working for the same firm until she met her late husband, the extremely wealthy Henry O. K. Marchant, who was in shipping, mining, timber and just about anything else that made money; his trademark was OK, and that's how he liked to be called; and that's how Ruth called him. He was the quintessential of the average man: average height, average face with thinning black hair and eyes to match; he was also twelve years older than Ruth. They just merged together, became recognised as a couple and on one of several occasions that he suggested they should marry, she agreed, with unexpected promptitude.

It is doubtful that genuine love played any great part in the proposal, certainly on Ruth's part, but a fashionable wedding duly took place in Bennington, marred only by a reluctance of his family to attend – they regarded her as a nobody, and not even American at the time, but attend they did and when, within a year she presented OK with a son, she was accepted with open arms, for the OKs were not a very productive species, and sons were especially rare.

The promptness of Damien's arrival after the marriage raised expectations that Ruth would produce many playmates for Damien, but there were no further births.

Now, in this new void in her life, her thoughts were focussed on the one man she had loved since childhood, and who had loved her in return … only, circumstances had thwarted their passions; marriages and missed opportunities, plus the fact that he was never at hand long enough to get to the altar; and that was not his fault either, for he was as eager as her to marry. All these factors had led her, instead, to OK. She'd written telling him of her widow status, not knowing where in the world he might be, and knowing him to be the most inconsistent of letter-writers that ever was, but months later she received a reply that was very definitely a proposal. She gripped her purse, for the treasured letter lay in it; she needed to read his lovely words very frequently.

She sighed his name dreamily. She knew him as Jarvis Brook, but he was known better to the rest of the world as, Robert Beard.

Chapter Three

The Omani Desert, 27 January,1959

Twenty minutes after Trooper Jones's radio message, a Whirlwind transport helicopter, escorted by two Venoms armed with rockets and 20-mm cannons, landed beside the gaping chasm over which the bridge had spanned and the first man to jump out was a young Army doctor, Captain Freddy Ashurst – newly qualified and even more newly commissioned.

Stray bullets, fired randomly from across the Saudi border, were whining through the air as he ran, ducking instinctively, followed by an RAF corporal with a stretcher and a body-bag. Occasional mortar shells were fired in their general direction, but all fell well short or wide, and exploded harmlessly, if noisily, even so the pilot sensibly taxied further out of range. Captain Ashurst was short, slim and very fair: his youthful skin had the rich pinkness of someone unused to a really hot sun.

"I've come for the body – Major Beard's," he told Sgt Piper, almost apologetically. "Over here, sir," said the sergeant, and he led the way to where Blossom was standing guard over the still form half hidden by the uneven ground. Beard's men had removed their Arab disguises as no longer serving any purpose, but Beard's long white robe had been pulled up to cover his face like a shroud. It was a bloody mask.

Capt Ashurst, after a cursory glance at the body's visible injuries, pulled away the shroud to look at the face it hid. He'd half expected to find it horribly mutilated, but apart from some severe grazing, a couple of minor cuts and some bleeding from an ear, the only damage seemed to be to the nose, which looked extremely broken. The face, which he could see had been baked almost to the colour of oak, was further darkened by layers of sand and sweat, and covered with the makings of a fine black beard. He frowned. He'd have expected the pallor of death to have been more apparent. The face should have been greyer, at least. The doctor, almost perfunctorily, leaned forward and pulled back an eyelid, and gave a start. He did the same with the other eye, and gaped in wonder.

"I thought this man was supposed to be dead," Capt Ashurst exclaimed in a shocked voice, staring up at Cpl Blossom who was standing nearby sharpening one of his knives.

"Well – he is, isn't he?" cried Blossom, staring back in amazement, hardly daring to believe the possibility of what the other was suggesting.

"Almost ... but not quite," answered the doctor, calm returning to his voice. "It's rather a good thing you didn't bury him, isn't it! Mind you, he's so very close to being so, it'll be a miracle if he isn't at any moment.

He's in a hell of a state. He'd be better dead."

"Don't say that, please, sir," cried Blossom desperately. "Not if there's any hope."

"Sorry, corporal," said Capt Ashurst, who had no experience yet of the bond that existed among soldiers, regardless of rank, who had faced death together, perhaps over a lengthy period. He then rushed to the helicopter for his emergency medical kit; he'd been so convinced he was merely coming to collect a corpse that he hadn't bothered to bring it with him before. He looked up, but otherwise ignored, a fresh flurry of whining bullets; he wondered, absently, if they had caused any fresh casualties, but as nobody else paid them any heed, he assumed not.

Now, kneeling beside Beard again, Capt Ashurst had to remind – and even convince himself, that he was examining a patient, and not a corpse. At first, he began to have fresh doubts, and pulled back an eyelid again to satisfy himself. He couldn't find a pulse, and as he searched over Beard's chest with a stethoscope his face grew more anxious and his frown returned; and then, at long last, he gave a long sigh and gave a small smile of satisfaction. There was a beat there: the merest murmur of one, irregular, but it was there. His patient was still alive. Just. But, for how long?

"Your major's still alive, boys," he cried to the little circle of incredulous faces.

"But he wasn't breathing, sir. There was no pulse at all," cried Sgt Piper.

"It sometimes happens when a body undergoes a massive shock – like this. He may even have stopped breathing for a moment or two – apparently just at the very moment you tried to find his pulse. At that moment, he was technically dead."

Capt Ashurst borrowed a knife from Blossom to cut away the Arab shroud and then slit the sleeves of the shirt Beneath; he'd been going to insert a saline drip into Beard's left arm but found this to be badly broken, and so put it in the right one. "Hold this up in the air," he told Sgt Piper, pushing the plastic bag into his hands. "Who put the dressings on his wounds – the major ones, that is?"

"I did, sir," admitted Blossom. "He was bleeding so much it seemed the right thing to do – I hope it was the right thing."

"It's probably the reason he's still alive – even if you did think he was dead when you did it!" returned Capt Ashurst, busying himself checking the worst wounds, and discovering a new one at the back of Beard's head where a piece of metal had buried itself. He cursed as one of the Venoms swooped low overhead and churned up a veritable sandstorm. A heavy burst of ack-ack fire from the sanctuary of the Saudi mountains discouraged any repeat performance for the moment.

"I did it as a matter of routine, sir," said Blossom, wincing at the unexpected praise. "There's some wounds, though, that I didn't dare even dress. I didn't touch them at all. There's the one his head and his back, sir, it's an awful mess. A great big bloody hole with 'is bones sticking out – an' one of his legs, the left one, looks like it's falling off. I put a tourniquet on … though it did seem rather pointless seeing as I thought he were dead. I suppose it should be loosened now that he ain't, or he will be, won't he?"

The doctor nodded understandingly, and immediately made the necessary adjustment. Even as he worked, he felt the likelihood of Beard still being alive when they got him to somewhere where he could be operated on most unlikely. He thought that any movement would tip the scale and that lifting Beard into the helicopter would assuredly kill him; the best, safest method was to strap the stretcher on to the frame for that purpose on the outside of the aircraft. Even as these thoughts raced through his mind, Capt Ashurst felt that death was only a moment away. Still, one had to go through the motions.

"What'll I do with these?" asked Blossom, holding out the scrap of shirt he'd torn off one of the dead Arabs to wrap the toes and bit of foot that had fallen out of Beard's boot.

"There's an ice bucket in the helicopter, we'll put them in there," said the doctor decisively after a quick examination of the items. "I shouldn't think there's an earthly that they can be grafted back on – but it's not my field. Trouble is, even if he survives, he's almost certain to lose his leg, so there won't be any need for any grafting." He knew that if Beard didn't die while being lifted on to the helicopter, he most certainly would if he didn't receive specialist treatment within the next few hours. After that it would be too late for anything; Beard's life was ebbing away – he needed a massive blood transfusion to survive, and a bloody miracle. He didn't even look up when three mortar shells came crashing in, creating short-lived sandstorms. Whoever was firing had still not found the range, but they were getting closer.

"Let's get him aboard the helicopter, he's not doing any good lying here," said Capt Ashurst determinedly. "We'll take him back to Shahjah, that's the nearest place – but medically it's little more than a clearing station. They won't have the facilities to deal with this. They'll probably just patch him up sufficiently and fly him on to Aden where at least there's a proper hospital. If we lose him on the way to Shahjah, so be it, it's his best – only chance. At least there's oxygen aboard to help him."

Capt Ashurst said there was room on the helicopter for the four soldiers, but the Arabs would have to make their own way back to Hamra to collect their pay. If he thought they would raise any objection, he was wrong; Salim and Walid were delighted, after all, they had a whole string of camels – the British ones and those that had belonged to the Arabs – to show for their trouble.

Beard's life, already in question, had all but ended even before Capt Ashurst delivered him to RAF Shahjah. There, he was stretchered into the wholly inadequate medical facility attached to the airfield, where the officer in charge, Flt Lt Terry Moorland, winced and shook his head.

His first concern was to assure himself that Beard was still alive. It took him some moments to find any pulse beat, and then he found it, barely a whisper, slow and irregular, but definitely beating. The doctor shook his head again, in disbelief.

"We haven't the facilities – nor the expertise to cope with anything like this," Moorland told Ashurst frankly after a superficial examination of the extent of Beard's wounds. "This is little more than a first aid centre. We can handle simple bullet wounds and stuff like that, but nothing on this scale."

"I brought him here because you were the nearest place I could think of," Ashurst said, with a shrug. "Perhaps he can be flown on from here to somewhere that has the capabilities."

But Moorland was already on the phone and speaking with the airfield's CO. In a cool, steady voice, he explained the situation and the urgency for Beard to be flown onwards to a place with a proper hospital. He suggested Aden.

Within an hour, Beard was transferred to a Pioneer transport aircraft and on his way to the Military Hospital at Khormaksar, Aden, with Moorland keeping him company. They had been able to do very little for him during his brief stay at Shahjah, beyond cleaning him up, repairing some lesser wounds, and changing the saline drip and adding a blood transfusion. He seemed to have tubes shoved in all over his body. The immediate diagnosis was that he was already more in the next world than this.

Col Oldroyds had been informed of this latest development and Beard's team was told to report back to another of their units, if there was one. They all knew they'd never see their major again.

Chapter Four

Aden, 27 January, 1959

After refuelling at RAF Salalah, the Pioneer went on to deliver Major Beard to the Military Hospital at Khormaksar, Aden, where the medical staff repaired some arteries, shook their heads over a score of X-rays, fed him drugs, and shoved more tubes into him – and sent for a priest, believing he would be of more immediate use than a surgeon.

In the event, after several hours of indecision, it was decided the climatic conditions of Cyprus were better suited to the patient, and he was flown to the military hospital at Akrotiri the following day.

It was here that surgeons first went to work on some of the twenty-eight separate wounds to Beard's body; the majority were fairly minor affairs, like his broken arm and ribs and nose, and some were simply deep cuts and gouges caused by flying debris, but some others were buried deep inside his body and needed to be dug out; these were the simple, straightforward operations that were carried out efficiently and, it was hoped, successfully.

But the major problems of his head wound, the shattered leg and spinal injuries remained. The piece of metal sticking out of Beard's head was safely removed, though there was speculation that there might be some brain damage that would need the attention of a specialist surgeon. Explorative operations on both the leg and back injuries were performed, but there was no great confidence on the part of the surgeons; it was simply a case of something having to be attempted if he was to survive, and in some form of physical normality. A feeling was creeping in, although it was never admitted, that it was really all a waste of time, but, of course, they would never stop trying.

Beard remained in a deep induced coma for several weeks: his injuries might have kept him unconscious, but morphine contributed to this condition. He remained in this state for well over two months – and every day of that period was regarded as a bonus, and a degree of optimism, hope, anyway, grew with the passing of each day. Those who believed in God, and even those who didn't, prayed for the young soldier's survival; perhaps, secretly, they also prayed for their patient to be put out of his pain.

And, in a way, their prayers were answered. It was discovered, quite by chance, that Sir Norman Blythe, the eminent orthopaedic surgeon, was holidaying on the island, and he readily volunteered his skills when approached. He was a man of courage who enjoyed a challenge; he was also a gifted surgeon, who didn't always follow the accepted rules. It was expected that his first action – which other specialists had been agonizing over for weeks – would be to amputate

Beard's left leg straight away; but he didn't.

Sir Norman justified this decision largely on the grounds that only the upper bones of the leg had been violently damaged; and this, he explained to assisting surgeons, some of whom voiced misgivings, was a field in which he had some expertise having been engaged for some years on the rebuilding of damaged limbs with the use of alloys incorporating such metals as titanium and vanadium, both of which were extremely strong, very light in weight and resistant to heat variations. The remainder of the leg, he pointed out, was not beyond microsurgery; the main arteries had already been successfully operated on, and while some others, and the muscles and tendons, had been torn and savaged, many were repairable or could be circumvented. The knee, he admitted, would have to be almost completely rebuilt – but it was all possible.

Of course, the spinal injuries were the key to everything: if they couldn't be repaired, nothing else would work; but, this area had been stabilised, temporarily, so it was a question of first things first: in this case, the leg.

Sir Norman set to work almost immediately. It was a long business, and only completed over many operations. He rebuilt the whole of the upper leg, fastening everything with metal pins, so that the limb resembled something associated with those of Herr Frankenstein; once the pins had been removed and the skin grafts completed, however, it would eventually look more normal. He also repaired the remains of Beard's left foot, but rejected out of hand the toes that Blossom had rescued.

"If they'd been frozen at once, and the operation performed immediately, there might have been a chance, but it's very doubtful – especially in the heat of an Omani desert. Even if all the conditions had been ideal, such grafts only have a fifty-fifty chance of success. They might appear all right for a short while," he told the medical team, "but the body too often ultimately rejects them. Gangrene is always the ineluctable threat. The major will have to make do with what's left of the foot. It shouldn't prove too much of a handicap, once he gets used to it. If he gets the chance, of course.""

He paused, and stared down at Beard. "We won't know anything until our young man puts his foot to use – and, of course, he may yet decide to die on us," he went on soberly. "One thing in his favour is – ignoring his present condition – his magnificent physique. He must've been as strong as Tarzan, and he'll need to be still if he's to get through."

It was decided to transfer Beard home to England as soon as possible for surgery on his spinal injuries and there was still concern over his head wound, and even as he was emplaned there was no certainty that he would survive the flight.

Chapter Five

Millbank Hospital, London, 17 *March,* 1959

Major Beard was flown into RAF Brize Norton in March, and was transferred by helicopter to Queen Alexandra's Military Hospital in Westminster. The hospital was known as Millbank, the name deriving from a mill there in the 1700s, which was demolished to make way for the vast Millbank Penitentiary from where convicts were transported to the far corners of the world. This in turn was demolished and the fetid marshes drained for the building of the Tate Gallery with, eventually, the Millbank Hospital as a neighbour.

It was there, in Room 601, purposely handy to an operating theatre, where he seemed to spend much of his time, that Beard remained – kept mercifully unconscious – while his body slowly mended.

His spine had been repaired: two nickel vanadium discs had been inserted at the lower extremity and several vertebrae replaced or repaired. There were other operations that needed to be carried out, but for the moment his body was recovering from those already performed. It was too early to say if all of these had been successful: that would only be known when Beard was able to put his rebuilt body to the test.

It was late into May before Beard gradually began to emerge from his deep sleep as the morphine drips were reduced. There had been earlier indications of a coming change in his condition, each sign of which was meticulously noted and recorded by the succession of nurses who maintained a ceaseless vigil at his bedside. They observed that he began to groan more often and more deeply, as though he was feeling the pains that had been with him for so long and which up to now his deep unconsciousness had smothered.

The fact that he was now clearly feeling his pain was regarded as a good sign – but, there was a limit to the amount of drugs they could give him to assuage them. Several times Beard uttered low screams in his dark torment; muscles twitched in his face, his body gave little jerks of protest, sometimes his mouth would form a scowl and deep frowns would crease his brow; and once, his head actually lifted off the pillow a few inches before falling back with an agonized cry, his whole body bathed in sweat. He sweated continuously, and his temperature fluctuated from very high to something near normal.

Something was stirring within him. He was still fighting in the only way he was able.

Then, at long last, some four months after the Oman explosion, Beard's eyes opened – but only for a moment. They saw nothing, and closed almost immediately. The nurse recorded: "Patient opened eyes 02.47 hours, 23 May."

It marked the beginning of the end of Beard's black nightmare: the start of his return to life. But it was a painfully slow business. Another four days passed before his eyes opened again, just for an instant, but soon afterwards they began to open almost daily, and sometimes they remained open for several moments, flickered, and then closed. "It's just his body waking up," the doctors determined, "he'll wake up properly when he's ready." And, of course, they were right. There came the day early in June, when Beard opened his eyes and they stayed open as he began to absorb what was within view. It was the middle of the night but there was a light nearby, and he saw the nurse staring down at him. He blinked at her several times.

"Ruth?" was all he could manage to say in a tiny whisper. It was only a word to him. He didn't really know what prompted him to utter it. It meant nothing to him. It was a name. He did not know whose.

The nurse shook her head slowly, her eyes bright at his first word. She knew all about Ruth. "No, major, I'm not Ruth ..." she started whispering back, when he interrupted her.

"Is that my name? Major?" he asked, in a voice he didn't recognise; the words, which he found barely audible, sounded strange and were difficult to pronounce.

Nurse Susan Willoughby frowned as she realised he had amnesia – possibly. Perhaps it was the shock of waking ... something episodical? She pressed a buzzer that would summon the night sister, and forced a smile as she whispered back, "No, sir. You're Robert Beard. The Major part is your rank."

She may have thought she was whispering, and probably she was, but to Beard her voice seemed extraordinarily loud compared with his own. He couldn't see much more than her face, which was round and plump and pink, with eyes that looked hazel and above them wisps of golden hair peeped from beneath the white contraption she wore on her head. She seemed to be looking at him terribly seriously. He blinked up at her in weary perplexity. Something was very wrong here, but he couldn't think what it might be.

"I'm in the Army, then?" he asked her, and this time he thought his voice sounded a little more natural, but it was still a very small voice and the words were hard to utter.

"Yes, major." Nurse Willoughby nodded her head, slowly, so as to emphasise the fact.

"And ... where am I?" he pressed ; he was hurting, and wondered why.

"You're in hospital, major. In London," she replied, her voice soft and warm. He liked it better than his own. "The Millbank," she added.

Beard heard the words, but they meant nothing to him. Hospital? He thought about this for a moment, and decided it didn't sound right, somehow. He didn't know why it should, but it did, which seemed crazy when he couldn't even remember his name. He winced as a spasm of pain shot through him with some savagery. It lasted only a moment, but it was a very long moment, and he uttered a low cry and felt the sweat poring over his body. He gasped out, breathing heavily as the nurse mopped his brow with soothing dabs, "I should be …" He had no idea where he should be, and really didn't care; he felt he was slipping back into oblivion. "Am I ill?"

"You were wounded, Major Beard, in the Oman," Nurse Willoughby explained,. "Go back to sleep now. You really shouldn't be talking."

"Wounded?" He thought about this for a moment, but didn't understand what this was all about. "Badly? When? How?" he pressed, ignoring her instructions to stop talking.

"You were wounded nearly five months ago," she told him patiently. "You've been here about three months. I understand you're recovering very well. Are you in real pain?"

"Christ, yes!"

"Where?" she could see his pain in his leaking eyes.

Like everything else, he thought hard about this for several moments. "Everywhere ... all over," he replied at length, and then gave a tiny shudder as a particularly sharp pain surged through his leg and stabbed him in the back. God, that was terrible! He gave a sharp cry and a gasp and knew that he must be crying because the nurse dabbed at his eyes, and he was able to see her clearer, except that he seemed to see her only in a watery way, and anyway he felt himself to be drifting away into another world. His leg seemed to be miles away, and hurt in several different places, but it was his back that he felt worst – and yet, although it couldn't be, or else he wouldn't feel it, it seemed to be numb, like other parts of him. It didn't make sense.

"I'll tell sister, and she'll get you something for the pain," Nurse Willoughby assured him softly. "In the meantime, you must rest. Try and go back to sleep." She looked up as a uniformed figure appeared at her side. "I think we've just lost him again, sister."

Beard was indeed already "lost." He could feel himself floating off again. In the background, a moment ago, he'd heard footsteps approaching, followed by whispering voices that were already fading. The silly things people said, he mused. Go to sleep, she'd said. It seemed so absurd. He'd been asleep apparently for four months, and the first thing the nurse says to him when he wakes up is, "Go back to sleep" and "All you need is sleep." It grew suddenly very dark and he knew he was about to return to his dark world and he fought to remain awake; he knew, too, that he was hurting terribly. Perhaps the pretty nurse was right, after all. At least sleep took the edge off the torture. And then he felt something rather lovely surging through his veins, and almost at once the darkness was complete: he was back in his pain-free world. At least there his brain didn't keep reminding him that he was hurting.

Beard slept for four successive days before opening his eyes again, but from that moment the continuous pain diminished and his recovery advanced with definite strides, very visible signs and there were no further serious setbacks. He realised, because it felt like it, that he'd had some further surgery. Of course, his eyes didn't stay open for very long at first: sometimes for only a few minutes at a time, sometimes for an hour or so, but he looked better. He still spent most of his time sleeping, but by degrees he came properly awake and began to take more of an interest in his surroundings.

He often murmured the name "Ruth" as he woke, without knowing why; indeed, having no idea if it referred to a real person. The nurses responded with pretty smiles and shakes of heads. He was still too weak to do much talking, but his eyes watched every movement among the staff he could see from his supine position. The nurses were too numerous for him to remember individually, save a very few; everyone of them looked absolutely gorgeous to him, even the stout, grey-haired one whom he took to be the Matron, or some such goddess. She always gave him a cheery smile and asked: "And how are you today, major?"

He couldn't remember ever answering with more than a blink: her visits generally coincided with him dropping off. She must be an exceptional nurse, he thought as the dark engulfed him.

Chapter Six

Millbank Hospital, June 11, 1959

Major Beard was wide awake. He'd heard their voices even before he regained consciousness, and there they were, gawping down at him. All three of them. So, it must be a Monday or a Thursday because those were the only days on which all three of them were there together.

"What's the date?" he jabbed at them before any of them could speak; he had no idea what prompted him to ask such a question; he wasn't going anywhere.

The question seemed to take them by surprise. They looked from one to the other, apparently lost for words, and then turned questioningly towards the sister standing alongside them. "It's June 11," she told them without hesitation.

"What day is that?" pressed Beard.

"It's a Thursday," added the sister, favouring Beard with an empathic smile.

"Of course," exclaimed one of the doctors, nodding wisely to his companions.

The trio of white-coated doctors – one or other of them always seemed to be hovering round Beard whenever he was awake – were gazing down at him now, all smiles, but with serious eyes.

They had no names so far as Beard was aware, but he had learned to recognise their different features and mentally thought of them as Doctors A, B and C, and categorised them according to the amount of pain they inflicted upon him.

Dr A. had a sharp, thin face with piercing little eyes and surprisingly thick hair – very grey: he was concerned with Beard's spine, and his ministrations hurt the most. Beard dreaded his approach, but often felt better after his visits. Dr B. had a pale face and very serious grey eyes – and was for ever making jokes, which never seemed at all funny: his main responsibility was for Beard's leg and, gentle as he was, he too inflicted considerable brief pain which lingered long after he'd gone declaring that "it's coming along very nicely." Dr C. was Beard's favourite: he inflicted almost no pain on him; this doctor, in fact, was the leader of the triumvirate, and it was he who carried out, or supervised, most of Beard's operations; he must have been satisfied with the results for, after studying their handiwork, he would always give Beard an encouraging smile ... and tell him to sleep!

There was a woman, too, who disturbed his peace of mind every so often – too often, he felt – leaving him exhausted and, sometimes, close to screaming: but, as with the others, he invariably felt considerably more alive after her ministrations. She was a physiotherapist: short and dumpy, fair-haired and jolly-faced; her name was Mrs Pearla Mussels. Her fingers were as tensile steel, but their touch was as soothing as a mother's ... even if they also inflicted pain as they rekindled life to dormant limbs. Her constant chatter and whole-hearted chuckles, served to take his mind off the physical side of her work. But she probably wouldn't be manhandling him today. Right now, he had the trio to contend with.

"How are you today, major?" The question came from Dr C. and came accompanied by a probing hand.

Well, Beard had been expecting that. It was their way of saying "Good morning," and was the prelude to a score of other questions concerning his well-being. And sometimes he responded by asking after Ruth, but his only answers were shakes and smiles, shakes and smiles. They knew about Ruth, of course, everyone seemed to know about her, but the consensus appeared to be that now was not the time to bring her into their discussions, apart from which her whereabouts weren't known beyond the fact that she was in America; plenty of time for talk of her when he remembered who *he* was; and so, for now, they pretended ignorance concerning her. For the moment, they were primarily concerned with where he was hurting most. Beard knew that question would come presently, when their explorations would add to his pain; but today, he reckoned he'd stick an oar into their routine first.

"I'd like to get up," he announced, with military crispness.

All three doctors actually laughed out loud in unison; even the sister smiled again; but the nurses hovering in the background looked alarmed, almost as though the major might actually try to get up – even though they knew he couldn't.

Beard sighed resignedly. It was to be another day in hell.

Later, once he became properly conscious again – that is, on a regular daily basis – and could watch what was going on around him, Beard appreciated the lunacy of his request. Every effort of his to move was frustrated; he discovered that he couldn't move above an inch or two: it was as though he was in a straight-jacket.

After ruminating over the reason for this, he realised that he was stretched out on the bed – and only now did he realise how hard it was, too! – with weights dictating his posture, if not his life; not only his left leg, but his back as well, were in some form of traction. He didn't know about his back, apart from the fact that it was in some kind of cradle, but his leg was in a sort of sling that was suspended from the lofty ceiling; so what with these obstacles, and a plethora of wires and tubes inserted or attached to various parts of his body, there didn't appear to be much possibility of achieving any sort of movement. He knew that the wires and things were connected to the machines with flashing coloured symbols which surrounded his bed. It crossed his mind that they might be keeping him artificially alive, in the same way as an iron lung, but he didn't pursue this theory – in case it was true.

One or more of the tubes must be feeding him because he was never brought any food to eat: perhaps it was contained in his pills; he wondered what he'd had for dinner today. The nurses brought him liquids to drink at clockwork intervals, of what he was uncertain. As far as he could make out, he was completely naked beneath a single steel-blue coverlet, but as the nursing staff seemed to be continually fussing over his body it didn't seem to matter. He looked forward to being given real food to eat : something solid : something he could see – even if he had to be fed.

On really bad days, he wondered if he'd ever get up and walk again. But he quickly reproved himself for such weakness of mind, and repeatedly told himself he would never stop fighting to achieve this goal; after all, he was supposed to be a soldier, wasn't he? And then he'd puzzle over his lost memory, and when he'd exhausted this topic – which was pretty soon since, as he didn't have any memory, there wasn't anything to ruminate over – he'd reflect on the unknown Ruth.

And then, one rainy day in July, Matron came striding in at twice her normal speed and, without preamble, exclaimed, "You have a visitor, major." She sounded excited.

"Who?" he asked, guardedly.

"She says she's your mother!"

Beard frowned.

He'd been told he was an orphan. Did orphans have mothers? Surely to God, he'd remember a mother, even if he did have amnesia? Drs A., B., and C., Matron and several nurses were on hand to watch his reaction. In fact, serious deliberations over the advisability of the meeting had preceded its authorisation, but in the end it was decided there was only the one way of learning anything, and no way were any of the doctors going to miss the reunion, if such it proved to be. It might prove to be the key that would unlock his mind.

And indeed, Beard's mind was in turmoil. "What's her name?" he demanded; then, in his next breath, "Is she Ruth?"

"No, major, I'm afraid not," came the firm reply. "She's a Mrs Queenie Fennell."

Beard frowned. "But shouldn't we have the same surname?" he exclaimed.

"Usually," agreed Matron, "but she may have remarried, and on the matter of names she claims you're someone else, too."

"Who?"

"Jarvis Brook."

Beard made a face. "What's she look like?"

"Formidable," said Matron circumspectly, but with a reassuring smile.

"So who's this Ruth? The only name I seemed to remember?"

The Matron gave a small shrug. "Perhaps Mrs Fennell will know," she suggested.

"Do you think she really could be ... my mother?" he asked doubtingly, yet hopefully.

"Let's find out, shall we?" replied Matron, almost as keenly.

Beard heard the nurse who was escorting Queenie Fennell into the ward whispering instructions like, "Now, you mustn't stay too long on this first visit, Mrs Fennell," "Don't talk too loudly, or touch him more than you have to," and "And please, don't let him see you cry." And, of course, she did all these things the moment she appeared at his bedside.

"Oh, Jarvis-lovey! Wot the 'ell 'ave they done to yer?" she cried, the moment she saw him stretched out on the bed with tubes and wires attached to him; and immediately grabbed at his hand and burst into deep sobs. A chair was positioned behind her and she was guided down on to it; she sank down readily, still clutching Beard's hand which she pulled to her and planted countless very wet kisses all over.

Beard, in no position to liberate his hand, stared at her with growing discomfiture, and some anxiety. Was this his mother? How was it possible? She evoked not the slightest memory, and yet he was clearly known by this woman, and with evident affection. He stared hard at the unknown face. He could find nothing in it to suggest any affinity between them: not a shade of likeness. He continued to stare at her without speaking. The small crowd of medical people who hovered around them appeared to hold their breath as they awaited his reaction to the poignant reunion.

Queenie, after her initial outburst, remained silent save for her continuing sobs, though even these became muted and less frequent; she simply sat on the edge of her chair staring desolately into Beard's face – the rest of him was covered – and holding on to his hand for dear life. She was a woman of substantial proportions : tall and, well, quite enormous all over: an unkind person might have called her fat. She had a face well-suited to the proportions of her body: it was large, and round and at the moment extremely red with emotion. Strands of tawny-grey hair stuck wetly across her forehead from under the wide-rimmed straw-sunhat that looked a strange companion to her crumpled navy raincoat and dripping rainbow-umbrella. It was hard to see the colour of her eyes through her tears but they looked greyish. Matron whispered to a nurse, and the latter relieved Queenie of her umbrella and discreetly mopped up the pool of water it had made.

"Hello," Beard murmured finally. It was a word, a beginning, perhaps a greeting. He'd almost called her Mrs Fennell, even Ma'am, but thought they didn't sound right – if she was his mother. He wondered about this name Jarvis she called him, but didn't pursue it for now; perhaps he had more than one name, and mother. Was that possible? 'Course not. He couldn't think of anything else to say in that moment, though he sensed his reply was inadequate.

This was borne out instantly by Queenie complaining, "Oh, darling, is that all yer can say arter all these years, when once we was all t' world to one another?" She wiped her tears with the back of her free hand and fidgeted with a button on her open-necked pink blouse until it burst free, landing with a tiny sound and then rolling away watched in mesmeric silence by everyone till it came to a halt, did a little twirl, and then lay flat on the polished floor. A nurse stooped to retrieve it and return it to Queenie. Then, all eyes turned back towards Beard to hear his answer, if he had one.

"I don't know what else to say to you, I really don't," came his response, dredged from heaven knew where. "I don't know who you are." He gave the hand that was gripping his a gentle squeeze, and was surprised at the strength of her response. "I'm told you are my mother, but I'm also told that I've been an orphan all my life." Queenie moaned, but did not interrupt. "If it's true that you are my mother, then I imagine it must be a wonderful thing and that we love one another. But I don't know anything, do I? I have no feelings towards you, no knowledge. What else can I say? I have no memory of anything prior to the explosion that put me here." He gave her a frown. "Didn't they explain all this to you, Mrs Fennell?"

She smothered a fresh sob. "Please call me Queenie, darling. You used to call me Mum – and I loved you the more for doin' so, but if yer can't remember nuffink, Queenie will 'ave ter do for now." She paused to give him a sad smile. "Your Mr Gibbs – 'e's a general, an' a Sir, for gawd's sake – 'e come an' found me at 'ome, an' 'e told me wot 'ad 'appened to yer. Said you was near killed someplace an' 'ad lost yer mem'ry, but 'e thought seein' me might jolt it back. But it ain't, 'as it?" Queenie shook her head, and let loose a few more tears. "I can un'erstand yer losin' a wife – wot yer 'ave done, or a sweet'art's love, like wot you've also done, but losin' yer mem'ry sounds plain barmy … careless … an' a load of old bollocks! You sure you ain't swingin' the lead?"

Beard smiled. "I hope not."

"Wot abaht Ruth, then? You've gotta remember 'er, at least."

"It's a name I keep saying, apparently. But I don't know her. I'm sorry."

"But yer love 'er, Jarvis," cried Queenie with passion.

"I don't remember anyone," repeated Beard, somewhat coldly. "If you really are my mother, I should love you above all. But I don't. I'm sorry. I don't know any of you."

For several minutes, during which time an orderly brought Queenie a cup of tea and she had to relinquish Beard's hand, they surveyed each other in silence. It wasn't until she'd finished her tea, and shucked herself out of her raincoat and removed her hat, that Queenie leaned back in her chair and spoke.

"I've knowed yer since yer was borned, Jarvis. I fink the best fing I can do is to relate yer life 'istory," she began. "Summat has ter ring a bell somewhere. Don't it? Wotcher say?"

Beard looked towards the Matron, who gave a slight shrug, but nodded. "It's worth a try – Queenie," Beard responded, with interest, if not enthusiasm. "Will it take very long?"

"A lifetime, possibly. I dunno. It certainly won't be told in a single session today."

"Well, I'm not going anywhere for a few months," said Beard with a small laugh.

"'Course, I don't know nuffink about yer soldiering, 'cept that you won some medals." She gave him a fond, proud smile. "I only knowed yer as a boy growing into manhood, and then going away for a soldier an' arter that seein' yer on a coupla leaves an' that time when yer bought me 'ouse."

"Just tell it as you remember, Queenie," Beard said encouragingly, and he really was as keen to hear her story as anybody ; more so, because, presumably, it was *his* story. And if it wasn't, well, it would help pass the time. So, he'd bought her a house, had he! Surely she had him mixed up with someone else?

"Then I'll start at the very beginning, 'cos that's when we first met," Queenie smiled back. "An' I'll try an' make it as interesting as possible. Just don't interrupt."

"Just remember all I know is my name, Robert Beard," he said hurriedly.

"Whatever it is, it ain't that, lovey," she sighed, but with a ghost of a smile.

And so she began, lifting the veil that shrouded that shrouded both their lives.

□ *And so the group of mainly medical people settled round Beard's bed, not really expecting Queenie's story to be very interesting or to last more than an hour or so. In the event, the narration continued over many sessions and spread over a period of weeks, with contributions from several narrators. Even so, on this the opening of the story, chairs were brought by the nurses for the doctors and Matron and a few others, and several nurses found excuses to be within earshot, but out of Matron's vision. And as the story progressed, there was an air of expectancy, even excitement, among the audience.*

Chapter Seven

St Giles, London, 25 September, 1925

Whoever it was lying there in bed, he'd never known his real name, and most likely never would. He'd been christened by Sam Trotter, a constable in the Metropolitan Police, who had found him abandoned in a carrier-bag left on the steps of The Seven Dials public house in St Giles, London; his attention had been drawn to it by some stirring from within.

So Queenie's story began – dismissing Robert Beard's name from the start.

It was chucking-out time on a cold, wet and windy September evening in 1925, and P.c. Trotter had been idling in a shop doorway, counting off the last minutes of his shift before making his way to Bow Street Police Station to sign off, when he became aware of the movement. When it was repeated with some desperation, he gave a weary sigh.

More soddin' kittens! His frown deepened as a thought stuck him. Hadn't he seen a woman seated there only moments ago? She must've left it – accidentally on purpose, like. If it weren't bleedin' kittens, it was bleedin' puppies, or sumffink bleedin' worse. He couldn't quite imagine what could be worse, less'n it was a bleedin' snake ... Gawd 'elp us!

For two pins, he told himself, he'd let someone else have the pleasure of discovering the bag, but when a tiny naked foot shot out of it, Sam moved from his shelter to investigate. He wasn't sure now that he wouldn't have preferred kittens – perhaps even snakes.

Arriving at the scene of the crime, for, of course, it was a crime to abandon a baby in this way, he paused and stared gloomily down. The bag advertised its association with Percy Buller & Co, vegetable, fruit and flower purveyor, who had their rat-ridden warehouse in adjacent Jarvis Brook, a ninety-yard sewer of a street with crumbling buildings leaning precariously towards each other.

Sam, carefully avoiding the kicking leg, nudged the bag tentatively with a boot, and it almost burst asunder, followed by an ear-splitting scream. He took two quick steps backwards and looked fearfully around, hoping for a sight of the child's mother, remembering only that the figure he'd fleetingly seen on the steps a few minutes before had been a tiny thing, but there was no one in sight who bore the slightest resemblance, nor anyone who looked suspicious – nor anyone eager to be of assistance.

It was at this juncture that Queenie Hoggins (as she was then called) appeared on the scene; a minor earthquake scattered the throng that was gathering around him, and from the resultant passage she emerged, and stood, arms akimbo, beside the constable, her great scarlet-bloused bosoms heaving in indignation as she glared at him, and everybody else around. The crowd fell back readily for they knew this was a woman whose voice could skin a cat when roused, and whose rough hands could punch as hard as many a man's. Queenie Hoggins was the landlady of The Seven Dials, and none of her customers took any liberties. It was said that she was twenty-eight – but it had been said for many years; it was also said that she took in lovers when the mood suited, booting them out when it didn't, but as nobody seemed too sure if she had one at the moment, they must have been discreet affairs.

"What's up wiv you drunken sods? Never seen a baby before? Christ knows you bastards spawn enough of the poor bleeders – an' yer can't even do that wivvout 'elp!" she railed, but with a yellow-toothed grin that was not unattractive. She gave her tousled, tawny mane a challenging toss, elbowed Sam unceremoniously aside. "'Ere," she commanded peremptorily, "let's 'ave a butcher's at the poor mite 'fore it does itself a mischief." And with a surprising agility, and even more surprising maternal dexterity, she swooped to pick up the baby, bag and all, and cradled the lot in her powerful arms. She poked a fat, work-worn finger into the bundle, and her fleshy face dissolved into quite a pretty smile, which was answered with a wail fit to wake the dead.

"Well, whatever it is, it's a 'ungry little bugger! See – it's trying to eat me finger!" chortled Queenie. She turned to Sam, who had been one of her discreet lovers over the years, and, grinning brazenly, enquired, "Not yours is it, Sam?" Sam gaped, almost speechless. "Certainly not!" he managed to say. Queenie smiled teasingly up into his face, murmured, "If you say so, love," then quickly added, "I'll take it inside outta the rain and cold an' clean it up. Mind you, it's probably more 'ungry than anyfink else. 'Ungry, an' cold."

It was a statement of intention, and fact, that did not require, nor seek, his approval. In a trice, she turned, ploughed her way like a dreadnought back to the pub door, and vanished within, leaving a relieved Sam to ponder what action he should take. He was still wondering if it wouldn't be in order for him to follow Queenie so that he might wet the baby's head, so to speak, and there was always the chance that she might invite him to stay the night, when his sergeant cycled up and demanded to know what was going on. He scarcely waited to listen to Sam's reply before clomping straight into the building to pursue his enquiries.

Sam – he had the stature of a giant: a forty-two-inch waist to go with six feet four of height, and a large, pink face perched above several folds of chin, and grey-green eyes that missed nothing – was left disconsolately outside to keep the peace, and ruminate on the injustices in life. At such moments, he generally contemplated on ways of escaping the wretched life he shared with his wife Lily in their home off the Pentonville Road ; she was a religious crank who, despite the church's strict teaching to the contrary, insisted that sex was a mortal sin, but being a staunch Catholic in all other respects clung on to him like a leech. She screamed at him whenever he was home, accusing him of having affairs and anything else that came to mind, but when he dared, mildly, to suggest a divorce, her screaming reached knew heights. It was a mortal sin, she screeched at him; the very word was anathema to her.

He was still pondering on whether he could simply leave her when, twenty minutes or so later, the sergeant emerged, wiping his mouth with the back of his hand and tweaking the ends of his moustache, followed by Queenie. She was now wearing a faded sailor's raincoat, a yellow sou'wester, and carrying the baby wrapped up in a carrot-coloured blanket, like a sack of flour in her arms..

"Right then, Trotter," said the sergeant, with an air of great importance, as befitted sergeants, "I wants you to accompany this ... er, Queenie, that is, down to Charing Cross Hospital and do the necessary. Give 'em the baby, see what they does wiv it, and 'ave your report ready first thing – er, well, soon as maybe," he added after consulting his watch. "It'll be best if Queenie carries the little blighter. You'd only drop the sod ... then there'd be more paper work. 'Sides, you'd look a real sight carrying it down the street, heh!"

Sam was past caring what he'd look like. His main concern by this time was that it was already long past his signing-off time – not that he was in any hurry to get home to Lily, of course, but at this rate he couldn't see any end to his shift. Blasted kids, he fumed, but without any real animosity; it was simply that he wanted to get his boots off, and sink a few pints in someone's kitchen – he might still be able to work something out with Queenie later on. Another thought crossed his mind, and he asked, with only vague interest: "Wot is it – a boy or girl? And, it ain't goin' ter croak on us, is it?"

"It's a boy," intervened Queenie, "and 'e seems fine. Least ways, 'e will be if 'e ever gets fed. I've give 'im a barf of sorts – on the bar counter, no less! I've wrapped 'im up warm – used a beer towel for a nappy, an' give 'im a few spoonfuls of warm milk which he guzzled like it were best bitter. Nuffink else I could do, were there, eh?"

"Proper blinkin' muvver, ain'tcher !" grinned Sam, and his eyes regarded her with a warmth that was close to being affection. Queenie, clearly pleased with what she regarded as a compliment, smiled back with a warmth to match his own. Sam, sensing that things looked promising, smiled back at her ... and thought the sooner they got rid of the baby, the better.

"Is there any name for the little feller?" he ventured.

"No name an' nothin' known," declared the sergeant boredly, like he was reading a charge sheet. "Not a perishin' clue about 'im. Nothin' in the bag. No bleedin' note. Nothin'. He was wrapped in a bit of sheet-thing, but it 'ad no laundry marks. The only bleedin' clothes the poor little basket's wearin' is a vest – an' that's got no markin's on it, neither."

"There's some sort of badge on it, though," interposed Queenie. "One of them religious fings. You know, wot Catholics go in for. A sort of cloth emblem. It 'ad a lady's picture on it. P'raps it's 'er ... the Madonna woman, I mean."

"Well, 'e ain't the Pope whoever 'e is," the sergeant growled irreligiously, and with this observation, he touched his helmet with a finger by way of salute and in a moment was pedalling hurriedly away with much needless ringing of his bell, for there wasn't a soul in sight, nor any other vehicle. Sam reckoned he simply wanted to get safely away ahead of any further complications, leaving him to do everything.

Sam, with Queenie trailing behind, creaked into the hospital some time after midnight. They were not in the least welcome, and even less so when the purpose of their visit became clear. The yawning auxiliary nurse who was holding the fort in reception when Queenie laid her bundle down, took a quick look at its contents, and fled in search of help. She returned long minutes later with the staff nurse, who took one look at the baby, touched him to see if he was real and grimaced when his tiny lungs told her that he was, and promptly sent for the night sister; and she, raising her eyes to heaven, decided a doctor should be called. A porter was despatched to fetch the duty doctor.

It was while this minor god was being sought, that the real God finally smiled on the baby, and sent him a champion.

Father Michael O'Shea, Roman Catholic chaplain at the hospital, was, even at that hour, prowling the wards searching for souls to claim and convert, when he heard about the baby. He was at the baby's side long before the doctor, and hugging himself rapturously at the sight of the Madonna sewn loosely to his vest.

"This baby must be baptised at once," he declared, almost desperately.

"He's not in any danger, Father," said the sister, smiling good-naturedly.

"Only God can say that with any assurance, sister," retorted the priest levelly, determined to claim the infant before his Protestant counterpart arrived on the scene.

Within twenty minutes, Father O'Shea had organised the service and pressed a startled Queenie and Sam into the roles of godparents, in the absence of anyone more readily suitable – which he thought would have been a real miracle at such an hour. The sister consented to hold the baby, though it seemed the child plainly wished to play no part in the proceedings and let his lungs voice his objection. There was a momentary hiccup in the brief service when the priest suddenly turned to

Queenie. "You are Catholic, I suppose?" he asked anxiously.

"I 'spect so, dearie," she replied, flashing him her yellow smile; she had a vague recollection of a Methodist background, or was it Baptist? Anyway, she'd been packed off to some sort of Sunday school as a girl: never been near a church since, of course.

Father O'Shea gave a little shudder, hesitated, looked hopefully up at the constable, who nodded with no great show of piety, and pressed on, with a nervous eye in all directions for the Protestant pretender.

Another pause. "What name?" he whispered urgently to the policeman.

What name, indeed? Sam knew there wasn't any known one, and he didn't know how to answer. He remained tongue-tied for several agonizing moments before inspiration came to him; there was only the single, impossible clue in the whole affair – the carrier-bag in which the baby had been found. On impulse, he growled back:

"Jarvis Brook!"

Father O'Shea, looking decidedly doubtful and ignoring Queenie's prolonged titter, glanced fearfully up as the chapel door swung open. The Protestant's dread Rev Simon Wellbeloved approached the group with a challenging glare.

"I baptise you, Jarvis Brook, into the Holy Roman Catholic Church," Father O'Shea rattled off, offering a grateful prayer for such timely opportunity ... and a benign smile to his brother priest.

At this point, Jarvis Brook was whisked away "to be looked at" by the doctor, the chaplains shuffled off together, and Queenie and Sam, their duties done, were abandoned to their own pleasures. It was still raining and they splashed their way back to The Dials, with Queenie tucking her hand possessively inside Sam's arm, both feeling that while others might win the plaudits, theirs had been the greater contribution in saving young Master Jarvis Brook for the world's pleasure.

Little could they know what the world had in store for little Jarvis, or the roles they'd play in his future.

As it was only hours before that he'd delivered Jarvis to Charing Cross Hospital, Sam might have felt that he had done all that could be expected of him, but Queenie had other ideas. Before he'd even given a thought to getting out of her comfortable, warm bed, she was on at him to see how "our godchild" was getting on.

And so it was, later the very same day, he'd returned to the hospital to enquire after the state of his godson. The first thing he learned was that Father O'Shea had been killed in the few hours since in a street accident while on his way to see the sisters at the Convent of Our Lady of Sorrows to discuss the baby's future. This seemed like a bad omen to Sam, but he was reassured by Dr Saul Levy, who greeted him with, "Ah-ha, come to see if we've lost your baby, hey?"

Sam grinned. "No, doctor, I just come to see 'ow 'e was seein' as 'ow I found 'im."

"He's perfectly sound," said Dr Levy, his plump round face becoming serious and professional. "I suppose there's no sign of a mother – or father?"

Sam shook his head. "Shouldn't think we'll ever see 'er. They don't often turn up."

"Quite so, quite so," acknowledged the other, who then went on, "Apart from having to circumcise him, your baby really is a perfect specimen. He'd been very well looked after, and I was surprised when the sister told me he'd been abandoned in the street the way he was. It always makes me so angry when I hear of such things. But, of course, we don't know the circumstances, do we? It's generally to do with money – or rather, the lack of it. Poor woman ... she must have been in hell to do such a terrible thing."

"P'raps she'd been abandoned, too. By the father," suggested Sam, who had dealt with many similar cases before, though never one in which he'd been so personally involved.

Dr Levy nodded, almost absently, and continued squinting owl-like through his pebble lenses at Sam. "Who knows what was in the poor girl's mind. She must have been desperate to abandon this handsome fellow. Well, at least she didn't drop him in the river."

"P'raps that's what she done wiv 'erself, doctor," said Sam thoughtfully. "How old do you reckon 'e is?"

"Well, the sister and I concluded he was about ten days old, possibly a day or so older. She said the baby had been baptised as Jarvis Brook, and that you'd provided the name. Where on earth did you dig that name up? One of your villains, I suppose?"

Sam gave a laugh and explained about the carrier-bag, and the doctor mused, "Well, I expect the sisters will change it to something more Christian."

"Oh, I hope not," said Sam, appalled at the suggestion.

"One thing we can decide, perhaps a little more accurately, is Master Jarvis Brook's birthday," said Dr Levy, scribbling some sums on an envelope. "Today is the 26th, and we think his lordship's somewhere between ten and fourteen days old. So, let's split the difference and say he was born on – we'd better make it the fourteenth, rather than the thirteenth; we don't want to wish any more bad luck on him, do we! So, there it is, Jarvis: September 14, 1925. And, in case no one's said it to you before ... a very happy birthday and a long life to you, Jarvis Brook."

"God bless," echoed Sam fervently.

"Amen," concluded the doctor.

With Queenie constantly demanding news of her godson and accusing him of dragging his feet, and even dereliction of duty, Sam –

who was quite as interested in Jarvis's future – called at the Convent of Our Lady of Sorrows only to be informed by the Mother Superior, Sister Beatrice, that, in pursuance of Father O'Shea's last wishes, the future of Jarvis Brook was already well in hand. A Sister Catherine had taken him in charge and was even now securing his official future as regards documentation and home. Sister Beatrice really didn't know a great deal more and told Sam he must look elsewhere for the answers.

He did so, and learned that Sister Catherine – Sister Kate as she was known on all but very formal occasions – had swept into Charing Cross Hospital like a shimmering explosion of sunshine, and immediately captured the hearts of everyone, dispersing an aura of goodness and joy all about her. She may well have been enveloped from head to foot in shapeless, repressive black, apart from her white wimple, but there could be no doubting that she was a real beauty – even if only her face was visible, and not much of that.

And Sam knew beauty could move mountains. Sister Kate, a State Registered Nurse and Midwife and destined to pursue a missionary vocation in Malaya, had been instructed to expedite the smooth transition of Jarvis Brook to the jurisdiction, and protection, of the convent, and she wasted no time. She had no trouble obtaining a birth certificate, the Registrar voicing little surprise at her request on behalf of a bastard child of the parish, and filling in the meagre details the certificate demanded. It seemed quite in order that the child should have a complete set of names, even that its birthday should have been determined, but that no scrap of information should exist concerning either parent; such deficiencies were all too common, the more so since the war. The production of a baptismal certificate was a real bonus.

Armed with these certificates, she arrived a couple of days later at the forbidding offices of the council's Social Welfare Board, off Kingsway, where, upon seeing their stony faces, she took a deep breath and proceeded to win over the hearts of a triumvirate of officials. It was as if she cast a spell wherever she went. The trio, representing as they did the full majesty of the Borough Council, decreed that Jarvis be placed in the care and protection and sole authority (under the auspices of the council, of course) of the sisters of Our Lady of Sorrows in perpetuity, or at any rate, until he became of age; in the case of orphans this was generally regarded as being about fourteen, but, in fact, was more often twelve or even ten. It all depended on the level of the child's intelligence and whether it could be apprenticed out.

Then, with extraordinary magnanimity, the trio further authorised payment to the convent bursary the sum of six shillings a week for the maintenance of the boy (the going rate was supposed to be a shilling a day, but the State, in its bureaucratic ignorance, assumed God took over the responsibility on the Sabbath), with the promise of an extra six pence weekly, annually awarded, in the event of the child surviving its tenth anniversary. Such generosity was rare, and Sister Kate gave a radiant smile of gratitude, bobbed a curtsy and tip-toed hurriedly away ... just in case there should be a change of heart.

Six weeks after his arrival at Charing Cross Hospital, Sister Kate removed Jarvis to Our Lady of Sorrows Convent's crèche. Both were about to start their separate lives: Jarvis was headed for a kindergarten at Hayes in Middlesex, and Sister Kate was about to begin her life as a missionary. A passage to Singapore had been booked for her, and from there she would make her own way to her ultimate destiny in the Malayan hinterland.

At the crèche, Sister Kate took a last lingering look at the baby who had become a very precious charge. For a few short weeks each had meant everything to the other. Now, she was about to relinquish her tenuous hold on Jarvis for ever. Instinctively, she bent and brushed his forehead with her lips in a feather touch. "Goodbye little Jarvis," she whispered. "Have a good life, little one."

She left him, asleep and blowing tiny bubbles, and resolutely refused the temptation to look back. "God bless you, Jarvis," she mouthed silently, squeezing back the moistness that welled in her so-blue eyes. She didn't suppose they would ever meet again.

☐   *Queenie admitted that from now on her story was almost wholly indebted to the remembrances of others, especially Jarvis himself; she had plagued many sources – his many homes, his teachers, anybody she could find – for the slightest intelligence concerning her godson. She was blessed with both being a remarkable listener and having an extraordinary retentive memory, plus the ability to talk endlessly – and tell a good tale.*

Jarvis was probably about four when he began to be conscious of his existence and to take notice of his surroundings. He knew his name was Jarvis Brook and that he came from London and was an orphan. He knew this word meant he had no parents, but this didn't mean much to him; since he didn't have any, he didn't miss them.

He was looked after by nuns at a convent called the Madonna in Hayes. They were very strict, and very religious. They seemed to like him well enough, even when they smacked him and made him cry for being naughty. Jarvis didn't properly know what being naughty was, but he thought he must have been very good at it.

Possibly his first real memory of life was of long rows of chamber-pots crowding out into the passageway from a large washroom, on which a score of toddlers sat straining each morning. It was a very serious business for them because, young as they were, they knew they would not be allowed to get up until they had done something.

Sometimes there would be tearful days when some simply could not oblige: then the sisters would ladle large doses of cod liver oil, or syrup of figs or some other horrid mixture, into their mouths and await results. Happily it seldom presented any personal difficulty to Jarvis.

Perhaps the main reason why four was such a landmark in Jarvis's life was because it was about then that Biddy was dismissed when she became pregnant – Sarah-know-all, who was eight – which seemed very old when you were four, told them this meant she was going to have a baby. They all sighed, because if Biddy had wanted a baby, couldn't she have picked one of them? Especially him. Biddy, who had been a lay helper, was a particular favourite because she was a pretty, jolly girl who used to laugh and play with them, and share their little secrets; instead of endless sermons, she held them spellbound with wondrous fairy stories. They all cried when she left, even Sarah.

However, life galloped on and Jarvis continued being naughty, and paying the price; the sisters said he was quite the naughtiest boy Madonna had ever known – and far from being mortified, Jarvis felt quite proud to have achieved such distinction.

The worst "really good hiding" Jarvis could remember, and it wasn't long after Biddy left, was when he ran away – apparently he already had a propensity for doing this. He was sure he had no real thought of running away – not in his slippers, but there it was, he found himself beside the village pond chatting to the ducks and who should appear beside him but P.c. Ernest Binns. Jarvis hadn't heard him approaching, but, all of a sudden, there he was blotting out the sun. Apart from giving him a start, he looked a friendly sort, if a trifle too large to be a real friend. Jarvis liked his smart uniform, and especially marvelled at his tall hat with its shiny badge. He seemed startled when Jarvis told him his name, almost like he knew him. "I'm looking for our Biddy. She's gone away," Jarvis confided, and he really didn't think he was telling a falsehood because he would dearly have loved to find her. P.c. Binns asked him lots of questions about what he knew about himself, which wasn't a lot, except that Jarvis now knew that he was born in St Giles in London; and in the end he hoisted Jarvis up on his shoulders, which Jarvis thought was great fun, and returned him to Madonna, and there was Sister Clare, the Mother Superior, to welcome him home; and what a reckoning followed, with Jarvis ending up howling in the corner.

Jarvis resolved there and then to be a much better boy in future, but he became very familiar with that corner. He seemed unable to stay out of trouble long. He was always dreaming up wonderful adventures that ended up with several of them visiting that little room. He was always the leader in these escapades and, really, it didn't seem to him that they were doing anything terribly wrong. But twice more P.c. Binns, who Jarvis discovered had red hair, returned him to the Madonna after further jaunts abroad. Jarvis couldn't help feeling that Mr Binns always seemed pleased to see him, and always asked lots of questions about how he was getting on, and once he asked Jarvis if he remembered someone called Queenie, though Jarvis supposed he meant the Queen (as if he'd know *her*!), and yet, they only ever met when Jarvis was in trouble.

When Jarvis wasn't standing in familiar corners, he surprised the sisters, particularly Sister Clare, who frequently expressed the view that he was destined to "come to a sad end" if he didn't mend his ways, by turning out to be very good at his lessons. Jarvis confounded everyone even more by showing a startling linguistic flair, which transpired quite by accident. Italian. It had been meant as a punishment – well, a means of keeping him out of mischief. Sister Natalie, who had come from Modéna in Italy thirty years before and still spoke with an accent, was cook there and they got along famously, with Jarvis turning out to have this language bent, and her feeding him tit-bits from her kitchen. By the time Jarvis left the convent, he was fluent in Italian.

But this private little Italian world of theirs was sometimes invaded by events claiming precedence, the most momentous of which was adoption. They all accepted being orphans as their lot in life and, in their hearts, none of them had any great expectation of any change in their status; but they did dream, and the chiefest of all their wildest dreams was to be adopted. *Adoption* ... they clung to this word as soon as they had learned its meaning; all their energies were directed at achieving it; they prayed, secretly and earnestly in bed, and whispered to God that just one parent would do if there wasn't enough to go round. Jarvis survived the heartache of being passed over three times at adoption line-ups. A dark melancholy persisted among them after each of these line-ups. They all learned to cry inside to hide their misery after each rejection.

In the seven years Jarvis spent at Madonna only eleven boys – he forgot the number of girls, except that Sarah-know-all was among them – were adopted. Actually, the total was twelve, but one boy, Robin Something-or-other, had been returned within a week by a young couple who said they'd changed their minds, and wanted a girl instead. Robin never recovered from the trauma of his rejection; he never spoke another word, and about a month after his return he was found floating among the ducks in the village pond. They were told he had fallen in while feeding the ducks, but no one believed that. Sarah whispered something about a broken heart. P.c. Binns appeared, looking very serious, and held long conversations with Sister Clare and others, before plodding away shaking his head. In the end, they all said lots of prayers for poor Robin and his broken heart, and duly forgot him.

The last of these bitter disappointments was two months ago, and now, there were new, more urgent, matters to hold his attention.

Jarvis was about to embark on the next phase of his life: he was leaving Madonna for St Hilda's Academy in Holborn in London. He was the only one being sent there. He wasn't told why and assumed, with a certain smugness, that it was because he was thought something of a bad influence and, therefore, best kept apart from the rest of the children. Whatever the truth of the matter, Jarvis was excited because he was facing something new: it was all high adventure to him.

The journey to London was made in a charabanc and, to Jarvis's astonishment, there behind the wheel was P.c. Binns, who apparently occupied himself at a variety of other jobs when he wasn't being a policeman. Today, he was their bus driver and was, therefore, addressed with rather less formality as plain Mr Binns. As Jarvis climbed aboard the bus, he favoured him with a broad grin, ruffled his hair and remarked, "On yer way 'ome at last, heh, Master Jarvis! Soon be among yer friends now." Jarvis had no idea what friends he meant, and offered him a brief "Morning" and a muttered, "Don't know who you mean, Mr Binns ... I don't know anybody in London," before disappearing to the back of the vehicle, while P.c. Binns laughed out loud as though Jarvis had said something awfully funny.

All too soon the ride neared its end. Jarvis waved farewell to his former playmates, each clutching a brown paper bundle that contained all their worldly possessions (the smallness of the packages showed how very little any of them possessed), who were dropped off like so many parcels of laundry at Gunnersbury Park where they were taken charge of by two nuns and marched away to God knows where, and then he settled his gaze on the last vestige of the past: the back of Mr Binns's head. He had just decided it was as much orange as red, when Mr Binns turned, gave him a wink and motioned him to come forward.

"Sit yerself 'longside of me, young Jarvis, we ain't got far t'go now," he said, in a conversational manner. Presently, he muttered "Almost there, we is. See!" He jabbed a stubby finger at a high, grimy wall. "That's yer new 'ome, boy! St Hilda's Academy, Holborn."

Jarvis had moved up alongside him as directed and as his eyes followed the direction of the finger, his heart slithered icily down into his boots. He stared, and the longer he stared the less impressed he became. There were spikes all along the top of the wall, and on its pitted face were any number of signs informing passers-by that bill-posters would be prosecuted. He felt immediately homesick for his lovely Madonna and the green fields that surrounded it. This looked alarmingly like a prison, and he supposed this was the real reason only he had been chosen to come here. His lower lip wobbled, but he clenched his jaw tightly, refusing to cry.

"An' 'ere's summ'ne come special to say 'allo to yer – an' bin waitin' blinkin' years ter do so," announced Mr Binns, rather dramatically, casting a wary eye up and down the street. "But be sharpish abaht it 'cos I ain't s'pposed ter stop 'ere fer nuffink, see." After another quick look around, he put a finger to his fat lips and gave Jarvis a quick, confidential wink. He seemed to be enjoying himself immensely, and Jarvis couldn't understand why.

The coach shuddered to a clanging standstill close to an entrance with a great iron gate, and Jarvis found himself gazing straight into the face of a woman he'd never seen before in his life. She looked very big, all over, and was almost bursting out of her drab green coat and was wearing a yellowish, wide-brimmed hat like a sou'wester with some multi-coloured flowers pinned to it. Jarvis was fascinated by the joyous expression on her face and supposed she was something to do with Mr Binns. But, it was him she was laughing at, and Jarvis stared back with even greater wonder at her mouthful of uneven yellow teeth. He decided that he quite liked her face: it was so downright happy. He gave her a small, hesitant smile, since Mr Binns seemed intent on ignoring her so far as civilities were concerned, and was startled when she thrust a little packet at him through the open window.

"'Allo, Jarvis, me precious boy!" she shouted up at Jarvis. "Gosh, ain't you growed!" she cried, her voice seemingly choked with emotion. "Ain't you 'andsome! I could hug yer!"

"Hallo," Jarvis replied, in a voice so weak it was barely more than a whisper. He clutched the packet she'd given him, but continued to stare mesmerized at the woman. She was a complete stranger, yet she acted like she not only knew him, but he was her best friend. How was that possible? How did she even know his name? Who was she? Could ... Oh God! could she be his ... he couldn't say the word ; couldn't even hold it in his thoughts, but his heart gave an almighty leap that was exquisitely painful. "Who are you?" Jarvis managed to gasp out after an age, but he couldn't be sure she heard him. At that moment, the iron gates swung open and a cassocked-figure waved the coach in. "We gotta go," cried Mr Binns, and shouted a "'Bye!" as the bus lurched noisily through the gates, which shut the moment they passed them.

"Gawd bless yer, dearie! Welcome 'ome, lovey!" bawled the woman who'd followed the bus as far as the gate, and now stood behind its prison bars waving her arms like a windmill gone mad.

Jarvis rushed to the rear of the vehicle to gaze back at her, and it was only then that he saw the little girl clutching tightly at her coat. She looked about three years old. She was a little wisp of a thing, with a white felt hat and a lot of dark hair pushing out from underneath. She waved at him with her free hand. They both waved, and continued to do so with great enthusiasm. Instinctively, Jarvis waved back, timidly at first, and then he was waving with no less vigour than them; and he threw in a wide smile for good measure, which he hoped they could see through the forbidding bars. Suddenly life didn't seem so empty any more. London didn't seem so awful after all.

Jarvis turned his attention to the momentarily forgotten package, tearing at the paper tied with blue ribbon, and pulled out a little wooden soldier. It was a guardsman, complete with busby, and about ten inches high; it was plainly handmade, and handsomely painted. He stared bemusedly at it, and then hugged it to him, gripping it tightly in his sticky fist. He loved it. And it was his! Well, he supposed it was. He'd never had a toy that was all his own before; he'd never had a real present, come to that, other than clothes around his birthday and a stocking of fruit and sweets at Christmas – but they weren't proper presents, really, were they? Toys, which were all shared, belonged to the Home and remained there. He carefully pushed the soldier inside the small paper parcel which contained everything else he owned.

Jarvis turned for another look, wanting to show his thanks to the woman for the wonderful gift, but neither she nor the girl was visible, only the formidable iron gates that looked determined to keep him their prisoner. He wondered who on earth they could be, especially the woman ; she looked a very motherly sort of person. He wished he knew if she were his ; but he knew he mustn't be silly about such things. Miracles didn't really happen. Only in the Bible book. But, if ... again he closed his mind to the thought and started to fold the wrapping paper that had contained his surprise present, and only then found the card that he'd missed in his excitement. One side was covered with flowers, apparently crayoned by childish fingers; on the other side, in a more mature but painstaking scrawl, was the startling message addressed to Jarvis Brook:

"If ever you need help, ask for Queenie Hoggins or Sam Trotter at The Seven Dials in St Giles."

The words were followed by a regiment of kisses.

□ *Queenie paused to dab at a couple of tears. "That were me, 'course. I were that 'appy to see little Jarvis all growed up, like. I 'adn't seen 'im since he were a tiny baby, just a coupla months old, though Ernie Binns give us a photo once wiv sev'ral kids in it, including our Jarvis." Beard looked up from his bed, and said, kindly, "And you think I'm this little devil?" Queenie gave him a searching look and smiled, "Oh, yes, lovey, you're my Jarvis all right." Beard returned her smile and said, "If so, I sound all right – so far. When did I become a soldier?" "Oh, not for years yet," chuckled Queenie, "there's lots to tell 'fore then." Beard stared at her, and frowned. "Is there a Ruth in this story?" "Good heavens, yes!" cried Queenie, laughing. "You'll meet her presently. Now, listen."*

And the story continued.

Chapter Eight

Holborn, London, 17 September, 1932

As Jarvis stepped down from the charabanc, hugging his parcel of belongings, he looked up at his new home, saw its faded red bricks and the three rows of windows, some of which had iron bars, and it seemed even more like a prison. The rows of curtainless windows stared glassily back at him. He sighed at their unfriendly faces, and sighed again as he remembered how eager he'd been to come here; he felt even more homesick for his dear Madonna, and especially Sister Natalie and her kitchen.

But he was given no time for wishful day-dreams, not even the opportunity to ask Mr Binns about the woman who had been waiting to welcome him at the gates. A voice asked if he was Brook, and when he admitted that he was – which he only did after a moment or two, for he had only ever been called Jarvis before and he'd almost forgotten this other name of his – it commanded Brook to follow him, and he found himself hurrying in the wake of a black-robed figure, without the chance of a backward glance nor even a quick whispered goodbye, although he was vaguely aware of Mr Binns calling "Keep yer pecker up, Jarvis," after him.

A few moments later Jarvis was standing before Father Hugh, the Rector, and was even more sure that he had been sent to prison. Jarvis was standing in the rector's study, and the smile which he had been rehearsing died before it could reach his lips, and joined his heart in his boots. Father Rector looked as gloomy as the two holy men in the prints on the wall, and it crossed Jarvis's mind that they might be relatives. He was tall and very thin; and apart from little grey tufts about the ears, he was completely bald.

Father Rector fixed Jarvis with his stern, grey eyes and, after a long minute, picked up a sheet of paper and stabbed a bony finger at it. "Now, it says here," he said, "that you're a mischievous boy. Is this true, Brook?"

"I s'pose," Jarvis sighed, hanging his head wearily. So, Sister Clare had reported his occasional misdeeds, he thought bitterly. He felt betrayed.

"No more!" the other retorted, loud and clear. "It also says that you are good at your lessons. You will continue to be so, d'you understand?"

"Yes, Father Rector," Jarvis cried, nodding his head furiously. So, Sister Clare was not so unkind after all; she had been fair, perhaps even generous. He felt so much better for knowing this. He didn't like to be thought of as wholly bad. Thank you, Sister.

Father Rector steepled his long fingers, pressing the tips together so that they became very white, and fixed Jarvis so hard with his gaze that he was compelled to settle his own eyes elsewhere. "I warn you, Brook, any transgression from the rules here will be most severely punished." He paused and plucked a willowy cane from a number in a large and highly polished brass shell case, which Jarvis hadn't noticed till now, and brought it down across his desk with a swish that set his loose papers dancing, and caused Jarvis to nearly jump out of his boots.

This reaction appeared to meet with Father Rector's approval for, after returning the cane to its holder, he parted his thin, colourless lips in what Jarvis took to be a smile. Whatever it might have been, it didn't last. In a moment, the fingers had resumed their steepling: the gaze had never wavered. After several minutes of silence, he rose to his feet, and Jarvis was amazed how much bigger he was than he had already supposed. In those halcyon days of long ago, Biddy used to tell them that the taller you were, the closer you were to God. It had been a sort of joke, but now Jarvis wondered. Father Rector stood about six-feet-five, so Jarvis figured he must be at least halfway to heaven. "Go off now, Brook," he said suddenly.

This, then, was Jarvis's introduction to his new home. He liked it even less the following morning when he was caned for the first time in his life: two swipes from a cane that was so willowy it seemed to wrap itself right round him. It stung horribly, even to the extent of squeezing a sob and several deep intakes of breath from him. And this was just for speaking during a Latin lesson. He'd only turned to ask a boy what it was all about because he'd never had it as a lesson before; he didn't even know it was a school subject; he thought it was something just for church. Jarvis slunk away, rubbing his backside and wishing the material of his trousers wasn't so threadbare.

He met Robert Beard in the playground the following day. He was bigger than him, bigger by two years, with cropped black hair and large bright black eyes with longish lashes. He was very thin – like him, but he still looked to Jarvis to be very sturdily built, being far better muscled than himself. Jarvis noticed this particularly because the boy was swaggering towards him in a very aggressive manner, and with a leer about his thin mouth which made him look exceedingly fearsome. Jarvis could have moved out of his way, but even at seven he could be quite stubborn when it came to standing up for himself and, besides, he didn't see why he should. In the next moment, it was too late anyway. The boy barged straight into Jarvis and then pushed him so violently in the chest that he toppled over on to his back. At this point he cheerfully informed Jarvis that he didn't like his face.

Jarvis was more cross than hurt as he sat panting in the dust of the quadrangle and, ignoring the crowd of boys who quickly formed a ring around them, refused to be intimidated by the huge frame towering over him. Jarvis picked himself up rather quicker than perhaps was wise, and confided, loudly, in case there should be any doubt in the mind of his antagonist, that his own face held no great attraction for him; he disliked it, too – and told the other so as firmly as he was able. The boy, who had commenced sparring like a boxer before Jarvis as soon as he was back on his feet, jabbing out threatening punches well short, like he was shadow-boxing, came to an abrupt standstill as Jarvis said his piece and stared back in astonishment; and then, his face clouding with rage at such impudence, he swung an almighty blow which caught Jarvis on the side of the head and sent him crashing to the ground again.

This time Jarvis was more wary in rising, giving his whirling head a chance to sort itself out. When he did move, he was like a pocket dynamo. As he straightened up, Jarvis butted his adversary so violently in the pit of his stomach that he doubled up, and as his head sagged, his mouth agape and whooshing air, Jarvis flailed at him for all he was worth, raining rights and lefts blindly. There was no science, and precious little power, behind the blows, many of which missed their target altogether, but by the time a strong hand forcefully parted them by the scruff of their necks, the other boy had a split lip, a bloody nose and an eye that was already puffing up, so the ferocity of Jarvis's whirlwind assault must have been pretty effective, if not lastingly damaging.

Still breathing heavily from their exertions, both were ordered to touch their toes while their backsides were stingingly dusted with a cane that fairly shrieked through the air, or perhaps it was they who shrieked and the cane merely whistled. Jarvis knew they both hopped and yelped as each stinging blow landed, and strove furiously to check the tears that gathered behind their clenched lids. At the conclusion of their punishment, they grudgingly complied – with as much ill-grace as they dared to exhibit – with the order to shake hands. Then, having spent several moments eyeing one another warily, each of them rubbing his smarting behind, Jarvis's fellow sufferer introduced himself.

"They call me Scruffy," he declared, with a boastful air.

Jarvis wasn't sure that he cared what *they* called him, but he thought he'd better make the best of things. "Brook – Jarvis Brook," he returned coolly, still on his guard. Scruffy was plainly a nick-name, though it suited him exceedingly well for his clothing was even more ragged than his own – but, then, he hadn't been in the sole care of nuns until a few days ago.

"It's not me real name, 'course. It's Beard: Robert Beard – but I always bin called Scruffy. I 'spect it's cos of me name – Beard. Get it?"

"Yes," Jarvis said, who didn't really get it.

"You fight good, mate," said Scruffy cheerily, dabbing gingerly at his nose, which was still trickling blood, with his shirt sleeve.

"Thank you, Scruffy," Jarvis beamed, his chest bursting with pride. "So do you."

They turned towards the main building, for Scruffy had been told to go to the infirmary to be patched up. "Wot they call yer – Brook, or Jarvis?"

"Jarvis, mostly," Jarvis replied, although they didn't seem to do so here.

Scruffy didn't care for either name. "I'll call yer Biffer – after Tommy Farr, the boxer," he declared.

"If you like," Jarvis muttered, none too impressed at this further change to his name. He'd never heard of Tommy Farr, but he thought he'd sooner be called Tommy than this ... Biffer-name. Still, he felt it'd have to do for the moment.

"Where you from, Biffer?"

"A Home in Hayes. It was called Madonna."

"No—oh, stupid!" snorted Scruffy contemptuously, "I mean, where was yer borned?"

"Right here, in London. I was found right here, so the sisters said," Jarvis answered indifferently, never having given the location of his birth much thought. He'd been told he came from St Giles in the Borough of Holborn, only he didn't know whereabouts in London this was.

"It's in t' Borough of Camden now, stupid," corrected Scruffy scornfully.

"It's still in London though, isn't it?" pressed Jarvis, uninterested in the name of either borough.

"'Course, stupid," snapped Scruffy.

"What I really meant, I s'pose, is where in London. I don't know if it's somewhere near here, or where it's at. I don't know anything about London. All I know is that I'm an orphan, same as you – an' ev'ryone else 'ere, I s'pose."

Scruffy seemed to be on the point of repeating his favourite "stupid" word, but instead muttered, "Well, I ain't got no parents – not now, so I'm a orphan, same's the rest of yer. But," he edged closer so that he bumped into Jarvis, and whispered, "I got an aunt!"

"Crikey!" Jarvis exclaimed, suitably impressed, and suitably jealous, too. He had no idea what an aunt was, but it did appear to be someone worth having. After a moment, he frowned and asked, all suspicious, "Why aren't yer livin' wiv this aunt of yourn, then?"

"'Cos no one can't find 'er, that's bleedin' why!" growled Scruffy, his voice full of annoyance, and menace. Jarvis took a precautionary step backwards in case Scruffy decided that he was to blame, but Scruffy only scowled at him for a moment, and then his face softened somewhat. "'Er name's Dolly," he went on, fairly composedly. "Don't know 'er ovver name 'cos she went an' got married, didn't she, an' nobody don't know who to. I ain't never seed 'er in m'life ... so far's I know."

Jarvis was unable to contain his curiosity any longer. "Scruffy, wot exactly is an aunt?" he asked.

"It's a sister of yer parents – a bruvver would be yer uncle," he replied, after giving Jarvis a long suspicious look as though unable to believe anybody could be that ignorant. "In my case, she were me Mum's sister ... an' she lives somewhere up north. Gawd alone knows where. We lived in Wapping, see, an' I was barely two when me Mum and Dad was drowned in the Thames. Ferry sank, so I was told. Anyways, there weren't nobody around wot wanted me – so 'ere I am."

Jarvis had never known anybody who might be able to remember their parents and he started to ask Scruffy about them, but Scruffy cut him short with a scornful "Naa–aah!" and a vigorous shake of his head. "But," he declared very seriously, "we're still lookin' fer me Aunt Dolly. We won't never give up. Never."

Jarvis was disappointed Scruffy didn't remember anything about his parents; he was clearly only interested in this aunt person. "Who's this *we* who's lookin' for yer aunt?" he asked hurriedly to hide his feelings.

"The Church! That's who, Biffer-mate," replied Scruffy importantly, and with a smile of satisfaction as though Aunt Dolly was just round the corner.

"Oh," Jarvis said, in a somewhat deflated voice. It certainly didn't strike him as being so promising, not if *they* didn't know the aunt's name. "How they going to find 'er, then?"

"Dunno," shrugged Scruffy, looking away. Then, in a confidential tone, and gently touching his bruised nose in a knowing manner and giving Jarvis a wink with his good eye, he declared: "They got their ways."

"Oh," Jarvis said again, no more impressed..

And so his term at St Hilda's began. He'd made a friend, and they remained friends until Scruffy was twelve and he had to be transferred to a more senior establishment. In the years between they formed a gang and called themselves The Bullets. There were six of them, with Jarvis the leader. They were chiefly concerned with having mischievous fun, generally in defiance of authority. It was a pleasure for which they paid the supreme penalty many a time, but they seemed to consider the excitement engendered by their escapades worth the brief pain; they simply took the canings in their stride as being part of everyday life.

Their pranks, Jarvis supposed, were silly and trivial – like glueing the chapel organ keys together on the eve of an important Feast Day, nailing a pair of long johns (and from the length of the legs they could only be Father Rector's) to the flagpole in place of the Papal flag, removing the clapper from the Angelus bell and letting off stink bombs at morning assembly to name just a very few – but they gave them a lot of fun. Of course, they exhausted and infuriated the priests and brothers, but that was part of the fun, too.

They survived to harass the brethren for two breathless years, and then, in a flash, their reign was ended by the simple expedient of breaking up the sextet. This came about, not by any sudden inspiration on the part of the academy's hierarchy, but because most of the gang's members simultaneously attained the age of twelve, which meant them being transferred to senior establishments. Jarvis was the odd one out, being under ten, and stayed behind at St Hilda's. The rest were despatched with unkindly haste across the Thames to Battersea: to a grimy complex with the somewhat whimsical name of St Boniface.

Jarvis saw a daguerreotype print of St Boniface (the building, not the saint) once in Father Rector's study (no need to say what he was doing there); it looked more like a Victorian prison than the real thing, and he subsequently learned it had been a workhouse until fairly recently. Jarvis felt quite sorry for poor Scruffy & Co – but only for a few moments. Jack Plant, who had been like his second-in-command, was sent to work on a farm after a few months, but Jarvis learned later that when still a month short of thirteen he disappeared on a horse, which was later found tethered outside a pub miles away. Jack then appeared to simply vanish off the face of the earth. Jarvis thought this was marvellous. He'd been a true Bullet, and Jarvis so envied his disappearing achievement.

If the Bullets hadn't been broken up in this way, leaving Jarvis all on his own, it is quite probable that none of the things that occurred subsequently would ever have happened; but there he was, alone at St Boniface, and those extraordinary events did take place; they had such an effect on his life that it was as if he were reborn.

Chapter Nine

Holborn, London, 12 August, 1937

After the break up of The Bullets, Jarvis was at a loss how to use up all his energies, for he could raise no enthusiasm for continuing his former escapades on his own. Of course, he still indulged in little bits of mischief, but the enjoyment he used to experience from them paled, and with the start of a new term he found himself turning his energies to his lessons.

After a brief interview with Sister Beatrice, the Mother Superior of the convent across the road, Jarvis resumed his Italian lessons under Sister Paula, and was glad to find he had forgotten nothing that Sister Natalie had taught him. In fact, because his Italian was so complete, and a young German lady, Fräulein Hildegard Schumacher, was teaching there, it was suggested that her language be added to his curriculum. And so, three days a week he learned German, and twice a week Sister Paula and he chatted away in Italian. It didn't leave him much opportunity to get into trouble, which he suspected was the whole idea.

These linguistic lessons had been Father Rector's suggestion, and he further decreed that since Jarvis had this flair for languages, he might add his mother tongue to the list. Jarvis didn't immediately grasp that he was being sarcastic. Be that as it may be, Father Rector soon had the boys' teachers drilling them, by rote, in the King's English. They shouted out the vowels as they'd never been heard before in a ghastly explosion of accents, and when their tutors had recovered from this cacophony, the boys started on the words: those words the priests thought suitable for their Catholic ears. They were at it more than a year, and though some of them did come to talk *proper*, they never quite lost the accents that they'd grown up with. And so there was Jarvis speaking Italian, German and English, but still saying his prayers in Latin, which he didn't understand.

Several notable things occurred in the year leading to his eleventh birthday. The most outstanding – well, that's what he thought at the time – was the realisation that from his tenth birthday he qualified to receive pocket money, at the rate of one penny a week. The rate would rise by a further penny each year up to a maximum of six pence, but he was told no one had ever been still in residence to receive such a whopping sum; all payments ceased the instant a boy, at whatever age, was apprenticed out or left the Home for any other reason. However, his initial excitement over how he'd spend his sudden wealth quickly diminished when he was told that acts of misbehaviour, of even the most minor sort, could reduce the allotment to nothing. Mostly, this was precisely what he received, and only once did he receive the full amount – he'd had chicken pox that week; usually, he was handed half-pennies, or farthings – but as he more often than not got nothing, he must have continued being a pretty mischievous boy. Whenever he was in possession of a copper or two, he entertained thoughts of becoming a banker.

There were ways of earning a little extra pocket money – by running errands for the staff. You didn't always get something, but on occasion you might be rewarded with a half-penny; more likely you got a thick ear if you were too long, as Jarvis mostly was. But he didn't mind, and he admitted it – he did dawdle. The trips gave him his only glimpse of the outside world and he made the most of them, to gape through the shop windows, his nose almost glued to the panes; to stare at everybody and everything, for they were all strange to him; and to listen to all the different sounds, especially the snatches of conversation he was able to overhear without a boot sending him crashing out of earshot.

Jarvis thought one of his biggest shocks on being allowed outside the walls of his prison was to discover there were so many people enjoying their freedom. There seemed to be millions – which was probably why he kept bumping into them and getting swiped at with sticks or brollies for his clumsiness.

One day, on one of these errand-running outings, he found a silver three-penny-piece standing on its side in a crack between the pavement slabs, and for a whole three days he clutched it in his pocket, not daring to let go of it, for the pocket was more hole than cloth and he didn't dare leave anything so valuable anywhere that lighter fingers than his own might get at it. The tiny coin occupied his thoughts for hours each day. In the course of them, he spent it over and over again, always on food – he forgot all about his ambition to become a banker. A chop, perhaps, though he gave no thought as to how he'd cook it : or some buns, big sticky ones : or some fruit, especially bananas, which he'd never seen. Never did a boy have better value for so small a coin than he did. However, the day came when he decided to spend it: safe-guarding it had become too much of a strain.

And then, he went and lost it!

In his excitement outside a shop exuding the tantalising aroma of piping hot eel pies which Jarvis found too tempting to resist, for he was permanently hungry, the coin slipped through his sticky fingers and rolled, ever so slowly, across the paving stones – and disappeared through a grating. He heard the sound as it plopped into the sewer, lost for ever, and his heart seemed to follow it. Jarvis remembered that he cried against an alley wall for several moments, quite unable to control his bitter anguish. But, he didn't think he cried for long, for hadn't he already forsworn such weaknesses? And besides, hadn't he had the pleasure of spending it time and time again in his dreams? He'd had his money's worth a hundred times over. It was his stomach that felt the loss most. Jarvis believed he was actually smiling, for all that he still stood with his head buried in his arms against the wall, when he heard a girl's voice behind him.

"What's the matter?" she asked, in a tiny but concerned voice. "Are you hurt? Is there something I can do to help? Please don't cry."

"I ain't cryin', you stupid fing! Bugger orf!" Jarvis snapped, wheeling round to face her, and quite forgetting his newly-learned *proper* English. She looked very small and very smart in her pale blue school dress and a sort of straw hat, kept in place by a piece of elastic under her chin; attached to a strap across her shoulder was a very small satchel, so small it was very little bigger than a purse. She looked about six, and had the sort of beauty that small children seem to possess as a matter of course, and which they still had even when they were angry. Right now she looked very angry indeed.

"Oh, you bad boy! That's swearing ... and very rude!" she exclaimed, in an outraged little voice, and stamping her tiny foot on the pavement. "That's a mortal sin."

"Push orf!" Jarvis jeered at her. "I'll bleedin' well sin if I wants. Wot's it to yer, eh?"

She stood gaping, her eyes large and round and her mouth wide open. Her face was quite white as she spluttered in a somewhat squeaky voice: "You'll go to hell and burn ... for ever and ever." And with that dire prophecy she hurried on down the street with her pigtails, black as the hell he was destined for, dancing just as angrily behind her.

"I 'spect so," he called after her, poking his tongue out at her indignant braids, and it was then that he spotted the wooden doll she clutched in her hand. He frowned, and couldn't immediately understand what exactly it was that puzzled him.

It was hours later that Jarvis realised what it was. He knew the moment he picked up George, his wooden guardsman and long-time treasured companion. George was almost the spitting image of the toy that girl had been holding. The only difference being that one was a soldier and the other a doll; they looked to have been carved from the same block of wood, and by the same hand. Quite suddenly, it seemed to Jarvis that he'd seen the girl before, too. Then, of course, he remembered. She definitely resembled that tiny thing standing beside Queenie that day he'd arrived at St Hilda's! He remembered wondering at the time if she was Queenie's daughter or something to do with Mr Binns, or both. He still didn't know.

It was no accident that Jarvis happened to choose that same route when next he was sent out to purchase something. He really did dawdle this time, continuously looking all round him, searching every little figure far and near, and sometimes darting down side-streets just on the off chance of spotting her, but he never did – although, on another occasion, he thought he had. He chased after her, pulled a pair of red-ribboned pigtails, and a perfect stranger turned and slapped his face, very hard. He responded by punching her in the eye and she set up such a hullabaloo – passers-by had laughed when she slapped him, but when he retaliated there were angry mutterings which he thought most unfair – that he dived down an alley, and subsequently kept well clear of the area; and duly forgot the girl and her wooden doll. Indeed, he gave poor George a few bashings for possibly being related to her.

In spite of his scholastic excellence, it was not in Jarvis to be good too often outside of the classroom, and there were several trips to Father Rector's study for the inevitable canings. There were other forms of punishment – like scrubbing floors, cleaning windows and other household chores – which were not nearly as acceptable; the one he particularly detested was having to sweep the vast courtyard out front all on his own.

He was engaged in this loathed occupation one hot summer's day when the dog-thing happened, and that would never have happened if the iron gates had been closed, as they should have been. The dog, that had the look of a wolf about it and colours, while mainly grey, that included some patches of black and brown, and even a blotch or two of leaf-green, evidently paint, trotted confidently, if not downright arrogantly, through the open entrance and, from a respectable distance, gazed circumspectly at Jarvis.

"Fuck off!" Jarvis told it conversationally, leaning on the brush he hadn't put to much use yet. The dog, encouraged, cocked a leg up and enjoyed a lengthy pee. "Piss orf, yer mucky sod!" Jarvis cried amiably, unconsciously lapsing into the sort of vernacularity that would not have pleased Father Rector. The dog, growing in confidence from the tone of his voice, padded forward a few paces, gave a friendly bark or two and promptly squatted down and crapped; and having done its business, as Jarvis stood mesmerised, it calmly wagged its much-mutilated tail and gave a bark of satisfaction. At this point, and with the realisation that he would have to clear up after it, his anger finally surfaced.

"Bastard!" Jarvis screamed at it, seething with resentment. "Get out of 'ere, yer filthy shit-bag!" he shouted, grabbing at the brush and hurling it at the dog, missing completely.

The animal retreated hastily, taken aback by the suddenly altered atmosphere. It eyed Jarvis quizzically, evidently unsure of its welcome, but as he maintained his menacing stance, it appeared to assume the worse for it bared its fangs and gave a series of snarls by way of retaliation. Jarvis responded by charging at the startled beast which gave an aggrieved whine, turned tail and streaked towards the gate with a final puzzled glance over its shoulder.

Jarvis pursued the dog through the gateway and chased it down the street. The dog, deciding that perhaps it was a game after all, wagged its tail and led him across Gray's Inn Road, to the vocal disconcertion of several motorists and a horse that was rudely awakened, over an impeccable patch of lawn, which gave rise to bellowed oaths and surly invitations to "sod off," through a maze of streets around the British Museum, and back along another jungle of tortuous streets, some of which were little more than passageways; and Jarvis finally lost the dog, and all interest in it, somewhere in the vicinity of Covent Garden.

After stooging around for what seemed ages, endeavouring to retrace his steps, Jarvis came to the conclusion that he was hopelessly lost; and further, that he hadn't the ghost of an idea as to the name of the street in which St Hilda's stood. It had never been necessary to know, and his few expeditions into the outside world running errands had not been wasted on reading street signs. Jarvis was contemplating what to do, even to the extent of wondering if it might not be appropriate to say some prayers, just to let God know where he was, when a policeman turned the corner and creaked towards him.

Jarvis swallowed his prayers and stared as the officer loomed nearer, briefly considered taking him into his confidence and confessing his predicament, then turned on his heel and hared down the street, darting down the first opening he came to. There was certainly no street sign here, but if there had been one Jarvis would have been too amazed to run any further, for it would have read: *Jarvis Brook*. He would have been even more surprised if he had known that the policeman from whom he was running as fast as his legs could carry him, was the very same Constable Sam Trotter who had found him a dozen years earlier little more than a hundred yards away on the steps of The Seven Dials.

But Jarvis knew none of these things then ... and he ran and ran like a frightened mouse looking for somewhere to hide, never knowing that he was running from safety towards terrible dangers.

Jarvis went on running until he ran out of breath. He stumbled to a full stop, gulping in air as beads of sweat raced down the small of his back and trickled into his eyes forcing him to blink, and leaned panting against a grimy wall. He looked wearily around, continuing to blink the wetness from his eyes, and peering through his straggly hair which cascaded damply over his forehead so that he could hardly see.

If Jarvis was lost before, he was doubly so now. He hadn't a clue where he was, but he realised quite suddenly that everyone about him was Chinese, which seemed crazy to him at the time. He was, of course, in Soho's Chinatown. But, he had no way of knowing that. His whole life had been confined within the walls of institutions, anything outside was an unknown world, and not to be trusted. He certainly didn't trust these yellow, slant-eyed faces around him: even the men had pigtails! And they wore long frocks, too! He ran for his life.

It seemed he had gone on running till it grew dark, and then he realised how hungry he was. God, was he hungry! His last meal, the thin morning porridge, was just a memory. He felt the knots gripping at his stomach and listened to the rumbling protests of his body, and decided that the worst of food was better than none at all. Unfortunately, this set him off thinking of food in general, especially the lack of it. Jarvis remembered when he'd first arrived at St Hilda's the porridge had been served with a ladle, a terribly small one; the younger boys got only one scoop, the older ones two. It had seemed exceedingly unfair to him, for he was certain his appetite was quite the equal, if not bigger, of theirs. As he himself grew older, he'd discovered that bigger boys did indeed need bigger portions, but he never did seem to get enough so, presumably, it was the portions that were inadequate; he was always hungry, even after a meal. Right now, having missed both dinner and tea, he knew he was starving. He gave thought as to how long he could live without food. Not very long, he decided.

Jarvis tore his thoughts away from food and turned his attention to the contents of his pockets. It didn't occupy much time, one pocket being completely bottomless and only kept together with a safety-pin, and yielding nothing of any immediate value; the other was like a bag of swag – 1¼d in sticky coins, a piece of string, two marbles, a crunched up pigeon's feather, a tiny lump of chalk, an empty sweet wrapper and a tram ticket he'd picked up while sweeping. He returned everything carefully back to his sound pocket, except the sweet wrapper. What had it been, what delicacy had it contained? Not having enjoyed its contents in the first place, he hadn't the faintest idea. Jarvis licked at the paper lingeringly, hopefully, endeavouring to savour its exquisite flavour, but could detect no hint of its former occupant, and finally discarded it as though with it went his last hope of survival.

Jarvis shivered. In spite of the heat of the day, it had turned quite cold and he had on only his grey shirt and short trousers. His knees felt positively blue with cold in the night air. He wished he had some socks to pull up, but these were only worn on special occasions – Sundays, and the like. After rubbing his legs vigorously, which brought only short-lived benefit, he retied the broken lace on one of his boots; his feet felt sore and cold inside the rough leather. He needed a new pair of boots, for his feet, like the rest of him, were constantly growing. But he didn't think he stood much chance of getting a pair of larger older boots, let alone new ones; might get some new laces, if he was lucky. He shivered again, and wondered what he should do. He knew he needed to find somewhere to sleep, and with this thought in mind he poked his head round the side of a shattered door of an abandoned building and ventured cautiously within. He emerged very much faster, having disturbed an army of rats that scurried about in all directions and squealed hysterically at his intrusion. He wasn't scared of rats, he suspected they contributed to his fare at St Hilda's, but he didn't particularly want to sleep with them.

His appearance was greeted with equal resentment at two other empty hovels; indeed, in one a great grey rat clung to one of his boots with such tenacity that he had to hit it with a piece of piping he picked up. The rat squealed hideously and dragged itself away, and Jarvis yelped too at the pain he had inflicted on himself, and hobbled off. Eventually, he found a costermonger's barrow with a sheet of tarpaulin on it standing at the entrance to a yard in a cul-de-sac. After kicking out its occupant, a tortoiseshell cat which arched its back in anger at being disturbed so unceremoniously, he crept beneath the covering, swearing as splinters pricked his knees in the process, and hugged himself against the cold. Quite oblivious to the many strange night sounds, and completely forgetting his night prayers, Jarvis was asleep almost before the intrepid cat stole back to reclaim its resting place beside him.

They were both rudely awakened shortly after four in the morning by a somewhat startled man who discovered them as he started pushing the barrow out of the yard. The cat, fearful for all nine of its lives, shot over the side of the barrow, streaked across the cobbled yard and disappeared up and over a sheer brick wall. Unaccustomed to such spontaneous propulsion, and not entirely certain that it was necessary, Jarvis reacted with the immobility of one with no idea of what action to take. Besides, he was sure he was close to starving and wouldn't have the strength to get far. Jarvis blinked the stickiness of sleep from his eyes, stretched his aching limbs, and began to feel at least half awake, even though the moon – looking so fat and round, and altogether too well fed – was a long way off retiring and the sun was nowhere to be seen, and offered the stranger a tentative smile.

He glared back, but it was more from a deformity of his rheumy eyes than any positive malice. Jarvis saw now, in the dismal light, that he was a little squirrel of a man, but with a depth and width of chest that promised compensatory strength. He had a small, ugly face, glowing white in the moonlight in spite of its unshaven aspect, with a thin, scowling mouth, and long tawny hair slicked down with some evil-smelling substance akin to fish oil. He wore a blue-check, sweat-grimed neckerchief around his scrawny throat, a much-stained black leather waistcoat that bristled with pockets bulging with assorted impedimenta some of which protruded into view, a collarless khaki shirt and bits of string to keep his baggy black trousers above his hobnailed boots.

"Well, matey, an' who might you be?" he asked, with more curiosity than aggression, perching himself on a shaft of the barrow.

"Brook, sir – Jarvis Brook," Jarvis replied, in a very subdued voice, wondering if this was an occasion for speaking in a manner fit for Father Rector's ears, or as it flowed. Before he had made up his mind, Jarvis cursed himself. He should never have given his real name, that he did know. But it was too late now.

"Wotcher bin up to, boy?" asked the man, suspiciously, leaning forward till his greasy head was only a touch away.

"Nuffink. Nuffink at all – 'onest, mister," Jarvis answered, the words tumbling out at a gallop. He noticed that the man's fishy head wasn't the only thing about him that smelled. His breath was heavy with a strange and pungent odour, which was more over-powering than it was repulsive. He learned later that it was garlic which he chewed incessantly in the form of bread, and that he chewed tobacco to smother its smell, and aniseed to get rid of that smell – and doubtless something else to lose that sickly perfume.

"Wotcher doin' 'ere then?"

"Nuffink," Jarvis assured him again. "Only sleeping."

"You run away, or sumfink, ain'tcher, boy?" the other quizzed, slipping into a more conspiratorial voice, and rising to his feet to give a quick furtive look round for a possible eavesdropper.

"Yes, sir," Jarvis confessed.

"Where from? Where's yer 'ome?"

"I ain't got one. I'm an orphan."

"For Christ's sake, boy," cried the man impatiently, "yer lives in some bleedin' place, don'tcher? Else yer couldn't run away, could yer? So, where'd you run away from?"

"I ain't tellin' yer," Jarvis said determinedly, having decided that the man was nobody with any authority and, even if he should be, that it was probably safer to say as little as possible anyway. Having come to this somewhat belated decision, he jumped nimbly down from the barrow, ready to run if need be, but growing in confidence all the time, especially as the man was scarcely any bigger than him. It even began to cross his mind that he might be up to no good himself, else he wouldn't be about so early. Jarvis added bluntly: "I don't even know who you are."

"Fair nuff," the other shrugged, and the slight smile he showed did nothing to improve his looks, only revealing a number of discoloured teeth. "I got several names." His grin widened, and Jarvis saw some more awful fangs – and gaps where others should have been. "But the one I uses most, an' which is more'n likely me own, is Simkin Maggs. Gawd knows who dropped that first name on me – some bleedin' parson, I s'pose. Deserves to end up in 'ell fer such devilry, if yer arsks me. Anyway, I never uses it. You can call me Maggs – if yer wants."

"Thank you, Mr Maggs," Jarvis said instantly, and, now that he knew his name – at least, one of his names, he found himself thinking the man wasn't such a bad fellow after all.

"Just Maggs, no mister," he corrected, unruffled. "Now, Jarvis Brook," he said quite pleasantly, seating himself down on the barrow again, "p'raps you'll tell me wot yer doin' 'ere ... in me barrer?"

"Sorry, Maggs. Didn't know it were anybody's. I 'ad nowhere to go. I never meant to run away, really an' truly I didn't. I was chasin' this dog, an' I got lost."

"Dawg! Wot dawg!" cried Maggs, jumping up off the barrow as if it had suddenly become red hot and looking anxiously round the yard, peering into the darkest shadows to see if the animal was lurking there.

"He got lost, too," Jarvis said easily, surprised and rather amused that a grown man like Mr Maggs should be scared of a silly old dog, but careful not to show his amusement.

"You mark me words, young'n," confided Mr Maggs, after yet another look all round, "'ave nuffink to do wiv dawgs'n cats – no, nor wimmin, neither. They'll all do 'orrible fings to yer if they gets 'arf a bleedin' chance. Claw yer throat out, or yer eyes, an' rob yer blind soon's look at yer. Mark me words, boy. Steer a wide berth of 'em all."

"I will, I will," Jarvis assured him hastily, wondering who or what had dared to leave him so fearful.

"Dawgs is even worse'n wimmin," went on Mr Maggs confidentially, moving a step closer after another quick look round. "They'll bark, see, or do summat just as 'orrible – anyways, they give yer away to the rozzers."

"Oh," Jarvis said softly, and gave a nod for he knew what the word meant. Of course, he hadn't had any dealings with such people himself, 'cepting Mr Binns, and he weren't bad – for a rozzer.

"So, wot yer plannin' to do wiv yerself, lad? I mean now that you've gorn an' run away. Anyfink planned, like?"

"No. Nuffink."

"'Cos I can use a boy like you. You're a big lad an' look strong 'nuff," declared Maggs, giving Jarvis's shoulders and arms a rough squeeze. He gave the yard yet another elaborate search, seemed satisfied, and then stepped even closer, gripping Jarvis's arm like a vice and whispering directly into his ear. "They calls me the Tin Man, 'cos that's me business. Metals, an' fings. I sells 'em, see? That's wot I am, boy; a dealer. Only, I does most of me work – collectin' like – at night, when the rest of the world's asleep, if yer gets me drift."

Jarvis vaguely got the man's drift, and pulled his arm free and rubbed it furiously to restore the circulation. Of course he knew what the man was on about. He was a thief! A thief in the night! The expression sprang to mind. It seemed to have a certain romantic, adventurous ring to it. Of course, Jarvis knew it was wrong – but presumably someone had to do it ... people had to live, didn't they? If there weren't people like Maggs about, poor Mr Binns would be out of a job – an' starving. This thought, in conjunction with the many smells of which Maggs reeked, all of which appeared to have some association with food, only served to remind Jarvis of his hunger. Unable to contain himself any longer, he confessed to Maggs, alias the Tin Man, that he'd had no dinner yesterday and was in urgent need of sustenance, or he'd probably die –

and be of no use to anybody.

"Don't do that, matey," said Mr Maggs earnestly, eyeing Jarvis afresh, plainly weighing up his usefulness to him. "I've a need for a strong kid like you. An' I'll play fair wiv you, Jarvis-boy, 'cos I fink we un'erstands each other. I'll put brass in yer pocket an' fill yer belly to the brim. Only first, me ol' sparrer, we got to shift ourselves an' move some goods 'fore folks starts wakin' up – an' lookin' fer things wot ain't there no more. See. So tighten yer belt, young'n, fer a bit longer an' just follow me."

Jarvis gave a silent sigh, and wished he had a belt instead of the braces that were part of his everyday uniform and which chafed his shoulders. He didn't want to be a thief. He wanted to be back at the Home where he belonged. But, he convinced himself, right now there wasn't a lot he could do about putting things to right. He'd have to play along – and see where it led. He watched curiously as Maggs prepared to set off. Maggs produced two pieces of black rubber with loops attached and told him to slip them over his boots "or yer'll wake the perishin' dead, let alone the rozzers." Jarvis noticed for the first time that Maggs already wore a similar covering under his own boots. As Jarvis fastened his rubbers, Maggs suddenly produced a hefty knob of darkish cheese from one of his waistcoat pockets and told him to chew on it and to keep up and, above all, to keep quiet. Jarvis, given no time to express his thanks, popped the titbit straight into his mouth; it was hard as a baked conker and grains of tobacco and other congealed foreign matter concealed whatever taste the cheese had, but he was grateful for whatever it was. After a moment, Maggs produced a crust of garlic bread from another waistcoat pocket and shoved it at Jarvis, who pushed it quickly into his mouth and was glad to find that it wasn't too stale. Then, after a final look around, they moved off, Maggs pushing the barrow and Jarvis chewing hungrily at his side.

Two things surprised Jarvis straight away: the first was the speed at which his companion propelled the barrow along seemingly miles of back streets, pausing only where they crossed others to cock an ear before racing on to the next junction; the second was the complete silence with which they progressed in the half-light of the early dawn. It was only after they had been travelling a good ten minutes, that Jarvis noticed the barrow was fitted with rubber tyres – much the same as we were. They trundled on, almost trotting, not a word passing between them, along endless streets, never seeing a soul, but twice wheeling abruptly down an alternative lane at the sound of not too distant footsteps. "Rozzer!" hissed Maggs warningly. Once, they saw – not twenty yards off – the figure of a constable plodding dejectedly away from them. "Constable Fogarty," whispered Mr Maggs knowledgeably. "'Is fancy bit must've kicked 'im out early. See wot I mean? Bleedin' unreliable, wimmin is. S'pose 'er ol' man must be on a new shift, poor bleeder." Jarvis wasn't quite sure whether his sympathies were for the "ol' man," who he assumed was the lady's husband, or the constable.

As soon as P.c. Fogarty was out of sight, they continued on their way, and never saw him, nor any of his colleagues, again. Indeed, the only incidents involved animals: two cats purring at each other and an extremely noisy, and nosy, dog. The cats were so engrossed with each other that they remained oblivious of their approach right up to the moment the barrow ran over them, when they parted with shrieks in opposite directions. The dog, a bull-terrier, intent on living up to its image as a guard dog, though what it was protecting Jarvis couldn't imagine, suddenly stirred from the gutter and proceeded to bark furiously and to snap at Maggs's ankles, and was hastily put to flight with a vicious kick (so vicious that Maggs ended up on his back from its impetus) in the face which considerably stifled its scream of agony. In those brief moments, Jarvis came to appreciate Maggs's aversion to such creatures. They were a downright menace – in his line of work.

Their journey took them at alarming speeds through the Aldwych, round the back of Fleet Street, even more rapidly across Farringdon Road where they saw their first signs of life, and up into Smithfield Market. Here, Maggs disappeared momentarily, squeezing between lines of vehicles all being frantically stuffed with carcasses of all shapes and sizes, and emerged presently with a bulging paper parcel under his arm and clutching half-a-yard of French bread containing two steaming sausages dripping with ketchup. He tossed the parcel under the tarpaulin and pushed the bread and stuff at Jarvis with instructions to "shove that down yer cake 'ole an' keep quiet." Jarvis obeyed both directions with gusto.

Almost before Jarvis was finished, and while still licking his finger tips, they were racing on again, swinging down to skirt London Wall until they were in sight of Moorgate. Here they moved with particular stealth through a couple of passages barely wide enough for the barrow, and finally stopped in a shadowy corner, shrouded by an ancient fig tree. They were in a small enclosed square with scores of tall windows staring accusingly down at them from elegant buildings. There was not a light to be seen anywhere, nor the faintest of sounds, save a distant hum of traffic. Alongside the corner in which they stood immobile, accustoming their eyes to the light of the square which even the fading light of the moon didn't touch, was a low brick wall surmounted with heavy steel railings. On the other side was a graveyard. In a trice, Maggs was perched on top of the wall. He removed a single loose railing, and wriggled through the gap.

"Wait 'ere, boy," he whispered down to Jarvis, in a voice so low it was barely audible. "When I 'ands you summat through this 'ole, grab 'old of it sharpish an' shove it outta sight under the tarp. Got it? Don't make a sound. Don't even breathe more'n you must. If yer 'ears anyfink, or sees anyfink, gimme a whistle like a jenny-wren – an' lie doggo."

Jarvis wanted to tell Maggs he didn't know what a jenny-wren sounded like, but he was gone, vanished with a silence in keeping with the surroundings. He reappeared as silently a few minutes later, stepping between the tombstones bowed down under a load of lead which he pushed, with some difficulty and much muffled profanity, through the opening. Jarvis took the load and all but crashed to the ground Beneath the great weight of it, but succeeded in shoving it reasonably quietly Beneath the tarpaulin. "Good," approved Maggs, who seemed to be breathing even heavier than Jarvis. "Heard anyfink?" Again, before Jarvis could speak, he was gone. The procedure was repeated three times. Each time he returned with three similar loads, all bulky and unwieldy, and it was quite as much as Jarvis could manage to stow each bundle adequately before the next was lowered to him. It seemed clear to Jarvis from the rapidity of Maggs's returns that he had been here before, maybe earlier that very night, and left the cache ready for collection.

"Just one more load," he wheezed, spraying Jarvis with his sweat, after his sixth trip.

Jarvis found himself constantly looking around, unconsciously imitating what Maggs did from force of habit to ensure self-preservation. Well, he was a thief too now, he told himself; and, he couldn't honestly say that the realisation greatly disturbed him. He convinced himself that a little larceny was only a little sin which God would understand and, hopefully, pardon. But, would the Law be as forgiving? And what interpretation would St Hilda's place on his awful crime – if they should ever learn of it? Jarvis shrugged and didn't bother to speculate further, and when a blackbird began its happy song in the tree above him, he wheeled round with a finger to his lips and uttered a "Shsssssh!" that was quite as loud as its voice. It briefly paused, relieved itself ... and gave Jarvis a second deafening verse. It sounded like Big Ben and he was certain it was telling every rozzer in London what they were about. Jarvis picked up a chunk of mortar from the wall, took careful aim, and hurled it at the bird. He missed, of course, and heard the shattering of glass close by. The blackbird burst into a fresh chorus quite unperturbed. Jarvis looked frantically about him expecting ... he didn't know what.

"Wot was that?" demanded Mr Maggs, his face appearing in the gap in the railings. As on every other occasion, Jarvis had not heard him approaching. He looked this way and that, trying to locate the crash he'd heard, and in the improving light Jarvis saw that the reason his face looked so very pale was that his whiskers were quite white.

"Milk bottle, I think – 'spect it were a cat," Jarvis suggested coolly, despite the pounding where his heart was supposed to be. It amazed him that he was able to lie so easily, and ably. The thought of Father Rector's reaction brought a cold smile to his lips. The poor man would have him on his knees for ever!

Maggs didn't look particularly convinced but, after another urgent look round and telling Jarvis to "keep awake an' stop day-dreaming," he lowered the first of three sacks which clinked with disturbing clarity. From the feel they were plainly filled with candlesticks, salvers, goblets and such like. Jarvis pushed them hurriedly out of sight as though they were red hot. They did seem to make his sin less venial, but, he thought, may as well be hung for a sheep as a lamb, though he didn't like the thought of being hanged for anything.

Once again Maggs darted off, leaving Jarvis to resume his anxious vigil. He returned moments later with an armful of flowers – multi-coloured sweet peas and dahlias, phlox and gladioli, and long-stemmed roses – still dripping with water, which he told Jarvis to spread out on top of the tarpaulin, after first ripping off the *In memoriam* cards. Two more trips and the barrow looked like a float in a flower pageant. "Whose funeral were they for?" Jarvis asked, feeling more guilty over the flowers than the other things. "Gawd knows," muttered Maggs, indifferently. He picked up one of the discarded cards, squinted at it in the shadow of the wall, and said: "Some bleedin' admiral, no less. Knight of the Pisspot, an' all that crap." His face contorted into one of his evil grins. The next minute, he carefully replaced the railing he had removed earlier and dropped down to join Jarvis beside the barrow. It appeared to be completely filled with blooms. "Well, 'e won't miss 'em, will 'e? An' they give us the best possible protection – in the form of camouflage," declared Maggs. "Come on now, let's bugger orf 'fore 'is bleedin' relatives turn up lookin' fer them."

Jarvis was doubtful, and his frown showed it. "But won't the flowers simply draw attention to us?" he asked in a very anxious voice.

Maggs gave a low chuckle, as he gave Jarvis a scrap of garlic crust and fed another piece into his own mouth. "You're right, Jarvis-lad," he allowed, spitting crumbs in all directions, "but that's all they'll see, innit. The flowers. They won't imagine there's anyfink un'erneath, will they? Folks almost always see only what you want 'em to see – but you gotta stick it right under their perishin' noses. Like wot we done. The flowers! If we was ter just push the barrer along wiv the tarp hidin' our stuff, they'd smell a rat straight orf."

Jarvis was impressed by this cunning, and wondered if he'd ever be as clever. What an asset to The Bullets Maggs would have been!

They left the quiet square as silently as they'd arrived, a bare twenty-five minutes ago, and, having shed their now conspicuous rubbers, moved as unobtrusively and speedily away as possible. The barrow was now very heavy and it groaned beneath its burden. Jarvis really felt that he was pulling his weight as he helped push the barely manageable contraption along. He was horribly afraid it might collapse and expose their ill-gotten gains to the whole world. But the barrow was a sturdy affair and well able to cope with its load. And Maggs had been right about the flowers. They attracted plenty of attention, but it was all of admiration, none of suspicion. Two women, hurrying to work, actually tried to buy some of the flowers, but Maggs, with suitably melancholy face, explained they were destined for a florist's to be used at a funeral being held the next day. However, he gallantly presented each woman with a single red rose saying, "I'm sure he'd've liked you to 'ave this, miss." He half-turned to give Jarvis a wink, and muttered out of the side of his mouth, "P'raps I should've got 'em to help us with the barrer!" Jarvis was hard put to stop himself bursting out laughing, and was only prevented from doing so by the sweat pouring down his face as they continued trundling along. He was beginning to wonder if Maggs was quite so averse to women as he would have him believe. His eyes seemed to stray – which meant that the barrow did, too – every time a pretty face came into view. Each time Jarvis was tempted to laugh out loud, but he smothered the impulses in case it should be thought unfitting for one engaged on so solemn a mission, and they puffed on, struggling to dodge the increasing traffic.

    Jarvis was left to wait in the shadow of St Paul's, and told to keep an eye out for trouble – which he supposed meant the rozzers, while Maggs disappeared with the barrow under an arch into a small square. For the briefest of moments, Jarvis wondered if Maggs might be seeking to ditch him so as not to have to give him a share of whatever he got, but dismissed the idea as being too mean for consideration.

    Jarvis found himself passing the time kicking at an old cigarette packet: every so often, probably by accident, someone would kick it back at him. It was when he was going through the motions of scoring a goal that trouble came: the cigarette packet went skidding over the concrete slabs, and unfortunately his boot went sailing through the air after it. By bad luck, it landed among a group of messenger boys, who proceeded to have great sport throwing it from one to the other as he chased frantically about trying to retrieve it yelling heatedly at the laughing boys – to the general amusement of other onlookers. The sport came to a sudden end with the return of Maggs, who deftly caught the boot in mid-air, sent the playful boys scattering with a mouthful of the choicest invectives, and gave Jarvis a cuff round the ear for drawing attention to himself. "It'll be the death of yer," he grated. "Merge wiv a crowd ... don't stick out like Nelson's bleedin Column, boy." But he wasn't too angry and, after he'd carefully looked about him, they moved off.

    Maggs had emerged from his business haggling after some twenty minutes, chewing hard and carrying his parcel of meat, but leaving the barrow in the isolated square. After his usual glance round, he gripped Jarvis's shoulder and steered him away. He told him he'd got a fair to middling price for the goods, after a brief difference of opinion concerning the current price of lead, but that he would have to come back later for the money because the man who handled that side of things, a Mr Nobbs, hadn't turned up yet. "Bit early for 'is nibs," sneered Maggs, "specially if 'e's got hisself an obligin' doxy." He gave a low chuckle and added as an afterthought, "Reckon we should've got a price on them flowers, too!" He came as near to laughing as Jarvis had heard him, evidently pleased with his witticism, and began rummaging through his waistcoat pockets. "'Ere, Jarvis, put this in yer pocket – an' don't lose 'er. It's a little sumfink ter keep yer goin' till we gets our money."

Jarvis goggled at the silver coin: a florin! Two shillings! It said so ... and so did King George, who stared benignly at him through his whiskers. "Crikey!" he gasped, incredulously, turning the coin over and over in his hand. "Thanks very much, Maggs. Gosh, I ain't never 'ad one of these in me 'and before. Never seen any silver money before, come to that ... 'cept a threepenny bit, but I lost that so it don't count, do it?" Maggs gave his evil grin, obviously well pleased with the world in general, including Jarvis; he thwacked him heartily on the back, propelling him several paces forward. "That's nuffink, boy," he said. "Stick wiv me an' we'll both be rich as lords an' live in a big castle. But fer now, we'll go an' get us some nosh."

They ate in a place called The Monk's Cellar. It was just off Ludgate Hill, to all intents and purposes beneath the railway viaduct, and, as Maggs remarked, "nice'n 'andy fer the lads when they're on parade at the Bailey." A flabby, unshaven man with an unlit cigarette in his mouth looked up from swatting blue-bottles on the counter, and greeted Maggs with an indifferent "'Lo, Alf," and then turned his black fish-eyes on Jarvis with even less interest before returning his attention to the blue-bottles. Maggs growled back a "Wotcher, Mario," glanced hurriedly round the room and stomped straight through, crossed an open yard out back and pushed open another door. It led to a slightly more pleasant room with a scrap of carpet and a number of cubicles that afforded their occupants a degree of privacy in which to do their plotting.

"Who's Alf?" Jarvis whispered, following Maggs into one of the cubicles.

"Me. That's me name 'ere – and don't ferget it. Alf Grout. If anyone speaks to yer in 'ere, say nuffink – just that you're wiv me ... even if I ain't 'ere. See?"

Jarvis nodded. He was far more interested in the prospect of eating than talking.

A tall, skinny and utterly plain woman with straight hair the colour of a sick parsnip appeared from somewhere, and flashed a row of blackish teeth at Alf (or whoever) in a macabre smile. He put an arm round her frail body, fondled the area of her chest – it was so flat it might have been a boy's – and, pulling her down into his lap, plonked a kiss on her open mouth. She uttered no sound, either of protest or pleasure, although her dull eyes did respond with a sort of vague twinkle. "This is Bertie," he announced, turning suddenly to Jarvis. "It's really Albertina, poor sow, but she's called Bertie ... an' she loves me!" Bertie, her head buried in Alf's shoulder, gave a strangled giggle. Well, it was a sound of some sort. Then Alf was whispering in her ear, and she looked across at Jarvis with quite sharp eyes, which he now saw were mostly green and didn't seem nearly so repulsive as they had done at first, and gave him a dark smile. For one terrible moment Jarvis thought he was expected to kiss her, or, even worse, that she was going to kiss him; but he sat there like a lump of stone and did nothing, and she made no move towards him. He had an awful feeling that she could read his thoughts; he knew he blushed, and then he saw her eyes were laughing, and he fixed his eyes on a tiny spider speeding across the table. Alf, who missed nothing, gave a mocking laugh, and thumped the table, annihilating the unfortunate spider. Then he gave Bertie the parcel of meat and she departed, encouraged by a playful slap on her rear which elicited another smothered sound.

"She's a good gel," Maggs confided absently. "Ugly as sin, of course, like me, but a good gel – an' a good cook, too. Heart's in the right place if nuffink else is. I usually gives 'er summat fer the kitchen 'ere 'cos they don't give 'er much else to cook – most likely summat from the knacker's yard! Bless 'er, an' I bet she'd make that tasty, too. 'Spect we've all ate a few nags 'fore now! She always looks arter me when I drop in, an' I do wot I can for the poor ol' thing. She's dumb, yer know."

Jarvis hadn't known, how on earth could he have done, and now that he did, he was appalled. The poor woman. Poor wretched Bertie. God hadn't given her much in the way of looks or anything; you'd have thought He'd give her a bleeding tongue, at least! But He hadn't given him any parents, had He? Strange the workings of God ... perhaps He was overworked, there were an awful lot of people that needed looking after. Jarvis felt desperately sorry for Bertie, poor soul ... but his thoughts soon turned to other things, like Maggs – or Alf Somebody-or-other for the time being. The more he came to know him, the less surprised he was about anything that happened – and he'd only known the old rascal a matter of hours!

"For someone who says he hates women, Alf, you seem to enjoy their company an awful lot," Jarvis observed, picking his words carefully so as not to give any offence, but eyeing his partner in crime with a mischievous grin.

"'Ate 'em! Lumme, boy, I doesn't 'ate 'em. Bless you, no. Don't trust 'em – not a one of 'em. But, no, I doesn't 'ate 'em. Lor, bless 'em. I *loves* 'em! That's me trouble. It could've been drink or dope, or a 'undred other evils, but wiv me my evil passion is fer bleedin' wimmin! Nuffink I can do abaht it, matey. I loves 'em all – more's the pity. Don't you 'ave no truck wiv wimmin, Jarvis m'boy. They'll break yer 'art an' chew the pieces an' spit 'em aht, straight, like wot they done to my poor 'art."

Jarvis couldn't help thinking that Maggs looked very far from being a man with a broken heart. But, by heaven, he looked a pretty sorry excuse for a Romeo! Jarvis gave an audible burst of very childish laughter, and fixed his gaze expectantly on Maggs, who did not disappoint him. Evidently in a rare expansive mood, probably because of their successful morning's work or simply because he had an attentive audience, Maggs, after a cautionary look round, admitted to having enjoyed half-a-dozen wives – at least! Not, he hastened to add as if this excused everything, that any of the relationships had been sanctified by marriage. "Now that would've been darft," he declared emphatically. He continued, reminiscently: "Christ! One of me gels was little older'n wot you is, boy! Gorgeous bit of crumpet, she were. Didn't know whether to love 'er or spank 'er – so I done both! An' I fink she loved t'one as much as t'other, bless 'er cheeky 'art. Then guess wot? The minx buggered orf wiv a soddin' miner from down Kent-way. Bet she finished up wiv a sooty arse, heh!"

His happy memories came to an abrupt halt with the arrival of their food, and for close on twenty minutes neither of them spoke, both applying all their energies to the business of eating; well, Jarvis was wholly absorbed. Alf had other distractions. He'd swept Bertie on to his lap and, in between spooning food into his mouth, he nuzzled up to her and whispered into her ear, telling her that he wanted her for afters – which struck Jarvis as peculiarly odd. Bertie kept disappearing and reappearing with something fresh to put on to their plates. Jarvis noticed that each time she brushed by Alf he would pat or squeeze a different part of her anatomy, which sent her mincing back to her scullery emitting some very peculiar sounds which seemed to keep him constantly amused. Jarvis was curious about their goings on, but he was far more interested in shovelling as much food as possible down him. He'd never had so much food on his plate before in his life. The meal was scrumptiously appetising, consisting of thick slices of red beef, little dumplings laced with herbs, and huge helpings of fresh vegetables, followed by an enormous gooseberry pie with cream that might just have been a bit off, and cheese and hunks of bread for good measure. To be honest, he thought he did most of the eating. Alf, now lolling back in the process of quaffing his second quart of porter, watched with impressive disbelief as Jarvis continued to devour everything in sight.

Later, as Jarvis belched and otherwise digested his voracity, Alf added further fragments of his history as it occurred to him, and he did seem to become more loquacious the more porter he downed. Yes, he'd gotten drunk once – well, he'd got drunk many a time, he admitted, but on this particular occasion he woke up on a steamer and eventually found himself in Buenos Aires, a pox-ridden place somewhere in South America. He'd spent seven years at sea following that drunken episode, and only managed to end up ashore again by missing his boat – yes, he'd got drunk again. Fortunately that'd been in London's Tilbury Docks, and he'd never got itchy feet again; not seawards, anyway.

Using his wits, and other people's property, he'd built up a fair livelihood and came to be known, and even respected, as the Tin Man because most of his works involved metal of some description, and he was involved in various other businesses which made him money in more senses than one. He didn't enlarge upon this but, as though thinking he had probably said too much already, gave a wry chuckle and closed the chapter on his life story by saying: "I bin caught a coupla times. Did eighteen-months down at Lewes, an' a five-stretch in Pentonville. But, I bin careful – an' lucky these last years. I don't fancy being sent down no more. Grub's terrible, an' no wimmin!"

He gave one of his indeterminate chuckles, and Jarvis added a low, respectful giggle of his own. For some moments they sat in silence, Alf with his nose in his pewter pot and Jarvis capturing crumbs off the table which had escaped his earlier attentions. He followed the progress of another brave spider across the table, and for no particular reason was inordinately pleased it made it to safety. Suddenly, Alf broke the spell, leaning towards Jarvis and staring him straight in the eye.

"Wot's gonna 'appen to you, matey?" he asked in an urgent tone. "You can stay wiv me, if yer wants – and I'd like yer to. But, I must be 'onest wiv you, Jarvis-boy. You'd oughta go back ... "

Jarvis had grown accustomed to keeping quiet as Maggs told him his story, but his words now startled him into speaking out. "But where – Alf? Where do I go? I've no idea where the Home is. Really. I wish I did. I'd be only too willing to face the music – an' you can bet yer life they'll beat me half to death."

Maggs shook his head in some agitation. Jarvis knew him sufficiently well by now to know that it would never occur to him to tell Jarvis to go to the police, who, doubtless, would easily find out where he'd run away from. Christ! they were probably already looking for him – and it shouldn't be very difficult with him in his present clobber. Jarvis felt he stood out a mile. But, people like them, Maggs and him, didn't have any truck with the Law. Maggs lived his own life, and wanted only to be left alone to live it ... if the rozzers would but let him. And Jarvis, he just wanted to be with Alf – well, he did for the moment.

"We'll 'ave to talk some more abaht this, Jarvis-boy. Later." Maggs stood up and followed Bertie to a door, turning before he disappeared to give Jarvis a meaningful wink, but he didn't comprehend its significance at the time. "I'll be busy for a while – you wait 'ere, however long it takes."

They vanished and Jarvis was left thinking what an odd pair they made. He wondered how they overcame the problem of her not being able to speak. Poor thing. Still, it hadn't appeared any handicap between them so far – if anything, it loosened Alf's tongue. He seemed to speak enough for the pair of them. Jarvis continued to ruminate over the day's incredible events, and examining his florin for the umpteenth time. It certainly seemed a very solid and shiny coin, not like his poor lost threepenny piece. Alf had left some cheese on his plate and Jarvis saw no reason to leave it there; he nibbled away at some and, on an impulse, shoved a sizeable wedge in his pocket. It was over half an hour before Alf reappeared, looking very pleased with himself. Bertie was close behind him, smoothing and straightening her drab frock, and Jarvis couldn't help thinking she looked extraordinarily self-satisfied, too.

"I'll just pop round the corner an' sort out me money," said Alf. "You meet me in abaht fifteen minutes where you waited 'fore – an' don't start no more footie matches or yer'll 'ave the rozzers blowin' their whistles at yer. Keep yer wits about yer an' yer peepers open, lad, then we'll go an' 'ave a butcher's at me crib." He leaned forward, speaking into Jarvis's ear so that there was no chance of anyone, even Bertie, hearing what he said. "I got me a diff'rent name there – Fred Guppy. Remember it, an' keep it to yerself. An' you better give yerself anovver name, lad. Yer can't go round wiv your own."

Jarvis couldn't think of any name; nothing he liked, anyway. Then, as he felt Maggs's growing impatience and hot breath in his ear, he thought of his wooden guardsman. "George King," Jarvis whispered back triumphantly. "Right. Don't yer go fergettin' it," returned Maggs, straightening up.

Maggs went directly, and almost as directly Bertie was at Jarvis's side with a chunk of sticky cake. She sat beside him and watched every mouthful disappear as pleased as any mother. It was soon gone, and he started counting off the minutes till it was time to go. Jarvis felt awkward, not knowing how to speak to someone who couldn't talk back. But it didn't seem to matter. Bertie suddenly placed her skinny arm round his shoulders and touched his forehead with surprisingly soft, warm lips, then stroked his hair, all the time making unintelligible sounds. Jarvis didn't really like her touching him, but he didn't want to hurt her feelings and so endured her caresses till it was time to leave. Then, he turned to thank her for all the lovely food and dashed off to keep his rendez-vous, pausing from the safety of the door to blow her a kiss in return. He felt he owed her something.

The first hint that something might be wrong was the sight of the Black Maria. Then Jarvis noticed the swarm of policemen and the growing crowd. And then he saw Maggs, almost hidden by the throng, handcuffed to another man, presumably the man he'd gone to see; the two men were bustled unceremoniously into the waiting van. For one fraction of an instant, when Maggs turned for a last look round, their eyes met. Maggs gave a tiny shake of his head, then his shoulders sagged forlornly, and he disappeared from view.

Jarvis blinked, but there were no tears. He didn't cry any more. Even so, his heart felt like some unbearable weight choking in his mouth as he turned away with the bell of the departing police van ringing in his ears. Jarvis had to force his legs to walk, and then close behind him he heard voices shouting.

"He had a young'n with him, officer," ... "Just a boy, he was," ... "All dressed in grey – just like that kid there, officer!"

And suddenly, Jarvis was running for all he was worth.

He didn't run all that far. For one thing he was too full of dinner, and felt rather sick, and for another there didn't seem to be anybody chasing him any more; and, rather more importantly, because he ran smack into the substantial body of a red-faced man wearing breeches and shiny, knee-length boots, a bright yellow tartan waistcoat and a black bowler. The man was clutching one of those long whips such as coachmen used to control their teams of horses, and he lashed out at Jarvis with it.

Jarvis moved agilely to one side, but not quickly enough to prevent the whistling thong cutting across his shoulders. He stumbled and fell to the ground with a sharp cry of pain. As he lay there a second blow caught him fully on his back and he screamed, and leaped to his feet. One of the men with the bowler hat man lunged at Jarvis with his fist, catching him high on his left cheek. The force sent him crashing down again, and once more the whip caught him across the shoulders. Jarvis uttered a whimpering cry, but in the same instant he was back on his feet and dodging through a group of men. Someone gave him a punch on the arm, someone else snatched at his braces – and clung on. Jarvis pulled with the strength born of terror in one direction, and the man in the other; his trouser buttons popped off in quick succession, and the man was left holding the braces while Jarvis was left holding up his trousers.

He scrambled about desperately looking for an escape route through the laughing men just as the whip stung his back a fourth time. He thought it must have been just at the limit of its reach for it didn't seem to hurt as much as previously, even so he couldn't restrain another sob. With an energy born of necessity, his back trickling blood and blazing like an inferno, Jarvis dodged and weaved round a man who aimed a vicious kick which left a searing furrow in his thigh, and then he was free ... and away, deaf to the laughter behind.

Jarvis ran like he was on hot coals, or as fast as it is possible to do when you're dripping blood, only able to see properly out of one eye and having to use both hands to keep your trousers up. If he'd been paying more attention where he was running, instead of tucking his head down to make sure his feet were keeping up with the rest of him, he wouldn't have trapped himself in a cul-de-sac. The dead end was the

Thames itself, with just a stone wall separating them, and the street offered no alternative escape route.

Jarvis had been joined on his frantic flight by a brown and black mongrel, and it was now yapping and leaping at his heels and making a frightful din. In that moment of desperation, he fully appreciated Maggs's aversion to such creatures; they didn't rate highly in his esteem, either. It was a dog which had got him into all this trouble in the first place. They *were* a menace, and he didn't want this mutt drawing attention to him. With absolutely no compunction, he swung his boot at it and the startled animal somehow clawed its way to the top of the wall, teetered momentarily, and fell with a splash into the river on the other side. There was no time for any feelings of guilt.

Somewhere, too close for comfort, he heard a police whistle and the sounds of raised voices and running feet. But, they didn't appear to be coming any closer and, having finally stopped panting, Jarvis clambered to the top of the granite wall to see what possibilities of escape the river side offered; he spotted a narrow ledge jutting out of the wall which seemed to offer a precarious route to a nearby footbridge. He noticed, too, a string of barges bobbing behind a puffing tug that would have to pass under the bridge. It looked like his only means of escape. It looked bloody dangerous, too. He could fall, and drown like the dog.

Jarvis eased himself across the wall, surprised to find the surface so rough, and lowered himself with infinite care, and great trepidation, on to the ledge which now seemed far narrower than it had looked from above; it was no wider than the width of a couple of bricks, and there was absolutely nothing to cling on to. He peered down, and wished he hadn't. The water looked a long way down, very cold and very dirty: and very uninviting. Even as he looked, it suddenly occurred to him that he had no idea if he could swim. He supposed he could. Why shouldn't he? It was in his mind to shrug but he decided there wasn't room on the ledge, and that he'd have to face up to the matter of swimming when it became a matter of necessity, if it did. Steadying himself on the wet and slimy surface and holding up his trousers with one hand while feeling his way along the wall with the other, he shuffled with dread care towards the bridge – which now seemed much farther off than he'd thought; too far, a voice inside cautioned him. But there was no turning back – he doubted if it was possible, anyway – and after what seemed an age, he reached the comparative safety of the catwalk just in time to drop, miraculously unobserved, at least he hoped he was, on to the last of the barges as it lurched below. He landed with a jarring thump on a heap of coiled ropes which felt like they were made of steel, but he did not appear to have caused himself any major mischief. There was a fresh gash above his right knee that was bleeding and a few more bruises, that was all.

He snuggled down, trying to make himself as small as possible, behind a bale of waste paper. It was only now that he'd stopped running for his life that he became aware of the whipping he had so recently endured, and with that memory the pains of his various wounds returned. No matter which way he twisted and turned, he ached all over. In particular, his back hurt agonizingly, like it was all torn open, but he sensed the bleeding from the weals had stopped because his shirt was stuck to the skin; and only a trickle ran from the tear in his leg where the boot had ripped the skin for several inches. His face throbbed terribly and he was sure the lump beneath his eye was still growing in size. He could barely see out of it, and at that moment he didn't particularly want to; he just wanted to fall asleep and wake up and find it was all a mad, mad dream and that he was back at St Hilda's, or having a German lesson at the convent.

Eventually, the movement of the barge rocked him to sleep, and he dreamed fitfully of being a pirate with Maggs, and woke up wondering if he was destined to turn up in South America, too? And be a sailor for seven years! However, his voyage proved considerably shorter. The tug came to a stop somewhat short of Charing Cross Pier, where the barges were fastened to several giant buoys beside the Embankment, and then chugged off. Jarvis spent the whole day, cramped and hungry, in his hiding place, not daring to poke his head out. He felt so sore all over that he came to the conclusion several things must be broken, and having made this painful diagnosis, he finally dozed off.

Dusk was already creeping up the Thames when he awoke, and his dreams of piratical adventures vanished and all his aches and pains returned with a horrible vengeance. After a while he managed to restore life to his limbs and ventured out of his hidey-hole on all fours, and he was exasperated to discover how relatively easy it would be to clamber ashore. Irritated because he would far sooner have done so hours before in the daylight; what he did not take into account was that he would only be able to do so now because of the exceptionally high tide, and besides, earlier, he would have been in plain sight of everyone – and that would have been curtains for him.

Once back on terra firma, and how much safer that felt, he immediately became conscious of his dirty and dishevelled condition, to say nothing for his battered appearance; there wasn't much he could do about his clothing, but he endeavoured to give himself a bit of a wash in a bird bath in the Victoria Embankment Gardens, only to have to abort his ablutions when a prowling park keeper spotted him and gave vociferous chase. It was a short chase, the keeper giving up at the edge of his territory. Being fairly certain still that most of his bones were broken, it surprised Jarvis that he was able to run as fast as he did. He came to the puzzling conclusion that perhaps nothing was broken, only dented.

Jarvis had already learned that a running figure drew attention to itself, whereas a walking one tended to merge with others; so, unless it was absolutely necessary, and then only for as long as it was necessary, he decided that he would walk at an ordinary pace like everyone else. He was sure Maggs – he thought of him as poor Maggs, but felt his old friend was probably safer in prison than he was outside – would have approved. So, Jarvis walked about haphazardly, without any idea where he was, but keeping a sharp look out for rozzers, and in this way found himself in Garrick Street, though this meant nothing to him. He was still lost. He shivered in the evening breeze and hunched his shoulders, ignoring the sound of his shirt tearing still further, and dug his hands deep into his pockets which both kept his hands warm and served to keep his trousers up – he had tried to use his piece of string as a belt, but the two ends refused to meet. He wondered longingly of St Hilda's; wondered if he was remembered there, and missed. He was at once ashamed of his thoughts – which then went on to think, wouldn't it be funny if he should stumble across St Hilda's again, all by himself. What a welcome he'd receive from Father Rector!

He sensed the man's presence even before he saw the fawn suède shoes, the immaculate spats and the impossibly-razor-creased trousers, clinging skin-like above.

"Hello, young man, you look like you've been in a fight or two. I hope you won," said the blond-haired man, in a soft, posh voice.

Jarvis had never seen anybody, certainly no man, look so – well, beautiful; that was the only word he could think of to describe the dandified man. He was tall and slim, and his so-smart grey suit fitted him like a glove; a gold watch chain peeped out of his waist-coat, and a pink carnation adorned his lapel. He carried a pair of grey kid gloves and a slim, silver-topped swagger stick in one hand. He had a middle-aged – well, thirtyish, bronzed face, clean shaven and with fat, sensual lips that were smiling down at him with frank delight. "You look a bit lost, my dear," he purred musically, lowering his magnificent head and gazing into Jarvis's face through twinkling blue eyes.

"Yes, sir, I'm afraid I am," Jarvis agreed readily, feeling very weary and convinced that he needed to turn to someone for help, and instinctively yanking up his sagging trousers.

"And why's that? A big boy like you?" the dapper man asked in a silky sort of voice, stooping down still further and giving Jarvis the benefit of some rare, and no doubt costly, perfume. He smelt absolutely beautiful, too.

"I run away, sir," Jarvis confessed, overpowered by his magnetism.

The man smiled: beautifully; everything about him was beautiful. Then, after a glance about him, he placed an arm round Jarvis's waist – he was surprised by this, but glad the man didn't touch his torn shoulders – and guided him off the pavement and into the entrance of what appeared to be an arcade. His hand moved up Jarvis's back, ever so softly, touching his skin where it showed through a big rent in his shirt. "Oh, you poor dear!" he exclaimed, continuing to stroke Jarvis's skin, "your poor back is all hurt and bleeding."

"It don't hurt all that much, not now," Jarvis insisted, flinching at his touch.

"Is that why you ran away – because of the beating?"

"No, sir, that happened after I run away," Jarvis answered, and hoped he wouldn't be asked to explain what had happened.

The man frowned, seemed about to pursue the matter, but didn't. "And do you know where you ran away from?" he asked in a voice as smooth as oil.

"No, sir; not really. It's an orphanage place ... called St Hilda's, but I've no idea where it's at – 'cept that it's round 'ere somewhere."

"Well, never mind, young man, perhaps we can find it together," he cooed, capturing one of Jarvis's hands and holding it in his own as he beamed into his face from only inches away. "What d'you say to that, heh?"

"I'd like that fine, sir. If it wouldn't be too much trouble to you." Jarvis was beginning to find the man's closeness rather embarrassing, and his scent almost intoxicating. He'd never known that men used such things. He knew that women bathed themselves in perfumes and stuff (Scruffy had told him: he knew about these things) but he'd never met one that did.

"No trouble at all, m'dear," the man assured him in a voice as sweet as honey. He moved back marginally, as though sensing his discomfort and Jarvis put this down to his breeding. Jarvis felt he was indeed lucky to have made his acquaintance. Now, if they could get on to the matter of food ... just the thought filled him with such hopeful pleasure that he was moved to give a timid smile. "We should all help each other in moments of trouble, don't you agree?" he went on, returning Jarvis's smile tenfold. "But first, I think we should introduce ourselves properly. My name's Oliver Roland, just like the two knights in Charlemagne's court – but maybe you don't know about them." – Jarvis nodded that he did – "Actually, I'm simply an Honourable ... but I'll be a Lord one day. And what's your name?"

"Jarvis Brook," he replied immediately; as he'd already mentioned St Hilda's it served no purpose to conceal his name. He hadn't been George King for long, he thought wryly.

"A capital name!" declared His Honourableness. "My friends call me Roley."

Jarvis would never have presumed to call such a fine gentleman anything so familiar; and he replied simply: "My friends call me all sorts of naughty names, I'm afraid."

"I expect quite a few of them call you 'darling,' don't they?"

Jarvis blushed at the very idea. "They jolly well better not ... or I'll bash 'em!" he cried fiercely. He felt like adding – but didn't – that he didn't much better prefer being called 'm'dear' the way His Lordship did, "Oh, no, sir; never. They wouldn't dare – not me mates."

"Oh, Jarvis, I love it! You really are a precious! You really do amuse me, you positively do," Roland laughed, very freely, and most attractively; almost like a boy himself.

Jarvis was glad that he was pleased with him, but wished his Honourable friend wouldn't keep his arm so firmly pressed against his back – almost as though he was afraid of losing him. Then he said the magic words, and there was no chance he'd lose him.

"Well, Jarvis," he said decisively, "I think the first thing we have to do is to get you something to eat." – Jarvis gave him a full-blooded smile and several nods, and his heart elevated him to the peerage at a stroke – "I'm sure you're hungry. My young nephews always are, especially after we've played some games together."

"I'm starving," Jarvis admitted, and gave his trousers a quick tug, just to satisfy himself, for they seemed to be continuously slipping.

"Righto! That's it then. First we eat. Then I think you'd best come home with me so that we can plan our campaign to return you to your – St Hilda's, was it? But before that we must have a look at your wounds, and then I think you could do with a hot bath and a good sleep in a soft, warm bed. St Hilda's can wait till tomorrow."

Without more ado, or waiting for Jarvis's approval, Roland piloted Jarvis – whose own hands were fully occupied with the business of holding up his trousers – out of Garrick Street, across another and into a rather sombre square which was made even darker than it really was by a vast church in the centre; the effect was to cast shadows in all directions. Roland, who had steered Jarvis through a little maze of laurel bushes which ornamented the island where the church stood, saying that it was a short cut to their dinner, suddenly paused, inclined an ear and looked hurriedly around. The next instant, he stooped, hugging Jarvis to him and raining kisses wetly all over his face, coming to rest on his mouth which he seemed intent on devouring; at the same time, one or both his hands were prying like tentacles inside Jarvis's trousers, the fingers stroking and searching everywhere with feverish intensity.

It took Jarvis a breathless moment or two to comprehend exactly what was happening. He had heard stories about such people (the boys back at the Home talked about such men – they were called homos) but never experienced, or even dreamed of, anything like this. Now that he realised this man's intentions, he wanted to scream, but was prevented by Roland's own insatiable mouth. Jarvis's initial feeling of panic gave way to revulsion, and finally to frenzied anger. He wriggled and struggled with all his might, but quite ineffectively for the other's arms were like steel bands round his body. The only result of his struggles was that his trousers slithered slowly down his legs to lie in a heap at his ankles, and with them went all semblance of self-control; as the trousers fell so too did his tears, large and scalding, rolling unstoppably down his cheeks and soaking both their shirts.

With his last scrap of dignity covering only his boots, Jarvis found that he couldn't move an inch; what with his trousers shackling his legs and Roland's arms pinioning his own, it was almost like being in a straight-jacket. Jarvis fought as best he could, but futilely, as the other's body became more urgently demanding. Something close to terror welled up within Jarvis. Overwhelmed by the sordidness and humiliation of it all, and by a growing horror of the sheer awfulness of his predicament, he retaliated in the only way left to him. He sank his teeth into Roland's tongue and held on for dear life, utterly insensitive to the hot blood in his mouth, the man's demoniacal cries or his flailing arms and thudding fists; and, quite suddenly, a tiny portion of the other's tongue came away in his mouth, and they were apart.

Jarvis gagged and almost swallowed the morsel of flesh in his mouth, before spitting it out on the ground. The effort sent him toppling, and he scrambled his trousers up as fast as he could as he climbed awkwardly back on to his feet. Jarvis continued spitting, determined to purge himself of every vestige of the man's vile flesh and blood. He looked for the scrap of tongue, it had only been the very tip, wanting to stamp it into the ground for ever, but couldn't see it in the gloom. He gripped his trousers with a fierce desperation as Roland lurched clumsily to his feet. His hands covered his mouth but were unable to stop the blood seeping through and dribbling over his suit, neither could he stem the flow of tears from his pain-filled eyes, nor still his anguished moans.

"You filthy sod!" Jarvis screamed with loathing. "Serve you bloody well right, you dirty bugger." Jarvis felt himself crying again in his terror and disgust. "I hate you, I hate you, you filthy swine!" He yelled at him.

It was only afterwards that Jarvis realised Roland probably couldn't see him clearly through his tears and that it was the sound of his voice that drew him in his direction. It was the worst possible thing he could have done. Jarvis saw his movement towards him and, keeping a tight hold on his trousers, swung his booted foot up savagely to meet the threat. More by luck than design, he caught Roland flush on his right knee-cap, smashing it with a sickening crunch – at least, it sounded like it. Jarvis heard something crack. Roland collapsed to the ground, an eerie howl escaping from his mutilated mouth. Even then he wouldn't leave well alone; he felt for, and found, his stick and lashed blindly out at Jarvis between racking sobs. Jarvis had no difficulty in evading the blows, nor in wrenching the cane from his hand, and in his turn, he belaboured the huddled figure on the ground unmercifully. Roland strove only to protect himself, especially his smashed knee, and even his sobs gave way to long, plaintive whining.

Jarvis continued flashing wildly down with the little stick, wishing it were more like the whip that had been used on him the previous day, until he began to have trouble holding his trousers up, and decided he wasn't going to risk losing them again. He flung the stick far aside and gave Roland a wild parting kick, not knowing where he kicked but having the satisfaction of hearing something more cracking followed by another howl, and then he was off at a steady lope, both hands firmly attached to his trousers. The church bells began a joyous peal as he ran off, but he was hardly aware of them. If he had paused to listen to them, he would have regarded their message as being a requiem for this vile pervert, and he would have begrudged him even this.

"Hope the sod dies in agony an' goes to 'ell!" Jarvis muttered to himself, as he darted down Long Acre, into Mercer Street ... and all of a sudden there was no pavement beneath his feet, and he felt himself falling helplessly. If he hadn't been clinging to his trousers with such grim determination, he might have saved himself; as it was, he just went on tumbling until his head struck something very solid ... and everything went black.

Jarvis didn't know how much later it was – nor even if it was day or night, for he wasn't sure he opened his eyes – that he heard the voice. A child's voice: a girl's voice. She appeared to be looking for someone called Rosie, who was evidently even younger than her for she was promising Rosie the most terrible punishments if she didn't come out of hiding "this very minute." There was no response from Rosie, and for several moments he heard not a whisper from the other girl.

This respite was shattered with dreadful suddenness by sounds that came in positive waves of thunder. First came a high-pitched shriek, then a clattering of small feet trying to keep up with the screams that raced ahead of them.

"Mummy, mummy!" she cried, and never did words contain more horror. "There's a body in the cellar! It's a boy ... he's dead!"

Jarvis didn't hear any more after that. Was she right? Was he dead? Well, he'd know, wouldn't he? Surely? On the other hand, it seemed more than likely. He could feel nothing, hear nothing, see nothing. Perhaps she was right. Perhaps he was dead. He hoped he wasn't, but ... it was blessedly quiet and seemed to grow even darker as he drifted deeper into unconsciousness.

□ *"This is where you meet Ruth, Jarvis," Queenie declared, her eyes sparkling.*

"Is she pretty?" asked Beard mischievously.

"Beautiful," Queenie told him "You'll probably recognise her."

"How? I don't even know me. I haven't recognised anyone or remembered anything you've related so far, interesting though it has been to hear. Enthralling, really."

"It'll come, darling," murmured Queenie. "Listen, now."

Chapter Ten

St Giles, London, 15 August, 1937

Jarvis knew he was neither dead nor dying the moment he opened his eyes. He'd been expecting, hoping, to find himself in heaven, or very close by – though certainly not in "that other place," and, instead, found himself enveloped in a voluminous garment and lying in a huge, soft bed and between crisp, cool sheets ... and a little girl was showering him with rose petals.

It was *her!*

The girl he'd almost come to blows with in the street when he'd lost his threepenny piece; and here she was again. She was about to release another handful of petals when she saw him looking up at her. Her face, which had been frowning, lit up instantly, and she leaned forward to kiss his cheek with the enthusiasm of one greeting a long-expected, much-loved visitor.

"I thought you were dead!" she exclaimed excitedly.

"So did I," Jarvis acknowledged frankly, with a tiny smile. "Where am I?"

"Silly boy! You're here – at The Dials," she laughed merrily. And when she laughed, the very real joy she felt was evident in her eyes, which were dark and velvety, like a pair of pansies: two large, darkly brown pansies. She looked about seven or eight, which made him feel vastly older at eleven. He had just decided she was quite pretty, when she jumped up, dragging her wooden doll carelessly by a leg, and plumped herself down on the bed.

"Dials? What's that?" Jarvis asked. He knew he'd heard the name before, but couldn't remember where or how.

"It's where you're at. It's my home. And it's also a public house," she explained in a quick rush of words. "You fell down the chute outside, right into our cellar where the barrels are kept. That's what Daddy says, anyway. It must've been sometime last night, 'cos we didn't find you till this morning – an' you've been sleeping like the dead all day. You didn't even wake up when Mummy bathed you – she said you were a mucky thing an' probably never had one before! And a doctor came and had a look at you and said you'd most likely live – if you survived the bath! But I think he was joking – about the bath, I mean."

Jarvis gave a tentative grin, not so certain of his survival. Apart from the ordeal of the bath, which came as a surprise to him, he didn't think he'd ever be the same again. His body felt as though it had been put through a mangle, and the weals of the whip seemed to hurt a hundred times more now, but, then, he hadn't felt anything while he was sleeping. Funny how that lump under his eye appeared to have vanished; still felt bloody sore, though.

"Mummy says you must've been fighting to get yourself in the state you were in – you were all over blood an' bruises, an' your clothes were all torn and filthy. Mummy called them rags," the girl babbled on, without a pause. "She was very cross, and unhappy too, over your terrible hurts – especially over the cuts on your back. Daddy said it looked like someone had whipped you. An' Mummy said it looked as if you'd been caned very recently. Oh, I do think that's beastly! Even if you were naughty. Were you?" She looked anxiously into his face – which must have looked dazed for he found it difficult to keep up with her torrent of words – and immediately shook her small, dark head, and rattled on. "It doesn't matter ... it's all terribly wrong, and horrible. Mummy put some ice on your eye. She said it would help the swelling to go down. It seems to have worked because it's not nearly so huge as it was – but it's an awful colour still. Daddy called it a black eye, but it's ev'ry colour but black!"

Jarvis began the makings of a smile but mention of his aching eye reminded him of its bruised state, and it immediately hurt twice as much, and, instead, he gave her a groan. This brought an immediate further expression of concern to her face.

"Mummy said your fall must've knocked you out. Gosh, you looked terribly dead. It was me that found you. I nearly died myself. I was looking for Rosie."

"Who's she? Your sister?" he ventured.

"Silly!" the girl cried merrily, standing the wooden doll up on the bed and straightening its crumpled red dress. "This is Rosie."

"Oh," he said simply. He recognised the toy as the one he'd seen her with in the street that day he'd lost his threepenny bit: it had a chipped nose. He said "Hello" to Rosie and took the opportunity to sit up: no simple feat in the encumbering shirt. It was like sitting in a bell-tent intended to accommodate at least half-a-dozen people of his size. "Is this your father's shirt?" he asked, incredulously.

"Yes," she answered, and laughed as she watched him floundering within the garment in question, only his hands and face visible while the rest of him struggled inside.

"He must be a giant," he declared, giving up his struggle with the shirt for the moment and resting his elbows on his knees.

"He is. He's a policeman."

Jarvis almost disappeared inside the shirt, emerging after a few stifling moments to stare at her in wide-eyed alarm.

"Don't worry, he's a darling! Wouldn't harm anybody less'n they were really bad. He's never ever raised a finger to me. I've only ever received kisses and hugs from him, an' Mummy says I'm the baddest girl there ever was – sometimes. I don't think she means it."

Jarvis could see that she was curious about his apprehension over policemen, but he wasn't going to tell her anything of his experiences, nor anybody else – and especially not her father, even if he was wearing his shirt. "We've met before, haven't we?" he said.

She nodded her head vigorously, and exclaimed "Of course we have. The first time was that day you arrived at St Hilda's, though I hardly remember that occasion being only three at the time. Mummy's told me about it – many times. The second time I remember very well. It was in the street not so long ago and, I'm afraid you were very rude – and threatening, which was why I ran off." Her words were sharp, but spoken with a smile.

"I'm sorry," he told her, genuinely so. On impulse he told her about the girl who'd slapped his face when he thought it had been her pig-tails he'd pulled.

"Served you right," she giggled.

"Sorry," he said again, as if it had been her who slapped him.

"That's all right, Jarvis."

He supposed he shouldn't have been surprised that she knew his name, but he was. Her mother would have mentioned it, of course. It was all tied up with that parcel he'd been given all those years ago. The one with his soldier toy and the note. He remembered now that it was the note that had said something about a place called The Dials, and mentioned someone called Queenie. "And what's your name?" was all he could think of saying.

"I'm Ruth," she cried, clearly appalled at his ignorance. "And I'm nearly nine."

He liked the name, but he only said, "I still don't know who you are, Ruth, or how you come to know me. We can't be related, or anything. And who is your mother?"

"Me!"

It was *her*! The woman who'd met him at the gates of St Hilda's and given George to him. He knew her instantly. He thought he even recognised the sound of her voice which, preceded by a creak of the old, oak floorboards, came booming in from the open doorway. She didn't look greatly changed, not to him. Perhaps there wasn't quite so much of her, but otherwise she was more or less just as he remembered her. And gosh, that was a long time ago. He was only seven then : it was the day he'd arrived at Hilda's. She was still fairly huge compared to him, of course; tall, large in the chest, broad in the shoulders and with a round face that was still fleshy, but not nearly so much so. There was something else about her face that tugged at his boyish heart. He thought she looked lovely.

"I remember you," he cried excitedly. "I remember you both now. But I never knew who you were, either of you – but now I know Ruth, and you're the lady who gave me my wooden soldier ... so you must be Queenie – Queenie Something. I'm awfully sorry, but I've forgotten the rest."

Queenie joined them on the bed, and smiled from one to the other, fussing with the skirt of Ruth's dress which had risen up above her knees, and ruffling his hair and quite ignoring his efforts to escape. "Yes, Jarvis, I'm Queenie – Queenie Hoggins, an' Ruth's my daughter," she told him, and though he didn't realise it her normally formidable bar-room voice had dropped many octaves. "You was found right 'ere on me doorstep – The Seven Dials, almost twelve years ago by Sam Trotter."

"That's Daddy," interposed Ruth breathlessly, bouncing up and down on the bed until a restraining hand stilled her.

"Don't complicate fings, darling," chuckled Queenie, heaving up a straying bosom as nonchalantly as though snaring a loose curl. "'E'll 'ave 'nuff on 'is plate tryin' ter follow fings as it is. Nah then, where was we? Oh, yes. Well, it were Sam wot finds yer, Jarvis, an' bein' a great, hulkin' man wiv no more brains'n a cockroach where babies is concerned, promptly 'ands you over to me. Right on chuckin' out time it were, too. An' you should've 'eard yerself, Jarvis! Wot a pair of lungs yer 'ad! Strewth, wot a blinkin' din! An' wot a right ol' pong, too!" Jarvis felt his face redden, but grinned anyway; Ruth had such a fit of the giggles that Queenie had to thump her on the back to stifle the resultant bout of coughing. "Anyways," she resumed, when they'd all settled down again, "I gives you a barf – an' judging by yer state this mornin' it were the last one yer ever 'ad, m'lad – right there on the bar of the saloon, an' we 'ad bleedin' carbolic in the beer for days after! After yer barf, me'n Sam 'ad to take yer dahn to the 'ospital so's some medical geezer could look you over, just to make sure you ain't got the plague, nor nuffink. Well, you ain't, so that's all right, but that was when the church people got their 'ooks into yer, an' they ain't never let go since. Mind yer, it were either them or the council, an' Sam reckoned you stood a better chance wiv the Catholic lot – but then 'e's one of 'em, so 'e would, wouldn't 'e? I don't s'pose there's much diff'rence between one orphanage an' another. Pretty grim either way, I 'spect. Though I 'ear they're getting' better nowadays. Are they, luv?"

She looked keenly at him, presumably expecting to find confirmation of what she'd said, but he only stared blankly back at her. "Any'ow," she declared stoutly, "it were my Sam wot give you yer name."

"Oh!" Jarvis was really surprised. Since he was an orphan, he'd always taken it for granted his name was one given to him by the sisters, or perhaps the council. He remembered Sister Clare telling him his birth certificate described his parents as being unknown. It seemed hardly fair to call it a proper birth certificate, for apart from his name and a calculated date for his birth, with the assumption that this had taken place somewhere in the parish of St Giles, which was then in Holborn and now in Camden, there was precious little on it. "How come?" he asked. "And how did he arrive at such a name?"

"It were at yer baptism, dearie. Me an' Sam was witnesses – godparents they called it, an' this vicar chap suddenly arsks wot yer name is – as if we knew! As if anybody *still* do! 'Course, nobody says nuffink, but then, out of the blue, quick as a flash, Sam comes up wiv *Jarvis Brook*! It were the address on the carrier-bag you was found in. It's the name of a street just rahnd the corner from 'ere. I fink it were very clever of Sam."

Jarvis wasn't all that impressed to discover he'd been named after some old shopping bag. Still, it did confirm that since this wasn't his true name, he had to have another elsewhere. What was it? Who'd abandoned him? Where did he belong? Could someone still be looking for him? Even now? This uncertainty set his poor head whirling; but where to find the answers? For the briefest of moments he'd thought that Queenie would have them ... might even prove to be ... but even this dream had been dashed.

"So, we're not related in any way?" he said in a small, lost sort of voice.

"No, lovey," answered Queenie, almost apologetically, shaking her head and wincing at the disappointment she saw in his eyes, and heard in his voice. "Not really. I wish we was."

"But, if we never met since that day you found me on your doorstep, how was it you and Ruth were waiting for me at St Hilda's that day?" Jarvis pressed determinedly, unwilling to let go of his dream.

"Well, Jarvis, me'n Sam always thought of you as 'our boy' 'cos we found you, and were yer godparents. We give you yer name even. We was only too sorry we couldn't keep you for ourselves, but we couldn't. The Church 'ad yer an' weren't ever gonna let yer go – not to the likes of us. There wasn't nuffink we could do abaht that, but we felt a kind of bond wiv you, knowin' you as we 'ad practically from yer birth, so over the years we sortta kept track of you. Sam, bein' a policeman, kept an eye on you, so to speak, through Constable Binns – who, I gather, yer got to know quite well in Hayes!" – Jarvis nodded, frowningly, into her amused face – "They'd bin doin' bits of business together for years – but the least said abaht that the better, if yer follow me." She tapped the side of her prominent nose meaningfully, and gave him a prodigious wink, followed by a hearty chuckle, before continuing. "A couple of rogues themselves, the pair of 'em, if yer asks me – bless 'em. Anyways, when Ernie – that's Mr Binns, was abaht to deliver you to that St Hilda place, 'e lets my Sam know – an' that's 'ow come we was waitin' for yer at the gates."

Jarvis stared intently at her for some moments, and he knew his face was unable to conceal his bitter disappointment. He'd been so sure he'd find some answers about his past from this long-dreamed-of woman, but it seemed a blank all round. After several moments sorting through his thoughts, he gave a long sigh and said, very quietly: "When I saw you just now ... just for a few moments, I truly thought that perhaps you might be my mother ... and I just couldn't understand why you didn't want me." Perhaps he hadn't really thought this at all, but he wished with all his heart that it could be so.

"Oh, Jarvis-love, if you was mine, I'd never ever let you go. Not in a million years," cried Queenie passionately, wringing her great, strong hands in her vehemence and then folding her massive arms round him and hugging him to her till he could scarcely breathe. Then she let him go, and carried on talking as if she'd never stopped. "But, no, lovey," she continued, "like I said, it just ain't so. I'm so very sorry, darling. I ain't yer Mum. I wish to God I was."

"So do I," Jarvis said with a wistful little smile, blinking through a misty haze. "I wish someone was."

Jarvis thought for a moment that he was going to burst into tears, and he was almost sure he would have done if it hadn't been for Ruth. It was she who rescued him in that awful moment. She suddenly took hold of both his hands, or a goodly portion of each for his were a good bit larger, and, with a wisdom far exceeding her nearly-nine years, said:

"You can share my Mummy if you'd like, Jarvis. She's big enough to love us both."

The quiet, simple words broke the spell which had threatened to engulf him. Jarvis blinked furiously for a second or two and found that the mist had cleared, and then his mouth, which had been trembling like a child's about to cry, opened fractionally and widened to form the outline of a smile – in fact, it may well have been a prince of smiles because Ruth responded with such a dazzling one of her own that it quite turned his head. Quite out of character but propelled by some force he could not comprehend, he leaned forward spontaneously to touch her lips with his own. It was more a peck than a kiss on his part, but Ruth applied such vigour into her response that they were both quickly breathless, and parted panting. Jarvis knew he looked red and confused; Ruth looked pink and radiant; and Queenie looked relieved and happy. Jarvis offered her a kiss, too; again, it was just a touch with his lips, but she returned it many times over full on his mouth. It was overwhelming, and wonderful; perhaps, too wonderful. He sighed, and shook his head. He couldn't help himself.

"It's awfully kind of you to be willing to share your mother," Jarvis said to Ruth when he eventually regained his breath, picking his words with extraordinary care, not wanting to offend anyone. "Only, it wouldn't be real, would it?"

"Well, Jarvis-dear, me an' Sam could be yer pretend parents – ar'ter all, we're still yer godparents. Least ways, that's what Sam says we was," declared Queenie, with another of her deep chuckles as she scratched her stomach energetically. "I thought it sounded rather grand –

a lot better'n bein' simply a witness, anyway. Though where the devil God come into it, I haven't an earthly idea. Come to that, I weren't any the wiser abaht me own role. I mean, I didn't do nuffink but stand there listenin' to you bawling. But I was so proud an' 'appy just bein' there. An' p'raps that was the important thing – simply bein' there ... doin' God's work, so to speak. Lumme! 'Ark at us!" She paused to enjoy another chuckle at the thought, and then asked gently, "It wouldn't 'urt you any to pretend, lovey, would it? It might even give you some real 'appiness. I know it would us."

"Oh, all right," Jarvis said, with no real enthusiasm. "If you like. It's jolly kind of you. Thank you – both of you. An' Mr Trotter, too" The words flowed without any feeling of sincerity, no sense of genuine gratitude, and he was afraid his voice might sound ungracious. All his life he'd had a succession of pretend parents – first the nuns, then the priests and the brothers. None of them had been real. And now he had a new set of make-believe parents. He had so hoped they'd be the real ones. He struggled with thoughts of what a godparent had to do with him; it had always seemed to him that God, too, had abandoned him to find his own destiny ... and then Ruth's voice broke into his bitter thoughts, and saved him again.

"And I could be your pretend sister," she cried eagerly.

"I'd like that," he said quickly, but thinking that sounded inadequate, he added a "Thank you, Ruth," to make amends for his probable insincerity. What the hell did he know about sisters – the sort that were supposed to be relatives? Beard had an aunt, and look where that'd got him!

Jarvis didn't look to see Ruth's reaction to his dispassionate reply; instead, as inspiration struck him, he turned to face Queenie and asked her if it wasn't time he got up.

"Up!" she cried, in something resembling mock horror, which would have been more realistic but for the twinkle in her eyes. "It's time you was *both* in bed!" Ruth's instant wail of protest was silenced as instantly by her mother's arms folding themselves round her, and the pair of them rocked to and fro on the groaning bed. "You, young feller, won't get up till the doctor says so," declared Queenie firmly, "and then, only if I approve."

"But I'm perfectly all right – just a few bumps and grazes," Jarvis insisted, but he already felt he wasn't going to win this argument.

"Orl right!" Queenie echoed. "You're lucky to be alive!" she declared, and then enjoyed another of her chuckles. "The doctor said you'd given yer 'ead a nasty crack an' it was a miracle it weren't broken. He didn't fink you 'ad a concussion, but 'e wants yer to lie still in bed for a coupla days at least to recuperate from your – er, adventures. An' so do I. Give me a chance to fatten you up a bit."

"Mummy says you're like a bean pole – all height an' no body," piped in Ruth.

"Skin an' bone is all y'are. Do yer get 'nuff to eat at that 'ome of yourn, Jarvis?" Queenie asked with a frown of concern, as she and Ruth resumed their rocking game.

"I dunno, do I?" Jarvis answered cautiously, not wishing to make any more trouble for himself in the future, for there was no doubt about him returning to St Hilda's. The only uncertainty was when. "I eat what I'm given," he said with a shrug. "It don't seem much. I'd eat more if it were there to be ate, but it ain't, so I don't. I s'pose it's enough, 'cos I'm still alive, ain't I?"

"Children – specially boys need plenty of food if they're to grow up big an' strong," commented Queenie doubtfully, eyeing the thinness of those parts of Jarvis that were visible, which wasn't a lot. She leaned forward, lowering her voice a fraction. "But I don't want yer puttin' on no weight till ar'ter tomorrer. I wants yer in bed tomorrer, an' lookin' as poorly as yer possibly can, 'cos someone from the 'ome is comin' to see yer."

"Oh, crumbs," Jarvis muttered, feeling genuinely poorly, sure that the visitor would be the Rector, "he'll skin me alive!"

"No. No 'e won't, Jarvis," Queenie assured him determinedly, and there was a glint in her eye that had him half believing her; but only half. "Sam's already been to the 'ome an' said wot's 'appened to yer, an' told 'em straight it weren't none of yer fault ... an' that there was to be no punishin' yer or 'e'd report the matter to the authorities, an' that'd mean an enquiry into the goings on there. Fair took their breaths away – 'im bein' one of them – a Catholic, my Sam said," she exclaimed proudly, before asking with some concern: "Is it awfully bad there, Jarvis?"

"I dunno," he repeated, carefully. It might be bloody awful if you were on the outside looking in, but if you were on the inside it was the only life you knew and so you just gritted your teeth and accepted its harshness, and if you prayed, like they were made to, it was generally for some means of escape.

"Are they kind to you?" pressed Queenie, in a voice that clearly expected to hear the opposite.

"I suppose – sometimes." Jarvis tried to remember some instance of kindness, but couldn't recall one. It seemed a silly question to ask, but he didn't want to upset her – nor make trouble for him. "It were better at the Madonna ... but that was only for babies."

"Aren't you 'appy at St Hilda's, lovey "

Jarvis gave a little shrug inside his tent-shirt, accompanied by a wry smile. What did orphans know about happiness? Survival was what they knew about: that was the extent of their lives. "I dunno," Jarvis answered yet again. "I s'pose. I don't know anywhere else, do I?" He leaned forward, avoiding Ruth's grasping hand, and said earnestly: "I'd sooner stay here with you."

"If only you could, lovey," said Queenie, with intense feeling, ignoring Ruth who gave a series of shrill "yeses" and jumped up and down on the bed clapping her hands excitedly.

Jarvis gave another invisible shrug; really, he hadn't been too optimistic. Miracles only seemed to happen in Bible stories. He'd never heard of one down here, not near him.

"I bin down to the 'ome, quite a few times, since yer bin there, Jarvis," said Queenie, taking hold of his hand as it emerged from the shirt to scratch his nose, "but they wouldn't let me see yer. Said it weren't allowed an' that it would upset yer, but I reckoned it was themselves they was thinkin' abaht. Upset their way of fings is wot they meant, if yer arsks me. I still went back sometimes to 'ave a look through them gates of yourn, 'oping ter 'ave a glimpse of yer. But, I never did – 'ad a few small cries abaht that." She gave him a little cheerful smile, but her eyes looked sad. "I wish they weren't so strict with you poor children," she sighed. "'An' don't tell me no fibs, lovey. I know they're free an' easy wiv their canes."

"Well, it weren't my fault – not this time. None of it. Not really," Jarvis insisted, thinking about his return to St Hilda's. Having never escaped an expected punishment before, he didn't really trust them to honour any promise to Mr Trotter. "It was all that dog's fault," he explained, and went on to relate briefly his skirmish with the wretched animal and how he'd got lost. "If only I'd 'ad that card you give me wiv George – that's what I called the wooden soldier you give me, but I didn't."

Queenie nodded knowingly. "You almost did find us. Sam said he seen yer only yards away from 'ere that first day yer run orf. Tuesday, weren't it? Three days ago," she said, sighing. "He didn't know who yer was, 'course; not then. Not till it was reported at the police station that you was missing from the 'ome – an' then 'e twigged. Sam said 'e only saw yer fer a second an' that the instant you clocked 'im, yer shot off like a bleedin' grey'ound."

"Cor! If I'd only known," Jarvis exclaimed incredulously, "then I wouldn't have done none of the things what I did."

"Like wot, Jarvis?" urged Queenie, fearful about what mischief he'd got up to while on the run. "What did you get up to, eh?"

"Nothing much," he replied, clamming up. He wasn't ready, or even willing, to tell about his activities. He had already decided he wouldn't ever tell a living soul about his experience with the Honourable Oliver Roland; the incident embarrassed him too deeply and he wished only to erase it from his memory. He winced with disgust and loathing at the very thought of him. As for the man with the whip, well, he didn't know anything about him except that he was a sodding brute with a whip. And as for Mr Maggs, he didn't ever want to say anything that might get him into trouble; more trouble, that is. All in all, the least he said about anything the better. "I don't remember nuffink," he said simply.

Then, after a searching look round for his clothes and not seeing them anywhere, he asked anxiously where they were.

"Clothes!" cried Queenie, clapping hers and Ruth's hands together, and looking pleased at the change of topic. "Rags, you mean! I wouldn't 'ave put 'em on Guy Fawkes hisself let alone a child. They fell apart the moment I started scrubbing 'em. Weren't much to start off wiv, were there? Torn, worn shirt; trahsers wiv hardly no seat to 'em, an' pockets full of 'oles; no socks at all, an' boots wiv string fer laces an' one sole 'alf orf. The only underfings you 'ad was pants, an' they weren't up to much, neither. They wasn't clothes, boy! Rags is wot they was – an' the boiler is where they finished up."

"What! My clothes! They'll whip me for sure! What'll I wear?" Jarvis cried in consternation, not for any love of his lost rags, but because he was fearful of having to face life in the voluminous shirt in which he hid now. Christ! He'd probably have to pay for them out of his pocket money – if ever they let him have any after this.

"You'll wear new clothes, that's what," announced Queenie, decisively, and with a beaming motherly smile.

"New!" Jarvis echoed the word and gaped back at her in wonder. He'd never heard of such a thing. No one he knew had ever had such a thing. Even their "best," or other set of clothing, had had many rough owners before ever it reached them. "New!" he repeated the impossible word, too speechless to say more; too flabbergasted even to feel excitement.

"Well, they'll be almost like new, Jarvis," said Queenie, and he noticed a catch in her voice which, at the time, he thought must be concern over the price of them. He knew better later. "Don't they give you any proper clothes at the 'ome? New ones, I mean?"

Jarvis shook his head, and thought it a daft question. St Hilda's view was that it didn't matter how old or thin a garment was, so long as it covered you sufficiently so as not to embarrass God. Queenie looked as if she was about to crush him to her again, and he was relieved that Ruth sat between them for his aching body already felt wounded enough.

"I suppose you're 'ungry, Jarvis?" she asked, smiling, suddenly remembering supper.

Jarvis's ears took on a new alertness. Food! He nodded his head repeatedly, his eyes widened and became instantly shining. "Always," he whispered, horrified at the thought of how many meals he had missed since that feast at the Monk's Cellar days ago.

Well, Ruth and he were given a proper beanfeast. The chicken broth was spooned into eager mouths and the bowls licked dry; the neat little chicken sandwiches disappeared even quicker, Ruth giving him half hers; dishes of raspberries and jelly, swimming in top-of-the-milk cream, slithered down throats like melting ice on fire; and everything was washed down with tumblers of lemonade. Then, when they were ordered back to their respective beds, he made do with splashing water at his face, rubbing a wet finger along his teeth and then drying himself on the tail of his shirt, which he had to gather up in both hands before rushing back to his bed. Ruth seemed to take ages before, wearing a pink nightdress and with her dark hair tumbling about her shoulders, she padded barefooted back to his bed, which she threw herself on, with the expressed purpose of giving him a goodnight kiss.

Beard had no experience of kisses, either receiving or giving them. Even so, he gallantly submitted his face to her searching lips and the kiss, when it finally settled on his mouth, seemed unnecessarily long and excessively wet. He broke away from her, gasping for breath and feeling all hot and bothered for all that he did not recall contributing anything to the kiss. A touch was all.

Ruth surveyed him with as much calmness as a nearly-nine-year-old could be expected to muster, clearly puzzled at his confusion, and, holding his hands, said very softly: "You haven't had many kisses before, have you, Jarvis?"

Jarvis was sure he blushed a bit deeper. He knew he gripped her hands so tightly that she gasped, and he let go like she was red hot – and she immediately grabbed him again. "No," he admitted, finally. "Not a lot. Not any, really ..."

"Don't the sisters ever give you kisses?"

"I expect they did when I was small. I can't remember. We only have priests and brothers at St Hilda's an' they don't give yer kisses. They only gives you the cane!"

Ruth gave him a smile which he quite liked, and then touched his cheek with a feather-soft kiss which he accepted without responding to. "I'll give you a kiss every day, Jarvis," she said in a small, earnest voice.

Not if I'm back with the priests, he thought grimly. He was half afraid Ruth was going to climb into the bed and sleep with him, but Queenie was having none of that. She lifted her protesting daughter off the bed, gave him a good-night kiss herself, allowed Ruth to give him a final one, and then they were gone ... and he wasn't sure but that he was not asleep by the time Ruth was put into her own bed.

Jarvis thought he must have had a nightmare during the night. He had no recollection of what it was about, but he imagined it was connected with that Honourable bastard Roland and his attempts to do things to him. He had a vague memory of screaming and of being soaked with perspiration, and of waking up to find himself enveloped in Queenie's arms. He must have been really soaked for his shirt-thing had gone and he was now wrapped in a huge pink bath towel. But he was hardly aware of this for his head was buried against Queenie's warm and comforting bosom, as she rocked him gently to and fro. He didn't enquire how, or why, he was there because … well, it was like being in heaven.

"Tell me about when you found me," he whispered after a while, his words hot against her warm breast. "About what happened after you left me at the hospital." He pressed himself into her, breathing in the perfume of her; this was his idea of perfect happiness. "After you'd done your godparenting bit, for instance. Didn't you ever see me again?"

"No." Queenie shook her tawny head and clutched him even closer to her warm body. "No, not till you arrived at St Hilda's – seven years later." She resumed her rocking motion, backwards and forwards, just as she had with Ruth. Jarvis loved it. "Tell me about those first days," he begged her, snuggling up closer. "I want to know all about those days I don't remember, and all about my … godparents."

Queenie demurred, even as she rested her cheek against his head. "It's late, dear. You need yer sleep. We'll 'ave a long talk in the morning." But, perhaps because, deep down, she knew she only had him for a very little while longer – perhaps only until tomorrow, that Queenie relented. She wrapped them both up in a blanket and they lay together on the bed.

"All right, my precious," she whispered, her breath hot against his cheek, "but it's really Sam's story so I'll tell yer like it was 'im tellin' it – 'cos that's the way 'e told it to me, like 'e were readin' it all from 'is notebook. In fact, that's exactly what it were like … a story out of a book. 'E's a good storyteller, is my Sam."

And there, in the still of the night, Jarvis learned at last about those first days of his life He clung to Queenie and to every single word of Sam's story, not daring to close his eyes in case he fell asleep and missed something.

Queenie's account of what Sam had told her over many weeks and with a lot of coaxing came to a sudden halt, and for some moments they lay there in silence. Then, Jarvis lifted his head an inch or two to look into her face, and said: "And Mr Trotter did keep an eye on me, didn't he? Even if I didn't know it – an' he never saw me."

She nodded. "Yes, lovey. Mr Binns always kept us informed about you while you was at Hayes. It's only since you've been 'ere in London, right on our own doorstep as it were, that we lost sight of you – temporarily."

"I wish I'd known you was looking, I'd have run away sooner," Jarvis murmured, returning his head to the pillow of her breast. He felt her chuckling beneath him.

"You'd better stop that lark, Jarvis," she cautioned softly, "or yer might get into real trouble. It were a miracle you 'appened ter fall into our cellar. Anyfink might've 'appened to you. Terrible fings."

Jarvis was about to tell her that terrible things did happen, but he thought better of it. Instead, he asked: "Did your Mr Trotter ever try looking for me Mum?"

"Good 'eavens, yes," said Queenie quickly, and hurried on to tell how very sorry Sam had been that he was unable to discover anything of Jarvis's background; he'd hoped to trace his mother, but though he creaked tirelessly through the streets asking endless questions, he could get no line on her, neither from hospitals or backstreet midwives. "As the weeks passed it became less likely that 'e ever would," continued Queenie. "P'raps, in time, she would surface, but Sam said that if ever she did it would 'ave to be a voluntary move on 'er part. She'd 'ave ter come out of the woodwork an' show 'erself, an' arsk arter 'er baby."

"An' she never did come forward lookin' for me?" Jarvis asked, his yawn probably an indication of his dwindling interest. He told himself, as he'd done so many times in the past when his parentage invaded his thoughts, that you can't really miss someone you've never known, not for ever. Still, it was nice to have learned something of his early existence, even if it didn't answer many of the questions accumulated in his head.

Queenie shook her head. Sam had not been optimistic, she said, but that had never stopped him creaking round pursuing his enquiries.

Jarvis felt close to falling asleep again, but there was one last thing he wanted to ask about. Sam and his wife, and her. "So where's Mr Trotter's wife then? Does she live here, too?" And before she could answer, he added, "When did you and Mr Trotter meet? Was it the night you found me?"

Queenie chuckled and made a low "shushing" sound. It was a minute or two before she answered. "It was certainly around that time, lovey. I'd known Sam for years before you was found, but it was only afterwards, an' while you was still in 'ospital waitin' for the convent people sort fings out, that 'e moved in 'ere with me. We've been togevver ever since, an' always will be."

"Doesn't Mrs Trotter mind?" he persisted.

"Lily? Yes, probably, I s'pose she do," declared Queenie forcefully, and suddenly breathing very hard, "even if she don't want 'im, not really. She was a nagging religious crank of a woman who made 'is life a misery. Even so, it was only after much soul-searching that 'e finally left 'er, an' moved in wiv me for good." What she didn't tell Jarvis until years later was that Sam's resolve didn't weaken when Lily refused to give him a divorce saying it would be a mortal sin in which she wanted no part; nor even when she demanded that he continue to pay her rent and insisted on him paying her a weekly allowance out of his meagre wages. He agreed to everything, but never wavered in his determination to leave her, or complained of the punitive price she exacted for his liberty. Good man that he is, he felt she was entitled to something in his place.

"He is the best man in all the world, and I wished we could be married," Queenie whispered as Jarvis lay in her arms that night. "I told myself that it didn't matter, but, of course, it did ... especially after a couple of years, an' I found I was pregnant ... and along came Ruth." She hugged them both at the memory, and added, "I love them both so completely, and now, I have you to love, too."

"How lovely," he murmured in reply, and fell asleep in the same instant.

Jarvis was hardly awake – it was his creaking that stirred him – when Sam looked in before going to work. They knew each another immediately – even though Sam wasn't wearing his policeman's tunic and had on only his trousers with the braces fastened over his vest. Jarvis recognised him as the policeman who had put the fear of God into him only a few days before. He looked a lot less frightening this morning. He was smiling.

"Just looked in to see how you was," he said amiably. "How are you today?"

"Fine – sir," Jarvis answered in a small, respectful voice.

"I'm yer godfather."

"Queenie told me. Pleased to know you, sir," Jarvis told him, blinking the sleep from his eyes.

"Likewise," Sam grinned back. He showed no surprise at seeing Jarvis wrapped up in a towel, and added: "You look very comfy."

"I'd like to get up."

"You wait till yer told, young'n," Sam said in a voice that did not encourage any argument. "Queenie'll tell you when."

"Yessir."

"I'm off to work now," Sam went on, in a milder tone. "Won't be seein' much of you durin' the day ... but we'll 'ave a chat when you're up an' abaht." And with that, he gave Jarvis a wave and creaked away.

Well, Jarvis thought, as he snuggled down in the bed again, that wasn't too bad. He'd thought Sam might be coming to arrest him. But as he lay congratulating himself, a new fear grew within him. Someone from St Hilda's was coming to see him today. He had no doubt that it would be Father Hugh himself, and that he would come armed with a cane. Jarvis wondered if he would insist on his returning to St Hilda's this very day, and thought that he'd probably never see Sam again, and that he'd be lucky if he was allowed to say goodbye to Queenie and Ruth, and all of a sudden he was kneeling up in the huge bed praying for all he was worth; praying that he'd be able to stay on at The Dials for at least another day, if not for ever. He prayed that God was awake at this early hour, and listening; please.

Well, perhaps God had been awake and listened to his prayer, because halfway through the morning, as he was lying with his freshly-scrubbed face and well-brushed hair peeping over the bed covers, he was startled when Sister Beatrice, the Mother Superior of the neighbouring convent where he went for his German lessons, was ushered into the room by a Queenie looking very matronly in a colourful, floral pinafore. He'd been so expecting Father Rector with the certain promise of a flogging to follow.

The arrival of Sister Beatrice in his stead was better than Jarvis could have dared hope for, and he was so pleased to be wearing the brand-new blue and white pyjamas Queenie had rushed out to buy him earlier. They were so much grander than Mr Trotter's rough shirt and, feeling that they were too beautiful to be hidden, Jarvis shot upright so as to display as much of them to his visitor as he considered decent, at the same time beaming a sincere welcome at Sister Beatrice, whom he had only spoken with once, but seen many times gliding along the convent corridors.

Sister Beatrice, who was short, big chested and with what he called a holy face, quite old, examined Jarvis intently from the foot of the bed. Jarvis suddenly remembering he was supposed to be looking as though he were dying, or recovering from the dead – whichever was worse, fell back against the pillow with a low moan and his face took on what he hoped was a death's door aspect.

Sister Beatrice, looking quite unmoved by this performance, took a seat beside the bed and extended her hand towards Jarvis. He grabbed at it so enthusiastically that he bruised his lips as he kissed her ring. Sister Beatrice remarked that she could not remember ever seeing a boy look so well, and shiny clean, and declared that she was delighted at his astonishing recovery having been led to imagine she'd find him laid out in the parlour awaiting the undertakers; and here he was alive and seemingly well, apart from his black eye about which she would not enquire, and looking quite as handsome as ever in the grandest pair of pyjamas she'd ever seen. Jarvis wasn't sure if she was being sarcastic or not, but it was gratifying that at least his gorgeous pyjamas had been noticed. Queenie, who hid her face momentarily in the folds of her apron, mumbled something about the recuperative powers of the young. "You know what kids is, ma'am," she added, with a knowing smile.

"I certainly do, Mrs Hoggins," conceded Sister Beatrice. (Jarvis had not heard Queenie referred to as Mrs Hoggins before and for a moment he wondered if there might be a Mr Hoggins somewhere, like that Lily Trotter woman, but he hoped there wasn't.) She gave herself over to a hearty burst of laughter in which everyone thought it prudent to join in, including the revitalised Jarvis.

Having cleared the air with her outburst of merriment, Sister

Beatrice held up an authoritative hand for silence and insisted on hearing Jarvis's version of events since his flight on the heels of his canine friend. Jarvis, frowning at this assumed friendship, then proceeded to give a very credible account of his adventures: or misfortunes, as he called them. It was a short story: short, and plausible, without being too convincing; in truth, it was so lacking in reality, it was more a fairy story. He did mention the whipping he'd so unjustly received from a complete stranger, and there were references to such actual misfortunes as being completely lost, hunger, loneliness and other associated hardships, but there was no mention of either Mr Maggs or Oliver Roland. In fact, apart from the whipping incident, the only really honest part of the whole story came in his concluding statement, " ... an' then I fell into this perishin' cellar, an' nearly croaked m'self!"

"We're all very pleased you didn't – croak yourself, Jarvis," declared Sister Beatrice, wondering if anything he'd said was truthful; she raised an amused eyebrow, and smothered a low chuckle.

"Did you know Queenie – er, Mrs Hoggins is my godmother?" Jarvis blurted out, beginning to wilt under the sister's steady scrutiny. He was quite sure he hadn't pulled any wool over those eyes.

"I do now," allowed Sister Beatrice, glancing round to give Queenie a slight bow of her head.

"And I've got a godfather, too. An' he's a policeman, an' all!" Jarvis felt quite proud: he was certainly excited. "An' there was me thinking I 'ad no one in the world."

"We all have a Father in God, and a Mother in Mary," Sister Beatrice rebuked mildly.

"Oh, yes, I know about them, Sister," Jarvis said with reckless impatience, "but these are real live people. I can see them, an' touch them, an' talk to them ... an' ev'rything. An', Sister, God never cooked me bacon an' eggs an' fried bread for breakfast! No, nor anybody else, neither."

Jarvis wondered if perhaps he'd gone too far. Had he been blasphemous, on top of everything else? He looked at Queenie, and found only the fondest of love staring wetly back at him; Ruth, who had crept silently into the room and was standing unobtrusively near the door, stared in wonder, marvelling at his daring, but evidently approving wholeheartedly as her nodding pig-tails showed. Jarvis returned his darting eyes to Sister Beatrice, who merely raised her eyes to heaven, and no doubt felt his visit to the confessional to be now even more imperative. Whatever her thoughts might have been, she disentangled her hands from her rosary, stabbed at the bed with a stubby finger, and said:

"Keep quiet, and listen to me, Jarvis. The doctor, whose judgement we must accept, says you've had a nasty bang on the head, but, while he doesn't think it's serious enough to pack you off to hospital, he advises that you have rest and quiet. He plainly knows nothing about small boys!" Sister Beatrice allowed herself another modest chuckle, which Queenie alone joined in. "Anyway, he doesn't want you moving from where you are – though for the life of me you look fit as a fiddle, but since Mrs Hoggins, good woman that she is, is agreeable, it's been agreed that you shall remain here for two weeks." Jarvis could scarcely believe his ears, nor, apparently, could Ruth, for he heard her give an exclamation of elation that matched his own. "That doesn't mean a holiday, m'lad. You're here to recuperate, though I don't doubt the good Father Rector will have his own thoughts about convalescing in such an establishment."

She turned again towards Queenie, and Jarvis thought she must have given her a wink – certainly Queenie gave one. "On the other hand, we cannot ignore the quite extraordinary coincidence that your hosts turn out to be your godparents, and so I've decided that a stay under their roof may be not only appropriate, but even beneficial. We'll see, won't we? In the meantime, you'll behave yourself and do exactly as you're told at all times; no fooling about, no shouting, no tantrums – and watch your manners and language. And don't be forgetting your prayers, and don't you dare miss Mass – at least on Sundays!" She paused, and fixed her steely green eyes on his wide-open, attentive, shining brown ones. "And, if you decide to run off again, make sure you're not caught – because you'll really be in trouble if you are! So, be a good boy ... and do try and remember you're not very well! Now, Mrs Hoggins and I have some matters to discuss, so I'll leave you with Ruth for company for a little while. No noise, mind, from either of you."

Sister Beatrice eased her plump frame off the chair, pressed something small and hard into Jarvis's hand, and mouthed a blessing that embraced both him and Ruth, who dropped a respectful curtsy, and then whooshed out of the room with Queenie at her side. Almost before they were out of sight and earshot, Ruth dived for the bed and belaboured Jarvis with so many kisses she had to stop to catch her breath.

"I'm quite sure you've told us nothing but a pack of lies about your adventures, my dear Jarvis," she declared cheerfully when she'd recovered, and then added, "I don't want to hear what you really got up to, if you don't want to tell." She paused, hopefully, in case he might want to, but he didn't. "Well, just don't ever do anything so silly again, Jarvis," she went on. "I was scared half to death when I saw you lying in the cellar. I was so frightened."

And she threw her arms round his neck and hugged him tightly to her again, and then burst into tears. Jarvis sighed, bravely ignoring the fresh pain she inflicted on his back. He'd heard that girls loved a good cry: silly things. He endured her embrace for some moments before disentangling himself, and, as Ruth busied herself with a scrap of hankie, he remarked, "Just imagine, though, if none of it had happened, I'd never have discovered I had godparents nor found you again. So, are you a godsister, Ruth?"

Ruth looked up at him and frowned, her tears gone as suddenly as they'd come. She wasn't sure if there was any such thing as a godsister ; she didn't think so, she'd have to ask Mummy. She shook her head to be on the safe side. "What did Sister gave you?" she asked.

Jarvis looked curiously at his forgotten hand, slowly opened it and they both stared at the little silver medallion.

"A St Christopher," exclaimed Ruth.

"She obviously expects me to run away again!" Jarvis cried gleefully, and received a pillow in his face followed by a shriek of laughter from Ruth. Then forgetting his wounds, they both indulged in a general free-for-all, till Queenie came back into the room and told them that Sister Beatrice was safely gone and that they could stop keeping quiet.

Jarvis didn't see much of Mr Trotter to begin with because he always seemed to be working. It wasn't till the fourth day that he and Sam (by then he'd got used to calling Mr Trotter just plain Sam) had an opportunity for their "serious" talk.

"Jarvis," Sam began, and though his voice was far from stern, Jarvis recognised in it the sting of authority which put him immediately on his guard, "in the first place there's nothin' to be scared abaht. You ain't goin' to be in no trouble, nor punished in any way – not by the Law. I promise you that." – Jarvis was at once suspicious – "But we – the police – well, we needs to tie a few fings up, like, which boils down to the fact that I've got ask you some questions – an' you've got to answer them truthfully, an' I know they teach you wot that is where you are. It's known as 'elpin' the police wiv their enquiries. You un'erstand?"

Jarvis sat staring across the table at the giant policeman, whom he had come, if not to love, certainly to like and to admire and to respect. He wasn't sure if that included trust – not in his present capacity. At this moment, his friend was also the enemy. Jarvis gave a single, cautious nod, determined to live up to the code of The Bullets. He wouldn't help the police in any enquiries that might involve either him or his friends, especially not Mr Maggs. "I don't know nothin'," he said resolutely.

"I 'spect you don't, Jarvis, but you might just know summat wivvout knowing it," replied Sam, in the warm and friendly voice Jarvis had come to know so well. "Let's see, shall we? Now, we're pretty sure it were a gent name of George Popple wot whipped yer. It's 'is style. He has charge of the City of London's ceremonial coaches an' 'orses, and finks 'e's God-almighty. He's known to be a bit free an' easy wiv 'is whip though he generally reckons he's got cause. He's got a quick temper, but 'e 'ad no right to whip you like that." Jarvis stared blankly, and said nothing. "There ain't much we can do abaht that, unless you make a complaint. No? Well, I didn't s'pose you would do. People never do, that's why 'e gets away wiv it. Thing is, one of 'is 'orses was stolen t'other night so he was probably in a worse temper than ever when ..."

But Jarvis didn't admit to being on the receiving end of that temper. "Seems a daft thing to go pinching horses," he said, sidestepping the clear inference behind Sam's unfinished words. "I mean, you can't hide a blinkin' great horse long, can you?"

"You might, in a field – mixed in wiv other 'orses," observed Sam, after considering the matter for a moment. "Surprisin' wot fings folks pinch these days – fings they ain't got no earthly use for." He paused to consider this fact while his great fingers scratched at the folds of his chins, and then continued, fixing his grey-green eyes afresh on Jarvis. "After the 'orses fing, we was wonderin' if yer might possibly 'ave chanced to run into the 'onourable Oliver Roland, who is known to us as a rather dis'onourable gentleman. A poofter, if yer knows wot that is."

Jarvis nodded. He knew. He stared grimly back at Sam, unblinking, his jaw clenched determinedly. Wild horses – stolen, or otherwise – wouldn't drag a word out of him. Never! He knew a moment of sheer terror at the thought – it hadn't bothered him previously, but then he wasn't being interviewed by the rozzers – that he might have murdered him, and the police were searching for his killer – *him*!

"Then you'll not be at all interested to 'ear that 'e 'ad a bit of a accident – the same night wot you 'ad yer own little accident an' fell into our cellar," said Sam, in an excessively casual tone. Jarvis could feel the perspiration forming on his forehead and he could feel the colour draining from his taut cheeks which must be another tell-tale sign of his guilt. "But 'e come off a lot worse, 'e did," added Sam quietly.

"He ain't dead then?" Jarvis cried, with such enormous relief he felt sure he was going to faint. He didn't and, as he felt the colour surging back into his cheeks, he wished he'd held his tongue, or at least kept the concern out of his voice. Impossible! It was such a relief to know he wasn't a murderer and not destined to be hanged, though he had to admit that he hadn't given that possibility much consideration till a moment ago. Did they still hang boys?

"Lor, save us, no! Not 'is nibs. Some scallywag busted 'is knee-cap an' broke a finger, is all. His 'onour said 'e bit orf the tip of 'is tongue to stop hisself screamin' wiv pain, an' while 'e were busy doin' that 'e were beaten wiv 'is own cane, so it seems. He claimed 'e'd been attacked by a gang of footpads. We finks the truth of the matter is that 'e approached some geezer an' bit orf more'n 'e bargained – in more senses than one! Anyways, the police 'as closed the book on 'im."

"I don't know him," Jarvis insisted, stubbornly. But he was sure his relief must be clearly visible to the world.

"I didn't fink so," smiled Sam knowingly. "Well, one person wot yer did 'ave dealings wiv, m'lad, is a gent who's got more names than you've got years on yer shoulders," he declared bluntly. "You probably knew 'im as Maggs, or Grout, or, as 'e's extremely well known to us, The Tin Man?"

"What makes you think I know him?" Jarvis whispered, terrified again, but ready to deny knowing everybody, and everything.

"Because of this 'ere coin, Jarvis," replied Sam gently, fishing deep in his cardigan pocket. He pushed the coin across the table.

Jarvis felt himself flinching away from it, but there was no escaping. He saw that it was a florin; he saw, too, that there was a hole neatly drilled through it near the edge. He picked it up and turned it over and over between thumb and fingers. He knew that the one Maggs had given him was missing – he'd assumed it had fallen through a hole in his trouser pocket – his old trousers, but his coin hadn't had a hole in it so this one couldn't be it. He didn't know whether to be relieved or annoyed that the hole made it useless. He looked up at Sam. "So?" he asked, the coin clenched in his fist.

"It's one of 'is," said Sam simply, "an' it were found on you, Jarvis."

"I've not seen it before. If I had a florin, it wouldn't have no hole in it. So?" Jarvis repeated, puzzled. "A coin's a coin. You can't just say it's his, nor mine, neither. Could be anyone's. Anyway, it's useless with a hole in it, innit?"

"You're not understandin' this, Jarvis. How'd you fink our Mr Maggs come to be called The Tin Man?" asked Sam patiently. "It were 'cos 'e minted 'is own money, lad. Your florin – that's it in yer 'and, it ain't real. It's a phoney. Just a lump of useless metal. It's counterfeit. He's made 'undreds of 'em over the years, the crafty beggar. All two-bob bits. But 'e won't be makin' no more. We found 'is workshop an' all 'is coin-making contrivances back of a Chinese tea shop in Greenwich. Silly blighter! He should've stuck to nickin' lead orf church roofs. Mind you, I 'spect these florins of 'is will go on turnin' up for years yet, an' I wouldn't be surprised if someone ain't holdin' a sackful for 'im. Probably some doxie – 'e fancied 'imself as a lady's man, it seems." – Jarvis immediately thought of Bertie, and hoped she'd be careful for Mr Maggs's sake; he squeezed the coin like it was an old friend. – "But there won't be any more of 'em, not now."

"He give it to me for helping him push his barrow the day he was caught," Jarvis said, feeling quite miserable. But it seemed rather pointless denying his association any longer.

"'Ave you got any more of 'em hidden away, Jarvis?" asked Sam, urgently.

Jarvis shook his head hurriedly. "No, honestly, he only give me the one. It was the most wonderful moment of my life. It was the most money I'd ever had in me hand at one time, an' I never got the chance to spend a penny of it – just like the threepenny bit I had, and lost," said Jarvis, bemoaning both losses, and not giving a thought to the fact that the florin wasn't genuine. Remembering Mr Maggs, he added sadly: "He'll go to prison, I s'ppose?"

"At least five years, I 'spect – p'raps seven wiv 'is record."

"Poor old Maggs. He was good to me, whatever else he's done. He fed me when I was almost starving – and he gave me this florin." Jarvis opened his fist and looked at the useless coin again. "It was his way of thanking me for helping him. And I did little enough – nothing, really, just helped him push his barrow. I didn't actually pinch anything, honest."

"I'm sure you didn't, Jarvis – an' like I said, you're not in any trouble," Sam said quietly. "We just needed to know how you came by the coin, an' if you 'ad any more or knew where any more was hid. It's a terrible serious offence is counterfeiting – an' you could be in big trouble if you even tried to spend that coin of yours. That's why I put a hole in 'er – so's you could keep it for a souvenir, like."

"Oh, thank you, Sam," Jarvis cried gratefully, renewing his grip on the coin. "I'll treasure it always. I'll wear it round my neck as a good luck piece. Mr Maggs should've worn one, too!"

They laughed together, and instinctively they hugged and, as only once before when in a similar embrace with Queenie, Jarvis knew complete safety and perfect peace; he felt both happy and loved, neither of which he had experienced before. He didn't want it ever to end. If he were to die at that moment, he would have been quite content with his life.

During the early days of Jarvis's "holiday" at The Dials, when he and Sam were getting to know each other, Sam – not realising that Queenie had already told Jarvis just about everything – told him about how he'd found him all those years ago, and about the others who had played a part in his life before he'd arrived at Hayes; people like Father O'Shea, Doctor Levy and Sister Kate, who was now in Malaya. Jarvis listened to Sam's version of his history with equal fascination for he loved to hear about those early days which were beyond his memory. It was unbelievably wonderful to belong to a family, even if they couldn't live together ; it was rather like being born again.

But, before he could even begin his holiday, Jarvis had to wait for permission to get up. First, a Dr Drinkwater called to examine him, which he did leisurely, talking constantly with Queenie, before proclaiming, as if there had been some doubt about it, "You'll live!" and adding that Jarvis could get up. Jarvis assumed this meant he could get up directly, but he'd reckoned without Queenie, who had her own views on the matter. "Tomorrer! That'll be soon enough," she declared. And there was no arguing there.

Next morning, the moment Queenie gave the word, Jarvis shot out of bed, determined not to waste an instant of his freedom – or convalescence, as she called it. The magic began right then with Queenie producing his almost-new clothes. New everything – well, she'd burned everything else; underwear, socks, shorts, shirt and a pullover. It was all the usual grey, but everything was so immaculately new it seemed a sacrilege to touch anything. There was also a pair of almost-new boots, gleaming like polished black glass. Jarvis felt like a king. He'd never felt so all-over smart and clean – except when he'd been dolled up for an adoption inspection, but even then not in *new* clothes; and to be wearing socks, and not even on some dead saint's feast day, now that was richness indeed. He was profuse with his gratitude, hugging and kissing Queenie repeatedly, and then dancing with her round and round the bedroom – with Ruth tugging at them and wanting her turn, which was very soon for Queenie started puffing and flopped down on the bed to get her breath back.

After this moment of ecstasy, or very soon afterwards, one of the first things Jarvis needed to get straight was what to call Queenie. He supposed he should call her Mrs Hoggins, or Mrs Trotter, or even Ma'am, but he wasn't at all sure which, if any. And so he asked her, with the bluntness of youth, and she said Queenie would be fine. But Ruth, who was like a shadow wherever he went, piped in: "I call her Mummy, so why don't you?" Queenie's eyes, meeting his, invited a choice with a warm, suggestive smile. "I'll call you Queenie, if that's all right," Jarvis said, for what was all right in a dream didn't count now. He shut his eyes to the disappointment in hers. She'd hoped, he supposed, that he'd call her Mum, but he couldn't. He wasn't ready for that – as much as he wished for it to be so. There was only one woman entitled to that name, and she'd abandoned him; but, she might turn up one day. "That'll be fine," she murmured quietly, and busied herself with a loose tawny strand of hair.

For the entire fortnight, Ruth and Jarvis were never apart, and seldom still, and even more rarely quiet. They raced up and down stairs, in and out of rooms, getting scolded all the time and frequently being threatened with getting "what for" knowing full well they never would. They were a plague to all the staff. There were quite a few of them when the bars were busy, but Jarvis only remembered the ones they came into contact with during the day. There was Mavis, the head barmaid, who turned out to be big and solidly-built, with a red, square face and a voice almost the equal of Queenie's; Millie, a sort of regular casual barmaid – he learned that she had several children but no husband, not even a pretend one like Sam – who was small and dumpy and very pale, with weak blue eyes and blonde hair which looked glued into a tight knot at the nape of her neck, and whom Jarvis always thought looked more in need of fattening up and a good holiday than ever himself; and then there was Hannah, who seemed just as much a child as they were – although she was, perhaps, fifteen or sixteen. She was the general dogsbody who did whatever she was told when she was told, and none of it very well; she spent most of her time washing up and scrubbing. She had no shape at all, her lanky body going straight up and down with no ins-and-outs to break the monotony, but above her thin, flat, magnolia-complexioned face was a mass of coppery curls that gave her a touch of beauty and femininity. Jarvis was not surprised to discover that she and Ruth played together in quiet moments.

The only other person Jarvis remembered was the potman, Fred Akers, who wasn't very tall but was as broad as a barrel of beer and terrifically strong – he was able to lift a barrel all on his own. He didn't have much hair on his head but he had great bushes of dark eyebrows, a round stubbly face, little green eyes and a set of very white teeth which he took out and popped into a tobacco tin when he felt like it. It was the first time Jarvis had ever seen false teeth. Akers was a grumpy, unfriendly chap and Jarvis was always scheming with Ruth to pinch his teeth, but the only time they managed it the blessed tin was empty – so they guessed he knew what they were up to, and gave up. Oh, and there was a Mrs Baxter who came in once a fortnight to do what was called "the big wash," and twice a week to collect dirty tea cloths and things and bring back clean ones. They all thought her a "holy terror" – Ruth's words – and kept well out of her way on wash days, and especially clear of the back yard where sheets billowed everywhere. Jarvis only saw her once (from a safe distance), and thought she had a jolly, rosy face. "Blowsy, yer mean," corrected Hannah, giggling.

It seemed strange at first for Jarvis to have only a girl as a playmate and companion, but they quickly became used to one another and, Jarvis had to admit, he found her company more and more agreeable, even to the point of looking for her on those rare occasions she couldn't escape doing chores for her mother. Well, why not? Why shouldn't he enjoy her company when his every wish met with her approval and compliance? Of course, there were times when it was the other way round, and even that gave him pleasure.

On that first day of liberty, Jarvis had grabbed Ruth's hand and dashed straight outside to absorb the sounds and smells of the teeming world, and began exploring every nook and cranny, much to the vociferous irritation of the street traders who didn't mind encouraging potential customers to loiter, but certainly didn't want any penniless kids under their feet. So, they didn't linger anywhere too long – just long enough to be shooed off. Jarvis was all for arguing with the stallholders, especially when their snarling threats were accompanied by a shower of rotted produce and, once, a kick that only just missed the seat of his brand-new trousers, but Ruth kept tugging at his sleeve, coaxing him away from trouble and reminding him he had to mind his new clothes

"or Mummy'll be cross and then you'll be for it – and probably me, too."
It was not a threat that would've daunted Jarvis normally, but in these
special circumstances, he was unwilling to put the probability to the test,
and so he yielded to Ruth's sensible counsel and they moved on till
something fresh attracted their attention.

Every day brought fresh adventures for them. They marched,
swinging their arms, beside a file of old soldiers shuffling along in the
gutter and creating an awful noise with their drums and whistles and
vainly rattling a tin cup; then their attention was drawn to the hurdy-
gurdy man and his monkey, but when the creature jumped on to Ruth's
shoulder, shoving a tin mug into her face and giving her pig-tails a
hearty pull, and making her scream, Jarvis promptly gave the brute's
own tail a hefty tug, and they fled; a barrel-organ was far more to their
liking and they joined a group of youngsters dancing and skipping to the
music while onlookers clapped their hands in time and donated an
occasional copper to encourage the sweaty grinder to keep turning the
handle. Afterwards, Ruth said she was learning "proper dancing" at
school, and said she would be ever so willing to teach Jarvis, if he liked.
Jarvis wasn't all that keen at first, but once they started he thought it
quite fun. Indeed, the pair got on so well together that Jarvis even
allowed himself to be taken on a visit to her school.

He had not been enthusiastic at her suggestion, but she looked so
eager herself that he let her lead him down some back streets and into a
rather mean alley which led to the rear of the establishment. A faded
notice informed passers-by that they had found not only St Clare's
Catholic Church and its infants and primary schools, but also a refuge
for the needy of the parish. Entrance to all of these was up three worn
stone steps and through a great iron gate. At the far end, which was
hardly any distance at all, stood a grimy, red-bricked building that was
evidently the school, and alongside, was the church of St Clare, whose
modest spire stretched through the polluted atmosphere in search of God.
Everything seemed to be squeezed into an impossibly small area, even
so between the two dismal buildings space had been found for a scrap of
garden where a few flowers struggled to live. A nun, who had been
tending this grave-sized plot, regarded their approach with some
surprise, it being a Saturday. When Ruth whispered to Jarvis that the nun
was called Sister Bertie, she had to explain that the sister had been
christened Benedicta by her grateful Italian parents. He still hardly
believed it. Sister Bertie, who had been on her knees, clambered
awkwardly to her feet, straightened up and surveyed them. She knew
Ruth, of course, but she eyed Jarvis with a curiosity not far removed
from wariness.

Ruth, with the confidence of one who felt herself at home,
dropped a customary curtsy, and introduced her companion. "Jarvis
Brook," she said, "he's from St Hilda's Academy, and he's staying with

us for two weeks. In fact, Sister, even though he's an orphan, he really belongs to us." She added, by way of explanation, "Mummy and Daddy are his godparents."

Jarvis, determined to be on his very best behaviour for Ruth's sake, bowed boldly, and said: "Hello, Sister. Lovely day, isn't it? I'm on holiday. Aren't I lucky!"

Sister Bertie invited them both into her private room, as she liked to call her mousetrap of a hidey-hole. It was really little more than a broom cupboard, with a pencil-thin stained-glass window that let in hardly any light, but it was her accepted retreat for prayer and meditation, and a place to discuss other people's problems without fear of disturbance. When they were all settled, she on the only chair, the two children on heaped hassocks, there was very little room remaining, but she managed to produce glasses of lemonade for them all and set Ruth to toasting slices of bread on a single-jet gas fire which they ate with home-made raspberry jam. Jarvis decided the visit had been well worth while.

And so the days of Jarvis's holiday rolled by: almost before he realised it, the first week had passed. They were lucky with the weather: only one day when rain kept them indoors. Queenie awarded herself a few days off and, with Ruth excused school, they all visited Madame Tussaud's where Jarvis caused great merriment to everyone else and some mortification to himself when he repeatedly asked an attendant where to find the Chamber of Horrors, only to discover he was talking to one of the wax models. The next day, they went to the Tower of London where Ruth oo-ed and ah-ed over the Crown Jewels while Jarvis gazed with equal rapture at the colourful ranks of tin soldiers drawn up on their battlefields. The following day they went to Regent's Park Zoo where, of course, they wanted to ride on everything, but their funds being limited they were restricted to one ride apiece. Ruth chose the llama, largely because it looked soft and woolly, but also because she adored its name, Esmeralda. After agonies of indecision between a camel and an elephant, Jarvis opted for the African elephant, called Big Bertha, but as it seemed to take longer to get everyone aboard than the ride actually lasted, he felt it all a bit of a let down.

A visit to the Alhambra Cinema House in Old Holborn was, to his mind, the highlight of the entire holiday – but as his opinion tended to change daily, this probably didn't signify very much. He had never seen a motion-picture film before, and thought it the supreme experience of his life as he sat tensely on the very edge of his seat gazing spellbound at the screen, yelling encouragement to Robin Hood who laughingly swashbuckled his way through continuous moments of certain death and miraculously emerged unscathed, and still found time to win the fair Maid Marian.

Sam Trotter only had one half-day off a week, so it stood to reason they weren't going to see a lot of him; briefly at breakfast (sometimes) and then again in the evening (their tea, his dinner) when he'd kick off his boots and invariably drop off to sleep in his chair. But it was he who took them to Mass at St Clare's on Sundays and gave them their two half-pennies each for the collections; Queenie would laughingly explain that God kept her company in her kitchen so she was excused going to church. No, Jarvis, she told him with mock severity, God wouldn't excuse his absence. A couple of times, Jarvis discovered Sam busy in his work-shed in the back yard. It was there, surrounded by all the tools of his craft, that he fashioned all manner of wooden objects, mainly toys for the local children. On the walls were rows of newly-carved Rosies and Georges, and Punches and Judys. Sam said they would find their way to different hospitals and charities for distribution at Christmas. He showed Jarvis how to use the various chisels and gouges without doing too much damage to his fingers, and together they made several wooden bowls. Jarvis loved these times with Sam, especially when they were by themselves. He imagined this was the way it was with real fathers, and he wished Sam were his and not just loaned to him by God.

On his half-days, Sam took them to the Kingsway Swimming Baths. On the first occasion, when Jarvis admitted that he didn't know how to swim, Sam laughingly said there was only one way to learn, and promptly threw him in the water. Jarvis sank like a stone, and surfaced just as quickly, gasping and spluttering, and splashing out frantically with arms and legs in an ungainly but quite effective sort of dog paddle. After that, Sam, towering like a colossus in the water, showed Jarvis what to do with his arms and legs – and how to breathe without swallowing half the pool, and in a very short time he had got the hang of it and was able to swim (or crawl, as Sam called it) in ever-increasing circles, until he was able to cross the whole width of the pool. There was no holding him after that, and off he set to complete a full length, with Sam idly cruising in his wake.

Jarvis quickly discovered that Queenie's cooking was a holiday in itself: an exciting and tasty holiday. Queenie couldn't follow a recipe to save her life, and probably wouldn't have trusted one if she could, but she had a natural instinct for cooking and, besides, she enjoyed eating good food. Her technique was to go shopping, buy the best food she could afford, and go home and cook it. Her kitchen, by any standards, was chaotic in its disorder; it was also spotless. There were bottles and jars, and tins and tubs, and dishes and pots scattered everywhere, but it was a kind of organised chaos, with the floor and work surfaces all spotlessly clean and the very air redolent with mouth-watering aromas. Pride of place, and her own particular joy, went to an Aga range, cream in colour, which was kept in constant use, for it fed not only the household but also its many scores of customers. The meals she cooked with her Aga were always a triumph; nothing too fanciful, but always homely and tasty.

Shopping with Queenie was an adventure, too; like expeditions. They would troop off, safari-fashion, Queenie in the lead gripping her purse and swinging an enormous string bag, Ruth and Jarvis following eagerly behind and clutching more carrier-bags, and sometimes, Hannah came too. Queenie seemed to know everybody, and Jarvis supposed many of them were patrons of The Dials.

She marched them into Smithfield Market where once, she told them like a tourist guide, they used to burn heretics, and said: "Beef today, I think, Willie," to a walrus-moustached man whose apron was splattered with blood. He produced the choicest of cuts which she examined minutely, lifting here, prodding there, before making a selection, while they all stood round her gazing in awe at her daring. "A nice clear colour, Willie," she observed knowledgeably. "I think we'll have some sausages, too." Several yards of savoury pork sausages were produced, approved with a regal wave, a snip was made – and four-dozen fat sausages dropped into a waiting receptacle. Money changed hands, change was counted and off they all went.

The next call was at Covent Garden the fruit and vegetable market – Queenie, who knew all there was to know about *her* part of London, said it had once been the site of a convent garden – where a skinny woman named Paula, in a green apron and a purple beret, rushed up to serve them. She gave each of the children a rosy apple, and then hovered at Queenie's beck and call, picking out the most perfect of produce as directed; each item, nevertheless, was thoroughly scrutinized before being consigned to one of the bags. Occasionally, something would displease Queenie and it would be returned with disapproving clucking sounds which appeared to mortify Paula. "These leaves is all wilted, Paula," Queenie would complain sharply; or she might have said, "Bleedin' 'orrible bruise on this 'ere apple, Paula." And Paula, with a half-smothered sigh, would exclaim: "Lor! It's me eyes, ducks."

Another time, they visited Billingsgate fish-market, a vast arcaded hall alongside the Thames near the Monument. Here, Queenie demanded of a man with a face like a full moon if a particular halibut was fresh; its eyes seemed a trifle sunken, she commented. "Strewth, Queen, the bleeder's still bleedin' breathin,' innit!" the man protested in a painfully injured voice. "It were 'avin' it away wiv its mate in the North Sea while yer was still in yer bed this mornin', that's 'ow fresh it is!" Jarvis didn't catch Queenie's rejoinder, but it brought a fishy smile to moon-face. "'Ere, boy, 'ave a eel fer yer tea, compliments of 'Enry Moffitt!" he said, passing Jarvis a superb specimen. Well, there was enough of it to be superb and he held it very gingerly in his hand for a moment, exceedingly doubtful if the thing was properly dead – it seemed to be wriggling, still. Jarvis, after uttering a hoarse "Thank you, mister," was going to drop the brute in one of Ruth's baskets, but both she and Hannah cringed away wanting nothing to do with it, so Jarvis had to drop it in one of his bags, keeping a wary eye on it and holding it well away from him – in case it might jump out and bite him. Queenie and Moffitt roared with laughter, and Jarvis's face reddened – but he was still ready to drop the bag should the eel poke its head out.

And then the holiday came to an end: abruptly and completely. The moment of departure came – Sunday, September 8, and Jarvis stood waiting by the back door with his usual parcel of possessions tucked under his arm, but this time it contained only presents – there was another set of clothing (everything had his name stitched to it on little labels) for what Queenie called "ordinary" wear, a big fruit cake, a bag of apples and an enormous bar of chocolate. He would be very popular with the other boys while his tuck lasted. He was waiting now for Sam, who had said he was going to walk him back to St Hilda's – Jarvis presumed to make sure he didn't get lost again!

Jarvis had said his sad goodbyes. He'd given Ruth a brotherly peck and told her that he'd never ever forget his best friend; Ruth responded by smothering him with kisses and then bursting into tears; and, in the moment he'd been dreading most, he found himself quite unable to speak to Queenie for the lump in his throat, and he'd simply thrown himself at her, burying himself in her and stretching out his arms as far as they'd reach, and she'd folded hers round him and hugged him to her. She whispered, "Be a good boy, lovey ... write, an' let us know 'ow you is," as they forced themselves apart, but he'd only stared back wooden-faced, not trusting himself to speak; not knowing when, or if, they'd ever meet again. He knew they'd both be sobbing indoors: Queenie frantically polishing the Aga, Ruth in her bedroom doubtless hugging Rosie for comfort.

Sam finally creaked up, and they walked slowly away from the building and down the street, not looking back and neither wishing to speak. Jarvis did softly thank Sam for clearing the way and making sure that he wouldn't be facing any punishment, and Sam muttered somewhat thickly that the way Jarvis was shooting up he'd be as big as him one day. At St Hilda's great gates, Jarvis pushed a crumpled piece of paper into Sam's huge hand with a barely audible "for Queenie," and quickly vanished inside.

As Jarvis lay in his old bed that night, hugging George for the first time in a very long while and fighting off tears, he pictured Queenie back at The Dials, with Ruth on her lap, smoothing out his note and reading out loud:

"Thank you for a really marvellous time. I'll never forget it – or you. You may be only my pretend Mum, but you're the only Mum I've got, and I love you very much."

Jarvis hoped it wouldn't make them cry, too much; and he turned his head and sobbed silently into his pillow.

□ *Queenie paused from her story to dab her eyes and blow her nose. There was a hush in the ward while she composed herself, her audience absorbed and eager for her to continue. Today's had been the third instalment of her story. Dr C. and the Matron had remained throughout all the sessions : others had stayed as long as their duties allowed. There had been pauses for cups of tea and a longer break for lunch, otherwise Queenie had told her tale to suit herself : her feelings and moods. Matron – Miss Ivy Flinn, and already Ivy to Queenie – had decreed that the story-telling must always halt for the day at teatime so that the doctors and nurses could "see to" the Major. Beard, the central figure, who had listened with great interest to the history of what they would have him believe was the history of his life, still had no memory of it. But he was as eager as the rest to hear more.*

And now Queenie continued.

Chapter Eleven

Battersea, London, September 8, 1937

The immediate consequence of Jarvis's brief absence from St Hilda's was that on his return he was sent for by Father Rector, and told that now he was almost twelve he would be leaving for St Boniface at Battersea as soon as arrangements could be made. "God knows what you will make of your life, Brook," he'd declared, mournfully. "Such talent ... such perversity of character. Such a terrible waste. I fear for your future."

While awaiting his transportation, Jarvis carried on with his lessons, and scarcely noticed the arrival of his twelfth birthday. But it had not gone unnoticed elsewhere. It had been arranged, through the influence of Sister Beatrice, that Jarvis should visit with Queenie once a month on a Sunday, and the first of these came on September 15, the day after his birthday. However, he was informed on his birthday the day before by Father Rector that he would be leaving for Battersea the following Saturday, and to be sure he had all his things packed ready. And so his visit to The Dials, so eagerly looked forward to, was not as happy as it might have been, as it was also to be his last.

Never was a dinner so grand, and so little appreciated; their tea party was the same melancholy ordeal. Everyone was convinced, that they'd probably never be together again. Ruth, never far from tears, hovered close all the while with a face full of woe and scarcely trusting herself to speak; Queenie, her heart weighing heavily in her breast, busied herself endlessly in a forlorn effort to control her transparent emotions; and Sam, desperately occupying himself (and Jarvis) chiselling at a lump of wood, kept muttering gloomily about an impending war. Farewells were speedy, lachrymose and almost wordless. The uncertainty over any future meeting was too intolerable to permit either discussion or contemplation; quick promises were made to keep in touch, and then the parting was complete.

The first person Jarvis met at St Boniface was Robert Beard, who was waiting for him at the old workhouse gates as the bus dropped him off nearby. As Jarvis hurried through the gates clutching his brown paper parcel of worldly belongings, Scruffy sprang forward and they hugged each other bruisingly and noisily, and at the height of their reunion his parcel burst open and his collection of things scattered all over the place, and they seemed to make even more noise retrieving them and retying the bundle. Jarvis was pleased to note that he'd outgrown his old friend, being now five feet five and a bit and threatening to grow a lot bigger. Scruffy resumed pumping his hand vigorously, gave him a friendly punch in the ribs and grinned amiably, displaying his superbly white teeth.

"'Allo, Biffer, you old bugger!" he greeted Jarvis. "I 'eard you was headed this way some days ago. Bin keepin' an eye open for you. Took yer sweet time gettin' 'ere, didn't yer!"

"Bloody hell, Scruff, I'm only just twelve," Jarvis rejoined, laughing. "I couldn't come any sooner, could I? Anyway, it's good to see you again, mate," he told him, and in that moment of sudden complete loneliness he really did mean it, as the warmth of his words must have shown. Jarvis gave him several playful punches in return to demonstrate his pleasure.

Scruffy took him to see the Rector, Father John Dullaghan, a cadaverous-looking man, with thin, silvery hair and weak-looking blue eyes. Father John, who looked altogether too frail to be alive let alone in a position of any authority, nevertheless was responsible for the running of St Boniface. He peered at Jarvis through his washed-out eyes as though he couldn't see him clearly and muttered, "Ah, Brook ... you've arrived safely."

"Yes, Father," Jarvis replied, wondering if he had expected him to get lost on the way, but concluding it was merely his way of welcoming him.

"I understand you have a gift for running away, Brook," pursued the other, still staring at Jarvis as if to make sure he was still there.

"Oh no, Father Rector," Jarvis assured him hurriedly, horrified that he should have heard of his unfortunate escapade. "It was all a – an accident, Father. Really."

"Let's hope so. Don't have any such accidents here, Brook," returned Father John in a voice that seemed to chill the air. "I don't tolerate such behaviour. If you did run away, you'd be very sorry when you were returned to us. Do I make myself clear?"

"Yes, Father," Jarvis cried earnestly. He had made himself perfectly clear, and Jarvis determined there and then never to provoke him. If he did, it would be another accident.

"Good," said Father John, in a tone that set in an immediate thaw; he even smiled, but that didn't really improve his looks, though it did something for the atmosphere. "There are excellent reports here about your school work, Brook, and we shall hope to see you advance in this direction. Learning is the hallmark of life: acquire it now, boy, because you won't get a second chance."

"I will," Jarvis assured him hastily, and sincerely. He wanted to learn; he always had.

"I see you already have a friend here," he frowned, staring at Scruffy with no great benignity, "make sure you're a good influence on each other."

"Yes, Father," Jarvis said quickly, thinking he didn't look very optimistic.

Father John nodded, apparently satisfied with him for the moment, and directed Scruffy to show Beard where the dormitory was, and they hurried off in case he should decide the occasion merited a longer lecture. "He don't look much, Biffer, does he ... but he can't 'arf lay it on wiv the cane," Scruffy told Jarvis softly as soon as they were out of earshot. "Even worse'n old Hughie back at Hilda's, so watch out." Jarvis made a mental note of this disturbing information, and renewed his determination to keep out of trouble as far as he was able, and certainly never to run away. Having found his bed and stowed away his parcel, Jarvis followed Scruffy to his secret spot in the boiler house where they could talk undisturbed.

"Any news of your Aunt Dolly?" Jarvis asked when they were settled.

"No; not a bleedin' word," muttered Scruffy. "I give 'er up. P'raps she's dead, like ev'ryone else. I dunno. 'Course, she might've emigrated, or summat like that."

Jarvis decided there was no way he could hold back all his secrets. "I found my godparents," he cried triumphantly, like he'd found a gold sovereign – even if there weren't none any more.

"No! Never knew you 'ad any," gaped Scruffy, hugely impressed, and then he frowned and asked scornfully: "Why ain't yer livin' wiv 'em, then?"

"Well, it's not a proper sort of relationship. There's no blood ties, so they've no real claim to me. They'd've had me in a flash, if they could, but they can't – so that's it. The Church has the sole right of guardianship, so I'm told. More's the pity. Don't know what would happen if my real parents was found, but that ain't likely after all these years."

"Well, the Church don't give nuffink away – nor back, neither," snorted Scruffy dismissively. "She ain't necessarily a good parent, but she's a bloody jealous one. Wot's worst is she's got the Law on 'er side – an' the Law's the biggest bastard of us all. So you've 'ad it, Biffer. You're stuck wiv the bleedin' Church for yer 'ome, same's me. We're 'ere till they kick us out to fend for ourselves – an' the sooner the better."

Jarvis was startled by Scruffy's outburst, surprised at the depth of his thinking. There was more to him than he'd imagined. He hadn't thought Scruffy capable of such reasoning. Of course, he'd known in his heart there was no chance of him being adopted by Sam and Queenie. Christ! they weren't even married ... and the precious Law insisted on having these bits of paper, all neatly tied up with red tape. Well, what did it matter, he'd probably never see either of them again – nor Ruth. He missed not having her around, always bothering him and trying to boss him, but always fun. No, he'd never forget them; never. After a brief, emotion-filled silence, he looked at Scruffy and asked if any of the old gang were around.

"No, only us," said Scruffy, brightening. "Remember Tim? Tim Hardy? He's in prison ... well, reform school, or summat like that."

"No!" Jarvis gasped, thrilled and impressed at Tim's achievement. "What'd 'e do to land there, then?"

"Got caught, didn't 'e," sneered Scruffy. "Broke into some place – a sort of club, it were, an' helped hisself to some bottles of pop. Only it turned out to be brandy, or summat just as deadly. The Bogies found 'im unconscious on the floor, didn't they? Silly sod! I 'eard they 'ad to pump 'is stomach out in 'ospital, an' then 'old 'im up in the dock in court. Wot-a-laugh! Bet 'e wished 'e were dead!"

"What about the rest of The Bullets?"

"Jarrett an' Mark Telford is apprenticed out. Jarrett almost as soon as we come 'ere – to a bleedin' cobbler, no less. An' Mark, 'e's wiv some Jew tailor bloke in Edgeware Road. I 'spect 'e spends all day sweepin' up the snippets. Soft bleedin' life, anyway."

"An' Jack? Jack Plant?" Jarvis asked eagerly, for Jack had always been his specially close friend of those long ago days. They had shared in some really hair-brained adventures at the time, generally just the two of them. It was a wonder they hadn't got themselves killed, but mostly they got away with not even being found out. They'd been great times: sometimes Jarvis missed them. He missed Jack, anyway. He couldn't picture him being apprenticed at anything, not unless it was something awfully exciting.

"Oh, yes, you two was always pretty thick, wasn't you. Lucky you wasn't 'anged, the pair of you! Well, Jack might well 'ave been by now – 'e never come 'ere, yer know. Went straight from Hilda's to some farm in Sussex, which was askin' for trouble, weren't it? I 'eard that our Jack took orf right away – on a 'orse! Can you imagine that! Our Jack on a 'orse – just like bleedin' Dick Turpin. That's the story I 'eard, anyhow. Don't know wot's 'appened to 'im since – probably still on the run."

"If he ain't been hanged – like Dick Turpin," Jarvis laughed, fairly confident his old mate would be surviving somewhere. "And Jimmy Dunne? He was always the clever one, when he wasn't getting into trouble with us. What happened to him?"

Scruffy's face clouded briefly before brightening with an evil grin. "You'll never guess, me ol' sparrer. Not in ten million years, you won't." Jarvis frowned impatiently, and told Scruffy to get on with it. "Got religion, didn't 'e!" snorted Scruffy contemptuously. "The priests got to 'im, an' now 'e's buried in one of their seminaries at somewhere called Shrigley in bleedin' Ireland! He's trainin' to be one of 'em – a bleedin' priest!"

"Christ!" Jarvis gasped, wincing at the enormity of such an earth-shattering step. "He was always going to confession and enjoyed the hymn-singing, but I'd never have dreamed they'd collar him. Mind you, he always was a quiet one," Jarvis reflected, "but bloody good in a fight. He'll probably make a good priest ... God help his flock! Wouldn't care to have him hear my confession!"

Jarvis plunged straight back into his studies and made an immediately favourable impression by passing the Oxford Junior School Leaving Certificate two years before was normal, and found himself in the same class as Scruffy. This close association did not bode well for the continued peace of mind of the fathers and brothers, leading as it did to innumerable pranks – the very least of which involved the pair of them getting sozzled on an extremely potent communion wine – which, in turn, led to dire punishments, either on the receiving end of a bruising, stinging cane, or learning, line-perfect, yards of hated prose, usually from the inexhaustible works of the detested Mr Shakespeare.

Father John tried to make sure Jarvis had as few idle moments as possible, and to this end his flair for languages was continued. Brother Karl was extricated from his duties as sacristan-cum-librarian three times a week to continue his German education, and his Italian tutelage fell on the shoulders of his confessor, Father Antonio, who visited St Boniface once a week to whitewash the speckled souls of the inmates and had been persuaded into staying on after these duties for an extra couple of hours or so to keep Jarvis up to the mark.

The routine was rather harsher at St Boniface than at St Hilda's; the rules were stricter, the canes heavier. In spite his workload of studies, Jarvis, together with Scruffy, was often in trouble. Even when they were kept well apart, they succeeded in getting together and slipping off somewhere. If there was no-one actually watching over them, they would be away. Jarvis didn't think they did any great harm, but there were constant complaints throughout the neighbourhood about them trespassing in gardens and empty houses. Well, they might have helped themselves to an occasional bottle of milk and a loaf or two from doorsteps, and fruit and things from gardens, but Jarvis was sure they were blamed for many things for which they were quite innocent. Once, they were escorted back by a policeman who clung to each of them by the scruff of the neck. The brute enjoyed watching them get the stick, urging Father John, who needed no encouragement, to "lay it on." However, there were lots of times when they didn't get caught and they thoroughly enjoyed their excursions into freedom and seeing how the rest of the world ticked.

St Boniface prided itself on its sporting aspirations, if not its achievements. Every morning, on a quadrangle that sloped deceptively towards the river, where much of its missing Tarmac lay, the boys endured twenty minutes of vigorous P.T. From the shelter of an ambulatory, Father Michael Fortune –　known to the boys as their

Misfortune – would survey the lacklustre display of callisthenics, which made up in groans what was lacking in motion; he was always on the look out for any sort of talent for his various teams. Father Michael had achieved a half-blue for hockey at Cambridge, and on the strength of this had reigned as undisputed (and unenvied) Head of Sports ever since. His honest efforts, in every field, met with singular failure. But he was nothing if not persevering, and quickly put each new calamity behind him, and turned to some new sporting activity – currently rugby was his mania. He spotted Jarvis straight away; well, he was a head taller than most of the rest and had the right build, and besides, he was the only one ever to put any effort into the morning exercises. Father Michael beckoned to Jarvis, and so started his sporting career.

Jarvis knew nothing about rugby, nor much more of other sports, but he was as keen in such activities as he was in his studies. He revelled in the rough and tumble of the game; what is more, he revealed an unexpected turn of speed which led to several tries – a rare achievement among the St Boniface players. His performances, and leadership, on the field inspired self-confidence to a team long accustomed to being steamrollered by all and sundry, and which now began to believe in itself, even to the extent of finding the will, and sometimes the ability, to win. But it was to be a relatively short-lived glory for Jarvis. It came to an end during a scrimmage when an opponent grabbed hold of his privates and yanked hard; memories of the loathsome Honourable Roland flooded back and Jarvis went berserk, sailing into the offender with both fists flailing until the battered boy was prostrate on the ground, and showed neither ability nor desire to rise. Father Michael's outrage was in no way mollified by Jarvis's indignant explanation that "the sod grabbed my prick!" and promptly gave him six of the most swingeing best there and then on the touchline, and, reluctantly banished him from the fifteen; reluctantly because the team's revived fortunes – they had won successive games, at once plunged to new depths of humiliation.

But, to his credit, Father Michael, having witnessed Jarvis's arms flailing more like a windmill than a pugilist, decided that if he wanted to fight he should become acquainted with the Marquess of Queensberry Rules, and referred him to Brother Andrew, who knew about such things. Jarvis thought that this was definitely something more up his street, but that was before Brother Andrew showed him his straight left, and he found himself sitting on the floor of the makeshift ring in a corner of one of the classrooms. Jarvis leapt back up on to his feet, his arms whirling furiously, and another straight left put him back where he was. Somewhat dazed, but more confused than hurt, Jarvis scrambled back on to his feet, a good bit slower this time, and aimed his own left with fierce determination. He struck only thin air, and walked straight on to yet another ramrod left. This time he remained squatting on the floor, holding his reeling, throbbing head, and when it had cleared looked up at Father Andrew with a bewildered expression.

And so Jarvis had his first boxing lesson. There followed months of more sparring lessons, in the course of which he came to understand the importance not only of the straight left, but the right hook and the uppercut, and bobbing and weaving and side-stepping out of danger, always lightly and quickly; and, most importantly, how to punch with his full weight behind each blow. He practised this continually on a large, sand-filled canvas bag that was suspended from a hook outside. By the end of the year, having spent as much time on his back as on his feet, he had the satisfaction of reversing their positions: Brother Andrew, having been nailed by Jarvis's straight left and a right cross, ended up on his sacerdotal behind, and gave his opponent a congratulatory nod. The lessons went on, and Jarvis learnt all about stance and how to roll with the punches that got through his defences, and how to move in general. He was amazed at the difference it made, and really felt he was punching hard. There were a score or more boys in the boxing class; they were all shapes and sizes, all older than him, and they were all hell bent on knocking seven bells out of each other, their only regret being having to box within the Marquess of Queensberry Rules, or not too far removed. Jarvis had many memorable bouts with them, acquitting himself well in the process, and certainly giving as good as he got.

There was, also, a brief excursion into rowing when St Boniface was bequeathed a clinker-eight by some well-intentioned parishioner. Jarvis was picked to be a member of the crew – selection proved an uncertain honour. First they had to carry the cumbersome craft a quarter of a mile to a suitable launching spot on the Thames, an expedition which afforded considerable amusement to pedestrians, providing they weren't in collision with the monster, irritated all manner of wheeled traffic, and brought suspicious frowns to the brows of several constables who were not accustomed to seeing such craft (upside down or not) on their beat.

Once arrived at the selected site, there was a brief blessing ceremony during which the boat, which had seemed to weigh a ton during the journey, was christened The Flying Arrow, and then it was realised they'd overlooked the need for a cox. It was decided that on this inaugural occasion, they could take to the water without one. Jarvis was first into the craft, taking the stroke's position without knowing, and the rest of the boys piled in behind him with some squabbling over places, but finally all was ready and The Flying Arrow was on the move. In next to no time, the craft had pulled away from the bank ; and in the same amount of time, it began to fill with water. In a matter of minutes it had sunk out of sight, and its crew were all splashing for the bank. There was no further interest in boating after that.

In his thirteenth year, Jarvis suddenly found his sporting

activities extended to include cross-country running. A questionable decision perhaps in view of his past propensities in this field, but Father Michael, remembering his speed down the wings in rugby matches, saw no reason why this energy shouldn't be let loose on a race track, and so Jarvis was set loose to run on grounds belonging to Battersea Wire Works Sports and Social Club, which the orphanage was allowed to use for a peppercorn consideration. Jarvis, who revelled in any open air activity, found himself in his true element when running; not so much in short races, but very much so over the longer distances. He seemed able to run and run without ever tiring or slowing and, once he'd been taught how to breathe correctly when pounding along, to swing his arms so as to give himself a smoother rhythm and to lengthen his stride while barely lifting his feet, he was like a racehorse let loose, and he ran farther and farther.

The way Father Michael greeted him on his return, Jarvis was sure the old devil suffered qualms each time he watched him disappear into the distance. However, his fears came to nought. Not that the thought didn't occur to Jarvis. But, where was there to run to? The Dials? They'd soon come looking for him there, and he didn't want cause any trouble for his "relatives". His only other friend was Mr Maggs, who was still in prison – where he'd most likely end up if he did a runner. So, he didn't run off; he just ran and ran and ran ... and kept coming back. Father Michael, seeing the way of things, and sensing that he might have discovered a real marathon runner of the future, gave Jarvis every encouragement, and arranged for him to do much of his running in Richmond Royal Park – where he'd really have room to stretch his legs. Father Michael seemed to think the twice-weekly tuppenny bus fare to East Sheen, the nearest entrance, well worth the expense. Of course, Jarvis seldom took the bus both ways, preferring to pocket the pennies as a nest egg for the future and just run instead.

None of Jarvis's various sporting activities was allowed to impinge on his scholastic progress, and he continued to excel in most subjects, and continued to enjoy his linguistic sessions with Father Toni and Brother Karl. All in all, despite occasional conflicts with authority and the inevitable punishments, this proved to be a very satisfactory period in his institutional life. He did not seem to be in trouble nearly so often: he supposed because he didn't have any spare time. Anyway, his good conduct must have been noticed, for when he approached Father John about the possibility of visiting his godparents on his fourteenth birthday, which just happened to be a Saturday, permission was granted – after an exchange of letters with Sister Beatrice, who assured him that Mrs Hoggins was an admirable woman with a young child of her own whose father was a policeman. Jarvis sure it was the "policeman" word that swung it.

The visit, from the Friday evening till Sunday evening, would be the first contact between them since just before he'd come to St Boniface. Theirs was not a relationship that relied on letters. Ruth sent Jarvis three letters. The first was a longish one in which she told him everything that she was doing at school and at home, all about the people they knew, and about Rosie who had been lost several more times. The next letter was considerably shorter and was largely a demand to know why he hadn't answered her previous one; the third, and last one, was short to the point of being curt. She thought he was hateful! Jarvis thought he might have replied to this one – but he wasn't sure. She said she never received one.

Jarvis disappeared straight away into the massiveness of Queenie, who hugged him unmercifully to her great body and didn't look as if she'd ever let him go. Poor Ruth, who had been nearly nine for so long and was now just ten – or in her vernacular "nearly eleven," was in agonies of excited impatience; she kept jumping up and down beside them, tugging at both in turn, and finally, in desperation, at both of them at once. "Me! Me! Me!" she cried petulantly. But it was several more minutes before Queenie loosened her hold of Jarvis, and he was able to breathe again; and then it was Ruth's turn.

She jumped up at Jarvis, her arms draping chokingly about his neck and her feet dangling several inches above the floor. Her arms tired after a moment or two, but she wouldn't let go; instead, she twined her legs around his thighs – and they both collapsed in a pile on the floor, where, undaunted, she continued to hug him as hard as she possibly could and splattered him with scores of little kisses, her lips pecking at any part of him she could reach. They happily ignored Queenie who stood above them, arms akimbo, laughing fit to do permanent damage to herself.

Eventually, Queenie announced, brooking no argument – not that she was likely to get one, that Jarvis needed fattening up; and further, that everything was ready and she wasn't about to see it spoil. They all retired to the much-loved kitchen which, due to the beloved Aga, seemed overly warm, but nobody minded. Queenie cleared a space at the table with a sweep of her arm, and turned her attention to the business of lifting lids off pots, sniffing at or tasting the contents, and peering through a cloud of steam into the oven, while Ruth and Jarvis sat and exchanged their bits of news, which didn't amount to much but went on and on.

Ruth only nibbled at her food declaring that she was far too excited to eat, but Jarvis devoured everything that was put before him. He did more than justice to dish after dish, ranging from carrot and leak soup, to braised lamb and bowls of piping hot vegetables, a great chunk of apple pie with a huge dollop of thick cream, and chose an enormous banana to finish off. It was more food than he normally saw in a month of Sundays and, there was Queenie saying, "That'll 'ave to keep you goin' till tea time, lovey."

Once safely seated in the parlour, Jarvis had to relate in detail all his adventures since they had last seen him – "since you don't never write an' tell us anyfink," as Queenie put it. But he told them only the good things: his successes at his lessons, specially the exam result, and sports. He glossed over the punishments he'd received feeling that they were behind him; and, besides, he did not feel unjustly used: he just shouldn't have been caught out so often. The arrival of Sam Trotter, vast and beaming, and playfully tooting on his whistle, causing a momentary panic among the pub's customers, gave Jarvis something of a breather. He rose politely to his feet and gravely extended a hand, but Sam boisterously swept it aside and gave him a bear hug that was quite the equal of Queenie's and Ruth's earlier efforts. He managed a squeak by way of greeting, and Queenie came to his rescue by saying, "Put the poor boy down, Sam, 'fore you damage 'im. He ain't one of yer villains."

Then, as they stood together, she exclaimed proudly: "My, Jarvis, ain't you growed! You're near as big as Sam!" Jarvis wasn't, of course, but at five-feet-eight and a whisker he was well on the way. Sam declared, "You'll be a giant 'fore you're done growin' – well over six feet, for sure. Tall 'nuff to make a policeman, anyways. Any thoughts yet abaht wot yer wants to be when you've done schoolin'?"

"Nothing definite. Sometimes it's one thing, sometimes another. I can't seem to make up my mind," answered Jarvis. "I wouldn't mind being a soldier, I think," he ventured, and quickly looked round to see how his suggestion was received. Queenie, with thoughts only of slim waists and gorgeous uniforms, nodded approvingly; Ruth, undoubtedly thinking she would then be very grown up and being taken to lots of exciting balls by the handsomest officer in the entire British Army, clapped her hands enthusiastically; but Sam, with the memory of four years in the trenches in the Great War, shook his head decisively.

"You don't want to, boy, not wiv all yer book learnin' an' fings," he said, seriously. "There's goin' to be another war with this bloke 'Itler. You mark my words. It'll come – an' it's comin' fast. You'll see. You wants to keep out of it, or you'll get yerself killed 'fore yer time."

"Fiddlesticks! They wouldn't dare," declared Queenie breezily, yet with a touch of uncertainty as she frowned at Sam. "We bashed the devils last time, didn't we? Them Boches doesn't want another kick up their backsides. 'Sides, we won't allow it to 'appen again, surely? Mr Chamberlain will soon send ol' what's-'is name packin' if he tries anyfink – you'll see."

"You can't trust no 'Un," Sam cautioned doggedly.

"Well, there you are then, this cove ... Mister-bloomin'-'Itler – 'e's a bleedin' Austrian, not even a German, so it's all right, innit?"

"All the bleedin' same, that lot," growled Sam. "Anyway, it's all part of Adolf's Greater Germany now ... an' you mark my words, 'e intends for it to become a damned sight greater. They say 'e's after Czechoslovakia now. Gawd knows who'll be next."

Jarvis was only mildly interested in this brief exchange; he didn't understand what they were on about, and whatever it was it'd all be long forgotten before it need concern him; a pity, really, he mused, thinking it would be fun fighting the Germans – or anyone. "Perhaps I'll be a chimney sweep," he said with a grin, and everybody laughed.

The day passed, and being so perfect, it did so in too much of a hurry. Bedtime came, but first Jarvis enjoyed the luxury of a steaming hot and bubbly bath all on his own, though Ruth had to be shooed away by Queenie with the warning to "leave 'im in peace, yer young baggage, or I'll smack yer bum!" Jarvis, left in peace, returned to playing with the boats Sam had made for him. Queenie, watching him as she leaned against the jamb of the door, said jokingly, "Don't forget to wash yerself while yer in there, lovey," and then padded away chuckling to herself.

Next morning, Jarvis was wished a happy fourteenth birthday by one and all, but Queenie said they'd celebrate it properly the next day when there'd be more time. On the Saturday morning, Jarvis and Ruth joined Queenie and Hannah in a quick sally through the local markets, marching from one stall to the next in single file, the children carrying the purchases like native bearers, and Queenie bawling for attention and then haggling with the stallholders. Afterwards, Sam took Jarvis and Ruth swimming, leaving Queenie free in the pub to torment her regular customers with the sharp end of her tongue, which they loved, and to indulge in her cooking. After dinner, they all went by Underground down to Kew Gardens. After ten minutes, Sam took off his boots, lay down on the grass and went to sleep with a knotted handkerchief over his face. Queenie, having sniffed her way dreamily through an intoxicating rosarium that stretched over acres, joined him, telling Jarvis and Ruth to run off and amuse themselves and not to get into any mischief while she sorted out their picnic – presently; she was snoozing, too.

Jarvis and Ruth scooted away determined to see everything, but in reality seeing only a tiny fragment of the huge gardens. Having run their feet off, they decided the jungles of the enormous hothouses might be more fun – until Ruth fell off the leaf of a giant water lily and got sopping wet, and they decided they'd earned their tea – and went and woke Sam and Queenie up.

On the Sunday, Jarvis and Ruth, each with a penny for the plate, went off hand-in-hand to Mass at St Clare's Church. Afterwards, as they walked home, Jarvis said he'd love it if Ruth would write to him

"Of course I will, Jarvis, and I have done," Ruth replied, "only it's not much fun when you don't answer."

Jarvis pulled a face. There wasn't a lot he could say in reply to that. "I don't get very much time to write letters, Ruth," he told her lamely. "I did write one letter to you, honestly I did, but – I didn't have any money for a stamp, and so it probably didn't get sent."

Ruth smiled, almost as cheerfully as if she'd received it. "Thank you, anyway," she said smoothly. "Perhaps I'll get one, one day."

"P'raps," said Jarvis, and they both laughed.

They were almost home when Ruth darted from his side to embrace a bundle of black rags wedged behind a giant basket of flowers in a sort of corner crevice between an ABC teashop and a jeweller's. The bundle was introduced to him as Mrs Molly, a woman of indefinite age, but certainly with a lot of years behind her. The years were to be seen in her wrinkled face; her skin was ash-grey, except for the cheeks which had yellowish blotches, and her red nose; there was a net of fine lines round her eyes, which were small and bright blue, and silvery bristles on her chin. She wore a huge black felt hat which was tied down with a black bootlace to keep the draught out of her ears. A long black frock-coat hid whatever shape she possessed; it hung far below her knees, between which she gripped her basket of flowers – when she stood up, she seemed even smaller and her coat reached her ankles. Propped behind her in the corner was a gigantic unfurled black umbrella. When Ruth had done kissing her and introducing Jarvis, Mrs Molly gave him a smile. It was quite lovely and brought her entire grey face to life.

"Is 'e yer sweetheart, Ruthie?" she teased in an unexpectedly strong voice, and immediately broke into a loud silly laugh.

Jarvis thought they both put the blooms to shame. Ruth went a delicious carnation-pink and he felt his cheeks burning as scarlet as any geranium. Ruth, the first to recover, explained that Jarvis was her "godbrother." Mrs Molly raised her grey brows and laughed so much her cheeks became even redder than theirs, and Ruth had to rub her back when her laughter turned to fits of coughing. It transpired that Mrs Molly (a regular at The Dials) and Ruth enjoyed little gossips each day as Ruth went to and from school. Mrs Molly gave Ruth a buttonhole of pansies and Jarvis a single red rosebud "to give to the one you love best" and they hastened on with her cackles ringing out behind them.

As it happened, Jarvis did give the rose to the one he loved best: Queenie. As soon as they were back at The Dials, he sidled up to Queenie, who was busy in her kitchen, handed her the rose, and whispered secretively: "Mum, could you lend me a penny so's I can ride on a bus back to Boneface? Then I could stay a bit longer. It took me 'bout an hour to walk here – an' I run quite a bit of the way." Queenie, who had stopped singing to her Aga to listen to him, gave him one of her suffocating hugs which he endured because he knew it was given with love, sniffed at the rose and whispered back hoarsely, "I 'spect so, lovey." Then she gave him a little shove out of the kitchen and, he thought, he heard her having a bit of a cry. He believed that was the first time he'd ever called her Mum; and he hadn't even noticed. It just came out that way – quite spontaneously. He supposed that was the reason for her tears. He hoped she wouldn't cry every time.

In the afternoon, Jarvis was given a "surprise" birthday party, because, as Queenie put it, "I don't s'pose you've ever 'ad one before even if it is yer fourteenth, an' Gawd knows when you'll get the chance of havin' anovver, so we best make the most of this opportunity." In addition to paper hats and balloons, there was a sumptuous feast complete with a birthday cake with icing and fourteen blue candles, and presents. Ruth, whom he'd never have dreamed could keep a secret from him, gave him two gigantic handkerchiefs emblazoned with his initials and embroidered with lots of tiny flowers, wrapped in tissue paper and tied with a green ribbon – which she demanded back because she needed it for school.

"Thank you very much indeed ... " Jarvis began, returning the ribbon and stuffing both hankies in his pocket after sniffing them to see if she'd put scent on them; she hadn't.

"You don't really deserve them, Jarvis, 'cos you never gave me anything for my birthday," declared Ruth bluntly.

"I don't even know when it was," he cried defensively.

"August 12. And don't you forget next time."

"No. I won't. Not ever again. Promise."

Sam's present was far and away the most marvellous of anything Jarvis had ever received in his life. It was a wondrous pen-knife, complete with such vital attachments as a corkscrew, bottle opener, a gadget for removing stones from horses' hooves, a file and two wickedly sharp blades. He was very effusive with his thanks, and then promptly threatened to cut off one of Ruth's pigtails with one of the blades. She ran shrieking to her mother for safety. Queenie's gifts were along more practical lines: a new shirt, and a shiny new florin. He made such a thing of examining the coin that Sam, snorting with laughter, assured him that it was a genuine one. "Not one the Tin Man made!" he declared. "Ooh! Thank you, Mum," Jarvis cried, hugging her. "Now I won't have to walk back to old Boneface!"

The wonderful day ended with Ruth coming and sitting on his bed and, preparatory to kissing him goodnight (an ordeal he had come to quite looking forward to now), asking if he remembered Mrs Molly asking if they were sweethearts. He nodded, cautiously. "Well, are we?" Ruth demanded, screwing up her face as she stared with fierce intensity into his eyes trying to divine his answer before he'd even had a chance to think of one, and thinking at the same time he had only to decide between two words. Jarvis took his time pondering and decided it was a daft, soppy question and was about to tell her so, but seeing the longing in her face, he hastily changed his mind and told her, "Oh, all right then, if you like." Her face immediately lit up and he was showered with further kisses. "Oh, goodie," she cried when she'd done, for the moment. "And we'll be married one day and live happily ever after in a castle," she added blissfully. "Well, I suppose we'll have to ask Mum first," Jarvis hesitated, thinking it better simply to remain as sweethearts. "Oh, Mum loves weddings," said Ruth enthusiastically, "and so do I, and so will you." A further flurry of kisses followed and then she left Jarvis, who dropped off into an untroubled sleep, with not even a dream to disturb him. By the morning, he'd happily forgotten his betrothed status.

As it happened, his florin remained intact for everyone accompanied him back to St Boniface, with Sam paying the bus fares. The journey seemed to last no time at all, and they all rode downstairs as Queenie said she could never climb up the spiral staircase. It was during the brief agony of farewells outside the forbidding walls of St Boniface that Queenie, clutching hold of Jarvis protectively, cried out: "Oh, Jarvis, it's more like a prison than yer ovver place!"

Ruth, seeing her mother's anguish, burst into tears. "A prison!" she echoed, and clung to his arm as tightly as if she'd been a wardress.

Sam, who alone knew what a prison was really like, regarded the building with a grimace, but observed pointedly: "It's got a good roof, an' it don't 'ave ter be no palace to be a good 'ome."

Jarvis, after giving Sam a look of sheer incredulity, agreed, more for the benefit of Queenie and Ruth than with any genuine conviction, and confirmed, "It's all right."

He then gave them all a last brave smile of reassurance, and vanished inside his prison before emotions overcame them all. Within a very few minutes, he was sweating at his sandbag; the sweat masking his feelings, and absorbing any hint of a tear.

If he had known what was to transpire before he saw them all again, he might well have let the tears flow.

□ *Oh, it were an awful place, Jarvis, Queenie declared, giving a shudder which amused them all. "I don't know how you could stay there all them years."*

Beard looked at her blankly, and wondered if it was as bad as she imagined. He didn't imagine this chap Jarvis had much say regarding his accommodation. A bit like the Army: you slept where your head lay.

Chapter Twelve

Little Warren Farm, Sussex, July, 1939

That weekend was the last Jarvis was to be allowed. In fact, he seemed to lose touch with The Dials altogether. Ruth sent him a flurry of little notes at first, but as she received nothing in return, these dried up until she was sending only one complaining letter a month.

They didn't have holidays at St Boniface. There were breaks between the terms, but lessons were merely replaced by hours of tedious work, the older boys being farmed out to do all manner of casual menial jobs – scrubbing floors, washing and polishing acres of windows, or hawking vegetables from door to door for local shopkeepers – when they had to contend with foul-mouthed housewives who boxed their ears, or brutes of dogs that regarded them as their sport (or meal) for the day and chased them out of sight. If any payment was made for their services, none of them saw any of it; the only thing they got was the cane (that never had a holiday) if there were any complaints about them. Jarvis, because he was tall for his age and looked strong, always seemed to be first choice for any heavy gardening jobs. The best "holidays" were the long summer ones, but only for the oldest boys: they were sent off to farms for six weeks at a time to help with the harvests.

Jarvis, who had longed for his turn, was chosen for such a holiday in July, 1939, and together with a number of other boys, who included Scruffy, he was despatched to a farm that they were told was beside the sea at Bexhill, in Sussex. Jarvis didn't know exactly where the farm was, and as for the sea, he never saw or heard it. The farm was called Little Warren, which may have owed its name to the local rabbit population. It comprised some 400 scattered acres, plus some woodland and an area known as Warren Heath, a furze-covered patch which was the headquarters of the rabbit colony. The farm didn't appear to be near anywhere, apart from a clutch of flint-stone cottages claiming to be a hamlet; they stood at the junction of two cart tracks which was called The Cross, and which was also the name of the pub there.

The boys were billeted in a barn, which they shared with all manner of rustling and itchy creatures, including a cockerel who wakened them well before dawn each day, and they ate at great trestle tables under the canopy of an enormous ash tree beside the main farm house. The food, compared with St Boniface's, was excellent and plentiful, and for that reason alone the "holiday" was always eagerly anticipated. They were paid a munificent sixpence a day (which somehow became half-a-crown at the end of a six-day working week) for a shift that began and ended with the coming and going of the sun, but as the money was paid directly to the bursar back at St Boniface, none of the boys expected to see any return for their labours. Jarvis had exactly 2¾d in coins tied up in one of Ruth's hankies, and he knew Scruffy had some money but he was very secretive about how much. They all had their secrets.

Harvesting was the hardest of work in those days, and no more so than at Little Warren which was reluctant and slow to change its traditional methods of working, hoping by being so that the revolutionary age of machinery, that had been sweeping over the land for half a century, would pass it by; a forlorn hope. Indeed, even here progress was creeping stealthily in with the hiring of a mechanical reaper, and a threshing-machine had long since been taken for granted to separate the corn from the husks. The scythe, even so, was still in daily use at harvest time; cart-horses, too, were still very much part of the scene, dragging whatever was attached to them, uncomplaining and amiable. But it was the mechanical reaper, its great sails whirling ceaselessly and tirelessly, that was the new king, unloved though it might be.

So far as Jarvis and the other boys were concerned, the harvest still depended on sweat: their sweat: buckets of it. They did a wide variety of jobs; some picked fruit (by far the most popular assignment), others lifted root crops, weeded vegetable patches that were acres in size, cleared ditches and drains (and lived in dread of disturbing whatever animal might be sleeping in them – especially snakes) and even helped with the milking; and there were others, like Jarvis, who were involved in the real harvest.

To begin with, he spent the entire day, stripped to the waist and wearing just his short trousers and boots on his feet, racing behind the reaper and binding the slaughtered corn into sheaves; hundreds upon hundreds, all stacked in bundles of a dozen or so which were called shocks and left to stand in rows to dry out like drunken soldiers on a battlefield; and all the while an overseer on the machine would be bellowing encouragement, like "Shift yer arse, boy!" "Wake up there, you dozy oaf!" "Tie that bleeding bundle up again!" How Jarvis wished he could be riding up there and that geezer was down here doing the work!

After the reaping and binding came the really punishing work, for now that the corn was dry it was imperative to get it safely stacked and thatched before the weather broke, and though the sky looked as though the summer would never end the whole operation was tackled as though it were a race against time. Hour after hour, day after day, and sometimes well into the twilight, horse-drawn vehicles were piled high with straw as the sheaves were pitch-forked endlessly up to the man building the load on the wagon. It was relatively easy at first, but as the levels grew higher and higher it became the hardest, almost impossible, work no matter how big and strong you thought you were; it became almost too much for Jarvis's youthful shoulders and sometimes it took two of them to lift the unwieldy load a dozen or more feet above their heads. Many a time Jarvis hoisted his long-handled pitch fork laden with sheaves to the dizzy top of the mountain, only to have it collapse and tumble all over him – which led to both roars of laughter and shouts of abusive sarcasm from all around. As the days passed it seemed like the harvest would never be safely gathered in, but, as in all things, it was completed, almost as an anti-climax, and the business of building the hay stacks proceeded.

But by then, Jarvis had vanished from the scene. In the beginning, they had been too physically drained at the end of the day to do much more than collapse on to their straw beds and sleep till roused by one of the farm hands. The cockerel that had performed this duty so admirably at first had been disposed of by Jarvis and Scruffy on the third night. There had been a lot of questioning by the farmer, but nobody knew anything, they hadn't really noticed the bird, let alone that it was missing – there were chickens all over the place and as far as they were concerned they were all one and the same thing. Jarvis didn't think the farmer believed them for a moment, but there wasn't much he could do. Scruffy and Jarvis, having made sure the cockerel's remains were safe from discovery by either man or beast, maintained an innocent silence about the whole affair.

There was no further interest in the fate of the cockerel, beyond the pleasure of its silence, and once the boys' bodies became attuned to their unaccustomed labours they began to indulge in more normal activities after the day's work, instead of flopping directly on to their beds. They played noisy, energetic games, and sang the bawdiest songs they knew and told scary stories round a blazing fire – which the farm foreman kept an anxious eye on and made sure was properly out when they'd done, which was when he decided. It was inevitable that Scruffy and Jarvis should become more venturesome and they took to exploring far and wide, finding the most perfect trees to climb, stone walls that they imagined were castle ramparts to leap from, an old quarry pit in which they could swim naked undisturbed, and wild fruit and nuts to gorge. Generally they roamed on foot, but once in a while they were able to sneak off on the back of one of the cart-horses thanks to a friendly farmhand. In this way, they discovered The Cross, for the horse knew its way to the inn.

It was there that Scruffy met Rose Ambler, the swineherd's 14-year-old daughter. After that, Scruffy lived in another world with Rose, who offered him a world of undreamed delights, and Jarvis saw precious little of him after their work in the fields. As soon as the evening meal had been gobbled down, Scruffy headed for the inn and his Rose's arms; and it was perfectly plain he didn't want Jarvis along. Jarvis was always asleep before Scruffy returned to the barn, but he didn't think Scruffy got much sleep.

On Sundays, it was customary for the St Boniface lot to be driven by cart to attend Mass at Middlefield, about five miles away. Attendance was expected among boys for whom it was a way of life, but it wasn't compulsory, and this was quite sufficient dispensation for Scruffy to decide to give Mass the elbow, evidently considering keeping company with Rose more rewarding than prayers.

And one Sunday, Jarvis decided that God couldn't begrudge him one day off to himself and, like Scruffy, he gave Mass a miss. Jarvis believed it was the first time in his life that he didn't attend Mass on a Sunday, and he couldn't in all honesty recall feeling very bad about it, even if it was a sin: a mortal one. The moment Scruffy disappeared in the direction of The Cross with a carefree wave, Jarvis took himself off across the hills heading nowhere in particular. It was weeks since he had been able to stretch his legs in Richmond Park, and his body fairly ached to be let loose to run free. As soon as he let himself go, letting his legs carry him as far as they wished, he felt an inner peace envelop him; all the niggling little problems of his life seemed to drain away, leaving his mind perfectly free to absorb the serenity of his surroundings; the lush meadows with their mixture of grasses and wild flowers, the stands of trees whispering in the warm breeze, the vivid yellow sweeps of the furze on the undulating hills, the shrieks of countless inquisitive birds, the startled flight of a family of deer in the distance and the constant bobbing of the little white scuts of rabbits that scattered myriads of butterflies from their pleasures on the long grass bents.

He must have run eight or nine miles when, topping a crest obscured by tall grasses and his vision drawn to four Scots pines, Jarvis suddenly found himself running pell-mell down a steep slope; his legs could barely keep up with each other as he raced downwards, quite unable to pull up. Jarvis, whose eyes were concentrated on his feet, had a momentary glimpse of a stream and several gypsy caravans far below, but racing up to meet him. Just when he thought he must stumble to the ground, his legs simply unable to maintain the momentum of his racing feet, he crashed, instead, into the very solid chest of a man who whirled him round in the air, and set him down on his feet, and held him firmly until he was steady.

"Whoa! Whoa there, matey," the man cried.

It took Jarvis several moments to gather himself together, to make sure his feet weren't still pounding like automatons. He looked back up the hill he had just raced down, and it looked more like a mountain with the quartet of Scots pines at its peak. His gaze next took in the five gaily decorated caravans, complete with smoking funnels, a collection of shaggy horses and fierce-looking dogs, a score or so of swarthy men and women in shapeless, dark clothing, and a whole swarm of assorted urchins splashing in the stream with hardly any clothes on at all. In the immediate moment, Jarvis's main concern on finding himself in the middle of the camp was about the dogs and their ferocious barking and snarling, and whether their ropes and chains were strong enough. Instinctively he took a step back, though as everyone, including the dogs, had formed a wide circle about him, this did not appear to avail him much. Again, instinctively, his hands covered his vitals, though as far as he was concerned all of him was vital. His protective action led to loud laughter around the circle.

"They won't bother you – not while you're with us," assured the man who had acted as a buffer in Jarvis's uncontrollable run towards the stream. He gave a sign to the others who uttered growls of their own to silence their animals. "They ain't kept to be friendly – not to strangers," explained the man, with a wide grin.

Jarvis turned to examine the man who had without doubt saved him from some serious mishap. Everything about him was dark, from the crumpled black trilby perched on his head to the solid black boots on his feet; in between, were black curly hair, greying at the temples, bushy black eyebrows, shiny black eyes that looked lost in a darker tunnel of their own, a thin, stubbly face and a shabby, black suit. The only relief from his blackness was a gold (or brass) ring dangling from his right ear, a sweat-stained red-checked kerchief about his neck, a collarless blue shirt and a patchwork waistcoat that was predominantly browns, blues and various shades of green. An easy smile that displayed two rows of very white teeth also helped to break the monotony.

"You're gypsies, aren't you?" Jarvis declared finally, and at once thought it a stupid thing to say. It was obvious the man was a gypsy. Still, they were the first gypsies he'd ever seen in the flesh.

"That's what people call us," acknowledged the other, his smile widening at the other's confusion, "but we're only travellers, really – not the devils they regard us as." And before Jarvis could get a word in, the man asked, "Where you come from, sonny? Running like that. You in training for something?"

"No, not really. I just like to run. It means freedom. Running sets me free and gives me a lift. When I'm set free, I feel I can run for ever, it feels so liberating." Jarvis could hardly believe that he'd said all these things out loud, and to a perfect stranger. They were the sort of private thoughts he kept to himself.

"You got a father, lad?" he asked.

"No, sir," Jarvis replied calmly.

"A mother, then?"

Jarvis shook his head. "No; not one of them either."

"You're an orphan, then?" said the other, shaking his head in his turn. "So, where d'you live? Who looks after you?"

"I live in Battersea – that's in London, in an orphanage run by the Catholics – priests and brothers."

"Is it all right? Do you like it there?"

Jarvis shrugged. "I suppose. They feed, clothe and educate me. I've been in a few of their homes now, but I reckon they'll keep me at Battersea – till they put me out to work."

The other nodded, understandingly. "I thought you might have been running away from someone, or something," he remarked, quizzically.

"No, I'm down here working on a farm for a few weeks," Jarvis said quite openly.

"So, not running away?" the man pressed.

Jarvis shook his head thoughtfully. "No."

"Ever think of it?"

Jarvis stared hard at the man, suddenly intrigued at the direction their conversation was taking. He'd never regarded his adventures with Mr Maggs as being connected with running away: that had been unintentional. "Possibly," he admitted, cautiously. Running away was easy enough, it was how to live afterwards that mattered, Jarvis mused, fingering the outline of the dud florin beneath his sweaty shirt. He always wore the coin round his neck on a piece of waxed string; it was his talisman.

"What's your name, son," the other asked softly, breaking in on Jarvis's thoughts with a friendly smile.

"Brook, sir. Jarvis Brook," Jarvis replied instantly, and not for the first time in his life he wondered if he should have kept his mouth shut.

"I'm Nelson," said the gypsy. "I don't know that I've got any other names. Nelson's what everyone calls me. It's a first an' last name. And you don't need to 'sir' me, ever."

Jarvis was ruminating over the word "ever" – it sounded like a long time, when Nelson interrupted his thoughts again and declared, "You've arrived just at the right time, Jarvis. We're just about to eat. You must join us. Be part of the family." With that, Nelson took Jarvis's arm and lead him towards a caravan while the others dispersed to their own places; even the dogs quieted amidst the movements. "You hungry?"

Jarvis nodded. When wasn't he! If he ran all the way back to Little Warren Farm right now, he'd still miss his dinner there, so he may as well tuck in here while he could, and then trot back to the farm – and face the music. But he was pretty sure Scruffy would cover for him, and he might not even be missed. He nodded his head, eagerly.

Nelson's wife had been given the name Ermyntrude; she had been born in a graveyard at Virginia Water and this had been the name on the nearest tombstone; happily it had a short form, Emma, and this was how she was known. Emma was a large woman: big-boned, anyway; rangy is how Jarvis would have described her, though with a bosom that caught the eye. It caught his eye, anyhow: he was starting to notice things like that, now that he was seeing a few more of them – women, that is, not just their bosoms. Her face, too, was large, with swarthily rosy cheeks and large, darkly bright eyes that gave it a wild beauty. Her dark hair was contained in a sort of string bag at her nape. She was wearing a dark green blouse, with the sleeves rolled up to her elbows, and a very full black skirt, and on top of this a voluminous floral apron, when Nelson and Jarvis climbed the steps at the rear of the caravan.

For several minutes they spoke together in some strange language (Jarvis learned later that it was Romany), Emma asking quick, short questions, rather sharply, Jarvis thought. As if she hadn't been watching their approach every step of the way, like the rest of the camp, she'd greeted Jarvis's arrival with a look, first, of utter astonishment, and then with a quick frown of suspicion, akin to hostility, which made Jarvis think perhaps he wouldn't be asked to stay for dinner after all. But, as Nelson continued talking, Emma's expression travelled through phases of disbelief, consternation, dissent, mistrust and, finally, she examined Jarvis more closely in a series of quick sidelong peeks.

Jarvis had remained hovering uncertainly on a step just outside the doorway, sensing that his presence might not be entirely welcome, perhaps even resented, and was prepared for instant flight regardless of the dogs prowling, doubtless hungrily, round the caravan. But his fears were needless. Emma made up her mind, and came to an agreeable conclusion about him. Her glances, which had been growing softer all the while, developed into little half-smiles until they blossomed into full-blown affairs that lit her face so that it shone like a harvest sunset. She turned to beckon Jarvis to her. When he came within reach, she opened her strong arms and folded them round him, hugging him close and whispering soothingly, if meaninglessly, in her foreign tongue, as though he had been a baby lying at her breast. Presently, she took his face between her large, rough hands and kissed him very firmly on the mouth.

"Welcome to your new home, Jarvis," she said, in a pleasant, if strangely accented voice. "Nelson's taken a shine to you an' wants you to live here as our son – so you're to be a member of our family – if you'd like, that is?"

Jarvis, still savouring her kiss, was startled almost to a state of dumbness at her suggestion; he'd been given no inkling of anything so momentous by Nelson – other than his nebulous "ever" word. It was almost too much to take in: that he would never have to return to Battersea; that he was to be part of a real family, with real parents; that he was no longer an orphan. And in those delirious moments of sheer wonder and happiness, to his shame he completely forgot that other home of his at The Dials, and even Queenie herself, and Ruth, too. The moment was too big for him to absorb anything else.

He nodded his head (which Emma still held) as vigorously as he was able and gave her what he hoped was a happy, grateful smile. Though, in truth, Jarvis was becoming more and more conscious of the stew he had seen simmering outside in a great blackened pot dangling from a steel tripod over a lazily crackling wood fire, and watched over by a vigilant little girl – God, was she now a sister! – wearing nothing more than a ragged petticoat and armed with a ladle almost as big as herself; the aroma from the pot pervaded the caravan, insinuating itself to his very taste buds and making him ravenously conscious of a great void in his stomach. It was dinner time: no time to think of running anywhere. He was here to stay.

Emma went on. "All right then, Jarvis, we're your family now, and Nelson's the head – not only of us, but the whole camp. Always do what he tells you; an' me, of course," she added quickly, giving Jarvis a brief glimpse of her homely smile. "If you don't, you'll likely as not get a clip round the ear!" She paused to give him another motherly smile, and a tighter hug. "Our own four girls will be your sisters, an' you their brother, an' I hope you'll come to love them as we do, and protect them always." Jarvis promised that he would, and she finally let go face and gave his hands an affectionate squeeze. He loved her at once, and made the profound discovery that it was easy to love when one was loved in return. Emma didn't seem at all bothered at having an extra mouth to feed, and in her next breath she won Jarvis's heart completely – for she talked his language! "First we eat," she announced. "It'll give you the opportunity of meeting the girls and, later, we'll talk some more."

The meal was everything that he could have wished: hot, tasty and plentiful. Jarvis was told that the meat was a badger that Nelson had caught, which didn't mean a great deal to him. Meat was meat, and he hadn't had enough of it to tell the differences. The food was eaten in comparative silence on his part for he didn't believe in disturbing his eating. There'd be time enough to talk when the food was gone, which is the way it happened.

In the course of the leisurely meal, Jarvis became acquainted with sisters, who appeared only mildly surprised, and not particularly ecstatic, at finding a big brother suddenly in their midst. The first was Vesta, who had been guarding the cooking pot outside; she was nine, dark like all her sisters and was a serious little girl, happier playing house than games. Her elder sister Matilda, called Tilly, was eleven, two years taller and had a riot of black curls tumbling over her face which revealed her mother's wild beauty when she laughed, which she frequently did; she had a neat little figure and was, without doubt, the prettiest of them all. Zita, who was seven, was the clever one; petite and vivacious, she spent her day, when her chores allowed, dancing and singing. The baby of the family, at five, was Fred. Her name had been chosen before she was born by Nelson in a bid to break the sequence of daughters; after her arrival the name was amended to Freda, but she was always called Fred, which seemed rather unfair. She wasn't even a tomboy. She was small, dainty and very feminine, with the round, happy face of a doll; she loved everybody, and was very lovable herself.

Later in the afternoon, it was close to evening, Jarvis was taken on a tour of the other caravans so that he could be introduced – Nelson proudly proclaiming him to be "our boy Jarvis." There were the Swanns and Butchers, the Browns and Wilsons, who between them numbered thirty-seven. They greeted Jarvis with varying degrees of warmth, some clapping him on the back, others ruffling his hair (which he still hated), some others who chose to poke him amiably in various parts of his anatomy, and those who made do with nods and smiles. Another significant meeting was with Granny Zilla – who became Madame Zilla professionally, a fortune-teller, who did not appear to belong to anyone in particular but was at present residing in the Butchers' caravan. She looked to be at least a hundred years old, but was probably no more than seventy. It was the wrinkled skin of her face, like that of a withered turnip, which aged her, and it was the only part of her that was visible – apart from her long, skinny and veiny hands with their evilly-long nails flashing like gold daggers. The rest of her was enveloped in black robes that seemed to be made more mysteriously dark by the mystical symbols and magical words in gold lettering emblazoned upon it, and a shawl with tassels that covered her head, except where a few strands of stringy white hair showed. Her deep-set black eyes glistened like lumps of coal in the still-bright sunlight and seemed to penetrate right through you, and when she spoke her voice emerged with the sort of hoarse, hollow cackle one usually associated with – witches! Jarvis was visibly startled by her and he felt her eyes burning into his back, searching his very soul, as he cringed away.

One way and another it had been quite a day, and Jarvis wasn't sorry when the time to bed down arrived. The sleeping arrangements were as surprising as they were reasonable; the parents and their two youngest children slept inside the caravan, everyone else underneath. Jarvis found himself jammed between Tilly, who was like an octopus, and two enormous dogs, a tawny lurcher with foul breath and something resembling a mastiff and both vying with each other for the privilege of either washing or loving him to death; what with their attentions on one side, and Tilly's marauding hands on the other, he didn't dare move a muscle, and slept like a log.

Nelson wasted no time setting about educating Jarvis in the ways of the outside world. On only his second morning, he touched his shoulder firmly, before even the sun was awake, pressed a finger to his lips and beckoned. Still almost drunk with sleep, or the need of it, Jarvis slowly disentangled himself from the embraces of Tilly and the dogs, who continued to cling to him like leeches. He was extremely reluctant to leave their embraces, and was dragged from their warmth by Nelson, who unceremoniously hauled him out into the dewy open. Jarvis gratefully pulled on a heavy green sweater Emma had provided him with and tied his boots, and, as he followed in the wake of Nelson, longingly wished that he had long trousers. His eyes were heavy and sticky with sleep, and he wasn't entirely sure if he wasn't sleepwalking. Their footsteps left dark prints on the dewy turf.

The very first thing Jarvis had impressed upon him was the need for absolute quiet, and it was with this end in mind that he was shown how to walk through the long grass and undergrowth without warning everybody and everything for miles around of his approach. "Don't be in too much of a hurry, always take care where you put your feet, an' don't be slow in stopping to have a listen, an' have a sniff of the air, too, to see if *you* can detect anything you can't see or hear. Your hooter ain't anywhere as sensitive as an animal's, but its purpose is the same, so use it," sniffed Nelson, whose feet barely left an imprint let alone made a sound. "When you walk, walk slowly with your weight on your back foot. That way you can feel about with the other, testing the ground, before transferring the weight, and so avoid hidden snags, like twigs an' roots. A snapping dry stick sounds like a bloody gun in the still of the morning."

Although Jarvis was still barely awake, he tried to absorb everything Nelson said and to put all his advice into immediate use, but while Nelson moved like a wraith just in front, his own footsteps were like machine-guns. By degrees, however, with continual practice, he improved to such a degree that Nelson was moved to nod approvingly – although he muttered, in case Jarvis should get too big-headed, "p'raps you ain't scared *ev'ry* perishin' rabbit off this side of the Ouse!" Jarvis's chest positively swelled with pride at such praise; he had yet to learn the agonies of sarcasm.

Nelson was an endless source of knowledge on every aspect of fieldcraft, and Jarvis found it well nigh impossible to retain every facet of every lesson he imparted; it was like a never-ending flood of information, a nugget here, a gem there, and then another snippet before he gave a casual wave at a tree or a bird, and proceeded to give a graphic history of whatever it was that had briefly caught his eye, and which Jarvis had missed altogether. Once Nelson came to an abrupt halt at the edge of a copse and whispered out of the side of his mouth, "That's one you won't see often." It was a fieldfare, which Jarvis hadn't noticed till it moved. Jarvis stared at the bird under discussion and, though it looked like an ordinary thrush to him, he found himself being infected by Nelson's enthusiasm, and so learned more.

The lectures continued like a river in full spate: details of flora and fauna poured forth in an endless stream. Jarvis never stopped marvelling at Nelson's font of knowledge, and as the days passed he began to assimilate more and more of what he was told, and his growing interest showed in the growing number of questions he asked about things. So his education progressed. Jarvis learned to read tracks on the ground, too; and, sometimes, to identify them though they might be little more than a smudged indentation, and days old; animal droppings also took on a new significance, as did trampled leaves and broken twigs that were still green and supple and where the dew and spiders' webs had been disturbed: all were pointers not only to the type of animal but, importantly, when they were made and, therefore, the likelihood of it still being around – possibly watching *him*!

There were occasional breaks from their daily instructional expeditions when Nelson would simply take Jarvis out walking – stretching their legs, as he called it – to find out where they were, and what was there; this was not as strange as it might sound, for they were now encamped in Hampshire, in an area known as Micheldever Wood, having had three other camps since Jarvis had joined them a scant fortnight previously. He had soon learned that these "look-see" jaunts were not the innocent strolls they might appear on the surface; that Nelson, always alert for possible deals, was really out foraging, and was at his most audacious when in a seemingly casual mood. Nelson had an eye and a head for business; if he saw the slightest trading potential in an article, and if muscle and ingenuity could move it, then that item was his, whether it be a brand-new, five-barred gate or a tin bath still warm from use; it was snaffled, transported and bartered probably before the owner missed it – and Nelson was over the hill and far away: and over the moon, too!

On one occasion during their slow journey across Hampshire, Nelson, with Jarvis and Tilly ambling as a shield behind him to conceal his activity, had strolled ever so casually through a farmyard dropping grains of corn (which he had just as casually helped himself to, of course) all the way to a point within easy access to their camp. The chickens quickly pecked their way along the trail and for two days they all lived on eggs, cooked every way imaginable. It was too good to last, of course, and eggs virtually came off the menu the day the caravans rolled on, but with them went the carcasses of several birds, so it was roast chicken for several days to follow ... and they made sure of not leaving a trail of their own.

Jarvis's education was not restricted to excursions with Nelson. He learned many equally useful things from Emma, particularly concerning plants and roots that were edible, the benefits of a wide variety of herbs, which hung in festoons about the caravan, inside and out, and the healing qualities associated with an endless string of other plants. A stroll down a lane with Emma and his new sisters, was like a walk through a well-stocked larder which he might have missed in any other company. The hedgerows were filled with delicacies, accord-ing to the season, like sloes, crab apples, elderberries, blackberries, rose hips, bilberries, wild mulberries, and, in secret streams where stretches of sparkling water had been dammed, either by accident or design, watercress by the bucketful could be found. Dotted here and there, and growing quite wild, were bushes of currants and gooseberries, and patches of thyme, parsley and sage for cooking, rosemary for flavouring, camomile and cowslip for tea-making, or if you didn't fancy either of them there was always tansy, which had the added benefit of repelling flies, or use dandelions to make coffee. Emma's larder was truly limitless. And, of course, there was always lavender or "lucky" heather for selling, for sometimes she did need a few coppers to buy things that Nature didn't provide.

Evenings spent relaxing round smouldering fires held a magic that had no equal, for young or old. There were home-brewed concoctions of varying potency to keep everyone happy, singing and dancing to the accompaniment of violin, accordion and flute (and sometimes a mouth-organ, but this depended whether or not the owner was sober, which wasn't very often), roasted parsnips or potatoes piping hot from the ashes to chew on, and there was story-telling by Granny Zilla which sent shivers racing up and down their spines as they sat, their hearts in their mouths, hanging on to every last word and hoping it would never end. Only when they were too tired to keep their eyes open did they retire, children first, to sleep like those proverbial logs.

A week or so later, Jarvis climbed into Granny Zilla's caravan – she was now accommodated with the Wilsons, the Butchers having been blessed with a new arrival – to have his fortune told. The session had been arranged by Emma who was a great believer in such things. It was dark inside the caravan, the only light being provided by two flickering red candles. Granny Zilla (she dispensed with the title Madame when among "family") sat on one side of a small, green-baize covered table on which stood a large crystal ball, sparkling and mysterious in the half-light. She wore her very special black, silk fichu with its gold symbols shimmering with a magic that reached out and sent squiggles of unease down his sticky back; the wavering candlelight that gave rise to this eerie sensation also gave her wrinkled face an awe-inspiring image. She extended a long, thin hand, palm-uppermost, towards Jarvis. He blinked back with reverential wonderment, staring at the white, veiny limb – and wondered if he was supposed to shake it, or even kiss it.

"You're supposed to cross my hand with silver," declared Granny Zilla, in a voice that sounded (to him) as far off as the grave.

"I haven't any silver," Jarvis whispered, swallowing hard, his voice emerging like a strangled squeak.

"You must give me something," she insisted, her dark eyes narrowing in the gloom.

Jarvis searched his pockets frantically, knowing they contained nothing of value, and eventually discovered a decidedly mutilated swan's feather.

"Will this do?" he asked, hopefully.

She nodded with great solemnity, and her eyes widened agreeably. Jarvis wasn't quite sure, but it did seem to him that those two great lumps of coal did actually twinkle; at any rate, the caravan appeared a good deal brighter. Granny Zilla, with an air of pomp and preciseness, placed the tattered and crushed feather very delicately on the table, and then placed a hand on either side of the crystal ball, her long nails (which today were painted a royal blue) flashing menacingly towards him. She lifted the globe off the table and stared straight into it with an intensity that threatened to shatter it into a million shards; occasionally she turned it reverently in her skinny hands, and several times she mumbled some inaudible incantation, at the same time swaying from side to side to such a degree that he feared she might topple off her chair, but she never did.

Suddenly, she seemed to have read rather more than she expected from the depths of the shimmering orb. Her face took on an even more ghostly, eerie aspect, her eyes acquired a dark glare; she gave a whisper of a groan, and replaced the glass ball reverentially on the table. "Give me your hands, boy," she muttered urgently. Almost without knowing it, Jarvis extended his hands and was amazed at the coldness of her touch. His own fingers felt like live coals. She lay her hands on his, palm to palm, the points of her nails resting on his wrists.

"You are not a true gypsy, my son, and you are not destined to remain long among us," she began, in a voice that sounded frighteningly remote. At her words, Jarvis made to snatch his hands away and to voice his terror for he thought she was telling him he was soon going to die, but she gripped his hands with an unexpected strength to still them and pursed her thin lips to utter a barely audible "Sssh!" to silence him, and then continued: "You will be taken from us by someone in authority and, presumably, returned whence you came. I see lots of uniforms."

Jarvis wondered if she might be referring to St Boniface, and the prospect of being forcibly returned there so filled him with bitterness and despair that, for a moment, it almost stilled his heart. It seemed so unfair that he should be dragged away from this new environment in which he had found instant happiness and contentment. At the same time, very deep down, he acknowledged that he would be equally heart-broken were he never again to see his friends at The Dials, for in the quiet of the night or in the early dawn just before he got up, he remembered them all : Queenie, his so-nearly Mum; Sam Trotter, the gentle giant and every child's idea of a father; and little Ruth, his special friend. It did seem likely that he wouldn't see any of them again if he continued in his present way of life. But, he'd be equally distressed were he to be taken from Nelson and Emma and his new sisters.

Granny Zilla clearly saw the agony in his eyes, and probably much more besides; a frown dimmed the light that shone in her own. "I see pain," she said. "A lot of pain, but that looks to be in the very distant future. However, I see great happiness for you, too. That, too, seems a long way off. I see a great, and enduring, love ... but many years will pass before you recognise it. You take many a wrong turning before finding the right path." She shook her head and peered yet again into the glass ball, and then back at Jarvis, and he thought she took on an even gloomier expression. "You will have success in life, but I can't see in what capacity. But, it doesn't end there." Again a dark cloud hovered over her face. "I see a great catastrophe ... and terrible pain ahead for a great many people, but ... the picture is fading now; my last impressions are of great pain ... tragedy ... and joy for you."

Jarvis did not linger when Granny Zilla came to the end of her prognostications. He had a zillion questions he was bursting to ask, but she prevented a single one, stemming the impending torrent by placing one bony finger to her lips and pointing the other towards the doorway ; he fled, in silence. Emma was hovering nearby, eager to hear of his expectations, but one look at his troubled face was sufficient to curb her curiosity, for the moment; and the moment was lost, for he never did tell what he'd been told about his future.

In fact, as soon as Jarvis had recovered from the frightening ordeal of the session, which didn't take very long, he began to doubt the plausibility of Granny Zilla's prophecies, and soon dismissed them as fanciful fairy tales. In any case, if they contained one grain of truth, he would soon know, for according to his fortune-teller his days as a gypsy were numbered; indeed, all but ended. He grinned wryly, and decided to await events; and as the sunny days rolled blissfully on, and nothing untoward happened or looked likely to happen, he convinced himself that Granny Zilla – the dear old bat! – was a fraud.

What powers Madame Zilla possessed may only be conjectured at, suffice to say that some of her prophecies came to fruition in an alarming manner, and very soon. August had seemed both to rush along and to go on and on, which Jarvis supposed meant that he was having the time of his life. On the very last day of the month their caravans had progressed into Dorset and settled for the night within sight of the wishing well at Upwey. After an early morning spent rabbit-netting, and with their booty dangling in sacks, the caravans were on the move, crawling sleepily along the road towards Martinstown and, eventually, a locality known as Black Down, and then it happened.

Their progress came to an abrupt halt on a bend where the road forked; one road wound round the hills to Dorchester, the other passed over a narrow stone bridge and struggled along to Martinstown. Nelson, in the lead caravan, had made a wide turn to line up his approach to the bridge, and then stopped. A strange clattering noise, not unlike a growl of thunder, was the first hint of impending disaster. As all eyes searched the sky for an explanation of the thunder, and thoughts even turned to the possibility of an earthquake, for the rumbling now seemed to be shaking the very ground beneath their wheels, an Army armoured tracked vehicle roared into view and smashed straight into Nelson's horse which was nibbling at the grassy bank as it waited patiently for the signal to proceed. The poor creature gave the briefest of heart-stopping squeals before it disappeared beneath the Caterpillars tracks. The low sound of its screeches continued for some moments before coming to a halt, and only the anguished sound of its laboured breathing could be heard.

The Bren-gun carrier – which was how the soldiers described their monster – was hastily reversed to reveal the mangled, but still twitching, animal. Nelson leapt down from the caravan, which had suffered no damage although standing askew as one of the wheels had slithered into a shallow ditch, and knelt beside the barely breathing horse. One leg had been half torn off, another was crushed and its body had been ripped open; fountains of blood shot up in the air and spattered everywhere. "Don't just stand there!" Nelson screamed at a white-faced corporal who appeared to be in command of the vehicle. "Shoot the poor thing!" The corporal, tearing his eyes away from the blood and mutilation, gave another retch before shaking his head. "Can't, mister," he cried, "we ain't issued with ammo."

Nelson railed contemptuously, "What! All them bleedin' guns an' not a bullet between you! What sort of a bloody army are you?" The corporal stammered his confused apologies, swallowed a mouthful of bile, blanched still further and, as Nelson produced a wicked-looking knife the size of a small bayonet, retreated several paces in dire terror of his intentions. Nelson, ignoring him completely, covered the dying horse's eyes and without the slightest hesitation plunged the blade into its jugular groove, and gave it twist. The horse was dead on the instant.

Once the corporal had recovered from his initial shock, and regained control of his stomach to a degree that his complexion was restored to something vaguely normal, he proved both helpful and competent. He posted a man to avert any further collisions, sent another to telephone the authorities, both civil and military, and actively assisted in the removal of the carcass from the shafts to an adjoining field. Nelson, having stripped the corpse of its shoes and various bits of harness, had a hurried discussion with his colleagues the result of which was that three caravans continued on their way taking with them certain items, including the rabbits, that might have been suspect in the eyes of the authorities and which, anyway, needed to be sold quickly. One other caravan remained waiting on the far side of the bridge and a fresh horse was fitted to Nelson's caravan so as to make it ready to follow. Nelson considered these wise precautions before the corporal finally took it into his head to order everyone to stay put until someone arrived to relieve him of the responsibility.

Meanwhile, Jarvis was clambering over the carrier, aiming its impotent gun longingly at all and sundry, and asking questions in quick-fire bursts that largely went unanswered; the youthful soldiers were too busy ogling Tilly who was playing the coquette (and diverting attention from Nelson's bustling activities) to shameless perfection. Jarvis had never seen a soldier close up before, and he was rather surprised to find they were mightily like ordinary people, like him. He'd expected them to be more like gods, and here they were in ugly khaki denims – and not a scarlet uniform in sight! Jarvis decided not to be a soldier after all – which didn't mean it wasn't all right to play with their tank-thing. He continued rat-tat-tatting with the empty Bren for all he was worth. But even as he played, his world was collapsing.

Sergeant Amos Pother of the Dorset Constabulary was the first official on the scene. Looking half the size of Sam, but still a well-fed figure, he arrived, red-faced and blowing hard, on a bicycle. After recovering his wind and mopping the sweat from his chubby, mottled face, he was quickly in control of the situation. He spotted Jarvis straight away. Only that week he'd studied a detailed description of him from the Metropolitan Police. It was just a routine notice about a runaway boy, one of many, but Sgt Pother's memory for such trivia was legendary. Having identified the face, he remembered its name. He decided not to act too heavy-handedly and, instead, beckoned over Policewoman Sadie Bold who had just arrived in a car with two other constables, and whispered some instructions to her. The officer unobtrusively took up a position behind Jarvis from where she could grab him should he try to bolt. For all Nelson's training, he never even noticed her.

Jarvis's attention was wholly focussed on a teenaged subaltern who had just arrived with a quartet of burly, red-capped military policemen. The lieutenant, having listened boredly to the corporal's excellent report, approached Sgt Pother, comfortably ensconced on a tea-chest and sipping a mug of camomile tea provided by Vesta, and said drily:

"I suppose you've heard about the war, sergeant?"

From the tone of his words, it was plain that he wished he were on some distant battlefield and not messing about with didicois and their wretched horses. In his opinion, which he voiced in a suitably loud tone, they shouldn't be allowed on the roads in the first place. Furthermore, if he had his way, they'd be the first to go over the top in the war.

Sgt Pother nodded. "Heard something about it on the wireless," he said flatly. It was clearly the limit of his knowledge ; that and the name Poland.

It was still more than the rest of them knew. The word "war" instantly attracted their attention. Quite incapable of concealing his excitement, Jarvis pushed his way to the very front of the throng and tugged at the officer's tunic.

"What war's this, mister?" he cried breathlessly.

The lieutenant, who had been holding his swagger stick in both hands behind his back in the best prescribed manner, flicked at his immaculate uniform where Jarvis's grimy hand had mauled it, smoothed it down, poked the boy away from him with the stick, and resumed his haughty posture.

"Germany has invaded Poland," he declared, in a tone that suggested the end of the world had arrived.

"Poland? Where the hell's that?" demanded Nelson, staring blankly.

"Eastern Europe," Jarvis spouted out, showing off the benefits of his geography lessons. "It's between Germany and Russia."

"That's right," said the lieutenant, scowling at the interruption. "The Fleet was mobilised last night and a general mobilization has been pro-claimed in the United Kingdom. Already, the Government's introduced Air Raid Precautions and ordered black-outs, and they've taken over the railways and started moving millions of people – women, children and invalids – out of the cities."

"Aha, that'll be this evacuation programme we've been told about," interposed Sgt Pother, who now had his honey-coloured eyes fixed on Jarvis.

It was then that the police began taking names and endeavouring to take statements from the gypsies. They gave whatever name came into their heads, swore they didn't know anything, hadn't seen anything, and shrank back. Jarvis was still listening to the lieutenant when Sgt Pother swung round to him and asked in a friendly, confidential sort of way:

"An' what's your name, sonny?"

"Jarvis Brook, sir," he said instinctively, catching Nelson's warning hiss too late. "Oh, God," he thought instantly, "what have I done!" Somehow, the memory of Mr Maggs sprang into his mind. Jarvis knew he would have been horrified at such a blunder; even speaking to a rozzer was a scandal more awful than even associating with "dawgs'n cats'n wimmin" in his book. Jarvis told himself that he was being silly, that the name Jarvis Brook wouldn't mean a thing down in this part of the world, but already he knew it wasn't so. This policeman knew. "Oh, God!" he muttered to himself again.

"And where do you come from, Master Jarvis Brook?" enquired Sgt Pother, his voice, while not unfriendly, now with the air of one who knows he has you by the goolies.

"Nowhere, sir," Jarvis cried, all flustered and helpless. "Nowhere at all. That is   ... I mean here, sir. I live wherever we're at. We're gypsies, see."

"No you ain't, lad. You've run away from a Home in London – Battersea, I think it was." The sergeant's voice became less friendly: more stern and formal. "They want you back, boy," he said quietly. "And, it's my duty to see that you go back."

"No! No! No! Oh, no! Oh, please, no!" Jarvis cried frantically, his voice almost a scream. He turned blindly to escape, but found his way barred by Policewoman Bold. She placed an arresting arm across his shoulders and slipped a restraining hand gently, but effectively, inside his arm. At the same time, she whispered in his ear, "Be a good boy. Don't make trouble for yourself." Jarvis didn't even try to break free. He felt too sick with the bitterness of his situation to be able to struggle. He said simply, but shrilly: "I won't go back! I won't!"

There was an angry murmur among the few gypsies remaining, but with Nelson and Emma to the fore, they surged forward menacingly, seemingly intent either to rescue Jarvis bodily or to create sufficient confusion to enable him to escape of his own accord; they seemed determined, at any rate, to have a punch-up with somebody. But they were halted in their tracks by Sgt Pother who faced them, calm and immovable, and addressed them in a tone that was not overly loud, but steady and unequivocal. It was the voice of authority, and of a man in command.

"Stand fast there!" he ordered the threatening group, instantly stilling their feet and silencing the menacing noises in their throats. "Don't you lot do anything silly. It's a very serious matter to interfere with a police officer in the execution of his lawful duties. You know that as well as I do. Any attack on a police officer, or even a simple obstruction, would land you all in the dock, and very likely in jail." He paused to let the import of his remarks sink in, but not so long that they had time to gather fresh impetus with which to press their cause. "The same dire penalties prevail," he continued sternly, "if you attempt to remove a prisoner from lawful custody. And ... and I'm sorry to have to say it, but this boy, Jarvis Brook, is under arrest – in his own interests. I don't know what he's doing with you lot – and we won't go into the matter; not now. He's a minor, a runaway orphan, and he'll remain in police custody pending his return to the Home he belongs to. And there's the end of the matter. I know it's a wretched business, but he has to go back."

There was a rising murmur of angry protest among the gypsies, but they stood fast. Nelson, his face grey with emotion, asked bitterly: "Why?"

"It's the law," said Sgt Pother, almost apologetically. He was well aware of the inadequacy of such a reply, particularly to people who lived – if not well beyond its limits – on the very periphery of the law. The law was not something that did much for them, and they tended to treat it with equal indifference. "The Home is entitled to have the boy returned to its care," he added weakly.

"But he's happy with us," insisted Nelson doggedly. "He's become one of us. We love him, an' I think he loves us."

"I do, I do," cried Jarvis, nodding his head desperately, a new hope welling in his breast, but though he struggled to free himself so that he could cling to Nelson, or Emma, or anybody else who didn't want to take him away, he could only wriggle futilely in the policewoman's hold.

"I'm sorry," said Sgt Pother, clearing his throat noisily.

"So you'll send the poor kid back ... an' they'll likely as not reward your efforts by flogging him," said Nelson stonily. "Is that what you want for him?"

Sgt Pother shrugged, but there was concern in his eyes. He was clearly under no illusion about Jarvis's reception on being returned to the Home; and neither was Jarvis. "It's the way things have to be, I'm afraid," he said firmly.

"It's not fair!" snapped Nelson.

"No," agreed the sergeant frankly. "It isn't. Life seldom is. But we make our own laws, and we have to abide by them – else there'd be anarchy. And it's often, like now, my sad duty to have to enforce these laws."

"He shouldn't be caged up in a Home," said Nelson bitterly. "He's like me: he's only alive out in the open – in God's real world."

"Remember that – and be sensible," warned Sgt Pother. "I'd hate to lock up someone like you. So don't go an' do anything silly." He drew a deep sigh, and went on: "We'll have to be taking him now. Does he have anything he needs to take with him?"

"We don't have anything but each other," cried Emma, her voice nearly broken as she strove to hold back her sobs.

Sgt Pother swallowed hard. "You'd best say your goodbyes then, and we'll be off," he said quietly. "Be as quick as you can – for everyone's sake."

It was one of the worst moments of Jarvis's life. He'd known that it had to come, and now that the terrible moment was here he just wanted it to be over before the pain became too unbearable. It was a moment very similar to one he had experienced when saying goodbye to Queenie. He steeled himself. He told himself he would not cry. For what seemed an age nobody made a move. Then Emma stepped sharply forward and placed her arms round him (the policewoman happily surrendered her hold), hugging him to her with such fierce determination that it seemed unlikely she'd ever let him go; she stroked his long, dark curls and laid her cheek gently on his head. "Is it like Granny Zilla said it would be?" she whispered, so softly he doubt if Policewoman Bold standing only a pace away caught the words. He nodded his head against the warmth of her suffocating breast. He wanted to lie there for ever. "Whatever happens in the future, Jarvis, know that we'll always love you as our own," she whispered again. Finally, she kissed the top of his head and hurried off in the direction of her caravan. Her shoulders were shaking convulsively long before she reached it.

Vesta, ever the little mother, stared after her mother with deep anguish, and then hurried over to Jarvis, lifting Fred up in her arms. "Bye-bye, Jar-wis!" prattled Fred, who only understood that he was going away. "Have a luv-erly time!" He gave her a kiss with lips that felt like sandpaper, and turned quickly to Vesta. "You've been just the brother we've always wanted to love," she cried, giving him a quick kiss before putting Fred down and darting away to comfort her mother. Zita rushed up, flung her arms round him and bestowed a dozen butterfly kisses all over his face, and rushed off without saying a word. Tilly, standing on tip-toes, whispered, "Who's going to keep me warm at night now?" She kissed him calmly, but with warmth and passion, and walked slowly away without looking back.

Nelson approached last and for several moments they just stood looking at each other, a few paces apart, and then they simply held each other without speaking for several more moments. "If ever you need us, Jarvis, any gypsy camp in the country will know where you can find us," Nelson said huskily. "We've loved you like a son, an' always will do. Please, come back an' see us one day, if you can." He gave a brief final hug and stepped back, and in that instant Policewoman Bold stepped forward and gently led Jarvis towards the waiting car. He didn't look back until they reached it. Nelson hadn't moved; he stood motionless and without apparent expression, but with eyes that looked to be drowning in grief.

The car pulled slowly away, and Jarvis continued staring back at Nelson until a bend finally parted them for good. Only then did Jarvis finally give himself over to his heart-break. He gave a sudden agonized cry of torment and flung himself against the policewoman. He gripped her so tightly she gave an involuntary gasp, and his sobs, in great racking bursts that swamped her breast, seemed to rock the car itself.

"Let it all run out, dearie," she said, holding on to him.

    □ *Queenie began crying at this point in her story and there was an adjournment while she composed herself; after she'd had dinner with the Matron, she was driven home and asked to return to resume her story when she felt able. She was back two days later.*

Chapter Thirteen

The Dials, 3 September, 1939

London was having its first air-raid alert as Jarvis's train arrived at Waterloo Station. It was a false alarm, but the curiosity and apprehension it engendered gave him the opportunity to slip the leash of his escort.

He had spent the whole of the previous day sitting dejectedly, and sullenly, in a locked room at Dorchester Police Station while steps were taken to return him to St Boniface. Because of the imminence of war and the bustling panic that attended its preparation – not least, the reception and movement of hundreds of thousands of evacuees arriving from all directions and having to be forwarded in as many opposite directions, his personal little drama attracted a very low priority. But, eventually, that morning, he was escorted to the station and put on a train (the very first he'd been on) to London. There was no police officer available to accompany him and he was placed in the care of an unfriendly train guard, who pointed to a distant corner of his van and told him to sit there and not move, nor speak either.

On arrival in London, where he was supposed to be handed over to a waiting policeman, the eerie wail of the air-raid siren and the absence of any constable, lured the grumpy guard out of his fortress to investigate. He very carefully locked the van door behind him, and Jarvis, just as carefully, nipped out of the opposite door, which he discovered was unlocked, and was away like a shot. He was vaguely aware of a strident voice screaming at him to "Take cover!" and demanding to know where his "bleedin' gas-mask" was, but he paid no heed, and legged it.

In next to no time, he had raced over Hungerford Bridge, bounded across Trafalgar Square and dashed up St Martin's Lane to St Giles. It seemed the most natural thing in the world that he should make his way there. Wasn't it more his real home than anywhere else in the world? Even more so than with his gypsy family? He darted in at the side entrance of The Dials, straight into the substantial figure of the woman he loved above all others, even including his dear Emma who had for a brief, happy spell occupied her place. Queenie's fat arms immediately encompassed him as he ran headlong into her. He lifted his head and met her smiling, reassuring eyes and a great weight of anxiety drained from him; the familiar feel, warmth, strength and, yes, even the smell of her, and the very largeness of her, filled him with joy, and peace; he was home, and he felt completely safe. Jarvis closed his eyes tightly to relish the moment, fearful of losing its magic; and then he looked up at her again, and whispered "Hello, Mum!"

Together, squeezed so closely they lurched like a couple of drunks, they made their way to Queenie's favourite retreat: her kitchen. It was in its customary chaotic disorder, but, as usual, everything was spotless; and the whole room was filled with the mouth-watering aroma of baking apples and cloves, and a joint could be heard sizzling slowly inside the blessed Aga.

"I s'ppose you're 'ungry, lovey?" she said, forgoing any question for the moment as to where he'd sprung from, and indicating a chair on one side of the solid, wooden table for him to sit on. Peering between the necks of several bottles and other such culinary accessories, Jarvis nodded eagerly, automatically; all of a sudden his meagre breakfast seemed too distant to be anything but a forgotten memory.

"I always seem to be," he cried, cheerfully.

Queenie grinned, not having expected any other response, and cut some slices (doorsteps they were, really) of bread and spread them thickly with darkly streaked dripping and piled them on a plate which she pushed through the chaos to him.

"That'll 'ave to keep yer goin' till dinner – which won't be all that long now," she said, seating herself opposite and plonking her great elbows on the table, cupping her chin in her enormous hands as she watched him pounce on the food.

They remained silent for several minutes – him fully occupied with the serious business of eating, Queenie, content simply to watch each mouthful disappear. Jarvis watched her, too, even as he ate. He could see that she was worried about something: him, he supposed. He was right, for as he pushed his empty plate away, his fingers searching for any missed crumbs, she said aloud:

"I suppose y'know the whole blinkin' world's bin 'ere lookin' fer yer! The police come sev'ral times, an' some monkey-face from that Boneface of yourn; dressed like a monk, 'e were, anyways! Scared the perishin' life outta me, straight up 'e did!"

"Garn!" Jarvis couldn't for the life of him picture Queenie being scared of anybody or anything; more likely it was the visitor who was terrified. He ventured a rueful smile. "I'm afraid I give 'em all the slip again today," he confessed. "At the railway station. I just saw the chance to run, an' I run. Straight to you – Mum."

"You'll run orf once too of'en one of these days, m'lad," scolded Queenie. She tried to look cross, but only managed a small frown which vanished almost as soon as it arrived; the twinkle never left her eyes. "Well, I reckon they'll be rahnd ag'in to drag yer back, lovey," she told him seriously, "an' there ain't nuffink we can do abaht it." She let that sink in, while she gathered up her thoughts and sorted them out; and then she went on: "You'll 'ave to go back, lovey, an' face the music. Sam's said that if yer was ter turn up 'ere, there ain't nuffink he can do abaht it – not even if they give you a beating. Oh, Jarvis," she cried, blinking her eyes hard and leaning forward to grip his hands tightly, "you'll 'ave to stop runnin' orf like this – specially now there's a bleedin' war on, an' all!"

Jarvis's face lit up, and he snatched back his hands and clapped them delightedly. "It's come? The war! It's started – really an' truly?" he cried excitedly. "I thought something must be up 'cos of the sirens and all the soldiers at the station. How marvellous!"

Queenie raised her eyes to the ceiling, and shuddered. She nodded grimly, not knowing whether to be angry or amused at him. "Yes, it's come – again," and her voice sounded sad and suddenly weary. "More's the pity. Gawd knows wot it's all abaht, or 'oo these bleedin' Poles is. That Chamb'lin bloke's bin spoutin' on the wireless – sayin' wot a 'bitter blow' it were to 'im! *'Im*, mark you! As if *he'll* be doin' any of the fightin' an' dyin' – or any of them other perlitical blokes. An' ain't it all 'is blasted fault in the first place? Gawd knows wot 'appened to 'is bleedin' bit of paper wot he brung back from bleedin' Munchin. Said it would save the bleedin' world, 'e did. Peace in our time, that's wot 'e promised!"

"What's going to happen, Mum?" Jarvis asked eagerly. He didn't want a history lesson right now – and certainly no talk of peace.

"Terrible things, lovey," Queenie replied, in a quiet far away voice. "Thank Gawd Sam's too old this time," she exclaimed.

"Where is Sam, anyway? P'raps he's gone off to join up to surprise you!"

"Not 'im; 'e's got more sense; 'e knows – 'e was in the last war, see. No, lovey, 'e was called in to do an extra shift. War work, they called it – an' that was 'fore we was even at war. I suppose it'll mean he ain't allowed to tell me wot 'e's up to. A fine state of affairs, I don't fink! Suppose there'll be a lot of this hush-hush nonsense now, specially for coppers."

Jarvis wondered, not very optimistically, if the war would still be on when he could join up. Not finding an answer, he asked by way of compensation, "And Ruth? Where's she?"

"At Mass – where you should be," retorted Queenie.

"I said a prayer on the train," Jarvis said, quite truthfully. "That should count."

"Ruth always remembers you in 'er prayers, Jarvis."

"That's jolly good of her," Jarvis exclaimed, not greatly impressed.

"She was in a terrible state when you went missing, lad. Cried all the time, an' prayed for you every day, too. She'll 'ave hysterics when she sees you back 'ere, all safe'n sound." Suddenly, as Jarvis pondered just how safe he'd be once they got their hands on him back at St Boniface, she leaned forward conspiratorially, her voice dropping to something of a hush although they were quite alone, and said: "Now then, young man, s'pose you tell me where you've sprung from – an' wot you bin up to these last two months; an' don't go tellin' me no fibs neither, you young devil."

Jarvis grinned, and launched forth into a fairly accurate account of his adventures. Actually, he didn't tell any fibs; he just didn't mention certain things – like his goings-on with the lovely Tilly. He gave a perfectly frank account of his farming "holiday" at Little Warren, even including Scruffy's affair with Rose. He explained that it was this "boring interlude" that had been the cause of him running off with the gypsies "because he was always with her, and I was left on my own."

"You should've done wot yer pal Scruffy done – found yerself a girlfriend to play with," chuckled Queenie, "then yer wouldn't 'ave got yerself in all this bovver wiv the police."

"There weren't one for me," Jarvis lied easily.

"Weren't there no gels among yer gypsy friends neither?" enquired Queenie blandly, a twitch of a smile playing about the corners of her plump mouth.

"Yes, I s'pose so, but I weren't interested in blooming girls," declared Jarvis, feeling himself reddening. He knew she could read him like a book, and guessed she didn't need him telling her what little boys got up to – if only in their minds. And still he tried to pull the wool over her eyes. "I was too occupied with other things to notice them properly."

He told her about the way gypsies lived, and how they kept to themselves – and were only too happy for other people, the *gorgios*, to do the same. He confided that although he lived with a particular gypsy family, he didn't sleep inside their caravan; no, he'd slept underneath, all alone, except for a pack of dogs. And he was sure this needless falsehood – the lie being one of omission, hadn't fooled Queenie for a moment; he hurried on to explain the many skills he'd learned in the way of fieldcraft and how this knowledge could be used to live, perfectly freely, off the land (providing you weren't caught by bailiffs and such like), but he skimmed over the poaching and foraging expeditions.

"Can't see as 'ow all this country know-how is goin' to be of much use to you 'ere in London Town," commented Queenie dryly when he'd done. "Still, I 'spect it all passed the time for you."

The difficult silence that ensued was shattered by a shriek as Ruth returned from her Mass. She'd spotted Jarvis the moment she came in from the street and came to an immediate standstill, allowing the door to slam behind her. She remained rooted to the spot for a moment or two her happy surprise flooding her face, and this gave Jarvis the opportunity to examine her. It was a year since they'd last seen one another and, apart from being a bit taller, she looked to be quite unchanged; the same skinny, leggy schoolgirl, all pigtails and ribbons. He didn't suppose she'd thank him for these thoughts, and he quickly decided that she was growing really quite pretty. She was wearing a pink cotton dress and cardigan, long white socks and shiny black shoes with big silver buckles, and on her head was a cream-coloured panama, with a red ribbon, which was attached by an ugly elastic band under her chin; at her throat, dangling on a chain, was a St Christopher medal, and she gripped a white glossy missal in her hands which were sheathed in little white cotton gloves that barely covered her wrists. Yes, he decided, she really was quite pretty; and growing up. It must be the dress!

The moment of shock having passed, Ruth, her face still effulgent with the excitement of seeing Jarvis, finally moved. Off came the hated panama and gloves, tossed with a careless unconcern at the hall-stand along with the prayer-book, and she was running towards him, pigtails and ribbons streaming like pennants, arms outstretched, laughing and shouting.

"Oh, Jarvis, Jarvis!" she cried loudly and breathlessly, throwing herself at him with such force she nearly bowled him over. "We ... we thought you'd been ... stolen!"

"Stolen! Who'd want to steal me?" he laughed teasingly, struggling against the force of her greeting, which was threatening to choke him to death; even so, he was hugely pleased at the warmth of her welcome, even to the extent of returning her countless kisses with an occasional poorly-aimed one of his own; his excuse was that he was too occupied trying to stay on his feet and loosening her arms from around his neck, where they seemed determined to make him the first casualty of the war.

"Oh, we would – Mummy and me ... especially me!" Ruth laughed happily in turn, and then delivered a further quick flurry of kisses on those parts of him that had so far escaped her attentions, before allowing herself to be pushed gently to arm's length so that they could examine each other more clearly.

"No one else would," Jarvis declared, grinning as Ruth stood pinkly, puffing and blowing to regain her breath..

"Wot you need, Jarvis, is for one of us to be lookin' after you all the time so's yer wouldn't ever want to run orf again," observed Queenie pointedly, looking from one to the other of them with her motherly smile.

"Oh, yes, yes. Let it be me, Jarvis! Please!" cried Ruth beseechingly, jumping up and down on tiptoes with such energy that one of her socks slithered down to her ankle.

"We've all been so terribly worried abaht you, lovey," Queenie put in hurriedly as Jarvis saw fit to ignore her daughter's plea.

Jarvis wasn't quite so indifferent to their concern over him as he appeared; he'd always imagined the only sufferer over his escapades was himself, and that had never bothered him unduly – a thrashing was quickly over and soon forgotten. It seemed quite extraordinary to think someone might actually care enough to cry over him when he was in trouble; he thought it quite unnecessary, and really not at all comforting.

"And please don't run away any more – unless you take me with you," urged Ruth.

"I'll wallop both yer backsides if ever yer does any such fing," declared Queenie forcefully, and Jarvis for one had little doubt but that she would, too.

"You've heard about the war, I suppose?" said Ruth, who knew her mother too well to feel under any real threat.

"Yes; Mum just told me," he cried enthusiastically.

"Father Daly announced it at Mass," said Ruth, breathlessly. "He gave us an extra long sermon on the strength of it, too, which I didn't think was very fair. Everyone was sad at the news, and I think Sister Bertie was crying. But the simply marvellous thing is that there's to be no Sunday school this afternoon because of it – the war, I mean. Father Daly said there'd be so much for everybody to do and he himself would be too busy visiting people who may be immediately affected by the war. I think he meant those families with men having to go off to fight. Perhaps there'll be no more Sunday school till it's all over?"

"Don't be daft," Jarvis retorted, dashing her hopes with a scornful laugh. "More'n likely get a double dose once they sort things out. I know we will at Boneface. Bet they'll even have us praying for the enemy – on the grounds that even they're God's children. Wonder if the Germans'll pray for us? Sounds stupid to me."

Ruth retorted somewhat impatiently that he was always in her prayers, though for the moment she was evidently more interested in the prospect of missing school, and this seemed to be more worthy of any extra prayers she had to undertake. "Surely with everyone being evacuated, they'll have to close the schools down," she suggested, but there didn't seem to be much optimism in her voice.

"Don't be daft," repeated Jarvis, grinning. "Do you think they want millions of kids running around the streets gettin' in everybody's way and nicking things from shops? Schools are the last places they'll shut, stupid!"

"Girls don't thieve things, silly," declared Ruth showing him the pink tip of her tongue and looking quite cross, for all of five seconds.

Queenie implemented an immediate armistice between them by announcing that it was dinner time, and that until it was over, and properly digested, both the war and their schools would have to get along as best they could without them squabbling – or else. In the same moment, Sam Trotter creaked into view, looking decidedly warrior-like with his row of Great War medal ribbons and brand-new respirator and tin hat. "Here's Daddy," sang out Queenie cheerfully. "Take more'n a bleedin' war to make 'im late for 'is dinner!"

Sam stared at Jarvis with astonishment, then smiled agreeably as he creaked over to slap him affectionately across the shoulders. "So," he declared, giving Jarvis a quick hug, "the wanderer's returned." That was almost all he had time for before Queenie bustled him off to wash before the meal. Afterwards, however, he whispered severely to Jarvis, "Told you there'd be a war, didn't I?"

Jarvis nodded excitedly. "Have you been to join up?" he asked eagerly.

Sam looked shocked, even horrified at the very idea. "I done my bit in the last one," he sighed, almost as if the memory of it was too painful to recall.

Jarvis couldn't for the life of him understand this reluctance to rejoice over the new war, but for the moment he was more impressed by Sam's medal ribbons, which he'd never seen before. Jarvis was certain that they bespoke unequalled heroics. He asked with eager anticipation: "Did you kill a lot of Germans in the last war, Sam?"

"Nary a one," he smiled, shaking his huge head. "No. Not one."

"Why ever not?" Jarvis cried, appalled at such dereliction of duty.

"I never seed one, that's why not," declared Sam, cheerfully. "I seed plenty of dead ones, 'course, but the only live Boches I seen was prisoners, an' they looked miserable enough wivvout bein' killed. I was a cook, see."

"P'raps you poisoned some!" Jarvis suggested, hopefully.

Sam roared with laughter. "I weren't that bad a cook!" he said, with a twinkle in his eyes. "Mind you, there was some wot might not agree! Still, I never poisoned any poor German. I only ever cooked for our boys – an' while I don't recall no compliments over what I give 'em to eat, they ate wot I give 'em readily 'nuff, an' I never 'eard of nobody dyin' from it, neither. If they did, they didn't complain!" He had another bout of laughter at this witticism.

"And you weren't ever wounded – just a little bit?" Jarvis pressed, ignoring Sam's joke in his desperation to find some instance of glory.

Sam frowned in feigned concern, and went through the motions of feeling himself in various likely places and counting off his limbs and digits; finally, his pantomime over, he shook his head and gave a loud sigh of relief, hiding a broad smile behind his huge hand. "Sorry – but no; not even a scratch," he announced soberly. "I was one of the lucky ones – millions weren't. Most was killed."

"So what did you get your medals for ... if you weren't killed or wounded, and never even killed anybody?" Jarvis demanded, almost accusingly.

"Just for being there, Jarvis," replied Sam calmly. "Just for being there – an' being lucky 'nuff to survive. It's them wot didn't that deserve the medals – an' a lot of good they'd 'ave done the poor devils."

The war, which had promised such breathtaking possibilities to his youthful mind moments before, lost its fascination for Jarvis for the moment, and they talked of other things, principally of his activities while "on the run," as Sam jokingly called it. Jarvis remained very circumspect over what he revealed, and Sam was too wise a policeman to press beyond the essentials. Later, as Jarvis blatantly eavesdropped, Sam telephoned his station to inform his sergeant that Jarvis had voluntarily surrendered, and he undertook to return him to St Boniface forthwith, and, yes sergeant, he'd make out a report in quintuplicate to oblige the Dorset Constabulary. Sam gave Jarvis a wink, whispered, "We'll try an' get you another day's liberty 'fore you 'as to go back to them priests of yours," and telephoned Father John, who Jarvis could just imagine flexing his caning arm – as if it wasn't always ready.

Sam quite excelled himself, being not only diplomatic and courteous, but efficient and authoritative. He told the attentive and compliant rector that Jarvis had been found and was in protective custody; however, because of his exhausted condition it was deemed advisable that he should have at least a day's rest to recuperate from his ordeal before being returned to their Christian care; yes, Father, he was physically all right, but starving and thoroughly worn out – and this business of the war had rather frightened him. Jarvis could scarcely control his hilarity at such an out and out falsehood – and to a priest!

"Yes, Father Rector, Gawd is indeed a wonderful protector," Sam agreed fulsomely, and went on to urge the holy man to show the same godlike compassion and not be too hard on Jarvis. "It's the opinion of the police that the lad weren't the master of 'is actions bein' in mortal fear of these gypsy blackguards. It was undoubtedly the 'and of Gawd – an' yer own prayers, Father – wot led the police to rescue the boy." Sam mopped his sweating face, gave Jarvis another wink and smothered a rising chuckle before continuing, "He's 'ad a bit of a scare an' that should be punishment enough – especially wiv this terrible war loomin' over us all. Yes, Father Rector, I'm sure Gawd'll protect us." Sam raised his eyes wearily heavenwards. No, he assured the Father Rector, there'd be no more running away; and yes Father, he'd bring the boy himself.

Sam soared to at least ten-feet-tall in Jarvis's estimation; definitely worthy of membership of The Bullets. Forgotten was any fleeting criticism over his not killing any Germans and failing to get himself wounded. They both gave themselves over to boisterous laughter over pulling the wool over the eyes of Father John, but Sam sounded a word of caution. "He agreed wiv me, but 'e didn't exactly say you'd get off scot-free, lad. So you may still be in for a hiding. You'll 'ave to be prepared for that." Jarvis nodded, and shrugged. He didn't see the sense in worrying about something till it happened; and, besides, he hadn't really expected to escape with just a blessing from Father Rector.

It was only then, although it had been deafeningly evident for some while, that Jarvis really took notice of the frightful din of shouting and singing coming from the pub's patrons, and Queenie emerged from the public bar, whose very walls seemed to be bulging, looking hot, breathless and very pleased with things, to replenish fast diminishing stocks from the cellar. "'Ark at 'em – all gettin' up Dutch courage to go an' fight old 'Itler!" she chortled. "At this rate we'll all be filthy rich by Christmas – if the war lasts that long!"

Sam, muttering "an' broke by Easter" under his breath, and Jarvis followed her down into the cellar and helped ferry crates of assorted beers up to the thirsty bars. Even Fred Akers, the potman, seemed to be in a good mood – as far as it was possible to tell, for his teeth were safe in his tobacco tin and it was difficult to be sure if a man who is all gums is happy. At any rate, he was working like a beaver down there, lifting empty barrels down and full ones up, tapping them with practised swings of a mallet and making weird noises which Hannah, who as usual was helping out wherever she was sent, told Jarvis was singing. He took her word for it, although he didn't recognise any tune or make out any words. Perhaps he was drunk! Millie, the barmaid with all the children and no husband, screamed down from the top of cellar steps "More gin ... whisky ... rum ... an' tonics," and rushed back to her bar where, she said, "they're all goin' mad." Sam and Jarvis raced after her with armfuls of bottles. It seemed hours later, although it wasn't, that Jarvis left Sam helping Millie behind the bar, although what help he was Jarvis couldn't be sure for he seemed to drink as much himself as he served to customers, and went off in search of Ruth.

Jarvis found her (and Rosie) in a private snuggery where it seemed they were about to enjoy afternoon tea, but all the little plates and cups and saucers and other necessary paraphernalia were swept aside on his appearance. Ruth announced that she would teach him how to play dominoes, or fives-and-threes, as she called it. Jarvis was never quite certain how, but he was sure she cheated, and he had the impression she made the rules up, changing them to suit her needs, as the games went on; she, in turn, looked exquisitely outraged and hurt by his insinuations, and blunt accusations, after she'd won – skilfully, as she contended with a magnificently wounded air – several games in a row. Even after he'd picked up the rudiments of the game, almost sufficient to cheat himself, he still couldn't win; and then, as tempers threatened to boil over, it was discovered that one of the dominoes was still in the box! Open warfare was only averted by the appearance of Queenie, who scolded them for making more noise than all the customers put together, and carted them off for what she called high tea, which meant, because time was getting on, that it was really their supper.

Later that night, while the customers were still loudly and volubly fighting long-ago battles they plainly knew very little about, and remembered less with every drink, and lustily singing martial songs the words of which they knew very little more about, Jarvis confided to Ruth much of the truth of his adventures on the farm and with the gypsies. He was sat up in bed, enveloped in another of Sam's enormous shirts for he'd already grown out of the blue and white pyjamas Queenie had bought on his last visit, and Ruth was curled up on top in her dressing-gown and nightie, clutching Rosie, her head on Jarvis's pillow and never taking her eyes off him. He mentioned Scruffy and *his* Rose, which brought a mischievous giggle from Ruth, but when he referred to his own temporary sisters among the gypsies, although not mentioning any intimacies, she remained studiously silent, and he was sure she conjured up all manner of romances – and broken hearts.

How long they spent whispering together, they never knew. Queenie apparently found them both fast asleep, and carried Ruth off to her own bed. Returning to tuck Jarvis in, she gave him a featherweight kiss which, nevertheless, seemed to touch some chord in his sub-conscious, for he suddenly smiled and opened eyes. They folded their arms round one another, and it was then that they had their "serious" chat.

She told him she was wondering if he wasn't growing up too fast and missing out on his childhood. She didn't mind that while not yet fourteen, he had the tall, broad frame almost of a young man; no, she was proud of his appearance. Jarvis made to speak, but she silenced his lips with her finger tips, and said he couldn't keep on running away and having the sort of experiences that he was having. She pointed out that he was only a child, and he should be playing games and learning his lessons instead of getting involved in such pursuits: he shouldn't be having to constantly scheme and fight to survive, not at his age. She searched his face with a worried frown, and shook her head slowly. Jarvis told her that his adventures, as he preferred to think of them, just happened, quite by accident, but again she shushed him quiet. He had no business chasing round the countryside with gypsies and other unsavoury characters, she told him seriously.

"You must first learn to overcome the problems of a boy if you're to succeed in tacklin' those of a man," she said, and gently kissed both his eyes as though he were a baby. "Don't be in too much of a 'urry to grow up, Jarvis darling. You'll be a man soon enough. Be a boy while yer can ... the longer you are, the more I feel you belong to me." After she'd gone, he dreamt he was in heaven – and everyone seemed very young, even the grown ups.

Next morning, having temporarily escaped from the possessive Ruth, Jarvis sidled up to Queenie, who was alone in her kitchen, and whispered, urgently, but quietly:

"Mum – have you any spare money?"

Queenie eyed him with a smile of curiosity. "Depends, lovey," she murmured. "'Ow much was yer thinkin' of?"

"Oooh – lots," Jarvis admitted, uncertainly. "A shilling – or, perhaps ... even more."

"Wot's it for, lovey – or shouldn't I arsk?" Queenie said gently, resisting the temptation to hug him as her hands were covered in flour.

"It's to buy Ruth a birthday present," Jarvis confessed. "I forgot it again even after promising her I wouldn't ever again. She never does mine, and I've got a whole pile of hankies she's give me. She hasn't said anything ... but I'm sure *she* hasn't forgot. Perhaps she won't be too cross if it's a bit late – what do you think?"

"I'm sure she won't, lovey," Queenie assured him, looking quite serious as she blinked away the moisture that gathered in her eyes, and which she blamed on the steam from a pot on the Aga. "It's a lovely idea, Jarvis. Very thoughtful." Queenie consulted her purse, and then shoved it back in her apron pocket. "P'raps we could put the bite on Sam, too. Men always 'ave more money than they know. Trouble is gettin' 'em to part wiv it!"

"I was going to ask him, only I thought he might give me some of Mr Maggs's money. You know, his dud coins!"

Queenie positively guffawed. "Oh, you're a caution, lovey! You really are," she said, and, when she had done alternately blowing her nose and dabbing at her glistening eyes, blaming both on the simmering pot, asked: "Wot did yer 'ave in mind for Ruth's present?"

"Oh, I don't know," said Jarvis, confusedly. "I've never bought a present before – not for anyone, and certainly not for no girl – and I expect they're the hardest to please." He'd no idea why he said that, but he was sure he was right. He hoped this present wasn't going to cost too much. "I never seem to have any money, anyway."

"It's a problem we all 'ave," Queenie allowed with a smile.

"Per–haps a ... necklace?" Jarvis ventured, catching his breath at the very notion.

"For a bob, yer say!" exclaimed Queenie, arching a brow, and then busying herself chasing several strands of tawny hair back into place in the knot behind her head, and from where they immediately escaped again. It was all a ruse to stop herself laughing.

"It might cost a bit more," Jarvis conceded. He hadn't the foggiest idea how much even the cheapest necklace might cost, but judging from Queenie's reaction it now seemed probable that it might cost more than a shilling: perhaps two. All of a sudden a necklace didn't seem such a good idea after all; or rather, it was just an impossible idea. Perhaps she'd have to settle for some hankies herself. "I might have some money – a little bit ... 'bout tuppence, if it ain't been nicked – back at the Home."

Queenie nodded, not trusting herself to speak.

Jarvis beamed. "And would you get it for me, Mum?" he begged her. "And ask the shop people to wrap it up nice, in a box – and tied up with a ribbon. Ruth'd like that."

Queenie stepped forward and gave him a gentle squeeze; more a touch, really. "I'll see what I can do," she promised, throatily, stroking his cheek with the back of her hand as softly as though she were touching fur, before he ran off to hide his confusion. Buying a present was a terrible ordeal, even when someone bought it for you, he decided.

Ruth and Jarvis dashed around outside searching for signs of the war, but for all they saw it might well have been over already. Everything seemed very much the same as always, apart from a sudden preponderance of uniforms; wide strips of brown paper across windows, which Ruth knowledgeably said was in case of bomb blast; and gangs of men feverishly filling sacks from mountains of sand dumped in the road. It was all very disappointing. Jarvis had expected to see positive signs of the war, with lots of explosions and shooting and screaming – but no one getting really hurt, of course.

The highlight of their tour of the "battlefront" was the brief glimpse of a huge gun being trundled behind an equally huge Army vehicle. "Anti-aircraft gun," proclaimed one bystander. "That'll teach them Huns!" cackled another, who looked about a thousand-years-old. This was more like it! Jarvis was very impressed by the gun – and a bit disheartened, too; perhaps it *would* be over by Christmas, after all. The only cheering sight after that was Mrs Molly, Ruth's flower-seller friend, whose customary black hat had been replaced by a helmet adorned with flowers. Behind her, concealing her brolly, was an unfurled Union Jack. She was doing a roaring business, but she beckoned them both over to give them a gob-stopper each, and a red rose for Ruth. "You can pretend it were given yer by yer sweet'art, Ruthie!" she said, with a wink at Jarvis. Once again they fled from her with flaming faces, though Ruth at least knew they were sweethearts, and remembered Jarvis admitting to it.

In the afternoon, they all went to the cinema – as Queenie put it, to get away from all the boring talk of war and have a good laugh. They saw King Kong, which had them far more frightened than any war, and set Ruth off shrieking so much Queenie had to take her to the Ladies. Later, back at The Dials, there was a double birthday tea party: one marked Ruth's eleventh of some months ago, the other was a premature celebration for Jarvis's fourteenth. Jarvis shot a questioning glance at Queenie, who nodded; and he wondered what he'd bought for Ruth! But first his own presents. There were the usual two handkerchiefs from Ruth, beautifully parcelled in tissue paper and fastened with one of her hair ribbons; a simply wizard telescope from Sam; then the most wonderful present he could ever have dreamed of from Queenie – his first pair of *long* trousers!

Jarvis dropped his short trousers there and then in front of them all, and lovingly pulled on the new ones, holding them up while Queenie

fussed around adjusting the braces. The new trousers were grey, too –
but what a difference. They were spotless and with razor-sharp creases
that seemed to go on down for ever. He felt ten-feet-tall – and almost
afraid to move. The material felt rough on those parts of his legs that had
always been bare, but it was such a manly roughness. He preened before
a long mirror Queenie wheeled in front of him, and was quite sure he'd
never seen anything quite so gorgeous. He moved first one leg a few
inches forward, and then the other; he tried a few tentative strides,
hearing the swish of the serge and feeling its luxuriance (forgotten was
its sandpaper touch against his skin!) against his limbs, and sighed
blissfully.

He gave Queenie a ferocious hug and a warm kiss, Sam shook
his hand in a very proper manner and called him "young sir," and Ruth,
clapping her hands with delighted approval, skipped round and round
him eyeing him with admiring eyes and finally stretched up and planted
a kiss on his lips. He didn't mind that, but when she wanted to stroke his
lovely trousers, he shrank back – fearing the damage she might inflict.
He knew he'd never be able to sit down in them for fear they may get
creased, and he was quite resolved to remain standing for ever – but that
was before the tea party. He had to sit down to that, didn't he?

But before that came the moment when Queenie announced that
Ruth, too, had a birthday present – from Jarvis, and that he hoped she'd
overlook the fact that it was rather a late one. She handed Jarvis what he
thought was a quite pathetically tiny package, but neatly wrapped with
crimson paper and a ribbon fashioned in the shape of a heart. It looked
gorgeous on the outside, at any rate. He ceremoniously proffered it to
Ruth, who snatched it with a squeal and excitedly tore off the ribbon and
ripped off the paper as though they didn't exist, to reveal the tiniest of
boxes; a box with a green velvet covering, but so very, very small. He
felt ashamed by its very littleness, certain that nothing so small could
contain anything worthwhile. Ruth lifted the lid with agonizing slowness
(or so it seemed, though he supposed she was even more eager than
himself to discover the contents); she dropped the lid to the floor, and
lifted a puff of cotton wool, which she also dropped; and then she was
staring into the box with a growing wonder and even greater pleasure.
Jarvis was still stretching his neck to try and see what he was supposed
to have given her, when Ruth launched herself at him – playing havoc
with his creases! For once she didn't drown him in kisses, but simply
hugged him. "Thank you, Jarvis," she whispered, loud enough for all to
hear. "It's lovely. I'll treasure it for ever."

It turned out to be a red coral necklace, and when Jarvis finally
saw it, he, too, thought it looked rather nice. He looked across at
Queenie and was pretty sure, from the way she laughingly raised her
eyebrows to the ceiling, that it had cost considerably more than his
suggested shilling. He'd probably spend the rest of his life paying for it!

But first, he was called upon to fasten the necklace round Ruth's neck, which was never still for an instant; it proved a feat so intricate, he had to call on the expertise of Queenie to help him.

It was a birthday party neither Ruth nor he would ever forget. Ruth, feeling so much older than her eleven years, wore her necklace until the moment she fell asleep and her mother gently removed it and placed it carefully in its box beside her bed. Jarvis, likewise feeling so very more mature than his almost-fourteen years, wore his beautiful trousers until the last moment before he climbed into bed, removing them only for fear of crumpling them – and with their removal, he felt he'd lost six feet in height; but in his dreams that followed he was restored to ten-feet-tall and wore a crown of red coral.

But then Jarvis came down to earth with the realisation that it was all over. Tuesday rushed up all too quickly. Goodbyes were brief and subdued, and then Sam led Jarvis back to St Boniface, and Queenie accompanied Ruth to St Clare's. Ruth had wanted to wear her necklace to school – indeed, she didn't ever want to take it off, but her mother demurred, saying teachers didn't allow such things, and so she consoled herself by keep looking over her shoulder until Jarvis turned a corner, and was gone from sight.

Carefully carrying his precious new trousers, and many other little gifts, including a shiny new shilling from Queenie, and eatables, Jarvis waved back as long as he could ... and then turned to face the front, and his uncertain future.

□ *"Oh, that was a lovely day, Jarvis. The best birthday ever. And you in yer very first pair of long trousers. It were the funniest sight ever, you dropping your old short ones and tugging yer new long ones up fast as yer could, and in front of us all. Oh, how we laughed."* Queenie fairly drooled over the memory. *"It made us forget, almost, that you had been recovered from the gypsies, and that we were at war once again."*

"I'm sure I wouldn't have behaved so shamefully," laughed Beard from his bed. *"It doesn't sound a bit like me. Sorry."*

Queenie gave him a fond smile, and carried on with the history of his life, whether he recognised it or not. She knew he would in the end, once he and Ruth were together. Ruth should be here ; she must set John to work finding her.

Chapter Fourteen

St Boniface, September, 1940

Almost at once he ran into Scruffy; or rather, Scruffy pounced on him the moment he stepped into the quadrangle, thwacking him across the shoulders enthusiastically, and demanding amiably, "Next time you decide to do a bunk ... take me with you!"

Jarvis grinned back, then briefly recounted his adventures, insisting that his runaway had been entirely unpremeditated. Then, although he had for some while doubted her existence, he enquired after Scruffy's Aunt Dolly, but his friend only shrugged and growled, "Not a bleedin' sausage!" After a moment or two, Scruffy added "If she don't find me soon, I don't know how we'll ever meet. It'll have to be soon, 'cos my time here is running out."

Jarvis, still regarding Aunt Dolly as being a bit of a cock-and-bull story, a wistful dream perhaps, stared at Scruffy in surprise. Of course, they'd all leave in time, but it had always seemed so far off – well, it still was for him. He'd been agreeably surprised when he'd reported to Father John and only been given a stern warning about the dangers of running away, especially now there was a war on. "I am advised by your Mr Constable that you have suffered severely as a result of your reckless behaviour, Brook, and I am moved to accept the probability he is right, so we'll say no more on the matter. Thank God for your deliverance, and make sure nothing like it ever happens again, Brook. Now, get back to your lessons at which at least you excel."

Meanwhile, the war continued to be a great disappointment to Jarvis: nothing happened. Once Poland, the reason for the war, had been overrun in a matter of three weeks, it seemed to be over so far as any fighting was concerned. In the spring of 1940, Cambridge won the Boat Race and life went on much as normal – and most of the evacuees found their way back home. But just as the boys at St Boniface had decided the war was probably over, the Germans suddenly moved in the West, overrunning first Norway and Denmark, then the Low Countries and finally gobbling up France – all of which made the English Channel the new front line, and Britain herself the battlefield.

The first real impact of the war on St Boniface (apart from the shrinking meals, and who'd have thought they could get smaller) was the extraordinary business concerning Brother Karl, Jarvis's German tutor. One lovely May afternoon, he was called from his library by Father John and told that a tribunal had declared him an undesirable enemy alien. Two days later, a Special Constable, complete with shiny blue tin hat, arrived to escort him to an internment camp. The boys sent him on his way with much jeering and whistling until silenced by menacing gesticulations from Father John and other priests. Jarvis was possibly the only boy sorry to see the forlorn figure being led away, although his feelings were largely selfish for his only concern was the loss of a German-speaking conversationalist. Nothing was ever heard of Brother Karl again, although it was rumoured that he was in a camp somewhere in Westmorland. If this was indeed so, he fared better than Father Toni; he, too, was detained some months later, and subsequently was drowned when the ship transporting him to Canada was torpedoed – rumour had it by an Italian submarine, but it was only a rumour. The boys were all very sad at his departure for his successor as confessor handed out far harsher penances.

Apart from these relatively minor incidents, life was little disturbed at St Boniface, apart from an increase in prayers, but a contribution to the war effort was made by reducing the fortnightly baths to once monthly (a sacrifice the boys bore with patriotic fortitude), and lessons continued with remarkably little disruption. Jarvis maintained his advancement both as a scholar and an athlete. He was now studying for his Higher School Leaving Certificate two years ahead of the normal age and, in Father John's prideful opinion, destined for high university honours, providing he won a free scholarship – and wasn't hanged first. Jarvis liked to think the Rector was joking when he said this. In sporting activities, Jarvis continued to excel to such a degree that Father Michael restored him to the rugby team. And he still worked out every day at his punch-bag and sparred with Brother Andrew, until the latter decided he'd taught his pupil enough – the truth being that *he* was getting hit too often and too hard now that Jarvis had grown to a height barely two inches below six feet and had shoulders and muscles like a professional boxer – and was still barely 15 years old.

And then it all changed. The Luftwaffe had been pounding London virtually non-stop since launching the Blitz on September 7, and on October 15, a Dornier 17, silhouetted in the moonlight and blinded by several searchlights, developed engine trouble and jettisoned its cargo as it tried to zigzag out of danger – only to crash on Hackney Marshes. Its shrieking bombs could have landed almost anywhere; they did so in Battersea.

As luck would have it the majority landed relatively harmlessly in the Thames. Two of the bombs, however, missed the river. One landed with a deafening roar on St Boniface's quadrangle making a huge crater and blowing in every window that side of the Home. The second bomb bounced on the irregular surface and collided with the building itself before exploding. The shattering blast appeared to pick up the building, already severely damaged by the first bomb, and give it a good shaking, before the entire wall facing the river gave a final shudder and collapsed with a roar in a cloud of acrid, choking dust that obliterated the sky. The roof closely followed suit, except that it slithered slowly, almost gracefully and with the minimum of fuss and noise – just a long, agonized, dying sigh, before crashing to the ground in a sudden rush that sent up another dense cloud of suffocating dust.

After the roar of the explosions and the crashing of debris, there were several moments of comparative quiet that seemed a lot more terrifying. Then faint sounds could be heard from beneath the rubble, moans and cries of pain, and frightened shouting among the boys, and then, ominously, a loud murmur as a boiler struggled for survival, before blowing up; yet more masonry and timbers crashed down, and yet more clouds polluted the atmosphere. Simultaneously, the first puffs of pungent smoke wafted up from the heart of the rubble, and almost directly flames were leaping everywhere. In the same terrible moment, the hideous screams from far below reached a heart-stilling pitch, louder, sharper and desperate in their agony, but only briefly; they quickly fell to whimpering sighs of intolerable pain, and then these, too, faded, and all was silent again.

Silent, save for the crackling of what was now becoming a pyre. There was a strong smell of gas everywhere ... and then came a final eruption.

Where they came from nobody knew, but as if by magic an army of rescuers materialized on the scene, and within minutes hoses were fighting the flames and bare hands were clawing at the rubble, lifting beams with infinite care and, every so often, pausing to listen for sounds of life beneath them, oblivious to the raging air-raid that continued all around. They were deaf to all sounds other than those below them.

By late afternoon only four boys were still unaccounted for; perhaps they had simply been blown into unrecognizable pieces; they were listed missing, presumed killed. For the moment, the bodies of the recovered dead lay in two long rows where the ambulatory had once stood; among them were Father John, and Brothers Andrew and Philip; twenty-seven boys lay beside them, covered with whatever came to hand. Another forty-nine religious and boys were injured, eleven so badly they were added later to the death toll. The 81 survivors, who included Jarvis and Scruffy, both unscathed, were swiftly shepherded away to an assortment of local shelters, the nearby convent, and other school or church halls. A Salvation Army lady appeared and provided them with mugs of hot sweet tea, but mostly the boys continued their disturbed sleeping, waking long after midday – when their first concern was that they'd missed breakfast, and possibly dinner, too.

The WVS, who appeared to have taken charge, quickly restored their spirits by providing bowls of steaming stew, with chunks of real meat in it, and a huge suet pudding with lashings of golden syrup and custard, and pitchers of fresh creamy milk – a nearby dairy had also been hit during the night and there was milk going begging there by the gallon. It was a feast the like of which they had never known at the Home, and for a while it took their minds off the grievous events of the night. But, as the hours passed, the shock and realisation of what had occurred took its hold, especially among the younger ones, and shrill voices became subdued whispers and small bodies trembled uncontrollably..

Still more ladies, some in real nurses' uniforms with big red crosses on their breasts and others in the less familiar black-and-white colours of the St John Ambulance Brigade, appeared; there was not much they could do to ease the psychological agonies that were now surfacing, but they comforted the distressed children as naturally as if they'd been their own: with the tenderest of embraces, the gentlest of whispered love, the very softest of kisses, and, when all else failed, the hushed crooning of a lullaby – few had heard the words before, but they helped to lull them back to merciful sleep. For most it was the first real evidence of affection they could remember, and some simply couldn't stop weeping over the sheer wonder of it; their tiny arms clung to their comforters as though to life itself – nor were the ladies less loath to relinquish their own hold.

Jarvis was horrified at the brutal way his friends' lives had been extinguished, but he wouldn't give himself over to any show of grief. Not so much as a solitary tear did he shed for his dead brothers; he dared not; a single tear would have let loose an uncontrollable flood, and he'd pledged himself that agonizing day he'd sobbed his heart out in the arms of Policewoman Bold, that never again would he allow myself to cry. He'd hide his feelings and mourn inside, alone.

It turned out that his group was accommodated in a furniture warehouse, Monty & Levy on Hangman's Wharf – within sight of the shattered St Boniface although a wide dock separated them; and there they stayed for three days before being broken up into small units, and billeted on local householders. Sister Penance – Jarvis was sure that wasn't her real name, and anyway, they nicknamed her Sister Penguin, to her evident delight – from the convent by the bomb site, which already had its share of the bombed-out boys, arrived on the scene with a retinue of nuns to organize things, and in particular to ensure they didn't wander too far from the narrow path of their Catholic upbringing; to this end, she at once shooed off all the Protestant women who had been feeding and looking after them so devotedly. She distributed rosaries, medallions and holy pictures from a capacious reticule as if she were some sort of Father Christmas. There seemed to be endless Requiem Masses as the toll mounted.

Sister Penguin came armed with a list of all the suitable families (they had to be Catholic to be suitable, of course, but others crept in on recommendation) in the district and very rapidly the boys found themselves being escorted to homes all over the neighbourhood. In twos, three and even fours they were absorbed into households, great pains being taken to keep special friends together. Jarvis and Scruffy (they insisted they were closer than brothers and couldn't be parted) were allocated to a Mrs Edna Bromley at 36 Grafton Street, in the shade of a gasometer – which didn't seem a very safe location, particularly as it was also uncomfortably close to what was left of St Boniface.

Mrs Bromley was smallish, squarish, plainish and middle-ageish; she also had a heart of the purest gold, and became as much a mother to the two orphans as she'd been to her own two sons who were now gone off to war. Nothing was ever said of any Mr Bromley, and it was assumed that, always assuming that he had ever existed, he was dead, serving a life sentence in prison or, simply, that he'd deserted her – which was the norm in those days. However, in a tortoiseshell locket that hung permanently at her throat was the faded print of a bushy-bearded man with large, dark eyes, who she admitted in a rare moment of nostalgic confidence, was called Norman; she would only ever describe him as "an ol' friend," but with such a lilt in her voice it was plain he was someone very much closer. As to religion, Mrs Bromley wasn't sure she had one, not one that was recognised. She believed in God, but not necessarily in one; she seldom visited any church and she didn't pray a lot – making do with little chats with whatever god came to mind when the mood was on her, as likely as not as she waited for the potatoes to boil, and definitely never on her knees. But she made sure Jarvis and Scruffy went regularly to their Masses and said their prayers at night because she was aware that this was what was expected of them – by those with the blessing of *real* faith.

Hers was a two-up two-down house and except when they were sleeping, they lived primarily in the kitchen, where sticky fly-papers hung from the ceiling and pots and pans dangled from nails, as did a print of Queen Victoria ; pride of place on a shelf above a small dresser were photos of her two soldier sons, Eric and Edgar. Apart from these photos, the most important thing in the kitchen was the range, on which a time-blackened kettle was always on the boil for Mrs Bromley was a tea-addict; she happily drank tea all day long.

Beard and Scruffy considered they'd definitely landed on their feet with Mrs Bromley – Mrs B., as they called her affectionately – and soon came to regard their new home as a little corner of heaven, and her cooking (rationing, or not) as simply out of this world. Both boys adored her and life was really grand in those weeks leading up to Christmas. The only fly in the ointment was that St Boniface was not the corpse everyone had assumed. Building experts declared that parts of the ground floor and the cellars were capable of being restored as a temporary expedient; and, indeed, work to this end was already in progress. The plan was to restore some of the classrooms and convert the cellars into sleeping quarters for the surviving priests and brothers. It was expected that the temporary accommodation would be completed in time for the start of the Easter term.

And, suddenly, Christmas arrived, and for all that Jarvis had been creeping there for years, he succeeded in soaring through the six-foot barrier. This was confirmed when he and Scruffy went to The Dials for Christmas, and Sam measured both of them and found little more than an inch difference, and that in Jarvis's favour. It was hard to believe there was a war on to judge by the feast that Queenie provided; no shortages there, of anything. She made Scruffy especially welcome simply because he was Jarvis's friend. Money was very short that year – except, it seemed, for the soldiers on leave who were buying drinks in the bars downstairs like there was no tomorrow – but while the presents were few, and very much of a practical nature, everyone got something, and some quite a lot.

Jarvis and Scruffy, who had 1s 4½d between them and no wish to use any of it, did all their shopping as they made their way to The Dials; they snatched an armful of flowers off a coffin (Jarvis knew Mr Maggs would have approved) standing momentarily unattended outside an undertaker's in Chandos Place to give to Queenie; Ruth got a quite handsome silver-backed comb (with a tooth missing) which Jarvis found during a brief exploration of a bombed building – it needed some scrubbing but came up looking shiny new, except for the gap left by the missing tooth which he explained had broken off when he tripped over and fell on it; Scruffy proudly presented her with an ostrich feather he'd rescued from a dustbin on the same site and which he'd wrapped up in a piece of tissue paper borrowed from Queenie; and Sam was honoured with a hardly-used tin of black shoe polish, which was also borrowed from Queenie and, therefore, already his own.

Ruth, flaunting, rather charmingly, her red coral necklace, received her gifts with the same childish wonder had they been gold, frankincense and myrrh. She, of course, gave Jarvis two more handkerchiefs, but she whispered that he'd have to give one of them to Scruffy because she didn't have anything else to give. Scruffy was most gratified with his share of Jarvis's present, and seemed to spend the rest of Christmas Day blowing his nose, till it looked quite red. In between putting his handkerchief to continuous, if needless, use, Scruffy and Sam talked together, while Ruth and Jarvis, with much shouting and shrieking, waltzed round and round the room making far more noise than the gramophone. Queenie sat back watching them with fond eyes as she beat time with one great hand and sipped mulled port from a silver tankard held in the other. Every few minutes she had to get up and wind up the machine and put on a fresh record : there was a choice of seven.

Sam, who had known all about the bombing of St Boniface but had learned straight away that Jarvis was safe and unhurt – in fact, he was even acquainted with Mrs Bromley through her sons, Eric and Edgar, who had both been Special Constables before joining up, nevertheless listened to Scruffy's version with some slight interest; it was clear, however, that he was far more concerned in topping up his pewter mug with frothy black porter from a jug held fast between his feet. However, when Scruffy inevitably mentioned his Aunt Dolly, Sam suddenly became all ears and voiced genuine interest, the more so since he vaguely recalled the sinking of the ferry in which the boy's parents were drowned. He was sure there'd still be a report on the incident down at the police station, and he made a mental note to look it up. He couldn't understand why it should be so difficult to trace the aunt.

"She 'ad to 'ave a name, didn't she? An' nobody can 'ide themselves now we got this 'ere National Register thing," he declared emphatically, though speaking as much to himself as to Scruffy. "It's got ev'ry livin' creature in the land in it – you can't escape it, no matter what side of the blanket you was born. It's like that Domesday Book thing, or even the Bible itself. It don't miss nuffink, an' it can't tell no lies, neither. So if you've got a name it's in the Register, an' if it's in there ... they've gotcher. There ain't anywhere you can 'ide. 'Course, there'll be some that escapes the net, always is, but not people like yer Dolly."

Scruffy didn't look too impressed, and probably wished he hadn't mentioned his aunt. He patiently explained to Sam that nobody knew her name, nor where she lived; that the Church had been searching for her all of his life, without getting a whiff of her. He suggested that Aunt Dolly could have emigrated to goodness knows where; that, anyway, she might not want to be bothered with him; and, besides, might be long dead – and laughing at the confusion she'd left behind.

Sam thought all this over very carefully, scratched his chins and finally emptied his jug. "Nobody can't just disappear – even if they is dead," he decided at length. "Not legally, leastways," he added after a further moment's reflection. "It's really simply a question of puttin' a name to a body; the rest's a piece of cake, as they says – just takes time, is all. Don't expect the Church put a great deal of effort into the 'unt, not really in its interest, y'see. But then, they ain't got the resources wot the police 'as. They ain't got our know-how. I'll see wot I can turn up. I ain't promisin' nothin', mind."

Jarvis and Scruffy were supposed to return almost immediately to Mrs B's, but there was a very heavy air-raid that night and Queenie wouldn't allow either of them to step a foot outside, and on the Sunday occurred what was called the Second Great Fire of London, caused by more than 30,000 incendiaries. Army engineers spent most of the following day dynamiting fire-gutted buildings, and still the raids went on. It wasn't until New Year's Eve that it was felt safe to venture outside, which after four days of sheltering in the beer cellars came as a blessed relief.

The streets were still in such a chaotic state that there was no hope of any transport, public or private, and they all set out to walk to Battersea singing songs that were loud in defiance, but which became considerably muted with the crump of each stick of bombs, both far and near, and each time the guns barked back at the invisible planes. They eventually arrived hoarse and jubilant at Mrs B's, where Sam promptly dropped off into a noisy sleep to everyone's equally loud amusement, and she entertained them with endless cups of tea. However, as midnight approached, she produced a bottle of port, at which moment Sam woke with a start, and smacked his lips; they all toasted in the New Year (the children's drinks being suitably watered despite their protests) and assured each other that this year must see the end of the war – but without being overly convinced or, indeed, being absolutely certain as to who the victors might be, but keeping such treasonous thoughts to themselves.

Finally, at one o'clock, or thereabouts, Queenie decided the time for departure had arrived; it came and went several times before being put into effect, and even then became an exceedingly protracted business. As usual, the farewells were brief and awkward, with no one wanting to say anything, but feeling they should and so ending up talking too long, and still saying nothing. Mrs B. and Queenie embraced like sisters, Sam all but toppled over as he slapped Jarvis and Scruffy on their backs, and Ruth cried as she kissed everyone goodbye; and then they were gone ... at the end of the street they heard Queenie bawl at an approaching lorry which screeched to a halt, and the driver helped haul Sam aboard and they all drove off together still singing lustily – at least Queenie was.

It wasn't till the following night, when they were both sitting up in their beds, that Scruffy remarked, almost meditatively, "I liked your girlfriend."

"Who'd'you mean – Queenie? She's my Mum – sort of," Jarvis replied, hardly giving the question any consideration; his thoughts, in fact, were focussed on Sam and he was wondering how many times he'd fallen down going to work that morning.

"Idiot!" snorted Scruffy. "I meant the girl. Ruth!"

"Idiot yourself! She's my sister – sort of," Jarvis retorted, frowning. The frown was because he was not too sure how to classify her; a friend, of course, a very special one, but certainly not a girlfriend, not in the sense that Scruffy meant. Was she? How could she be?

"Are you sure?" pressed Scruffy, in a disbelieving tone.

Jarvis stared at him, growing irritated. "'Course," he snapped back.

"I don't think she regards you as a brother, not the way she looks at you!" Scruffy said with a sarcastic grin. "More as a sweetheart, I'd've thought!"

"Rubbish!" Jarvis said heatedly. His cheeks felt like they were on fire, and he couldn't understand why he was so flustered. Mrs Molly had called them sweethearts, but then she was a bit crackers. Even so, Ruth had said they were sweethearts, but then she would. But, hadn't he agreed with her, sort of? "We're – she's just a very special friend. And, since she's my godparents' daughter, she is a sort of sister, too."

"I see," said Scruffy, unconvincingly. "Well, I still like her," he declared, grinning.

"You just keep your mitts off her, mate; she's *my* sister!" Jarvis laughed.

Scruffy didn't reply, not audibly, but Jarvis thought he distinguished the word "Balls!" He grinned, felt safe, and in the ensuing silence pushed all thoughts of sisters and girlfriends from his mind and dropped easily off into a sleep that was undisturbed by dreams of them.

The classrooms of St Boniface were restored in double-quick time. The rest of the Home was still missing, apart from the warren of cellars below the patched-up classrooms. It was a wreck, but it was functional, and it was there amid the ruins that lessons resumed that Easter term with a new Rector, Father Paul Neame, to breathe life into the carcass. There was so little of Father Paul, he might have been one of the boys himself; but, though he stood barely five feet tall, he had the heart of a giant. He had a thin patch of grey hair, bright greeny eyes that winked through thick lenses and a round face that was always kindly, understanding and forgiving. He was an historian of some repute and instructed each class in the subject.

It was a very smooth and gentle introduction to the new way of things, the only interruption to the routine coming shortly before Easter with the visit of Captain Harvey Peregrine Rawley-Smith, of the 21st Bengal Lancers in the Indian Army, to address the older boys. Resplendent in immaculate uniform complete with the most polished of Sam Browne belts, dazzlingly colourful shoulder-knot and patches, and a row of campaign ribbons, he saluted his young audience as smartly as if he were on parade.

He then sat informally on a desk, and, tapping the ribbons on his chest with his swagger stick, proceeded to tell the boys exciting stories – with the emphasis on duty and courage – of how they had been won serving all over the sub-continent, and beyond; he took them through cavalry charges, desperate marches to relieve beleaguered colleagues, night journeys through jungles at the head of a column of elephants, ambushes and treachery in the mountain passes, and not forgetting the colourful life of India itself.

It was well done and the boys were enthralled, nor did their interest wane when the heroic captain dived briefly into a history of the British raj's glorious, and gory, achievements in India, beginning with Clive's victory at Plassey, continuing through the subtle wisdom of the East India Company, surviving the infamous mutiny of 1858, and reaching the zenith of its greatness today – all without ever mentioning the fact that the entire sub-continent dreamed, prayed and plotted the withdrawal of their infidel masters.

The boys had sat in rapt silence throughout; now, they took their cue, and, rising to their feet, cheered and cheered; and when they were too hoarse to shout any more, they thumped their desks and stamped their feet to continue their deafening display of patriotic fervour. This was the moment for Captain Rawley-Smith to reveal the purpose of his mission. It was evidently an oft-repeated address and he knew his lines by heart. He, too, rose to his feet, and silenced them with a single gesture of his hand.

"Lads," he shouted at forty excited faces, just in case they should have been deafened by their own applause "Lads," he roared again, "the British Empire needs you! India needs you! I need you!"

Thunderous cheers broke out again; and were silenced again. They sat there agog, with open mouths and thumping hearts, impatient for more of the same.

"I want to take some of you back to India with me," continued the captain, adopting his well-rehearsed warlike stance. "I have with me application forms for emergency commissions in the Indian Army. You, too, can serve your King in the richest jewel in his empire ... and live like kings yourselves!"

More cheers, but at a lower pitch as the boys' cunning minds began searching for the inevitable snags; they didn't seem immediately recognisable, apart from India itself, even so the signal for silence was almost unnecessary.

"Of course, only the very best of you will go," went on the captain, noting the diminishing enthusiasm; he was evidently used to that, as well. "There will be selection boards, and only the most promising, physically and scholastically, will be chosen. But, for those of you selected, the future will be golden indeed."

More cheers, but subdued: more polite than enthusiastic; they stopped of their own accord.

"Those of you selected will do your initial training over here, attached to an English line regiment – the Queen's Royal Regiment. On completion of battalion training, you will embark – at which moment you commence drawing pay equivalent to that of a sergeant – for India to complete your training and be commissioned as second lieutenants in one of the crack Indian Army regiments, ready to serve wherever you're sent."

Captain Rawley-Smith paused to test the water, so to speak, and found his audience had grown decidedly chilly; their temperatures were not those of potential heroes – not any more; their applause was scarcely enough to call polite. But in a final fling, probably knowing that he was wasting his time, he told them: "It really is the grandest opportunity ever offered a boy. A very, very rare privilege. A commission in the Indian Army. An opportunity to be officers and gentlemen."

Possibly because it was clearly the end of his talk, something of the initial enthusiasm returned to the cheering, even so it was patchy. It seemed the majority of the boys had given this rare opportunity their instantaneous consideration, and decided against it; and Jarvis was quite definitely of this view. India, after all, was a very long way away; too damned far to go and get yourself killed; they could do that more comfortably at home! He had a little smile at that. He didn't want to die here, either! The captain didn't linger long; he chatted briefly with a small knot of boys, whose interest appeared to revolve solely around elephants and tigers, distributed some literature, left the application forms, and was gone.

A couple of days later, as they were seated at Mrs B.'s kitchen table finishing dinner, Scruffy pushed his well-scraped plate away, glanced about him, almost furtively, and blurted out: "I'm jolly well going to have a crack at this Indian Army thing!"

Jarvis was flabbergasted. He'd been aware of Scruffy's preoccupation since the lecture, but hadn't associated it with anything of consequence; least of all volunteering to join up – in either the British or Indian Army. "You must be mad!" Jarvis declared, leaning back from the table so that his chair tilted on two legs, until a sharp admonition from Mrs B. brought him down square again with a clatter. "What on earth for?" he demanded.

"Yes, why?" echoed Mrs B., turning from the range where she was making tea (she was always making tea) to scrutinize Scruffy, who squirmed under their combined gazes.

"Well," he said, with a helpless sigh after frantically searching their two faces for some sign of encouragement, and finding none, "I'll be eighteen soon, and I'll be called up, anyway. I don't particularly want to be a soldier, of any sort, but if I must, I might just as well make the best of a bad job – and go for an officer. And how else could I be one, an' right from the start, heh?"

Mrs B. pulled a wry face and nodded, but didn't say anything.

Jarvis had to admit it, not that he did, not out loud, but Scruffy did have a point: a very sound one. What other way could he ever hope to become an officer? "I wouldn't believe everything that captain chappie told us," he said circumspectly; "probably got all his medals playing polo – that's their game out in India."

Scruffy ignored the gibe. "I've been reading up all that bumph he give us," he went on, with a rare determination, "and it all seems to make a lot of sense to me."

"'Course it will, you dope," Jarvis cried sarcastically, "that's what it's suppose to do, it's like adverts on hoardings, isn't it? Doesn't mean any of it's true though, does it?"

"Well, it offers me a responsible job," argued Scruffy defensively, "and one with a future ... "

"But it doesn't," Jarvis interrupted. "Read it again. It's only an *emergency* commission. What happens when the emergency is over? And you stuck out there in heathenish India with no money – and, knowing you, with six wives to boot."

Mrs B. threw up her apron and covered her face as she laughed herself into such a fit of physical jerks that she sent the tea pot flying, whereupon she started to cry as well. Jarvis leapt down to pick up the shattered pieces and mop up the tea, and comforted Mrs B. by kissing her through her apron, and whispering in her ear, "If we can get rid of him, let's make sure we keep his ration book!" This brought on another bout of convulsive laughter, which he treated by rubbing her back rather vigorously. After she'd recovered somewhat, Mrs B. produced another teapot and busied herself making a fresh brew.

"Well," insisted Scruffy, when he saw that he had their attention again, "who's to say how long the emergency will last? It may go on for years and years. And by that time, I'll be a general – and filthy rich!" He paused as Mrs B. started shaking again, but this time her mirth was more under control, and short-lived, and he added: "And if I'm none of these things, well, at least I'll have seen India which is more than I'd ever be likely to do under my own steam, would I? I'll learn to play this polo game of theirs, go pig-sticking ... and then, when I've had enough of that, I'll write books about the place like that Rider Haggard fellow."

"He wrote mostly about Africa," Jarvis observed dryly. "Perhaps you mean Kipling – he was the bloke who wrote about India. *Kim* an' that stuff."

Scruffy, who plainly hadn't the slightest intention of writing a book about anywhere, and most likely was unfamiliar with Kipling too, shrugged disinterestedly. "Whoever," he muttered.

Jarvis was silent for a moment or two as he considered Scruffy's plans for a military career, however brief. The more he thought about it, the more he thought it might not be such a stupid idea after all – for *him*. "Perhaps you're right," he said, carefully. "It could even be a heaven-sent opportunity. I don't suppose there's any harm in applying, anyway." He paused, and added with a broad grin: "Wouldn't mind having a bash myself!"

"Hush up, Jarvis," cried Mrs B., almost crossly. "You might be a big boy for yer age, but you're still a boy – an' yer shouldn't even fink of such foolishness. The very idea! Heavens, lad, you're barely old enough to be a Boy Scout let alone a soldier!"

Mrs B. bent forward to fill the second pot of tea and, placing it on the hob to draw, turned her attention back to Scruffy. "Jarvis is obviously too young to be thinking about anything but 'is lessons – even if 'e is bigger'n you, an' you, Master Scruffy, aren't a whole lot older," she said. Jarvis could tell, the way she looked from one to the other of them, that in many ways she thought he was really the older; he'd always been the leader, making decisions for the pair of them. "But, as you say, you'll soon be eighteen, an' I suppose that makes you almost a man, as far's the Army's concerned – which goes to show what a foolish lot they really are! Still, I suppose there's some sense in what you say."

"Of course there is!" agreed Scruffy excitedly. "It's only a matter of filling in a form for the present – an' then we just see what happens. By the way," he turned abruptly to face Mrs B., "Father Paul said you had our birth certificates and other things. I have to send mine with my application form. You haven't lost 'em or anything, have you?"

"No, love. I've got everything safe – birth certificates, identity cards, ration books; there's talk of clothing coupons, too, but we ain't got them yet. P'raps they'll give us some money to buy the clothes wiv, too – some 'opes! I 'ad to use your birth certificates to get your new ration books when you come to me."

"Father Paul said to tell you to hang on to all our documents because there's no proper facilities for keeping such things at the Home at present. No office, or anything."

Mrs B. nodded. "Just let me know when you want it, love," she said, pouring the tea.

"Thanks, Mrs B.," said Scruffy, with a triumphant smile. "You're a brick! A solid gold brick!"

"What else did Father Rector have to say?" Jarvis asked, sarcastically, surprised that Scruffy had managed to keep it all a secret. It seemed quite extraordinary to him that Scruffy had had the gumption, or even the boldness, to tackle the Rector on his own; they normally discussed such assaults together first, and then it was always him who went in first. Once again Scruffy had surprised him. This Indian Army lark seemed to have given him new spirit.

"He gave me a marvellous reference," beamed Scruffy, pleased as Punch to be the centre of attention. "Said I was one of the brightest and most popular boys; intelligent, industrious and honest!"

"Only a man of God could get away with such lies!" Jarvis declared, laughing out loud. "Father Paul hardly knows you – or any of us yet."

"Just as well, isn't it!" Scruffy grinned. "Good thing it weren't Father John: his testimonial would've put me in clink!"

"So, how old do I have to be before I can apply to join?" Jarvis demanded, rather dispiritedly, feeling as if Scruffy had already deserted him. But, there was nothing he could do about his age.

"Well, you can apply during your seventeenth year, like me – in case you need a deferment to sit an examination – again, like me; but you've got to be eighteen when you actually join the Colours, which begins when you take the oath of allegiance."

"Crikey! And I'm not even sixteen," Jarvis moaned. "And I'm sitting the same exam as you. It's not fair! The whole damned shooting match'll be over before I'm that old!"

"Let's 'ope so, love," put in Mrs B. fervently.

Jarvis pulled a face at her, but he could never stay mad at her for more than a few seconds at a time; his peevish glare disintegrated as suddenly as it had formed, and he burst out laughing. Perhaps there'd be another war for him later on!

The weeks rolled by, with incredible speed at first and then more leisurely. Scruffy had received a formal printed acknowledgement of his application, together with the return of his birth certificate, and after that – nothing. Nothing at all. He lived in torment waiting for further news; an interview, a medical, a directive to go somewhere, anywhere; but, nothing. His torment became a burden for them all.

He plagued the ancient postman, pressed into wartime service, who crawled snail-like on his rheumaticky legs along their street delivering letters; he pounced on everything that fell into their letter-box; he spent hours pacing up and down or with his face pressed against the pane waiting for the next delivery; he cursed the postman for his lameness if he was late, which he often was; and he all but tore his hair out when the poor old chap limped by without making any delivery at all. The worst days were when they were invited, in a score of circulars, to save every blessed thing under the sun, to give up every little thing that made life just bearable, and to donate what was left, right down to their last drop of blood. Scruffy devoured every leaflet before throwing it furiously aside, incensed that so much paper should be wasted when all he wanted was a single sheet inviting him to give his all for his country; well, India, in his case. But, no such call came. His life, it seemed, was not wanted.

After a fortnight, his impatience waned appreciably. The postman came and went (or didn't), at his own best pace, in comparative safety. After another week, Scruffy resigned himself to the fact that there was not going to be a letter, but that did not entirely stop him remaining alert for the sound of the postman's familiar shuffling footsteps, just in case. He imagined every possible calamity that could have befallen his precious letter – and gradually gave up expecting anything.

Scruffy tried to convince himself that he wasn't really bothered and, although he still stomped around with a face as grim as November, in the end, almost succeeded in believing it. At any rate, life became a little more relaxed in Grafton Street, as he sat back and waited for his ordinary call-up papers – as a private. Jarvis had long ago given all thoughts of the Indian Army the elbow, and now found he didn't have to give his mate such a wide berth; and Mrs B., happy in the knowledge that one son was safe somewhere in East Africa and the other equally secure somewhere in North Africa, was relieved that she didn't now have to walk so lightly round Scruffy, and to see his appetite on the mend. In fact, both Jarvis and Scruffy forgot everything for a while except the business of their Higher School Leaving Certificate examinations, which suddenly loomed up; they both assured one another that they'd passed easily, and then tortured themselves with doubts as they went over the papers time and time again. It would be many weeks, perhaps months, before they knew the results, which made it worse.

Then, on the morning of May 10, following a particularly ferocious night raid that saw both the House of Commons and Westminster Abbey badly damaged, rail traffic virtually halted, hundreds of streets blocked and thousands of fires raging the length and breadth of London, the postman's rheumatism appeared somewhat easier as he threaded his way through debris that littered Grafton Street. He stopped at their house, seemed to take an age peering through the bundle of letters in his hand, and then pushed two fat envelopes through the letter-box, gave the door a resounding rat-a-tat-tat, raised his cap to an anxious-eyed Mrs B. when she emerged to discover the reason for the commotion, frightened her even further with a toothless grin, and shambled on whistling with rare jollity.

Mrs B. frowned after him, and then stooped to extract the two letters from the wire-cage. Her hands trembled as she turned them over and over in her hands, staring at them in wonder. One envelope was printed in a neat, but still sprawling, hand; the other, buff-coloured with the dread OHMS legend, was type-written and looked horribly officious.

Both were addressed to Robert Beard; one with the addition of an Esquire.

Robert Beard, Esquire, stared at the two envelopes agonizing over which to open first. After all this time, he did not for an instant suppose the military-looking one contained anything but confirmation of his rejection. Mrs B. and Jarvis sat on the opposite side of the kitchen table, their eyes watching both him and the letters. He toyed with the envelopes, weighing them in his hands, feeling them tremulously. As far as Jarvis knew, Scruffy had never received even one letter before, and here he was with two. And fat ones at that. And one calling him an Esquire, no less. Jarvis could tell that it was this grandiloquence that decided the matter. Scruffy picked up the official-looking envelope, and opened it, hardly daring to anticipate anything but the worst.

"Perhaps they're sending me a medal," he grinned.

"Fool!" cried Jarvis, "only the Yanks get medals before they get their uniforms."

Scruffy ignored this gibe and continued shaking the documents out of the envelope, and it was, indeed, the long-awaited communication from the India Office.

It contained an order, from a Brigadier Grenville Pummery, for the addressee to attend a weekend selection board at 174a Marylebone Road, starting at 08.00 hours on Saturday, May 31, 1941, and concluding at 09.00 hours the following Monday. The itinerary would include a medical examination, various aptitude tests, films, lectures, discussions and PT sessions. The addressee was instructed to bring his own shorts and plimsolls, and, of course, the usual toiletries. Punctuality throughout was not only stressed but underlined – in green ink. There were several leaflets and a detailed outline of their future course for the successful candidates. His face told Mrs B. and Jarvis that the contents of the letter were exceedingly satisfactory; his words added the wholly unnecessary confirmation.

"They want me! I'm to be an officer!" he exclaimed, in a voice of incredulous disbelief and joy. "You'll have to start calling me Sir, so's I can get used to it." He pushed the documents proudly over towards Mrs B. and Jarvis, and, after an equally excited perusal of them, and noting that far from being immediately elevated to officer status he was only being called for a preliminary examination, Jarvis observed, with an evil grin, that its coldness was tantamount to an invitation not to come!

But Scruffy was already deaf to such witticisms, and blind to everything else. He had neither eyes nor ears for anything save his second letter. It evidently made the first irrelevant: inconsequential: unimportant: a nothingness; it banished everything else from the face of the earth. He continued to stare at it dumbfounded, incapable of speech, or any rational thought. His face, drained of colour, took on the aspect of a wax effigy; a sheen of sweat covering his brow became minute pearls that gathered force and rolled down into his eyes, raced along his nose and dripped unheeded on to the precious pages of the letter. His dark eyes, afire with some mysterious inner light, pored over the flimsy sheets of paper, and he devoured their words, over and over again, seeming never to have his fill, his mouth hanging open as he formed the words. Finally, his eyes now shining with a sort of madness, a joyous madness, he clutched the already crumpled pages to his chest; a smile took over his face that looked to contain all the magical wonder of Christmas; at the same time tears galloped down his cheeks and gathered at his chin, from where they splashed on to his shirt and the letter; and then he folded his arms on the table, rested his head on them, and sobbed with complete abandonment; one fist yet clutched the letter with the determined strength of a miser.

Mrs B. and Jarvis stared at each other with a consternation that was a mixture of alarm and bewilderment. Mrs B., with the advantage of being an experienced and caring mother, was the first to move. She went to Scruffy's side and took his head in her arms and pressed it against the warm and comforting softness of her small body, her fingers playing with the tangled knots of his unruly hair; presently, she tried to extricate the mystery letter from his grip, but at that moment no power on earth could have prised loose the tentacles that clung so tenaciously to it. Perplexed, and fearing something dreadful had happened – what, he couldn't for the life of him imagine – Jarvis also tried to comfort his friend. He caught hold of Scruffy's free shoulder and asked, in his gentlest voice, "What is it, mate? What's happened, Scruff? You can tell us." But Scruffy hadn't done crying yet; he had to drain himself of emotion before he could reply. It seemed to take a long time but, as his body finally stopped its convulsive heaving and the tears exhausted themselves, he lifted his head and croaked:

"It's Dolly!"

"Dolly!" Mrs B. and Jarvis repeated the name together, she having absolutely no idea of its significance, he knowing full well, and disbelieving.

Scruffy nodded, sitting up straight and wiping his tear-stained face with the backs of his hands, but still gripping the letter for dear life.

"Your Dolly, d'you mean? Aunt Dolly?" Jarvis gaped, incredulously. He hardly believed his ears, even then.

"Yes," Scruffy nodded his head again, this time more energetically, his eyes shining with a sort of agonised excitement and the colour beginning to creep back into his cheeks. "My Aunt Dolly!"

"No!" Jarvis gasped. He tightened his grip on Scruffy's shoulder, and wondered if his news meant she was dead. Over his head, Jarvis whispered to the alarmed Mrs B. about who Dolly was, and only then realised that all he knew – all anybody knew, was that she was Scruffy's aunt and that she'd been missing all his life. It seemed enough, for Mrs B. bent to kiss the top of Scruffy's head and then moved towards the range. Mrs B.'s infallible remedy for every crisis was a pot of tea. She busied herself with the preparations, but Jarvis knew she never missed a word of what was said – and nor would she miss an opportunity to chip in with her sixpenny-worth at opportune moments.

Again Scruffy nodded, too excited to speak, looking again at his letter which he now commenced to smooth out on the table with his hand.

"She ... she isn't dead, is she?" Jarvis pressed, uncomfortably. He knew as soon as he'd got the question out that she wasn't. Scruffy wouldn't be looking so damned pleased with himself if she was, would he? It was clumsy of him.

"No! Idiot!" boomed Scruffy, thumping the table with his fist and making the pages of the letter jump. "She's written to me, hasn't she?" He smacked one of the dancing pages to indicate her letter. "Pages and pages!"

"But how?" Jarvis exclaimed, not without some irritation, for he couldn't imagine how it could have happened – and Scruffy was being damned slow about offering any explanation. "How's she suddenly come to life? We both thought she was dead after all the years of searching for her. How'd she learn where you were living, heh? We've only been here since we were bombed – less'n eight months ago."

"That copper friend of yourn: your godfather – you know, Ruth's father. He found her, and told her everything," explained Scruffy, who seemed about to burst into tears again but, instead, decided to laugh.

"Sam! Sam Trotter!" Jarvis stared at him in amazement. "But how? How'd he know about her? And why didn't he tell us he was looking for her – let alone that he'd found her." A chilling thought struck him. She might be a murderess or something, and locked up in prison. Sam could presumably find her easy enough if she was in one of them. But Jarvis didn't voice this line of thought, and simply asked: "Where'd he find her, then? Just where is this Aunt Dolly of yours?"

"Hathersage!" declared Scruffy, referring to the letter. "That's a place up North, in Derbyshire."

If he had said the Moon, Jarvis would have been no more astonished. Hathersage meant as much to him as any other satellite, and Derbyshire very little more – except that he thought it was more in the Midlands than the North.

"And why's she writing to you now – out of the blue," Jarvis asked, frowning, as if in fact she had just returned from the Moon, or somewhere equally remote.

"P'raps she never knowed you was alive till now," suggested Mrs B.

"That seems to be exactly right; she didn't," Scruffy confirmed, picking up the letter again and scanning through it. "She had no knowledge of me – till now. Not till Sam Trotter told her."

"And yet, you've known about *her* all your life," Jarvis said, with growing doubts. It all sounded a bit too far-fetched for his liking; decidedly iffy.

"I knew I had an aunt because it was in some papers in my mother's bag which was found after she drowned, but no one was ever able to find her – my Aunt Dolly, that is. We didn't know if she was still living – or even if she'd been on the ferry, too," insisted Scruffy, refusing have his joy dampened. "It was even worse for her because she didn't even know I existed. The moment Sam Trotter told her about me, all she wanted was to see me. She's written to say she wants me to come and live with her for good. That I've to think of her as my mother! Oh, Jarvis, isn't it simply too wonderful for words. It's what I've dreamed about all of my life. A *real* home with a *real* relative! All my very own! Oh, it's more than I ever dreamed was possible!"

Mrs B. placed cups of tea on the table, sat down and asked: "Can we see your letter, dear?"

Almost reluctantly, Scruffy loosened his hold on the letter, and grudgingly nudged it towards her. Jarvis was particularly curious to learn Sam's role in the matter and peered over her shoulder; they read it together. It was written in ink with a cheap pen, and the paper was of a very poor quality. The letter, containing innumerable blotches, was a jumble of disjointed thoughts, but throughout the message was clear; she was overjoyed at the discovery of an unimagined nephew, and wanted nothing more than to be united with him and to take the place of his dear mother, her sister.

The letter left Mrs B. breathless, for she had read it all out loud, but she was still the first to speak for Jarvis remained too astonished to say anything. In fact, apart from being immensely impressed by Sam's sleuthing, there seemed to be so much left unsaid that he didn't know what to think. Scruffy, having listened agog to every word as though each was added confirmation of the marvellous news, simply beamed with delirious joy – and carefully gathered up the pages of his letter and thrust them deep into some secret repository within his shirt; he patted it, for safety's sake, and sighed with blissful contentment.

"She sounds a nice woman – lonely, too," was Mrs B.'s cautious verdict when she finally recovered her breath. "It don't really satisfy a body's curiosity, though, do it?"

Jarvis agreed, and also agreed wholeheartedly with Scruffy's observation that the only person who knew the answers to the questions hanging on all their tongues was Sam Trotter. There was nothing for it, they simply had to go and see Sam – and straightaway.

The pot of tea was left untouched, and they all made their way directly to The Dials where, miraculously, they found Sam unencumbered by his womenfolk, apart from Mavis who, in the absence of Queenie, was in charge of the bars, and Hannah, who appeared to have been promoted for she was painstakingly engaged in adding measures of water to long rows of assorted bottles; she greeted them with a broad grin and made no attempt to conceal her activities. She told them simply: "Queenie said the stuff were too strong fer them wot's got to go an' fight in the war!"

Sam, when they told him about Aunt Dolly's letter, which he read extremely slowly and without a word or a single expression of surprise, seemed strangely reluctant to tell of his part in discovering her whereabouts, and Jarvis believed that if it hadn't been for Scruffy's desperate pleading he wouldn't have told them anything – or, at least, not nearly so much. Even then he played down the "miracle," as Scruffy insisted on calling it. He led them all to the quiet corner where he was accustomed to reflect and drink in peace, though today he said it was because he didn't want any eavesdroppers; he peered round conspiratorially, but only Hannah was in sight – and she merely waved to him when she saw him looking, and carried on watering the bottles and softly singing to herself.

"There's nuffink really to tell," he insisted, settling back in his chair and looking round at the eager, expectant faces. "I done nuffink miraculous. It were just ordinary police work – an' a bit of luck."

But Scruffy would have none of this. "Tell us, tell us, Mr Trotter!" he begged, with impatient excitement. "Please! How was it you were able to find Aunt Dolly so quick when the Church couldn't after a lifetime of looking?"

Sam smiled benignly. "I don't fink they looked very 'ard, son. Probably too busy sayin' their prayers an' lookin' arter you!" he said, with a wink at Mrs B., whose eyes twinkled in return. "Like I said, there weren't nuffink to it, not really. It were all there just waitin' to be found. Ev'ryfink's writ down in documents ... it were simply a matter of lookin' in the right places."

"Go on," cried Scruffy as Sam paused, as though he had come to the end of his story.

"Can't tell you an awful lot, Master Scruffy," Sam continued, and he seemed to be concentrating very hard with his memory and picking his words very carefully. "In the first place, there ain't a lot to tell, and in the second ... well, some of it's concerned wiv police business an' it ain't for your ears. I ain't allowed to tell you. You un'erstand?"

"Tell us what you can, Mr Trotter ... please!" implored Scruffy, almost beside himself with impatience.

"Please, Sam," Jarvis urged, feeling he should support Scruffy's plea.

Sam looked uncomfortable, and Jarvis honestly couldn't understand why he thought it necessary to be so secretive over such a matter. After all, it wasn't as if the security of the country was being endangered: the only person it concerned was Scruffy – and, of course, his Aunt Dolly. Perhaps Sam came to the same conclusion for after a few moments he began telling them about his search.

It seemed that Sam had had little difficulty in discovering Dolly's maiden name. A study of the police report on the ferry disaster of 1923, in which her sister Violet (Scruffy's mother) was drowned, revealed that the sisters had been brought up at Grays in Essex where they were remembered, with no great fondness, as the two Burton girls – although there did not appear to be the same ready recollection of any Mr Burton, but, then, the name was one of many borne by their mother, Sarah, who had long since been buried under that of Potter. The trail seemed to end with this discovery and, if it hadn't been for a stroke of good fortune, it might have died there in Grays for no one appeared to know, or care, what had become of her. The good luck was that Dolly met a certain Fred Pickle and fell in love; well, she got married anyway, Sam grinned.

"If it hadn't bin fer this little ceremony, I might never 'ave picked up 'er trail again," he went on, after emptying a tankard of ale and bawling to Hannah to bring him another. "They were now documented, yer see," he continued after his empty pot had been replaced with a brimming one and Hannah had skipped away. "The 'appy event took place at Balls Cross in Sussex – though what they was doin' there – apart from gettin' spliced, I ain't got no idea. Mind you, they done a runner soon's the ceremony was over ... leavin' the parson, an' others, unpaid."

The happy couple simply disappeared, and if Dolly hadn't been widowed three years later, Sam doubted if he'd ever have traced her again. "It seems that 'er 'usband, poor fellow, was blown to smithereens in a coal mine explosion at Highcroft in the West Riding of Yorkshire. That was in March, 1922 – the year 'fore you was born, Scruffy." Sam paused to take a long swig at his beer before continuing. "Gawd knows wot 'e did before, but I got the impression that this mining work was Fred's first-ever job. Unlucky bleeder, weren't 'e! 'E should've stayed single!" He paused again, seemingly to sort out his story.

"Go on," said Scruffy fretfully.

"What 'appened next, Sam?" demanded Mrs B., equally curious.

"That were the trouble, weren't it? Nuffink 'appened, not so's you'd know," declared Sam, frowning. "A year or so after Fred was killed, Dolly seemed to simply disappear – again. She'd apparently been very ill for a long time. I discovered she'd bin in the local infirmary – summat to do wiv 'er lungs ... pneumonia, consumption, summat like that, though there was talk of other worse fings – but afterwards she upped an' vanished. She'd made friends wiv a woman called Martha Longley who 'ad some nursing experience an' looked after 'er. Although I got the impression Dolly weren't expected to survive 'er sickness, it seems she did, 'cos she and 'er friend Martha moved away from Highcroft – and that was the last anyone ever 'eard 'em."

"But you found her, Mr Trotter, didn't you!" cried Scruffy excitedly.

"Yes," admitted Sam, in a subdued voice. "The records concerning 'er 'ad come to a full stop, but as there was no death certificate wiv 'er name on it, I figured she must be alive somewhere." As he had some leave due, Sam decided to spend it in Yorkshire; a sort of busman's holiday, he'd told Queenie. Of course, there was now no trail for him to follow. It was about seventeen years since the records (those he had access to) lost track of Dolly, and Sam wasn't entirely sure what he expected to find. He wasn't a great believer in miracles, not here in England, but he thought he'd need one if he was to find her. But, he'd got the bit between his teeth now, and spent nearly two weeks creaking round the mining communities, always asking questions, chatting to estate agents and trades people – and in the end he found his miracle. He found Dolly ... or rather, he found the long-retired solicitor who'd handled the sale of her home in Highcroft and was able to point him in the right direction; first to a cottage in Conisbrough, and then, after more nosing around, to her present residence.

He found Aunt Dolly, or Mrs Pickle to give her proper name, hoeing in the kitchen garden of a stone cottage which was as close to Hathersage as it could be without being part of it. There was a boundary stone just beyond the cottage wall that put its position some feet inside what is known as the Peak District. Dolly was tall, thin as a broom-handle, with a thin circlet of hair that was now more grey though there were still strands of gold that told of its former colour. She'd looked up as Sam appeared at her gate, regarded his huge figure thoughtfully for some moments, and then gave him a tentative welcoming smile.

"We got along like a 'ouse on fire," said Sam finally. "You're a lucky young man, Scruffy. She's a fine woman, your aunt. You'll love 'er."

"I always have, Mr Trotter," said Scruffy simply, his eyes brimming happily.

"'Course you 'ave, boy," acknowledged Sam. "She's a lovely lady ... an' a marvellous cook, too. You won't starve wiv 'er, lad. Naturally, she didn't even know of your existence, an' when I told 'er ... well, she said all that in 'er letter, didn't she?" Sam blinked his eyes and cleared his throat. "I'll tell you one thing, she likes a talk! I was wiv 'er for two days, and I don't fink we stopped rabbiting once! I come to the conclusion your Aunt Dolly don't get many opportunities for a good chat, so when someone does visit 'er she likes to 'ave 'er money's worth!" Sam looked up at Scruffy and added: "She promised she'd write, which she 'as ... an' she give me a quick peck as I was leavin' though I 'spect she meant it fer you – but I fink I'll keep it for myself ... Queenie won't mind!"

When they were all back in Grafton Street and seated round the kitchen table sipping the inevitable cups of tea, their heads were swimming with a million thoughts about Sam's revelations, but not one of them could find a single word to say. They were too engrossed with the history of Aunt Dolly's disappearances to wish to break the spell. It was Mrs B. who brought them all down to earth again.

"It seems to me, Scruffy ... well, don't you fink you might be a little old to go gettin' yerself all in a lather over an aunt you ain't never seen?" she asked, so gently it was impossible to take offence. "Isn't it rather too late for such things? A child don't want to be adopted when it's all growed up, do it? Ain't it the same wiv this aunt of yourn? Ain't it too late for such things – at your age?"

"Oh, no, Mrs B. I've been wanting to belong to someone all my life," Scruffy cried earnestly, staring at her with such intensity that she had to lower her eyes and fix them on a tea leaf floating in her cup. "It wouldn't matter if I was a hundred years old. It's what I've always dreamed about. She's all I want. All I've ever wanted. Only another orphan can understand how I feel now that my Aunt Dolly's been found."

Jarvis nodded. He couldn't find any words to say just then, but he understood. He'd been there himself. But he'd found Sam and Queenie, and Ruth, and though they weren't blood relations, like this Aunt Dolly to Scruffy, he loved them as deeply as if they were real family. In the absence of any real aunt, he was perfectly content with his pretend family. And then there was Nelson and Emma and their girls: he loved them all, too, but differently.

"Yes, dear; even so, don't go doing nuffink in a 'urry," cautioned Mrs B.

"I've been patient eighteen years, Mrs B. There's absolutely nothing to be said about it. I'm going to her," declared Scruffy, with quiet determination. He sat there with his arms folded on the table, a smile touching his eyes; he seemed to be a million miles away, or however far away Derbyshire was. Jarvis guessed his heart was there already.

"Well, give yerself a few days to fink it all out, at least," urged Mrs B. "Write to her first, like she done to you. Tell 'er abaht yerself. You don't want to go meetin' like strangers, do yer? She may need time to prepare for you, too. It's been a shock for 'er as well, love. Give it a few days to sort itself out. Don't do anything impulsive."

But she might as well have been speaking to a brick wall. His mind was already made up; he was going to follow his heart. Then, suddenly, Jarvis spotted that *other* letter still lying on the table, and quite forgotten. The sight of it at last loosened his tongue.

"And don't go forgetting, matey, you belong to the Army now!" Jarvis exclaimed, with some concern.

Scruffy, back among them at a stroke, looked startled for a moment, stared back at his friend and then at the letter on the table, and then snapped scornfully: "The Army! I'm not interested with *them* – not now!"

"I shouldn't think you have any choice in the matter, Scruff. You don't have any say about it, not with a war on. Remember, you've signed documents. You're committed. And," Jarvis reminded him, "you're under orders to attend that Selection Board thing at the end of the month."

Scruffy glared angrily at Jarvis. "Well, I simply won't turn up," he said crossly. "I'll just tell them it was all a mistake."

"Yes, but it's your mistake," Jarvis said levelly. "I can't see the Army letting you just walk away. It's like the Church, once they've got their hooks into you, you're theirs – till *they* say otherwise."

"Well, they won't know where I am, will they?" countered Scruffy, but there was a trace of doubt in his voice. "Unless you two spill the beans!"

Mrs B. smiled, grimly, and took a sip of tea. "You know we wouldn't never tell anyone anyfink, love – not for all the tea in China," she assured him, pouring more tea – Indian tea. "But you can't go ignoring the Army, lad. Like Jarvis says, they're the Law. Martial law they call it now. You won't be able to hide from them – not for long. Not wiv the war going on an' on. Not wiv all the bleedin' documentation we got these days. They'd find you – easy."

"The redcaps'd simply come and drag you off," Jarvis added seriously.

"Well, I simply won't go with them!" declared Scruffy defiantly, but his eyes lacked the confidence of his words. After a longish pause, his lower lip buckled, and he asked in an agonized voice: "What am I going to do? I want to go and live with my Aunt Dolly more than anything in the world ... but, I don't want any trouble with the Army, either."

No one had any solution to offer and after a lengthy silence, Mrs B. wisely suggested "Let's sleep on it." She held her cup in both hands and stared hopefully into it as though she were reading the leaves, but she didn't appear to find any answers there either. "Give it time, Scruffy," she said, repeating her earlier advice. "You've waited eighteen years – give it a day or so more – an' then write an' explain the position to your Aunt Dolly. Get fings straight in yer own mind first – an' get this Army fing sorted out. They might give you some sort of deferment – or even compassionate leave."

A bomb fell fairly close by and shook the house, rattling all the windows, and they all looked up – up at the ceiling as a shower of plaster dust fell, but nobody spoke. It took another pot of tea before they finally retired – to "sleep on it," in Mrs B.'s words.

Chapter Fifteen

Grafton Street, Battersea, May, 1941

In fact, they "slept on it" for several days, during which Scruffy mooched around looking as miserable as a cod on a slab, before Jarvis had his brainwave: the perfect solution. He spent the remainder of the day thinking it all through. It seemed foolproof, and simple. He was amazed at the simplicity of the plan, and only surprised it hadn't occurred to him earlier. He called a council of war for the three of them.

"These Army people," Jarvis said to Scruffy when, once again, they were gathered round the teapot in the kitchen, "they've no idea what you look like, do they? You didn't have to send them a photograph, did you?"

Scruffy shook his head. "No," he said, looking bewildered, "they didn't ask for one. I just filled in the form – you know, you saw it. You dictated most of it."

Jarvis nodded, impatiently. "Well then," he declared, with the air of one unveiling some momentous enterprise, "what's to prevent me from taking your place in the Army, leaving you free to join your precious Aunt Dolly up in – where was it? Yorkshire?"

"Derbyshire," corrected Scruffy, absently. He stared, boggle-eyed at Jarvis, clearly unsure if it was the silliest of ideas, or a brilliant one. "We couldn't possibly get away with it, could we?" he asked finally, his voice tense with excitement.

"'Course you couldn't!" snapped Mrs B., looking horrified. She stared at Jarvis so hard she missed her mouth with her cup of tea and dribbled it over her apron.

"Why not?" Jarvis demanded, a roguish smile spreading right across his shiny, eager face. He thumped the table with the flat of his hand as an added emphasis. "It only takes a bit of cheek, don't it – and I've always been accused of having too much of that."

"Stop talkin' such rubbish, Jarvis! It's ridiculous!" cried Mrs B. vehemently, banging her cup down in its saucer so hard the handle snapped off. "I never heard of anything so scatterbrained. Do yer fink they're all fools in the Army – like you!" she exclaimed shrilly, snatching at Jarvis's hand which was still on the table. "Jarvis – for pity's sake, you're just a boy … a fifteen-year-old boy! You frighten me sometimes, you really do."

"And you're an old worry-guts, " Jarvis laughed gaily, taking the broken handle from her and kissing the back of her hand before she could retrieve it. At the same time, Scruffy leapt to his feet to replace her cup. "Remember, Mrs B., the rest of the cadets will be just boys as well," Jarvis argued, immediately serious again. "I doubt if many will be bigger, most will be a lot smaller; some will look older, even if they aren't – and some will look younger, even if they aren't. I know everything that Scruffy knows, and possibly more. And I'm bigger and stronger than him."

Scruffy was too impressed by the logic of these arguments to take exception over this last remark – which he knew to be true. "Just supposing we got away with it – you in the Army as me, and me in Derbyshire as you. I don't see that that necessarily helps us. If we both disappear, they'll know that Robert Beard is legitimately in the Army, so the hue and cry will be on for you, Jarvis Brook – and sooner or later they'll trace you up in Derbyshire, only they'll discover it's me they've got 'cos I'll have your Ration Book and Identity Card! And then they'll start wondering who the Army's got! I don't see how it can work, damn it!"

"'Course it can't!" echoed Mrs B. sharply, picking up the fresh cup and eyeing the two of them over its rim. "They'll simply arrest the pair of you, tan yer backsides and then send you back to the Home. Either that, or you'll both end up in prison!"

"But why should anybody look for either of us at your Aunt Dolly's place?" Jarvis queried, archly. "The authorities don't know of any link between her and us. We three are the only ones who know this Mrs Dolly even exists."

"An' that Sam Trotter – an' 'im a copper!" Mrs B. blurted out. "An' I shouldn't fink 'e keeps any secrets from 'is Queenie – an' even though I love 'er like me own, I doubt if she's kept a secret in 'er life!"

Scruffy paled under a deep frown. "No copper's to be trusted!" he muttered.

"Sam is," Jarvis insisted. He'd missed this aspect in his scheming, but even now he felt it reasonable to assume that Sam could be trusted with their secret, and Queenie wouldn't ever do anything that might endanger him. "I'll explain things to him," he said confidently. "He won't let us down – and he could be a useful ally."

Scruffy looked doubtful, then nodded, slowly. The frown took a while to clear, but he evidently thought things were looking promising again for after a moment he managed a small smile. A fresh frown quickly wiped the smile away, however, as his thoughts returned to the matter of documents. "But my papers – identity card, ration book and so on, they'll give me away, won't they? They'll be in your name, and sooner or later some busybody's going to tumble to what we done. I'll be identified by someone from the Home and packed off to God knows where – probably to prison, like Mrs B. says; and they'll boot you out of the Army – if they don't shoot you first! There, clever Dick!" railed Scruffy bitterly, but with more frustration than anger. "You didn't think of all the bloody documents we have to have these days, did you?"

"Aha! 'Course 'e didn't!" exclaimed Mrs B., almost triumphantly.

Jarvis stared from one to the other of them, giving each what was meant to be a supercilious smile. He was in no hurry to shatter their convictions, and rather enjoyed keeping them dangling. When he did reply, he did so with a cool cocksureness that was intended to irritate them further. He felt very smug.

"You're both wrong," Jarvis told them calmly. "Of course I thought of these things. And I promise you, Scruff, you'll be perfectly safe with your documents – because, my friend," – he paused with the dramatic timing of an actor – "you'll be neither you nor me, but have an entirely new identity ... and, what's more, have perfectly genuine documents!"

Mrs B.'s hands shook so much she had to put her cup down again; she sat and stared at Jarvis with a faintly mocking incredulity. "Nah!" she exclaimed. "It ain't possible."

"How the devil can it be?" demanded Scruffy, but more curious than disbelieving.

Jarvis kept them waiting for an endless moment longer before launching into his explanation. "Remember, just after we were bombed, Scruff, that WVS woman who was fussing around us tying labels to everybody, filling in forms by the bucketful, constantly ticking names off on her lists and trying to put faces to names – and immediately forgetting them?" Scruffy clearly didn't remember her at all, but he nodded impatiently and growled at Jarvis to get on with it. "Well, who was it who was constantly at her elbow, helping her? It was *me*, weren't it! It was me who hovered round her, providing her with the names of all the boys, and even pointing some of them out, weren't it? And she was very pleased to have my help and said I was a good boy – and gave me a barley sugar for being so helpful! The next thing that happened was this bloke from the Ministry of ... Something coming and ticking off all the names on the list, and there was me again pointing out a boy each time he called out a name. We did it a few times because the boys were always moving around, on purpose. Anyway, in the end he gave us all brand new ration books and identity cards and things, again carefully ticking off the names on her list as he did so. Only, it was the list I'd helped to compile."

Scruffy looked bewildered. "I don't see how any of that helps us," he argued. "Those documents still identify us, don't they?"

Jarvis shook his head with deliberate slowness. "Don't you see " he asked, assuming an air of surprise. "I never gave the woman all the proper names, did I! It struck me even then that it would be mighty handy to have some spare papers – if ever I decided to run away again. If I had papers saying I was someone else, there wasn't much they could do about it – except send me on my way. And then I thought you might want to come along, too, so I got papers for you as well. And I added two extra spares in case we ever needed them. I never dreamed at the time what we'd end up using them for. Thought I'd be joining up with my gypsy mates again, not the Army! See, it pays to Be Prepared!"

"You're a rogue, Jarvis – or whatever you fink yer name is now," declared Mrs B., shaking her head and staring at him as if she'd never seen him before; but she was chuckling.

Scruffy was frowning, but his face was a lot brighter and there was a hint of a sparkle in his eyes. "What names are on these phoney papers of yours, then?" he asked, plainly still puzzled.

"Well, they're not actually phoney, Scruff. You know them as well as me. They're those of the four boys who couldn't be identified after the bomb blast. You'll be Robert Parkin, and if ever I need to escape from the Army, I'll have a choice of three identities won't I – I fancy John Charter," Jarvis declared cockily. "You'll remember the four bodies were never recovered – well, not so that they could be identified as such. Their identities were only presumed and Father Paul told me the authorities didn't even name them individually on the death certificate, calling them simply 'unidentified victims of an air-raid.' An' that's how they were buried. So, you see, the names are genuine enough – and what we have, matey, are four *bona fide* aliases that'll stand up to any amount of scrutiny."

But Mrs B., far from voicing any praise for Jarvis's ingenuity and scheming, only   continued shaking her head. "Those poor children," she murmured sorrowfully, and with a final shake and a long sigh, added cynically, "Talk abaht dead man's shoes … you'll be dead 'fore you start, seems to me."

Scruffy stared hard at Jarvis, still sorting out what he'd said in his head. After a while, his face visibly relaxed and the beginnings of a smile formed at the corners of his mouth as comprehension sank in. "You're a cunning old sod, Jarvis!" he cried, his voice ecstatic with excitement. "A blinking genius! If you're not careful, you'll end up a bloody general!"

"Better'n being shot, I suppose!" Jarvis agreed with a return grin, and feeling quite extraordinarily pleased with himself.

"Wait a minute, Mr General," cried Mrs B. in a sort of scoffing tone. "What abaht the documents they give me when you come here?" demanded Mrs B., who clearly hadn't grasped all the ramifications of Jarvis's plotting. To conceal her confusion, she got up and busied herself shelling peas; she had to do something with her hands because they shook too much to hold a cup and she simply had to occupy them some way. "They're in yer proper names – Jarvis Brook and Robert Beard. I 'ad to produce yer birth certificates when they come up for renewal."

"Of course," Jarvis told her, beaming hugely, "they're genuine, as well."

"How ..." Mrs B.'s baffled voice trailed off into nothingness, and a stream of peas escaped unnoticed across the floor.

Jarvis grinned teasingly at her. He really was feeling on top of the world. "Simple," he announced expansively. "When I was helping the WVS woman with the list of names, I included those of our four dead mates, and as soon as the man from the Ministry had provided the WVS woman with a pile of official documents matching her list, I took the opportunity, while busy helping her, of swiping the four that shouldn't have been there in the first place. The poor woman didn't have much of a memory for faces – nor names, and I was always having to produce the boys she wanted. I think the other lads were a bit puzzled at her sometimes calling me John, but she didn't seem to notice, and of course we weren't together all that long. Old Penguin came and took us over and we never saw the WVS again. Naturally, I made myself indispensable to Sister Penguin as well, in the course of which I pointed out that Scruffy and I seemed to have been overlooked in the distribution of new documents, and she, good woman that she undoubtedly is, went sailing into some council office – it's amazing how no one ever shuts a door on a nun! – and emerged in double-quick time with brand-new ones, *and* a voucher to get us new clobber! Well, it wasn't exactly new, but I got a good pair of trousers, some underpants ... oh, yes, and a cardigan that turned out to be a girl's! Don't know what happened to it – I 'spect Penguin nicked it for herself! But those documents of ours you've got, Mrs B., the ones with our real names on, they're the cat's whiskers; they're the ones Sister Penguin got for us. I'll be using Scruff's when I join the Army as him. And he'll go up to Derbyshire as Robert Parkin – I've got all the documents up to date and safe and sound, including the spares."

"Been busy ain't you, matey. You're a bleedin' genius!" declared Scruffy again, giving a gleeful whoop.

"You've got a criminal mind, Jarvis, an' you'll probably 'ang," Mrs B. said in a shocked voice, but her eyes were smiling. She sat with the tips of her fingers pressed together and raised them to her lips, as if in prayer, gazing disbelievingly at Jarvis, and occasionally shaking her head very slightly in a further expression of wonder, and then she gave a little gurgle and burst into a merry peal of laughter, in which both boys joined in. Having abandoned her peas, Mrs B. set about making a fresh pot of tea (actually she merely filled the kettle and placed it on the hob while Scruffy, uncharacteristically, volunteered to do the necessary) and then moved to where Jarvis sat. She took his head between her hands and gave him a succession of loud kisses, before returning to her seat and saying:

"I shouldn't be listening to your scheming, Jarvis, let alone giving it me blessing. I don't like the thought of a boy your age joining the Army, not wiv the war on an' all, though India's a long way off from that, but, y'know," she paused, and grinned almost guiltily, "I really think you boys might get away wiv it. You certainly seem to 'ave thought it all through, love – 'cept ... well, I fink Scruffy'll be safe in 'is Derbyshire bolt-hole – nobody knows of it, an' it'll be assumed he's away in the Army anyway; no, I'm not so worried abaht him as I am abaht you, Jarvis." She stared at Jarvis with pain in her motherly eyes. "As Jarvis Brook, you'll simply be a runaway boy so far as the p'lice is concerned, but they'll soon find out you and Scruffy was mates and go checkin' wiv 'im – that is Mister Soldier Beard, an' then the game'd be up, wouldn't it! Don'tcher see? It'll be you, not 'im, they'll find."

Jarvis considered her words for a moment, calmly and not really worried. "P'raps you're right, Mrs B.," he conceded. "Personally, I don't believe they'll go to all that trouble looking for a runaway kid – not with all this bombing going on, but I have already considered this possibility and come to the conclusion we need a diversion of sorts. And the only one I can think of involves my friend Nelson, if only I can find him. He'd be able to lay a trail that'll keep the police going round in circles for ever. I'll get word to him somehow – and after I've gone, Mrs B., you've got to be suitably surprised if you get a few strange postcards purporting to be from me; surprised, and know nothing. The cards'll be from Nelson – and they could be from almost anywhere. Wales would be my bet!"

"Who's Nelson?" asked Mrs B. suspiciously.

"It's better you don't know," Jarvis answered with a wink, and tapping the side of his nose significantly, in the manner that others had been doing to him as long as he could remember. He was enjoying himself hugely.

Mrs B. leaned forward and squeezed his arm affectionately. "I think you'll probably end up in the Tower of London, Jarvis," she told him, with a touch of pride, "that is, if you ain't 'anged first! But, if they don't catch up wiv you, I don't know if yer mightn't amount to something – pr'aps even a general, like Scruffy says. A hero, at least." She stopped, and stared earnestly into his laughing eyes. "I just 'ope you ain't a dead one!"

In the three weeks before he attended the weekend selection board, Jarvis busied himself tying up all the loose ends to his plans, which he and Scruffy rather pretentiously christened Operation Double Bluff; being the only ones cognizant of all its ramifications, it was probably the best kept secret of the war. They were too scared to breathe a word about it. Of course, the one exception was Mrs B., whom they weren't really in a position to hide anything from, but whom they were sure would protect their secret for ever. Of course, Sam would have to be told something of their plans, but only what was necessary.

Jarvis tackled Sam at the very first opportunity; and he tackled him head-on. Jarvis told Sam straight that it was really all his fault in the first place for finding Aunt Dolly. Jarvis said it was only to be expected that Scruffy would want to be with his aunt now, and no longer had any interest in joining the Indian Army. It was just as natural, Jarvis insisted, that he should want to do everything he could to help his friend – even to the point of taking up his place in the Army under his name. Jarvis didn't tell Sam the full story: he didn't think he should – not with him being a policeman. He felt that the least Sam knew about some aspects of his scheme the better – for both of them. So, he didn't tell Sam about the other identities he and Scruffy planned to use.

Sam heard Jarvis through with barely any show of surprise, except in his eyes which seemed to grow brighter as he stared intently at him. When Jarvis had said his piece, Sam remained quiet for several moments before speaking. He began by saying that he was not entirely in favour of the scheme, but that he understood the reason behind it; he accepted that Scruffy's only ambition now was to be with his aunt; he didn't even mind Jarvis's apparent impatience to go off to war in his place, that was only to be expected, even admired, in lads of his age – as he said, they were both too young to know better! As a policeman, he would not condone or approve of the Law being broken, or even dented. He conceded, however, he wasn't so much concerned with the venial transgressions – he wasn't without blemish in this sphere himself, he admitted – and he'd decided that Jarvis's plan fell in the same category.

"There are some sins, like white lies, that do more good in the eyes of God than perhaps the Law allows," he concluded with a smile.

Sam's main concern was how Jarvis expected to be able to pass for an eighteen-year-old, but Jarvis assured him he looked no younger than Scruffy, and was taller and stronger and would easily pass in a crowd. Sam shook his head, and said he was probably right.

"And, Sam, please, promise that you won't breathe a word about it to a living soul – not even to Queenie," Jarvis urged anxiously.

"So far as the rest of the world's concerned, yer secret's safe wiv me, Jarvis-lad," declared Sam, "But, I don't 'ave no secrets from Queenie, none whatsoever. I tell 'er ev'ryfing. I'd've thought you'd've knowed that. 'Sides, you'll learn you can't keep nuffink from wimmin – even if yer wants."

"I'm sorry, Sam. Truly. I just didn't want her to be worried about me," Jarvis said.

"She'd be a whole lot more worried if you just done a runner an' she didn't know where you was at – nor wot you was doin'," said Sam pointedly.

Jarvis nodded, understanding, and feeling contrite and embarrassed over what he'd said. "You're right, of course; sorry," he said again, this time with a wry smile. "What about Ruth?" he asked. "If she knows, she'll be babbling it to everyone. You know what girls are like!"

"That's summat you'll 'ave to decide fer yerself, Jarvis," said Sam quietly. "She'll know summat's up. She'll get to know you ain't at the Home, or wiv yer Mrs Bromley ... an' she'll be pestering us wiv questions, and in the end she'll find out somehow and 'ave to be told the truth. An' why not?" Sam paused and gave Jarvis a steady stare. "Ruth loves you completely, Jarvis. And I don't mean as a child. She'd protect your life wiv 'er own any day, you've no call to keep secrets from 'er."

Jarvis remained purposefully silent, but the slight colouring of his cheeks was answer enough for Sam, who gave him a paternal smile; he knew the affection was mutual, if more unrestrained on Ruth's part, but that was the usual way of these things. "I still fink you're terrible young to be goin' orf to be a soldier-boy," he said reflectively, toying with his chins. "I wouldn't be fooled, straight." Jarvis was tempted to point out he'd be going off to be a pukka officer, not a soldier-boy, but held his tongue. "Mind yer, I s'ppose, bein' in India-land the most dangerous fing you're likely to see will be a tiger – or one of them cobra snakes!"

This reminded Jarvis to swot up on India in readiness for the selection interview; he presumed he'd be expected to know something of the country – besides its tigers and snakes. He also decided that he ought to do something about making himself look a bit older. He fleetingly considered greying his hair, but decided – after a brief experiment with ashes – that perhaps this might be going too far. He didn't want to go looking twenty, did he? Then someone told him that shaving regularly in cold water would do the trick. So he acquired a safety razor and scrounged a single blade off one of the priests, and set to work. Twice a day, he lathered his face – quite the smoothest to be found in all the land – with laundry soap ... and shaved it all off again. His only real achievement was the removal of a considerable quantity of skin from his face, with the result that the lather acquired a distinctly pinkish hue – and his face was scarred all over with painful and bloody nicks. Mrs B., hard put to control her mirth, carefully dabbed his wounds with iodine (grinning at, but ignoring, his protests that she was drowning him with the stuff) and stuck cotton wool where the bleeding persisted. The first treatment gave him the colouring, almost, of a real Indian; the second gave him the appearance of having contracted some rare form of measles whose manifestations were in some way connected with snow flakes.

With the completion of each session of first aid duty, Mrs B. would scurry off to let loose her giggles in a cup of tea, leaving Jarvis to gaze forlornly at his speckled reflection. Once, he spotted a solitary hair, and was about to let loose a whoop of joy, when he realised that it was one of Mrs B.'s – and a white one at that. He persevered with the shaving for two weeks, daily agonizing over his image for any sign of ageing; there was none. If anything, he seemed to look even younger: Mrs B. said this was because his face had never before undergone such relentless cleansing. Jarvis stared at her aghast, and the shaving ended forthwith – together with any unnecessary washing. He resolved to leave his age for others to bother about.

Scruffy, who like Jarvis was impatient for the adventure to begin, set Operation Double Bluff in motion ahead of its actual launching, by keeping Father Paul informed about his forthcoming selection board and his expectations of being called up soon after. Father Rector wished him success in his ambitions and said he would be remembered daily in their prayers.

So, the thing was in motion: the great adventure set to begin.

The next thing was for Scruffy to write an especially careful letter to his Aunt Dolly. After his initial desperateness to write to her, the urge to do so had lessened daily until he found himself seeking excuses to put it off. He could not explain why this was, unless it was a fear of being rejected, though in view of *her* letter this had to be considered simply too unlikely for worlds; more likely, and it was the explanation he chose to accept, it was due to the uncertainty of this Army thing – and how everything could fall flat should it fail. The very thought of such a calamity terrified him. Both Mrs B. and Jarvis watched from their seats by the range as he struggled over his letter at the nearby table. Neither of them uttered a word during his ordeal, and for a long time Scruffy sat staring helplessly into space with the paper and pen lying unused before him.

Scruffy had never written a proper letter before and, as he finally overcame his fear and put pen to paper, he wondered if he would be able to do so now; but he need not have been concerned. As soon as he had written "My Dear Aunt Dolly," the words flowed in a never-ending cascade; it was as though he were chatting to her across the table. He told her how he had known of her and longed for her all his life, how he'd dreamed of meeting her one day, never daring to hope that he might actually do so; he told her what an enormous impact her loving letter had had on him, how he had cried over its pages and wanted to rush straight to her and never lose sight of her; he explained that he must continue to be patient a little while longer, however, because there were formalities to be sorted out which he didn't properly understand; he couldn't even tell her when he expected to be free to come to her – he didn't tell her it was because he and another boy had to act in unison, and that everything depended on when he was called up; but he did tell her that his name was now Robert Parkin and not Robert Beard, and that he would explain the change to her when they met and that in the meantime it might be better if she said nothing about it to anyone and simply got used to thinking of him as Robert Parkin – and that he was known as Scruffy, anyway. He repeated that he would explain everything to her when they met ... very soon, he hoped; and he concluded by telling her, in a sort of whisper, how hearing from her had been the happiest moment of his life.

Both Jarvis and Mrs B. were curious to know what Scruffy had written, but his lips were sealed even tighter than his envelope – which didn't stop him from begging a stamp off Mrs B. He gave them just a general outline of what he'd written and ignored every question, saying only, "It's private ... it's *family* ... between me and my aunt." Jarvis smiled. He could understand this secretiveness: it was the same between him and his pretend family. There were things orphans didn't ever want to share: they found love so rarely it made them selfish.

But for the moment, Jarvis had other things on his mind which pushed such needs unceremoniously into the background; for one thing, he was urgently trying to get used to being called Robert Beard; and for another, the moment of truth (for want of a better word) had arrived. It was the selection board weekend.

The venue, 174a Marylebone Road, turned out to be in the middle of a long row of massively-built houses whose undoubted elegance was hidden behind great bulwarks of sandbags and boarded windows. Inside, as he would soon discover, the entire row of buildings comprised a massive transit camp, capable of accommodating a whole brigade. With Mrs B.'s battered cardboard attaché case in one hand and Scruffy's papers in the other, Jarvis marched boldly up the wide stone steps, nodded cheerily at the sentry who ignored him, and presented himself to an acne-riddled corporal seated in solitary gloom at a trestle-table just inside. A hand-printed sign bearing the magic words *Indian Army* sat on the table beckoning all comers.

"Robert Beard reporting, sir," Jarvis declared, handing his documents to the corporal, who smirked as he ticked off the name on his list, glanced briefly at the papers and tossed them back at him in a manner so casual as to be insolent.

"Up the stairs, second floor, Room 82; present yourself to a Sergeant Pryor," he said in a bored monotone, before adding, with something of a sneer, "By the way – sir, I'm a corporal," – he tapped the chevrons on his sleeve, and gave Jarvis the suggestion of a two-fingered salute – "you don't call me 'sir' ... just plain corporal."

"Thank you, corporal," Jarvis replied, coolly, "As a civilian, I was being polite. When I'm in the Army, I'll know better, won't I?"

Corporal Acne blinked back. "Yes – sir," he stumbled, taken aback by Jarvis's authoritative tone. But Jarvis didn't linger: he was already halfway up the stairs. He was pleased that he'd found the words that he had, and spoken them so curtly, but he was angry, too, that he'd allowed himself to be goaded. A fine bloody start to his military career, he fumed. If he expected to become an officer, he had to learn self-control first. But that was very nearly the only hiccup throughout the weekend.

The exception occurred within ten minutes of his arrival and meeting the first of his companions who, on learning of Jarvis's Battersea background, exclaimed contemptuously, "Good God! has it come to this? Are gentlemen expected to share quarters with bastards!"

Jarvis had no doubt that he was a bastard, and the fact didn't bother him in the least – he'd read in his history books that half the occupants of the thrones and clerical palaces of Europe (and especially in England) shared his status, but it was the first time he could recall being called one in quite such an offensive manner. He reacted spontaneously. Not being a gentleman, he punched the fellow full-bloodedly in an ungentlemanly area, and the boy doubled up and fell to the floor. After a brief while, he recovered sufficiently to offer Jarvis an apology. It was not the best of starts, perhaps, but from then on the weekend progressed smoothly. Jarvis found it more interesting and entertaining than an ordeal. Really, it was not unlike being at school. There were lectures, interviews and a lot of exercising and drilling all of which he took in his stride. And when on Monday the sixty-odd potential cadets were let loose into the sunshine again, Jarvis marched with a soldierly gait back to Battersea confident that he'd been accepted. Robert Beard, that is.

Scruffy was far more anxious about confirmation of this for until it came he could not make plans to join Aunt Dolly in Derbyshire. He had wanted to dash off there and then to be with her, but Jarvis stamped on this idea promptly. Both of them had to continue exactly as they were until Jarvis's acceptance was confirmed and he had a date on which to report to start his training, he pointed out firmly. If Beard were to disappear before then, all their plans would come to nothing. "We must both disappear on the same day, you up North to your Aunt Dolly as Robert Parkin, and me to some OTC camp as Robert Beard," Jarvis declared forcefully. "Neither of us must attract attention to ourselves before that day," he added explicitly. "We simply act as normal until we're told the date."

Of course, they were both impatient for news. Scruffy was quite beside himself; and a further lovely letter from Aunt Dolly only added to his frustration. Mrs B., treading carefully between both of the boys, sought her usual refuge reading cup after cup of tea-leaves; they provided small comfort and no clue concerning their future. Their exam results arrived; they had both passed their Higher School Leaving Certificate, but only Mrs B. appeared in the least excited at the news.

Then, two weeks following the selection weekend, the rheumaticky postman returned, and another buff-coloured OHMS envelope fell through the letter-box. Mrs B. picked it up, examined it and returned to the kitchen, tapping the envelope teasingly against her nose as though sniffing its perfumed contents.

"Which Robert Beard wants to open this?" she asked, mischievously, wafting the envelope high above her head.

Scruffy snatched it from her hand, and read out loud: "Robert Beard, Esquire." He passed it over to Jarvis with an excited shout. "It's from *them*, Biffer!" he cried. "It's come! It's what we've been waiting for all these weeks! You open it, mate – it must be for you!"

Mrs B. sat down and retrieved her cup of tea, but though she lifted the cup to her lips she didn't drink; she simply gazed over the rim, never taking her eyes off Jarvis, who slit open the envelope without ceremony and withdrew a sheaf of papers, including a railway warrant, which was a give away: it told him all he needed to know. After a moment's scan, Jarvis grinned, looked at the two faces regarding him with such tense expectation, and let them out of their misery.

Robert Beard was informed (Jarvis read out to them) that he had been accepted as a candidate for an emergency commission in the Indian Army; he was instructed to attend at Northumberland Avenue Police Station at 11.00 hrs on Monday, June 23, 1941, to take the oath of allegiance; and further ordered to report at the guardhouse of Maidstone Barracks at 14.00 hrs on Monday, September 1, 1941, for enlistment into his holding unit, the Queen's Royal Regiment. The warrant was a one-way ticket from Victoria Station to Maidstone.

"Not exactly in a hurry to get their hands on you, are they?" complained Scruffy with a frown, as he frantically worked out how many more days he'd have to wait before he could join Aunt Dolly. He made it 44 days. It seemed an eternity.

Jarvis shrugged; it didn't seem all that long to wait – not to him; in fact, almost no time at all. In truth, beneath his veneer of calm, he was excited. "I suppose it takes time to organize these things," he pointed out. "There must be scores, possibly hundreds, of recruits in the pipeline. Funny when you think of it – all us chaps so eager to go to war."

He was glad he hadn't said something like "rushing off to get ourselves killed," as he'd had half a mind to, because right at that moment Mrs B. burst into tears. They both looked up with a start and stared at her in dismay. "Don't worry about me, boys," she sobbed, dabbing her eyes with a handful of her apron, "it's just the thought of losing you both just when we was all gettin' on so well togevver. An' you know how I miss me own two lads."

They both rushed to place their arms comfortingly round her heaving shoulders. "Don't you worry, Mrs B.," Jarvis consoled her, "you won't really be losing us because we'll write so often it'll be like we're still with you, and then you'll think you've got four sons – and you won't be lonely because Father Paul will send you some more boys to look after, once they realise we've really and truly gone." Scruffy chimed in, "That's right, Mrs B., we'll both be writing and because we've both got the same name, you'll think you've got twins!"

Of course, they all knew these letters couldn't be sent or all their careful plotting would be wasted. Scruffy was talking nonsense. Jarvis told himself to remember to warn Scruffy that he must never ever use his real name in any correspondence; he must forget that such a name had ever existed; and whatever letters he felt compelled to write should always be posted well away from where he lived, preferably in another county. Mrs B., even knowing that letters would be impossible, seemed brightened by the thought of them and, with a final dab of her apron and a hug for each of them, she rushed to replenish the teapot knowing that it would always provide the cup to cheer. She looked back at the table; Scruffy was already scribbling furiously, impatient to tell his Aunt Dolly the latest marvellous news; Jarvis met her gaze, and winked.

"I'll send you a ton of tea from India, Mrs B.," he called over to her.

Mrs B. blinked her moist eyes, smiled back at him, and turned quickly to her teapot. She couldn't stop the tears running down her cheeks – and Jarvis was grown up enough to let her enjoy her weep without interference. He shook his head and gave a wry, if very boyish, smile as a thought struck him.

"Christ!" he reflected, "I'll still be under 16 when I join the Army!"

Jarvis had been impatiently ticking off the days until he was due to take the oath of allegiance, and now the day had come. He arrived at Northumberland Avenue Police Station half-an-hour early, and a quarter of an hour after the appointed time, a police sergeant appeared, called for silence and close attention, and ticked off their names on a list he had clipped to a board. Jarvis answered to the name Robert Beard, loudly and clearly, without a thought that he could be shot for doing so. The oath itself was probably the biggest anti-climax of all; the sergeant mumbled some inarticulate phrases, they all spoke their names and mouthed the appropriate responses as directed, and it was all over; each of them signed their name where indicated, and then they were shown the door ... and told to make haste, quietly.

Jarvis (God! he must start thinking in the name of Robert Beard) marched home feeling rather depressed about it all, but before he was halfway there he was grinning quite cheerfully. No one had so much as mentioned his age, let alone questioned his identity. With these last obstacles removed, all he had to do now was to wait. He swung his arms as he marched, and whistled. He was already a soldier. He wondered if he was being paid.

And now the days really did drag – especially as it was now the school holidays. Both Jarvis and Scruffy got the feeling that the moment of their deliverance was growing more distant rather than nearer; of course, it wasn't, but in their youthful eagerness, Time, if it didn't actually move backwards, seemed to creep along so slowly it was as though it had come to a definite standstill. Then, almost unnoticed, zero-hour (they thought it fitting to adopt military terminology) was only a week away, and the days suddenly seemed not only so much shorter, but to race past us.

They began to scramble about putting the finishing touches to the arrangements for their respective departures. Jarvis's own preparations were negligible. He knew from the documents he'd received that the Army would provide all his needs and, not having much in the way of personal possessions, he planned to take only a few toilet necessities (including the still superfluous safety razor), a change of underwear and a clean shirt, some of Ruth's handkerchiefs, the super pen-knife Sam had given him, and the red-white-and-blue braces Queenie had given him at Easter. Jarvis was able to pack all his belongings quite easily in Mrs B.'s attaché case which he had now taken permanent possession of – with her blessing.

Scruffy, who had been ready and packed to go for the past week or more, now unpacked everything in his excitement, and started again. His packing was an altogether more formidable affair, and God alone knew how or where he had accumulated everything; he was one of those who couldn't bear to throw anything away, and he was determined to take all his treasures with him – no matter whose it was; among these was a tiny silver cup Jarvis had won (and lost) for boxing. Jarvis warned him against nicking anything belonging to Mrs B., for he would not have put it past him to take some spoons or even a sheet or two to present to his Aunt Dolly. Though he was sure Mrs B. would have willingly given him anything had he asked for it. She gave him her one and only suitcase, which had an extending lid, and he crammed it to bursting point; Mrs B. and Jarvis had to sit on it while he wound a clothes-line (heaven knows whose) round it for safety's sake. Scruffy then started making parcels of carrier-bags, which had to be tied with string. There were four of them.

That same day, they emptied their pockets and searched various likely, and not so likely, hiding places, and discovered their combined wealth totalled 3s 7d – and two French coins of very minimal denominations. It didn't seem much for two fellows to pit themselves against the world with, but they were accustomed to having empty pockets and had the optimism of youth that they'd make out. Scruffy haggled skilfully (he thought) with a pawnbroker and got 2s for Jarvis's silver cup, which the old misery said was more a thimble. Well, they thought it was a jolly good exchange, anyway. Mrs B. came up trumps and gave them each half-a-crown. It was a lot of money to her, and it would leave her short for a while, but she gave it willingly and with a lot of love – and they certainly didn't give her any opportunity to change her mind! This brought their assets to 10s 7d, and Jarvis told Scruffy he'd better have it all since he had to buy a train ticket to Sheffield, and then needed bus money, or perhaps another train, to Hathersage.

"It might not be enough, but it's all there is," Jarvis said, with a philosophical shrug. "You might have to walk some of the way; who knows, you might be lucky and get a lift. Don't forget to ask for a half-price ticket – tell 'em you're only 13 ... " – Scruffy glared belligerently at Jarvis and screamed he looked twice as old as him, but Jarvis ignored his outburst – " ... and being evacuated. I'll be all right because I've got my travel warrant to get me to Maidstone. Mind you, I could still do with a few coppers, I suppose ... I might be able to scrounge something off Sam."

With the passing of his latest exams, Jarvis was now a free agent so far as the Home was concerned. Under the benign regime of Father Paul, their new rector, the boys were not sent out to scrub floors and such like and were free to amuse themselves as best they might – probably to the consternation of the local residents. All things being equal, Jarvis should have been preparing himself for university (for which he was qualified in everything but age), but the times were not equal, and, of course, he had plans which had nothing to do with further education. In the meantime, until zero-hour arrived, he kept a low profile and did very much as he pleased. He passed his time reading German and Italian books, and speaking the languages when he could find someone to converse with.

He continued to keep himself fit, sometimes joining in the PT exercises that continued on a haphazard basis during the holidays, but more generally keeping to himself, pounding his sandbag or going for long runs on his own. One day, he ran only as far as The Dials and found Sam sunning himself on the front step – the very place they'd first met almost sixteen years earlier. Sam had a knotted handkerchief on his head and looked like a well-fed Beau Geste. For the moment, Jarvis forgot about his need for funds; instead, he squatted beside Sam and asked him where he'd be likely to find some gypsies.

The very word clouded over Sam's sun-drenched face, his grey-green eyes glinted with suspicion and hostility. But he quickly blinked away these thoughts, remembering that Jarvis had enjoyed a brief, but meaningful, rapport with a group of the outcasts. So, when Jarvis explained that he needed to get a message to Nelson, and that it was vital to Scruffy's departure up north to his Aunt Dolly and his to parts unknown in the Army, Sam didn't press for further details; instead, he commented drily, that gypsies could usually be found making mischief somewhere in the vicinity of Epping Forest, way beyond Shoreditch and such like, out in Essex.

Jarvis's ears pricked up when Sam suggested that a bicycle would come in handy searching the highways and byways that criss-crossed Epping's bit of so-called forest. "It's really little more'n scrubland," snorted Sam scornfully, for he had seen the great forests of Germany, and beyond, when he'd been a soldier; real forests that went on and on for weeks, not a few paltry miles. "But they likes to stick to the ol' names – even if a forest over 'ere only consists of a paltry dozen or so trees." He added, after a snorting chuckle, that Jarvis was welcome to borrow his official bike "to go an' look for yer friends." Jarvis jumped at the offer and was astride the elephantine machine and straight away pedalling away like mad with Sam's bellowed exhortation about not letting "them bleeders steal me bike" ringing in his ears, and Queenie's softer scream to "take care" as she leaned perilously out of an upstairs window, both going unanswered.

Jarvis, without really knowing where he was headed, succeeded in losing himself several times before finally emerging from Shoreditch and heading for Clapton, where a milkman stopped talking to his horse just long enough to point him towards Woodford Green. Later, discovering himself near Chingford and veering towards Loughton, he began to pick out gypsy signs in the manner Nelson had taught him, and finally found them: four caravans, whose occupants had been eyeing his progress for some time.

Once Jarvis had presented his credentials, so to speak – Nelson's name was passport enough, and explained the purpose of his visit, he was readily accepted by Dandy Hanks, the headman, who was dark and big-boned, though gaunt with it. Jarvis felt immediately at home, but he knew that he was only there for one purpose, and that was to get his letter delivered to Nelson. He had worked carefully at the letter, not wanting to give anything away in case it should fall into the wrong hands; it didn't mention his military plans, nor even Scruffy, but it did say that it was important the authorities were given the impression that he (Jarvis, though by then he'd be Beard) had gone to ground somewhere far away, and to this end it asked Nelson to send a few postcards to Mrs B. (Jarvis gave him her address because he had to, though he was loath to involve her); it asked him to keep up the pretence for as long as he could – several months, if possible, by which time he figured that the authorities would have lost interest in him, or that he might even be on his way to India.

Jarvis handed the letter to Dandy who called over a youth of about fourteen, gave him the envelope, which disappeared somewhere in the region of the boy's crutch, and muttered some instructions in his ear. The youth nodded, turned and scampered away; in a minute, he'd left the camp and was out of sight. "Your message is already on its way. Young Errol will hand it to a caravan headed for Glastonbury," said Dandy casually. "I know Nelson was somewhere near Plymouth two weeks ago. Anyway, our folk at Glastonbury will see he gets the letter – probably a lot quicker'n by post these days!"

Jarvis pleased everyone by joining a group going off to set traps in woods on a not too distant estate. They only saw one gamekeeper, but he gave them no trouble, being old and more concerned with his pipe; they set their traps and then bagged half-a-dozen or so assorted birds, using a net technique Nelson had showed him, but their greatest success came when Jarvis and one of the men, having crawled snake-like through the undergrowth with never the whisper of a sound, pounced on a pair of plump ducks. Together with several baskets of fruit and vegetables – including most of a row cabbages that had stood proudly in line under the protection of a scarecrow (which itself suffered the indignity of losing its entire wardrobe) – and a pail of eggs, they all decided it had proved a most rewarding expedition, and they returned to camp by a circuitous route with a feeling of great satisfaction.

It felt wonderful to be eating out in the open again (although the cooking had to be done on ranges inside the caravans now because of the blackout regulations), and Jarvis would have been content to live such a life for ever; but he knew this couldn't be even as he lay back in the trampled grass contemplating the serenity of the sky and its myriad twinkling sentinels. The mournful droning of unseen enemy bombers, greeted by dazzling fingers of light searching them out and the shattering explosions of anti-aircraft shells being fired with blind optimism, brought him crashing down to earth from his celestial reveries. First thing in the morning, Jarvis climbed on to his bike again, gave Dandy and those of his companions who were astir a fraternal wave, and headed back to London – and the ugly, real world.

After returning the bike to Sam, Jarvis promised Queenie – who insisted on stuffing the equivalent of breakfast, dinner and tea down him before he left – to return on Sunday, the day before he had to leave for Maidstone, for a farewell party. He'd blanched when she'd mentioned this, and hissed, "It's supposed be a huge secret, Mum!" But Queenie simply smiled and said it was; it was *their* secret. "The rest fink it's just a knees-up." Jarvis grinned back, kissed her fondly and left for his other home with Mrs B. He walked slowly, for apart from his swollen stomach, he was also carrying several bundles, but safely arrived back in Grafton Street, Scruffy greeted him like he'd been missing longer than his aunt, saying "It's been deadly here without having you ordering us about! We were worried about you."

Presenting Mrs B. with his bundles, which included half a dozen brown eggs and an assortment of cabbages and apples, Jarvis explained his cycling mission into the country. "It's all aimed at covering our tracks once we're gone," he said. "Especially mine! But, honestly, I can't see the authorities breaking off from winning the war to go looking for the likes of me – especially if they think I'm somewhere down in Devon, or even Wales. 'Course, the most perfect place would be if they thought I'd somehow got away to Ireland! Anywhere out of their reach."

The following day, Saturday, Jarvis and Scruffy sauntered round to St Boniface; the idea was for Scruffy to say his farewells, and for Jarvis simply to be seen. Scruffy remained to chat with Father Paul, while Jarvis gave his sandbag a series of farewell punches, and with each punch he muttered his new name : *Robert Beard.*

The sun rose early next morning and was already hot when Jarvis and Scruffy, with Mrs B. beaming proudly between them from beneath an enormous fruit bowl of a straw hat, and all of them in their Sunday best, made their way to The Dials. They arrived so early they met Ruth being shooed on her way to Mass at St Clare's on her own, which meant Sam was working. Ruth, who had been sulking under her hated panama, brightened at once on espying them and begged Jarvis, and Scruffy if he wanted, to accompany her to church, in which prayer she was vociferously supported by Queenie and Mrs B., who said that their domestic duties prevented them from going, too, but asked to be remembered in their prayers.

Jarvis believed both he and Scruffy had had high hopes of escaping this duty on this of all days, certain that the ritual prayers they had been mouthing as long as they could remember were enough to last the rest of their lives. But Queenie was insistent: they needed all of God's protection in their coming adventures – perhaps she guessed that neither of them was likely to see the inside of a church again for a very long time. So, on his last day as a civilian – Jarvis could still hardly believe that from tomorrow he'd be a uniformed soldier – off they went as directed with Ruth laughing happily as she skipped between her reluctant escorts, her hands tucked inside their arms.

Both boys made the best of things, though Father Daly's fearsome sermon on the evils of coveting their neighbour's wife did nothing to raise their spirits. They reluctantly dropped their smallest coins in the plate even though they desperately needed every penny for their own needs; they had bravely ignored the first collection but Ruth created such a to-do when they tried to do the same with the second that they felt obliged to dig into their pockets; and that's when they got rid of the French coins. Ruth went up to receive Communion looking for all the world like an angel, and when she returned, with the expression of a saint in heaven, she hissed, "You should have gone, too – you bad boys!" Jarvis reddened, and hissed back, "We just 'ad a whopping big breakfast, didn't we!"

Once returned to The Dials, all thoughts of angels and saints were quickly forgotten. The day really and truly began; faces that had been so solemn and bored in church, now relaxed in laughter. For a few hours, even the war was forgotten. There was roast beef and Yorkshire puddings for dinner, with trifle and cream for afters, and over a protracted tea – which was more a sort of buffet – there were hot muffins and cinnamon toast, ham sandwiches and pies, cakes and a huge red jelly, plus an assortment of drinks, both intoxicating and otherwise. Nobody concerned himself with wondering how such a feast was possible at the height of the harsh war-time rationing; this was not a day for feelings of guilt nor of recriminations, it was a time to eat, to gorge, to forget everything in its brief pleasures – even the ladies, who professed bird-like appetites and smaller stomachs, did so to repletion.

Jarvis went in search of Ruth and found her in her bedroom putting the finishing touches to a tiny, flat package tied with a rather worn piece of pink ribbon. Jarvis pushed a little parcel of his own at her: it was clumsily wrapped in newspaper.

"Will you look after George for me, Ruth?" he asked. "I can't take him where I'm going, and I think he'd be happier with you than Mrs B." He felt a little guilty as Mrs B. had carried the parcel in her bag from Battersea and had just reminded him about it.

"Of course, Jarvis," Ruth answered readily, her fingers already tearing at the paper. She withdrew the brightly-painted wooden soldier Sam had made all those years ago, and gazed fondly at it before giving its cheeky face a little kiss and laying it on her pillow beside Rosie. "Perhaps they'll fall in love and get married, like us," she giggled. "Of course I'll keep him safe for you," she added warmly, as Jarvis remained silent. Ruth turned to pick up the package she'd been tying and handed it to him. "Here," she said, "it's for you – for your birthday."

Jarvis felt a pang of embarrassment; just as he never remembered, she never forgot. It contained the usual pair of giant handkerchiefs; he would have been surprised had it been anything else; they represented a sort of special bond between them. Ruth told him that he could give one to his friend Scruffy if he wanted, because she hadn't anything else at all to give, but he shook his head. "Not this time!" Jarvis declared firmly. Scruffy would have to look to his Aunt Dolly for any future hankies.

Jarvis sat down on the bed beside her. For some reason he was especially pleased to see that she was wearing his coral necklace, but it also made him feel terribly selfish, and mean. It was the only thing he'd ever given her, and even then it was really more Queenie's gift than his. "I'm afraid I forgot your birthday again – and I haven't anything to give you even now. I'm most awfully sorry."

For just a fraction of a moment, she looked sorry, too. Then their eyes met, and she smiled up at him. "That's all right, Jarvis. I know you don't mean to be forgetful. Mummy says most men are – and have to be reminded. Tell you what," Ruth cried, and a sparkle lit her dark eyes as she smiled serenely up at him, "you could give me a kiss as my present – if you like!"

Jarvis was startled by her suggestion, and he felt his face must have shown something of his puzzlement. A kiss. He'd already given her one that morning. It seemed a strange request since she'd always had so many from him regardless of her birthday. Still, if that's all she wanted, it seemed an easy way of discharging his duty. But, as he leaned forward to bestow his gift on her nearest cheek, she leapt to her feet before his lips reached her, so he had to stand up, too.

"What's the matter?" he asked her. "Changed your mind?"

"Certainly not," she retorted, and added quickly, "I want you to give me a proper kiss, Jarvis. Not one of your usual pecks that are over and done the instant they're laid. I want a proper kiss, Jarvis, as befits a sweetheart."

"Sweetheart?" repeated Jarvis; there was that word again, and he then remembered Mrs Molly's teasing gibe, and gave an unexcited grin. "You're my sister, sort of," he told her.

"No I'm not, Jarvis. Not of any sort. I'm your sweetheart, you admitted it, remember? And I want a proper kiss," Ruth insisted determinedly. "It's the least you could give me for my birthday."

"What do you consider a proper kiss, then?" he persisted, disregarding the ones he'd received from Tilly beneath the gypsy caravan ; exciting as they'd been, especially when her fat tongue had reached down to his tonsils, she did much the same with her dogs.

She stared challengingly at him, disbelieving his ignorance in such basic matters. "Not the sort you've always given me, Jarvis," she answered tetchily. "You've pecked at my ear, my cheek, my nose and even my chin, when really kisses should be bestowed on the lips."

"I've kissed them, too," objected Jarvis, becoming flustered.

"You've pecked at them, darling," Ruth returned in a gentler tone. "You have to put more feeling into your kisses. I won't break if you press hard. Now then, Jarvis, a proper kiss, if you please – and a girl shouldn't have to ask for one, darling, not from her very own sweetheart."

Jarvis swallowed involuntarily, still unsure of where he'd gone wrong with his kisses in the past. A proper kiss, she demanded. Bloody lucky to get kissed at all. He blinked. What the devil made a kiss improper, anyway? A kiss was a kiss, wasn't it? Apparently not. Well, he wasn't going to kiss her like Tilly! In the past, if he'd had to, he'd usually aimed his lips in the general direction of a pink cheek, content to plant his offering on which ever was proffered, but Ruth was having none of that today. She wanted more. He took a half-step closer to her, at once wondered if he was improperly close, shrugged away the thought, planted his feet firmly on the floor and squared his shoulders. He was ready for battle.

Ruth gave him no time for second thoughts. She was at him, standing on tip-toes and with her hands anchored round his neck. Her eyes closed as her pink mouth closed on his, and Jarvis discovered something of the reality of kissing as her mouth opened wide in welcome and seemed determined to swallow him whole. Well, she'd never done that before. Jarvis, fearing for his tonsils, felt he was going to choke, and there wasn't a thing he could do about it – nor, he discovered, wished to do. He was transfixed: pleasurably so, even if he could scarcely breathe. Jarvis felt Ruth's tiny tongue dart in and out of his mouth, exploring its entirety, and the sensation was an experience altogether too exciting and wonderful to bear – and so utterly different to the assaults by Tilly. He was quite over-whelmed by the thrill of Ruth's passion: exquisitely so, and pressing hard against her, not wanting to lose any of the searing tremors stabbing up and down his spine as though electrical talons were devouring him. He couldn't understand it. Surely the simple communion of their tongues couldn't produce such a difference? But, yes, apparently it could, and he didn't want it ever to stop. He was conscious that Ruth had taken complete control of their embrace the instant their hot lips had touched, which he thought was only fair since it was her present. For his own part, he simply clung to her. His head was whirling, but he wanted the moment to go on for ever.

Hours later, they parted. That's what his heart told him, but, of course, the kiss lasted barely a minute or so. Once the brief touching of their tongues was over, he stood back from her, staring at her – and breathing as hard as if he'd just run up a thousand stairs. In the past, he had never thought of kissing as being anything more than a tiresome duty; something polite, like making an apology or saying "thank you," and the quicker it was over and done with, the better. Not now. Not any more. He had never known such ecstasy. He hadn't dreamed that such pleasure could be derived from a simple kiss. Oh, there was nothing simple about their kiss. It was something sublime. When, he'd finally moved his face from hers (and how his head still whirled), compelled by the urgent necessity to take in air, he could still feel their hearts pounding against each other, and he was sure his raced the faster. He opened his eyes to look at her, and the first thing he noticed was that she was a lot taller than he remembered; yes, very definitely bigger, and developing a very definite shape. She was growing up – and he'd never noticed. He heard her sigh, ever so softly, like a child in its sleep, and he swallowed hard without relief.

"Happy birthday!" Jarvis exclaimed, feeling himself returning to normal, though still tingling all over, giving her a grin of cheeky triumph as though he had done something extraordinary, instead of the other way round. He sat down on the bed, sitting straight and sure his face must be some deep scarlet colour.

"Thank you, Jarvis – and to you," Ruth exclaimed with a joyous little laugh, dropping a little curtsy before leaping on to the bed beside him.

In that moment, she did not seem at all grown-up. She was a little girl again ... or was she? Would she ever be again? Jarvis was not positively certain but he thought he was a little frightened at that moment – and him about to go off to be a soldier! Of course, it was all to do with the magic of their kiss. And all he could think of to say as he turned to look at her, and she sat with shining eyes staring up at him, was to ask: "How old are you now, Ruth? Thirteen?"

"Nearly fourteen!" corrected Ruth, a little indignantly, though there was laughter in her eyes.

Jarvis nodded, and felt on more familiar ground. "Of course," he murmured.

"So, you're leaving us," Ruth said suddenly, very softly, her eyes still fixed on his face.

It was a statement rather than a question, but its suddenness took him by surprise. It seemed too generally known that he was about to go away, but Ruth plainly had suspicions as to where he was going. What had she heard? Jarvis felt tongue-tied. "Yes," was all the answer he could find, nodding his head again in a bid to give the inadequate reply more substance. It had been given out that today's celebrations were largely to mark Scruffy's departure to join the Army, but obviously it had to be known that Jarvis was going away as well. "Yes, you know I am – everybody knows," Jarvis added, trying so hard to sound casual. "You all know I'm off to start working – on the land."

"Daddy says you're going to Kent on government service ... and Mummy that you're going to Maidstone to do some sort of war-work. Everyone tells me something ... all except you," she pressed, in a quiet, accusing voice. "There's something going on, something you're all keeping secret from me. Even you – and we've always shared our secrets. You never even mentioned any of this to me."

"I'm sorry," Jarvis muttered dully, sorry now that their moment of rapture was giving way to normality, and noting her reproachful tone. "I've not exactly had much opportunity to tell you anything, have I? I haven't seen you for weeks."

"Is it true? You're going to Maidstone?"

"Yes, of course."

"Liar!" The word flew from her lips like an arrow, but there didn't seem to be any barbs attached to it, though it was followed at once by a sharp accusation. "I don't believe you! None of you!"

Jarvis frowned, but remained silent.

"People don't normally tell me things – grown-up things, so when they do, I know something's going on that they don't think I ought to know about. All right, so they think it's safe to tell me you're going away somewhere in Kent, and drop hints about you going to work on a farm – but I don't believe that for a moment."

"What do you imagine I might be doing?" he teased, wondering if she knew anything or was just guessing. Of course, she might have overheard her parents talking. Kids had bigger ears than elephants!

"You're running away to join the Army with that Scruffy, that's what! Admit it!" she cried breathlessly, her eyes ablaze with the conviction of her accusation.

"Don't be daft," Jarvis replied stonily. Blast the girl; she'd got it half right, somehow. Of course, she was just guessing. "I'm not running anywhere, you silly girl!" he countered, "I've got a railway warrant for Maidstone Station, so there, Miss Know-all!"

"You're still off to be a soldier – admit it!" she insisted, dismissing the warrant as if it didn't exist, or, at any rate, was irrelevant.

"Absolute rubbish!" Jarvis declared.

"Admit it!" she cried again.

"It's just childish nonsense," he protested weakly, squirming under her scrutiny.

"Admit it!" Ruth repeated shrilly.

"No," Jarvis said, but there was no strength in the word, and it vanished altogether as he blustered on. "Stop it, Ruth. I can't ... I mustn't ... it's secret."

"Admit it, Jarvis! Admit it! Admit it!" she sang out repeatedly, her voice becoming stronger as his grew weaker, her eyes never wavering.

In the end, he silenced her by placing his hand gently over her mouth. She reacted, first, by giving his hand a little nip with her teeth, and then, by giving his palm the softest, wettest of kisses. He laughed, and snatched his hand away.

"All right, all right, I'll tell you," Jarvis said, jumping up; and he did. He told her almost every blessed thing, holding back only the details he'd kept from Sam. "There now! I hope you're satisfied!" Jarvis felt angry – at himself – for yielding, and telling her so much. It would serve him right if he was caught and locked up in the Tower of London. He wondered, though with a grim smile, if they still stuck heads on spikes there. He thrust his hands deep into his pockets and stared down at her from several paces away. He wondered if he mightn't have made a terrible mistake in telling her his secret, but he knew in his heart of hearts that he hadn't been able to help himself; knew, too, that it was a relief to have confided in her. He didn't believe there should be secrets between them. Not if they were really sweethearts, like she said. "Now you know the lot. But ... " Jarvis told her warningly in the most serious tone he could conjure up, " ... if you breathe a word ... "

"As if I ever would!" she broke in, bristling at the very suggestion.

"If you did I'd spend the rest of my life in quod," Jarvis declared flatly, convincing himself that either Sam or Queenie would probably have told her everything as soon as he was gone.

"And I'd come to visit you every day and bring you hot meat pies and baskets of fruit and lovely flowers – and, of course, files and things like that. And we could have long kisses through the prison bars."

Jarvis burst out laughing. He didn't imagine any prison would hold him long with Ruth knocking on the door. He found it hard to think of her as a child any more, and it was that kiss that still hovered in his thoughts when he looked at her. "Let's hope it won't come to that, heh!" he said cheerily. "Really, I'm tremendously looking forward to being in the Army."

"I'll write to you every day, Jarvis," Ruth cried passionately.

"No, you mustn't," Jarvis told her sharply. "Not until I'm safely out of the country and in India, anyway."

Ruth looked so disappointed that he thought she was going to argue again, but she only asked: "How long will that be?"

Jarvis shrugged. "I'll be in training here in England for about six months, and then there's the voyage to India. God knows how long that will take. Say, another three or four months. Then there'll be more training there. So I should think it'll be a good year, maybe more, before I'm settled down safely somewhere in India."

"Gosh!" exclaimed Ruth, clearly regarding anything longer than a week as a lifetime. "You'll have forgotten all about me by then."

"Never!" he assured her.

"And you will write back to me?" She seemed not to appreciate that he would have to write to her first since she wouldn't know where he was stationed.

"On my honour!" Jarvis promised her faithfully. "Every chance I get," he added, to be on the safe side. "And you must remember my name's now Robert Beard, so don't address me as Jarvis Brook or I'll never get it. And you'll have to learn to be patient, like me. You must understand, Ruth, I won't be able to write until after I've left England – and we'll both have to be very careful what we say."

She nodded acceptance of this requirement, and to his agreeable surprise she seemed satisfied with his assurances, or as satisfied as a girl can be when she knows she's about to be deserted, possibly for years. The thought seemed to prompt another question. "How long will you be away, do you think, Jarvis?"

"I've no idea," he admitted, truthfully. "Years, I imagine. It'll depend on when the Army's done with me, I suppose – and the war, of course."

A week, a month, a year – it was all the same to Ruth; it spelled out a long, long time.   "You'll come back to us, won't you, Jarvis?" she asked, simply, but her eyes seemed haunted by the fear that he mightn't.

"Of course, you ninny!"

"And we'll always be sweethearts – like we said?"

"Always," Jarvis replied, rather too quickly. Sweethearts? What did that really mean? It was a childish, girlish thing. The word was unknown at the Home where there we no girls. Besides, this was no time for such silliness: her still at school, and him off to war. They'd have to do with being "best friends," as always. Safer that way. On the other hand, his mouth was still so warm and bruised from their kissing, he wasn't so sure. Still, was he really expected to marry her sometime in the future? Was he really and truly committed? Would it be so terrible? His mind was in turmoil as the questions kept on coming.

"I'll pray for you, Jarvis, every day of my life so that you'll come home safe and sound to us," Ruth whispered so earnestly she looked in pain.

"With such protection what on earth can happen to me?" Jarvis said, smiling.

"Mind you don't go falling for any of them Indian princesses! I don't trust girls who wear veils over their faces ... I'm sure it's a snare to trap the unwary – people like you!" Ruth looked to be teasing, but Jarvis wondered if she might not be warning him, too.

"I shall return to you alone!" he said with a majestic bow, and a twinkle in his eyes.

Ruth clapped her hands, apparently feeling satisfied with the state of affairs for the moment. She was in the process of curtsying in her turn, and making something of a pig's ear over the attempt in that she finished up sitting on the floor, when a hubbub downstairs reminded them that there was a party in progress. They felt recovered enough to rush down to join in, and it really was a wonderful end to a truly memorable day. A day crowded with happy incidents, comic moments, fun and laughter and lots and lots of kisses – though none the equal of that earlier one! Would there ever be? In the weeks and months that followed, Jarvis often felt himself smiling as he recalled fragments of memories of that last evening.

He remembered Scruffy being taught to dance by several girls and impressing them with his light-footedness; he remembered Queenie and Mrs B., both exceedingly jolly after savouring several alcoholic beverages, falling off their chairs when they pulled a cracker, and laughing like drains as they sat in a confused heap on the floor; he remembered Mrs Molly appearing in her shabby black garments but brightening the occasion with her flowers, which she showered among them; he remembered skinny little Hannah looking quite lovely in a dress borrowed from Ruth and her copper hair flying as she danced round and round with anybody who asked her, and by herself when they didn't; he remembered Millie, the barmaid with all the children, with her blonde hair for once freed from its confining knot and entertaining them all with her delightful voice; he remembered Fred Akers looking almost handsome with his new set of teeth which he kept flashing at everyone; he remembered Sam, the lovable giant, who for once didn't seem to be creaking, toasting everybody present, and many – including Winston Churchill (thrice), Roosevelt and "that Frog de Gaulle" – who were not, and eventually dropping off into a stertorous sleep from which he occasionally emerged to offer some strange toast (both Dick Whittington and his cat came to mind) or to render a few muddled lines of a song – *Run, Rabbit, Run* seemed a favourite.

And, of course, there was Ruth. He remembered she kept commandeering him for a dancing partner and, as they whirled gracefully together, thinking she fitted very comfortably, and contentedly, in his arms. Indeed, her contentment had been so infectious he was moved to ask her, while the record was turned over, "Have you forgiven me?" She looked up with puzzled eyes. "What for?" she asked in turn. "For not telling you I was leaving to join the Army. You see, I was so afraid you'd blabber about it at school."

"Oh, Jarvis," Ruth whispered back, not moving out of his arms nor moving her eyes from his, "I'm not a child. I'd never do anything that might bring danger to you. I'd die first."

"Don't do that!" Jarvis cried, with mock seriousness, and then grinning broadly. "And, Ruth, I won't forget to write – I promise."

Ruth, smiling as though he had just delivered a whole sackful of letters, stared almost fiercely up into his twinkling eyes and declared in a voice that was both calm and passionate: "Oooh, Jarvis! If only I were a man, too! Then, I could come with you. Gosh, it must be simply super to be a man and be able to go off to war whenever you like and fight battles! I'd love to do that ... beside you, of course."

"I think I'd sooner know you were safe at home – waiting," he laughed out loud, and on an impulse he planted a kiss firmly on Ruth's delighted lips declaring, "That's to make up for the birthdays I forgot!" Then he remembered surrendering her to Scruffy and then galloping off with a happily hysterical Hannah, followed by many others.

Jarvis took care not to get involved in any further discussions of a serious nature and, with this in mind, danced with anybody to hand, ate whatever was presented and generally made a point of always being part of a group. He also embarked on a brief experiment with bitter beer under the tutelage of Queenie. She allowed him a half-pint of some dark brew, and threw up her hands at his immediate expression of distaste. "Straight down, lovey!" she instructed. Jarvis obeyed, and was grateful to see the empty bottom of the glass, thinking the ale quite the vilest concoction he'd ever tasted. Queenie at once insisted on the second half and, producing a somewhat paler draught, gave the command "Bottoms up, lovey!" He did precisely that ... and just made it to the kitchen sink, where he brought it all up.

"There now, lovey!" said Queenie, amiably, bustling around, clearing up and placing a pint of iced water before him. "Get that down you – slowly." She watched him as he sipped obediently at the glass, the sips getting gradually longer. "There's nuffink wrong wiv booze, Jarvis-love," she told him, "but never be in a hurry wiv it. Always remember, whatever she is, she'll be stronger than you. Be patient, lovey. The day'll come when yer wants a drink ... even need one. When the time comes, you'll know it. No need to jump the fence. Now, finish yer water – it's got summat in it wot'll settle yer tummy."

Then, as if it was something she'd just thought of, she added with a quiet intensity, "You an' trouble seem to 'ave walked 'and in 'and all yer life, Jarvis, an' mostly it's bin yer own fault – yes it 'as, lovey," she smiled, squeezing his hands. "Only, just remember, where you're goin' now, you've got to be twice as careful as ever you was in the past. So, don't do anyfink silly … don't go being too brave an' getting yerself 'urt." She blinked wetly, gave a wretched smile and walked off hurriedly – and Jarvis determined not to get himself killed. She'd never forgive him!

When the time came to disperse, everyone did so speedily and with a minimal display of emotion. It was very much a night for stiff upper lips and no fuss. Queenie briefly crushed Jarvis before tucking a ten-shilling note into the brand-new wallet the staff had given him; she was quite unable to say a word, having to make do with a mouthed "Gawd bless yer, lovey!" in his ear. Ruth gave him a single, dry, peck of a kiss, forced a heartbreak of a smile and fled upstairs followed by her mother. Sam, who probably hadn't been as asleep as he made out, woke up as if on cue to place another note – it turned out to be a whole pound – in the wallet, and stood in the doorway silently waving good-bye as Jarvis departed with Mrs B. and Scruffy. Almost as an afterthought, he called after them: "Keep yer head down, Jarvis!"

□   *"That were Sam's battle cry," murmured Queenie, "he insisted Ruth included it in all her letters to Jarvis, an' she did, bless 'er. It's a good thing Jarvis kept every one of them she sent over the years. Dozens of 'em. Wonder how many he sent her."*

"Not many, I bet," said Mrs B. "Only a couple come to my place."

"I 'spect she's 'ad a few we don't know abaht. Be nice if she'd share 'em with us," Queenie mused out loud. "But they'd be love-letters, wouldn't they. Girls don't share them. Still, be lovely if she read them to us." She turned to take hold of Beard's hand. "Is any of this ringing any bells, Jarvis? It's largely 'er letters you've been listening to. If it weren't for them we wouldn't know nuffink. Me an' Mrs B. just filled in the gaps. Didn't that kiss bring anyfink back? She told me abaht it so of'en."

Beard stared hard into her beseeching grey eyes, striving for some sign of recognition, but finding nothing. "I'm sorry, but no. I don't think I'm the lucky chap. Nothing is coming back to me," he told her gently, but bluntly, adding wryly, "I like to think I'd remember a kiss like that, but I don't. It's just a rather lovely story. Perhaps, if Ruth were here …"

"We're desperately trying to find her," Queenie interposed. "She lives in America now, but …" She let go of Jarvis's hand and turned towards her husband, seated beside her, and queried, "What

about it, John? We need Ruth here, now."

"She's in America still," he reminded her. "Don't know where."

"Well? They claim to have invented the phone. Call her!"

"I keep trying, and they tell me she's touring and out of reach at present. I'll call again later – it's the middle of the night there now."

"Stupid country!" muttered Queenie. John grinned, and kissed the back of her neck.

"Well, we come to the Army part of the story now, Jarvis, perhaps something here will jog your memory while we hunt for Ruth," declared Queenie to the others, "but I'll hand over the story-telling to the general here, that's his side of things."

But it was Mrs B. who stepped in first to see both Jarvis and Scruffy off in search of their destinies.

Chapter Sixteen

Grafton Street, Battersea, September, 1941

Operation Double Bluff moved into its final phase later that same day for, of course, it was well past midnight before they were back in Grafton Street. It began early because Jarvis and Scruffy were both far too excited to lay in bed, sleep being out of the question. They were up well before their usual time; long before they needed to be. For the umpteenth time they checked on their possessions, but really there was practically nothing for either of them to do. Even Scruffy found it unnecessary to pack and unpack as a matter of course; he was content simply to count his bits and pieces: one crammed suitcase and four near-to-bursting parcels. It wasn't that he had much in the way of possessions, merely that what he had was excessively bulky when it came to containing them.

Jarvis had no such problems. Everything he was taking fitted into Mrs B.'s little cardboard attaché case. Sam had given Scruffy a large slab of bacon hacked from a carcass delivered, wrapped in cheesecloth and draped over a delivery bicycle, in the backyard of The Dials the previous day by man wearing a green bowler. Jarvis just happened to witness the delivery, which Sam had explained as "salvage from a blitzed warehouse down on the docks." Scruffy squeezed his slab into his case for Aunt Dolly. Jarvis's "share" had been given directly to Mrs B. who, even now, was cutting slices for their breakfast.

When they had exhausted their pretensions of completing their packing, they sat on one of the beds while Jarvis meticulously sorted out their personal documents and, as diligently, gave Scruffy his. Next, he took out his wallet, still exuding the magical smell of new leather, and extracted the various notes he'd been given. Two pounds in total! Scruffy stared at it and whistled softly; then looked at Jarvis with some suspicion. It did seem an enormous sum – it was for someone who had seldom had two pennies at the same time. Even as Jarvis wondered when he would ever be so rich again, he decided to give most of it to Scruffy, keeping back only a few coins in case he needed some small change for a bun or some such thing.

For about half-an-hour they rehearsed their new identities for the very last time. Scruffy became Robert Parkin for good and all, and Jarvis became Robert Beard – and hoped to remain so for an equally long time. It was all very confusing, even comical, for a while, with questions being tossed from one Robert to the other and being variously received, and sometimes being greeted so blankly it was tantamount to being ignored altogether. All in all, it was not a very good rehearsal, and did not augur well for the future – with the curtain about to rise, and the play to begin.

Jarvis thought they tried too hard – and got into a muddle as to who was who. They were sure things would improve once they were really living their roles, but Jarvis believed they were both relieved when Mrs B. called them down to eat.

In the event, breakfast was an uncomfortable affair. Their minds were too full of a million other things to spare thoughts about food; they ate mechanically, hardly knowing what they ate. Poor Mrs B., suffering a hangover from the previous night's celebrations, was close to tears at their imminent departure and hovered wretchedly about the table making mountains of toast that no one had any stomach for. She busied herself – between endless cups of tea – making piles of sandwiches for their journeys and, afterwards, they passed an hour playing rummy at which, for once, neither Jarvis nor Scruffy could raise sufficient spirit even to attempt to cheat. Finally, it was time to go, and mightily relieved they all were, each for different reasons – Mrs B. because she couldn't hold back her tears a moment longer. They hugged and kissed her, promising faithfully never to forget her and assuring her she would always be their extra special aunt, and left her to fill her teapot with her tears. And then they were off ... Scruffy, looking for all the world like a Sherpa porter, practically hidden beneath his voluminous packages, while Jarvis carried his weighty suitcase and his own little attaché case.

At King's Cross-St Pancras Stations, by the time they'd discovered which was the one Scruffy wanted and bought his ticket, which wasn't as much as they'd feared, his train was almost due to depart so they were spared a protracted farewell. They piled all his belongings somewhat precariously on the luggage racks and then stood on the platform looking rather self-consciously at each other, and each secretly wishing the whistle would blow. Finally, it did, and they shook hands, formally at first and then rather more vigorously, before flinging their arms around each other and hugging one another just as hard as they could.

"Do you think we'll ever meet again, Biff?" asked Scruffy, in a very small voice.

"We'd jolly well better not!" Jarvis retorted, with a forced laugh.

"Oh, no. Of course not," agreed Scruffy, nodding his head. "So, this is it then?" he muttered, breaking loose and moving towards his compartment. He turned after only a pace and, trying to appear composed, said: "Cheerio, Biffer, old mate. Don't get yourself shot or anything like that, will you!"

"I'll try not. Good luck, old Scruff. Give my love to our Aunt Dolly," Jarvis called after him.

Scruffy still hesitated. "You're sure you'll be all right, Jarvis?" he asked, suddenly anxious. "I know you've always been a hard nut ... never scared of anything and always fighting someone ... but this is the real thing, mate. I couldn't live with myself if anything happened to you. I'd feel terrible, I really would."

"I wouldn't feel so clever myself," said Jarvis casually, then, seeing the other's seriousness, he grinned and added, "'Course I'll be all right, Scruff. If I ain't, it won't really matter, will it?"

It probably wasn't the cleverest thing to say in the circumstances. Scruffy looked increasingly wretched. If you start blubbing, mate, I'll wham you one somewhere that'll bring more than tears to your eyes, Jarvis grated to himself. Aloud he told him: "I'll be fine, Scruff. It's what I've always dreamed of doing. Don't you worry about me, matey. Just look after the aunt. I bet she'll be lovely."

Whistles shrilled with fresh urgency and Scruffy, his moment of panic gone, seemed to recover his equanimity. He gave a tentative smile as an elderly porter shepherded him towards the train, and called back: "We'd both better shut up and remember who we're supposed to be, otherwise we're both likely to be shot right here on Platform Nine!"

He climbed aboard, slamming the door behind him as the guard blew his whistle one last time and waved his green flag. "Goodbye, Mr Parkin!" Jarvis shouted. "Good-bye, Mr Beard!" yelled back Scruffy. The train began to move, the great engine belching smoke and hissing out clouds of steam which immediately hid the carriages from view. Jarvis continued waving with quite violent enthusiasm even though he couldn't see the train, much less Scruffy, and went on doing so until even the smoke had disappeared. The train had vanished, too. It was only then that Jarvis felt that a very vital part of his life was gone; gone with that train. Suddenly the station seemed a very quiet and lonely place, and he turned and hurried away, gripping his attaché case like it was the only friend he had in the world.

It was a long walk to Victoria Station and he briefly considered taking a bus, before deciding he'd better conserve his money. Jarvis arrived in good time, patted the inside pocket of his jacket (this had been bought only last week by Mrs B. at a bring-and-buy for sixpence) to feel his railway warrant and the envelope containing his orders, and marched confidently across the concourse, his boots (exquisitely shiny) echoing resolution with every stride. It crossed his mind that some of the young bloods hurrying alongside him might be destined to be his comrades-in-arms, and the thought filled him with pride and eager anticipation. Instinctively, he straightened his back, thrust out his chest and held his head high as he approached his platform, delighted to observe that he towered above the two young redcaps standing at the gate.

His train was already waiting and he clambered eagerly aboard, impatient to discover his destiny. Whatever might happen, he felt that this was what he'd been training for all his life, and even the recollection of Grannie Zilla's prophecy of "something terrible" happening to him in the distant future failed to diminish his enthusiasm, for he also remembered that she'd said he would be a leader of men. Well, he was off to war, and he was excited at the prospect. Hitler had better watch out if they ever met – though this seemed unlikely since Jarvis was headed for India, and Hitler only wanted all of Europe, for now.

Jarvis began munching the sandwiches Mrs B. had packed for him, and it seemed to him he could already hear distant guns calling his name. Be patient. I'm coming. Jarvis Brook ... oops! shouldn't that be Robert Beard! ... Robert Beard is coming as fast as he can.

In fact, Robert Beard was asleep before the train pulled out.

□ *And so Mrs B. concluded her contribution to the Jarvis Brook saga or, as both she Queenie, declared "This were the moment when we accepted you'd become Robert Beard, Jarvis." Queenie added in a strained voice, "But you was always my Jarvis ...still is."*

"I'm sorry to belie your belief, ladies, but as far as I can recall, I've had no other name," said Beard softly, adding a small smile. "I'm told I am Robert Beard and my papers confirm it. I'm sorry."

"Oh, Jarvis – Mr Beard, I'm so sorry, too," Queenie whispered back.

Beard had lately been allowed to sit up for short spells and been promised a change to exercises out of his bed – "But not quite yet, you understand," Dr C. had told him last week, or was it the week before? The promise had come with a nodding smile, which Beard had learned to mistrust. No, he didn't understand. He wanted to leap out of the bed now and hug this woman who claimed to be his mother, or something like one. He didn't know her from Adam – oops, that should be Eve, he corrected himself, but he so wanted to. He felt like some alien creature being known by so many, and him not recognising a soul.

"But," he told her, and there was sincerity in his words, "I'm enjoying your story, and coming to like your young man, Jarvis." Her eyes thanked him. "Please go on," he said.

"My part is almost done for the moment, dear," Queenie said, explaining that so much of what she'd related belonged to the letters Ruth had written to him, and which had survived in better condition than himself. "Now, these gentlemen must take over. I know nothing of what you got up to in yer soldier life. You never told us nuffink over the years."

The gentlemen beside her had the look of military men: one was Beard's age, the other old enough to be their father. The young one answered to the name of Bertie: his once golden hair was greying and thinning and there were lines around his amber eyes and he had a stiff leg, perhaps a false one, but when he smiled he lit up the room. The other, sitting as though at attention, was known still simply as Gibbs: he wore a suit of grey, his hair was grey and his luxuriant moustache was grey: his craggy face provided the only change of colour – purplish; the grey eyes, however, were as alert as ever behind the spectacles.

Bertie it was who took up the story – after Queenie had accepted that as Jarvis Brook had adopted the name of Robert Beard at this point in his life, that was how he should be referred to in future: the foreseeable future, that is.

Chapter Seventeen

Maidstone Barracks, 1 September, 1941

Robert Beard was still fast asleep when the train juddered to a halt at Maidstone: his station; and was still in this somnolent state when the train screeched to a halt at Dover, the terminal. A prodding by the guard returned him to consciousness, and after relating his tale of woe to a thoroughly unsympathetic RTO lance-corporal, he was sent on his way back towards Maidstone three hours later with the derisory recommendation that he remain awake for the next hour, at least.

This was not the spectacular start to his Army career he'd envisaged. However, when he finally arrived at Maidstone Barracks and presented himself to his platoon sergeant, he was greeted quite amiably. "Glad you decided to join us after all, Beard. It's not often one of our young gentlemen goes AWOL before he's actually arrived!" said Sgt Jack Bone, who was tall, almost distinguished-looking and seemed to think his remark terribly witty. His grey-blue eyes actually sparkled as he added, "Lights out in 20 minutes, so if you want to write to anyone to let 'em know you've arrived safe and sound an' think the Army's bloody marvellous – which it is, be sharp about it."

Beard shook his head. "Not me, sergeant. I don't have any relatives. I'm an orphan," he declared quite cheerily. He would dearly have loved to have been able to ascribe Queenie and Sam as his own, in any capacity, and Ruth, too, but they weren't, none of them. They all belonged in a different life. Jarvis Brook's life, and he was now Robert Beard – and God help him, and Scruffy, if ever he forgot it for a moment.

Sgt Bone, pushing open the door of the barrack-room which was next-door to his own quarters, uttered a gravelly sound that might have been a chuckle and muttered, "That's a bloody change, anyway. Most of the chaps I get here seem to come from ruddy big castles an' have more bleedin' relatives than Old Nick." He evidently thought he'd said more than enough for the moment for he shut his mouth with a suddenness that threatened to bite his tongue off. He frowned, and jerked a thumb at the top bunk of a two-tier contraption that didn't look particularly stable and which creaked prodigiously as the occupant of the lower berth moved. "That's yours." And, giving Beard a nod of dismissal and giving a scowl round the rest of the barrack-room, wheeled about and marched noisily away.

Beard surveyed his bunk: on it were a crumpled, doubled-up palliasse, a lumpy mass that represented a pillow and three grey blankets – all laying on the metallic mesh that served as the bed's springs. It didn't look very comfortable, nor particularly safe, but Beard was sure he'd slept on a lot worse. Just so long as it didn't collapse on the poor sod underneath! And, of course, at that moment the "poor sod" poked his out from the lower berth to introduce himself. "The name's Huntington-Hartwell. Neville Humbert de la Bare Huntington-Hartwell, actually," he proclaimed, extending a thin, manicured hand that contained surprising strength. "Terrible mouthful, isn't it? The Army seems to have settled for just plain Hartwell, but my friends call me Bertie."

"Hello," cried Beard, greatly impressed by the formidable mouthful of names, and determined to be counted among the other's friends. "I'm Beard. Plain Robert Beard." He looked the other straight in the eye, and added with a grin: "I don't know that I've got any friends outside the orphanage, so you can call me anything you like."

Bertie gave a carefree chuckle. "Then I shall call you Bobbie."

"Thank you – Bertie."

Bertie's face, a little older than his own, was crowned with a wavy halo of fair, almost yellow hair that gave it the added appearance of belonging to some Greek god; a golden-tanned skin gave further credence to this unlikely theory, as did the sparkling, amber eyes and the so-friendly smile.

Beard subsequently learned that Bertie was the scion of a barony whose seat was Highways, which was in Dorset, Wiltshire and Hampshire: it really depended on what part of the estate you happened to be standing. But Bertie was most unlikely to inherit the title. He had two elder brothers: Edmund, the eldest of the trio, was a captain in the Royal Hampshire Regiment and serving somewhere in North Africa; and Simon, the middle one, was a lieutenant in the Wiltshire Regiment – only he'd transferred to the Commandos, and it was anybody's guess as to where he might be serving. There was also a sister, Perdita, who, happily, was better known as Poppy. She was a year younger than Bertie, who described her as stunningly beautiful, horribly spoilt, and dearly loved. She was something or other in the Red Cross, but only when the weather was fine and it suited her.

Adonis unwound himself and emerged from the lower bunk. He was of the size befitting a god, which in earthly terms made him a whole inch shorter than Beard, slim and well-proportioned. He was wearing sky-blue silk pyjamas with a monogram on the breast pocket and smelt divinely (if you liked such things, which Beard didn't particularly, having never had the pleasure before) of talcum powder and the like, and the tantalizing scent of some heavenly after-shave (Beard was madly jealous). Together they made up his bunk, and were safely in their respective bunks when the lights went out without warning.

Beard, content to lie there in his underpants – as he'd always done, was musing on Bertie's silk pyjamas, when, presently, a faint sound beneath him broke into his eager thoughts, and he cocked an ear. "Well, well, well ... I didn't know gods snored!" he grinned, and immediately fell into an untroubled sleep.

        This was the beginning of a friendship that endured throughout their training. Both took naturally to soldiering, and the Army reciprocated. It was the uniform that set Beard on the road. The moment he put it on he felt himself no longer a boy: the uniform was his mantle of manhood. From that moment he took everything in his stride, from the complexities of parade ground drilling to firing off five-pounders and Boys anti-tank guns. He quickly showed leadership qualities and it was no surprise that he emerged as one of the top three cadets of the intake when their initial training was completed on November 29 : the rest would be completed in India. But first would come two weeks' embarkation leave.

        Bertie had prevailed upon Beard to spend his leave with him at his family's home, pointing out that Beard had no place of his own to go, nor any family – and that, besides, he'd be lost without his company. Beard, after the briefest show of hesitation, agreed most willingly, but he was determined to sneak a last glimpse of Mrs B. – and perhaps Queenie and the rest before they reported back for embarkation, and insisted he must have a couple of days in London at the end in which to say a proper goodbye to his old landlady. Bertie, certain there must be at least the hint of a girlfriend, had raised an elegant eyebrow, but had said nothing beyond saying, "Of course, old man." Their train seemed determined not to move for the duration of hostilities, but finally the engine puffed into life an hour late, and they were on their way – at a snail's pace, and stopping at every excuse.

        Upbridge Halt, where they finally descended, was a nothing place. No shops, no church, no school, not even a pub; all these were at Upbridge proper, out of sight behind a sprawling wooded hill and about seven miles farther down the track. There was a single row of twelve stone cottages which stood in pairs and were branded with the baron's coat of arms: they stood in a respectful line opposite the station; and at a respectful distance, too.

        It was snowing quite steadily, although not settling, not to any great degree anyway. As the station's sole attendant, Ray Smithens, had locked everything up and left a note to the effect that he was on duty with the Home Guard, Bertie had no qualms about marching up to one of the cottages and asking to be driven up to Highways. He did it so pleasantly, and so naturally, that the householder invited "young Master Bertie" and Beard inside for a drink in the warm while he went off to harness Snow White to a trap. Beard was very impressed: it was his first experience of the way things were done when his lordship required a favour.

        The house came into view between stands of silver birch, and the occasional giant oak or beech, all standing gaunt and naked and bowing as the relentless winter wind directed them, long before they swayed up the gravelly drive. It was a massive house of many parts: its several additions over the centuries had made it a rather unattractive pile. The central Tudor portion, complete with oriel windows perched on massive timber supports, had a battlemented tower on top with two flag-poles. Bertie said that in happier days, and better weather, a Union Jack and a gold and silver flag bearing the family arms always hung there; the custom had had to be suspended *pro tem* following repeated machine-gun attacks on them. In the background, surrounding the house in a sort of protective way, were much larger hills, now being fast buried beneath the driving snow, with extensive woodlands protecting them in turn. Good poaching country, was Beard's immediate thought. Nelson would be happy here, he smiled inwardly.

Bertie dismissed their driver with two half-crowns and the season's greetings, and, having announced their arrival by lifting the giant knocker and letting it thunder the message far and wide, lifted an equally large catch on the massive, heavily-studded door, which swung open with surprising ease. Both men rushed inside out of the cold and wet, the door slamming shut behind them with the crash of a cannon. Their first impulse, after shaking themselves reasonably dry, was to dump their rifles, kitbags and other burdensome accoutrements with an unceremonious clatter on the flagstone floor. Then Beard had his first chance of seeing the grandeur in which the gentry lived.

It didn't exactly take his breath away at first glance, apart from the sheer spaciousness of everything, because some areas had been boarded off for the duration; even so, to a boy raised in an former workhouse, it was still rather grand. The hallway, with its magnificent sweep of twin staircases with banisters of burnished oak that was black with age, was the size of a railway station – that being the yardstick by which Beard gauged anything of real size. There were massive paintings of men with silly wigs and women with even more bizarre hairdos on the panelled walls, gloomy tapestries hung here and there, impressive in size but doing little to improve the scenery (in Beard's estimation), and bits of porcelain and glassware crowded various recesses. The centre of the hall was dominated by a vast shining mahogany table on which stood a huge urn covered with gaudily coloured dragons, snakes, pagodas and such like. Beard thought it hideous, like the paintings, and assumed this meant it was priceless.

Bertie, after "Hallooing" in vain to someone called Stafford – "our ancient butler … something of a family heirloom," he explained, led the way through wide corridors towards the family quarters, and gave a rat-a-tat-tat on a large cream-coloured door that proved to be the drawing-room. His parents were seated round a gigantic fireplace – it was big enough to accommodate a cart-horse and had seats on each side in the inglenook – where a substantial log fire blazed and crackled, spitting out sparks for all it was worth, as he and Beard entered; their two faces were already peering round the shoulders of their large leather seats to see who was there. They gazed, startled, at the two figures, and then wonder sprang into their eyes, and for a moment they were incapable of movement, but only for a moment.

Lady Pamella, for so the mother was known, was the first out of her chair. With a cry that was almost a shriek, she flung herself at Bertie, who stepped nimbly forward and caught her tall but slight frame in his arms. Mother and son swayed, locked in a frenzied embrace, she moaning and laughing and crying all at the same time, but still trying to talk to him as she pulled his head down and endeavoured to kiss every inch of his face, and ran her fingers feverishly over those parts of his body she could reach as if to make sure he was all there; he simply stood there, absorbing her joyous assault, and laughingly exchanging kisses and whispered endearments, while she had her fill. Finally, satisfied for the moment, she pushed him from her, but barely more than arm's length, so that she could examine him properly; and he stood there like an attentive child waiting for her nod of approval.

Instead, she frowned. "What have they done to your hair, darling?" she cried out in anguish, stepping forward to run long pianist's fingers through his shorn locks.

Bertie laughed out loud, almost with relief that this was all she could find to complain about. "They're keeping it for me till after the war," he joked.

"And are you a captain yet?" she asked in all seriousness, examining his uniform and vaguely wondering why he wasn't wearing any pretty medal ribbons.

"No, mother – not even an officer. And I haven't won any medals either – they don't give you any for serving in the snowdrifts of Maidstone!" he smiled, guessing her thoughts from the way she fingered the unadorned area on his breast. "We're both still only cadets, darling." He turned and led Beard forward. "Let me introduce you to Robert Beard, mother – or Bobbie, as I call him. He's my very best friend, and was the best of all the cadets – and I think he may well be a general one day."

Beard stepped forward with a polite smile and outstretched hand, but she would have none of that, not today, not for her Bertie's best friend, and insisted on planting a motherly kiss on both his cheeks.

"Pretend my kisses are from your own dear mother," she gushed breathlessly, all excited by the occasion, and feeling like crying and laughing in her happiness.

"Thank you," said Beard, deciding on the moment not to mention he was an orphan. He exchanged warning glances with Bertie, who looked up from exchanging bear-hugs with his father. This was followed by a considerable amount of backslapping and most unmilitary saluting on Bertie's part which the other hugely enjoyed. Then it was Beard's turn to meet the father, who introduced himself as Lord Thierry and explained he'd inherited the name through some ancestor's indiscretion in being born in France.

And so their leave began – and it began on a low note because, inevitably, one of the first questions asked was whether they'd be home for Christmas. "Sorry, Mother," cried Bertie, pulling a face. "Our leave ends December 15 and I expect we'll be on the high seas while you're all tucking into turkey and plum pudding." And Beard didn't improve things when Poppy – tall, golden-haired and utterly gorgeous – appeared just as winter darkness descended outside early in the afternoon. She spotted the familiar, beloved figure of Bertie the moment she entered the room, uttered a little cry of delight, and jumped at him, delivering a real smacker on his lips, and several more on either cheek. For several minutes they hugged each other and boisterously exchanged the banter of brother and sister, mostly about boyfriends and girlfriends. And then it was that Beard, who had been mildly jealous in that he wished he'd been on the receiving end of such affection, dropped his clanger.

In the moment of their introduction, she asked, "Do you ride, Mr Beard?" and he'd had to admit he did not, and then compounded his shortcoming by saying he wasn't particularly keen on horses, or any other animal, come to that. He was hardly aware of his words, wishing only to have her attention as long as possible. He could have bitten off his tongue as he saw the frown leap into her eyes, and she snatched her hand back into her own safe keeping and turned abruptly away. "Really, Mr Beard," she remarked icily, "horses are far better company than most men I've met." Beard, who had thought her quite the most beautiful girl he'd ever seen, felt very chastened, certain that he'd never love again, though instantly revived by the arrival of Stafford, "the family heirloom," with a tray of high spirits. He grabbed the nearest glass to hand, and the world seemed a lot friendlier.

As Bertie was wholly preoccupied with his mother and Poppy had moved to join them, Beard and Lord Thierry chatted away, mainly about the state of the war. Lord Thierry was briefly curious about his guest's home and background, but Beard, apart from vaguely dropping the word London and giving the suggestion that his family were "something in the police," wouldn't be drawn in case he should let something slip that might create problems. He didn't dare relax his guard for an instant. He must always remember that he was Robert Beard, and no one else. Jarvis Brook didn't exist any more; he was dead ... at least, for the foreseeable future. So he quickly turned the conversation to other topics, though his inquiry as to there being any gypsies in the district was a clumsy mistake. He should have known that few, if any, landowners regarded gypsies with anything but hostility. Lord Thierry was no exception. He gave Beard a quick hard look, and growled

"There'd better not be!" Beard closed his mouth abruptly and nodded in serious agreement; but, inside, he was smiling, and wondering on whose land Nelson was foraging.

After several drinks, pressed on him by Bertie, whose laughing eyes suggested he was perfectly aware of his friend's torment, and an excellent dinner washed down by several bottles rescued from Stafford, Beard felt a lot more composed (actually, he was rather tipsy; he must be, or was it simply in his imagination that Poppy smiled at him several times in the course of the evening?) and decided the world wasn't such a bad place after all.

On waking the following morning, he found himself with a thick head, but with his heart intact; the snow had moved on, and a sun of sorts was shining; in fact, all was right with the world, and he was reasonably sure he could survive the loss of Poppy. The ten days of their leave galloped by and the delicious Poppy, far from avoiding Beard (possibly to repair the wounds of their initial meeting, but more likely so as to give her mother more time alone with Bertie), sought him out like an extra brother and proceeded to instruct him in the rudiments of sitting on a horse without falling off too often. This sounded safer than falling in love, he thought – but it wasn't, of course. Getting on the beast was an art in itself, staying on was plain scary. He was an ungainly sight perched perilously high on the horse's back and gripping its mane for dear life, but he told himself he enjoyed the lessons even if he didn't exactly master them and occasionally managed a rueful grin before sliding off to finish up sitting in a puddle – which sent them both into fits of laughter.

Their friendship blossomed still further one morning when Beard's mount took it into her head to take him for a gallop, and away they went with Beard yelling at the animal to "Whoa!" and Poppy standing, hands on hips, quite unable to stop herself laughing. She found the pair of them, some half an hour later, at the Laughing Pig at Upbridge – and Beard insisted he'd simply gone where he was taken. "I imagine she was thirsty – good thing she knew where to go," he grinned, as Poppy rode up. "I hope they don't put you in the cavalry when you get to India, Bobbie!" she giggled, dismounting. "You might do better aboard an elephant!" Leaving their horses guzzling at their own trough, they disappeared inside the pub to quench their own thirsts.

Sometimes, Lady Pamella commandeered both boys, tucking an arm inside both theirs and marching them all over the place – fearful of letting them go, and never ceasing to chatter. Bertie and Poppy squabbled incessantly, but in the playful manner of siblings. In the evenings they played piano duets together, going mildly mad as they thundered at great speed through such things as *The Robin's Return*. Poppy was by far the more accomplished pianist and some of her solo performances were extraordinarily good, if Beard did but know it; but he had eyes more for her than ears for the music.

When the weather permitted, and Beard wasn't falling off horses, there were also walks over the estate with the host. Lord Thierry was amazed, impressed and thoughtful over Beard's skill in setting traps; he was thoughtful because he wondered how and where the boy had learned his skills. He was delighted, however, when, as often as not, the snares yielded something for the kitchen. In a moment of confidence, when they walked back to the house with several rabbits dangling from a stick, he told Beard that the reason Smithens was so seldom to be found at his place of work at the Halt had nothing to do with the rarity of trains, nor with his Home Guard duties either, but was because – he was quite convinced – the confounded man was everlastingly poaching ... and mostly on *his* land! "He's a clever devil, too," allowed his lordship. "Never been able to catch him red-handed, of course. But, you mark my words, it's Raymond all right! I'm not sure the cheeky blighter doesn't sell the proceeds of his thievery back to me." Beard was suitably impressed, and stayed impressively silent. "Monstrous!" he exclaimed to Lord Thierry.

There were, too, other visits to the Laughing Pig, for Lord Thierry believed all soldiers should be acquainted with the benefits of strong drink in order that they should fight the harder in battle. It was a theory expounded to him by Stafford, but he saw no reason to doubt its efficacy. On one such visit, Beard had a barmaid called Bunty discreetly pointed out to him. "That's our Stafford's lady-love!" whispered Bertie, his eyes smiling beneath their lashes. "She who bore his love-child a couple of years back."

There was a low, mocking burst of laughter round the table. "Well, if it weren't his, he got the blame – or the credit of it!" declared Lord Thierry in a hushed, gravelly voice. There was no need for whispers though, for Bunty (fat, fortyish and oozing amorousness) came sidling up to their table and straight off enquired after her inconstant lover. "The sod hardly ever comes to see his son," she complained, with a wide smile, addressing herself largely to his lordship. "We called 'im Oliver Stanley – after them two film comics, mainly 'cos we all thought it a bit of a laugh at our age!" She gave a long hoarse cackle, thinking her remark terribly funny. His lordship produced a small grin, Beard just looked amused, but Bertie laughed wholeheartedly, and patted the woman's bottom comfortingly. "Hardly ever gives me anything for the poor mite, either," she went on, giving Bertie an encouraging glance. Lord Thierry produced a ten-shilling note which disappeared in a flash into the cleavage scarcely concealed by her scarlet blouse; Bertie discovered a half-crown which he dropped into the same receptacle, and Beard entering into the spirit of the occasion donated a florin, hoping it wasn't one of Maggs's! "Now then, Bunty, bring us some more drinks so's we can toast the health of this scamp of yours," said Lord Thierry, amiably. "Which one do you mean, yer lordship? There's another warming up in the oven!" declared Bunty saucily, mincing off.

Beard gave Stafford a closer look when the next opportunity presented itself, but saw only a tallish, slightly bent man, extremely lean and almost completely bald, with rubicund cheeks that suggested either an affinity to strong drink or a serious heart condition in an otherwise white and unremarkable face. Generally, his gait and the richness of his breath supported the former theory. Certainly a pair of thinly blue eyes peering through thick lenses gave no hint of the womanizer behind. And the man must be well into his sixties, if not beyond. Smiling, Beard shook his head: he was amazed, impressed. He decided Stafford must have an amazing line in chat with the ladies.

But Beard was about to discover a little more about the way of the world himself. Without a doubt it would prove to be the high point – or low point – of his stay at Highways. It happened at the party held on the last night of their leave when everyone danced to records played on a radiogram and drank whatever Stafford could be enticed into releasing from *his* safe-keeping. Beard was quite a success on the dance-floor. "I'm surprised at this, Bobbie," Poppy cried archly in his arms as he whirled her about during a fast-moving waltz, "I imagined you boys in cloisters" – she had wheedled from Bertie the fact that Beard was an orphan – "led such a dull life." Beard grinned and said smoothly, "There was a convent close by where we were obliged to partner the girls." This was only partly true; he'd learned most of his dancing on Ruth's feet. "They taught you very well," smiled Poppy, and she wondered what else these convent girls had taught him.

It was all very noisy and gay, with lots of uniforms and pretty girls in their prettiest frocks, and Beard suddenly became aware that he seemed to be continuously in the company of the same girl: and he didn't mind a bit. Miss Georgina Challinor was pretty and blonde, with very red lips which she kept moistening with the tip of her tiny pink tongue, grey cat's eyes that seemed never to leave him, and she wore a tight-fitting red dress that displayed her firm, erect breasts in a most aggressive manner. A bit of all right, as he and Bertie would have labelled her. The thought made him wonder, fleetingly, if perhaps he'd been set up by Bertie – or even Poppy – but he brushed the thought aside, deciding that Georgina had obviously picked him out as the handsomest unattached male in sight. It's the uniform, he told himself modestly. Wait till I'm a proper officer!

After a certain amount of clinch-type dancing, during which they barely moved off the same spot on the floor, Georgina suddenly took hold of Beard's hand and led him at fox-trot pace away. She was plainly familiar with the layout of the house, for after leading him up the main staircase, she took him along several long corridors, up another stairway and along another corridor, and finally into a bedroom from which no sound of the party could be heard. She turned the key in the lock and, still holding his hand, pulled him straight over to the huge double bed where, without any preliminaries, she proceeded to devour him with her red mouth. Georgina's lips were in constant motion and her scalding tongue almost choked him with its frenzied gyrations; it was like an electric eel gone berserk. He tried to pull away, but didn't seem able to find the strength – or was it that he didn't have the will-power? And then, the pair of them breathing in deep bursts through open mouths, she pulled away of her own accord, and her hands ran lasciviously down his body pausing only to squeeze the throbbing bulge in the area of his groin. They appeared to groan in unison.

"Let's do it, shall we, darling!" she whispered urgently.

Without another word they both began throwing off clothes in a sort of wild desperation; at least, she did. Beard, beside himself in his ecstatic pain, couldn't believe the speed with which Georgina undressed, but of course once her dress had slithered with the merest whisper to the floor, he saw that she wasn't wearing much else – and that little was soon gone. "Hurry!" she panted heavily as he sat staring at her with his fingers still fiddling with his tunic buttons. "Of course," he whispered back thickly, his eyes mesmerized by her nudity. Tilly hadn't prepared him for this! It wasn't fair, he seemed to have far more clothes to take off than her. Georgina lay back on the bed and watched him struggling feverishly out of his uniform, impatient at his slowness and hating every button that kept him from her, but finally the fumbling was done and he was ready for her; as naked as on his natal day. She stretched her arms wide to receive him. "Lover!" she cried throatily. "Come and love me!"

He came at her like a greyhound out of its trap, except that he was more like a bull in a china shop. He really had little idea how to go about the assault, and Georgina finding his approach altogether too rough to be pleasurable, especially when an elbow came close to blinding her, gathered her strength and pushed him off her before he became too aroused and spoilt everything. "You have got a ... something, haven't you, darling?" she panted, anxiously, alarmed about the bruises she was certain he had inflicted upon her already. And then came the body blow, for her. He didn't have a contraceptive: didn't even seem to know what one was – and there he was growing larger by the second. By the time Georgina had dived among her clothes on the floor and retrieved the condom she kept in her bra for such emergencies, it was too late. Beard was all spent and limp – and remained so. Georgina gave a little scream of frustration. "You useless bastard!" she spat out furiously. She flung herself off the bed and began pulling on her clothes again; and when she had done, she stormed out of the room without a backward glance, nor a single word, slamming the door behind her.

Beard sat on the edge of the bed for some minutes, just staring at the panels of the heavy door. At first he had blushed so deeply he thought his head would burst into flames, but he'd cooled down now and this prompted him to dress – which he did almost as quickly as he'd undressed. He wasn't used to failure, and even less to incompetence, but the truth of the matter was that he'd been out of his depth here. The priests at the Homes had never told them anything about sex – only that even thinking about it was a mortal sin; and it was the one thing the Army assumed he knew all about, since it was the one subject they didn't have a manual for. He'd be bloody well properly equipped next time. He fled from the room and made his way back to the party area, certain that all eyes were on him and knew his secret. He glanced quickly all round for Georgina, but she was nowhere to be seen. He breathed a sigh of relief, and found Bertie at his side proffering him a glass of champagne.

"And what have you been up to, Bobbie-boy, to make our Georgie leave so hurriedly?" asked Bertie casually, his laughing eyes never leaving his friend's face, which immediately turned quite red again.

"I think I upset her, a little," said Beard quietly, trying to appear casual.

Bertie laughed gleefully and slapped Beard on his back as they moved to the bar for refills. Beard was pretty sure his friend knew what he'd been up to, and confessed, "She knew more about you-know-what than I did!" He sighed. "Even so, I almost managed it." Bertie laughed so violently he splashed them both with champagne. Beard gave a wry smile of his own, his face returning more to its normal colouring. He drained his glass, and whirled away to dance with the first free girl to cross his path. She just happened to be Poppy.

"Did you hit Georgina, Bobbie?" she asked straight away, and he wasn't sure if she was accusing him or mocking him.

"No. Of course not," Beard protested, amazed at the very idea, but relaxing when he realised she was only teasing.

"She had to leave ... all of a sudden ... said she had a terrible toothache," said Poppy smoothly, her eyes sparkling and the corners of her mouth twitching in a merry laugh. "Her face did look a little swollen – especially round one eye. Looked almost like a black eye."

"Perhaps she walked into something – a door, maybe," suggested Beard, who really was unaware of any injury except to her pride. He added with a wink, "I think I might have spoiled her evening ... unintentionally!"

Poppy laughed out loud and pulled his head down to plant a warm kiss on his lips – the same lips that Georgina had been devouring so recently. It was incredible how different Poppy's lips felt. "Don't look so unhappy, you silly boy," Poppy told him, squeezing his hand. "I do believe she terrified you!" she giggled.

Beard wasn't sure she mightn't be right. One thing he was certain of, he felt far safer and happier in Poppy's arms ... and just then the music stopped, and she darted off to make someone else happy.

The day of departure came and Lady Pamella's farewell of her son was very moving, and quite painful to witness. Beard was pleased to be distracted by Poppy, the warmth of her farewell being all that he could have wished for. She clasped her hands around his neck and whispered, "Are you sure you don't want Georgina's address?" He could only blush and shake his head in reply. She gave him another kiss. "Don't go and do anything silly – like get yourself shot!" she smiled up at him, and then dashed off to repeat her farewells to Bertie.

It was as if they would never part, but suddenly they were and then they were all in a horse-drawn carriage and clip-clopping down to the Halt. There, on the platform, Mr Smithens waited to hurry them on their way. A tiny man, with a face like a wizened owl, he looked quite smart in his uniform in spite of the shiny patches at the elbows. He was fussy, efficient and servilely respectful to the party from the big house, constantly bowing his short frame and touching the peak of his cap, but all the while impatient to blow his whistle. Fortunately the train was on time, and Lady Pamella didn't have to hold back her tears any longer as the two aspiring heroes sped away towards distant battlefields.

But first, Beard had those two days he'd allowed himself in which to see – from a distance if must be, his own loved ones. He felt reasonably safe in the name of Beard, who, after all, was quite entitled to spend his leave in London, or anywhere else he chose; so long as nobody saw him as shouldn't.

"Can you amuse yourself for a couple of days, Bertie?" he asked urgently as soon as they arrived in London. They had slept on the train which had been diverted and halted for hours due to air raids, and it was now almost seven on Saturday morning – and they didn't have to report in until Monday, December 8. "I'm duty-bound to say farewell to my dear landlady – she was like another mother to me." Beard stooped to gather up his kit, and added, "And there's others I want to see, if I can."

"Aha, so Georgina did give you her address, you rotter!" laughed Bertie. "But, yes, of course I can amuse myself, there must be several fiancées dying to love me. The family has a flat in Brewer Street, Soho. I'll be staying there. Here, I'll write down the address for you. Guard it with your life." Bertie hastily scribbled down the address and handed it to Beard, who read what was written, nodded his head, and tucked the leaf of paper safely away in his breast pocket. "Whatever you get up to, Bobbie, you must be at this address on Monday morning no later than 8 o'clock, and bring a taxi. Remember, if you're late, I won't be there."

"I'll be there, never fear," grinned Beard, hoisting his kitbag over his shoulder. "Don't keep me waiting, Bertie. Have fun."

"You give that Ruth of yours a kiss from me," Bertie said with twinkling eyes.

Beard blushed; he hadn't been aware he'd even mentioned Ruth, certainly not to the extent that Bertie would remember her name, and in terms of affection. God! he'd have to watch his mouth better than this. He hadn't given little Ruth a thought in a month or more. "I will," he promised Bertie, not knowing who he'd be kissing before the day was over, but expecting she'd be among the lucky girls. "I will," he repeated.

"Make sure you do – leave Georgina for me!" cried Bertie, laughing so heartily he startled a flock of pigeons into flight.

The two men shook hands outside the station, and strode off in opposite directions.

It was as though she had been watching out for him. The moment Beard turned into Grafton Street the door flew open and out rushed Mrs B. shrieking "Jarvis!" still drying her hands on a tea cloth. Her arms flew up, the tea cloth went flying, and she flung herself at him, and burst into tears – the echoes of that forbidden name still filling the street.

Beard raised his eyes in mock helplessness. Would nobody remember! He retrieved the tea towel and propelled Mrs B. back into the house, sat her down in her favourite chair beside the immaculate, sputtering range, and made her a cup of tea while she enjoyed her cry. Presently, when she'd calmed down, he told her gently: "You simply must remember, Mrs B., that I am now *Robert Beard.*"

"Even when there's just the two of us?" she protested.

"Always," he insisted firmly. "It's true what they say: Walls do have ears! And it'll only take a whisper from one Nosy Parker to land me in it. It's best to be always on your guard. You never can tell who might be listening. Careless talk does cost lives, so let's try and make sure mine isn't one of them!" They both enjoyed a little laugh, and Mrs B. – muttering "Well, I won't call you Scruffy!" – had another cup of tea before he continued. "Now, give me all the news. Has there been much of a hue and cry for me? Any news of Scruffy? What about Queenie and the rest at The Dials? And what about your two boys – are they safe and sound?"

She couldn't keep up with his flood of questions, and burst out laughing, slopping tea all over the place – mainly herself. While Beard mopped up, she told him her sons were still in Africa, but now in Egypt – or it might be Libya, and wrote to her when they could – "They're good boys," she smiled dreamily – to say they were well and enjoying the sunshine and the warm waters of the Mediterranean, but were terribly bored and homesick. The poor dears! No, she hadn't heard a word concerning Scruffy, but she presumed this in itself was good news for that had been the plan, hadn't it? Beard nodded, but still wished there'd been some sort of news about his old chum. Christ! was it really only three months since they'd parted? It felt more like three years.

It seemed nobody had been particularly concerned over the disappearance of Jarvis Brook, which pleased Beard in one sense, but disappointed him in another; he felt entitled to be missed: it was his right! Father Neame, the rector at the Home, had made the loudest noise, but his voice muted appreciably once the council's allotment in respect of Jarvis Brook was withdrawn. The police had shown virtually no interest in the matter at all. This was doubtless due to Nelson. Two days after Jarvis had vanished, Mrs B. had received a postcard showing an unpronounceable Welsh slag-heap on which Jarvis (yes, it was positively Jarvis Brook's writing, both Father Neame and Mrs B. assured the already bored police) had written that he was having a lovely time and wasn't coming back. A week later, there had been a short letter from Cork in Ireland in which he said he was hoping to get on a boat for Australia as a deck hand, and then came another card with a picture of lots of boats on the River Shannon from Limerick with the cryptic message: Nearly there! For several weeks after that there had been no word, and Mrs B. had begun to wonder if perhaps he really was there – in this Australia-place. Then, one morning, not long ago, the last of the picture postcards had arrived – from America! The picture was of an enormous and bustling Lake Patacong and it had been posted in Paterson, New Jersey, in the United States of America! Nelson, who hadn't stirred from his caravan site near Guildford during the whole of the winter, had done Jarvis (alias Beard) proud, ensuring that all sorts of friends posted everything on carefully chosen dates. The card from America was the deciding factor. The police, whose search had been very superficial from the start, lost interest in Jarvis completely. He was the Yanks' problem now. As for Robert Beard, nobody had ever needed to look for him; he was in the Army where he should be, and doing very nicely, according to a casual enquiry.

Beard clapped his hands enthusiastically. Oh, well done, Nelson! And from one brief family, he turned to one of longer standing. "And Queenie?" he asked eagerly.

"Oh, wot a one she is!" exclaimed Mrs B., breaking out into a merry laugh. "We've become very close friends since you've been gorn. We goes shopping togevver – an' in some very strange places ... backs of huge lorries, down dark alley-ways an' in odd little corners, whopping big ware'ouses – an' even on barges! Tell you one fing, Jarvis – or whatever I'm s'pposed to call yer, I ain't never bin short of anyfink since I knowed 'er, an' that's a fact! An' nobody arsks me for no coupons – nor 'ardly any money, neither. But I fink I've got yer Queenie to thank for that ... she's a love!" Mrs B. had instinctively lowered her voice as she confided these activities, but now she raised it again, and her eyes twinkled.

"You haven't even mentioned little Ruth's name, you bad boy," went on Mrs B. "I seen a lot of her, too." Mrs B.'s smile widened at the sudden light in his eyes at the mention of Ruth. "'Course, she ain't so very little no more; shootin' up like I don't know what – a proper little beanstalk. Be a big gel by the time she's done growin' – like 'er farvver!" She started chuckling with her face deep in her tea cup, and emerged spluttering and spraying tea at Beard, who danced back out of range. When she'd recovered, she exclaimed: "But, she don't arf rattle on, that little miss! She never stops arskin' after yer, Jarvis – like she wants to be the first to know if you've 'ad yer 'ead blowed orf! Bless 'er. Gawd knows wot she'd do if you 'ad – break 'er little 'art, it would. Break all our bleedin' 'arts, an' that's a fact."

"It wouldn't do mine a lot of good, either," laughed Beard, leaning forward and giving Mrs B. a comforting kiss – which set her off crying again! "Tell you what, Mrs B. Since nobody seems to be looking for me – an' I've got papers to prove I'm Robert Beard and that I'm on legitimate leave, let's take a chance ... an' pop round to The Dials tonight and surprise 'em all. What do you say?"

"Oh! They'd be so 'appy, Jarvis. An' I know it'd make you 'appy, too."

"OK. It's settled," decided Beard, who couldn't bear the thought of going away without seeing Queenie and the rest. Not when he was so close to them. And, the more he thought about it, the risk did seem positively non-existent since it was supposed he was in America, thanks to the crafty Nelson – God bless him! Still, he wouldn't take any unnecessary chances – not with just tomorrow to get through. "I'd best take all my gear because they're certain to insist on me stopping there the night. We'll wait until just before opening time," he told Mrs B., "then you'll have to nip in ahead of me to prepare them. I'll go in the back way and go straight upstairs – but, for heaven's sake, be discreet – and remind everyone it's Robert Beard that's visiting them, not ... you-know-who! And *you* remember it, too!"

"Yes, Jarvis," replied Mrs B. without thinking, and they both laughed loudly.

"Fine pair of spies we'd make!" declared Beard, raising his eyes to the ceiling in mock despair.

They arrived without incident at The Dials; it had been dark since early afternoon, and the blackout made it darker still. As Beard, kitbag sitting atop his back-pack and his rifle shouldered, loitered near the back entrance, Mrs B. disappeared inside through another door with much bustling excitement. Almost immediately, Queenie came crashing out the front door screaming, "Jarvis! Where the 'ell are you, Jarvis!" in a voice that could be heard the length and breadth of the street, and probably as far as India itself.

Beard felt himself go cold all over, but, horrified though he might be at her deafening use of his name, he couldn't prevent himself from laughing either, and, as Queenie came out one door bawling out his name to the world, he moved swiftly in through another ... and there on the stairs was Ruth, standing perfectly still, her mouth wide open. She had heard Mrs B.'s excessively loud whisper that Jarvis was outside and hadn't dared to believe her ears; and now she hardly dared to believe her eyes. But the shock lasted only a moment or two, and then a glow of supreme happiness suffused her incredulous face and she jumped the remaining stairs in two bounds and ran straight into his widely spread arms joyously screaming "Jarvis! Jarvis! Jarvis!" at full pitch.

Beard gave a shudder, and for the moment gave up the impossible struggle to insist that his name was Robert Beard. Nobody appeared to be in the mood to pay any heed to such a directive, being quite happy to throw caution to the wind – and him to a firing squad! Hannah's coppery head appeared from somewhere and she shrieked "Jarvis!" too, and so did Millie, who poked her white face out from one of the bars, only her cry of welcome was at a considerably lower pitch. Beard wondered if he really cared at that moment; he felt so deliriously happy to be home with his own loved ones, his pretend family, no matter for how briefly. These two days might have to last him a lifetime. Gathering up all his gear again, Beard strode upstairs with Ruth at his heels. He had barely had a chance to dump everything on to her bed before Queenie pounded into the room, puffing and red-faced, but with shining eyes and laughing mouth. "Come'n give me a hug an' a kiss, Jarvis-lovey!"

Beard moved straight into his dear Queenie's arms; and, after she'd crushed him half to death and left bruises all over his face with her fierce kisses, he had to stand there like a wayward schoolboy while she held his hands in a vice and bombarded him with questions. Was he well? Was he warm enough? Was he on leave, or on the run? Was he sure? How long was he staying? Only till tomorrow! (A stifled sob came from Ruth's direction, which Queenie echoed with a prolonged sniff of her own). Were they feeding him properly? Was he sure? Was he keeping regular? (A snigger from Ruth was rebuked by Queenie with a "You'll get yer backside properly walloped in a minute, miss!") Why hadn't he written to let her know he was alive? Was he hungry? Well, of course, he was. When hadn't he been? Anyone could see he was starving! With that, she grabbed his hand and led him off to her kitchen and the sacred Aga, and as he was being dragged through the door he turned to wink back at Ruth, who showed him her tongue – and then immediately mouthed a "Hurry back," and sent him on his way with a child's kiss borne on the palm of her hand and wafted after him with tiny fluttering fingers.

In the kitchen, where Mrs B. was already sipping a cup of tea,

Queenie pushed Beard into a chair at the familiar table, crowded as ever, and busied herself checking the contents of the stove, in particular a simmering stew; she added a few extra titbits. "You'n Mrs B. can eat wiv Sam when 'e gets in – which shouldn't be too long, less'n there's a blinkin' air raid, then Gawd knows when he'll be in." She gave him a huge cup of coffee and a jar of biscuits to keep him going, while she prepared endless more vegetables for his benefit. He didn't mention that Mrs B. had made him a huge omelette stuffed with bacon and mushrooms for lunch, and various other titbits during the afternoon.

But Beard was a good trencherman and Queenie could not fault the way he tackled the heaped plate she set before him: the stew was enlarged with at least six different vegetables, and this was followed almost immediately with a huge portion of rhubarb and apple crumble and custard. He declined repeated offers of seconds, and they spent the rest of the evening in noisy talk. When they could scarcely keep their eyes open, Beard retrieved his kit from Ruth's room to his own old one, she following behind carrying his rifle. If she had any thoughts of lingering there, they were dispelled by the appearance of Queenie who told her kindly, "Kiss 'im good night, love, then get off to yer own bed."

The next morning, Beard had thought he'd be the first downstairs, but there in the kitchen were both Queenie and Mrs B., cups of tea in hand; and it was only quarter to six.

Queenie, on her feet immediately, gave him a gentle morning kiss, then chided him, "You should've 'ad a lie in, Jarvis. Don't 'spect yer get much chance of one in the Army."

"I always wake up at the same time. It's in-built. Whatever time I gets to bed, I still wake at the same time," said Beard, with a shrug and a smile.

Queenie was already cooking bacon for him, and as this was frying she put a mug of tea in front of him as he sat beside Mrs B. "I'll do you a coupla bacon sarnies fer now, love, and that'll 'ave ter keep yer goin' till dinner-time," she told him. "We'll 'ave a huge feast around midday an' later on a bit of a party to send yer on yer way."

"Sounds good to me, Mum," he told her cheerfully. "Where's Sam? I haven't seen him since I arrived. Is he still asleep?"

"'E ain't bin 'ome, yet," Queenie sighed. "Must've got 'is 'ead down at the station for a bit. Don't know what kept 'im on duty so long, though. Didn't 'ear no air raid in the night. Ah, 'ere comes Ruth – must've smelled the bacon."

Sam arrived about ten full of excitement. "You 'eard abaht this new war wiv the Japanese?" he asked, plonking himself beside Beard after divesting himself of respirator, helmet and things.

Four blank faces stared at him. "Japan," repeated Beard slowly, placing the country in his mind, and showing vague interest. "When did this happen?"

"During the night – only it were morning-time in Hawaii, which is somewhere in the Pacific ocean – near China, it is," declared Sam knowledgeably. "It's bin on the wireless. It seems the Japanese has sunk the American fleet there using hundreds of planes from aircraft carriers. It's awful. Wonder if it'll affect you, Jarvis? Get you into the fightin' long before you – or any of us expected?" he said, making no attempt to hide the concern in his voice.

Beard shrugged. "Shouldn't think so," he said calmly. "Probably be over in a few days. And anyway, won't it be more an American thing, and nothing to do with us?"

"Not a bit of it. Them Japs has invaded all our places out there – Malaya an' Burma, and Hong Kong, too," retorted Sam. "An' that were before they declared war on us – cheeky devils."

"India's a vast country," Beard returned, dismissively, "with lots of other vast countries between it and where the Japanese are fighting. It won't affect me. I'll be sipping tea on some lady's shady veranda in far away India." He ignored Ruth's hiss at this suggestion. "This Japanese thing is billions of miles from India, Mum," he declared breezily, turning to smile at Queenie. "I'll be lucky if I ever hear a gun fired in anger – so stop worrying. You'll be in far more danger back here with the Blitz than me!"

Queenie wasn't convinced, and in her heart she did worry, for all of them, but there wasn't anything she could do about things. She smiled grimly back at Jarvis, whom she loved as dearly as if he had been her own flesh and blood. She shook her head in bewilderment. "You don't even shave, lovey," she accused him, as though this was a sound reason for boycotting the war, or at least a reasonable excuse for him staying out of it.

"He's bin tryin' ter for ages," grinned Mrs B., looking up from her empty cup. "Only nuffink won't come ... not a whisker!"

"I can't help it," Beard smiled apologetically at her, and stroked his smooth chin, "I'm doing my best, honest."

"How old are you, really, lovey? Wot wiv this new war and all, it's so 'ard to remember everyfing wiv yer runnin' arahnd pretendin' to be some'n else – an' 'im years older'n wot you is," exclaimed Queenie fearfully, disconcerted by his so-boyish smile.

"He's just sixteen, Mummy!" announced Ruth, staring at him with her chin in her cupped hands and her elbows spread on the table. She boldly added: "And he should be at school – like me!"

"Sixteen and a quarter!" corrected Beard with a superior toss of his head.

"And you forgot my birthday – as usual," she cried sharply.

"Well, I couldn't do much about it, could I?" he said defensively.

"We did agree not to communicate till I was safely out of the country. It's only because nobody seems to be looking for me – thanks to my brilliant planning, I might say, that I risked coming here today ... because I missed you all so much!" He paused to let that sink in, seemed moderately satisfied, and then turned to Ruth and asked teasingly: "So, how old are you now – twelve?"

"Fourteen!" she shouted furiously.

"That means you're only just turned thirteen," he joshed.

"And two whole months, you horrid thing!" she flashed back resentfully, adding, as he burst into laughter, "I hate you!"

"Stop it, you two. We've only got Jarvis wiv us till tomorrer mornin', an' I won't 'ave 'is visit spoilt by this silly nonsense," broke in Queenie sternly, but with a twinkle in her eyes. "Stop it at once, or ... or I'll pack the pair of you off to bed – wivvout no dinner!"

"I only want to keep him safe at home with us, Mummy," said Ruth, with a quiet intensity.

"I know, darling; we all do," said Queenie, gently, sniffing over a steaming pan. "But there ain't a lot 'e can do abaht fings, not now. 'E's in the Army, an' 'e's got to do wot 'e's told. Be good practice fer when 'e's wedded!" She laughed at this, Mrs B. cackled and Ruth simply smiled dreamily, and coloured softly. "An' anyway, it's summat 'e's set 'is mind on, an' 'e ain't abaht to change it, even if 'e could, for nobody – even for us wot loves 'im," Queenie continued, shaking her head till she was in danger of unwinding it. "All we can do is wait till it's over an' done wiv. It's wot wimmin spend their lives doin', ducks ... waitin'!"

"Waitin'," echoed Mrs B., her voice coming through the steam of a fresh cup of tea. "We spend our lives waitin' 'and an' foot on 'em ... 'cos we love 'em so."

Beard felt a bit of an ogre, but he kept silent – deciding he'd only put his foot in it if he said anything.

"When can we call you Jarvis again?" Ruth asked earnestly, for all the world as if she'd ever called him anything else.

"When it's safe," he replied simply. "Until then, you must all carry on calling me Robert Beard – Bobbie, if you prefer."

Ruth grimaced. "Yes, Jarvis," she said pointedly. "Don't forget to send us your address so we can write to you."

"Yes, of course I will," he assured her, "but I won't have a proper address till I'm settled in India, so you must try and be patient a good bit longer. And if you don't address me as Robert Beard your letters will never find me – and for heaven's sake be careful what you say in them because all letters are censored."

"Outrageous!" vociferated Queenie, who'd never written a proper letter in her life. She sat down heavily at the table and distributed steaming fingers of jam tart between Beard and Ruth, and licked her own fingers with relish.

"I shall expect a photograph of you with your elephant and wearing your poshest scarlet uniform and all your medals," insisted Ruth, in between sucking at her fingers.

Beard nodded cautiously. He didn't think scarlet uniforms were worn any more, and he was sure no medals were awarded for elephant-riding, and doubted if he'd qualify for any for simply holding the fort in the vast peace of India. He concentrated on his piece of tart, hoping for more; there wasn't.

Ruth disappeared, ostensibly to wash her hands, and returned in a twinkling, rather self-consciously, wearing Beard's famous coral necklace; everyone noticed it, and studiously made no comment on it, content to exchange knowing winks and secret smiles between themselves. Out of the corner of his eye, Beard viewed the colourful little necklace bouncing at her throat, and felt well pleased with his – or rather, Queenie's, purchase. He thought it suited Ruth very well. She, meanwhile, bustled around giving the impression of helping her mother with the final preparations of the meal, until Queenie somewhat impatiently suggested that she keep from under her feet by laying the table. Easier said than done. There was not a vacant inch of space on the surface, and Ruth stared uncertainly at the battlefield. Queenie, seeing her dilemma, gave her a quick hug by way of encouragement, and swooped everything up in the table-cloth and dumped the lot with a crash in an already overcrowded cupboard; there was a further crash fro within; a series of flicks with a tea cloth and a quick sweep with her ham-fist at anything she'd missed, and the table was cleared. A fresh table-cloth was produced and Ruth commenced laying out the cutlery very precisely; she then found serviettes and serving mats, and retrieved such condiments as she thought might be needed from the cupboard floor ... and all the while she was hoping and praying that she'd be allowed to stay up very, very late so as not to miss a moment of Jarvis's brief stay.

Sam having shed his boots and most of his uniform, returned (still creaking) with two foaming pints of bitter and led Beard into a quiet snuggery where they could talk in peace. "You 'ave learned to drink, I presume, young man?" he grinned. Beard nodded, and they spent upwards of half-an-hour toasting each other, their regiments and several others, the King and Queen and a great many of their subjects, by which time they were deep into their second pints, and Beard was grateful that Bertie had patiently, and knowledgeably, tutored him in the manly art of drinking. Even so, the call to dinner was a welcome respite.

Dinner was eaten in comparative silence, apart, that is, from the noise of eating itself. But towards the end of the meal, remarkable at that period of the war for its prodigious proportions, let alone the wide assortment of goodies on offer, Sam elbowed Beard and remarked, "So, you got away wiv it, heh Jarvis! There's not a blinkin' soul in the world lookin' fer you, s'far's I know. 'Course it were all yer schemin', I know – a proper bleedin' villain you'd 'ave made! – but I reckon yer Mr Nelson deserves a 'eap of credit, too. Lov-erly picture cards 'e sent!" he snorted in admiration of the rogue – and all of his fellow conspirators. "Are you plannin' to stay bein' Robert Beard for good'n all ... or will yer become yerself again? I 'opes yer become our Jarvis again, 'cos it ain't easy rememberin' yer new moniker."

Beard shrugged off the questions, making a non-committal response, but they were ones that he had given much private thought to – without reaching any definite conclusion, other than one day, when the right moment presented itself, he would revert to his rightful name: Jarvis Brook. Well, it was certainly more his right name than Robert Beard, and he didn't imagine he'd ever find a truer one. However, for the time being at least, his only concern was to safeguard the supposed identities of both himself and Scruffy; and already far too many people seemed to know, and be involved in, the secret. The sooner he was safely out of the country, the better. He hoped Scruffy was well hidden, too.

When everything was eaten, the washing-up done and they had sat digesting their dinner – digested, too, the latest news of the war which didn't sound very good, they forgot it all over a bit of a sing-song and this merrymaking set the pattern for the night, which developed into something of a knees-up: noisy and jolly. Numbers were boosted by some of the pub regulars who, Sam assured a momentarily appalled Beard, were the last on God's earth ever to assist the police in their enquiries, so his identity was safe. It seemed to Beard that half London was there, but there was nothing he could do about it and, with a shrug to the consequences, he determined to have a good time while he could. If they shot him at dawn, so be it.

One of the very first on the scene was Mrs Molly, complete with floral helmet and her customary black frock-coat, who distributed what flowers she had left from her great wicker basket, drank two glasses of stout and then deposited a big kiss on Ruth's cheek, leaving an equally large frothy witness of the event. Mrs Molly, her red beak ablaze, then demanded to see Beard and promptly gave him a smacker, too. "My two love-birds!" she trilled, taking hold of Ruth's hand and watching with delight as colour flooded her cheeks and then breaking out into a loud cackle as Beard's broad back disappeared in the throng.

There was lots of talking, with many tall tales told; singing of old favourites that brought tears to the eyes of some of the older ones, which they just as eagerly sought to hide by burying their noses in tumblers of what they fancied; and dancing to Henry Hall records on the gramophone which everyone seemed to enjoy immensely despite the clumsiness of their movements. When the pub officially closed, the bar staff joined in the revelries, together with several transient Servicemen determined to utilize every second of their leaves.

Ruth, steadfastly refusing to admit to tiredness, danced almost incessantly with Beard, releasing him from the crowded floor only to monopolize him in any corner they could squeeze into, and where she still had to almost shout to make her whispers heard; she relinquished him, grudgingly, only to Queenie and – but only because they took no notice of her objections, to the barmaids Mavis and Millie, and even Hannah tugged at his sleeve and insisted on her turn. Beard also partnered a sprightly old woman, known as the Mafeking Widow; in spite of her energy (which seemed limited to the one dance) there appeared to be nothing of her beneath her widow's weeds, which included a boa and an ugly black hat with part of a colourful peacock's feather stuck in it; Beard, afraid that she might crumble in his arms, danced a most gentle waltz with her watched and applauded by everyone.

"Good boy," whispered Queenie, as pleased as Punch, tucking her arm through his before Ruth could steal him away. "That's Mrs Gunning – or Tibby, as she's known. Lost 'er third 'usband at Mafeking an' bin a widder ever since. Must be turned ninety. First time I seen 'er dance since the Coronation, gen'rally too pickled! You watch yerself, lovey, I 'ear she's still lookin' fer a new 'usband – anybody's!"

"That's horrid, Mummy!" cried Ruth, quite crossly, snatching Jarvis away and remaining deaf to her mother's bellowing laughter. But it wasn't very much later that Ruth fell asleep during an interlude, and Queenie carried her off to bed – returning some time later with a tray piled high with bacon sandwiches. Once they were gone – and they soon went – the party began to break up, and at 3 am, after innumerable "last toasts," Beard practically fell into his bed; he was asleep instantly and dreamt that he was being chased down the nave of a great cathedral by the Mafeking Widow, clutching a bouquet of daisies and buttercups in one hand and a blood-dripping knitting-needle in the other.

Beard woke up with urgent suddenness an hour later and, having checked himself for murderous needle wounds and found none, he discovered Ruth curled up on the top of the bed in her dressing-gown. She looked very peaceful and beautiful in her sleep, her pink lips slightly parted as if she were about to kiss someone, and her long black lashes resting like wings high above her pink cheeks; she looked very much like his notion of what a little angel looked like, except that he knew she was anything but a real one! But, he also knew that he loved her – in a big brother sort of way; and wondered often if it went deeper. He leaned over and kissed her waiting lips, and she murmured a sigh and turned over with a child's smile. He pulled a blanket over her, and then dropped off at once into an untroubled sleep.

He woke at his usual time, just before 6.00, and slipped out of bed without disturbing Ruth, who didn't appear to have moved a muscle since he'd touched her lips two hours earlier. Nor did she stir as he lightly kissed her again, on her cheek, except, perhaps, that she gave another tiny sigh through her parted lips.

Beard found Queenie already astir in her kitchen, for she had had to send Sam on his way at 5.45. She gave Beard a cheerful good morning smile, but there was no joy in her eyes for she knew that very shortly he, too, had to be off – and he wouldn't be returning in the evening like Sam; he'd be gone for years: possibly, for ever. The thought brought real pain to her eyes and a dead weight to her heart. But, he was still hers for a little while longer, and she stuffed him full of breakfast with the air of one firmly convinced that it would be his last. She watched him lovingly as he attacked the mountain on his plate.

"Sam 'ad to go orf to work," she told him, conversationally, anything rather than having to listen to her own thoughts. "'E said to tell yer to 'Give 'em 'ell ... an' keep yer 'ead down, Soldier!'" Beard nodded, his mouth full. "Ruth still asleep, I s'ppose?" He nodded again. "She was so 'appy last night," Queenie went on dreamily. "We all were, Mum," he told her gently, smiling. "And we will be again – very soon. You'll see." Queenie clenched her jaw, and then asked quietly, "Wot time do yer 'ave ter leave, lovey?" "Seven-thirty," he told her, and then they all busied themselves.

There was so little time and what there was raced by and it seemed Beard hardly saw Ruth, before he was kissing her goodbye and jumping into a taxi. Ruth had been so cross with herself for not waking up with him (cross at him, too, for not waking her), for she hadn't wanted to lose a moment of the little time left for them to be together. As soon as she was up and about and had made a pretence (at Queenie's insistence) of breakfasting, Beard had grabbed her hand and dragged her off to Mr Liebenberg's tiny camera shop round the corner; fortunately he was up and about though still blinking sleep from his eyes, but knowing Beard was away for a soldier, he obligingly took half-a-dozen or so photos of them. Ruth promised faithfully to send him the best of the lot – just as soon as he let her know where to send them. After that, Beard produced a tiny, almost-silver bracelet – and threatened to take it off her if she didn't stop crying at once.

He had then given her one of his two precious £5 notes – they were huge and white and the very first he'd ever seen let alone possessed – and told her to buy something nice for Queenie. "I'm no good at that sort of thing," he told her quickly. "You'll know the sort of thing she likes ... a hat, or something. She likes a splash of colour." He pressed the second note into Ruth's hand, too, saying, "This one's for you to buy yourself a real grown-up frock with ... to welcome me home in when I come back. You'll be all grown up by then." Ruth looked as though she was going to burst into tears again, but stemmed the flood. "It's not your money we want, Jarvis," she cried, tightening her grip on the two notes, "it's you – only you!" He swallowed a lump in his throat, and said with forced nonchalance: "Look after George for me, will you?" She nodded. "Of course." She added with a sad little smile, "I think he's getting rather fond of Rosie!"

Then the taxi arrived. It was time to go. There was no time for protracted goodbyes. Beard wished he was already gone as he was smothered in a flurry of kisses. Pecks, really, though Ruth did manage a real hurried kiss. "I do love you so, Jarvis," she whispered against his chest, clenching her eyes shut and holding tightly to his arms. "Please, please come back safely. I think I'd die if you didn't." Mrs B. said, "God bless you and keep you safe." The only words Queenie could find when her turn came were "Take care, lovey." She hugged him to her and made moaning sounds between dry kisses.

In the taxi, Beard fought to recover from the ordeal of his final farewells, and the elderly driver, who evidently doubled as an ambulance driver for he was still sporting his tin hat which proclaimed the fact, looked back and said kindly, "It's hell, ain't it, mate!" Beard nodded numbly, and turned to wave one last time, not knowing if anybody could see him, and seeing nothing himself, but guessing they would continue standing there until well after the taxi was out of sight. He arrived at the flat in Brewer Street and was relieved to find Bertie ready for their leave was running out fast. Bertie was the devil of a long time saying goodbye to a dark-haired girl who didn't fully emerge from the building, but finally they were in the taxi and away.

"Who was the girl?" Beard asked, more for something to say than any real interest. "Her name's Maud," answered Bertie with sigh. "Special?" queried Beard, teasing. "I think so," said Bertie softly. "And how's your Ruth?" Beard gave the littlest of sighs as his eyes squeezed tightly in memory of her. "She's growing up," he said simply. And they both remained silent for the remainder of the drive.

At Chatham House, in Horseferry Road, they were given railway warrants for Liverpool and told to report to Transit Camp B-4. This turned out to be a tented city on Aintree Racecourse. It was pitch-black and freezing cold when they arrived, but they eventually found their correct tent – and were re-united with the rest of the chaps belonging to their intake. It was a pretty grim place, cold and wet, with long queues for the mess tent and mile-long hikes in squelching mud to primitive, inadequate latrines. To make things worse, it started to snow. They shivered there for nearly a whole week.

On the fourth night, there was a heavy air raid on Liverpool Docks in which an ammunition ship blew up and inflicted more damage on neighbouring transports than a whole pack of U-boats. It seemed likely that their ship was among the casualties for the following night, Beard and his companions were entrained and shuttled south to Bristol where, two days later – one of which they spent marooned in a siding seemingly unloved and forgotten – they marched somewhat cheerlessly aboard the SS Standen Castle, designated for wartime purposes as Troopship No 1107. Two Lewis guns appeared to be its only armaments.

Beard and his companions sat aboard the Standen Castle, as they all preferred to call the ship, for two further days during which there were innumerable air raid alerts, none of which developed into anything serious. The cadets, who by now fully expected to be disembarked and sent elsewhere, argued endlessly as to where this might be. Plymouth and Southampton were the favourites, with London the rank outsider.

Finally, late at night on December 23, 1941, the Standen Castle slipped away from the quay and joined the silhouettes of a tiny convoy – and came to a stop. Several hours later, however, there was a sudden commotion on deck and a clanging of bells, which some know-all said meant "Full ahead!" but more probably meant "Slow ahead!" – there was even one wag who suggested it meant "Abandon ship!"; at any rate, the ship moved purposely forward at a very modest speed out of the estuary and towards the open sea.

"Bet our first landfall will be bloody Liverpool!" declared Bertie drily.

It wasn't; but neither was it India.

Chapter Eighteen

Somewhere at Sea, December. 1941

The voyage was slow and boring, apart from constant alarms over U-boats and aircraft which never materialised, but which nevertheless entailed tedious hours at boat stations, and further tiresome boat drills. By the time they were steaming alongside Africa, most of the ships that had left England with the Standen Castle had dropped off, most heading towards the Mediterranean, others towards the Americas: only seven vessels continued southwards to Cape Town.

Lieutenant Ian Stokes, the Indian Army officer in charge of the 60-odd cadets, tried to keep them occupied with daily PT exercises on the deck, courses and lectures, and even started up Urdu classes. Beard got along quite well with this – though conversation was a bit impracticable with only Lt Stokes to practice on, and him always busy; Bertie, raised on classical Greek, was rather less enchanted with the language, especially when told that Hindi was another major language among the 22 spoken in India. Beard concentrated on the one, learned some useful knots from one of the seamen, and how to play bridge by Bertie.

The most noticeable thing was that it was getting decidedly warmer; that and the fact that three of their tiny convoy had been torpedoed off Southwest Africa's Skeleton Coast: a fourth had already limped towards Freetown, Sierra Leone, with engine trouble. The remnants of the convoy ploughed on relentlessly, and finally, one night, a bearded sailor remarked to Beard and Bertie, who had come up on deck in search of some fresh air, "There it is, gentlemen – Cape Agulhas!" Beard peered in the direction the man's gnarled finger was pointing, but all he could see of this landmark was a darker mass in the blackness. "You mean we've reached India at last?" he queried in some surprise, for he had understood their destination to be still some way off. "No, sir," chuckled the other, "it's the southern-most point of Africa!" Beard might have been more impressed had he been able to see this promontory, so he confined himself to an impassive "Oh." Bertie commented, "I bet if we'd gone through the Med we'd already be in India." Their knowledgeable sailor grunted, "More likely at the bottom of the Med, sir!"

The convoy was reduced to one when the Standen Castle's two remaining companions dropped off at Port Elizabeth, and then the Standen Castle herself was suddenly re-directed to Durban, in Natal. It came as an even bigger surprise when all the troops aboard were ordered to disembark – the only explanation offered was that the vessel had been commandeered by "higher authority." Two days later, Beard and his fellow cadets, still in the care of Lt Stokes, found themselves in a desolate camp several hundred miles inland, towards the north. The crews of the lorries that dumped them there had orders to deliver the party and return, and they were extremely eager to return to civilisation; they deposited the cadets at the gates of the largish military camp, laughingly warned them to check for snakes, poisonous spiders and "other horrors" in the buildings, and sped away in a cloud of red dust.

As far as the eye could see there was only bare red baked soil, the only relief being that provided by the rows of barracks, which were ugly in their uniformity. Their first thought was that they had been abandoned to wither and die under the blistering sun. But they weren't. Within a few days, a rather large Indian Army colonel arrived by plane, together with a number of men who turned out to be instructors, and assured them, "India needs you!" He told them that while there was no transport available to take them on to India at present – he mentioned that the Standen Castle had been torpedoed to bolster their spirits, the situation with regard to the Japanese was becoming so desperate that the completion of their training had taken on a fresh urgency. It had been decided, therefore, to press ahead with their course right here on the spot – up to the point of commissioning if the circumstances dictated, and go on to India as and when it was possible. The colonel had a lengthy discussion with Lt Stokes, but he didn't appear keen to linger and was soon on his way back to endure the temptations of Cape Town.

The camp did not have a name, just a number: Z 14. The barracks, too, were identified simply by numbers – although Bertie quickly christened the one he and Beard shared (17) Bleak House; the name adequately described its comforts, but it was to be their home for the next several weeks. During this time they marched over what seemed like half of Africa, built bridges across impossible obstacles – and promptly blew them up, studied map reading, learned something of logistics and the rudiments of leadership, and generally engaged in mock battles that became tiresomely unreal.

"The next man I shoot had better stay dead or I'll strangle him," Beard declared wearily, as his latest victim rose from the dead and trotted off to his next assignment in the exercise. "All this continual pretend stuff is playing havoc with my morale as a marksman!" Bertie, never lost for a repartee, commented: "Well, that gazelle-thing you shot last week stayed dead, didn't it?" Beard grinned back, "Bit of a fluke that shot, if you ask me ... the way it was leaping about like a kangaroo. One of the Kaffirs told me it was a springbok."

Then, quite suddenly, just like their training in Maidstone, it was all over: the cadets' crash course was completed. Friday, May 1, 1942, marked Commissioning Day. The fat colonel returned, accompanied by a lean and lanky major-general who took the salute as the 56 surviving cadets marched past in splendid order. And as soon as the necessary formalities were completed, these worthy gentlemen fled away, leaving the cadets to celebrate on their own. The newly-labelled officers and gentlemen spent several glorious days saluting one another but, gazetted though they might be, as the weeks passed the solitary pips on their shoulders soon lost their glamour, and they wondered what was to become of them. But, nobody seemed in the least bit interested in them; they appeared to have been completely forgotten, however serious a threat the Japanese posed. This, in spite of repeated signals sent off by Lt Stokes.

It was a month, which seemed like a year, before the world was reminded of the shiny new young officers whiling away their time in the wilderness, and this only came about   when fate stepped in with a bang one dark night. An ammunition store blew up demolishing half the camp and slightly injuring two men. The spotlight was suddenly very much on Z 14. Senior officers arrived by the plane load, and the provosts stared suspiciously all round. It was decided on the spot to close the camp; the problem was what to do with these very new-looking Indian Army subalterns. After much dithering, nobody wanting the responsibility for them, it was decided that since they were essentially a British affair, let the British sort it out; and since the British were being chased backwards and forwards across Egypt, why not put these blighters on a train for Cairo – and send the Brits the bill. They'd be getting the bill for the destruction of the camp, anyway – whoever was to blame.

The cause of the explosion was never discovered, though Beard felt that the authorities held him responsible if only because he'd been duty officer on the night in question. He was careful to express no opinion on the matter, not even to Bertie, beyond suggesting that it was an act of God.

And so they were entrained and, after numerous adventures – like going big game hunting during which Beard shot a lion when the train driver walked off to visit his family for a few days, and the fact that several lengthy portions of the railway lines were missing, they arrived in Cairo on Sunday, June 21. The fact that their arrival coincided with the fall of Tobruk may have had some bearing on them being given a week's leave with immediate effect; time for a soak in a bath, a sleep in a real bed, a few decent meals, and for Beard an opportunity to send a carefully-worded letter to Mrs B. knowing that it would be read by all at The Dials. It was a short letter; he told them simply that they had reached Africa on the way to India, that the voyage was smooth and that it was very hot. The reality of things came when they reported back at a transit hotel and were shepherded into a small hall. They were told there was still no transport to get them to India, and this was followed by a more dramatic shock. A Colonel Angus Bruce, tall, red-haired and with cheerful blue eyes, told them they had been chosen as the nucleus for the first Indian Army airborne unit. They were leaving at once for Ramah

David in Palestine to learn all about parachuting.

His announcement was greeted with somewhat shocked silence. He chose to interpret this as a sign of enthusiasm; perhaps youthful excitement. "Bloody hell!" muttered Bertie under his breath, nudging Beard and giving him a look of horror. Beard shrugged and pulled a face, but managed a small grin after several moments. He'd been prepared to fall off an elephant in India if the worst came to the worst – but, to fall out of an aeroplane … and on purpose! The idea sounded positively absurd – and bloody dangerous! "It might be fun," he grinned at Bertie, who winced.

Col Bruce, wondering about the white faces gazing back at him, gave a loud and jovial laugh (the faces seemed to grow whiter) and said it was a very great honour for them all. What's that? Ye–es, strictly speaking, he believed it was supposed to be a voluntary thing ... but there was a war on, he reminded them with a forced smile. There was only time for duty and patriotism, he added coldly. Altogether, five men, defying the colonel's withering glare, rose and declined to share in the honour. Beard, who was beginning to doubt if he would ever really get to India, broke the strained silence that followed to ask: "Couldn't we do this parachuting business when we get to India, sir?"

"Don't believe there are any chutes out there, m'boy – and you wouldn't want to be jumping without one, would you?" He paused for the laughter which he felt his remark merited, but it was very slow in coming and muted at that, so he scowled and hurried on, "And besides, there are no instructors out there. As it is, we have to rely on the RAF chappies at Ramah David."

It was not the answer anybody wanted to hear, and it did nothing to bolster morale. Bertie nudged Beard and whispered, "Do you suppose the Nips have already overrun India?" Beard pretended to look shocked, wondering at the same time if they had.

It was already September when Beard and his fellow officers – all proudly sporting their brand-new parachute wings – returned to Egypt, and were directed to the old Commando depot at Geneifa, on the Bitter Lakes. "Sit tight, and await orders!" they were told by Col Bruce, who promptly disappeared in the direction of Cairo.

Beard, lazing alongside Bertie whose nose was buried deep in the pages of *Vanity Fair*, wondered how long they would be left to languish there – being baked by the sun and ravaged by flies. They'd already spent a fortnight there, their physical training continuing daily under the merciless shouting of PT instructors who seemed to imagine they were all Commando personnel, or so it seemed to Beard. He anticipated a long wait, for he had already learned that the Army did nothing in a hurry whatever the crisis – which was only to be expected since the generals' orders were issued by politicians far, far away in the safety of their Westminster clubs. A shadow put an end to such treasonable thoughts and, looking up, Beard met a pair of steely grey eyes set in a craggy face staring down at him. It was another colonel, spare but well-formed and heavily-tanned; he wore a cap with a general staff badge. At least, that's what Beard thought it was as he was about to leap to his feet.

"At ease, gentlemen, I'm Colonel Gibbs – Ozzie Gibbs," he introduced himself, squatting down on the ground facing the pair of them with an open, friendly aspect.

"Morning, sir," said Beard, warily. He wondered if he oughtn't to have leapt to his feet and saluted anyway, but it was too late now.

Bertie, quite unfazed, raised his golden head from Thackeray's golden prose, gave one of his sunny smiles together with a brief nod, marked his page and closed his book.

"Been looking for you two chaps," said the colonel conversationally, taking off his cap and running strong fingers through his thick fair hair.

"Ah," exclaimed Beard, anticipating a movement order to India.

"Have you found us a boat, sir?" asked Bertie, shading his eyes.

Col Gibbs, tweaked his military moustache, arched his eyes questioningly, but ignored both questions. "How did you boys enjoy parachuting?" he asked instead, his keen eyes fixed on the pair of them.

"It was all right, sir," Beard replied cautiously, thinking this didn't have the sound of India about it. "Too late for second thoughts once you've jumped, isn't it? If it don't open, there's no time left for worrying."

"Best part was feeling the ground beneath ones feet again, especially on the night drops," commented Bertie, putting his book down on the ground.

"What's your interest in us, sir?" asked Beard bluntly. "It's not India, is it?"

Col Gibbs grinned, but his eyes remained serious. He shook his head as he looked from one to the other of them, and said in a voice that was both authoritative and quiet, "No, I have other options for you, gentlemen. I'm selecting men with your sort of qualifications for teams I'm putting together. I think I can use you two."

Beard frowned, his eyes narrowing as he regarded the colonel with fresh interest. It felt strange, and irregular, to be squatting like this on the ground with a staff officer. Bertie folded his arms and looked from Beard to the colonel, whom he eyed with disquiet.

"Teams for what, sir?" enquired Bertie quietly, thinking this did not sound good.

"You'll have to talk to a Colonel Bruce about that, sir," pointed out Beard. "He seems to be in charge of us at the moment. We're waiting for a posting to India. Transport, that is."

Col Gibbs just smiled back, lazily snatching a fly out of the air as he did so.

"Who exactly are you, sir?" Beard asked, with uncompromising directness.

"Have you got the right chaps, Col Gibbs?" asked Bertie, more politely.

Once again Col Gibbs ignored their questions. Instead, he rose to his feet, looked about him and beckoned to them. "Let's take a stroll, shall we, gentlemen?" he said quietly, walking slowly away from the canal towards the open desert. Beard and Bertie followed, both feeling the suggestion had been more an outright order. When they were out of earshot of any possible eavesdropper, Col Gibbs halted and turned to gaze afresh at the two young officers. "Let's squat down again, shall we?" They ranged themselves on the gritty sand, Beard and Bertie on either side of the colonel. Beard was beginning to wonder if this mightn't be some elaborate hoax, when the colonel began to expound. "Gentlemen, you will not repeat this conversation to anyone, is that clearly understood by you both?" He searched their faces intently, and they both nodded their heads, and responded solemnly, "Yes, sir."

"I'm with a department of the Foreign Office and empowered to recruit men, carte blanche, for missions beyond the normal parameters of any of the Services. You both have the competence, if not the experience, that I require. Of course, any wartime job has its hazards, but I think I can promise you action beyond normal soldiery. I guarantee you will acquire all the active service, and more, you'll ever want. How does that strike you, gentlemen?"

Foreign Office! Beard immediately thought of secret things, and that this fellow seemed fond of calling them gentlemen – which, of course, they were, especially now they were commissioned. "Are you asking us to become spies, sir?" he asked, frowning.

"Certainly not," exclaimed Col Gibbs, looking horrified at the suggestion. "That's an entirely different business." He gave a little squirm of distaste.

"We'd be in uniform, then, sir?" queried Bertie pertinently.

"Of course," retorted Col Gibbs, swatting at a fly hovering near his moustache, "after all, you'd still be British officers, wouldn't you? Naturally, if a situation arose and an officer thought a disguise of some sort might save lives, then that officer would use his discretion. Chances have to be taken when operating behind enemy lines. After all, we all want to come out of this alive, heh?"

"Of course, sir," said Beard readily, "but if you were to be caught behind enemy lines out of uniform, you'd be liable to be shot as a spy, wouldn't you?"

"You'll find the Germans are liable to shoot you whether you wear a uniform or not," observed the other, with just the hint of a smile.

Beard nodded : he believed that, anyway. And what he was saying had a certain appeal to a young chap ready to do his bit ; this bit about operating behind enemy lines certainly sounded exciting enough to warrant at least hearing more. "Well, it sounds all right to me, sir," he added, "but how is it possible? I'm not even sure we're in the British Army! We're supposed to be in the Indian Army – if ever they find a boat to get us there. That's why we're kicking our heels here. Do you really think they'd be willing to release us just as we're about to be of some real use to them?"

"No problem," the colonel assured him airily, dismissing Beard's concern with a carefree sweep of his hand. "As I said, I have carte blanche to select where I please."

"Well, count me in, sir," Beard replied, giving Bertie a quick glance; anything was better than idling about here at Geneifa. Might see a bit more of the world, at least.

"We would retain our commissions, I presume, if we joined your lot?" put in Bertie pointedly. "We've only had them about six months, and they're the main reason we joined the Army in the first place. I'm sure we don't mind where, or even who, we fight, but, speaking personally, I feel I'd do it better as an officer than a private!"

Beard nodded his wholehearted agreement. He'd grown accustomed to being an officer, receiving salutes and being called Sir (on rare occasions), and even if he hadn't yet had the opportunity of giving any orders, he wouldn't surrender his commission for any cause.

"Yes, of course you would," Col Gibbs said blithely, expecting that he was right.

"When would you want us to join you?" pressed Beard, suddenly concerned that they might be on a boat to India before arrangements could be made for the transferral, and so miss what sounded like the opportunity of a lifetime. It certainly sounded more promising than anything India had to offer ... particularly since they couldn't even get there.

"What's wrong with right now?" suggested Col Gibbs, arching his brows persuasively. "When it's done, it's done. Get your kit together and we'll move out right now. I'll require you both to sign the Official Secrets Act, of course, but once you're with me, I promise you there won't be any repercussions from your Indian friends. Tell you what," he said, climbing to his feet, "you have a little chat between yourselves about it and, if you haven't changed your minds, we'll meet by the main gate in an hour – with all your stuff, and I'll take you to meet your new commander, if I can find him. Anyway, I'll take you to your new camp, where, in time, you'll discover your real capabilities and learn things about guerrilla warfare that you never dreamed."

As soon as he'd walked off, Beard and Bertie held a whispered conference. "I suppose he is genuine?" said Bertie. "Why shouldn't he be?" retorted Beard, adding with a grin, "But if he isn't, we can always double back – and say we got lost in the desert." Bertie grinned back and said, "They might believe us if we said we got pissed in a bar somewhere, or, better still, in a brothel!" They laughed like a couple of schoolboys, but their minds were already made up and they were waiting for the colonel when he appeared.

They met their new commander, Major Milburn Yeo, in the rather splendiferous Shepheard's Hotel in Cairo – the place seemed overflowing with very senior officers and Beard, at least, was suitably impressed, if not overawed; Bertie, being accustomed to such richness, took it in his stride. Major Yeo, a solid, square-faced man with short black hair and alert almond-coloured eyes, had evidently been briefed about both men. "Right, gentlemen," he said to Beard and Bertie after they'd been formally introduced by Col Gibbs, "enjoy yourselves tonight, this might well be your last civilised meal for a long time." And apart from a few pertinent questions at the outset, the meal developed into something of an orgy, of eating and drinking. At any rate, Beard was feeling quite legless by the time they arrived at their new camp in the Canal Zone in the early hours of the following morning after a hectic drive along (and frequently off) the desert road at breakneck speed with Major Yeo at the wheel, and the rest of them hanging on as best they could.

Beard woke with the devil of a hangover at 5.45, after barely three hours' sleep. In fact, he was wakened, none too gently and certainly with no consideration for his condition, by an Army PT corporal who invited him very loudly, and repeatedly, to join – "in ten minutes, if you please, sir!" – in a little light exercise. "You too, sir," the corporal shouted, giving Bertie's cot a shaking. Bertie's eyes slowly focussed on the man, and shuddered. He rose feeling very fragile.

The *little light exercise*, preceded by an hour's PT, turned out to be a jaunt of some six miles into the desert weighed down by a load – and it was meticulously weighed at the start and end of the march – of 40 lbs. It was the beginning of a period of training that was too painful to reflect upon until some years had safely passed. At the time, it was enough – indeed, it seemed a miracle, simply to survive.

There was an almost round-the-clock training programme. The PT instructors, who went to work on their victims very nearly before they were properly awake, extracted the last ounce of flesh from the men's bones. A former Glasgow police sergeant, whose face was scarred by various razor slashings, taught them more ways of killing with a knife than even the Arabs knew; his frequently repeated counsel about giving the knife a "wee twist" as you sank it into some suitable area of your adversary, was never to be forgotten. And there was another former policeman, from Hong Kong, who instructed them in the art of unarmed combat and showed them a dozen or more different ways of killing with the bare hands by means of chops and straight-finger jabs at various pressure points, plus, of course, the breaking of necks. "But this can be quite a noisy business," he said, with sober concern. "Apart from the actual sound of the snapping, the body convulses quite violently in its final spasm ... so, gentlemen, use your loaf when you apply this particular means of killing – there's so many other lovely ways, all absolutely soundless. Let me demonstrate on ... would you care to join me, Mr Beard?"

The marches into the desert became more frequent and the distances extended from 20 to 40 miles and, occasionally, to 60 miles; and the loads were increased to 75 lbs. India and its elephants sometimes seemed a most attractive alternative to Beard, but deep down he was really enjoying himself – especially when he had moments to catch his breath. Bertie's enjoyments were restricted wholly to the rest halts, when he would console himself with the thought that his Commando brother Simon was most likely enduring far worse. Sometimes, in the course of three-day exercises, during night marches there would be a lecture on reading the stars and familiarizing themselves with them – and then they would jog 20-odd miles back to camp. It became more and more exacting even for athletes like Beard, and those other men with Commando backgrounds. But, pushed to the very limit though they were, most won through, so perhaps those hated instructors really knew their stuff.

By way of a break from the physical side of things, great emphasis was impressed upon them on the importance of map reading, the stripping down of every known make of gun, including those of the enemy, constant firing practice on the ranges and in endless battle exercises, various methods of demolition, intelligence gathering and the art of infiltrating the best guarded of positions, communication by wireless, Morse, semaphore and, just as importantly, hand signals. To complete their training, there were lectures on the most advanced medical matters, even to the point of performing minor operations.

There seemed no end to the pace and range of the training, but, almost imperceptibly, it must have eased for Bertie found time to pursue the scheming Becky Sharp in Vanity Fair, and Beard, having learned to swear in a couple of Arabic dialects, decided to risk writing another letter, this time to Ruth, again using Mrs B.'s address. Actually, the letter consisted of a few scrawled lines on the back of the photo which Bertie had taken of him posing with his foot on the lion he'd shot; it showed as much of the lion as him – and he wouldn't have sent it if Lt Stokes hadn't assured him that there was a breed of lion indigenous to India.

Beard wrote that he was well and hoped she was too, and that he'd been commissioned and that she'd better call him "sir" in future – "Sir Bobbie!" that is. He made no mention of his being in Africa instead of India, saying simply that it was awfully hot and leaving her to think what she chose, knowing that the Army postal system would leave her in ignorance. He wished her a happy fourteenth birthday, late as usual and knowing, anyway, that she'd be furious as she'd now regard herself as being at least fifteen, and told her not to forget him and to give his love to Queenie and Sam and Mrs B. – and printed his name, ROBERT BEARD, and underlined it twice; he added a clumsy X for a kiss, as an afterthought. It was hardly the sort of letter to set a young girl's heart pounding with excitement, but he told himself he still had to be mindful of the censors, and that anyway she was too young to be receiving letters at all, being still a schoolgirl. He smiled at this, and added another kiss.

Then, out of the blue, as they sat in the officers' mess which they shared courtesy of the nearby naval station, HMS Saunders, Bertie confided to Beard that he had applied to join an outfit called the Special Boat Service. In fact, he said, the idea had originated with Col Gibbs who had learned Bertie was sufficiently experienced with sailing ships to take part in such nautical jollities as Cowes Week. "He said he'd discussed my expertise with Lord Jellicoe who is apparently running the Boat Service show. It's something that developed from a Commando canoe section. Now it has sail and MTBs. Sounds promising for those of us that go down to the sea in ships. Gibbs gave me an introduction and – well, old man, I've orders to report to his lordship at his base at Athlit, just south of Haifa in Palestine. Gibbs, it seems, having discovered where my talents lay – including my knowledge of Greek, thought they could be put to better use in boating than whatever horrors he's got planned for you."

Beard was surprised at the news, and disappointed to be losing his only real friend in the Army. "Well, you kept all this close to your chest, Bertie," he said, forcing a grin. "I never had a clue. I suppose I could learn to be a sailor, too!"

"No, Bobbie, not you, you're a soldier through and through," laughed Bertie, "you'd be lost at sea. You'll make a better general."

Beard gave momentary thought about volunteering for the Boat lot anyway. However, he already knew enough about the Army to know that if there was any volunteering to be done, the Army would do it on your behalf. Wasn't that really why he was here with Gibbs' secretive group? He wondered where all this training would lead him.

"Trust the Army to terrorize me into jumping out of aeroplanes, and then decide to make a sailor out of me!" Bertie complained, though clearly the idea of messing about in boats seemed a far more attractive proposition than tramping over the desert in a temperature of 110 degrees with a ton of gear on his back.

So, the two friends said their goodbyes, with long, vigorous hand-shaking and each swearing to keep in touch with the other without knowing if this would be possible. "If we lose sight of each other out here, which we will, remember that you'll always be sure of a welcome back home at Highways," Bertie assured Beard. "And be more generous with your letters to that sweetheart of yours!"

Beard felt himself blushing more like a schoolboy than a lover at the other's teasing, and then Bertie was gone, and neither was sure he'd ever meet the other again.

☐ *At this stage, the narrators took a break for a couple of days, while the nursing staff gave their patient a "sorting out," and when they all reconvened Bertie, having completed his contribution for now, yielded to Gibbs, whose turn it was to search his memory.*

Before he opened the curtain on his portion of the scene, Gibbs explained that he was indebted to those letters made available to him and the contributions of many of Beard's surviving colleagues who were able to provide the minutiae that completed the picture, and told the story. Official reports gave only the salient details of Beard's exploits, as ever, it was those who shared them who are able to bring them to life.

"I'll try to emulate Queenie and make my part as interesting as hers," added Gibbs, turning to give her a warm smile. "But, she knew the boy: I only know the man."

"And I don't know anybody," declared Beard, "not even myself."

Gibbs grinned amiably. "I sent you on your first mission," he said quietly.

"The first?" exclaimed Beard. "You mean, this wasn't it?"

"No, Robert, there were many of them," replied Gibbs soberly. "This was the first."

"Tell me about it."

And so the chronicle continued.

Chapter Nineteen

Somewhere in Tunisia, December, 16, 1942

In a part of Cairo that might be described as semi-posh there were whole streets set aside as billets for officers when duties permitted. Beard, who had been allocated quarters in one of these to go with an unexpected two weeks' leave a fortnight or so ahead of Christmas – which meant he wasn't going to have Christmas off, was half asleep on the verandah swinging on the sun-lounger, and wondering whether he oughtn't write a letter or two.

When he had an opportunity to relax, like now, he often thought of his *family* back in England – Queenie, who as far as he was concerned was his Mum and had a heart big and good enough to be the real queen of that land; Mrs B., who was like a second mother to him; and, of course, little Ruth – well, he supposed, she wouldn't be so little now, would she? Nearly grown up, even. Good Lord! – who was always telling him she loved him more than anybody. He smiled each time he remembered her, which admittedly wasn't very often, not these days; mostly, he remembered that special birthday kiss of theirs! A letter? No, too dangerous. A card, then? Yes, space for fewer words: less dangerous. But even this littleness she never received.

A sound penetrated his ear and disturbed the blessed quiet of the district. Moments later a Jeep came to a noisy stop at the house, and Beard had a premonition that his leave – and he was only four days into it, was about to be cancelled. Surely they wouldn't do that to him for yet another 300-mile exercise? He stretched languidly, watched a fly tip-toeing along his bare feet, flicked it away to make room for another and gave his visitor a somewhat sour look. "Lieutenant Robert Beard, sir?" enquired Cpl Allen, who knew perfectly well to whom he was speaking. "What is it, Tom?" asked Beard warily. "I've orders for you, sir," answered the corporal, handing over a sealed envelope, then waiting while it was read; and as soon as he saw Beard's expression, he added, "And I've orders to take you to wherever you need to be – and to impress upon you the need for urgency, sir."

Beard gave the corporal a glare, and muttered, "I'm not going anywhere without my boots, and then I intend to wash and make myself thoroughly presentable."

"By then I'll have been court-martialled and shot, sir."

"I shall send flowers."

Both men grinned, and the corporal heaved Beard up from the swing. "Any idea what it's about, sir?" asked Cpl Allen as he began humping Beard's gear into the Jeep. "I know as much as you, Tom – that I have to be where I'd sooner not be at this moment. I anticipate a call to arms as my Christmas present." Cpl Allen, who was tall, solid and dark haired, frowned and said, "We'd better get to it then, sir." "Of course, it might simply have something to do with Christmas entertainment," suggested Beard. They both laughed loudly as the Jeep roared into life and took them to find out at a reckless speed.

Half an hour later, Beard stood before Col Gibbs in his office at GHQ Middle East. "Take a pew, Mr Beard," directed the colonel as he continued shuffling through maps and papers; he scarce glanced up as he waved Beard to a seat and parcelled up the documents and penned notes. It wasn't quite the same as preparing presents. Beard hid the amusement the thought provoked. Major Yeo, seated at another desk studying maps through a massive magnifying glass, looked up, gave Beard a half-smile of greeting, and resumed his spying.

"How would you like to get away for Christmas, Mr Beard?" asked Gibbs softly, smiling benignly across at the smartly-dressed officer.

"Where have you in mind, sir?" returned Beard cautiously, but eager to learn where his destiny lay. He had thought *fate*, but decided *destiny* sounded better.

"I think we have found a little something to occupy you, Mr Beard," Gibbs answered with quiet disingenuity after a minute or two. "So, your days of loafing are over, sir."

Loafing! Beard was about to protest and indignantly bring to mind the months of training which had awakened and tortured every muscle in his body, but in time he caught the twinkle in the colonel's grey eyes which now joined the almost full smile beneath his moustache. Beard stayed silent, and waited to find out where his commando training abilities were about to take him.

"You are no doubt aware that the war in North Africa is coming to an end," continued Gibbs chattily. Beard nodded, circumspectly. He only knew what the likes of the colonel thought he should know, which was as little as possible; otherwise, he relied on the myriad rumours and indiscreet remarks that abounded everywhere, the difficulty being to distinguish fact from fiction, and that included whatever bulletins the BBC broadcast.

"With the Torch landings in Morocco and Algeria, Rommel is being squeezed into a corner – Tunisia, from the west and the south. The Germans are a stubborn lot – a bit like us. They'll fight for every inch of Tunisia. They have to: it's their only way back to Europe," the colonel emphasised. "The Americans are new to the war and will take time to find their feet, but the British 1st Army is there to lead, and Monty's 8th Army has just smashed through at El Agheila in Libya. Monty's next obstacle will be the Mareth Line which defends the Gabès Gap and the Tunisian heartland." He explained that this was a fortified belt between

Tripoli and Gabès, built before the war by the French to deter Mussolini's ambitions in that direction. "Of course, he's got to take Tripoli yet. As you see, there's a lot more fighting ahead so anything we can do to expedite a German surrender, we are instructed to do. This is where you come in, Mr Beard."

He gave Beard an expansive smile, and beckoned him to come round and have a look at various maps, reports and signals that were being continually added to by a steady stream of clerks. Beard peered over Gibbs's shoulder and studied a map showing a large portion of Tunisia: the eastern coast, from Bizerte down to Sfax. In between was the port of Sousse, which was circled in red. Far to the south lay Libya, but the 8th Army was still a long way from Tripoli and no immediate threat to Tunisia. This, he supposed, was the likely area for his insertion (he disliked this term, it sounded rather indecent, but this is what they called these parachute drops), though the Gabès Gap, which was where the coastal plain narrowed to just a few miles between a large sea of salt marshes and the Mediterranean, might present a problem.

Beard stabbed a finger at the red-circled Sousse and asked its significance.

"We thought it presented a good target for you, Mr Beard. What do you think?" asked the colonel conversationally.

Beard studied a larger map intently, looking for any expanse of open ground. There wasn't any. It was almost all built-up, with railway lines and main roads, and mountains. The only possible spots were already airfields. "I don't see any feasible place for a drop, sir," he pointed out politely, but with an anxious frown.

"Oh, you won't be parachuting in – quite impossible terrain," said Gibbs airily.

Beard looked relieved.

"We plan to land you by submarine," continued the colonel.

Beard looked shocked.

Submarine! He paled as the word circulated in his brain, and evinced surprise and perhaps even horror. Suddenly, leaping out of a plane into the void and taking a chance on where he landed seemed so preferable to having that empty space replaced by water, blocking out both light and air. He gave an inner shiver even as his lips, so tightly closed, opened sufficiently to murmur, "I see, sir," adding, after a long swallow, "When, sir?"

"Oh, right away, Mr Beard, or you'll miss the boat. Time and tide wait for no man, as the saying goes," declared Gibbs firmly.

A million questions crowded Beard's head, but the only one he managed to get out was, "You're not planning to land me at this," he stabbed at the map again, "Sousse place are you, sir?

Gibbs gave what is often ascribed as a condescending smile, even as he shook his head. "No, Mr Beard, that is one question I can answer – in the negative."

In view of this negative answer, it seemed pointless to ask "Where then?" Perhaps it was not to be in Tunisia at all. On the other hand, Libya looked impossible – presuming it was to be behind enemy lines. Instead, Beard pressed, "Is this to be a lone operation, sir, or do I have company?"

"Answers to all your questions, and many others are contained in sealed orders, at present under lock and key aboard the submarine, whose name I can tell you is HMS Jellyfish. You and the captain will open them once you are under way, and not before. Read, digest and shred them before you leave the sub." The colonel added, almost as an afterthought, "There are three of you in the team, Mr Beard. You will be in charge."

"May I know who the other two men are, sir?" asked Beard, with some determination.

"Major Yeo, who will escort you to the sub directly, will introduce you to the others at the quayside. All your necessary gear is already aboard," explained Gibbs with something of a flourish, before adding cheerily, "You are holding up the war, sir."

Beard nodded, wondered if he should smile and, instead, rose to his feet and saluted smartly. It was clear the briefing, such as it was, had ended. And he didn't even know where he was being inserted by the sub; and what a ridiculous name for a sub, Jellyfish! Evidently everything had been arranged beforehand. What he was supposed to do remained a secret. All he knew was that whatever it was he had to make it all work, and survive. Especially that. And that bit wouldn't be in any orders, either.

Gibbs returned the salute with an informal gesture and, as Beard turned to go, pushed out his hand and shook Beard's warmly. "Good luck, Robert," he said gruffly, "Remember, there's been a first time for us all. It's a learning game. You'll enjoy Tunisia."

The colonel smiled, Beard smiled in return, and then he was gone. On the drive to the docks, Major Yeo murmured softly, "You have to understand, Robert, when Gibbs says he's instructed to do something, his orders probably come from Churchill personally. Sometimes they may seem bizarre, but they usually work out."

Beard, whose mind was so full of what was happening to him, particularly in regard to the unknown mission ahead, was sufficiently stirred by this intelligence to look surprised.

"Gibbs has been watching you keenly over the months, Robert," went on Major Yeo, "All of you, of course, but you in particular. He feels, because of your – shall we say, singular upbringing, you will be more cunning and tenacious in moments of danger. He picked you out as a leader straight away during your training. Be assured, he's immensely proud of you, and has every confidence in you."

If this was meant to pep him up ahead of the mission, it worked, though Beard only countered, "The one thing that concerns me is how the devil does he expects us to get out of Tunisia once we've done our business – whatever that entails."

"Don't think he hasn't given the matter thought, Robert. He has faith that you will devise some method. He's also given you two exceptional men – seasoned soldiers, rogues both, to keep you company."

"Well, let's hope the Navy feeds us on this voyage," said Beard, hiding his interest concerning his colleagues, "because I missed my dinner today."

On this note, Beard finally went to meet the enemy: Wednesday, December 16, 1942.

The Navy proved generous and helpful hosts. The moment Beard stepped aboard, he was escorted to a cabin where he found the two men who were to accompany him. Both men were dressed up in Arab attire. He knew them both of course, Sgt Jack Trumpett and Trooper Tim Cole; they had all trained together. Beard knew he was in good hands. Sgt Trumpett, a village postman in peacetime and in his late twenties, was a tall and powerfully-built man who understood the need for discipline in war and was skilled in its arts. Trooper Cole, a Cockney cab driver from Shoreditch in his early thirties, was stockily built in a compact way and a veritable genius with all things mechanical, and his specialist weapon was a knife. Both men, who were dark-haired, were unshaven to a degree that they could be said to be bearded. Beard, whose daily shaves were still largely unnecessary, felt naked and jealous. The two men were tucking into plates of dumpling stew as he entered.

"We was afraid you'd missed the boat, sir," grinned Cole, his mouth full, looking up.

"You look very well dressed for going to war, sir," said Sgt Trumpettt, raising an eyebrow questioningly. Where are we going, it asked.

Nothing had been said to Beard about dressing up as an Arab, but it made sense, and he was sure he'd find suitable clothing among the gear brought aboard. "Hello, you two," Beard greeted them. "We'll make a fine team." He broke off to thank a steward who placed a steaming plate before him. When he'd gone, and he'd tasted a couple of mouthfuls, he continued, "The reason I'm dressed up is because about two hours ago I was on leave, suddenly hauled off a verandah swing, and driven at break-neck speed to GHQ for a briefing with Col Gibbs, who suggested that this diversion of ours would be good experience for me." Beard grinned, a little embarrassed. "I can't tell you anything at this moment. I don't know anything. The captain of this boat has sealed orders for me which we cannot open until we're at sea. All I can tell you is that our destination is Tunisia."

"Should be nice there this time of year," murmured Cole.

"It's their winter so it should feel just like a summer at home," observed Sgt Trumpett, with a tiny smile.

A double tap on the door preceded the appearance of a lieutenant, who, addressing Beard, said "Welcome aboard, sir. Do you have everything you need?" Beard nodded. "We'll be under way in ten minutes, gentlemen. I'll come and collect you then and take you to the captain so that you can do your sealed orders business." He grinned, and with a theatrical whisper behind his hand, said, "The crews' money is on Sardinia." Beard gave a chuckle and said, "So long as your captain knows where he's taking us."

The Navy lieutenant, who clearly knew their destination and had expected Beard to confirm it, put it down to innate Special Forces secretiveness, and added, before departing, "Oh, all your equipment is secured aft. You'll be wanting to check it over in due course. Anything you want, just ask your steward, Griffin. Meanwhile, sit back and enjoy the cruise. I imagine you've a couple of days' rest ahead of you at least."

Two days later, Beard and his team were in a dinghy paddling the last hundred yards or so towards the Tunisian shoreline, just to the north of Hergla which jutted out into the Gulf of Hammamet between Sousse and Nabeul. Behind followed a second dinghy, laden with supplies. Ahead, an occasional double red-white signal led them to a narrow gravelly beach beneath a low cliff where they met their contact, Pierre Rouget, who was leader of the clandestine resistance movement in that area.

It was 01.40 on Saturday, December 19, 1942.

The two rubber boats bounced heavily against each other as a brisk cold wind got up and created a fury of waves just as they ground on to the beach. Everyone was out on the instant and began the unloading, and this was when Rouget emerged out of a crack in the cliff and approached them. He, as were Beard and his men, wore Arab robes and headdress, and looked as though he belonged in them. He was French, but born in Tunisia, dark-skinned, middling height and inclined to portliness. He addressed Beard, who came forward to meet him knowing that Trumpett would have a weapon trained on the man, in German. "Hurry," he cried urgently, as he shook Beard's hand, "We've a long way to go and a lot to do before daylight."

"You have transport nearby, I hope," said Beard, returning at once to help with the unloading. He'd hardly had a chance to get used to the long flowing robe he was wearing, and found it too cumbersome to move as quickly as he'd have liked.

"Of course," returned Rouget, hastening forward to lend a hand.

It was fifteen minutes before everything was piled at the foot of a path that led to the top of the cliff. The path more resembled a goat track, but Beard declined the sailors' offer to help hump the stores to the top. "No," he told them firmly, "you get back to your boat as quickly as possible, and thank you for your help."

"Good luck to you, sir, and your chaps," one of the sailors said as the dinghies pulled away.

"Safe journey," called back Beard, and turning round saw that the other three were already struggling up the cliff laden with boxes. He picked up a box grenades and followed in their wake. It took them close on twenty-five minutes to stack all their equipment – weapons, ammunition, explosives, food and the rest – on the lorry and cover it all with a blanket of fruit and vegetables.

Rouget, who was even more clean-shaven than Beard though much older, explained that he had a vineyard farther north, behind Enfidaville, and had an arrangement with the Germans to sell them fruit and vegetables, and of course keep them supplied with wine "which the bastards seem to live on." In return, he enjoyed minimal privileges, including a meagre allocation of petrol. "I have a permit which entitles me to drive at night as I have to visit several plantations after the curfew," he added. "I have to fill in details of times and routes, but it is always the same. They may check my mileage, but I help myself from their fuel dumps." Beard warmed to the man even as he stared grimly ahead.

They hurtled along the empty coast road towards Tunis, Beard seriously wondering if Rouget would do the Germans' job and kill them all. But he kept quiet, gritted his teeth and fixed his eyes on the darkness ahead, expecting any moment to be challenged at some road block. Rouget, sensing the turmoil in Beard's head, grinned and raced on, determined to make use of the main road as long as possible. The lorry rumbled along at breakneck speed in almost complete darkness, for Rouget had on only sidelights. He knew the road so well they were all he needed and, besides, there was already a sort of half-light: the first suggestion of the new dawn.

Then, as the lights of an approaching vehicle appeared in the distance, Rouget swung off the road with only a minor reduction in speed, and carried on along a narrow, rutted, jungly track which at times proved barely wide enough to accommodate the lorry's passage. They bounced precariously on, sometimes forced to come close to a stop by a tree in their path, and crashing on over undergrowth and snapping off branches of other overhanging trees. Every minute, as they swayed from side to side or rolled over an obstacle, Beard half expected the arsenal behind him to explode and obliterate them all. But it didn't and they eventually juddered to a halt behind a low-roofed house on the edge of a community of sorts. The nearest neighbour looked to be about a hundred yards away, but it was still too dark to see clearly through the trees.

Beard and his men jumped to the ground and stood looking about them while their limbs recovered from the ordeal of the drive. But Rouget quickly stirred them all into action. "Don't stand about," he muttered at them. "get cracking and empty the lorry. It's got to be back at my place almost immediately, or there'll be bloody questions asked." As he spoke in German, Beard had to translate for Trumpett and Cole. "Unload," he said simply. It took them twenty minutes to unload the vehicle and restore the flowers and vegetables. Rouget told Beard to get his own stuff stowed away out of sight in the house, and suggested he and his men kept to the house for the remainder of the day.

"I'll see you all this evening, about six o'clock. We'll have a pow-wow and you can decide your plan of action," he said amiably, climbing up behind the driving wheel. "I'll help you whenever I can, or get one or two of my men to help out. We'll shake the bastards up, *nicht*?" Then, giving a wink, he roared away.

By the time they had all their gear under cover, some in the house, the remainder hidden in outbuildings, it was full daylight. After they had eaten, Beard told Sgt Trumpett and Cole, "Right, we'll stick to Army rules, four hours on, and four off. Get your heads down, I'll take the first watch."

They were all slept out by the time Rouget returned, with a huge bunch of bananas, a small sack of dates and some bottles of wine. "A gift to help you face the hazards ahead," he told them with a grin. Beard wondered if the man had had any chance to sleep himself, and thought he'd probably only managed to steal a few naps among his vines. After they'd eaten and drunk several toasts to the success of their mission, Beard called them to order, and outlined the purpose of their mission.

"In brief, we are directed to set Tunisia ablaze from end to end," he declared.

"All of us!" exclaimed Cole, with a hint of sarcasm.

"*Nur wir beide!*" gaped Rouget, his eyes suddenly large.

"Yes, sir," said Sgt Trumpett calmly.

Beard, having cleared his throat with some more wine, gave them a grin and went on to explain the situation. He raised a small cheer when he pointed out that they could leave the mountainous west to the two Allied armies converging on it, though the Atlas Mountains stretched right across Tunisia in the north. The Americans would find their way through eventually, and the British 1st Army would target the northern ports, with Tunis as their ultimate goal. But 1st Army had a long way to go yet, and the Atlas foothills might prove an obstacle to Beard and his men. Disregarding this, that left the eastern coast and all the rest of Tunisia down to Libya for the three of them to operate in. He discounted Rouget because the Germans made use of him during the day and would become suspicious if he was absent too often from his vineyard. He would carry on as usual, and help out as circumstances allowed. In any case, they'd have to rely on him up to a point over transport. But, he warned Trumpett and Cole, there was a lot of walking ahead of them – and in sandals.

Beard, ignoring the groans, went on to tell them what he proposed. Destruction was their priority. Gibbs had supplied details of a number of targets, and Rouget had already added to the list, and doubtless they'd find plenty of others themselves. The targets were purposely spread right across the country to cause the Germans maximum insecurity. But, if they started blowing things up right from the start, Beard pointed out, Jerry would quickly be aware there were saboteurs in their midst and concentrate on hunting them down – and there weren't an awful lot of places they could hide and still be an effective force, and achieve what they had been sent here to do.

So, what he proposed was that they locate suitable targets and leave delayed action charges. They'd start operations as far north as they could get; in Tunis itself, if possible. They'd leave explosives timed to detonate up to two months later, gradually reducing and staggering the times depending on the Allied advances, decreasing them sharply as they withdrew south towards Libya and its sheltering desert. Gibbs had said it would probably be two to three months before the 8th Army were properly into Tunisia, unless there was an unlikely German collapse. Hopefully their explosions would coincide to help the Allied advances. They'd need to rely largely on Rouget to provide news about the Allied advances.

They went to work on their second night in the country. Rouget had provided sketches, which he admitted might be out of date, but which showed certain German sites worth a visit. After they had buried the bulk of their supplies in various hollows in the foothills of the Aurès Mountains, Beard sent Sgt Trumpett and Rouget off in the direction of Béja, with the instructions to get as close to the coast as they were able, though Rouget would only be able to put the sergeant on the right road before returning to his vineyard to allay any suspicions Jerry might get that he was up to something they should know about; meanwhile, Beard and Cole strode off over the Atlas foothills towards Tunis itself. Beard knew that Sgt Trumpett was more than capable of operating on his own. They planned to rendezvous in ten days, by which time Beard expected they'd have exhausted their supplies of explosives and needed to return to Rouget's house to rest up and re-stock. Rouget was their only link with HQ.

Beard was conscious that this would be his first sight and contact with the enemy, and a deep thumping of his heart warned him against recklessness. He was also aware, with boyish pride, that this was his first command. It was a small command, true, but it was his; he was responsible for the lives of the men with him; he was responsible for giving them their orders, and making sure they were the right ones; sensible, at least. He had no fears for himself, and doubted that either of his men had any for themselves, but he felt a concern for them that he did not feel for himself. Perhaps it was apprehension of the dangers ahead, perhaps it was something all leaders felt before a battle. He gave himself a wry smile, for he could hardly call what they were hoping to achieve a battle; yet, it was more than a game of hide and seek: they could still be killed in what lay ahead. But he hurriedly brushed aside all such negative thoughts, and concentrated on the business in hand.

He could have wished he was in uniform and wearing boots instead of open-toed sandals, but they went with the Arab clothing they were obliged to wear if they were to move around in daylight. Beneath the ankle-length robe, known locally as a *thobe*, he and Cole wore local cotton trousers, purchased by Rouget, and all their weapons, explosives and other necessary supplies were strapped about them. It was inevitable that they should both look rather overweight, and move somewhat awkwardly. But, however unwieldy they might feel, they moved at a good pace through the night, moving in a sort of north-easterly direction, certain of finding suitable targets on which to leave timely reminders of their visit.

Beard thought it might be pushing their luck if they went into Tunis itself, but in the event they found it relatively easy. On their third day, they managed to tag along behind a string of camels plodding through one of the mountain passes and, eventually, having slept the remainder of the day in a thick wood that could well have been a forest, emerged and without difficulty found themselves in the port of La Goulette. From there, Tunis was but a stone's throw. They ambled along the Avenue Habib Bourguiba, which ran through the new city from the clock tower to the Cathedral of St Vincent de Paul, where it turned into the Avenue de France which lead into the medina, the old city, with the Zaytouna Mosque at its heart. Beard instinctively made a mental map of the streets so that he and Cole would know where they were in night-time sorties. Earlier, Beard had thought they were on the Cap Bon peninsula, a good bit to the south, and he didn't want to make that mistake again. Anyway, it had afforded them a glimpse of what had been Carthage, but they weren't there for sight-seeing purposes. As might have been expected, there were a lot of German soldiers moving around but Beard and Cole mingled with other Arabs, and no one paid them any heed.

Later, as the real dark descended, they successfully laid their first explosives beneath three oil containers, and set to go off in nine weeks' time. They tried, unsuccessfully, to move on to Khereddine which would have given them access to an airfield and Carthage. The Germans were simply too thick on the ground and there were checkpoints everywhere. Beard and Cole settled for placing charges beneath two bridges over a canal, in spite of sentries stomping overhead as they trod their beat. They set these charges to go off in nine week's time as well, feeling that if they left them any longer they would be sure to be found. They placed four further charges in the port ferry area the following night after watching an almost ceaseless flow of Germans commuting to and from Sicily and Italy. As soon as they had extricated themselves from both the bridges and the ferry terminal operations, they withdrew back into the woods to eat food they'd bought in the medina souks and to rest up.

And that was the way it went until it was time to rendezvous with Sgt Trumpett and Rouget. Beard and Cole worked well together. Cole was very efficient as a soldier and noticed everything. For a peacetime London cab driver, well known for their garrulity, he was remarkably taciturn, offering almost no conversation except concerning their work. Every now and again he would growl that he missed his "fucking boots," and they'd both smile and move on. Beard found this all quite satisfactory as it afforded him the necessary quiet in which to think and plan their movements and operations. He knew he could rely on Cole to work on his own as well, and in this way they were able to attack twice as many targets.

They spent most of a week "touring" the Cap Bon which had mountains, forests and lots of harbours. It also had hot springs and they found a small isolated pool and decided to risk having a bath as they were beginning to smell unpleasantly. They took it in turns, one standing guard while the other stripped off and wallowed in the luxurious warmth of the water. A bar of soap would have been beneficial, but they couldn't expect everything. They would like to have washed their clothes, particularly their Arab garbs, but had to settle for a change of underwear. Still, it had been wonderful feeling the fresh air on their naked bodies for a few minutes. But this idyllic interlude was short-lived, and within an hour they were laying small limpet mines to a network of jetties and other naval installations – and grateful to be rid of the cumbersome things, and then it was on to search for fresh targets; and there were plenty of them. A dozen or more fuel and ammo dumps, and various military buildings, were targeted, the timers now being set at eight weeks. The most difficult part of their work was to place the charges so as they would be well nigh impossible to be seen or found. This extra precaution took time, adding to their danger, but it was necessary.

Their reunion with Sgt Trumpett and Rouget provided a welcome, if brief, interlude to exchange news. Rouget, with his access to a wireless, gave them the latest war news which was all good, though it seemed the 8th Army was having a hard time of it and advancing very slowly on Tripoli. Sgt Trumpett reported reaching the port of Tabarka, close to the Algerian border, and leaving several "parcels" due to explode in eight weeks' time in the port area and inside some large warehouses; he'd also mined a bridge and several roads at Béja. Beard added this report to his own activities and, together with a brief note to Gibbs, handed them to Rouget to forward to HQ. It was only when Rouget – who had casually mentioned that Gibbs had spent two months in Tunisia earlier in the year setting up his network of agents – said that the British had captured Sirte on December 25, that Beard realised they had missed Christmas Day entirely, and here it was almost the new year: 1943.

Their supplies were intact and having replenished their needs, Beard and his men, after being dropped off at a suitable point by Rouget, set off again on New Year's Day. Sgt Trumpett was quite agreeable to continue carrying on working alone, and it was agreed to meet up again on the 14th. Beard and Cole headed for Hammamet, a fishing village which had been one of Rommel's headquarters, and found themselves instead in Nabeul, a small trading port. There were several more targets there; and so it went on. They adopted no regular routine for sleeping; they slept as the opportunity presented itself, taking turns. They would have preferred to sleep by day, leaving them free to work throughout the night, but it was often necessary for them to travel for long periods in daylight, and so they slept when they could, and when it was safe. Their priority was to select targets and set their charges. Mostly they bedded down in one of many small forests or some lonely mountain gully.

Beard thought they enjoyed amazing good fortune. Granted it was the last thing they wanted to do, for their own safety, but there was never an occasion when it was necessary for them to kill either a German or an Italian – nor even to immobilize one, for this would have had the same effect of drawing attention to themselves. There were a few close calls, like when a German soldier addressed a remark at Cole, who didn't comprehend a word. Cole had had simply glared at the soldier and spat on the ground, and the German had gone on his way laughing. And then there'd been the time, in Sousse itself, when they'd sheltered overnight in a shed during a rainstorm, and there'd been a knock on the door. Both men, anticipating an invitation to surrender, had been prepared for a shoot-out and possible death: at best, capture with the same end after torture. Instead, there in the doorway had been an Arab offering them a large jug of hot coffee and a plate of freshly-baked bread, hunks of cheese and slivers of meat. His dark eyes shone a smile and, having handed the food to Cole, who hastily put away his knife, placed a finger to his lips, mouthed a "*Bon chance*," turned about and returned to his house. So, their presence had been observed; fortunately by a generous friend. However, even as they'd gobbled down their feast, Beard determined not to place them in such danger again. Henceforth they would avoid built-up areas for such purposes and rely on woods and mountains to provide their shelter.

Throughout January, they continued to enjoy this good fortune. They linked up with Sgt Trumpett on the 14th as arranged and had a good long talk about how they were doing, and simply enjoying a break from the constant tension and having a gossip together. Two days later, all stocked up with their lethal loads, it was back to work. And on the 28th of the month, needing to replenish their supplies of explosives – and replace their sandals, they were back at Rouget's house when he came rushing in to tell them that the 8th Army finally had captured Tripoli five days earlier. A week later, news filtered through that the British had entered Tunisia itself, and quite suddenly there seemed to be millions of Germans in the south of the country; too many for comfort, anyway. In the midst of this German build-up, Sgt Trumpett materialised with reports of further successes, including an airfield.

With the realisation that the earlier explosive charges they had set in the Tunis area would shortly be going off, Beard decided that the three of them would work together from then on as they were having to move south rather faster now to keep pace with the Germans, who were racing to block the British advance up from Libya. Beard did not want to lose sight of Trumpett as the time approached when they would need to seek safety in the desert and wait for the British to arrive.

The three moved as best they could, sometimes being obliged to remain hidden in one spot for days at a time as huge convoys of men and guns rumbled past them. When they were able to emerge, they moved far and wide leaving lethal reminders of their passing. The explosives they planted now were timed to go off within two to three weeks: and towards the end, within a matter of days. They spent a week in the port of Sfax where German shipping was busy coming and going; they would have left earlier but the place was so crammed with troops and their vehicles, it was simply impossible to extricate themselves. It was the same all the way along the coastal plains, with military traffic stifling every road. It seemed cheeky, and perhaps reckless, but Beard decided to take advantage of this huge build-up of vehicles, mostly in open spaces, to help himself to one. And, after Cole, the ex-cabbie and expert mechanic, had disabled as many as they had time for him to fix, that's what he did, driving away with only a German forage cap and a scowl for disguise.

Beard appreciated that a lone German scout car would attract the attention of the Germans, but it gave them a respite from the walking they'd been doing for close on three months, and Beard was able to tune in to British and German news bulletins on the wireless. He would have liked to get into the ports of Skhira and Gabes, especially the latter, but there were road blocks everywhere and even German vehicles were being checked, so it made sense to swing away from the coast where the enemy was massing and, in the event, they were never challenged, and Beard went on driving until the vehicle ran out of petrol. The jerrycans they'd thought contained petrol were filled with water, so, having pushed the car off the road, they all had a good drink and took to walking again. They were in the comparative safety of hills and mountains, and they rested up in the forest region of Bou-Hedma.

It was now the middle of March, and Beard knew from listening to news bulletins in the car that only the fortified Mareth Line guarding the Gabès Gap held the 8th Army at bay. Beard felt sure Montgomery would soon be crashing through there, and then would have an open road north to Tunis. He decided it might be time to get out of the firing line altogether and simply leave the armies to it. He'd done all that could be expected of him in that area, and he didn't want to be squeezed between the two opposing armies. Of course, there might be other opportunities elsewhere, for the Germans seemed to be everywhere, even where he was hiding up.

As March drew to a close and the temperature rose, Beard and his men found themselves near the oasis fortress town of Gafsa, where there were phosphate mines, Roman pools, palm trees, an airfield – and Germans; lots of Germans. He remembered Rouget had warned him against going south where there was the great salt lake and the nightmare sand dunes, hundreds of feet high, of the Grand Erg ; even so, the desert appeared to offer him the best refuge to bide his time and wait for the 8th Army to break through Gabès, and meet them on the road north.

And once they were within sight of the desert, Beard decided it was safe enough to discard their Arab clothing. Apart from the increasing heat, it served little purpose now. They saw no one, and they were heading towards their own lines. They were all delighted to put their feet into boots again and Cole, especially, couldn't get out of his thobe quickly enough – "frock," as he called it, with real distaste. However, they all retained their Arab headgear as being the best protection against both the broiling sun and swirling sand.

Two days later, as they approached what passed for a road in that scrubland region of desert, they saw some strange silhouettes in the distance and, advancing cautiously, found the sprawling black mass to be hundreds of fuel drums expertly concealed beneath acres of camouflage netting. It was further protected by sentries who prowled round the area, occasionally kicking at a stone that got in their way. The British trio were grateful for the date trees that afforded them some cover. Further exploration as the dusk developed revealed that this was part of pretty largish camp; and it appeared they had wandered right into the middle of it. There were rows of camouflaged tents of varying sizes on either side of a broad central track as far as the eye could see, which admittedly wasn't all that far. Presumably off-duty Germans were resting in what shade there was. There were many others moving about, but as the dark descended they retired, leaving only the bored sentries to be seen.

"We'll have a go at this," Beard said softly. "Probably be our last job. We'll use up whatever explosives we have left."

Suddenly, Sgt Trumpett gripped Beard's arm very tightly, and whispered right in his ear: "There's a sentry over there, sir; to your right!"

Beard turned his head very slowly and stared at the German about ten yards away ; he had a rifle slung over his shoulder, and was whistling softly to himself ; he was facing the three of them, but never saw them ; he looked very young, and bored. They waited for him to move, which he did after an age, and as soon as he showed them his back, they all veered off even more soft-footed to the left, only to spot a second sentry sheltering glumly between two tents. This one, also with his rifle slung over his shoulder, was looking directly at them: in their direction, at any rate. Not for the first time, Beard was thankful they shunned any recognizable uniform. They all wore sheepskin-lined leather jerkins over nondescript khaki uniforms, and fortunately had exchanged their kuffiyehs for navy woollen headgear as night came on. They needed to get hold of some German Army forage caps for use in moments like this, he thought, wishing he hadn't left the one he'd had in their abandoned car. They might look a pretty motley trio in their pseudo-uniforms, but they did not look too obviously English nor immediately threatening, excessively well-armed though they might appear. "Keep walking," Beard instructed his companions. "Give him a grin."

Beard, with Sgt Trumpett and Cole following, strode purposefully on. Trumpet, who was in front and first to meet the sentry's disinterested gaze, gave the man what could only be described as a leer, Cole simply scowled at him, and Beard only nodded. Not a grin from any of them! Beard had unobtrusively released the safety on the Schmeisser (a captured MP 40 which he hadn't yet had the opportunity to use) cradled across his chest and was well aware that Cole had one hand within an inch of the Luger at his side while the other one already held his knife. The sentry grunted something to them as they passed and Beard, lifting his free hand, half-turned and growled something back in a sort of complaining whine without really looking at the man, who gave a snigger as they disappeared into the darkness. "What the hell did you say to him, sir?" muttered Cole, returning the knife to its hidden sheath. "I told him we'd been drinking date wine and had the shits!" explained Beard, and now he grinned with relief. "I could do wiv a bleedin' drink!" said Cole, with a sigh. "I told him we were trying to walk it off – and hoped to bag a gazelle or something for the pot in the process." Cole gave the beginnings of a smile and muttered, "At least that might explain why we're all armed to the teeth."

Ahead of them they saw two more sentries marching to and fro together, and they ducked between some tents – carefully stepping over the guys and pegs – to circle round them. It was quickly evident what the sentries were guarding: thousands upon thousands of artillery shells. They soared out of a great pit but though they were hidden from the air by miles more camouflage netting they were in plain view to Beard and his men, who were now on their bellies examining the area from a distance of barely 40 yards. Cole was all for dealing with the sentries there and then, but Beard shook his head urgently. "Those sentries are in plain view of the rest of the camp," he whispered. "If they were to disappear suddenly, someone'd be sure to notice and come over to investigate. On the other hand, as long as they don't see us, those sentries are *our* protection."

After a few minutes' thought, Beard made up his mind. "We'll split up," he said carefully. "I'll see what I can do about destroying these shells, while you, sergeant, have a go at that fuel dump we saw." He turned to Cole and said precisely, "See what else you can find, Tim. And remember, this is not a killing spree. We leave one body behind, and Jerry will know they've had visitors. Let's set the primers to go off tomorrow. We don't want to be anywhere near here when the place goes up." He knew Cole would be pleased at the use of his first name, just as he guessed the man would die rather than admit it.

Beard fixed a rendez-vous, allowing them 35 minutes to accomplish their objectives. He wished them both good luck, adding, "If you're rumbled, scarper. Leg it into the desert ... eastwards, towards our boys." They nodded, and in a moment Beard was on his own.

Moving forward, silent as any snake, Beard couldn't help but think his gypsy friend Nelson would have approved. The sentries were a good 50 yards away, and moving farther away, as Beard wriggled behind the protective screen of shells and climbed down into the first of a series of pits. It took less than the 20 minutes he'd allotted himself for the task to push the lumps of plastic, each with its time fuse and pencil-thin blasting cap, as far as possible in among the shells and out of view. Moving from one pit to the next, he shoved a charge in at irregular intervals along the entire 100-yard-plus length of the arsenal. He used up the last of his plastic, and so once these were in position he saw no reason to hang about.

Beard moved away as rapidly as prudence dictated, intending to make straight for the road and safety, but almost immediately he came upon a bowser which, from the way a sentry was smoking surreptitiously in its shadows, very evidently contained neither aviation fuel nor petrol. Beard assumed it contained water and decided he had time to cause the enemy some further aggravation.

By good fortune the sentry decided to go on walkabout as Beard neared, so he turned his attention wholly on the slowly dripping tap and found that it was indeed water. Beard had a good deep drink, filled his own water bottle and another that he found hanging there, and then casually turned on all the taps he could find – just enough so that the water would drain away into the sand, but not so that it would attract attention doing so. This little bit of sabotage had taken barely four minutes, and now Beard moved purposefully towards the RV. Sgt Trumpett, who was already there, gave him a wide grin and a thumbs up. A few minutes later, Cole turned up – wheeling a motorcycle-combination.

He explained to the others that, being a professional mechanic, he had sought out the camp's motor pool and found a scrapheap of vehicles. Among these he'd found one perfectly functioning machine – "wiv a few bits from here, and a few more from there," and exchanged it for a really sound model. He'd collected several jerrycans of petrol which he'd loaded into the sidecar, and then wheeled it all the way here. "And bloody hard work it were, too, sir," Cole declared, wiping sweat from his brow. "And I never seed a sentry the whole time," he added. Sgt Trumpett, who had picked up a couple of Jerry field caps, slapped him soundly on the back, exclaiming, "Well done, mate." Beard grinned and said, "Well, we'll push the thing along for a mile or so, then see if it works."

It worked very well, though they frequently had to turn sharply off the road and hide as German transports swept by. In this way they progressed several hundred miles, though sometimes not in the right direction, and when the machine finally died on them somewhere near Zagrata, from where the sounds of battle sounded just around the corner, it was the last day of March. They hid up in a hollow that seemed to mark the beginnings of the desert proper, and watched the endless flow of retreating German lorries, tanks and whatever else moved on wheels. The distant artillery barrages gave way to machinegun-fire, and then came the distinctive sound of rifle shots. Infantry mopping up, suggested Sgt Trumpett. Beard thought that now might be the really dangerous time. They didn't want to be shot by their own side by accident. They just stayed put, scarcely moving, hardly making a sound. Doing nothing to draw attention to themselves.

Then, on Friday, April 2, they heard a vehicle nosing around and eventually Beard identified it as a British reconnaissance Jeep, and moved out with his hands raised holding something nearly white and shouting that he was a British officer.

And it was over. And not a shot fired, nor a German killed, smiled Beard. Though what havoc his bombs had caused, he could only guess. The last of them should have gone off by now. He hoped they had, for he didn't wish any to inflict casualties on their own men.

☐ *There was a moment's silence as Gibbs concluded this Tunisian episode, then Queenie found her voice and exclaimed, "You never told us anyfink abaht this, Jarvis." Her words came over almost like an accusation: or complaint.*

    "It's all news to me, too,"   declared Beard from his bed. "Exciting, isn't it!"

    "You could've got yerself killed," cried Queenie.

    "Perhaps I'm a ghost," suggested Beard, grinning.

    "Oh, you're no ghost, major," said Dr C. assuredly. "Ghosts don't bleed!"

    With a wry grin, Gibbs resumed.

Chapter Twenty

Somewhere in Sicily, April, 1943

Three days later, they'd been flown to their base camp in the Canal Zone, where there was some lengthy debriefing, some congratulations and promotions. Beard was made up to acting captain, Trumpett to staff-sergeant and Cole to corporal. And they were each awarded a week's leave.

"I'd give you longer, Robert," Gibbs told Beard, "but that's all I can spare. I want you back doing some serious training. You're horribly out of condition after your saunter through Tunisia."

Beard controlled his feeling of outrage with what he felt was masterly self-control. At that moment, he could envisage no more arduous training than what he and his team had endured during the past four months. He felt thoroughly trained and in peak condition. What he needed was about three months R&R.

"I hope our efforts there served some useful purpose, sir," he retorted, a trifle more frigidly than he intended.

"You all did very well, Robert," Gibbs assured him, with a twinkle in his grey eyes. "Your work was of great importance. Apart from denying the Germans a very considerable quantity of vital supplies, your delayed-action bombs did a lot to undermine the confidence of their troops. Nothing instils terror more than not knowing where or when an explosion is going to occur. And you didn't fire a shot, you say. Amazing. Yes, very well done, sir."

And with this last compliment, Gibbs sent Beard on his way with the suggestion that he get pissed or laid. But first Beard had his extra captaincy pip sewn on to his tunics, and then he discovered he had mail awaiting him. Three letters, all from Ruth.

In the privacy of his quarters in Cairo, Beard lined up his letters as though they were soldiers; he changed their positions according to the dates on them. Dear Ruth. He easily recognised her neat, childish hand; and there was her name and address on the back to confirm their origin. The letters appeared to have been written at intervals of several months, the last being dated some three months previously. He supposed there were hold-ups with the mail like everything else. He didn't know. These were the first he'd received since leaving England. Come to that, they were the first proper letters he'd received in his entire life. He fingered the first of Ruth's letters excitedly: it seemed to be quite thick. Finally, he tore it open with the feverish eagerness of a small boy opening a present.

Out fell a photograph, one of those taken on the last day of his embarkation leave. It was not a very good one, doing neither of them any favours, it even seemed slightly blurred, and he couldn't help thinking that if this was the best Ruth could pick out, the photographer (who was Polish, or something) must have been pickled on vodka still – even if he had taken their photos at the crack of dawn. But, perhaps he and Ruth were really the ones to blame; he remembered they hadn't been all that co-operative, being more concerned with laughing at one another, or pulling faces, and rarely sitting still or doing what was required of them. Poor Moishe Liebenberg, who was 76, tiny, bald and spectacled, was continually scolding them as he peered hopefully through his thick lenses. They'd both been too keyed up – over his imminent departure – to concentrate on the birdie! He remembered that at any rate! Ruth's face was turned away from the camera, her gaze fixed somewhere in the vicinity of his right ear; and he was staring straight in front of him (though not in Mr Liebenberg's direction) and looking very stern indeed. He recalled that he had intended it to be a martial pose; now, he thought he looked rather idiotic – simple, anyway. Gallantly, he decided that Ruth looked rather lovely even if he could see only half her face; and, anyway, he didn't need a photograph to remind him what she looked like: he knew it too well, and he'd always thought she looked all right – for a girl. He smiled at her image, thinking that perhaps she was pretty after all, and pulled her letter out of the envelope; he was pleased the censor hadn't violated any of her loving, innocent words.

"*My darling,*" she wrote, " *– and before you start protesting, Mummy said it was all right to call you this lovely word, since you insist on keeping your own perfectly adorable name a national secret. Daddy calls it hush-hush, but I think it's all plain barmy – just like this silly war. And anyway, you're very lucky to be getting a letter at all, whoever you think you are.*

"*Just when I'd decided you'd forgotten all about me, and I began to think I hated you, along came your letter. Even then it wasn't a proper letter, only a few words scribbled on the back of a photo (the lion looked rather sweet – poor thing), but at least you enclosed an address at last for me to write to – so I love you, once again. Of course, I never really stopped. I never could – not for long, even when you were beastly, as you so often were! Oh yes, darling, I do love you. Please take great care of you – for me.*"

She explained the disappointing quality of the photo by saying that dear Mr Liebenberg's lean-to studio had been devastated by an incendiary bomb, and almost everything had been lost in the blaze. Only four of their negatives had survived and she was assured this one was the best of the bunch; she dreaded to think what the others had looked like. Anyway, they had to make do with what they'd got – which was one print each. Of course, she hinted, he could always have a nice one taken wherever he was – and, please, not with another poor dead animal as the main attraction, and send it to her in a silver frame. She added that poor

Mr Liebenberg had gone to live with a cousin − "I think it's a pretend family like you and me." − in Whitechapel.

"I saw him on the day he left − all huddled up like a little bag of bones on the back of Mr Levy's horse-drawn cart with his one suitcase tied with yellow twine and clutching his gramophone for dear life. It was awfully sad. And he was crying; and I wondered if he could see me waving to him through his tears." (Beard could sense a pause here, and he didn't doubt that Ruth had cried, too.) *"I think it hurts more to see a man − and especially a very old man − crying than even a child. But so many people seem to be crying these days as the war drags on. Sister Bertie said it would be all right if I included him in my prayers even though he is a Jew, and so I do, alongside prayers for your protection − and an early letter. A long one."*

The letter went on to relate her tiresome days at school, and reams more about the super dresses she and Queenie had bought with the fivers he'd given them. It was all terribly boring stuff and he skimmed over most of the details, noting only that Ruth's was a green something or other with accessories and Queenie's a lovely something else and all red and flouncy; the words "divine" and "heavenly" cropped up repeatedly. In all honesty he couldn't raise much enthusiasm over their purchases, the only thing that did strike him being that £5 was a hell of a lot to pay for a frock! Still, if it made them happy ... Ruth said that she wore her new silver bracelet, and the coral necklace, every Sunday at Mass because it made her feel closer to him; and she hoped that he remembered to go to church when he was able. She concluded with another desperate plea for a proper letter, adding that Queenie sent her love and an earnest prayer that he was getting sufficient to eat and keeping out of bad company, and there was a brief postscript in which Sam urged him to keep his head down.

Letter number two repeated, several times, her resolute demands for a letter. Apart from that her only real piece of news was that Sam had been promoted to sergeant, although she wasn't sure if this was just for the duration. They were all very proud of him, anyway, even if Mummy did say it was only worth an extra bob or two which, with prices the way they were, didn't amount to much. Still, as she also said the war looked like going on for ever, it would seem Daddy was going to be a sergeant for a long time to come. Ruth went on to roundly accuse him of not loving her any more, or he would surely have found a way of getting a message to her before this and telling her he did. Her injured feelings did not prevent her from ending the letter with scores of kisses − at least he hoped the crosses represented kisses, and not markers for his grave! Queenie's concern regarding his diet was repeated, and Sgt Sam's advice was also repeated.

The third letter was excessively short, being angry and blunt. *"My darling,"* it said, as usual, *"Just let me know you're not completely dead, and haven't entirely forgotten me – you beast!"* And that was it, apart from a whole string of postscripts, including the usual anxious inquiry from Queenie, and Sam's more practical exhortation; and there was a sad one, too, about Mr Liebenberg being found hanged in his cousin's shed, having used his beloved gramophone for his step into the next world. There followed the usual array of kisses and a final PS: "Rosie and George are so in love they're getting married ... doesn't that give you any beautiful ideas – darling?"

It certainly did. He resolved not to follow suit until he was at least a hundred! He didn't doubt that he loved Ruth; he was sure he always had, and possibly always would, but wasn't it in a strictly brotherly sense? He was perfectly happy to love Ruth; it gave him a warm sense of belonging; but he wasn't so sure that his conception of love had anything to do with marriage. It had been dear old Mrs Molly and her endless chatter about them being sweethearts that had put the idea into Ruth's head and she had eagerly perpetuated the myth with its ultimate conclusion of marriage ever since. That really did seem too drastic: final, anyway. Besides, he'd always felt comfortable thinking of her as a sort of pretend sister. He knew, deep down, that this was only so when it suited him – like now. Well, he felt certain that there must be all sorts of love, and he was quite sure his didn't call for such a sacrifice.

And whatever interpretation he chose to put on his love for Ruth, he felt that he was nowhere near old enough to go making permanent commitments like marriage. Hell, he wasn't even eighteen yet. And what about Ruth? She was still a schoolgirl. But he was worldly enough to know that a girl became a woman one second before she was born because that's when she first opened her mouth; her plans for marriage probably began one minute later! Some introvert had told him this back in England (was it Scruffy?) and now Beard smiled wryly at his own cynicism, and blew an apologetic kiss in the direction of an imaginary Ruth. He smiled again. How could she expect him to entertain thoughts of marriage – not that he did, he told himself hastily – when he got the hots for almost every girl he met! Like Poppy, albeit momentarily, and ... well, he wasn't sure if Georgina qualified for inclusion; as he remembered, she'd scared him half to death. Anyway, he had to admit, he liked girls in general, when he got the chance to meet any. But that didn't mean he'd like to marry them all: a very sensible Law forbade such happiness!

Beard decided it was as well he was half a world away from his darling Ruth. There was a sort of comfort in distance, at times. He wouldn't have dreamed of calling her a "darling" had they been together – it would have been something far less gentlemanly! He also decided to be circumspect in his reply, which didn't necessarily have to be too prompt. He winced at his own beastliness, and spent his leave doing very little more than living the life of a tourist: sightseeing by coach, eating well, drinking too well, and sleeping extremely well. One of the things he did was to have "holiday" snaps taken of himself at every opportunity, with particular emphasis to the pyramids of Giza, camels and such like as backcloths, which he thought he'd send to Ruth to let her guess his whereabouts. And then another plaintive "My Darling" letter arrived, and he decided it was time to send her his photos – and a letter.

He made repeated starts to his letter, beginning in turn "My Darling," "My Dearest," "My Dear," "Dear Ruth" – and eventually settled, dispassionately, for "Hello Ruth." He then plunged straight into it, thanking her for her "most welcome" letters and excusing the long delay in his reply on the war. He used the war as a further excuse for being unable to say either what he was doing or where he was doing it, simply that he'd been in action for months and this was the first opportunity he'd had to write a letter. Honestly. He could just picture Ruth screaming "Liar!" before adding, in a whisper, "darling!" Tongue in cheek, he went on to say he hoped she was well and, deciding not to enquire how she was doing at school, he rushed on to say he was sorry he'd missed her birthday yet again – what was she now? Fourteen? Or, nearly 15! – and it looked like he wouldn't be seeing her again this year, or even the next. "We'll probably both be very old – twenty-something, at least, when next we meet – and won't even recognize each other!" He meant it as a joke and hoped she'd accept it as such. Then he thought it might even be true, and he shrugged and hurried on. "Anyway, happy 15th birthday in advance!" He grinned, knowing that the instant this landmark was reached she'd be "almost sixteen." Which made him think: "And I'll be 18 in just a few months' time – and then I'll be safe from them all!"

He concluded hurriedly, saying he hoped she liked the photos he was enclosing, expressing his genuine distress at the death of Mr Liebenberg and spent the remainder of the letter describing his promotion. Once again he printed his name: ROBERT BEARD, and sent her a single kiss. As an afterthought, he added a PS: "Love to Queenie – and congrats to you, Sergeant Sam!" After a long moment, he added another PS: "Please don't ever stop writing, Ruth. You know I love you." He added another solitary kiss, hurriedly sealed the envelope and rushed out to post it – marvelling at his extraordinary daring, or was it simply foolhardiness?

Back at camp at the end of his leave, Beard was handed a letter from his old friend Bertie. He wrote saying he'd heard a whisper that Beard had been in action, and wanted to know the worst. "If you don't reply immediately," went on Bertie, "I'll assume you're missing, a prisoner or on the run." Bertie briefly mentioned that he'd had some lovely letters from Maud, and couldn't wait to get home to see her. Beard, struggling to remember who Maud was, scribbled a hasty reply to the effect that he was quite well, and neither missing nor captured, and would tell him all about it when next they met. "Isn't it rather dangerous for you to be getting serious over Maud?" he enquired, recalling the other's advice about safety in numbers where girls were concerned. He didn't mention his own letters from Ruth.

Beard, who had resumed his gruelling training routine right through into July, was thinking about Ruth, wondering if it was too soon to be writing another letter to her, when the duty officer poked his head round the flap of his tent and said that Gibbs would appreciate his presence. Beard reached for his cap, straightened himself up and hastened to the large tent that doubled as Gibbs's office and quarters. He rapped on the canvas with the flat of his hand, entered and saluted smartly.

"Ah, Beard, I thought you'd left us," said Gibbs, smiling as he looked up from his crowded desk. His grey eyes studied Beard for some moments before he waved him to a nearby chair. "You look rested enough, captain," he declared cheerily, almost as if he was a doctor speaking to his patient. "I've another little job for you. Shouldn't take you more than a day or two. Just a long weekend, really."

"Yes, sir," responded Beard cautiously, his heart thumping in anticipation of another mission. Where to? Rumours were rife of imminent landings on mainland Europe: Italy and Greece were favourite. At least he wouldn't have to wear a "frock" in those places.

"You're flying to Philippeville in Algeria immediately Robert," the colonel continued, still smiling as he riffled through some documents, and extracted a blue sheet of paper. He studied the flimsy for some moments and then, leaning forward on his elbows, the rictus smile vanished and his face became serious as he said quietly, "This information is for your eyes and ears only. You understand?" Beard nodded instantly, and thought "Oh God, it is back to frocks." Aloud he said simply, "Of course, sir." Gibbs nodded in his turn, and went on, "It's Thursday today, you'll be in Philippeville tomorrow and you'll take part in Operation Husky, the invasion of Sicily, which is set for the following day, that's July 10."

He went on to explain that Beard's sole task in this business was to get to the port of Augusta and capture, or kill, a Major Klaus Brandt of the Hermann Goering Panzer Division; who, in reality, was an SS officer: Sturmbannführer Karl Pffinkel. He also claimed allegiance to an Intelligence unit, in the name of Albert Pröhl. "I expect there are several others," said Gibbs coldly. "The man is an animal. He deals in murder, torture and mass extermination of people. The War Crimes people have him in the top half of their list. They want the bastard, alive or dead. They'd sooner have him alive, but" – Col Stubbs gave a small shrug – "so long as there's a body."

Beard wondered if his role was to be an executioner. The notion sent a chill through his body. He hadn't killed anybody yet, but was quite prepared to do so if it became necessary – as was his duty, if only for self preseravtion. Still, this sounded an odd way to do it. A thought struck him. Perhaps the fellow would surrender – or shoot himself.

"This man is evil, Robert, and must not be allowed to escape. Intelligence tells us that Pffinkel, to give him his true name, who has been operating throughout the province of Syracuse for the past year, has his HQ on the island of Augusta – in fact, he resides and works at the port's Grand Hotel on Corso Umberto. Get him, Robert."

Gibbs added that he was giving Beard four men "just in case you need to defend yourself." And his final words were, "Don't forget your 'chute."

Beard's team was waiting for him in the map room from where, armed with various maps and charts, they were driven to the RAF airfield of Heliopolis, just outside Cairo. They were all well-known to each other: they had all trained together in various conditions. In addition to the newly-promoted Cpl Cole, there was Sgt Earnest Hall, tall, lean, with dark alert eyes, who, in more agreeable days, or rather nights, had followed a more promising career as a safe-cracker; and Privates Alan Thompson and Norman Webb, both known as hard men. Both had the dark menacing look of street fighters. Thompson, the heavier of the two and immensely strong, had been a railway worker in civvy street. Webb, a peace-time window cleaner, was lanky with sharp eyes and quick feet. He had a scar down his left cheek, the relic of many a street fight and was known to favour a knife; he was also an excellent marksman with a rifle. Both men had done time for petty thefts and brawling, but had proved to be excellent soldiers. Beard felt that he was very well protected.

The airfield at Philippeville was like a sprawling Little America. The flag hanging lifelessly from the makeshift pole was American, the planes so neatly lined up far into the distance were American, the acres of transport with their left-handed steering wheels were American, the personnel moving unhurriedly about their business were American – and the English they spoke was American. And the plane that landed Beard and his four-man team there was an American Dakota.

"You guys the Limey paratroopers?" drawled an enquiring voice as they disembarked.

Beard stared up at the man, who must have been close to seven-feet tall. He noticed the man's boots, shining clear as glass – not a grain of sand blemished the shiny perfection, and here they were in a desert. He counted the stripes on the fellow's arm and knew he was some kind of sergeant. Mind you, he was so immaculately uniformed with creases and a pale blue silk cravat at the throat, he might well have been a general, but the MP armband suggested otherwise.

"Yes, sergeant," declared Beard, smiling quite amiably, "we are indeed those ... guys." He wondered if Americans saluted officers of different nations, and turned away as a voice addressed him by name.

"Captain Beard, is it? I'm Major Tommy Hunt of the SAS. I understand you'll be travelling with us." They exchanged salutes and handshakes. "The sergeant here will take you to your quarters and see to your every need. Food, mail, ammo ... you name it, they've got it. They're very well organized. There's an officers' briefing connected with our mission given by an American major-general called Washington-Brown. I'll send someone to collect you. As you can guess, security's pretty tight round here. Get some sleep if you can. We go in the first wave in two C-47s. We leave here at 00.27 hrs tomorrow. Our Zero Hour over there is 03.15 hrs. That'll be about the time we'll be dropping you off." He gave Beard a small grin. "Do you need someone to check your chutes?"

"No, we do our own," said Beard firmly.

"Quite right," grinned Major Hunt. Then, as he and Beard moved away a pace, he gave another grin and remarked, "I thought we were the secretive ones – the SAS, I mean. But I know nothing about you chaps ... who you are, or what your job is. I only know that our orders concerning you came direct from GHQ Middle East – and that is to kick you out in the region of Syracuse while my lot fly on to deal with some heavy guns."

Beard said nothing immediately. He simply smiled, the way he'd watched Gibbs. His smile gave nothing away, nor invited further discussion on the matter. The smile, and those steely eyes, were all the answer anyone got from Gibbs in such circumstances. Beard, while happy to emulate his superior, relented only to say, "It's a need-to-know thing." He had no intention of telling anyone that his was a very small affair compared with the overall operation – which entailed thousands upon thousands of men being delivered by ships, planes and gliders to several parts of the Sicilian mainland.

Their guardian, the giant sergeant, identified as Master-Sergeant Kaiser Jefferson, led them to tents where they unloaded their gear; they then followed him to a PX where goodies in the shape of fruit and candy, condoms and booklets in Arabic, French, Italian and Greek containing phrases to meet a wide range of needs were freely available; then followed him to a mess-tent the size of a football pitch and ate steaks the size of footballs with French fries and green salads, followed by peaches and ice-cream, washed down with unlimited coffee – tea was an unmentionable word. Beard, looking round at the busy jaws, thought, "One thing about the Yanks, they certainly know how to go to war!"

M/Sgt Jefferson said they could attend a film show in the camp (Betty Grable was showing off her legs, he informed them), attend church services of their choice, or simply get their heads down. The majority chose to rest, but first everyone checked and packed his own parachute in a giant canvas hangar; and no man let his chute out of his sight after that. Beard, having attended the conference with Gen Washington-Brown, explained to his team how their mission would fit in with the main event, and wished them all good luck.

Beard retired early, and was somewhat miffed to dream not of heroic deeds in battle, but of Ruth shooting kisses at him with her hand.

M/Sgt Jefferson had said they would be flying out at 0027 hrs – and he undertook to call them in good time. He duly did so, looking immaculate as ever, and escorted them to their plane, calling "Good luck" after them as Beard and his men clambered aboard.

"Hi, buddy!" greeted the pilot as Beard poked his head into the cockpit, with Sgt Hall peering over his shoulder. The pilot's soft hat, with its eagle-badge seeming out of all proportion, was pushed back from his forehead, and an unlit cigar was jammed into a corner of his mouth, which was made larger than it really was by its enormous grin of welcome. It was a young, fresh face and his lean body was encased in a flying-jacket that hung open to the waist. "I'm your chauffeur, boys. Welcome aboard."

Beard grinned back and breathed a "Hello." Sgt Hall only frowned at the informality.

"I'm Lieutenant James Humfrey Maxwell 111 – but just call me Max." He indicated the gum-chewing man seated alongside him: the man looked up from reading a paperback edition of Little Dorrit and gave a nod and a wink by way of greeting. "An' the professor is Hank Schneider, my co-pilot ... he does most of the work around here, when he can tear himself away from his books!" He laughed enthusiastically at his own joke, and added, as a screwed-up ball of a face appeared and cast a small shadow among them, "An' this, gentlemen, is Sgt Arney Saunders – an' he really runs the whole shebang, according to him! The sarge answers to the name of Buck – and a lot else besides!"

There were quick nods and handshakes all round, then Sgt Hall accompanied the small but heavily-moustached Buck to superintend the men and their gear.

Beard sank into a vacant seat behind the pilots, and asked eagerly: "When do we go?"

"You in a hurry, Mac?" asked Max, looking quite horrified.

"You bet," returned Beard enthusiastically. "Made plenty of jumps in training, but I've never jumped into action before."

Max shook his head. He examined his watch, then the instrument panel before him, and said in his lazy drawl: "Wa-al, you'll haveta wait a bit longer 'cos we can't take off till we get the word, pal. There's about a million planes up in the air tonight for this Husky lark, so it's a question of waiting our turn – and then making bloody sure we don't stray out of position, 'cos if we did we couldn't help but hit another plane." He enjoyed a loud laugh, rolling the unlit cigar around in his mouth. "Once we get the green light, I promise you we'll be out of here faster'n you can yell Hallelujah!"

The sky – although they could hardly see a thing beyond the Plexiglas windows – was crowded as they approached the coast of Sicily; there were bombers toing and froing from softening-up raids, fighters swooping around, score upon score of C-47s towing Horsa gliders crammed with infantry, guns and supplies – and somewhere in the middle of this was the plane carrying Beard and his team. The crossing from North Africa had been uneventful, though the weather had been foul: but the word was that on Sicily itself things would be perfect for the invasion, whatever that meant.

When they were about a dozen miles from the coastline heavy anti-aircraft batteries made their presence known, and felt. Even in the half-light the flak could be seen bursting above and below and in the midst of the armada of aircraft droning relentlessly to an orderly landfall. Planes shuddered from near misses. As the volume of flak intensified, and increased in accuracy, Beard could sense the struggle some pilots were having to hold their machines steady on course. Several didn't manage it, and their planes plummeted into the sea, sometimes colliding with other aircraft on the way. All over the sky blazing C-47s careered about causing quite as much destruction as the AA guns. Wings of other planes were chewed off by propellers, or simply sheered off cleanly in collisions or by ground-fire, and still more fell victim to tow ropes left flapping freely behind tugs preparatory to being jettisoned; they wrapped themselves round gliders' wings, sometimes wrenching them off, sometimes flipping a glider over on its back. And then it was their turn to fly the gauntlet.

Beard was just thinking "perhaps we'll be the lucky ones," when the C-47 ahead of them received a direct hit and blew up. The glider it was towing, snapping free from its tow rope, turned a cartwheel and landed on top of Beard's aircraft. This coincided with a deafening, and jarring, explosion in the cockpit area that led to a hurricane of wind, dense acrid smoke and debris tearing through the body of the plane wreaking havoc as it went and leaving everyone dazed, blinded and choking – and, some injured and two men dead. The plane itself gave a fearful judder and continued to shake itself almost to pieces before tilting sideways and dropping like a stone for several hundred feet. It was then, as Beard was still struggling to his feet and yelling to his men to be ready to jump, that the miracle occurred. The plane suddenly levelled out with a jar that sucked the breath from Beard's lungs. Miracle? his mind asked. If so, it was a miracle that required someone to be flying the plane.

Beard raised his head from the floor cautiously, and peered anxiously about him. He could scarcely see anything through the smoke apart from a jumble of arms and legs. Beard struggled to his feet shouting "Get hooked up, and wait!" conscious that an American voice was shouting the same instruction to anyone who was able to hear above the uproar. Beard knew he had to reach the cockpit to find out what was happening, though getting there was like fighting an obstacle course, with bits of plane and injured men blocking the way, while bits of everything were flying around. He clambered over wreckage to reach the cockpit, and in the same instant something new and heavy smashed into the plane. But though the plane juddered alarmingly, it steadied out again and flew on. It seemed – well, like the miracle was continuing. Beard, pressed on, the miracle apparently shielding him from the lethal debris flying all around, thinking to himself, "A chap could get killed here."

Then he found himself face to face with real death, and for several long moments he stopped thinking.

There was hardly any of the cockpit left: it was open to the elements like a veranda, nothing recognizable, only unutterable destruction. The whole of the front was gone, smashed inwards by the glider that had catapulted into them, and an AA shell that had scored a direct hit almost at the same moment. The wonder was that they were still flying. Perhaps it was all part of the miracle. The port engine had exploded and, like the glider, hurled itself at the pilots and come to rest a foot or so above Max, held up only by two metal struts that showed signs of buckling at any moment. Still strapped to his seat, Max was skewered by two blades of the propeller. The blades, or rather shafts from them, had passed right through his body – one in the chest region and one through the stomach, and then burying themselves in the seat. Blood spouted from Max like geysers from a dozen wounds; it gushed from fearful facial gashes, and an eye looked to have been torn out of its socket. Schneider, too, still sat trapped in his seat. Another blade had mercifully decapitated him in a single blow, and freed him from any further pain. His head lay in his lap together with Little Dorrit.

Miraculously – perhaps, cruelly – Max was still alive: even conscious at intervals. He seemed unaware of any great pain, and Beard assumed this was because most of him was paralysed. Max couldn't see anything nor move his head, although his arms – his fingers and hands, anyway – seemed to be functioning, after a fashion. Max felt, rather than saw, Beard as he reached his side and bent over him.

"What ... a lark, eh!" he whispered, and the barely audible croak released a steady dribble of blood.

Beard knew that there was nothing to be done, although he thought a bullet might provide blessed relief. He cast an anxious eye at the engine suspended above the pilot, flinched fractionally away, and then found his attention held by the man's hands. Incredibly, they still held the control column and, apparently, it was those hands alone that were holding the bucketing plane up. This was their miracle. But the miracle was dying fast. Already Max was passing in and out of life for several precious seconds at a time. What would happen once Max released his grip on the joystick? Beard instinctively grabbed at Max's hands as the plane dropped sharply, and heaved on the column. He didn't know what else to do, but it seemed to have the desired effect: the plane gave a wobble and levelled out. Beard sensed that Max was conscious again and was mouthing the word "Go," followed, he was sure, by "What a lark!"

Knowing that time was running out, Beard returned to his men to tell them to dump everything and jump, and saw that another officer and Sgt Buck were already organizing things. Beard didn't know the man but they exchanged grim nods, and together hurried the exits. He wondered how far they'd have to swim; wondered, too, how high they were. His own four men were waiting for him by the exit door, which made him both pleased and alarmed. "Strip off every scrap of equipment you can ... grenades, ammo, weapons, packs ... the lot. But hang on to your chutes!" Sgt Hall gave a stolid grin, but for the most part the men were already too busy shedding everything that unfastened. Beard rushed on, "Don't know how far we'll have to swim ... tie your boots to your belts, or anywhere else where it won't hamper your swimming. It might be a long swim so stick together. On your way, boys – NOW!"

They were the last to jump, but instead of following them, Beard returned to the cockpit with the intention of ending Max's agony with a bullet, only to find him already dead. Beard, conscious that the plane was well ablaze and plunging, hastened to the exit door, unbuckling things as he went, and hurled himself through the door with no idea what height he was at, nor how far he'd have to swim. He pulled the ripcord, and prayed.

The water was cold, and filthy. Beard had no time to see where his plane crashed; the sea had rushed up to meet him almost immediately. He'd slapped his quick-release button and fell from the harness of his parachute only feet from the water. It seemed an age before he spluttered to the surface, conscious of having swallowed something distasteful, and it was then that he realised how intensely cold the water was. His descent had lasted no time: just a matter of seconds; he reckoned probably less than 600 feet.

He looked around him, conscious of a strong smell and taste of fuel oil in the water, studied the distant shoreline for several minutes to make sure it wasn't a cloud, and decided it was about a mile off, possibly a lot less: it was hard to be accurate with your head level with the water and waves bobbing you up and down. He realised now that despite his orders to others, he'd had time to divest himself of very little before leaping from the plane; all he'd managed to get rid of was what was on his back and some of the webbing at the front, which still left him with his boots, water-logged uniform – and his pistol, which seemed nailed to his body. There were several men splashing about nearby, a few floating face down, but most were swimming. He saw a group of men clinging to a large section of a plane's wing and struggled over to join them, and together they kicked towards land.

Almost the moment Beard crawled ashore, still spewing out mouthfuls of polluted water, a familiar voice greeted him. "That you, Mr Beard?" And it was Sgt Hall, stripped to his underpants, who came over and helped heave him to his feet. "Gone native, sergeant?" Beard queried, still dripping and spitting out sea water. "Seemed the best way to get dry, sir," grinned the sergeant. "Cole and Thompson are drying off back among the rocks," he added, "but we haven't seen Webb yet."

Pte Webb made his appearance some two hours later looking more dishevelled than the rest of them. He'd apparently clung to a piece of timber that had drifted considerably further up the coast, but his main complaint was that he'd lost his "fucking trousers" in the water, and he didn't intend invading anywhere in the nude. He'd eventually taken a pair off a floating body and now appeared, almost presentable – in so far as a man wearing trousers suited to a man twice his girth could, with his boots dangling round his neck. Beard noticed, with some approval, that the man still had a knife sticking out of both his socks.

As far as one could see along the beach there were groups of men in various stages of déshabillé, recounting unlikely stories of their survival. There was nothing much they could do. The sounds of war were all around them, but at a distance, and for the moment Beard was content for it to remain so, but he knew they had to get off the beach as quickly as possible. He led his group to the top of the cliff and, about a quarter of a mile inland, in the shelter of some wooded hills, saw what was left of a shell-hit house. It was surrounded by a confusion of mulberry trees, oleanders with scarlet blooms and orange and fig trees, and it was on these that they hung what clothes they possessed. The sun seemed a long time getting up that morning, but when it did, it was high and hot and quickly dried and warmed them all, though their clothes took a bit longer, and were eventually put on still on the damp side. Beard was the only one with a gun: his revolver, which he was busily drying as best he could with one of Ruth's wrung-out hankies.

When they felt dry enough, Beard thought they should make an effort to rejoin the war and, a dozen or so miles later they topped a second rise to find themselves looking down on Syracuse – another twenty-odd miles away. Syracuse itself was already crowded with men of the 8th Army's 5th Division, and the harbour was full of Allied ships disembarking ever more troops. It was already past midday, but Beard decided they'd set straight off for Syracuse, where at least they were assured of being fed. So, in the heat of the day, they set off and it was their own sweat that now soaked their near-dry clothing. They kept coming across the bodies of German soldiers, and stripped them of whatever clothing and weapons they needed. In this way, Beard, the eternal forager, acquired a Luger pistol, a Schmeisser and a pair of excellent night binoculars; and Webb exchanged his trousers for a better-fitting pair, and those needing shirts took them, too.

So, it was a dishevelled, but well armed, group that finally reported in at Syracuse that evening. In the efficient way of the military, they were given hot food, hot showers and an exchange of clothing, as well as being allocated sleeping quarters, all of which Beard thought was pretty good going for an army that had landed only a few hours earlier. It seemed absolutely delicious to strip off his clothes, especially his boots, and stretch out naked beneath the blanket, oblivious of what other life shared his bed. He was asleep almost before he closed his eyes.

He was beginning to dream of faraway things like Ruth and cricket when a MP sergeant shook him awake to hand over orders relating to Augusta. He and his men were to report at the port office at noon; a Jeep would collect them at the billet at 11.30 hrs. Beard was further instructed to replenish what explosives and weapons they'd lost. The MP undertook to escort Beard to the nearest depot to arrange this.

Beard and his men were no sooner arrived in Syracuse docks than they were whisked aboard a non-descript former cross-Channel ferry named Wych Cross, but now allocated the number 1307, and just as hastily stowed below with instructions to stay put until their target had been secured. Their hosts, the SAS, had orders to capture and hold the port till relieved by the main army fighting its way overland.

Augusta, they had all been assured, would be a doddle. What they were not told was that the Royal Navy had, only the previous day, been sent packing by six-inch coastal guns sited in the hills surrounding the harbour when it attempted to intimidate the garrison into submission. But as the Wych Cross moved slowly out into the Ionian Sea and proceeded at full steam towards Augusta, picking up an escort of two destroyers and a cruiser as she went, it would seem that the Royal Navy's appearance the day before had had its desired effect – when all was over it was found that the coastal guns had been destroyed by its gunners, who had then fled. Only a few gun crews had officers with backbone enough to stay and make a fight of it, and theirs were the guns which opened up now, but even their resolve wavered as the guns of the British warships replied and quickly found the range.

The sea was calm and the sun still pleasantly warm as the duel of the big guns screamed overhead with the Wych Cross in the middle, impatient to add her terrier's yap with her little 12-pounder. Occasional shells were directed at her but were no real threat, and the Wych Cross pressed forward, eager to discharge her business and then be free to hurry out of harm's way. Beard and his companions studied the shore line, and especially the harbour, through binoculars with increased intensity as it loomed closer, examining the installations and adjoining buildings, scanning town landmarks, like the citadel and the all-important bridge that linked it to the mainland, searching the waterfront for any offensive activity. They fully expected something to come out and attack them, but nothing did. There was no sign of life; the whole place appeared deserted.

"Maybe they're all dead," muttered Thompson to no one in particular. "Make sure you don't join 'em, then," growled Sgt Cole. "There's none so dangerous as an enemy you don't see." Beard nodded, but otherwise ignored the banter. He was searching for any building that might resemble the hotel where Sturmbannführer Karl Pffinkel was supposed to be holed up. He thought he'd located a place suitably grand to be ascribed Grand Hotel, the man's residence. It was not all that far off. "If I was Pffinkel, I'd be long gone," Beard mused. "I hope there's a proper pub ashore," said Webb to no one in particular, though they all laughed.

The Wych Cross opened up with her pop gun as she closed on the harbour, but she did not appear to do anything more than frighten some seagulls. The Wych Cross herself continued to bear a charmed life in that not even a bullet violated her body. Presently, it was just after 1930 hrs, she reached a point about a quarter-mile off the outer boom, and proceeded to lower the LCAs which wasted no time in heading for the shore. Once there, they came under concentrated enfilade fire from heavy machine-guns sited on either side as they entered the deserted harbour at their best speed. Mortars were also brought to bear on them. As far as Beard could see none of this fire had any effect on the SAS, and as soon as an LCA was available Beard ordered his team aboard, and they were soon ashore.

The Navy's bombardment appeared to have knocked out most of the enemy's batteries by now, but a few guns still roared defiance till, one by one, they too were silenced. The battle was carried on by the heavy machine-guns and mortars both in the town and on the mainland, and snipers seemed to be everywhere. Even as the shelling and shooting continued, Beard darted into the town and down an alley, shouting over his shoulder "Follow me."

Beard's study of the town through binoculars stood him in good stead for he seemed to have an unerring instinct for knowing where he was. Even so, after moving cautiously along passages and streets for twenty minutes or more, he called a halt in the shelter of a long stone arcade, and warned his team, "We're close to our target, the Grand Hotel. It should be down the next street and overlooking some sort of square. I know you've all done this sort of thing before, but I want no heroics. We grab this chap – if he's still there, and scram back to the dockside as quickly as possible." He added bluntly, in anticipation of queries, "We're not part of the fighting that's going on elsewhere around us, though obviously we will defend ourselves if provoked. But remember, our job here is not the fighting but to secure our prisoner before he does a bunk."

They came under sniper fire almost as soon as they entered the street leading to the square, and it was quickly evident that German troops still occupied several of the houses. Automatic fire was sprayed randomly down the street from several windows. Beard quickly decided to about turn, and ten minutes later they arrived at the rear of the Grand Hotel, which was still flying both Italian and German flags. Leaving Thompson to watch the back, with instructions not to let anybody enter or leave the building, Beard led the way into the hotel after telling his men to use silencers on their weapons so as not to give Brandt any warning. It was as well, for they met and shot several Germans as they made their way to the front entrance. There in the foyer were several more Germans and Italians, all with guns in their hands, anxiously discussing the gunfire outside; they were summarily despatched, for Beard was only interested in taking one prisoner. Outside were sentries and machine guns behind sandbag shields; they, too, were eliminated silently.

Beard left Webb to keep watch on things at the front entrance, while he made a thorough sweep of the ground floor with Sgt Hall and Cpl Cole, but found only bewildered, cowering staff and a despondent manager whose fat and oily face immediately brightened at the sight of fresh uniforms. The manager approached them with an air of cautious reverence, rolling his fat hands lovingly together as he bowed, as far as his cumbersome stomach would allow, and welcomed Beard with sickening smarminess. Beard, ignoring him completely, walked away to peer into various nooks and crannies, and eventually it was left to Cpl Cole to enquire, "What's he prattling on about, sir?" Beard, coming up to them, listened to the manager for a few moments and, giving a shrug, replied: "I think he's offering me the keys of this hostelry ... or Augusta ... or both." They both laughed, and the manager continued to babble as though pleading for his life; and after a few moments Beard gave the man cause to be fearful by prodding him with the muzzle of his pistol, at the same time putting a finger meaningfully to his lips and growling "*Silenzio!*" In the sudden silence that ensued, Beard demanded the pass keys for the upstairs rooms and the visitors' book.

Salvatore Rossini, for so the man identified himself and assured "his excellency" that that the hotel had virtually emptied overnight – "the invasion, you know" – but that, of course, His Excellency the *Colonnello* could have anything he desired ; and, moving behind the reception desk, he produced both book and keys. At the end of several minutes, Beard, ignoring his elevation in rank, roared to the man to be silent, and turning to Sgt Hall, said wearily, "He says there's nobody left, but we'll make sure. I don't trust people when they're too helpful." He told the manager to lead the way, and one by one the first floor rooms were checked. Sgt Hall ticked the names and room numbers off in the visitors' book as they went. In one room were an elderly Italian couple hugging each other in terror: Beard simply said, *"Mi scusi!"* and closed the door. In a second room they found two teenage boys, also hugging each other: Beard simply growled *"Continuare!"* and slammed the door.

It was on the second floor that Signor Rossini became noticeably more agitated and had to be physically dragged along by Cpl Cole, whose rough attempts to calm the man's fears largely served to increase them. When they came to No 7, Signor Rossini shrank back and looked about to faint, but Cpl Cole held him firmly upright. The door was found to have a key already in the lock – on the inside, and Signor Rossini, weak as he was, made as if to knock on the panelled door but his arm was arrested in mid-air by Beard, who smiled menacingly and shook his head. Beard turned the handle noiselessly and pushed gently: the door was unlocked and opened readily and soundlessly; if it had been locked, Beard had already made up his mind to shoot the lock out and charge in – shoving the manager ahead of him. All four moved quickly and silently into the room – Signor Rossini being propelled by Cpl Cole's sub-machine-gun jabbed sharply into his back.

It was Signor Rossini – of course – who made their presence known, endlessly repeating *mi scusi*! in a panicky voice that yet clung to the hope that the room might be empty. But the moment he began his excited ranting up popped a girl's startled face from the rumpled bedclothes. It was followed almost at once by her naked torso. She gave an initial tiny squeal of surprise, but otherwise made no sound. There was no hint of alarm in her face. She just sat there, motionless and erect, like a queen on her throne, staring back at the intruders; perhaps there was a suggestion of indignation in her eyes, it certainly wasn't fear; there was something indefinable there, but whatever it was, she made no attempt to cover up her nakedness – for which Beard, for one, was most appreciative.

She really was a joy for the eyes of mankind: a real beauty. She was a robust-looking girl, probably in her early twenties, or even late teens, with raven hair tumbling over her shoulders, the glossy tresses threatening to conceal her thrusting breasts which looked so firm and full. Her skin was a blend of olive and bronze, and smooth as silk like the emerald sheet which was bunched about her middle, looking not unlike a classical tutu; her face was round, with a short blunt nose, a large red mouth, and the whole dominated by her large, dark, bold eyes. They were so deeply dark they might have been black, and they gazed with an intensity that transfixed them all.

Beard was one of those so paralysed; and blissfully so. He had been wondering what she was doing still in bed with the sounds of battle all around, now it seemed the most natural place for her to be at any time, and he wished only that he might join her there. He stared straight back at her, absorbing every voluptuous curve on view, and trying to visualize those that weren't. After a very long inspection, or so it seemed to him although a moment was all there was, the magical interlude was shattered by a voluble outburst from Signor Rossini which brought Beard crashing back to reality. Signor Rossini and the girl suddenly began shouting furiously at each other, he angrily waving his podgy fists, and she hurling abuse back at him. Cpl Cole, tearing his gaze from the girl, turned to Beard and shouted above the din: "What's going on, sir? Ain't she paid 'er bill, or summat?"

Beard shrugged with magnificent imperturbability, and answered just loud enough to be heard above the shouting match: "On the contrary, I shouldn't think she's ever had to pay a bill in her life. Too used to having such things looked after by someone else. My guess is there has to be a man around here somewhere." He tore his eyes away from the girl, and told Cpl Cole, "For God's sake shut this bugger up somehow – gag him or shoot him, I don't much mind which. Just make it quick, and permanent."

As things transpired, Signor Rossini and his tiresome voice became a matter of some irrelevance. Beard, exasperated beyond endurance as the girl joined in the shouting match, fired a single shot into the ceiling, which had the effect of silencing both their tongues, Rossini's and the girl's, even before the plaster reached the floor. Then, the event that put the seal on the silence for good and all, came as Beard stepped towards the girl – whose name, he now gathered, was Didi – and he saw, on the far side of the enormous tumbled up bed, a German officer's uniform neatly draped over a sort of Sicilian version of a chesterfield.

The soldier in him was alerted instantly. He whirled round, his eyes everywhere, his gun searching out the darker recesses of the room, fully expecting to find the owner of the clothes lurking in the shadows. Finding nothing, he shouted warnings to his two men and turned his attention back to the bed, where Didi, seeing she was no longer the centre of attraction, decided it was time to consider her modesty, which she endeavoured to do by covering herself with totally inadequate hands. The movement disturbed the sheets, ever so slightly, but it was sufficient to reveal to Beard a single blue eye watching him; it was peering from behind the girl's back: round the curve of her bottom, to be precise – and in that one glimpse he realised why she was still bed. He should have guessed she wouldn't be alone there.

Yelling to Cole and Hall, Beard dived for the bed, shouldering

Didi rudely aside and, seeking and finding one ankle while Hall grabbed the other, hauled her suddenly very vocal companion from beneath the sheets. The German – blond, blue-eyed and complete with duelling scar – came to rest with a thump sitting on the floor, as naked as his partner. He looked to be in his late thirties, not awfully tall, but lithe and strong. He might have been quite a handsome man, despite the scar, had he been able to control his indignation. He could not, and his face crimsoned, as if he was having a fit, as he gave vent to his outrage with a torrent of apoplectic words. The words, whose blasphemous translation – but not their meaning – were lost on Cole and Hall, were brought to an abrupt and savage stop as Cole whacked him across the mouth with the barrel of his Schmeisser. The man gave a howl of pain and clapped his hands to a mouth already gushing blood. He continued to sit there swaying and moaning, the blood oozing between his cradling fingers, dribbling down his body and splattering on to the carpet where the stains grew like the circles on water. After a moment or two, he made a cup of his hands and spat a couple of teeth into them. The whites of his so-blue eyes seemed to turn pink as they glared at the corporal.

Beard knew straightaway that this was the man he'd been sent to capture. He answered exactly the description, inadequate though it might have been, Gibbs had given him. No matter what he was calling himself now, this was undoubtedly Sturmbannführer Karl Pffinkel.

Didi, seeing she was no longer being admired, took the opportunity of seeking refuge behind a bolster at the top of the bed, her pillow having fallen to the floor, from where she peered at the German with something approximating disappointment. She spat out the single word, "*Bastardo!*"

Beard, having carefully gone through the officer's clothes, and emptied the pockets, flung them over to Sgt Hall. "Let the bastard dress, sergeant," he instructed. "He doesn't look all that attractive as he is. Watch every movement he makes. We don't want him taking any suicide pills, do we?"

"Can't we just shoot 'im, sir?" Sgt Hall urged, eyeing the German with fresh repulsion.

But Beard was too preoccupied examining the German's papers to reply immediately. The documents, which included map sketches, appeared to identify the man – just as Gibbs had spelled out in Cairo – as Major Klaus Brandt of the Hermann Goering Panzer Division; they also identified him as an SS officer in a different name and rank: Sturmbannführer Karl Pffinkel. There was also a pass claiming allegiance to an Intelligence unit – this in the name of Albert Pröhl. Beard knew he had made an important capture. Well, of course he had, that's why he'd been sent to get him. Brandt seemed to be a man of many parts – perhaps too many. Intelligence would have a field day with him. Perhaps, after all, the real credit was Gibbs's: dammit, he'd even had the fellow's address.

At length, Beard shook his head. "I'm afraid not, sergeant. We need to get him to Intelligence as quickly as possible, I'm thinking," he told Sgt Hall seriously. "Don't take your eyes off him."

"Do you think he's some sort of a spy, sir?" asked Sgt Hall.

Beard shrugged, and then nodded his head slowly. "Something like that, sergeant. At any rate, he's the fellow we came for, so all we have to do now is find a way back to Cairo. Intelligence need to see these papers as soon as possible."

Sgt Hall regarded the prisoner – whatever his name – with renewed interest, possibly even awe. He'd never met a spy before. "Why the devil do you suppose he didn't escape with the others while he had the chance?"

Beard looked across at Didi, and gave another shrug. "Had other things on his mind ... and left it too late, didn't he?"

Sgt Hall grinned. "Not very professional behaviour, is it? Not for someone in his line of work. He should have shot her, and got the hell out of here." He glanced momentarily in the direction of Didi who was almost hidden by a pillow she was clutching to her. "Will they shoot him, do you suppose, sir?"

Another shrug. "Tie his hands behind his back, sergeant," he directed. "And put something in his mouth. We don't want him dripping blood all over the place – or we'll have every rabid beast for miles dogging our tracks."

Sgt Hall, who would far sooner have been slipping a noose over the man's head, made the man wince as he tied his hands, and he shoved one of the German's own socks in his mouth to staunch the blood. He then pushed the man into a chair, and stood guard over him.

Beard turned back to the half-hidden girl, and knew she'd need interrogating by experts, too. And he thought how terrible it would be if they had to shoot her as well.

Didi peered furtively round the edge of her shielding pillow once again, glanced from Beard to Sgt Hall and, after some deliberation, demurely asked if she might get dressed. Beard shrugged, and nodded, with well-concealed reluctance. Cpl Cole emerged from searching the connecting bathroom and they all watched her as avidly as if she'd been a performer on the stage of the Windmill Theatre in London as she pushed aside the bolster. Whatever modesty troubled her appeared to vanish as she discarded this final protection for, with a contemptuous toss of her head at Signor Rossini and a saucy smile at the soldiers, she swung herself off the bed and minced – with delicious indelicacy – across the room to a wardrobe; and Beard for one was convinced that each delicate pink buttock beckoned to him in turn as she wiggled. He knew he was getting a hard on as he watched her with aching eyes and thumping heart, hardly daring to breathe as he licked his dry lips, not wanting to miss a moment of her nakedness as she moved over the carpet with the slow grace of a ballet dancer.

His eyes were still glued to her – and for the moment it was her voluptuous bottom that was on display – as she fussed inside the wardrobe among a rainbow of garments and selected what appeared to be a patch-work bathrobe, and slowly turned towards him. Beard's head was too full of lascivious thoughts to see, till ... too late, the tiny mother-of-pearl-handled pistol in her hand as it emerged from a pocket of the robe.

It was pointing straight at him.

There was no time to leap aside or to reach for his own gun: there was only an instant in which to move fractionally sideways so as to present the smallest possible target as she fired. The bullet struck him high on the head, just above his right eye, but because he was in the act of moving, it was only a glancing hit; it grazed the bone beneath the brow with quite a thump, and bounced away. He felt it scorch along the length of his eyebrow, hurting excruciatingly, and then he was conscious only that his eye lost all vision and thought, as he fell to the floor, that he'd lost the eye – although he was only aware of a stinging hurt above the socket. Even before he hit the floor, he was aware of another infinitely louder burst of gunfire, obviously from an automatic weapon, accompanied by a single strangled scream, and then another burst of sub-machine-gun fire. He must have blacked out for a moment or two at that point for he didn't remember anything more.

Cpl Cole had pretty well cut Didi in half with a prolonged burst from his Schmeisser right across her chest, she barely had time to scream; he had then emptied the magazine into Signor Rossini for no better reason than that the man made the mistake of moving – perhaps only to stretch his hands higher in the air. Automatically kicking both bodies to make sure no miracle had saved them – a needless precaution since there was a gaping hole where Didi's heart had breathed, and Signor Rossini's stomach gaped open as if he had committed hara kiri – Cpl Cole now knelt beside Beard and, with surprising gentleness, turned him over.

Beard's good eye opened almost immediately, and straight away he knew that his other one was still in place, and functioning, for he was aware of a distinctly pinkish blur; he guessed it was blood, and the fact that it was *his* blood did not unduly alarm him: he was content enough for the moment to know that the eye was still there, and functioning. He gave several involuntary gasps as Cpl Cole gently examined the wound, clamped a wet towel over it and kept dabbing at it, ignoring Beard's repeated sharp intakes of breath and occasional savage oaths that escaped his clenched teeth.

"You'll live, sir," declared Cpl Cole, rather too casually; "it's really not much more'n a scratch."

Beard could have punched the man, but he didn't even struggle, just lay there docile as a child while the corporal continued his ministrations. Beard knew he was in good hands.

The bullet had carved a furrow along the brow; it was a nasty cut and rather more than Cpl Cole could cope with; it needed stitching and he was not up to such delicate work, not near eyes. "Hold this towel in place, sir," he said quietly and then tore out of the room and raced down the stairs to tell Webb to find a medical chap, and just at that very moment a soldier with a red cross armband passed, and Cpl Cole grabbed him. "My officer's been 'it in the eye," he explained simply.

Cpl Tim Wheeler followed Cpl Cole up the stairs and was told laconically by Sgt Hall, "Two dead, corporal, and one man wounded. And he isn't so very badly hurt – more stunned than anything. It's Captain Beard." Cpl Wheeler busied himself examining Beard, and nodded agreement. "You're about right, sergeant. A few stitches is all he needs," he said, and proceeded to make rather a meal of cleansing the wound; he inserted three stitches with the grave air of one doing petit point, each of which had Beard gritting his teeth; painstakingly counted off eight tablets into the patient's palm with the advice not to take them – unless he was in particularly severe pain, in which event he should report to the MO anyway; and finally put on a dressing.

"He can take the bandage off tomorrow if he likes," Cpl Wheeler said for general information. "Fresh air is the best therapy for everything – that and cleanliness."

He paused while he packed his instruments and things, then added: "No real need for convalescence, Mr Beard, but I'd avoid the rough stuff for a day or two if you can – which seems likely as I gather the business here is just about over. Just a matter of sitting tight till the boys come up from Syracuse. Matter of hours – that's the word, anyway." He gave Beard a professional glance as the latter stirred into a sitting position. "Still, sir, you were bloody lucky. Another hair's breadth, as the saying goes … "

He smiled amiably at Beard as, with Cpl Cole's help, he lifted him on to his feet and sat him on the bed. Beard, feeling more dead than alive, grunted his appreciation as Cpl Wheeler departed.

As Cpl Wheeler had intimated, the real action was largely over. The port of Augusta had been secured, the SAS controlled the only bridge connecting to the mainland, and the only task now was to hold on to it. The Navy was now in contact with the advancing 5th Division and reported that forward elements of the 17th Brigade should be relieving the defending force before dawn.

Beard was able to send a radio message to Gibbs, courtesy of the Navy, to the effect that Brandt had been secured intact, together with some papers requiring immediate attention. Almost at once, a signal came back ordering Beard to hold on to both prisoner and documents and make his way back to Syracuse and wait at the airfield which was already being made serviceable.

Well, there was nothing they could do until Augusta was relieved and, the Navy being so cooperative, Beard arranged for them to secure Brandt for the night. At the same time, an obliging ship's photographer offered to photo-copy Beard's collection of documents, and so these too were locked up for the night. Beard felt sure Gibbs would appreciate having the extra photos for his own purposes. This left Beard and his men with a free evening.

Those soldiers not engaged in defending the bridge were already whooping it up. The bars did a roaring trade – or they would have done had anybody been paying; it was the happy hour gone mad. The men soon spilled out into the rubble-strewn streets where fires, continuously fed, provided quite sufficient light for their energetic parties. Beard, having decided that *vino* was as good a panacea for his throbbing head as anything else, told his men to enjoy themselves and not get lost. "We'll be staying at the Grand tonight," he grinned.

Beard moved on, stopping every few yards to exchange greetings and drinks with the revellers, and then sauntering on and, in a little leafy square, he spotted Sgt Hall seated at a table with a dazzling array of bottles; he had his arm round a voluptuous female with masses of black hair cascading down her back, and an exceedingly tall topper on his head. He was evidently endeavouring to teach her the Henley Regatta Boat Song, with comically hideous results, and Beard, not wishing to intrude, turned down a side street; his head was in no condition for such goings-on. He wondered what Cpl Cole was up to – and then thought it better that he didn't know. "Probably plotting somebody's assassination," he mused gravely, but almost at once reprimanded himself. After all, the man had saved his life that day.

And then his ears picked up the first rumours. They began as the tiniest of whispers, and spread like wildfire into a flurry of furtive activity, all in the space of a few minutes. There was wholesale looting going on. No one seemed sure how it all started, nor even whether it was sanctioned by anyone with any authority – there were those who swore blind that it had been, but they chose not to remember by whom. No time was wasted. Men of all ranks, fanned out in search of treasure, and Beard told himself that if there was anything to be had, he was going to have his share.

There wasn't much to be had. Presumably the Germans had had first pickings, then the Italians, and now the cupboard was virtually bare. Even so, men could be seen darting in and out of buildings and hurrying off with mysterious, and often quite bulky, bundles. Bolts of silk and other fabrics, carpets, paintings, candlesticks and huge vases were trundled through the streets back towards the dock area, and Beard doubted they'd get any further. There were, however, experienced looters; wiser, more selective men, who knew where to look and chose their loot with an expert eye; it had to be small, and valuable; something that could be easily carried, and was readily saleable. Into this group – if only by chance – fell Beard. He wrestled with his conscience for a whole minute before deciding that he didn't have one and that, besides, he was entitled to his share of the booty. Three times he came across safes that had been expertly opened and rifled – Beard wondered if Sgt Hall had abandoned his young lady and got there first. But in an upstairs office of some questionable mercantile marine company (questionable because apart from the name on the door there was no evidence that any business was done there), Beard found a safe in a dusty cupboard that had either been missed or ignored by the experts – and, and with a degree of expertise of his own, blew it open with no great expectations concerning the contents.

He was to be agreeably surprised.

The safe contained mainly faded documents, but beneath these Beard found an envelope, more a package really, that age had left colourless; inside were a couple of dozen or more round and chunky objects, presumably coins or tokens of some sort. Beard knew nothing of numismatics, but he could decipher pieces of names that suggested Roman emperors and one that spelled out Charlemagne, and all had quite clearly defined heads imprinted on them – even if Charlemagne's nose was missing; he imagined the coins had belonged to some collector, or, and more likely, had been stolen from a museum; he supposed, since they were obviously very ancient, they were of some value, perhaps even great value, and he quickly decided that whoever they had been, they were now very definitely his ... like it was treasure trove, only this time it was going into his pocket, and not the King's. Begging your pardon, sire, he muttered as he slipped the envelope carefully into an inside pocket, and resumed searching – and immediately found more treasure.

There was a tiny bag of black chamois leather containing a two-string pearl necklace, a smallish silver-framed painting of a remarkably ugly woman with a long neck, and a rather squashed cardboard box holding a hand-painted brooch, a cameo of someone's head, and a ring. The moment he saw the ring, Beard said to himself "That's for Ruth!" He couldn't for the life of him imagine why he should think of her at that moment of thievery, having been perfectly content not give her a thought for a very considerable time, but he did so now quite spontaneously. Perhaps, really, the ring would be a sort of peace offering for forgotten birthdays. And having satisfied himself on the point, he turned his attention back to the ring. It winked back at him in the dim light afforded by the bonfires outside, and he felt doubly reassured that all was well. It was a pretty ring with a square diamond of the palest blue surrounded by tiny brilliants. He'd always thought that diamonds were colourless, but the square stone definitely had a bluish tinge about it so perhaps it was something else. It didn't really matter what it was, did it? He didn't suppose Ruth would be bothered; he was sure she'd be over the moon to get anything; still, it looked rather large for her. Perhaps she'd prefer the pearls. The cameo and brooch he'd give to his dear Queenie, and that was everyone taken care of, except Sam; he'd have to settle for a pint – unless Beard could lay his hands on something else, which was quite on the cards. He'd have to ... because he suddenly remembered he'd forgotten Mrs B., which would never do.

All he had to do now was to hang on to his spoils until he could get them safely home ... and from the commotion outside things were beginning to stir in that direction even now.

As dawn was lazily blinking its eyes open, the 17th Brigade, in the shape of an armoured battalion with a heavy artillery unit, linked up with, and promptly relieved, the SAS. Even before then scores of Allied ships had converged on the harbour, and the lengthy business of ferrying ashore thousands of men and their equipment, plus tons of stores, was already under way.

First ashore among these men was a provost marshal, Major Nigel Such, who quickly located Beard and said he'd been ordered to escort his party to an airstrip even then being constructed just north of Syracuse. Beard hurriedly gathered his team up and collected his prisoner and documents, and in next to no time the major had commandeered transport and they were racing southwards and there, at a place called Priolo Gargallo, or thereabouts, their plane was waiting. Beard celebrated the moment of boarding by having his bandage replaced with a wide strip of plaster; he then promptly fell asleep and woke up as they were coming in to land at Cairo.

As the plane came to a halt, Sgt Hall sidled up to Beard's seat and, after a quick stare at Major Such, began searching one of several capacious pockets of his bulging combat jacket. When the hand emerged, it was thrust straight at Beard.

"Here, sir," said Sgt Hall, in an affectedly casual voice, "I thought you might like to 'ave this ... it's more yours than mine, anyways."

It was the little mother-of-pearl-handled pistol Didi had shot him with. Beard automatically checked the safety-catch and breech, and then weighed it in the palm of his hand. It didn't seem possible that such a pretty little thing could have threatened his life ... but it bloody well had done! He couldn't even identify the weapon, probably some sort of Beretta, possibly a made-to-order job to meet the special requirements of a particular lady, whatever her occupation. The pistol could only hold two bullets at a time: it still contained one bullet, so she'd only got the one shot off. It was so small it would fit unobtrusively in her handbag, or almost anywhere about her person ... or in a bathrobe pocket!

"Thank you, Ernest – sure you don't want it?" said Beard, sufficiently moved by the moment to use the sergeant's first name. Now this *was* a trophy to cherish.

Sgt Hall shook his enormous head vigorously.

"I'm surprised Cole didn't grab it for himself – after all, the other bullet was probably meant for him," said Beard, with a smile that died on his lips. Death was no cause for mirth.

"He was too busy fussing over you. I picked it up 'fore he had the chance," declared Sgt Hall. "Mind you, I don't think that manager chap had much of value left on 'im by the time our Tim had done rifling his pockets!"

Beard nodded, and this time he allowed a slight grin to escape his clenched lips. Pocketing the pistol, he turned in his seat to stare round at his team. They looked like a band of pirates with all their weapons, and bearded faces. He touched his own chin – still as smooth as any girl's! – and not for the first time felt embarrassed, and annoyed. It simply wasn't fair – he shared the same dangers as these men, didn't he? You'd think the extra responsibility of his rank would provide him with the fiercest, bushiest of growths. He swept his hand right round his face without encountering a solitary whisker, and sighed. Whoever heard of a beardless leader of men?

□ *"Oh Jarvis, you and your women, they'll be the death of you yet," shrilled Queenie.*

And they all laughed, especially Beard.

Chapter Twenty-one

Somewhere in Poland, September, 1943

Gibbs hailed Beard with a "Well done," and then spoilt the moment by adding, "I heard you'd been near mortally wounded, but I see it's only a bit of a cut. Still, you'd better have a bit of leave." But first he had to write a detailed report of his Sicily adventures, and go over Brandt's documents with the Intelligence people, and when he finally started his leave six days later, he wondered if this was a continuation of his interrupted leave, or a new one.

In the end it turned out to be a very generous three weeks, and on his return to duty, he was greeted warmly by Gibbs, who asked most considerately, "I hope you've had enough time to recover from your Sicilian affair?"

Beard was at once on his guard. "Barely, sir," he replied, and then, not wishing to appear impertinent, he asked, "Did that Brandt fellow prove cooperative?"

"Oh, yes, our Intelligence chaps can be very persuasive – they learned a lot from the Gestapo's methods, not that they can't be just as inventive themselves," said Gibbs darkly. "Once the fellow's smashed jaw had been treated, they were amazed at his readiness to talk. They were surprised and impressed by his volubility, and what with what he told them and those detailed documents you collected, they were able to give information to 13 Corps in Sicily that will save many lives and shorten the campaign there. Everyone at Corps HQ is delighted with the results – and there are suggestions that a decoration might be in order for the man responsible. But I shouldn't hold your breath. Those responsible for such things are mean and slow when it comes to recognizing the gallantry of others, and then they generally manage to honour the wrong man."

"I'm happy enough to have escaped virtually unscathed," declared Beard stoutly. He'd never given a thought of being courageous; he hadn't really done much, nothing heroic – except get almost shot in some poor girl's bedroom. He'd better not mention that fact to Ruth either, he reflected

"Quite so – as I said, just a scratch," agreed Gibbs, and then added with some severity that Beard was partly to blame for letting himself to be shot in such ridiculous circumstances. The woman, declared the colonel, should never have had access to a weapon.

"How the hell do you search a naked girl?" Beard protested, but more amused than indignant.

"Very slowly!" answered Gibbs tongue in cheek, then adding quite sharply: "Never trust a woman, Robert, naked or otherwise – and especially when she turns her back on you." He gave a piratical grin, and went on: "You should've searched that bloody cupboard before letting her ferret around inside it ... good thing she didn't have a grenade hidden in there!"

The colonel roared with laughter at Beard's look of consternation, and told him to resume his training activities.

But Beard didn't mind, not really; he enjoyed physical exercise, especially the long runs. And every so often he could return to the sun-lounger on the verandah of his billet, and enjoy a good sleep, a long bath and several good meals. And one morning, having enjoyed a hearty breakfast, he was swinging contentedly on the sun-lounger, when Cpl Allen, who was still enjoying his mail detail, screeched up, and waved a package at him.

"Ah, are you returning me to the war, Tom?" cried Beard, pretending to scowl.

"No, sir, I've brought your mail," replied Cpl Allen, grinning. "Someone must love you."

"Bring it here, you lovely man!"

"So glad you weren't killed after all, sir," said Cpl Allen, dropping two letters and a somewhat large and soft parcel into Beard's lap. "We'd started a collection for you."

"What for?" cried Beard with a grin.

"The piss up, sir," the corporal grinned back.

"Bugger off!" shouted Beard, laughing.

When he was alone, Beard turned at once to examine his mail. The parcel contained a 10-yard-long scarf of many colours – just what he wanted in the burning Mediterranean heat! He tied it round his middle, and turned to the letters. Naturally, they were both from Ruth. Bless her! He turned to the first letter.

"*My Darling*," it began as usual, and went on to call him all manner of unladylike things for not writing to her – and then thanking him for his "teeny-weeny" note which accompanied his photos of camels and sphinxes and things. "*You looked absolutely gorgeous in the pictures*," she admitted, though Queenie thought he looked "dangerously thin," and added accusingly in the next breath that Sam had said that the sphinx, at least, belonged to Egypt and not to India, so you must have taken them an awful long time ago if you hadn't even reached India. In view of this, Ruth said he very definitely owed her a letter, a very long one, explaining this, and would he PLEASE send it before she died of her "*aching heart*." The rest of the letter was full of puerilities, but at least they were friendly and she closed by sending her undying love – and a photo of herself in her new green dress. It looked lovely, as did she, though her image was spoiled by her very solemn expression – trying to look all grown-up, the little booby, grinned Beard affectionately. Ruth added the usual postscripts from Queenie and Sam, the one reminding him to eat properly, the other urging him to keep his nut down. Ruth added yet another PS repeating her love and her concern for his safety – and telling him to wrap up well with her scarf at nights.

The second letter was very brief (for her) and told him that Sam had been awarded the George Medal! "*And the old darling never said a word about anything to us,*" she wrote, and he could sense her excitement. "*The first we knew was when the letter came from the War Office telling of the award, and saying what he'd done to win it. Apparently, Daddy found this unexploded bomb ticking away – in Chandos Place, right behind the hospital, and just hoisted it up on to a casualty trolley with the help of two ambulancemen – they've got awards, too – told everyone to 'keep their heads down,' and simply trundled it down to the river and tipped it in, trolley and all. He said he was afraid he might be accused of stealing the trolley, but I think he was only joking! The bomb didn't go off for hours but that didn't make it any the less heroic, did it? We're all so terribly proud of him. And Father Daly spoke about his bravery during Mass and said it was an inspiration to us all. And there's a possibility Daddy may receive his Medal from the King himself at the Palace! If so, Mum and I will be there to see him getting it – and we'll wear our posh new frocks for the occasion. Oh, my darling, we're over the moon with excitement and pride.*" Beard was quite as excited and proud, so much so that he forgave her for adding, "*This doesn't mean that you've got to go dashing off and doing something idiotically brave just so's they give you a medal, too! One hero in the family's more than enough – we want you safely home with us, and all in one piece. A thousand medals aren't worth a drop of your blood, my darling.*" There was more of the same, and silly bits like Queenie putting up the price of whisky and things to the Yanks "*because they've got more money'n they know what to do with – which ain't fair when our boys is doin' all the real fightin' and ain't got two pennies to rub together for their pains*"; and the fact that the air raids were easing off – "*except that just when you think they're finally over, back they come and blow the place to bits again.*" There were the inevitable PSs about being careful what he ate – but not to miss any meals, and about keeping his head down.

Beard was sufficiently moved by the letters, which he read over and over again, to go inside there and then and write one of his own in reply. Even so, he was careful about what he said. He did tell Ruth that he was no longer in the Indian Army, but now a captain in the British Army, though he decided against telling her that he was a parachutist (she'd die of fright!) and, indeed, telling her nothing about what he did, saying only that having had a spell of building sandcastles in North Africa, he was now enjoying a spot of leave.

"We're having loads of fun sunbathing and swimming, drinking lots of lovely wine, eating lots of gorgeous food, and helping ourselves to lots of delicious fruit," he told her, as if quoting from a travel brochure. Then, in case he got carried away and mentioned things better left unsaid, he got a colleague to take some snaps of him with plenty of innocent atmosphere in the background, persuaded someone else to develop them and posted the whole lot off – before he changed his mind. There, she could have no complaints now.

His training, meanwhile, continued relentlessly, and every day he half expected to be summoned by Gibbs for some sort of assignment, but there was none. The training exercises continued, and as he sweated, marching miles into the desert, clambering up cliffs with the usual 60lbs of gear about his body and doing many parachute jumps from various heights, he told himself he was being hardened up for the Second Front in Europe. There had been a lot of talk about the coming invasion, with all sorts of suggestions as to where it might take place. An optimistic choice was the beaches at Nice in the South of France, but more realistically they knew it had to be somewhere along France's coastline in the English Channel. Many of Beard's colleagues had already slipped quietly back home to prepare for activities in that area, and Beard grew impatient to be among them. He was getting bored with the sand, flies and heat of Egypt.

But, throughout August and into September, during which the Sicilian campaign ended and the invasion of Italy had taken place, he continued with his training. He had thought that with his knowledge of Italian, he would have been sent there. But, no, he remained in Egypt, fuming at his inactivity, thinking occasionally of Ruth, and talking to camels.

And then it happened.

An official note was delivered at his quarters by an MP corporal ordering him to present himself to Gibbs at Middle East GHQ. Beard hugged himself, saying this was it – his posting back to Blighty for the invasion. His chance to see everyone at the Dials. What sort of leave would they give him once he got there? A long one, he expected; and he felt quite nostalgic for the sounds and smells of old London Town.

But his dreams were dashed the moment he saluted Gibbs. "Sorry to break into your training schedule, Robert, but you can't expect to escape the war indefinitely."

It was a poor joke, and Beard didn't bother to smile: he simply nodded. Gibbs got down to business immediately. Beard guessed it was something dire; unpleasant, anyway.

"I would like to have given you more time to recover from your Sicilian mishap, Robert, but the matter is urgent," he said, and his voice impressed the fact. "Besides," he added with a half smile, "you're the only experienced officer I have to hand. The rest of my officers are –

well, they're away, so there it is." He gave a shrug, toyed with his moustache for a moment or two, then added, "We have to attend a briefing with a Brigadier Charington who is something big in the War Office and, I suspect, the Government. Whatever, we answer to him."

"When, sir?" asked Beard, who really wanted to ask where he was being sent.

"Now."

There were several officers already present in the vast room to which he was directed, among whom he recognised Capt Arthur Kemp and Major Donald Pitt, who were on Gibbs's planning staff. The room was bustling with activity: a sense of urgency pervaded the air: everyone seemed to be rushing about, or making what appeared to be desperately urgent phone calls, or poring over maps and scraps of paper. Beard saluted as a matter of course, but to nobody in particular, and nobody in particular – apart from Kemp, who gave him a brief friendly nod – paid him any immediate heed, though after a few moments a voice from the mêlée round the long table invited him to sit down – and wait.

"Ah, there you are at last. You are Mr Beard?" The question was tossed suddenly in his direction from somewhere in the middle of the table. The voice seemed to contain an element of surprise: even doubt.

"Yes, sir," returned Beard, somewhat taken aback by the question. He had been examining his boots and wondering if he shouldn't have given them a wipe over before coming, and looked up now with a guilty start. Oh God, he thought, had they discovered his true identity after all this time? He leapt to his feet and stood rigidly to attention, his heart thumping wildly as he half expected to be told he was to be shot at dawn, or at the very least that he was under arrest and about to be transported home in chains. Then he remembered they wanted him for a mission, and felt he might live a little longer; he felt safe again.

"Sit down, Mr Beard; sit down," ordered the unknown voice; and Beard sank down, feeling somewhat weak about the knees. "You're very young to be a captain, Mr Beard," drawled the voice, which now seemed a lot less threatening. Beard located the speaker, as a brigadier complete with the red tabs of a staff officer. He was completely bald, with a thin, bony face and a long, skinny frame to match; he sat ramrod straight examining Beard, and was introduced as Brigadier Peter Willoughby Charington – and Beard didn't doubt that he was as tough as old boots.

"I cannot imagine why or how it is my face doesn't keep pace with my years, sir," declared Beard, in as calm a voice as he could conjure up. "It must be the open air life I'm living." Christ! He hoped he wasn't being cheeky. He really should keep his mouth shut, and stop volunteering unsolicited information.

The brigadier gave the faintest of smiles, but it disappeared almost immediately. "Whatever your years, you must be an exceptionally competent officer for I'm told you're just the man we need. We have an exceptional mission for you, captain."

"Yes, sir," said Beard, ignoring the surge of excitement in his chest.

"It's in Poland," said the brigadier, in a voice so smooth he might have been asking Beard if he was interested in going to a cricket match.

"Yes, sir." The words emerged almost of their own accord. Beard had been expecting, hoping for something momentous. But, Poland! Bloody hell! He stared back at the brigadier, and then at some of the other officers at the table, and then back to Brigadier Charington; for once in his life, Beard was at a loss for words. He hadn't heard Poland mentioned since the beginning of the war. He had to think for a moment as to where exactly it was, and the thinking didn't inspire any particular desire to go visiting there. Were there planes that flew that far? He gave his dry throat a quick swallow, and added another "Yes, sir," hoping his voice wasn't lacking in enthusiasm.

"Excellent," declared the brigadier in the same casual voice, his piercing deep-set greenish eyes boring into Beard from beneath thin, untidy brows.

"Yes, sir," repeated Beard, lowering his own eyes from the other's relentless gaze, and glancing instead at the upside down maps strewn across the table. It took him a moment or two to locate Poland, and didn't like the look of it: too far from anywhere friendly: too many mountains. And how the hell was he expected to get back from there? Yes, how?

"Your mission is to bring out a Polish scientist. And time is of the essence," declared Brigadier Charington. "With the Russians now attacking on all fronts, now may be our only chance to snatch this man. It's really an SOE initiative. Their man on the spot, known as Blue Bear, already has our scientist under wraps. Your task, captain, is simply to rendezvous with this man, collect our scientist and any papers he may have and bring them back to us before the Russkies get their mitts on them. Clear?"

"Yes, sir," said Beard once more; there didn't seem to be any other response he could make. "This scientist, sir," he ventured, "where exactly is he?"

Brigadier Charington, having learned all he wanted from Beard's face, turned his gaze on the map before him, hovered over it with a long, bony finger, and then brought the digit down like a diving bird in the south-eastern corner of the country. "There!" he said, and kept stabbing at the spot. "Come round this side and have a look where you're going, captain – you can't see anything from there," he said, and offered Beard the makings of a smile, which made the invitation rather less inviting. "It's really quite a lovely country – lots of forests, meadows, rivers, pretty villages and things."

And Germans, thought Beard as he came round, elbowing himself between the brigadier and a major, and leaning over the table. Poland didn't look any more attractive when seen the right way up, he decided. The brigadier's finger seemed to be buried in the Carpathian mountain range; the finger crept up a fraction and pointed at a place called Przemyśl. "He's there," said the brigadier. "Close to there, anyway. It's on the San river."

It sounded a bit vague. Beard peered with fresh intensity at the map. Przemyśl looked to be almost part of Russia: almost in the Ukraine, anyway. And the war was being raged in that country.

"Aren't the Russians fighting there, sir?" queried Beard, with concern.

"No, they haven't got that far yet," said Brigadier Charington assuredly. "That's why we have to move fast. Tonight, in fact."

Beard had seen this coming, even so, now that it had come, the imminence of his departure shook him. He dredged up a smile, and murmured a "Yes, sir." It seemed to be his password for the day.

"There will be five others in your party. You may need them," went on the brigadier coolly. "You'll tag on behind some Wellingtons destined for the Ploesti oilfields in Romania, and then break off to continue your journey alone. At your destination, you jump after exchanging signals with your reception committee."

"Yes, sir, I follow that," said Beard, almost apologetically, "but … er, I don't quite see how we are to return. This place … Przemyśl, looks to be in the very heart of enemy held territory. Will we be air-lifted out? It's such a distance …"

"It's all been worked out for you, Mr Beard," interrupted the brigadier, a trifle too airily to be entirely convincing. "The man who'll meet you when you land, Blue Bear, or more likely one of his associates, has it all arranged. He'll give you all the gen. After you've collected your scientist, Blue Bear will have seen to it that your exit from Poland is arranged through the Carpathians with a guide into Hungary and transport through that country into Yugoslavia, and on to the coast where we'll send a submarine to collect you all. Couldn't be easier, could it? Bit like a Cook's tour, what! Shouldn't take you much more than a week. The mountains may prove a bit of an obstacle. No telling how long it'll take you getting through them, but you're all trained for that sort of thing, aren't you. Trouble is you chaps never get the opportunity to really use your legs; bit of exercise will be good for you. All that lovely mountain air. But I'm pretty sure Blue Bear will have an easy, pleasant hike planned for you. The only unknown factor, as I see it, is the scientist himself – whether he'll be physically up to this mountain jaunt."

"Yes, sir," said Beard, falling back on his normal reply, and wondering if it shouldn't have been "No, sir," this time. And, if this was going to be such a cakewalk, why did it need six men to bring one old fellow out? He assumed the man would be someone of advanced years. Scientists usually were, weren't they? A thousand other questions hammered away in his head, and he didn't know which he should ask first or, for that matter, if he was entitled to ask any of them. "How am I to recognise this scientist, sir?" he ventured.

"He'll be identified to you when you meet him," answered Charington tersely.

"And what if he's changed his mind and refuses to leave Poland?" Beard pressed.

"Shoot him!" returned the brigadier instantly, his voice cold and blunt. "But make sure you collect all his drawings and any other papers."

Beard stared back, trying hard to hide his shock at the order which came at him like a bullet. "Am I allowed to ask the name of this scientist I am to shoot, sir?" he asked, his own voice sounding less calm than he could have wished..

"Ask him first before you shoot him, Mr Beard!" cried the other, and Beard wasn't too sure he was being reprimanded or not. "It's better that you don't know his identity till you have him physically under your protection, captain. For the moment," said Charington, with a humourless smile, "let's simply refer to him as Buttercup – which is the name of your operation."

Beard smiled, and warmed towards the unknown scientist – the poor sod! "What about the SOE contact?" he asked.

Charington raised one of his untidy brows, and his eyes actually twinkled. "He'll make himself known to you if he's around, and if he's of a mind to. He was headed for Kraków earlier in the week, so it may be you won't actually meet him. In that event, you'll simply make use of his network of contacts among the *Armia Krajowa* – that's the main Polish resistance movement, and there's many of them – and the escape routes he's set up."

"Yes, sir," said Beard automatically, though his mind was still conjuring with the name Buttercup, and wondering how he could be expected to shoot someone with such a name. "So, who do I rendezvous with, if not him?"

"He'll make himself known on the ground, using the Buttercup code-word."

The brigadier abruptly declared that they had better get down to the finer points of the briefing. "The nitty-gritty, as Major Pitt calls it," he added. After that, everyone was very serious and busy as the details of the mission were gone through, maps poured over, equipment and supplies listed and discussed. Any question Beard asked was answered promptly: if it wasn't readily known, someone was detailed to find it out; anything he asked for, he was given – after a nod from Gibbs, who supervised everything. The most important of his requirements was men, and he wondered which five men had been chosen to accompany him on this madcap mission. He'd have thought it more a one-man job. Perhaps the fellow had a lot of luggage, he grinned to himself.

Of the four men who'd been with him in Sicily only Pte Thompson was available, the remainder being otherwise engaged – most likely back in England, on leave, Beard thought ruefully. He would miss Cole especially; they had established a good relationship. The remainder of the quintet comprised Staff Sgt Jack Trumpett, who had been with Beard in Tunisia: tireless and dependable to the nth degree; Cpl Harry Jenkins, slim, fair-haired, although his head was cropped almost bald, thin-lipped and with grey eyes that were never still: a first-class soldier: an instinctive killer, who favoured knives; L/Cpl Aidan Felbridge, the R/T man, also tall and slim, who could march for ever beneath the combined weight of his radio and an assortment of other gear, while determinedly keeping his hands free for his rifle, with which he was a Bisley accredited marksman; and the fifth man was Pte Tom Hill, a short, but clearly very strong man, who had the look of an uneven parcel, being a square and angular person, especially about the face: formerly with a Reconnaissance unit, he had the look of a real soldier.

Arrived at the airfield, Gibbs pushed out his bony hand at Beard and said heartily, "Good luck to you and your men, Robert." He had half turned away when he added: "Do be assured this mission of yours is of paramount importance. Your scientist is more an aviation engineer really. He designs aircraft, and the word is he's come up with a revolutionary type of engine that'll make our present planes obsolete. We mustn't let the enemy get their hands on his designs."

"The enemy including the Russians, I presume?"

"Of course," agreed the colonel, in a lowered voice, "allies are always more dangerous than our enemies. We know who they are. It's the unknown where the danger lies."

Beard nodded, and gave a grim little grin. The more information he was given, the less promising the mission sounded.

"Felbridge is the one we'll be protecting closest, sir. If anything happens to him, we won't be able to contact the submarine, or anybody."

The colonel managed a small smile as he nodded agreement. "The order for this operation came direct from No 10 itself."

Beard was not greatly impressed. He looked down at his papers, and saw the date was Thursday, September 16, 1943. It struck him at that moment that he'd been entitled to vote for two whole days now. This thought did not impress him either.

The flight seemed endless, and cold. At some point, their

Lancaster parted company from the rest which flew on towards the Ploesti oilfields, and straight away a feeling of abandonment was added to their burden of discomforts.

There had been very little time, an hour was all, for Beard to confer with his men, but, as he had known they would, they had taken things in their stride and their good spirits further raised his own. As the plane thundered through the air, he gave up the unequal struggle of shouting further instructions above the engines, and subsided into a series of catnaps. It was the cold that kept waking him. He peered round the dark interior of the plane. Jenkins was the nearest to him. Beard knew the man would be bristling with knives, and hoped he didn't cut his own throat when he landed. Felbridge was stretched out – one hand resting on his radio-transmitter; he seemed to be singing or humming, but Beard could hear nothing above the roar of the plane's engines. Beyond him, lay the formidable length of Trumpett, who looked to be dead to the world, though Beard didn't doubt he'd be alert beneath the surface. And somewhere opposite, almost invisible in the gloom, lay the figures of Thompson and Hill. Beard, wondering if any of them was really asleep, closed his eyes again to shut out any secret fears, knowing everything would be all right when the time came.

The dispatcher kept them informed of their progress and, with minutes to go, he called Beard aside and told him the pilot had reported no ground signal as there should have been, and did Beard want to jump anyway. Remembering the importance of the mission that had been impressed upon him, Beard nodded his head without hesitation, knowing it would mean the huge plane making a fresh run. The men were already fitting their leg bags, which contained all their personal arms and necessities, and then the routine orders were bellowed: "Stand up ... hook up," and they shuffled under the weight of their cumbersome loads towards the yawning exit. Here Beard turned and shouted at his companions, "No dawdling in the doorway looking at the view!" It was meant as a joke, to bolster the men's morale, but nobody laughed. Only the dispatcher grinned, as he shouted "Three minutes to go, gentlemen!" Then a bulb above the door flashed a warning red, and almost immediately its green companion lit up. "Go!"

Beard flung himself out as the lights changed, heaving his kit bag up in the same movement. He was vaguely aware of Jenkins hurtling after him and then felt, rather than heard, his static line slapping against the open doorway, and then he was falling like a stone and hanging on to the rope attached to his leg bag like grim death. After what seemed an eternity, there was an almighty jerk and he was catapulted upwards, spinning and twisting, as his parachute opened and spread out above him. Beard gave an unconscious sigh of relief and peered about him in the almost total dark as he continued his descent at the mercy of the slender silk cords, and thought he could make out Jenkins far above him and a shadow that might have been someone else: it should have been Felbridge, as the next man in the stick.

Below it was even darker. There was no sign of a recognition signal, and Beard wondered what sort of reception there would be for them. Had he been right in his decision to jump? They'd find out within seconds.

Chapter Twenty-two

Operation Buttercup, 17 September, 1943

Beard was searching the blackness beneath him for any sort of a light that might be the missing signal, but saw nothing. Then, just as he was about to snatch at the quick-release for his leg bag, he saw out of the corner of his eye and a good bit to his right, something winking through the trees and instinctively veered in that direction. As a result, he and the heavy bag landed together, one on top of the other, but at least they managed to overshoot the forest of pines, only clipping a few where the trees thinned out.

Beard had barely climbed to his feet than he was blinded by a powerful torch being held no more than twenty-odd yards away. "Turn that fucking searchlight off," he cried out urgently, jumping to one side and whipping out his revolver in the same movement, and whoever was holding the torch switched it off immediately. The blackness that followed was even more intense than before, and while he stood blindly searching ahead, it occurred to him that his English had been understood … perhaps. He tightened his grip on his revolver.

When he'd blinked some vision back into his eyes, Beard peered intently in front of him and almost instantly a shadowy figure stepped out from behind a thick fir tree. Beard stared harder, disbelieving what he saw.

Before him stood a boy, no more than fourteen, with a thin, white face and wearing a black peaked cap from beneath which a pair of sparkling, dark eyes stared back. The boy, who was enveloped in a thick jacket much too large for him, started to flash his torch from side to side.

"Stop doing that," snapped Beard sharply, returning his gun to its holster, as he disentangled himself from the rigging lines and collapsed the billowing canopy of his parachute and gathered it in. The torch went out at once, but after a moment or two resumed its signalling, and Beard somewhat belatedly realised the boy was not alone, and he nodded and muttered "Carry on." But, as the boy began flashing the torch in circles as large as his arms could stretch, Beard growled, "That's enough, for God's sake!" Then, as he moved towards his weapons bag, his eyes still watching the boy, he gave a series of signal whistles so that his men could locate him. There were three immediate responses. Beard having retrieved and checked over his weapons, turned with a frown towards the boy.

"Who the devil are you?" he demanded, his voice stern with suspicion, turning his attention back to the youngster.

"Me, Jan … I say for you … Buttercup," the boy answered, struggling with his English. "We go … Przemyśl. We go fast … still dark."

The boy faltered, his vocabulary exhausted, but Beard was cheered to hear him use the Buttercup word; he must be genuine. Just then, Beard's five men appeared from several directions, together with another man who turned out to be the boy's father. He was a shortish man, very wide, and looked menacingly strong. He had several days' growth of beard with grey eyes to match, and wore a black woolly hat and a long brown leather coat. His eyes gave warning of some adversity, and Beard's heart sank to his boots. Had his man, this scientist chap, died, or had something equally fatal to the mission occurred? Had he come all this way for nothing? More to the point, was his escape back still on?

The man identified himself as Wladyslaw Jasienski, then asked circumspectly, "Buttercup?" Beard nodded, with growing relief. "Force 301?" pursued Jasienski rightly. "303," corrected Beard, impatiently eager to know the worst. The man's face visibly relaxed and some vigorous hand-shaking ensued, and then, with an arm holding his son close to him, Jasienski spilled out his awful news.

Only the previous day, the man who should have been their reception leader, Józef Szajna, together with several of his group, had been detained by the Germans in Leszno, about ten miles from Przemyśl. It appeared to have been a random sweep by the SS and they probably had no idea at present who they had netted, and all might be released after the weekend when the interrogations would probably start. If the Gestapo got involved it might be a different story. Jasienski gave a forlorn shrug, and hurriedly assured Beard that his mission was not compromised.

"We're different units and only a few leaders are known to each other," he explained. "I'm fully cognizant of the purpose why you're here, and will take over Józef's role and see you through the mountains safely and pass you on to your next contact, if that's agreeable."

"Of course," said Beard immediately, having little option over the matter and really not giving a damn who acted as his guide. He was far more concerned that the Germans were likely to be alerted far sooner than might have been hoped; and, besides, he certainly had no desire to be marooned here in Poland. "You speak excellent English," Beard observed, grateful for the fact. "We learn at school," said the other dismissively. Beard smiled, and thought how lazy the English were in this respect – except for him, of course. "How many of you are there?" he asked looking around, for he didn't imagine he'd landed conveniently at the feet of just the father and son. "In addition to ourselves, and we're pretty laden, we've brought you three loads of supplies – probably socks and stuff."

They both smiled at the joke. It all helped to relieve the tension both were feeling. "Thanks, our feet get cold in the winters," said

Jasienski; then, his smile fading, he added, "There are four others strung out. Sorry about the signalling, we had difficulties with our torches – damp batteries, I think. We were afraid you'd abort when you didn't get any signal, but praise God you didn't. We glimpsed your chutes just before you landed. My colleagues will already be pilfering through your presents, for which I thank you on behalf of us all. God bless your Winston Churchill," he beamed hugely, then added, "My men are humping everything to the lorry which will take us all to Przemyśl."

"How far away is that?"

"About thirty kilometres."

"And this man I'm collecting – I've not been given his name, he's ready and is aware of the hazards ahead?" Beard asked bluntly.

Jasienski shrugged, and smiled. "I'm sure he is. Stefan Mickiewicz – that's his name, is used to the mountains, and walking in them. He's been used to both all his life – says that's where his inspirations come from. He knows his journey with you will be a hard one." He paused, then added hurriedly, "We'd better get going. Anything that moves at night is liable to be stopped and searched by the Germans. I'll take you to Stefan's home directly, and leave with the lorry to go on and disperse your goodies. You'll have the whole of tomorrow to discuss details with Stefan. Oh, silly me," he exclaimed with a titter, "it's already tomorrow, isn't it! Friday, I mean. Well, after you've had something to eat and a bit of sleep, you'll be able to talk things over with Stefan later today. My advice is that you all eat and sleep well. We start your journey home at 6am on Saturday – which *is* tomorrow. You'll need to be ready at five o'clock – and wear things so as to look like you're going for a weekend's hike in the mountain foothills."

Beard managed a grin. "We won't look much like hikers with all our weapons."

"You'll have to carry them in suitable holders – there'll be plenty at Stefan's," assured Jasienski, "and suitable clothing." He then added with some concern, "Now, we really must be on our way to meet your host."

Stefan Mickiewicz lived in a big, old house, and this aptly described the man himself, for he was tall, solidly built and his wrinkles gave him the look of being much older than he really was, which Beard thought was no more than sixty. His complexion was more that of a woodsman than a scientist, Beard thought, mindful also of the man's powerful handshake : the hands, too, were calloused and rough ; but he'd never met a scientist before, so perhaps this was the way they were. The man had greeny eyes: sometimes gentle, sometimes intensely sharp. His head was round with straggly greying hair swept fiercely back to cover the beginnings of a small bald circle, like a priest's tonsure. His face certainly had colour enough to confirm his mountain life, or a healthy indulgence in the local brew which, of course, was vodka. It was a friendly face. His powerful hands, weathered like his face, were wide, with long tapering fingers. Beard noted that the smallest finger of the left hand was missing, and it looked a recent amputation.

Beard and his men were introduced and there followed more handshaking, and then several rounds of drinks as toasts were drunk to each other, their countries, the Carpathians, and whatever else occurred to them. A meal of some sort of stew had been prepared for the visitors and as soon as this had been consumed, Stefan returned to his bed for a few hours' more sleep and Beard and his men stretched out where they could, taking turns to keep watch.

As soon as they had breakfasted, Jasienski appeared and they all got down to business: maps were poured over, routes discussed, rejected and agreed. To begin with, it was all about the Carpathians, their first hurdle. There were several closer routes to the border and those mountains, but, with personal knowledge of them all, Jasienski assured Beard the safest and quickest was the one that had been decided upon by the underground organisers.

It would begin by train on the main line from Przemyśl to Kraków. They wouldn't be going that far, he said. "Too many German security guards, the buggers swamp the place and pounce on civilian travellers at random. The bastards search you very thoroughly … right down to your balls if they feel like it," Jasienski growled. "No, we'll be off the train well before Kraków. Don't know exactly where yet, but it'll be either Tarnów or Bochnia. The conductor of our train is Tomasz Jasiński, who belongs to one of our groups. He'll be told as we travel where's safe and where isn't. He'll keep us in touch with things."

It all sounded very straightforward, thought Beard; perhaps too much so. They faced a journey of some hundreds, perhaps thousands, of miles through various occupied countries, and it all began with a mountain that might take several days to get through. He began checking his weapons, putting aside a knife and pistol and several clips of bullets which he would carry hidden on their journey. Stefan's precious documents, which comprised quite a bundle, were sealed in waxed paper and, together with some of the tools of his trade, packed into a wooden container that fitted into the bottom of an already fat satchel. This was then placed in the custody of Sgt Trumpett. Beard could think of no safer place. Apart from this satchel, all that Stefan was taking from the house he had lived in his entire life was contained in a single haversack. He said that it contained his memories, and that he would carry it himself to freedom. Beard nodded understandingly, and tried to imagine its contents. Lots of family photos, he guessed; and a few books, and perhaps a sample of his homeland earth.

It was then, Stefan dropped his bombshell. He declared, quite casually, that when it came to walking, and obviously there was going be a considerable amount, they would have to pace themselves according to that of the slowest of them. "The children haven't the endurance or stamina of mature, seasoned campaigners like ourselves," he added, with an expression of sadness.

"*Children!*"

Beard stared in disbelief. However well their journey had been prepared, he knew that it would test the strength of the best of them. He had no wish to be encumbered with a parcel of children. Christ, no! And were women to be added to the exodus? He shuddered, and cursed Charington and the rest of them back in Cairo for giving him no inkling of such an impossible millstone. He had, of course, been aware of others in the house apart from his own men and Jasienski and his son Jan. He'd seen a couple of women in the background who seemed wholly involved in cooking and preparing foods for the journey ahead – and there'd also been several children running around, and continually being shushed, but he hadn't associated them with the elderly Stefan. Beard considered bringing one man out across thousands of miles of enemy-controlled countries was hazardous enough, but with the added burden of a flock of kids … it was impossible, and unfair.

"I was told there would only be you to bring out, sir," Beard said stiffly, trying to hide the depth of the shock he felt.

"I know, and I'm sorry for having deceived you – all of you," Stefan returned in a severely apologetic voice, his eyes full of pain. He spread his hands out wide and asked, "What choice did I have?"

"How many are there?" Beard asked, his voice cold and resentful of the position in which he was being placed.

"Three," answered Stefan, some of the grimness easing from his face as he sensed a softening in the other's stance.

"What ages?" demanded Beard.

A ghost of a smile lit Stefan's green eyes. "Jadwiga is the eldest. She's eleven, and so beautiful. Then comes Piotr, who is nearly nine, and the youngest is Vanda, who is nearly eight." The smile spread to his lips and widened with the mention of each child. "I'm their grandfather," he added, seeing Beard's puzzled face.

"Oh, no, this is not possible," insisted Beard "They couldn't manage the mountains, and God knows what's in store for us beyond them."

Stefan beckoned Beard to follow him into another room, and once there he shut the door and they faced each other, the scientist and the soldier.

"You are not married, I think?" Stefan began, and the smile on his face made him look quite young himself, if silver-haired and wrinkled.

Beard shook his head, and briefly thought of Ruth, and

wondered if one day they might be; he shook his head again, slowly.

"You're too young yet, my friend," said Stefan, his green eyes sparkling. "And, if I may say so without offence, possibly too young yet to have the responsibility you do."

"We grow old very quickly these days," returned Beard evenly.

Stefan chuckled, then stared hard at Beard. "The children are all I have, and I am all they have," he said calmly and slowly after a moment's pause. "Jan, their father, was my son. He was a captain in a cavalry regiment and killed defending Warsaw in the first days of the war. His two brothers, Marek and Jakub, died with him. My wife, Monika, their mother, died in the bombing of Kraków where she was visiting, and Jan's wife, Elżbieta, was killed here in Przemyśl together with another son, Karol, by Russian bombers. Fortunately, I had this place on the outskirts of the city and we've all lived here ever since – courtesy of the Nazis for whom I am forced to work."

"I am very sorry for your losses, sir, but ..." began Beard.

Stefan grabbed at Beard's arm and, pushing his other hand forward, said, "See that finger!" He pointed to where his missing finger should have been, and went on, "The day the Germans swept the Russians out of Przemyśl, the Gestapo burst into my workshop in a building behind this, and without any explanation or preamble grabbed hold of my arm and one of them simply hacked off my finger without any form of anaesthetic. I think I fainted. I'm sure I did because one of the swine threw a bucket of water over me, or perhaps he did it just for fun. Anyway, their leader told me that I now worked for them and that each time they found I'd tried to sabotage one of my designs, I'd lose another finger."

He paused, and for one terrible moment Beard thought he was going to cry, but though his eyes went glassy, there were no tears, just an awful look of fear, and then he went on. "I'm not a very brave man, but I'm afraid I tried to be, or silly enough anyway, to point out that without my fingers I'd be unable to work for them. The bastards grinned in my face, and said the children's fingers would do as well. And if I tried to disappear or run away, each time they'd cut the throat of one them."

Stefan paused again, and stared unblinking at Beard. "I will not leave without them, captain. You may take my papers and anything else, and welcome, but I'll not leave a single one of my grandchildren behind to be tortured by those animals."

Beard did not hesitate in his reply. "The children go with us," he said simply.

In the early dawn of the following day, they all ate to repletion, the children chattering excitedly all the while, for all that they were still half asleep. Beard examined them, as one does view children, and he was experienced enough to note that though they appeared normal on the surface, their young faces showed the strain the war had left on them, and it was to be seen in their eyes, and the nervous movements of their bodies at sudden sounds. They missed their mother in the way that very young children do; they missed their brother, Karol; they missed their aunts and uncles; they missed their right to the simple joys of childhood. They lived, without understanding, in daily fear of the lives and were visibly growing old before even attaining teenage. Beard knew he was right to take them away from this terrible shadow on their lives, though he did wonder if they'd be rid of the scars of their experiences so easily.

Beard then inspected his men, and liked what he saw; no garish reds or bright yellows, but quieter browns and greens, much like when they'd landed in the country for, naturally, they had not arrived in uniform. Beard himself wore black trousers, a green-check shirt and a dark brown waistcoat with many useful pockets, and felt rather like a pirate. They all carried weapons secreted about their bodies, but the remainder of their considerable arsenal was contained in several innocuous ski bags and other containers. One way and another, they were pretty heavily loaded – it was the ammunition that weighed them down, but they were used to that; it was like their suit of armour, it protected them.

Their departure was delayed several times as the women fussed over the dressing of the children, but finally all were ready, with Beard and his men looking their parts as ramblers and picnickers and, of course, not a weapon in sight.

Then, just as they were moving outdoors, one of the women, who had already kissed the children a thousand times, rushed forward and enveloped Beard in her arms. She squeezed him hard and whispered [Jasienski translated her words] "Our Lady bless you for what you're doing ... be safe, all of you," adding after several sobs, "You're so young you should be home in your own mother's arms."

Beard blinked, thought of Queenie, and wished he were. Returned to reality, he plonked a kiss on the woman, plundered a cheery smile from somewhere and followed the rest outside.

All went very well, to begin with. The train was punctual: it was also short and very crowded. However, the Blue Bear escape plan was so well organized that it included a reserved compartment, and into this piled Stefan and his three grandchildren, Jasienski and two of his men, and Beard and his five men, plus all their baggage which more than filled the luggage racks. To put it mildly, it was too much of a squeeze, and several men at a time had to take it in turns to stand in the corridor, though in reality they were doing guard duty, keeping alert for any possible threat. The children, after their initial burst of excitement, resumed their disrupted sleeps.

The train was cold, noisy and the seats hard, but it soon warmed up as the sun burst into flames, and the train ambled along at a steady pace, spewing dark smoke, and stopping at every station. Beard, seated after a spell of duty in the corridor, eyed the children, who had certainly been no problem so far. Vanda was still asleep in her grandfather's arms. Piotr, still half asleep, hugged the red-and-white football he had so nearly left behind at Przemyśl, as he stared disinterestedly at the passing wooded hills in the distance and the meadows in between. Jadwiga, having tired of fidgeting with her own clothing, which had something of the colourful Polish tradition about it, was now undressing her rosy-cheeked doll, called Lucja, and evidently giving her a good scolding. Beard smiled, and thought: yes; so far, so good.

The first hint that their good fortune might be about to change came in a whispered conversation between Jasienski and the train's conductor, Tomasz Jasiński, another member of the resistance movement. Apparently, Jasiński had been warned of unexpected German activity near Bochnia, their intended destination; so, instead, they'd have to leave his train at Tarnów and catch another down to Nowy Sącz, which was an alternative and longer way to the mountains. They all held their breath as the train puffed its way into Tarnów and screeched to a halt.

Beard and his party disembarked in several small groups to appear as inconspicuous as possible, for there were eyes everywhere; but, of course, it was the children, noisily tugging their grandfather along, who attracted whatever attention might be drawn, for it was as impossible to keep children quiet as it was to avoid smiling at them. Thankfully, they all remembered to speak Polish.

Jasiński made several hurried phone calls to advise those underground links involved of the change in plans for, of course, he had to continue on with his own train. Before blowing his whistle, he turned to Beard to say that all had been arranged. They'd end up at the same place, but from a different direction. "You'll have a bit of a wait for your train from here because it's a special train, sort of," he gave Beard a wide, rascally grin that suggested the train somehow had been diverted especially for him. "If all goes well, the train will take you on beyond Nowy Sącz down to Nowy Targ, well into the Tatras. The train will continue down towards Zakopane, but you'll have to get off before then – too many Germans enjoying themselves there – and carry on by foot to Lysa Polana. This is where you cross the border into Czechoslovakia. It'll be a bit of a hike, but you're in good hands. Wladyslaw Jasienski will see you safely through."

Beard shook the conductor's hand warmly, words did not seem appropriate just then. At least, he could not conjure up the right ones to convey the depth of his gratitude to a man who had done so much for them, and might well have saved the lives of the whole party. The man smiled understandingly, murmured the Polish equivalent of "Best of

British," and turned to signal the driver to proceed with a furious blast on his whistle. He glanced back to give a final wave but in a matter of moments had disappeared in a cloud of black smoke as the train gathered speed with a series of evil-smelling belches.

  For two hours it was easy to forget that there was a war on: that they were sitting plumb in the middle of occupied Europe, with battles raging all around them. The long winter was still a long way off. Today, the sky was blue, the sun was shining, birds were chattering cheerily, and there was a murmur of a breeze that was like a kiss. The children played in a field beside the railway station, watched over by their grandfather and Sgt Trumpett, who had attached himself to the quartet as their particular guardian: Felbridge, astride a log, was acting as sentry, though his ears were more alert than his eyes, which were absorbed in the beauties of the panorama that surrounded them: Thompson and Hill were stretched out in the grass, for all the world as if they were at a cricket match: and Cpl Harry Jenkins, having taken it upon himself to watch his officer's back, did so as he honed a succession of knives. Beard, Jasienski and one of the latter's men (the other was patiently pacing the station platform), having traced half a dozen possible routes through the mountains, prepared a picnic. Yes, for a little while, life was good; very good; peaceful.

  But their peace lasted just the two hours. Then, there was a shout from the platform. Their train was in sight, and nerves that had been at ease were once again at full stretch. They were all quickly aboard the "special" train, which turned out to be a freight train with a single car for passengers, and from then on everything went like clockwork. About three hours later, the train made an unscheduled stop some half-dozen miles past Nowy Targ, and Jasienski said this was where they had to get off the train and "walk a bit."

  They were in a mountain valley with gentle open meadows that gave way to thick forests of beech, which gave way to fir and above these was more wild, rugged terrain to the top. They set off in the foothills of the Carpathians, through a green and hilly region. Beard and Jasienski led the way, discussing details of what was to happen beyond Lysa Polana. The magnificence of the scenery would have had them all staring in open-mouth wonder had they been permitted the opportunity to stop and stare, but Jasienski trod resolutely on and so the rest were too occupied viewing the ground ahead to look at the beauty all around them.

  Stefan's energy impressed Beard. The "old man," who otherwise kept company with each of his grandchildren in turn, talking and encouraging them, frequently caught up with the leaders and though he might be puffing a little (and who wasn't?), he was always cheerful and mainly concerned with when they would be stopping for the day as he had elected to see to the preparations of their meals. If he had an ulterior motive in this offer, it was to ensure that the children ate regularly, and rested often. Beard thought this reasonable enough if they were to continue their mountaineering trek. But he also agreed with Jasienski, who thought they should keep these halts to a minimum, and told Stefan so very firmly, though in soft tones so as not to alarm the children. In the end, Jasienski reluctantly agreed to the pauses as long as they were only long enough to allow time for a light snack. He explained he was anxious for them to be out of sight among the trees as quickly as possible, and he kept urging them on, though the terrain became gradually steeper and the going tougher. So, what had started as a game for the children quickly became an ordeal beyond their endurance.

Still Jasienski pressed forward. But it had been a long, wearying day, and after an hour's trudging up ever-steepening and rough ground, the children simply stopped and flopped down. The girls insisted they couldn't walk another step and begged to be taken home, and Piotr, still clutching his football, who had manfully kept going without complaint, suggested they continue their walk tomorrow – after a good supper and a night's sleep. But again Jasienski relentlessly insisted they must keep going, at which point Vanda started to cry, and Jadwiga, although eleven, felt obliged to join her. The only solution was to carry them, and so they were shared among the already heavily-laden men. Vanda actually fell asleep perched high on Sgt Trumpett's shoulders and clutching his ears.

Beard and Jasienski maintained a steady pace, allowing a ten-minute break every hour. "How far do you reckon we have to walk?" Beard asked his companion. Jasienski thought for a moment, did some sums on his fat fingers, and replied, "Possibly forty miles, maybe more – perhaps nearer fifty." Beard looked impressed. "It'll take us a couple of days on foot. If we'd been driving from Kraków, we'd have done it in little over two hours," muttered Jasienski.

Beard was less impressed. Jasienski's grey eyes grinned at him, as he continued, "No matter what obstacles we meet with on the way, we have to complete it all by Tuesday evening, because first thing on Wednesday you have to be at Lysa Polana to catch the weekly bus for Poprad in Czechoslovakia, the next leg in your journey. We have, of course, fixed things at the border and your seats have been booked on the bus." Jasienski paused for a moment to scratch his developing beard, before adding, "To be honest, captain, we may have to cover some sixty miles or more, and some of it will be hard going."

Beard shrugged. He and his men, laden as they were, could take anything in their stride; in a single day if need be. He guessed Jasienski was thinking of the children. They all knew the children could never manage anything so gruelling, so the men would have to continue carrying them, and that couldn't go on for ever and would mean more frequent halts. They strode on relentlessly, and after four hours they had covered some twenty miles and were well into a forest of firs, and made camp in one of those grassy clearings always found in forests. Almost as soon as they'd eaten, they settled down for the night, Beard arranging sentry duties and taking the first watch himself.

The dawn seemed to come very early, with the sun immediately warm, and with it they were all astir. The children, sinfully happy to be missing Mass on a Sunday, seemed to have forgotten the ordeals of the previous day, and from an early hour were bounding over the limits of the clearing with little shrieks and shouts.

With two more days of trekking and climbing through the mountains ahead, Beard was all for pressing on as soon as they had breakfasted, but Piotr was happily kicking his football around with some of the men, and so he allowed them to carry on for a little while longer. This indulgence, however, was to prove their downfall. Piotr gave the ball a prodigious kick which sent it flying up in the air and out of sight beyond a mound at the edge of the clearing. Piotr gave a cry of delight, and started to run and retrieve the ball.

And then it happened.

The ball came flying back, and following it came a grinning German soldier: his grey forage cap with its *Edelweiß* insignia identified him as an *Alpenkorps* soldier. His eyes took in the scene in a single blink and in the same instant his grin disappeared. He opened his mouth to shout with his hand already at his pistol. But he uttered no sound other than a gurgle, nor did his hand get any further. He staggered a pace or two and then fell forward, the hilt of a knife protruding from his throat.

Even as Jenkins was retrieving his knife and ensuring the man was dead, Beard was whispering orders. He told Jasienski to press on quickly and silently with Stefan and the three children. "Get as far ahead as you can, don't stop for anything," he instructed. "Sgt Trumpett and Felbridge, our radio man, will go with you. The rest of us, including your two men, will sort things out here, and catch up with you shortly." Beard sensed the protests of both Trumpett and Felbridge but he silenced them with a compelling glance. "Our mission is our priority," he reminded them. "I need you, sergeant, to take charge of this party, and without Felbridge and his wireless you'd be stranded. Now, get them all moving, and keep them quiet. We'll catch up with you before you know it. Now, push off."

Piotr looked terrified and about to shout out or scream, perhaps both, but Beard's serious face choked back any such sounds. Beard, shaking his head slowly, continued to hold a finger to his own lips, silencing them all with a low shush as they were hurried on their way by Trumpett, who whispered to the children that it was "a silent game" and they "mustn't wake the sleeping fairies."

Beard still winced at the noise the "silent" children made, watching almost a whole minute until they were out of sight, and sound; then he wheeled round to give directions to those remaining with him. They had all shed their large and heavy backpacks, and Beard hastily removed his own. Then, without a sound, using hand signals that had been practised a hundred times in exercises, he sent Thompson, Hill and one of the Poles off to the left, indicating that they were to encircle the Germans and use only firearms fitted with silencers; his mouth told them that no Germans could be allowed to escape, and that no prisoners were to be taken. He, Jenkins and the remaining Pole then began moving off in the opposite direction, spreading out.

Incredibly there was not a sound in the air. Even the birds had stopped singing, as if knowing something terrible was about to happen, and waiting for it to be over. Beard was wondering about the stillness, thinking it might make the Germans suspicious, when a German voice, exclaimed irritably, "Dieter! Where the fuck are you? We're moving out."

The utter silence persisted, only it seemed deeper, and more threatening. The sun was already hot, and Beard felt the sweat gathering in driblets and coursing down his spine. He was kneeling on one knee between two fir saplings that effectively concealed him, ready to spring into action. He held his pistol, fitted with a silencer, in his right hand and was conscious of its slight tremor. The silence was their best protection, but it was also nerve-wracking. He knew that any shooting would attract attention far and wide, and that would almost certainly be the end of them all. He sweated on, breathing softly so as not to make a sound. And then, suddenly, the quiet was shattered by the sound of heavy boots stomping through the undergrowth. The peace ended, and the war resumed, all in a trice. Again that German voice thundered out to the dead Dieter.

"Fuck you, Mielke," the voice cried, "stop playing with your fucking balls and get back here. We're off."

The figure of a burly sergeant finally came into sight and stood standing, scratching his own testes, looking around him, almost immediately above where the body of his comrade lay. It was a moment or so before his eyes focussed on the dead soldier, and in one of those moments, Beard shot him through the heart. He leaped forward to catch the body to lessen the sound, but in the event they both crashed down – and made twice the noise. It did not seem to matter. The quiet returned, but not the peace. Beard breathed quite heavily, giving up the idea of silent breathing. Perhaps the sergeant's men weren't so eager to leave. Well, hopefully none of them would ever be leaving, Beard thought grimly. At that moment, Jenkins appeared beside him and whispered, "There's eleven more of 'em left, sir. Just lounging about. There was a guard – at least I suppose that's what he was, he was the only man holding a rifle, but I've dealt with him."

It didn't seem to take any time at all. Beard gave a double-whistle signal and those with silenced pistols opened fire: two bullets for each victim. The two Polish resistance men accounted for a soldier each with their long, double-bladed knives. And that was six down with five to go. In fact, it turned out to be six more because just as they thought they'd done, a soldier emerged from the depths of a bush still adjusting his braces, and it was a matter of conjecture as to who actually shot him, suffice to say four bullets were found in his chest. The little massacre had taken less than three minutes, and except for the slight plop of the pistols and the falling bodies it was as silent as such killings should be. "I wonder if he knew what was going on while he was having his crap," murmured Hill. "Well, he does now," declared Jenkins, giving one of the bodies a kick to make sure it was dead. He'd always found a kick on the side of a knee was an infallible test.

Beard and Jenkins searched the twelve bodies for anything useful but found no papers of any significance and very little else other than a couple of maps, which they kept. At the same time, the two Poles, having stripped the bodies of anything else, were industriously collecting the Germans' weapons and ammunition and piling them into waterproof sacking. "You'll never be able to carry all that load," observed Beard, helping himself to half a dozen magazines. "We'll bury them somewhere nearby and collect them another day when there's more of us," returned one of the Poles, smiling. Beard nodded, and said they'd better get the Germans' bodies out of sight. "It might give us a few more hours before the balloon goes up and they come hunting for us," he said thoughtfully. They found a shallow hollow, needing very little further digging, not too distant and spent nearly an hour carrying the bodies to their resting place and then covering them over. The Poles, meanwhile, had returned having buried their loot to their satisfaction.

It was easy for Beard and his men to follow the trail, and as they did so they lay false ones of their own; they were trained in such things. Beard was surprised at the distance Jasienski and the rest had covered, and guessed Trumpett was pushing them hard. It took Beard an hour and a half to catch up with them, and after only a brief pause for a drink from one of the many waterfalls, they all continued on their journey. Beard, after detailing Hill to watch their rear about a quarter-mile behind, joined Jasienski in the lead and stepped up the pace on being told they probably had another fifty miles to cover. Beard began to give serious thought as to whether Jasienski knew distances in miles, but so long as he knew the way to Lysa Polana, they had to be satisfied.

And so they bedded down for their second night on the Tatras, and with the sun gone and them being considerably higher, it was very cold, but if there were any inquisitive lynx, chamois or even brown bears around they were not disturbed.

Another morning came and tired bodies stirred and stretched, and were soon on the trail again. It was not long before Vanda had had enough, and took her place on Trumpett's broad shoulders. Jadwiga and Piotr struggled on determinedly, but required frequent pauses to rest, and as the day wore on and their limbs ached and their pace flagged till they almost came to a standstill, they too had occasional lifts on shoulders, the men taking turns, though there were times when the children had to be put down and led by the hand round rocks jutting perilously over high precipices.

It was obstacles such as these that slowed them down most, though when in the valleys they all pressed hard to make up for lost time. With each footstep Beard half expected to hear the Germans, with their bloody dogs, noisily chasing them. But, no; there was never a sound, though an eagle paid them unwelcome attention as it circled high above, and sometimes swooped down to the tips of the giant firs. Beard scowled at the bird, concerned that it might act as a marker for any far off marksman. But, with no apparent hue and cry, Beard wondered, hopefully, if the German *Alpenkorps* soldiers might have been on a weekend exercise and so wouldn't be missed till today, or even tomorrow.

With this optimistic thought, he called a halt, leaving them with less than twenty miles more to cover on the Tuesday. They had sighted Lysa Polana through the trees, and though Jenkins had insisted it was at least fifty miles off, Jasienski assured them it was nearer twenty, and Beard concurred.

The sweat continued to pour off them long after they'd shed their loads, human and everything else. After washing themselves in a cooling little stream, then preparing and eating a substantial meal, the adults sat down and watched the children scampering around chasing the football that had so nearly led to disaster. Sleep was sweet after the exertions of the day.

They arrived without incident at Lysa Polana early on Tuesday afternoon and were met by their next contact, Petr Zahradnik, a smallish, wiry man with a bushy, black moustache, very blue deep-set eyes and a smile that lit up an otherwise dour face. "You made good time," he said, shaking Jasienski's hand like it was a pump. They all clambered aboard the bus and, after what seemed an age, though it was still light and very warm, duly arrived in the early evening at Poprad where they descended.

Zahradnik, with an all-embracing wave to the rest, stooped to pick up Vanda and led them all to a large house standing beside a small hall. Inside the house, which had a balcony and wore a coating of winter logs, they were met by Eliška, Zahradnik's sister, and two other women all of whom were effusive with words and effulgent with the sheer delight at seeing the children, who were whisked away to be bathed, while Beard and his men were shown rooms and where they could shower.

"We run a hostel for hikers and skiers in their appropriate seasons, as do many of the neighbouring houses," explained Zahradnik, "so overnight visitors are the norm – except we don't get to see many kids as young as yours, so you'll have to excuse the ladies for being over the moon. Besides, the hostel serves as a good cover for my other activities." He smiled enormously at them, contriving a wink at the same time. "Give me your clothing – underwear and things, and they'll be washed and ready for you by morning."

It was sheer bliss to stand naked under the steaming hot water and wash away the grime accumulated over the past few days of living in the open. The dirt seemed to peel off in layers and when the skin was properly bared, then the water felt really scalding, and that felt like heaven as well. As they waited their turn beneath the shower, they talked of their journey so far, of the brief, silent skirmish with the Germans in the mountain forest, and of what lay ahead. "You've got to hand it to these Polacks, their organisation is first class," asserted Jenkins. "Well, so far so good," allowed Thompson cautiously.

Beard, watching the men shave, those that wanted to, gave a wry grin. He still had no real need to shave, but he went through the motions anyway. He felt it was expected of him as their officer. Perhaps he'd grow a whisker one of these days. Later, all glowing pink and with the smoothest cheeks a girl could have wished for, he considered their position. Here they were plumb in the centre of Europe, and wholly dependent on an organisation of untrained amateurs to see them through a minefield of obstacles. On reflection, perhaps it was unfair to think of them as untrained amateurs; every day they were gaining in experience, and paying with their lives for the slightest mistake. Surely that made them professionals? Certainly Beard and his party could have no complaint, thus far. There was no doubting their courage, and they had been fed and led through enemy territory by these *amateurs*. The Poles had been superb. They had to hope the Czechs, and the rest, maintained the standard.

At least their bus arrived on time: it was uncomfortable, dirty and, more to the point, it was late in departing because the driver had some shopping to do. This made the protracted farewells even harder to bear, and not just among the women they were leaving behind. Beard had formed a close friendship with Jasienski, and found it especially hard to say goodbye. But eventually, both had tired of making small talk and shaking hands, and Beard had taken a last look into Jasienski's grey eyes, and expressed the hope that the repercussions of Stefan's disappearance, with his entire family, did not fall too heavily on those left behind in Przemyśl, and that Blue Bear survived his ordeal, and then climbed quickly on to the coach.

When he looked back, Jasienski was gone.

☐ *Queenie, momentarily stunned to silence, clapped her hands in wonderment as Gibbs paused in the story. "Christ! Jarvis, you could've got yerself killed playing games like this! Don't you dare do anything so dangerous again, lovey," she cried, gripping his hand. "No wonder we never got no letters!"*
And they all laughed. Only Beard looked puzzled.

Chapter Twenty-three

Somewhere in the Balkans, September 22, 1943

"Today, we cross Czechoslovakia and, perhaps, into Hungary," Zahradnik confided as he plonked himself heavily down beside Beard. "They're both as bad as the other. Both Nazi puppet states. But, perhaps, not by choice."

"Is it so easy to cross borders in these times?" queried Beard, wondering at the casual way the other talked over their hazardous journey.

"Sometimes. If you know where, and know the right people, and have luck," replied Zahradnik, and his splendid moustache danced as he winked at Beard. "Luck is your best ally. We have a very long ride ahead of us, be lucky if we get as far as the border tonight. We only ride in this bus because it is the recognised bus. The official one. It will take us through the mountains – and faster than I'd care to drive, and put us down at Muráň where, God willing, we will find another vehicle waiting for us – and that the driver knows that instead of a few there are a lot of us. He will have been told which roads are safest and will have several options as to where to cross the border into Hungary."

Zahradnik paused to scratch his moustache. "Wherever he stops, he will confirm his instructions, but we'll be very lucky to make the crossing tonight. My bet is that the driver will follow the River Rimava until we join the main Bratislava-Košice road, and get off it as quickly as possible – probably somewhere near Lučenec, and then wriggle our way to the border and cross as advised. It is generally not a problem – we have contacts everywhere. But, wherever it is to be, we need to be close to Rétság – that's just to the north of Budapest. Naturally, it boils down to everything going smoothly, and not running into any roadblocks – and not losing anyone." He paused to stare gravely at the children, counting them, and then smiled. "By the way, you're supposed to be looking for farm work on the Nagyalföld – that's Hungary's Great Plain. Stretches from the Ukraine in the east to Croatia in the west."

Few of the places mentioned meant much to Beard. Apart from the fact that they were in the Balkans and on his maps, he felt quite adrift of the world and could see no early end to their journey – and hadn't Charington said they'd probably be back in a week, a fortnight at the most? Well, the first week was ended, and their prospects of getting back inside the next did not look promising. He smiled at the other's explanation of their presence. "Wouldn't get much work with three children in tow," he observed.

"Oh, in this part of the world the whole family comes along," declared Zahradnik affably, "and they all work."

"We should have brought along some women then," grinned Beard.

"Always," agreed Zahradnik, his moustache dancing furiously. "But with such a distraction you'd never have got out of Poland." They both enjoyed a small laugh, before Zahradnik added soberly, "I think we're already a big enough party without such attractions." The moustache gave a final waggle before Zahradnik continued, with more urgency, "Once we reach the Duna – that's the Danube to you English; it has half a dozen names as it flows through Europe – once there, the plan is for you to proceed hidden on a barge and later to go on by train into Yugoslavia, and then you're home and dry! Of course, circumstances may change the plan. Train journeys can be very dangerous, especially in that area, so perhaps you'll end up on another coach – maybe several different ones. But you'll be safe all the while." The moustache grinned. "You might have to climb a mountain or two on the way."

Beard gave a slow smile. It sounded easy enough in words, he doubted it would be as easy in the doing. He did not feel comfortable having everything taken out of his hands. It didn't feel right. He winced. It was these very people, already suffering the bitter pill of occupation, who were taking all the risks, making all the decisions. He hoped their reward would not be death. Well, he supposed they all risked their lives, but he'd feel far easier in his heart if he had a greater share in their extra danger. He felt altogether too much of a passenger. Of course, his brain, which was more in control of the situation, told him this was the way wars were conducted. Sometimes you led, sometimes you followed. No doubt true, but it was of little comfort. He knew there was a great distance to go yet: hundreds of miles of danger. He shrugged, and found himself staring at Stefan whose face already showed a deepening pinkness from their brief open-air life together; he sat calmly, serenely even, close to his grandchildren, apparently telling them a story. The shadow of the huge Sgt Trumpett embraced them all. Beard smiled, comforted by the family scene, and felt reassured about their future.

And well he might be. For, it was as Zahradnik had anticipated: or very near. They crossed the border next morning near Koláry, duly drove through Rétság and clambered aboard a huge wheat-laden barge which, several hours later, lurched its way up the Danube to Gyor. This was really taking them away from where Beard thought they needed to be, but Zahradnik explained that they had to avoid the more direct route, via Lake Balaton, because that whole area was like a German playground.

At Gyor, a rather sinister-looking man whose sole name appeared to be János took over from Zahradnik, although the latter was to remain with them until they passed into Yugoslavia. János was like a black shadow. A tall, thin shadow with wiry black hair, black eyes, black stubbled face, black suit and black boots: and his white shirt looked a close cousin. But, despite his looks to the contrary, he was friendly, energetic and good with the children; he was also very well organised. He had their next transport waiting for them.

As Zahradnik had thought likely, train travel was considered too much of a risk with every civilian being rigorously checked at the train stations, and security police travelling on many of the trains as well. So it was decided they were still to travel on water, but on a different river: the Rába; and instead of a barge, a small boat, about the size of a fishing vessel. It was loaded with assorted vegetables and planking, but below decks there was a whole new world for the children to explore and run about in, for the crew were underground members and so they could do as they pleased – so long as they kept below and out of sight of curious eyes. Stefan and the tireless Sgt Trumpett watched over them like a pair male nannies, only allowing their charges on deck for fresh air when it was absolutely safe. And when they weren't entertaining the children, Beard made sure his men had weapons to hand.

It really was most pleasant chuffing leisurely along the winding river through what was called the Kisalföld, or Little Plain. Farms stretched endlessly in flat steppes towards the great Bakony Forest that separated the lowlands from Lake Balaton. The river, never terribly wide and well shaded by trees – and farther south by gentle hills and shady forests, flowed quietly on its way and they passed through scraps of habitation, too small to be thought of as being villages, or even hamlets, but where their passage was marked often by friendly waves. Stefan and Sgt Trumpett, the latter by now affectionately, if secretively, known as Big Papa to the three children, would hold tightly to them as they leaned over the sides, always pointing, always asking questions, always insisting they had spotted a fish; and once, Big Papa was able to point out a pair of white storks in the distance.

And then, abruptly, they were reminded of the ugliness of life.

It was as they tied up at the close of their first day on the river, close to a small wooded bend, that several shots were fired across their bows. The suddenness of the attack took them all by surprise, but only for a moment. Beard snapped "Get below!" to the children and their guardians, which they were already doing, grabbed up a Sten gun and moved to the shelter of the gunwale to search for their attackers. He saw them straightaway but even as he took a sight on them, János shouted out, "Hold your fire, Mr Beard." János, together with Zahradnik, was already talking to the gunmen who came into view on the bank close to the boat, their arms outstretched but still holding their weapons.

After an anxious exchange of shouted words lasting close on quarter of an hour, it transpired that the two youths, for that's all they were, had only wanted to steal a few bags of vegetables. Perhaps because he was relieved this was all they wanted, or perhaps simply to get rid of them, János had a couple of bags tossed ashore, but in the midst of expressing his thanks, one of the would-be pirates recognised a crew member and asked where they were headed. Zahradnik intervened to shout back "Szentgotthárd!" This was only partly true: the boat was going that far to deliver its cargo and take on board a fresh one of grapes to bring back, but Beard and his party would leave the boat at Körmend, the stop before.

The "pirate," after fumbling in a small sack, produced a small parcel which he tossed to his friend, Milivoj, begging him to deliver it at the Customs House at Körmend. Milivoj, catching the round object deftly, held it gingerly and cried back, "What is it? A bomb?" The youth gave a laugh and replied, "No, it's a Christmas pudding for my Mum!" Feeling the package with a more respectful care, Milivoj called back, "OK, Jan." Beard and his men joined in the merriment when Zahradnik explained matters. "Bloody cheek," muttered Jenkins when he'd finished laughing.

Early the next morning, as they were negotiating a series of tricky bends and still well short of Körmend, the utter quiet of the day was shattered as machine-gun fire sprayed the length of the boat, killing a man standing in the bow and wounding another amidships. Beard recognised the sound of the Schmeisser as it raked the deck again, and leapt once again to the side of the boat for protection. Behind him followed Jenkins, Thompson and Hill and they all spread out and awaited developments. There was a rattle of rifle fire, but few of the bullets actually hit the boat, so Beard guessed they were meant as warning shots to keep their heads down. The boat, momentarily lurching freely, brushed against a submerged branch, and ran aground in some shingle at the water's edge. Beard heard Zahradnik and János dragging themselves across the deck and signalled them to keep low, and then gave Jenkins a nod and the pair of them went over the side into the water. It was surprisingly cold, but they were barely in it than they were out again and advancing through the screen of trees that came right down to the edge. They saw the enemy almost directly.

"They look like deserters," whispered Beard, frowning as he noted the men's ragtag appearance. Two of them were actually smoking which no disciplined soldier would dream of doing in such a situation when the last thing was to draw attention to themselves. The smell of tobacco had been the first thing he'd noticed as he entered the wood.

"Still Germans," pointed out Jenkins, the scar down his cheek glowing menacingly as his hands embraced his armoury of weapons.

"They must have transport nearby," hissed back Beard. "Let's find that first, cut off their line of retreat … and then we'll take the rest on – making sure we're not hit by our own chaps on the boat."

They discovered the truck within a hundred yards of the river attracted by another smoke signal. The single guard was quickly dealt with by Jenkins and, as Beard snatched up the man's Schmeisser, they both turned to move silently back towards the river and the remainder of the deserters. There appeared to be seven of them. They made no attempt to conceal their safe positions, shouting to one another as if they'd been on a picnic, except that they kept taking potshots at the boat. Beard and Jenkins wriggled closer through the trees, then Beard tapped the other's arm, indicated the use of silenced weapons, and sent him to the left while he worked his way to the right. Beard came across his first victim sooner than expected. It was an extra man, the eighth, and Beard had been attracted to the unpleasant smell of him before discovering the man squatting bare-arsed doing his business. Beard put paid to his efforts with a single shot, and lowered the body, with some distaste, using one hand. "Get on with it, Sepp, you're stinking us all to death," whispered a nearby voice in German, and he was Beard's next victim. The trees had thinned out enough at this point to give Beard a glimpse of the boat, and between them he saw the German with the Schmeisser, and he became victim number three. At this moment, Jenkins sidled up to him, his grey eyes as steady as ever but with a near smile on his lips, and muttered gravely, "I've accounted for five of the bastards, how about you, sir?"

"Only three," confessed Beard, with equal gravity.

Jenkins did some mental sums, and his grin widened. "Found an extra one, eh, sir?"

"He was having a shit," explained Beard; he shrugged and then gave a lame smile.

"They're a shitty lot, the Krauts, aren't they."

"I expect it was only our cargo of greens they were after, really, like those kids yesterday," remarked Beard thoughtfully, and then added quickly, "We'd better alert the boat and let 'em know the shooting's over or they'll be picking us off. Then we'll see if there's anything useful in their truck, and check over the bodies and collect their weapons."

They arrived at Körmend early in the afternoon and Beard and his party said goodbye to the boat, which continued on to Szentgotthárd to discharge its cargo. The first task was to discreetly dispose of the dead crewman into the care of a priest, and to leave the wounded man with a local family with access to a trustworthy doctor; and János, who handled these matters, did not forget to leave the Christmas pudding at the Customs House for the mother of the erstwhile pirate.

As soon as they had all found their land legs (that's what Zahradnik called it when the children asked why Big Papa kept them marching up and down as soon as they got off the boat) and eaten well, they returned their limbs to sleep and clambered aboard two lorries and began what they were told would be the last stage of their flight from Poland. If it sounded euphemistic, Beard was content to accept its possibilities. The children were becoming more and more fractious, and Stefan himself looked to be wilting under the constant strain of their ordeal; and there were days of more wearying miles into the unknown ahead of them before they reached their goal. Their tension grew as the ending neared, fearful that they might be caught in sight of success

There had to be two lorries now because of the loot – ammunition, weapons and such like, which the freedom fighters had looted from the Germans at the river ambush and had no intention of abandoning, and the lorries had to be seen to be carrying something other than themselves. In their case, they hid behind cargoes of cabbages in one lorry and casks of wine in the other. Beard travelled in the front of the wine lorry alongside János. In the rear were Stefan and his three grandchildren, Sgt Trumpett, Jenkins, plus Zahradnik and two of his confederates, both alert and determined-looking, and neither more than twenty. Everyone else, including three more resistance men, was piled into the second lorry with the cabbages.

Beard asked János if he'd had any news filtering back from Przemyśl about the flight of Stefan and his family, but János only shook his dark head and whispered back that the Germans had seemed slow to grasp that Stefan had vanished with his entire family; almost two days, in fact, and while they were dithering Józef Szajna (alias Blue Bear) and his companions had been released from custody on the Monday and, likewise, disappeared instantly. In fact, while there would undoubtedly be one of the usual repressive searches for Stefan, it did not appear it was being pursued with any immediate vigour beyond Poland, so for the moment it looked as if they might have got away with it. At least they were out of Poland, which must be considered as the danger zone, and were well on their way to where they needed to be. He himself did not know their ultimate destination as he was being directed by couriers as they went.

Well, this was all very promising news, and if the Germans weren't all that desperate to recover the runaway scientist, Beard began to wonder jut how close the Russians were to Poland. But he knew, too, that the German web, particularly that of the Gestapo, spread far and wide, and didn't doubt that there was plenty of time yet for them to come up against unexpected dangers before they were really in the clear; safe, and away. So, perhaps Stefan was right to be anxious.

They drove all day, along a variety of tracks, keeping off the main roads as much as possible, always southwards. It was hot, without any relieving breath of wind, and conditions inside the lorries, where the temperature was probably in the 100s, were close to unbearable; the sweat coursed along unknown creases in their bodies and at times the air was so heavy it was hard to drag in sufficient to stay conscious and focussed on their situation; but they did, of course, it was the only way to stay alive. And the heat went on growing.

Beard thought the endurance of the children was marvellous: they suffered in comparatively stoic silence; and he felt sure a lot of credit was due to Stefan and Big Papa. The only moments of relief, and they were short, were the stoppages for personal reliefs and something to eat, and a chance to exercise tortured limbs. There were inevitably other stops, for punctures; these were many for the roads were riddled with potholes, and the tracks along which they relied were littered with unkind rocks and sharp roots. In these instances it was a case of all helping out for their worst fear was to be caught immobile out in the open. The land was mostly flat and agricultural, with sunflowers as far as the eye could see, but with occasional extensive woods which provided some relief from the blistering heat. The further south they went the more hills they had to contend with: gentle hills with their slopes mostly crowded with tiers of vines and other fruits, and in the background white-capped mountains came into view.

It was already dark when they crossed the border into Slovenia, and once well inside stopped for the night. It was then after one o'clock in the morning and everyone was dog-tired; the children had long been asleep, though fitfully, their eyes opening with every bump of the road. Between them, Beard and János set up guards and took their turns at sleeping. Beard slept deeply for about two hours when his turn came, then woke with a start, and learned that two Yugoslav partisans had materialised and were devouring maps with János and some of his party. They spoke in a dialect that even Zahradnik found difficulty in comprehending, though he did manage to convey to Beard that the newcomers would be taking over the direction of movements from that point. Prvoš, he added, was the leader of the two men, who both wore the Red star of Communism on their caps and had bandoliers of bullets across their chests and various weapons about their bodies. Both were villainously ugly, and Beard was glad to have them on his side – if they were.

And they certainly proved to be, as did their comrades who materialised along the way with warnings of enemy troop movements in the area and directions as to which routes to take to avoid them. Beard discovered that Prvoš spoke a more than passable German, and so they were able to communicate personally, though Prvoš proved to be as taciturn as it was possible to be, even when giving directions or snapping orders. Towards evening, they had crossed the River Mura into Croatia, which Prvoš described, in a voice to match the ugliness of his looks, as yet another German puppet state where nobody was to be trusted. They pressed on eastwards, avoiding Zagreb and the Medvednica mountain range to the south, Zahradnik, who was leaving them now to return home, explaining to Beard that since the Allied invasion of Italy the Germans had been pouring more men and equipment into the country, especially along coastal districts, in case of another invasion there. Beard wondered how it would be possible for him and his party to get to a point from which they could set off to rendezvous with their submarine, but he kept his thoughts to himself. First they had to get through several mountain ranges before they could even get a sight of the coast, let alone a sniff of the briny.

The following day the little convoy turned sharply south and all that day and most of the next they threaded their way through narrow valleys with thickly-wooded mountains rising on either side, and sometimes there would be extensive meadows with flowers and cattle with tolling bells round their necks.

It was more than ten days now since their mission had begun, and Beard began to have visions of another week of travelling. That sod Charington had said it might take them a fortnight, at the most. He'd said it would be just like a Cook's tour, whatever that was; and he'd also mentioned that mountains might be a bit of a problem. Well, he'd got that right, but even if almost everything had been done for them and, apart from a couple of minor actions involving the enemy, they'd simply followed their conductors, their *tour* looked like lasting a lot longer than a fortnight. The mountains seemed to block their escape route to the sea.

Beard could see no end to these mountains. It took hours of twisting and turning through bumpy, rock-strewn valleys that combined to make their journey both tortuous and torturous. Beard smiled inwardly as he remembered having the difference in the meaning of the two words drummed into him at Battersea. It was bloody right, too, he thought grimly. The trouble here was that there seemed to be one mountain after the other. He'd given up trying to keep track of where they were on his map. He had only a rough idea, and then only after Prvoš had told him that they had just by-passed a place or were nearing another. Right now, he said they were safely in Bosnia-Herzegovina and on flatland approaching Prijedor. Beard found the place on his map, and kept his finger on the spot. It looked a long, long way from the coast, with yet more mountains to contend with, but at least they appeared to be on a plateau of sorts. "We're almost there, captain. Soon be home now." Prvoš had the gall to suggest, albeit with the suggestion of his unsightly smile.

But almost immediately he was proved wrong.

The sound of its engine and the splintering of trees preceded the heavy half-track vehicle as it burst out of the forest that extended on either side of the wide track they were travelling along. The vehicle came to a halt in the middle of the track and one of several men, all sporting the Red Star emblem, jumped down and rushed up to the lead lorry and spoke with Prvoš. Almost immediately Prvoš was shouting orders and making urgent circular movements with his arms indicating that their two-vehicle convoy should turn about, and in next to no time they had manoeuvred round and were chasing after the half-track back the way they'd been travelling.

Forty miles later, Prvoš explained in his usual terse manner to Beard the reason for their desperate retreat. It appeared that thousands of German troops, complete with artillery and all the motorised accompaniment they needed, were engaged in some major exercise and heading straight towards them. "About two hours off," declared Prvoš shortly, displaying little concern over the threat. "Just a nuisance," he added sourly. "Delay us a few days, perhaps." Beard nodded, knowing the other would not appreciate any further words on the matter.

In fact, three days passed – during which they were severally halted or diverted, before their little convoy was stopped for good by a formidable band of Red Stars whose company included senior elements of the partisans. Prvoš took part in a lengthy bout of discussion, then returned to Beard with a scowl that was nowhere near as offensive as usual, and declared dramatically, "We're here, Captain Beard! From here we march for one day, and the next you will fly home!"

"Fly?" exclaimed Beard incredulously. "How? Where on earth can we take off from? There's not a flat, open piece of land anywhere near. It's all mountains and forests."

Prvoš ignored the questions with an air of sublimity. "Fifteen miles – well, perhaps twenty-five on foot – from here we have located a tiny German airfield. It is completely isolated from any community. The only access is by a single road – as you'd expect in the mountains. It is used by the Germans mostly for private flying amusements and for their spotter planes. But there is at present also a Junkers 52 transporter. It is a recent arrival, and it is this that will fly you home." Prvoš came to an abrupt stop, seeming overcome by this rare and long speech. He started coughing, and then indulging in a series of deep breathing exercises. His discomfort lasted only a few moments and then his face lost its redness, and was as ugly as ever.

Beard, who had occupied the moments of Prvoš's distress to digest his information about their flight home, knew a moment of concern himself. "You make it all sound very easy, my friend, but do you imagine the Germans will let us simply walk in and take it over – long enough to fly a plane out? And once we were in the air, we'd be the target for every enemy plane in Jugoslavia," he protested. "We'd be shot down within ten miles."

Prvoš shook his head. "Do not worry, captain. The moment you are in the air, the whole of Yugoslavia will go up in flames. It is all planned … attacks on airfields, gun sites, radar and communication centres. The Germans won't notice a single plane – and particularly not one of their own – in the chaos."

Beard hoped he was right.

"Of course, we have to capture the airfield first," added Prvoš calmly.

In spite of the assurances of the major diversions given by Prvoš, Beard had serious misgivings at the thought of attacking, holding and flying safely away from an airfield hidden among mountains and surrounded by an alert, well-equipped enemy. On the other hand, if it was their only way home ... These misgivings persisted during the day-long trek through thick woods of oak, then fir, and almost entirely uphill. Beard, laden and fully armed again, took it all in his stride; he was trained for such endeavours, and trod doggedly in the footsteps of the Red Star man ahead. Behind him followed his own team, similarly loaded like Sherpa porters, with the addition of the children, Stefan and a veritable army of Red Stars.

Beard's feelings were only slightly lifted when he was able to look down on the airfield; in fact, he was almost level with it. At a distance of some three hundred yards, he thought it looked small; very small; too small. It was about the size of two, maybe three, football pitches, and he wondered if it was big enough for a plane to take off from. Well, obviously it was, for there were half a dozen small aircraft parked in roofed bays, a Storch – and nearby was the Junkers 52 which was to be their ticket home. Beard pursed his lips, and wondered. The plane looked as enormous as the airfield looked miniscule.

Before bedding down for the night, Beard and his men, together with Colonel Antun Miroš, leader of the fifty-plus partisans, went into a huddle over the final details of the attack on the airfield the next day. Col Miroš, who was more a political man than a soldier, was pleased to defer most of these to Prvoš and Beard, who was probably the only real officer present. Miroš, tall, skeletal and with sharp pale blue eyes, said little – and missed little. He and his men had had the airfield under surveillance for weeks and knew the routine of the place by heart and the function of every building. Beard impressed upon them all that it had to be a silent attack: no gunfire or explosions until the plane was up and away; then they were free to blow the place up to kingdom come before making their own getaway.

Zero hour had been set at 20.40 hours, Saturday, October 2. That was the time set for the diversionary attacks throughout that region of Yugoslavia. It would also be the moment of Beard's take-off. The attack on the airfield itself would take place shortly before.

It was a pity, he thought, that everything had to be accomplished in broad daylight, but this was because of the mountain peaks all around. A take-off in the dark was considered too dangerous, and Beard was inclined to agree; indeed, he did so readily.

Beard, Jenkins and Felbridge circled the entire airfield the following morning, looking for weak spots: danger spots. At one point, a security blind spot, they were able to crawl right up to the barbed wire and confirm that it was not electrified, as Miroš had assured them. It was nearing midday, and already the camp looked positively deserted. There were several watchtowers, but apparently only two were manned at weekends

"It's the weekend," Miroš explained when the leaders met for a final briefing. "Half already away for a dirty weekend. Rest will be away by noon, leaving just the necessary number to do sentry duties, cook meals and sweep the floors. About forty-fifty men, tops."

"We'll move in twelve minutes ahead of zero hour," Beard said decisively.

Felbridge, the accredited marksman, set the ball rolling, taking out the two sentries in their watchtowers with his rifle fitted with a silencer. Simultaneously, Beard and the rest of his team were at the fence, cutting wires. As soon as they were through, they headed for the main gate from the rear and took the two sentries there completely by surprise. Neither made a sound as they were lowered to the ground, one with his throat cut and the other with his neck broken. Beard pointed to the guardroom, and the only sound that emerged from there was a smothered scream. At this point, Beard waved Miroš and the rest of the partisans to come in and do their butchering.

"You Aiden, dismantle the radio room – no calls in or out, but don't sever the electric cables entirely, we may need some power for the plane – fuelling, for one thing." It wasn't often he used first names when addressing his men, but when he did he felt a certain warmth inside, and he knew it gave his men a fillip – the pity was these rare lapses in procedure only occurred on the battlefield, but perhaps that's when it counted most. Beard knew he was always secretly delighted when Gibbs called him Robert, even if it wasn't his true name, but then most of his names were borrowed ones.

In the end, it wasn't much of a battle, except that whoever was on the base died, mostly at the hands of the partisans, though Jenkins was sure to have had his share and Beard, using a silencer, shot a man with no trousers who was wielding a sword as he tried to escape, and a dog that had its teeth in Miroš's leg and wouldn't let go.

The whole affair was over inside twelve minutes, for it was then that continuous explosions could be heard in the distance as Yugoslavia was "put to the torch," as Miroš had predicted. Beard nodded approval, and called for one of the partisans to tend Miroš's leg. Miroš grimaced as a man with a red cross badge sliced through his trousers and swore as the man trickled some liquid over the area of the wound. "You should get a penicillin injection," grinned Beard, adding conversationally, "or you might get rabies." Miroš tried to smile but couldn't make it, instead he muttered, "Bugger off and catch your fucking plane, captain." Beard proffered a very correct salute, and said, "Thank you for all your help, colonel. Now you'll be able to get on with your real war." Miroš, leaning on an elbow, handed Beard a scrap of paper he'd dug out of a pocket and retorted, "Ask your Mr Churchill to help us fight the war by sending us the wherewithal to fight it. Here's where." Beard glanced at the coordinates and stored the slip of paper carefully in his breast pocket. "I'm sure he won't let you down, colonel," he said correctly. "Good luck, sir." Miroš waved him away.

Beard rounded up his own men and then collected Stefan and his three grandchildren who had remained protected in the woods until now. They looked little the worse for their recent ordeals as they rejoined Beard and the others; Jadwiga hugged her doll Lucja, Piotr clutched his red-and-white football, and Vanda sought and tightened her hold on Big Papa's hand. Beard, with all his responsibilities safely secured, then sought out the ugly and often brusque Prvoš who, even so, had done so much to ease their journey, and for once he showed his human side: still ugly, but infinitely brighter, even his dark eyes sparkled. The two men hugged in silence; when they parted, Beard smiled, Prvoš nodded, and that was it.

Finally, Beard and his company turned and headed towards their plane which had been towed into position ready for take-off. They boarded without delay, the children being very excited at this new adventure, and Beard left them in the care of Big Papa in the rear while he and Stefan went to the front of the plane and sank with relief into the two pilot seats. Having strapped himself in, Beard stared with some trepidation at the array of dials, and turned to Stefan, who was regarding his parachute with some curiosity.

"Right, Professor, fly us home, if you please," Beard called out cheerfully.

Stefan turned, perplexed, and as the true meaning of Beard's words registered, his green eyes widened in horror. "Me!" he cried, his voice cringing as he shrank back in his seat. "I can't fly a plane!"

Beard, already frowning at the other's look of terror, stared back, disbelieving his ears. The man simply had cold feet. He was in a panic. "Of course you can," he replied as calmly as he was able, "you design the bloody things, Stefan."

"Yes, I've designed planes, lots of them," Stefan replied weakly, apologetically. "But I don't fly them. I don't know how, and that's the truth. I've only *flown* twice before – as a passenger." He added the last bit desperately. His normally white face, which had acquired a lightish pinkish tan over the past weeks, now turned almost grey with fear.

"This is ridiculous," exclaimed Beard incredulously, staring with renewed awe at the galaxy of meaningless dials, knobs and instruments. "You must have some idea of how to start the thing."

"Sorry. No. I can't even drive a car, let alone an aeroplane," said Stefan, biting his lower lip in his agitation.

"Well, I can drive a car, and I don't see why flying a plane should be more difficult. One way or another, we're going to fly this thing – it's our only way out, and I'm due for some leave." Beard spotted a key hanging on a hook and, assuming it was the ignition key, took a deep breath, inserted it and turned it. Immediately the plane's engines roared into life, delicious spasms of life, everything throbbing from the vibration. Then, as suddenly, the engines gave a judder and died. Beard could hear the children laughing hilariously behind. "What the hell," he muttered to himself, "can't be much different to driving a car. Probably wants a bit of choke, is all."

Before he could locate anything resembling a choke, Stefan, leaning across to nudge him, pointed to a figure racing across the airfield towards them. It was Prvoš. Beard frowned and, opening his window, shouted down to Prvoš, who was panting below, "What's up? Do you want to come with us?"

Prvoš ignored this and shouted, "Get out of here fast. We're about to blow up all the buildings – runway's next!"

Beard felt sick, which was silly since they hadn't moved an inch. He swallowed hard and shouted back, "I'd love to. How do you start these things?"

Prvoš looked momentarily sick himself, but shouted up, "Have you switched on the fuel supply? You have to do this before anything, and make sure the electrics are off. You turn the engines on later, I think."

Beard examined the panel in front of him afresh, and some other overhead switches, and then saw one that said fuel. He turned this on, and the engines came to life with a roar." Beard felt a lot better, and more so when Stefan discovered a manual and began explaining some of the instruments and reading out the proper starting sequence and pointing out the appropriate switches as they came up. Beard decided it was all rather easy when you had someone telling you what to do, and where things were; and finally, he got to use the ignition key. Even then he wasn't quite sure how it all happened, but Stefan, whose eyes had been fixed on the engine gauge, tapped his knee, pointed to the throttles, and shouted "Push them forward about a quarter!" Beard did as he was told and then sat back while the engines readied themselves, and after a while Stefan himself adjusted the wing flaps and then made a forward gesture with his hand and screamed above the din, "Go!"

Beard instinctively pushed the throttles as far forward as he could and the plane surged forward to its take-off speed. He had no idea what this was, but Stefan shouted out that he'd reached something called rotation speed and indicated that he should pull back on the control column, which he did hurriedly. Almost at once he felt a difference in the plane's behaviour and then, just as he became fearful that they might run out of runway, the nose began to lift and he realised they were airborne. His sensation of thrill plummeted as for several seconds the plane dropped into emptiness, but as he pulled back on the controls in some desperation the plane lifted and they were soaring up in the air and above the neighbouring peaks, and then Beard, having decided not to be sick after all, finally got the hang of how to level out the aircraft, and he had a sense that all was right in the world. The world certainly looked wonderful, clean and empty, up here: it was a different world.

"Piece of cake!" he told the ashen-faced Stefan, who was furiously studying the manual, certain that they should have done something, but hadn't. "I knew you could fly!"

Beard's confidence in his ability to fly the plane was growing, at least when it kept on a level keel; his self-assurance fluttered with each sudden dip of the aircraft. He was recovering from a particularly sharp fall when he felt a tap on his shoulder from behind, and Felbridge was shouting in his ear, "You're going in the wrong direction, sir."

"I'm just getting the feel of the beast, for Christ's sake," Beard snapped back into his headset, more startled by the unexpectedness of the voice than irritated, though inwardly he was somewhat shocked at the information; on the other hand, for the moment he was glad enough just to be up in the air, and staying up there. He gave Felbridge an apologetic grin, and added, "I'll have a go at trying to turn the thing round. I suppose it's achieved through the control column."

"You have to put your foot down on the right pedal rudder and move the control column to the right," chipped in Stefan, delving into the manual again. "It's a wide, slow business."

Beard nodded, and presently they had turned about and were heading north. "Isn't this the way back to Poland?" he demanded, frowning.

"You continue on this course for about fifty miles to avoid a string of mountains, then turn sharply south-west and keep going," answered Felbridge, examining the map in his hand. He was drawing a course with a pencil, which wavered from side to side in an uncertain manner. "I'll tell you when, sir."

"Where does that take us?" pressed Beard, who was experiencing some difficulty in holding the plane steady due to sudden cross winds.

"Hopefully to safety. Perhaps Cyprus or somewhere in the Lebanon."

"That's a hell of a distance," protested Beard. "Find somewhere nearer."

"Are we OK for fuel?"

"You'll know when we fall out of the sky," Beard replied, with a nonchalance he was not truly master of. He examined the fuel gauge, tapped it, and felt rather more optimistic. "We're all right for the moment."

Felbridge frowned, but forced a grin.

"Try and raise our chaps – by radio or Morse. Any British base, the nearer the better, and warn them we're flying a German plane. We don't want to be shot down by our own lot after all our efforts. They'll probably send up fighters to escort us in." It was a wonder Jerry hadn't come up to investigate them, and he attributed this to the fact that the partisans' blitz was occupying all their attention. He paused as the plane suddenly dropped a couple of hundred feet, and yanked on the control column to send it climbing again. The sooner they got out of these mountains the better, he thought, but then he remembered that Yugoslavia was practically all mountains – except the coastal regions, and that's where the Germans were thickest. Perhaps their best route would be across the Adriatic Sea towards Italy. As this thought struck him, Beard wondered how far the Allied invasion there had progressed.

"We might be able to land somewhere in Italy," he suggested. "Find out what the state of play is over there. And the RAF may be in the air over Yugoslavia tonight, see if you can contact them, and advise them of our predicament – if you can do so without telling Jerry all our secrets."

Felbridge gave a wry grin, and turned to get to work.

"And, Aidan, we've travelled close to a hundred miles towards Germany and I don't fancy going any closer, so I'm turning south-west now as you suggested." Beard set in motion the process with the feeling that he was really getting the hang of things, even if the aircraft did bucket about rather disconcertingly. "And try and get me a proper bearing, old chap. This south-west business is a bit vague."

An hour or so later, Beard broke off from chatting with Stefan as Felbridge returned with a clipboard in his hand and a big smile on his face. First he gave Beard a new bearing and once the necessary adjustment had been made, he gave his news. "We're headed for Bari on the Italian coast – or rather the nearby Foggia airfields, which we captured a week ago. The RAF has been alerted and when we come within range we will be escorted in and a pilot on the ground will talk you down. Apparently we're doing marvellously well in Italy. Don't know about anywhere else."

Beard nodded his appreciation of the news, but his mind was already immersed with the prospect of landing in the dark. He and Stefan had been studying and discussing the procedure with the help of the manual, Beard thanking his lucky stars that he understood German. It seemed a fairly straightforward routine, and would be a lot more so if he was being talked down. He felt calm about it. It was something that had to be done, and he was the one who had to do it.

They seemed to have been flying for hours; well, they had been flying for hours, nearly three. Beard knew they were flying over the

Adriatic, he could see glimpses of light on the ruffling water. In spite of the noise of the engines, it felt peaceful all alone in the air with just the far away stars for company; it was like being in a different world; a vast space of complete emptiness.

Then Felbridge came up with a new course, and it was back to earth again. And half an hour later, he became aware of another plane flying unpleasantly close to him, but then he realised it wasn't all that close at all. He could see the RAF roundels and recognised the aircraft as a Hurricane, and in the next instant the pilot was speaking to him, giving him instructions and telling him they were fifty miles from land and that there was nothing to worry about.

And there wasn't. Presently a new voice, identifying itself as George, came over his headset and from that moment virtually took over the flying from Beard. It was a very calm, precise and authoritative voice, and it was very welcome. Beard did exactly as he was told, lowering his height and speed, remembering the flaps and landing wheels, and finally making a very creditable landing at Foggia. And it was all over.

Five hours later, having showered, shaved and eaten to repletion, they were all back in the air, this time in an uncomfortable Dakota, heading for Cairo – and Beard was very content that someone else was doing the flying, and didn't for a moment believe Stefan when he insisted that Beard was an instinctive pilot: a natural. Beard told himself he'd flown his last plane: he was a one-flight pilot.

□   *"You flew an aeroplane! Don't you ever do that again, Jarvis!"* cried Queenie, *amazed and horrified at the same time, and then breaking into a chuckle.* "And you don't even know how to fly! You'll get yer wings soon enough, don't rush it, lovey!"

"Apparently this Jarvis of yours can fly ; I can't," observed Beard. *"The more I hear of this chap and his exploits, the more I'm positive there are two of us – him, and me."*

Chapter Twenty-four

On leave in Cairo, October, 1943

"I suppose having spent nearly three weeks gallivanting round the Continent you feel you've earned a spot of leave, captain?" smiled Gibbs as they sat opposite one another in his now familiar office at Middle East GHQ after their drive from Cairo airport.

"That would certainly be most rewarding, sir," agreed Beard, very quickly.

"Well, you've probably earned it," conceded Gibbs, "but first you have to be de-briefed, and then you have to write up a detailed report on your mission, and that'll most likely occupy several days. The Intelligence boys have already spirited Stefan Mickiewicz and his family away, and we'll probably never see any of them again. So, you go off to that billet of yours, gets some rest and some decent food inside you, and report back here 0900 hours on Tuesday. Then, once everyone's finished with you and you've completed your report, we'll talk about that leave. Go on, be off with you."

Beard was thankful to be released to his bed so promptly; it seemed ages since he had enjoyed the luxury of anything so comfortable, and with the promise of an undisturbed sleep. Brigadier Charington appeared to have taken over the airport when they landed. They'd all been herded into a hanger, and almost immediately Stefan and the children had been whisked away in a convoy with military police escort to some secret destination, but not before Sgt Trumpett had been relieved of Mickiewicz's precious box of documents, with barely an opportunity to do more than wave to the children to whom he would always be Big Papa. The brigadier had then squeezed Beard's hand and uttered a perfunctory "Good show, Mr Beard –told you it would be a doddle, what?" a sentiment that embraced the entire team; and, just as he was stepping into his staff car, he turned to remind Beard not to delay his detailed report on his mission. Beard's men were as promptly driven off to their camp, while Beard accompanied Gibbs to GHQ.

A quiet return home, Beard reflected. But then, he hadn't expected a brass band or shouts of Hurrah! A low profile: that was their way of life.

And at the end of the week, everything accomplished, reports in triplicate, Beard was given three week's leave. It felt sheer bliss to be free to do anything he wanted, but the euphoria did not endure long. After the first few days of liberty in Cairo entirely on his own, Beard began to find his leave a very dull and wearisome business. Time hung very heavily on his hands; he yearned for anybody's companionship. But

Cairo was being drained of men for the more active theatres of the war.

The only other chap currently in residence at his billet was a Lieutenant Cuthbert Curtis of the Royal Engineers who was awaiting a posting, and for the space of five minutes Beard had dared to hope that they might team up for the duration of their leaves. But there was an insurmountable snag that robbed him of even this companion. Curtis, a small, red-cheeked man with sleepy green eyes was freshly out from England; on the voyage he had met Mildred – ATS, or something similar, and they had fallen in love – Curtis had, at any rate ... utterly. He wanted not the smallest part of Beard, not with his beloved Milly being so conveniently, and tantalizingly, stationed in Cairo. It was enough that he had to sleep in the billet, instead of in her arms; he begrudged even the few hours he slept, and was away before Beard stirred to patrol first the barracks where she slept, then the building where she worked – until she was released to him for a few ecstatic hours.

Beard, who decided the man was a complete imbecile, had never felt so fed up. He found himself eating meals he didn't want, just to pass the time – and he seemed to be the only person in the world who was entirely alone; he drank till his head swam dizzily and he all but fell down; and he trudged himself round in all directions, without the slightest interest in anything he saw. About the only thing he remembered was kicking at a dog – what the hell an Airedale terrier was doing here on the streets of Cairo, he couldn't imagine – that got in his way; he remembered because he missed the mutt and fell flat on his back to the great amusement of passers-by – and some old crone had flayed at him with her parasol, screaming words of sadism and cruelty to animals. He'd broken her parasol in half and then sought refuge from her, the heat and teeming streets in the cool stillness of a church, not caring what denomination it gave allegiance to; but fled within minutes as he espied a priest with a strange hat making a beeline for him. So much for the peace and solitude of churches, he thought, making his escape.

He resorted to writing more letters, and it was then he realised how very few people he knew well enough to write to. Top of the list, and almost alone, was Ruth, and he wrote her another cool and carping letter, full of complaints as though she were to blame for not being there to play with him; he wrote plaintively to Bertie as if it were his fault that he was footloose with no one even to talk to; he even thought of writing to Scruffy, but managed to resist such a mad impulse – even anonymously. Instead, he turned his boredom on the offerings of the many cinema establishments – they were mainly ugly great halls with rows of seats only slightly softer than concrete and screens that constantly collapsed. On his first visit, Beard was entertained to a double helping of Deanna Durbin – and promptly fell in love with her; next he was introduced to Ginger Rogers – and he loved her, too; and then he was transfixed by Greta Garbo in Camille – but because she took such a long time dying in the film, he decided that she was best left alone, as, apparently, she wished to be. All in all, he decided to remain true to Deanna Durbin; he wondered if he should write to her and tell her of his love, but because of events that were about to unfold he never got round to it.

Garbo's was the last film Beard saw that first week. On his sixth night on the loose in Cairo, he went on a bender that he knew less about as the hours staggered by. Starting at Groppi's – he was physically encouraged to leave an hour or so later for abusing a waiter who had insisted corned beef wasn't on the menu or ever likely to be, and progressed rather unsteadily through a fog of numerous hotel bars and other less savoury establishments. As he lurched along the crowded, humid streets, he found no one who was willing to share his company for long, and his aggressive attitude and general drunkenness ensured that he was constantly being directed to seek his pleasures elsewhere. So it was that, in the very early hours of the following morning, he found himself in a first-floor drinking den, barely able to stand, or drink for that matter; he crashed hither and thither, being roundly cursed for his clumsiness, and finally sprawled over the bar counter, propped up on either side by unwilling (uncooperative, anyway) sailors, unable to speak coherently but still endeavouring to abuse the skinny Sinhalese barman, who grinned amiably and incomprehensibly back.

It was the extremely sudden and urgent need to find somewhere suitable to be sick – the sailor to his right hastily grabbed his cap out of harm's way, and gave Beard a vigorous push in the opposite direction. This propulsion sent him sailing through a tinkling screen of glass beads and bamboo, straight into the very substantial body of a glisteningly black woman in a bright red dress. Beard clung to her desperately for support, and as she struggled to free herself from him, he was sick all over her. She screamed hysterically, and shoved him from her with such violence that he was sent tumbling down the flight of stairs. He came to rest – for want of a better word – out in the street, where he was further cursed by people who were compelled to step over him, and at least one person gave him an unkind kick in the process of doing so – possibly to see if he was still alive, but more probably for the sheer hell of it, the resulting grunt satisfying both possibilities.

Beard's thoughts were a confusion of rambling ideas as to what was happening to him. He told himself he should try and get up, and then became concerned as to whether he would ever be able to move again. He lay immobile in an untidy heap, arms and legs stretched out like a puppet's whose mechanism had failed. He wondered if he was damaged, and decided it didn't matter – not any more. His head was spinning, so fast he felt he had no control over himself. His eyes were shut and he wanted only to sleep: to sleep for ever – except that he felt too ill to do even that; he wondered if he was dying.

And then, he felt a cold hand gently touch his forehead, and he knew; he'd arrived in heaven – or the annexe, at the very least..

"Are you all right?" asked a voice. It was a woman's voice, gentle and concerned: soft like an angel's kiss.

The absurdity of the question was lost on Beard as he struggled to open his eyes. He forced one heavy lid open, and then the other, painfully and cautiously, and after a moment something that restored his thoughts of heaven came into focus – a dimpled white knee that hovered just above his face. It was a very white knee, and nicely rounded, too. He raised his gaze to feast on several inches of even whiter thigh visible beneath a denim skirt. Up and up strained his eyes, regardless of the pain caused by the effort, till the teasing whiteness turned to mysterious, exciting blackness. He tried to swallow, but found he couldn't. He tried again to penetrate the darkness, looking for her wings, but though his eyes opened a little wider everything was a blur.

"I'm'fraid I mebbe slightly dead," he slurred thickly, and was quite surprised even by that unnatural sound for he hadn't supposed the dead spoke out loud; so, perhaps he wasn't properly dead after all. This unexpected intelligence gave him no particular pleasure; if he wasn't dead, he felt he should be. Oh, Lor! he moaned.

"You're drunk, m'lad!" declared his angel firmly, but with the loveliest of smiles. "Pie-eyed, you silly-billy!"

Beard stared up at her, as though in disbelief; his mouth sagged into a sort of gormless grin and for an instant it looked as though he might try to speak again ... but the effort proved too much, and he passed out.

"You're going to hate yourself when you wake up," the angel told him with a sober grin.

But Beard only snored in reply.

When he woke, Beard did hate himself. His head – he felt sure there must be more than one – not only hurt, it throbbed as though there was a steamroller at work inside crushing everything into tiny pieces. He groaned, not daring to move in case he stirred some dormant pain into life; but, after lying lifeless for a long, long time, he finally risked opening his eyes – just a crack at first, and gradually more and more; his eye-lids felt like they had been sandpapered. Fresh waves of pain hammered his head, but by degrees he overcame his deep nausea to take stock of his surroundings.

The first realisation was that he was lying in a bed; a soft bed, with silky Nile-green sheets and entirely enclosed by a mosquito-net hanging from a frame fixed to the ceiling. Somewhere an electric fan whirred ... but what brought an instant frown to Beard's aching brow was a subtle but pervading fragrance of – he didn't know of what, but he imagined it to be some exotic perfume. Perfume! That must surely indicate the presence of some female! He shot up in some consternation, and immediately wished he had been more circumspect, for the movement cost him dear as his various heads crashed against each other in protest, stoking up fresh bolts of pain. Once the pain had subsided somewhat, he discovered that the bed was a double one and that, though he was now its only occupant, there was the tell-tale hollow of where another body had recently lain beside his; and very closely, too.

He was still digesting this, plus the fact that he was completely naked, when he heard a sound and saw his angel of last night approaching – at least, he assumed it was she for he hadn't been able to see very clearly before. He still couldn't see any wings. She was wearing a floral kimono of leaf-green silk which showed even more leg than he remembered seeing earlier. It struck him as being strange apparel for an angel; she didn't seem to be wearing anything else under the robe. He felt a warm flush creeping over his cheeks, and somewhere below, he was aware of a stirring, and something hardening. Oh God, he thought to himself.

"How's our corpse feeling?" she greeted him angelically.

"Barely alive," he retorted, his voice sounding as thick as his tongue felt.

"Here, drink this," she instructed, handing him a glass tumbler from a tray she carried. The glass was half-full of a whitish liquid.

"What is it?" he asked suspiciously, sniffing at it with frank distaste.

"Never you mind, my hero! It's best you don't know ... just get it down you, and all in one go," she commanded, in a voice which suddenly didn't sound very much like that of an angel. "You'll feel a lot better."

"Or dead," he muttered, regarding the glass doubtfully; but, deciding that it could hardly make him feel any worse, he did as he was told, emptying the glass in a single long swallow. Its benefit was not instantaneous, but then nothing ever was – except poison! He almost gagged at the thought, but the liquid continued on its way to his stomach ... and presently not only his stomach felt easier, but his head seemed restored to singleness and things seemed to lose their blur. He gave a little shudder, still unsure of his recovery.

"Where am I?" he asked her guardedly, but with only mild concern; he was perfectly content to be wherever he was.

"You're in my flat, and in my bed," she answered him with an angelic smile.

Did angels have beds? "And who are you?" he pressed, desperate to know her better.

"I'm Gillian – Gillian Crumpet. I'm supposed to be a sort of lieutenant, but I'm really simply a nurse at the American Hospital here."

"Are you American?" Beard frowned, puzzled. "You sound English ."

"Good heavens, no! I'm from Swaffham in Norfolk, you know, where the sugar beet grows," laughed Gillian; and when she laughed her whole face seemed to share her pleasure; it was still pink in spite of the African sun and positively radiated happiness from her huge cat-green eyes to her firm round chin. She tossed her long reddish hair and continued at a gallop. "The hospital's owned by an American organisation, but the staff's almost entirely English – and all our patients are British soldiers, although I suppose that'll change now that America's in the war. But for the moment at least we live in our own palatial quarters – no sharing with half a dozen girls, and we have a sentry marching up and down outside, like it was Buckingham Palace. We're so much better off than nurses in British hospitals, the poor dears. The Americans pay for everything, and there's a canteen at the hospital where the food is free – it's excellent, too."

Beard digested all this with his bloodshot eyes fixed fascinatedly on the narrow patch of white where the kimono was teasingly parted: on either side a breast lay barely concealed, although each symmetrical mound was clearly visible in shape. He was drooling over these shapes … and suddenly was reminded of his own nudity.

"Where's my clothes?" he demanded, hastily looking down to ensure that he was decently covered; he couldn't do anything about his growing erection down there.

"I've washed most of your things," she informed him. "I sent your uniform to the cleaners. It'll be ready tomorrow."

"What'll I wear till then?" he asked, somewhat disconcertedly, though immediately thinking it was a damned stupid question.

"Do you need to wear anything?" she asked archly, smiling at him through long lashes.

He stared back at her, hardly daring to believe his ears and not knowing what to think, or say. Since he was plainly not in heaven, not the promised one, there was no imagining her to be an angel now. He didn't say anything, but after a very few moments, he gave her a smile: a very boyish, excited smile. But he remained tongue-tied.

Gillian raced on. "I found your leave pass in your pockets – I've put all your possessions in a bowl on the table," – she waved a hand in the direction of a window, "and I called your billet in case they were concerned over your absence. I told them you'd run into some friends from England and would be spending your leave with them ... I said you'd let them know."

"You seem to have been busy," he said with blossoming affability, his smile spreading to his eyes at the thought. It occurred to him that without any clothes he didn't have much option but to stay put. He felt pleasurably delirious at the thought of her *invitation*. "How on earth did you manage to get me here?"

"It wasn't easy. You're quite a size, and heavy, Mr Beard. Too heavy for me to handle on my own. I prevailed upon two passers-by to lift you into a taxi, and the driver and the sentry outside – he's a darling, and you must say something nice to him when you see him – carried you in; fortunately, we're on the ground floor." She gave a little giggle at the recollection. "You've been sleeping all day ... you started waking up an hour or so ago. And now," she looked up at him with a mischievous gleam in her eyes, "it's early evening, and time for bed again!"

Beard breathed rather deeper than usual, not quite certain if he was expected to say something, and if so, what he should say. He was so confused, he found himself half-stifling a yawn, reddened as he realised how this might be interpreted ... and then they both burst out laughing.

"I'm sorry to have put you to all this trouble, miss," he murmured.

"Gillian, please, darling," she smiled, "only teachers get called 'miss,' and then only by children when they're naughty."

Beard gave her a naughty-boy grin. "Yes, miss," he said impishly, and then more seriously added, "I've never been drunk before ... not passed-out-drunk, anyway."

"It doesn't matter. We were plainly meant to meet, Bobbie – I may call you Bobbie, mayn't I? – because I've only just started on leave, too," Gillian gushed. "Why don't we spend our leaves together – here?"

Beard could think of no good reason why not. Heaven knows he'd been miserable enough on his own the last few days. Security momentarily crossed his mind, as it should do considering the type of soldiering he was involved in, but he dismissed it; he couldn't conceive that he was in the presence of any Mata Hari – and he didn't have any secrets to tell if she was. Besides, he was beginning to believe that nothing would be farther from their minds than the war in the immediate future. "And what do you propose we do with ourselves on this joint leave of ours?" he teased her, hoping he sounded more worldly-wise and confident than he felt; a lot more so.

She stared at him, her large eyes showing surprise. "Make love!" she told him simply.

"All the time?"

"Oh, yes please!" she sang out with happy laughter, and then seeing a whisper of concern, perhaps even doubt, at the corners of his perfectly adorable mouth and in his dark, beautiful eyes, she quickly added: "No, silly; not *all* the time. We must conserve our strength ... and ration our love-making. In between, we'll walk and talk, and swim, and play lots of tennis – because I'm good at that! – and go dancing, and I'm good at that too, and eat out in quiet, romantic restaurants, and go shopping, of course – I want to buy you something beautiful, and cheap; perhaps a pretty silk tie, or a wallet."

"Camel-skin, of course?"

"Certainly not – crocodile! You can dive into the Nile and pick out your own! And then I can jump in to save you ... or the croc!"

"No! We'll have him for dinner," grinned Beard. "I've never had a croc steak before!"

They laughed together, just like a couple of excited children on the verge of a great adventure, and Gillian leaned forward to touch his cheek with the gentlest of palms while she brushed his mouth with her lips with equal softness. It was only a touch, but it had the thrill of the most passionate of kisses. It was a declaration of love, and in that moment Beard fell in love ... forgetting all previous loves.

"But you mustn't wear yourself out, Bobbie. We have to save ourselves for the main event – love!" she whispered, moving closer to him and speaking almost into his ear, which she honoured with the tiniest of delicate nips hastily followed by a compensatory kiss.

"You make it all sound too wonderful for worlds," Beard murmured pleasurably, tingling all over at her touch, never dreaming that he could ever be jealous of his ear! And to think only yesterday he'd been bored out of his mind, and only two weeks ago he'd been killing people, and near to being killed himself. If he had to die, this was where he'd choose it to be! "I've been so desperately lonely these last few days ... that's why I got so drunk ... and fell at your feet." She shushed him, but made no other attempt to silence him, "I'm terribly afraid of being a disappointment to you. I'm not very experienced at ... love – in fact, not at all." Again she hushed him, but with a tiny smile of understanding as she looked into his so- serious face. "I've never done anything like this before – never had the chance," he went on, taking it for granted that she had, "so you'll have to be patient with me."

"Sssh!" she repeated, holding his head against her shoulder and planting little kisses where she could reach. "Patience and women are close acquaintances," she assured him. "Love is an experience we'll share by learning together. I'll teach you what I know and we'll progress from there, like all lovers. But, my dearest, promise me that when we make love, it will be with love in your heart, not simply lust. Only love is real."

Beard nodded his promise but remained silent, not entirely trusting himself to say the right words, and was quite startled when she suddenly detached herself from him, saying that she must prepare something for them to eat "to give us the strength to love," and he must have a bath to wash away the memories of his previous day's excesses. Adding that he'd find a housecoat of sorts big enough to cover most of his essentials, she went off singing towards the kitchen, turning on the bath taps on the way – and he couldn't help noticing, in his lecherous state, that she had quite sturdy legs, an attractively broad bottom ... and that her hips swayed with a delicious sensuality that sent his senses reeling.

After several minutes of quite randy thoughts, he pattered over the tessellated floor, tested the water in the bath, turned off the taps, and then sank, with a sigh of pure pleasure, into the steaming, bubbly, scented water. He would probably have fallen asleep and drowned quite happily had Gillian not appeared, slipped the kimono off her shoulders with a provocative twirl, and stepped into the bath with him. After giving him several quick kisses, she proceeded to guide his willing hands in bathing those parts of her she couldn't easily reach, and, of course, returning the favour. The water was quite cool when they emerged – and they didn't get round to eating anything until long, long afterwards.

It seemed that they were seldom out of bed in the ensuing days, but they must have done, for, in between their bouts of feverish love-making, they did all the things that Gillian had said they would – except, she wouldn't let him dive into the Nile because she thought it looked too polluted with oil and filth, and there was always the probability of crocodiles. However, she did buy him a present: not a leather wallet, but a powder-blue sharkskin suit – because, she insisted, it was too much of a torment to her having him constantly either bare-skinned or in the same uniform as a million others; he bought her a necklace of malachites to go with her eyes. She was so delighted with her present that she wanted to wear it in bed, but they both found it a hindrance to their activities and Gillian herself agreed the treasure was superfluous in that place where all that was needed for perfect happiness was each other – accordingly, she consigned the necklace to her bedside table where it winked through the night at their goings-on.

Gillian, who was nearly five years older than Beard, seemed to be experienced far beyond even her years in the ways of love, and her delight in passing on her knowledge was like that of a very young girl; certainly she taught him all he needed to know, and possibly a good deal more besides. If she was a good teacher, he was an equally responsive pupil, the proof of which lay in the intimacy that so speedily developed between them; indeed, theirs was a most mutually satisfying relationship. In moments of relaxation, to which both had recourse to recoup spent energies, they would lay in each other's arms and gossip like an old married couple. Lying there with her long russet hair spread over the pillows, she laughed so compassionately when he confided his ignominious experience with Georgina. "Poor girl, she must have been so disappointed," she whispered. "So was I!" he confessed.

Beard never again had any difficulties with French letters, as she called his condoms. In the course of his tutelage, he discovered the importance of foreplay and of the absolute necessity of protracting his actual love-making; she sulked and scolded him quite heatedly when he came and went in the same breath on one wretched occasion. He'd never felt so awfully inadequate. Well, he had of course, with Georgina, but that experience did not bear comparison. Gillian was patient and he learned, and with constant practice and an urgent desire on both sides to please the other, their orgasms became a shared climax: a sublime moment for both of them.

Towards the end of their leaves – and how the time seemed to flash by – their love-making became less desperate, though just as satisfying. There seemed more time to do other things, or simply to lay quietly together and talk. Gillian disclosed in one of those moments when even the most secret of secrets are confessed, that she had come out to Africa not so much to follow her nursing vocation as to be near her fiancé, Crispin Thomas, who was a captain in the Royal Artillery. But he'd been listed "missing, believed killed" after a fearful battle near Sidi Barrani even before she landed, so she'd never had the chance of seeing either him or his grave. Fortunately her work tending the wounded kept her fully occupied, mentally and physically, leaving her little time for private grief, and as the months had passed and the ache inside her eased, she came to accept his loss as something permanent – unlike the War Office, which was unable to alter his listing; and so, gradually, she had started to live again, and, because of her great capacity for sexual passion, to love again – when the urge was there. And the night she'd met Beard, she was in need of love.

"Once I'd accepted that Crisp was dead, life didn't seem so awful any more," she said with a far-away expression.

Beard, in his turn, told her something of his orphanage days; he didn't reveal his true identity, nor mention Scruffy in any way, but he made those far off days sound more exciting than wretched, except that day he'd cried his heart out when he hadn't been chosen for adoption; he told her of the times he'd run away and of the great adventures he'd had dodging the rozzers; and he told her especially of his dear Queenie, whom he spoke of as his pretend mother, and he didn't hesitate to include Ruth in his history. In fact, without realising it, he talked at great length about her, and the longer he went on the warmer his voice grew. Gillian, who had alternately laughed and felt close to tears, and sometimes anger, as he poured out his recollections, wondered about the even more terrible things she felt sure he'd left out. But when he paused, she simply nodded her head thoughtfully.

"You're in love with her, of course; you know that, don't you?" she said gently, taking hold of his restless hands and clutching them to her chest.

"Who? Ruth?" he demanded, sitting up, ready to deny her if necessary.

"Of course Ruth," she returned equably.

He stared at her in astonishment, bewildered and even irritated.

"Ruth!" he echoed derisorily. "She's just a child ... a schoolgirl!"

"I don't expect she thinks of herself as such," Gillian smiled, in a knowing sort of way. "Love makes a woman of even the youngest of girls. Remember, Juliet was only thirteen when she died for her love."

"That's fiction – just a silly old fairy story," scoffed Beard, "and, anyway, Ruth's no Juliet. Can't see her plunging a dagger through her heart over me, nor anybody else – and I'm damned sure I wouldn't over her! Anyway," he cried, snatching back his hands so that he could clench his fists and have some control over his topsy-turvy emotions, "where'd you get the crazy idea that I was in love with her?"

"From you, Bobbie. It's the way you speak her name ... it's in your very breath, darling. There's a special warmth in the tone of your voice at the very mention of her – and it's there for all to see in your eyes ... nakedly so. You'll deny it vehemently now, but it's there in your soul, and always will be. It's all rather lovely ... nothing to be ashamed about, Bobbie."

"But it's *you* I love, Gillian!" he insisted desperately, grabbing at her hands and holding on to them with the same desperation. "Truly! I've never loved anyone as I love you – and I never will."

"No, Bobbie, my dearest. What we've shared is sex. We've made love ... been lovers, and it's been beautiful, darling, but it's not the same thing as being in love. You'll discover this yourself when you're with your Ruth again."

Beard stared, dumbfounded, shattered. Was it true? Could it possibly be? Oh, why should it be! And yet, now that he gave the matter thought, he remembered that others had kept telling him the same thing. Why was everybody trying to marry him off to Ruth? Mrs B. had been one, and even Bertie – and he'd seen the same dream every time he looked deeply into Queenie's loving eyes ... and now his darling angel, his marvellous Gillian was repeating it ... like she was reading the banns. Oh, it wasn't fair! Of course he loved Ruth – she sent him letters; but he was sure he had no thoughts of marrying her. Sure, *she* had thoughts about it, but girls – especially schoolgirls, were always thinking such nonsense. And for a moment he wasn't sure he didn't hate her for causing him this grief; but it was only a momentary anger.

"There'll never be anyone else but you for me, Gillian," he cried out, almost despairingly. He released her hands again, and thumped the bed as though to emphasise his words. "I'll never love anybody else. I don't love Ruth in the way you mean – she's nothing but an old playmate. I love only you, Gillian."

"And I you, dearest – at this moment."

"I want to marry you," Beard declared bluntly, almost aggressively, as though he already knew it was hopeless.

"No, Bobbie," she said firmly. "Let's not spoil what we've had. Ours wasn't the sort of love that leads to marriage. Beautiful as it was, our love was only a transitory affair. It was something we both needed. I have the normal healthy physical needs of a woman just as you have yours as a man. It was a new experience for you – and you'll go off and have others; but that's all they'll be – experiences. And I like to think that one day your Ruth will be pleased you had these little affairs because, deep down, no woman likes her man to be entirely inexperienced."

"I must have been a great disappointment to you, then," he exclaimed bitterly.

"No, Bobbie. We were good for each other. You filled a void in my life at a time when I needed love ... and I filled the same one in yours. It did us both good, and there was no wrong in what we did."

"You talk as though it were all over between us," he retorted accusingly.

"It was only going to last as long as our leaves, Bobbie. Heaven knows where you'll be posted to next. We'll possibly never meet again," she whispered seriously, yet not without passion. "But you'll always occupy a very special corner in my heart. You're very, very dear to me, Bobbie. You've given me more happiness than I ever believed possible after the loss of Crisp ... and I do hope you'll remember me with affection – even after you and Ruth are married!"

"That'll be the day!" he ejaculated, but the bitterness had already dropped from his voice. He had calmed down as suddenly as he had boiled over, and now, as he remembered Ruth, and acknowledged that neither of them was a child any more, even the idea of marriage didn't sound quite so preposterous – only highly improbable. He flinched as the thought whirled around his brain. He wasn't very sure of anything at that moment, except that Ruth was too much a part of him for him to be cross with her for long, or for her to be far from his thoughts for long, come to that. Perhaps Gillian was right. It did seem that, after all, she talked a lot of sense, even if her words were unbearable to accept. He couldn't believe that their great love was about to end, or that they might never meet again. "If I'm ever in Cairo again, will it be all right if I come and see you?" he asked in an agonized voice.

"Of course, Bobbie. I'd be very sad if you didn't look me up. After all, we have been lovers – and are still, and lovers shouldn't fall out even if their paths go in opposite directions. We'll always be very special friends. But," she gave him a coy smile, "it might be best if you give me a ring first – in case I have another ... visitor."

Beard gave a grim smile of his own, as he nodded understandingly. He guessed that after he'd gone, there'd probably be other soldiers who needed comforting and loving, and it really wouldn't do for their paths to cross in those circumstances. And there was no feeling of jealousy in his thought.

"I won't write because I'm not much at letter-writing," she added, but she knew it was because letters would be too painful ... and letters, too, could be dangerous.

"Me neither," Beard admitted, and now, finally, as they relaxed in each other's arms, he accepted that their liaison was about to end. The realisation brought neither anger nor regret, not really; it had been wonderful while it had lasted, and the memory of it would stay with him for ever, but in his heart of hearts he believed he'd known from the start it couldn't last – certainly not for ever, as true love should. Still, he was grateful for the – experience, as she'd called it; and he'd certainly be a better lover in future!

They made love one last time just before the alarm went off at 5.30; she had to report back at her hospital at 7 o'clock, and he was expected to return to the war. Gillian smiled at Beard through the stickiness that blurred her vision, and she had to blink her lashes several times before the green of her eyes peered through. She kissed him quickly on the lips, tossed her tangled hair from her face, and then she was pattering off to the shower to properly wake up. Beard joined her briefly under the cold jets and for a few moments longer they enjoyed the feel of each other, their mouths in energetic union, and then they were busy climbing into their respective uniforms.

Beard had expected to see her in some form of military outfit, KDs at least, but she wore her nurse's uniform of blue cotton with its traditional belt and silver buckle and the distinctive scarlet tippet about her shoulders, which he thought seemed a little incongruous out here in Africa – but very fetching. She wore no head-dress nor make-up, and he thought her mouth seemed much wider and thinner without its splash of paint. Her gorgeous hair, now in severe restraint, was tied up and hidden behind her head. She looked almost strict, in a pretty sort of way. For a longish moment they stood staring at one another, drinking in memories for the future.

"I've never heard of your regiment before, Bobbie," Gillian said softly, moving forward and stretching up to touch his cap badge and then tracing the parachute wings that adorned his sleeve, and the medal ribbons on his chest; she looked thoughtfully at them, and then shook her head slowly. He told her few people had because it was supposed to be a secret one, and she at once placed a finger over his lips to silence him, and whispered, "Let's leave it a secret, darling."

They left the flat in silence, and the same silence accompanied them all the way to her American hospital. It was a silence that neither wished to break, for it seemed to draw them closer together for these last precious moments. At the hospital, Gillian, taking her holdall from him, stood on tiptoes to kiss him most decorously on his cheek, at the same time whispering throatily into his ear, "Take care of yourself, my love"; and, after a tiny pause, "Be good to Ruth, d'you hear!" And then she was running towards the entrance, without a backward glance.

Beard stared after her and gave a little salute at her vanished figure; and then he turned and marched away. Once again, he felt like a soldier ... but how lovely it had been not to be one for just a little while. The war would seem a strange world after his little peep into heaven.

☐   *"I certainly have no recollection of this lovely lady," cried Beard, laughing, and manoeuvring himself to look the general squarely in the face, "but if you have her phone number, I wouldn't mind making her acquaintance – for old times' sake!"*

"Sorry, Robert, no number," smiled Gibbs.

"And just supposing I am this lucky chap of yours, how the devil do you come to have such intimate details of this ... alleged relationship?" asked Beard bluntly, if with a twinkle in his eyes.

"From you, mostly," returned Gibbs, with mock gravity. "I have questioned as many men you served with as still survive and this two-week affair of yours was not the secret you may think. Remember, it was in Cairo and you were seen together in many places – you did not spend all your time in bed. And there was a letter from the lady in question that told all. Additionally, Robert, in the course of your lengthy periods of induced unconsciousness you talked out loud at times, giving the nurses, who recorded your every word, information far removed from your medical state, entertaining though it was. I have endeavoured to piece it all together and present as interestingly as possible."

"If only you'd sent poor Ruthie more letters, Jarvis," Queenie intervened. "She wrote you so many ... and they were beautiful, but you hardly ever bothered to reply. That was so unkind, and mean. She waited and waited for the tiniest word from you. She loved you so much."

"I deny everything," declared Beard jocularly. "I suppose you're now going to tell me that I shot the Gillian lady and dropped her in the Nile for the enjoyment of the crocs?"

"No, you returned to duty," replied Gibbs soberly, "and her letter followed you."

Chapter Twenty-five

Letters from Ruth, 25 October, 1943

Beard still had a week left of his leave, thanks to an accumulation of days owing which had been added on. He was still thinking of Gillian, and wondering how he could possibly do without her, when a man from his camp delivered a batch of letters – together with a warning that Gibbs was looking for him. Beard thanked him, then promptly forgot both Gibbs and Gillian, and turned to his letters.

They were all from Ruth, of course; who else wrote to him? Her letters always arrived in numbers, though, if fault there was, it was his since these days they simply gathered dust until his return from one of his missions or training exercises. As was his wont, he stood the letters in a military line according to their dates, and eagerly opened the oldest one first.

"*My darling – oh, Jarvis dearest* ... " – Blast the girl! Can't she ever remember my name, swore Beard under his breath; and immediately forgave her everything as he read on – " *... I have some terrible news to tell you. Terrible and sad. I wanted to keep it from you, but Mummy said that it wouldn't be right and that I must tell you.*" Beard sensed an enormous pause before she continued. "*Daddy has been killed in an air raid.*" There; her terrible news was out, and he felt another long pause. "*It was on the night of August 23-24. We don't know for sure exactly when it happened. There'd been some scattered bombing all around, but it seems a lone bomber simply dropped its load right on poor Daddy – it was in that street just this side of the Opera House. I think it's called Flower Street. Do you know where I mean?*" Beard shook his head, and read on. "*The Opera House wasn't touched, but the rest of the street was blown away. It disappeared – and Daddy with it. That was the worst thing. They never found anything of him – not enough for us to bury. Just a little paper bag of bits of bones that could have belonged to anybody. It was horrible. His Police Station arranged a memorial service at which a lot of strangers said a lot of very nice things about him, and Father Daly said a Requiem Mass for him and promised that prayers would be said for his soul for ever. Everyone's been very kind. I never knew Daddy was loved by so many people. I honestly thought we were the only ones. A week after he died the notice came about the investiture at the Palace. That brought our tears flooding back, as you can imagine. Mummy says Daddy's medal will probably be sent on to us in time, but it isn't so important any more.*" Beard could almost see the tears running down her cheeks, and felt that he was waiting for her to recover so that she could continue. "*We're* *broken-hearted, but learning to live with our terrible loss. But it's as if our world has gone. Smashed to smithereens with him. And there's nobody left to lean against – only you, and you're so far away, and now, dearest, we're both so dreadfully frightened for your safety. Please, please ... oh please do come back to us – safe and sound, and very soon. We need you to help us pick up the pieces."*

There was a hurried postscript saying that a horrible witch of a woman – *"I think she was mad, too,"* declared Ruth – had appeared on the scene claiming to be Sam's real wife and saying she was entitled to his police pension! She added that Queenie had walloped the woman across the face with a mackerel she happened to have in her hand and chased her down the street waving someone's brolly and hurling things off barrows after her. *"Mummy must have chased her clear across London because she had to come back in a taxi. We haven't seen sight or sound of the woman since."* Ruth added, and her brevity added to the mystery, that Queenie seemed to know the woman. There was a final PS in which Ruth begged him to hurry home. *"We need our loved ones with us at this time,"* she said.

Beard was absolutely shattered by the news. Surrounded though he was by death every day, he was, nevertheless, shocked that it should touch Sam back home. It seemed, somehow, most unfair. But, of course, it was happening every day. Civilians back home were probably more in danger than he was – most of the time. Beard shook his head, sadly, and with some bitterness. Sam was the nearest thing to a father he had known, and, although they hadn't spent a lot of time together, he'd grown to love him, in the way of a child. Sam had been like a special friend: always there when needed, always ready with sensible advice and warm encouragement: someone to be trusted, always. Beard had thought of him as being indestructible. Now, with his death, it was like discovering that God didn't exist after all, else how could it have happened? He dashed the blasphemy from his thoughts: this was no time for such heresy. Beard wished – deep down in his heart he wished it, and the ache was an added pain – he had shown his affection more, but he knew that his upbringing had not equipped him to be demonstrative in his feelings. However, he consoled himself with the belief that there had been a close bond, an inner understanding, between them that made this display unnecessary. Oh, he hoped this was so.

From Sam, Beard's thoughts returned to Queenie and Ruth whose love, he was sure, was far deeper than anything he felt; they were part of Sam's family, his blood, whereas he was really an interloper, like a stray dog taken in and given a bone. But they all shared Sam's love in varying degrees. Beard wanted to comfort his dear adopted kinfolk, but did not know how at that distance. It had to be by letter; but how to begin, and what to say? Again and again, he started the letter. Finally, he settled for "My Darlings," as Ruth had done so often, and rushed on. The words flowed easily, like a small boy's tears – or those of a man who only knew how to cry inside, and he hoped that they would provide some measure of comfort; the fact that he felt comforted by writing them made him think they would. He could do no more to lessen the distance between them than to let his heart speak for him, and it overflowed with happy memories of Sam, who had been so special to each of them in different ways. He sent the letter off as soon as it was completed so as to hurry his words of comfort to them.

And then he picked up Ruth's next letter, which appeared to have done almost as much travelling as he had, judging by the various stampings it bore. He settled down with the eagerness of ... perhaps a lover

"*My Darling*," she wrote, quickly adding "*I love you, I love you, I love you*," and underlining each lovely word, before launching into a lengthy, and apparently tearful – at least, he supposed the blotches were tears – complaint about his not writing to her for simply ages and ages. At this point, presumably having paused for breath, she thanked him for his last letter with the lovely photos of Sicily; she placed a question mark after the name of the island for he hadn't identified the place, supposing the photos would do this. Beard grinned; he'd sent the letter only about three months ago, which wasn't really so long ago, was it? She couldn't expect a letter every week, could she? But she did; of course she did, and she accused him of having other distractions and not having the time to think of her. It was the same back home, she wrote. Every day she saw soldiers chasing after girls and flirting with them in public, and she supposed they all had sweethearts dying for a few words of love in a letter (Beard wondered if she meant the boys or the girls).

"*My darling*," she wrote in a whisper, returning to her own love (and here the blotches looked larger), "*please don't forget me altogether, and do please let me know that you are safe and well, and that you love me*." She added that she died a little more each time a new battle was announced on the wireless – it didn't matter to her where it was or who won the stupid thing, only that he might have been hurt in it; only a letter from him could mend her poor bruised and empty heart. After a brief reference to how lonely life at The Dials was without Daddy, and about Mavis being head over heels in love with some ghastly GI, Ruth repeated her demand for a letter – a long one, and a loving one – and finally added Queenie's postscript about eating properly. Beard felt a pang that there was no directive from Sam about keeping his head down.

The next letter was a very different affair: a lot less complaining, and more interesting – entertaining, anyway. The prayer for a letter was repeated again and again, but Beard found it easy to skim over these, for suddenly his interest was wholly taken up by Ruth's story of how she and her mother had had to go to court over Sam's widow Lily. Ruth had mentioned the woman briefly in a previous letter, but apart from being amused at the thought of Queenie slapping the woman across the face with a mackerel and then chasing her across London, Beard hadn't paid much heed to the matter. He did so now, for the woman stood in the dock answering to the name of Mrs Lily Mutton; she was charged with bigamy and fraud.

Ruth appeared reluctant to say so, but Beard got the impression that she thought Lily quite a handsome woman – for her age, which was given as 45; she was fair, with a pleasant face, apart from a rather too-sharp nose and beady little hazel eyes that never stayed still, and she had a figure that was too big for her body. Yes, Ruth thought the woman must have been quite attractive in her long-ago youth, and even now wasn't entirely unattractive. Ruth said the proceedings were terribly complicated – and boring, too, for she had fallen asleep wedged between Queenie and Mrs Molly – and she hadn't understood half of what was said.

What was clear, however, was that Lily was a much married woman – at least, she had gone through marriage ceremonies one after the other ever since 1916. But that first marriage, on August 4, 1916, to Bombardier Arthur Mutton of the Royal Artillery, at Our Lady of Victories Church in Kensington High Street, had been her only legal one. None of the others counted.

"*I'm awfully glad she wasn't really married to Daddy, but it's terribly sad that because he believed he was, he couldn't ever marry Mummy,*" wrote Ruth, and Beard could almost see the tears welling in her velvety eyes. "*Not that I could ever love either of them more if they'd been married a hundred times, and if that's a sin – then Father Daly will simply have to forgive me when I go to confession. I really cannot understand this woman, Lily. She was a sort of religious crank, and a frightful hypocrite into the bargain ... she went to Mass almost every day, spent half her life on her knees praying, surrounded herself with holy pictures and statues, and yet she happily went about marrying all these men and drawing pensions and allowances in all their different names – even from poor Daddy, almost as if she was engaged in doing God's work. She was such a religious nut that she insisted on marrying in church (I wonder if she wore white!) and always refused point blank to even consider a divorce. She must be mad ... a mad, evil woman.*

"*I can't imagine how she remembered all the names, but it seems she did; each husband had his own folder with all his details, and once a week she'd have a day of reckoning – collecting money from her unfortunate men, who all thought they were still married to her and only wanted to make new lives for themselves, whatever the cost. I didn't know it myself till now, but she even made darling Daddy call on her each week to pay his dues. But it was this money business that finally led to her undoing. It came about when the authorities investigated her application for a pension when Daddy was killed, and one after the other these other husbands came to light. She was already drawing five widows' pensions, five that were known (Mummy said there must've been others after Daddy) – and there she was singing at High Mass every Sunday and going to confession regular as clockwork, like a good Catholic wife. Mummy said the fact that she didn't have any children meant that God had at least drawn the line somewhere."*

Ruth said she couldn't remember all the names of the men involved. The first, after Arthur Mutton, had been a Roland Corker in Richmond – and that had been before the Armistice, and while Mutton was still at the front. As Corker's name had been mentioned, Queenie, sitting uncomfortably close to the dock, had stood up and screamed *"Slut!"* at Lily, who stared vacantly back and continued reciting her rosary. Queenie had been admonished by the judge, who wagged a cautionary finger at her. The roll call of husbands continued, and when the fourth was mentioned – a King's Cross railway engine driver named Ron Clarke – Queenie could contain herself no longer; she was back on her feet shouting words like *"Bitch!"* and *"Hussy!"* at the top of her voice and swinging her handbag in Lily's direction. The judge, a very understanding gentleman, shook his head at Queenie; his warning to her this time was rather more stern. Queenie had subsided back into her seat, bowing her head at the judge, and remained silent, though breathing very heavily, as the name of a Lambeth postman, Kenneth Pitcher, was added to the list, and remained doggedly mute ... right up until Sam Trotter's name was mentioned.

"Mummy leapt to her feet with a shriek and ploughed through everyone till she got to the dock," continued Ruth, and Beard wondered if she was as breathless as he was. *"She grabbed hold of Lily's hair with one hand and slapped her about the face repeatedly with the other until the court officials were able to pull them apart. In the course of the struggling the beads of Lily's rosary scattered all over the floor, and Queenie and two policemen slipped on them and fell down."* Beard burst out laughing as he pictured the scene: in fact, he laughed so much tears blurred his vision and he had to wipe his eyes before he could continue reading. *"When order had been restored the kindly judge, who was now quite angry, had Mummy brought before him. 'Madam,' he told her, 'you are in contempt.' And he ordered her to be taken below to the cells 'to be dealt with later.' I was very frightened at this and I'm afraid I started crying quite loudly, and had to be taken out of the court by Mrs Molly. We didn't go back until the case was over. We were told that Lily, who had been sent to prison for seven years, had crossed herself when sentenced and asked if she could see a priest first. Mummy was brought back before the judge, who was now looking both stern and kind. He told her that he had considered sending her to prison, too, but had decided to impose a fine of £25 instead. Seeing the look of consternation on Mummy's face, he smiled down at her and said she wasn't to worry as*

someone had already paid the fine. We were never told by whom, but I do believe it was him – the judge! Wasn't he a love!"

Beard read this second letter again, and then a third time. It really was a most intriguing story. He wondered how much Lily had collected from her husbands over the years – and what had happened to it all. Perhaps she'd spent it all on church candles! One thing was certain: there must be a lot of husbands breathing a lot easier now that she was safely locked away. Such women, he mused, did not encourage a chap to enter lightly into the battlefield of marriage.

With this thought in mind, he resolved to be careful in reply to her letters. He expressed his amazement over the Lily business and said he hoped she and Queenie had recovered from the ordeal. It seemed, he told her, like a nightmare that was best forgotten. *"Be happy with what you have, Ruth. At least you have had a father, and you still have a mother,"* he wrote. *"For me the most wonderful thing was that, for a little while at least, I was allowed to share Sam with you. I still think of Queenie as a mother, and know you will continue to let me share her."* And because he felt such a surge of emotion at that moment, he weakened and said that he loved both her and Queenie. He felt there was safety in numbers and, besides, he expected it was true.

A warm glow of well-being embraced him, and he hurried on with the letter, hardly mentioning the war but giving a glowing description of the beauties of Italy, suggesting that the war looked as if the tide had turned in England's favour at last, and that if this was so that he might be coming home soon. He wasn't sure if the censors would allow him to be so optimistic so, to make up for the anticipated deletion, he concluded by telling her again that he loved her – it was easy to be brave at this distance – and signed the letter with a whole army of kisses. There! What more could the girl ask for?

He posted the letter straight away, afraid that if he didn't, he'd tear it up and never get round to writing another.

First thing the following morning – it was just after 4 o'clock, to be precise – word, in the shape of a Provost officer, reminded Beard that Gibbs wanted to see him at headquarters immediately. So, once again his leave was being terminated prematurely, though as the officer informed him, stiffly, that there'd been an alert out for him several days, perhaps he was lucky to have enjoyed as much of it as he had.

The officer, who was politely uncivil, said his orders were to escort Beard directly to Col Gibbs at GHQ Middle East, but Beard was unperturbed, even excited. This time, the cutting short of his leave must mean he was being sent home to UK to join the rest of his comrades in preparations for the Second Front.

Please.

□ *"Oh, that was a terrible time for us, Jarvis. Sam's death was the worst moment of the entire war for us," cried Queenie, breathing hard to stem threatening tears. "Your letters, few as they was, were lifesavers – the only fings wot kept us going. They gave us hope. Our only fear then was that sumfink might 'appen to you."*

At this point, the tears broke through and Miss Flinn, the Matron, who had contrived never to miss an episode of the Jarvis/Beard saga, placed an arm round her shoulders and signalled a nurse to bring a cup of tea – at which point, Mrs B. inevitably raised her hand for one, too. In the end, a lengthy recess was called for afternoon tea.

"He sounds an exceptional man, this – son of yours," said Beard quietly, glancing round the circle of faces, and finishing up gazing at Queenie. Their eyes met through her tears, but there was no recognition on his part. He supposed this Jarvis of hers had been killed somewhere, and he had the misfortune to be his lookalike. It really was a ridiculous situation, the more so since it was being taken seriously – by this lady, Queenie; and, really, the whole lot of them. There could be no substance to their claims, he'd know it if there was, surely? And yet, they seemed so sure.

"You are, Jarvis," she whispered back.

Gibbs broke the unsettling atmosphere by announcing that he had best take up the reins again, and proceed with the story though, truth be told, he was beginning to wonder if it would have the effect of jolting Beard's memory back. Well, there wasn't an awful lot more to tell, so here goes.

Chapter Twenty-six

Somewhere in Yugoslavia, October 27, 1943

But, no; he wasn't going home. Gibbs waved a friendly fist as he motioned Beard to the seat opposite his desk which, as ever, was strewn with papers, maps and books. "Where the devil have you been hiding yourself, Robert?" he demanded briskly. "I've had men scouring Cairo for you for the past week."

"I've been on leave, sir," replied Beard levelly, and added pointedly, "I still am."

"Cancelled – days ago," retorted the colonel smoothly. "War is hell, isn't it, captain! And you're supposed to remain in phone contact even on leave."

"I was with a lady," Beard explained unabashed. "I assumed she'd said where I'd be when she rang my billet to explain my absence."

"She didn't," smiled Gibbs, sensing Beard's gratitude at this apparent oversight.

"Oh," said Beard, adding his smile to the occasion. "I doubt if either of us would have got out of bed to answer the phone, anyway."

"You were in bed the whole week?" exclaimed the other, impressed.

"Almost a fortnight," amended Beard, smugly, even if it was stretching the truth.

"Soldiers have no right to enjoy themselves in this way in wartime, no wonder they have no strength left when they go into battle."

"But it's good for our morale – sir." The *sir* came dangerously late.

Gibbs stared hard at Beard. "I thought you had a steady girl – a fiancée, at home, Robert? Do you confess these peccadilloes to her?"

Beard blushed, and shook his head urgently as Ruth's honest, loving face came to mind. Heaven save me, he thought; and quite suddenly, he felt an urge to hold Ruth tightly in his arms, feel the firmness of her body and let her knew he loved her, and only her. And then he wondered : were these thoughts being whispered in his ear by Gillian?

"Definitely not, sir. But, I have committed a million mortal sins in her eyes this leave," declared Beard soberly, relieved to find himself freed from his impossible thoughts.

"Well, you haven't time to go to confession now," laughed the colonel, "because you're needed for another job before you see Blighty again."

Beard hadn't imagined his leave had been cut short for nothing, still he was conscious of the usual surge of excitement in his breast now that it had been confirmed.

"Where?" he asked simply, yet the word contained an element of urgency.

"It's Yugoslavia again, Robert," Gibbs told him.

"Oh," said Beard, and for once in his life he was completely lost for words for several seconds. He had been expecting somewhere nearer home with the Second Front looming. Poor Ruth would have to wait a little longer, it seemed; strange how his thoughts were now filled with her, and Gillian already relegated to the forgotten past. Or was it Gillian who was still controlling his thoughts concerning Ruth?

"Won't take you long. Be in and out before you know it," declared Gibbs, giving his moustache a tweak.

"Yes, sir," said Beard, who remembered the same words from Charington prior to his previous mission. Well, that had come very nearly within the parameter of the brigadier's estimation. He glanced down at the top map on the desk. Yugoslavia. His eyes darted all over, absorbing every ugly inch of the country, looking particularly at the vast range of mountains. He remembered them, and the fact that they'd probably be feet deep in snow by now. He didn't really fancy parachuting on top of those peaks in these conditions. The thought of deep snow was not appealing. He was better attuned to the heat of deserts.

"Our allies over there," Gibbs continued, "have asked us to blow up a bridge for them. It links a railway line that runs smack through two mountains and is the only means by which the Germans can move speedily from north to south in that area. Our friends have tried for months to destroy the bridge, but they haven't been able to get near it. The SOE have tried twice, without success. We've tried bombing it from the air – but the mountains make it impossible. The plain fact is only a ground force can hope to do the job – so we're sending you in to see what you can do."

"Yes, sir," said Beard again, still staring at the upside down maps. His missions all seemed connected with the activities of the SOE, but he never actually came in contact with them; they seemed an even more secretive bunch than his own lot. It did strike Beard, fleetingly, that if the SOE had had two goes at this bridge, and failed, it must be a very formidable, if not impossible, job. Well, he'd have to see, wouldn't he? It wasn't an option.

"Excellent, you seem to have a flair for the impossible, which is why you were picked for this job," exclaimed Gibbs, giving his moustache a gentle pat. "By the way, you've been made up to acting major for the job to give you extra authority in the eyes of our allies."

"Oh," said Beard, and immediately assumed it was an honorary promotion ; either that or he wasn't expected to survive!

"Time is vital," Gibbs went on, a touch of emphasis creeping into his voice. "We need the goodwill of these people with a Second Front in the offing. They'll be impressed if we can rid them of this thorn in their backyard – we're hoping that they'll be sufficiently impressed to be more inclined to fight the Germans instead of each other, which is a sort of national pastime. The more Germans they can hold down the fewer will be facing us when the time comes."

"Yes, sir," said Beard once more; there never seemed to be any other response he could make at these briefings. "This bridge, sir," he ventured, "where exactly is it?"

Gibbs stared at the map before him, lifted it up and, after briefly examining a couple underneath, pulled out another and nodding his head, exclaimed "This is the best one. Come and see for yourself, Robert." The invitation came with the makings of a smile, which made it rather less inviting. "It's really quite a nice country." Charington had said the same of Poland, and of course he'd been right, reflected Beard; it was a lovely country – or it would have been had he been there as a tourist in peacetime; it was a cruel and dangerous place at this time.

"Once you got out of the mountains, it was a very nice country indeed," Beard thought to himself; but in war it was just another battlefield. He stared down at the blue-circled area where the colonel's finger was buried, somewhere in the Dinaric Alps, or, more precisely, on Mt. Dinara itself; the finger crept forward a fraction and pointed near its base. Apart from a narrow coastal strip, where Split looked to be the only place of prominence, there seemed to be nothing but mountains – and even they appeared to have precious few passes. There were long valleys running parallel to the Adriatic coast, but hardly any transverse valleys, and Beard could see that this must make travelling inland something of a nightmare. Well, he knew it was, he'd been there before, hadn't he? He bent closer to the map, but could see no sign of a railway line or bridge.

"It's not marked on this map," explained Gibbs, answering the query in Beard's raised brow. "It wouldn't exist at all if it wasn't for the war. The Germans are largely responsible – they developed the existing caves and had the track built. Probably feel a lot safer from partisan attacks. The line links Split with Dubrovnik in the south, goes a long way towards Sarajevo in the west," – the colonel showed each place to Beard with a stab of his finger – "and is supposed to go north to Banja Luka ... though I don't think that part's built yet. But as you can imagine, this bridge is important to the Germans."

"I remember mention of that Banja place from my previous visit, but I don't think we got anywhere near it," murmured Beard absently, then, feeling he should show rather more enthusiasm for this new mission than he honestly felt, observed, "It's a regular Clapham Junction, isn't it?"

"I suppose," replied the colonel, tonelessly. "It's called D-17, so far as we're concerned – don't ask me why."

"Yes, sir," said Beard, falling back on his normal reply. "When did you have in mind for this operation to take place, sir?"

"You'll be eating lunch in the air today, major," replied Gibbs calmly, giving Beard a smile that was meant to be encouraging, but fell somewhat short. "You'll be leaving within the hour, almost. You fly first to Italy. You leave on your mission from Bari at 2310 hrs. You parachute in, of course – a sub will bring you back when you call. There'll be four others in the party, so you won't be lonely."

Beard had guessed it would be sooner rather than later, but the immediacy of it rather took his breath away. As ever, it was the getting back part that concerned him. He didn't want to take up flying again. From somewhere, he dredged up a grin.

"Yes, sir," he said; it was his usual password on such occasions.

After that, everyone was very serious and busy as the details of the mission were gone through, maps pored over, equipment and supplies listed and discussed. Major Pitt, who Beard knew was on the colonel's planning staff, congratulated him on his promotion, and in the same breath produced detailed maps of the local area involved, so far as mountains can ever be described as having a locality, since they tend to spread themselves over half a country, and beyond. Beard was told about the displacement of German forces in the area, so far as they were known, but he knew that this information could not be relied upon as any occupation troops were constantly being shovelled about. He spent some time discussing codes and call signals. The operation, he was informed, was to be known as Force 142.

"The local language is Serbo-Croat," remarked Gibbs conversationally. "I don't suppose by any chance that you speak it, Robert?"

Beard resisted a temptation to say he'd never heard of it, and shook his head instead. "I'll probably pick up a smattering as I'm parachuting down!"

The colonel grinned. "Make sure that's all you pick up, Robert, the country's riddled with pox."

Beard responded with a grin of his own, but remained silent.

"Well, language doesn't pose any real problem, Robert," said Gibbs, returning to the matter in hand. "You'll be met at the DZ by the local partisan leader, a Major Borisav – that's all the name we have for him, but I'm told he speaks adequate English."

Beard nodded circumspectly; he guessed this probably meant the man had six words of the language – five of them swear words, and the sixth "No!"

In a brief quiet moment, Beard grabbed Major Pitt's arm and whispered, "Tell me, Donald, when did the SOE last have a try at this bridge?"

"Two nights ago," replied Pitt, after a quick look round. "We understand that they were caught. At any rate, there's been no news concerning them. And, of course, the bridge remains untouched."

"So the whole area is alerted," observed Beard bluntly.

"Jerry probably assumes that that's it, at least for the time being," smiled Pitt encouragingly. "You'll most likely get bored with your own company."

Beard gave a return smile. They both knew the Germans would be swarming all over the district assuming that there would be other saboteurs on the loose. Beard, who had been told to ask for anything he wanted, wondered if he shouldn't have asked for his leave to be restored.

He met his team at Cairo's military airport: Sgt Ray Stubbs, recently returned from an operation on Crete – the man had many qualifications, not the least of which were his talents as a field doctor; Cpl Harry Jenkins, the killer with the knives, who had watched Beard's back on their previous visit to Yugoslavia – hopefully, they'd continue keeping each other alive. L/Cpl Aidan Felbridge was back again with his rifle and radio equipment, and the fourth man was L/Cpl Jimmy Simms, a man of immense strength and an experienced climber. It was a good team.

"Don't forget, Robert," said Gibbs, as the two men shook hands, "there are two main factions in Yugoslavia, Tito's army of peasants – they're the Communists, and the group you'll be dealing with, and the Cetniks – they're mainly officers and men of the former Royal Yugoslav Army led by General Draza Mihajlovic who want their King to return to power when the war's over. Both lots are our allies and it serves our interests to arm them both, but if they spent half the time fighting Jerry as they do each other we might get some value for our money. But we don't, and don't imagine for a moment that you can trust anybody."

"Our allies sound more dangerous than the enemy," commented Beard, feeling he'd had this conversation before with someone. Still, there'd been no treachery on his previous trip, when the Communists had been his hosts – and kept a very watchful eye on him.

"They generally are, major," retorted Gibbs, who went on to add heartily "Good luck to you and your men, Robert. I shall expect you all back in nine days time – though the sub will be available for longer, if need be. Just let us know when you want to come home." He had half turned away when he added: "Oh, by the way, you've been awarded a Mentioned In Despatches – not sure exactly what for, your peregrinations in Tunisia, or your lecherous behaviour with that poor woman in Sicily."

Beard grinned. "Thank you, sir."

"Don't thank me, Robert. The citation was the recommendation of Charington. He thought the way you performed in Tunisia, scattering bombs the length and breadth of the country, showed remarkable courage and leadership. And, of course, capturing that spy Pffinkel in Sicily was an outstanding achievement in view of your distractions."

Beard, coloured slightly at the reference to the gorgeous Didi who had come so close to killing him, but grinned again. He knew where the recommendation originated.

"Do be assured, Robert, this latest mission of yours is of paramount importance," Gibbs said with some earnestness. "It was Churchill's own idea. He's very keen to have this bridge destroyed. He hopes that it may make the Germans think the Second Front is going to be in the Mediterranean, maybe even in Yugoslavia – but I suspect the real reason is as a sop to King Peter. You know, by the way, that it was on Winnie's personal orders that a Sunderland flying boat was deployed to rescue the king from Kotor on the Montenegrin coast as the armistice was being signed in Belgrade?" Beard shook his head respectfully, but showed no real interest in this piece of intelligence, and the colonel went on, "Anyway, you know that a suggestion from Winnie is the same as a Papal edict, so when he raised the business of this bridge, something obviously had to be done."

Beard nodded, gave a wry grin, offered a last salute and boarded the plane.

Even before the plane was airborne, Gibbs was shaking his head, wondering if Beard would get anywhere near the bridge. No one else had. There was a chance of course; there was always a chance, but in this case he thought it might require a miracle to pull this off. "Good luck, Robert, and God bless you," he whispered after the plane, and then walked quietly away.

It was as well Beard was not privy to his colonel's doubts for the success of his mission, for, deep down, he was not bursting with conviction himself. However, being an inveterate optimist, Beard hastily overcame any incipient doubts and resolutely told himself that nothing was impossible. At least, he'd give it a damned good try. Whatever happened, he'd leave his mark in some awesome form. The thought lifted his spirits.

He'd been given no opportunity to discuss things with his men; just a few words in each man's ear before the roar of the plane's engines made communication impossible; besides, he gathered they'd had a longer briefing than he had. Of course, he'd been otherwise occupied with the passionate Gillian and already felt more inspired than any briefing could lift him, but his men's good spirits raised his own still further and they all stretched out – and it was only the cold that kept them awake. It penetrated the many layers of their clothing, even including the lined, white parkas and the extra thick trousers they'd been issued with, and crept into their bones. Beard shivered, and wondered what the hell it would be like when they were sat among the mountains. Probably too cold to move. He studied one of the maps Gibbs had given him. Where the bridge should be, but wasn't shown, was a red cross – drawn faintly between two mountain tops. He wondered how far apart they were, and how high. Be funny if they landed on the damned bridge.

They didn't. Beard led the way, jumping blindly. He couldn't be sure of anything; it was black above him, and milky white beneath. In between, it was just plain freezing. And, just as had happened in Poland, there had been no signal from below. But, as before, they'd jumped anyway, the pilot assuring them they were exactly where they should be. Everything was white as far as he could see. He assumed he was falling on some level portion of a mountain, or a plateau in between. He couldn't tell. It all looked the same down there. He had only his altimeter to indicate his height. It seemed to be racing. He continued searching feverishly for any sort of a signal from their reception committee, but there was nothing to be seen, only the blinding whiteness, and now, as the ground stretched out its white arms to embrace them, the dark patches of forests. Beard experienced a moment of panic before he got a grip on himself. What if the pilot had made a mistake? What if they'd missed the bloody mountain and they were floating down on some frozen lake? He tried to remember if there had been a lake anywhere near their mountain. He couldn't remember one. Christ! he hoped there wasn't one. If the ice was thick he'd probably break his legs, at least; if it was thin, he'd drown in the icy water, unable to save himself because of the weight of his equipment.

These and a score of other dire thoughts raced through Beard's mind as he tumbled earthwards. He spotted the tips of the conifers with barely enough time to snatch at the quick-release device for his leg bag and only just managed to guide himself clear of a particularly tall fir with its white canopy, before landing heavily in a snow drift. The snow was so deep and soft it had been virtually impossible to roll as he landed, as he would have done normally. However, he was reasonably certain that he was undamaged, and with this comforting conviction he lifted his face out of the snow, breathed a quick sigh that was really a prayer of thanksgiving, and at the same time began disentangling himself from the rigging lines and collapsing the billowing canopy of the parachute and gathering it in. He retrieved his leg bag, checked over his weapons and searched around for his men and their supplies. The first man he saw was Jenkins, who was quartering the area for any sign of life, his Schmeisser swivelling round and pointing in every new direction.

"Wasn't there supposed to be someone meeting us, sir?" he asked, with a deep frown, as he walked towards Beard, his eyes still searching. "A Major Borisav?"

Beard looked up from opening one of the supply canisters.

"Someone should have been here ... there should have been landing lights, too," he agreed. "We're bloody lucky to have escaped with our skins intact landing blind like that on a mountain and at night. At least we weren't impaled on the blessed trees and landed on fairly level ground – or rather, snowfield. Must be a plateau of sorts. Are we all down safely?" he asked as an afterthought.

Felbridge and Simms were seen struggling up a steep incline carrying one of the supply canisters between them. They found Sgt Stubbs twenty minutes later dangling upside down from a tree, having crashed through innumerable branches before reaching this undignified position. He was making such a devil of a racket that Beard snapped that he'd shoot him if he didn't shut up, which had the effect of silencing him but causing considerable noisy mirth among the others. Once they were assured Sgt Stubbs was unhurt, they all set about roughly massaging his bruises, happily ignoring his protests, as though they were having a romp after a Rugby match. This was before they discovered the only thing they'd lost in the drop was most of their food and that they'd have to rely on the emergency supplies they each carried – unless, of course, their hosts were able to feed them. But first they had to find their hosts, preferably before daylight which was still some hours off.

"We'd better spread out and see where these partisans are at," declared Beard. "Some sod should have been here to meet us. Makes one feel sort of unwelcome. We'll take a different direction each and rendezvous here in, say, twenty minutes. Give a whistle if you find someone, but keep the noise down just in case we're not among friends. You, Felbridge, stay here and watch our things."

They were about to move off when Simms, swearing softly, elbowed Beard in the side and nodded his head in the same direction that the muzzle of his Sten was pointing. Beard froze. Fifty yards away, just clear of the dense, snow-laden trees, stood a dozen or more men. They had evidently just emerged from the shelter of the trees and were in the process of spreading out in a semi-circular line, their weapons and faces pointing with equal menace at Beard's group. They wore white camouflage uniforms of sorts, with German-style boots to their knees and thigh-length jackets made of assorted animal skins, and on their heads they wore fur hats that covered their ears and much of their faces, something like what the old-time Cossacks wore; each hat bore a badge which appeared to incorporate a crown. The men's bodies were festooned with bandoliers and stick grenades. It was clear these men were not the reception committee Beard's force had been expecting, but neither were they Germans. So who were they?

Beard, his eyes never moving from the men, curled his finger round the trigger of his Schmeisser while his thumb released the safety catch. He caught the faint sounds as the others followed suit. He was wondering who was going to break the impasse of silence, when Jenkins nudged his elbow and indicated behind them with his head. Beard swung round, and froze again, for there stood another row of similarly heavily-armed men, their weapons trained purposefully. Beard resisted the comic-book temptation to order his men to fling themselves flat in the belief that the two opposing rows would open fire and wipe each other out; it didn't work that way in the real world. And in that real world, Beard appreciated that they were completely surrounded, remained perfectly still – whispering to his men to stand fast, but his brain was in overdrive. The trouble was that he could find no answers to the questions that raced through his head. The only thing he did comprehend was that he and his men were in a most alarming position. They stood no chance, but the thought of surrender was anathema to him; but, he had his men to think of. He needed to think fast, but his thoughts became blurred : frozen, perhaps.. He had just become aware that it was bloody cold standing immobile on the snowy mountain when a voice broke the stillness, in English, and he felt his heart pounding furiously – and suddenly the cold didn't seem to hurt as much.

"Who are you?" demanded the voice: an authoritative voice.

Once again Beard about-faced, repeating his order to his men to "Stand fast!" as he sensed Jenkins, and doubtless the others, was about to explode into action. He looked ahead at the imposing figure who had stepped forward from the line. The man, who had an air of courtliness even in his shabby clothes, wore a pistol at his hip and had a pair of binoculars resting on his chest; he looked distinguished rather than handsome, and as scholarly as he did soldierly. He was tall, his tallness accentuated by his thinness, with a long, white, thin face, and pale grey eyes that sat in dark sockets and stared out imperiously, never blinking.

"Major Robert Beard – British Army," answered Beard carefully, stepping forward a couple of paces himself, and standing erect. There was no point in pretending to be anyone else. He thought of offering the man a salute, but as that would have necessitated moving his hand from his gun he decided against such courtesy. "And you, sir?"

"Colonel Petar Zdravko – of the Royal Yugoslav Army." He seemed to grow several more inches as he proclaimed his allegiance.

Beard stared back, his face a blank, but his mind in a turmoil of confusion. This was the wrong lot! These were Cetniks, the enemies of the Communist partisans he was here to meet. Where the devil was Major Borisav? Had this lot wiped out the people who had invited him here? If so, his position was impossible. His mission was over without ever getting off the ground. How bloody ridiculous ... and on top of a mountain. Better get it over with before they froze to death. He drew in a deep breath of bitterly cold air, and expelled it in a cloud of steam. What to do? And because, for the moment, he couldn't think what to do, he slid back the safety catch on his Schmeisser and gave a belated salute, adding a polite "Sir."

"Is this all of you?" the colonel enquired, with more concern than hostility, returning the salute.

"Yes, sir," replied Beard, guessing the other probably knew this.

"No casualties, then?"

"No, sir. Thank you."

"What are you and your men doing here, Major Beard?" asked the colonel. "I don't imagine you're part of an invasion force come to liberate us?"

Beard, noticing for the first time that the man spoke faultless English, didn't see any point in concealing the object of his mission, but he wasn't going to volunteer the fact that he was here at the behest of Tito's lot. Too much of a red rag to these royalists! "No, sir," he replied, carefully. "I've been ordered to destroy a bridge that connects a railway track running through two mountains. I presume we're standing on one of those mountains?"

Col Zdravko's pale eyes showed a spasm of amusement even, as comprehension dawned, but it may well have been only a reflection of the moon which showed itself briefly before being enveloped by the clouds again. "Actually, no, major. I'm afraid you've landed on neither of the right mountains. The ones you want are a little to the north of here."

It was Beard's turn to show slight amusement.

"Who has told you to do this thing, major?" asked the colonel.

Beard frowned. It seemed a senseless question. "I take my orders from my superiors ... like any other soldier," he replied, a trifle stiffly.

"Of course you do, major, we all do," acknowledged Col Zdravko with quiet dignity. "This bridge you talk about is important to the Germans. The narrow gauge line is known among us as The Subway and its destruction would be a blow to their prestige – and morale. We've all been trying for a long time to destroy it, including your own people, but without the slightest success. Personally, I don't think it's possible. What makes you think you can succeed where we've failed?"

"I don't know that we can, sir," declared Beard evenly, "but I've been ordered to try. I'll need to examine it very carefully first."

"I imagine you were expecting to be met on the ground, eh, major?" said the colonel, in a conversational voice. "Someone has asked you to come and have a go at destroying the bridge? You expect someone to act as your guide and interpreter in this business?"

"We'd naturally be grateful for any assistance," admitted Beard cautiously. "After all, we all want the same thing – the defeat of the Germans, don't we?"

"Of course," agreed Col Zdravko, conjuring up a smile which fleetingly softened his face but failed to reach his eyes. "Unfortunately, the mountains on either side of this bridge are in an area under the influence, if not full control, of the Communist partisans. I think you were expecting to be met by them, were you not?"

Beard remained silent for a moment, then nodded his head and said, "Yes, sir. I think that's about the size of the matter."

The colonel nodded his head in acknowledgement. "I'm rather afraid, major, that your friends are waiting for you on the mountain opposite." He turned to point airily into the darkness behind Beard. "We have watched them, and they are doubtless watching us."

Beard had already come to this conclusion, but he was still startled to have his worst fears confirmed. "Oh," was all he could manage by way of an immediate response, and the colonel took advantage of the silence to continue speaking.

"This mountain we're standing on is called Number Nine, owing to its geographic position. The one you want, and where your friends are waiting anxiously to welcome you, is on the other side of a long and very steep gorge and about twelve miles distant – as the crow flies, but three times that since you are not equipped with wings! The two mountains that connect your railway line are known locally as Romeo and Juliet because they lean so affectionately towards each other. This is one of the reasons your bombers have never been able to hit the bridge: it is completely hidden and protected by the – er, lovers leaning towards one another! That is, if they can even find the right mountains ... so don't feel too badly about your pilot dropping you off on the wrong one."

It sounded a very pretty story: it also sounded very plausible. Whatever the truth of the matter, Beard thought they were in a ridiculous position – and that the sooner they disassociated themselves from the Cetniks and found the right bunch of guerrillas – and the right mountain, the better. "I imagine the Germans patrol these mountains, sir?" he pressed thoughtfully.

"You may be sure of that," confirmed Col Zdravko. "And be assured your partisan friends weren't the only ones waiting on the mountain for you."

"Can't you lot work together against the Germans?" asked Beard, frowning. He didn't suppose the British government enjoyed having either the Americans or Russians as allies, but in war, surely, you learned to get along with anyone willing to fight the same enemy as you. You needed each other, and anyone else of a similar disposition.

"Do the British trust their allies?" countered the colonel. "You don't even trust the Irish – and yet half your generals are Irish ... the good ones, anyway!"

Beard didn't doubt the truth of this, but he chose to ignore it. "Well, sir, we're allies – and I hope you won't prevent us from going about our business. We're only concerned with the bridge ... your squabbles with anyone other than the Germans are your own affair, but I trust you will not let them interfere with our mission."

Col Zdravko remained silent for several moments, before saying

"*Ne*," and walking towards Beard with his hand extended. Beard shook the hand with feelings of relief tinged with suspicion, but there could be no doubting the colonel's sincerity – even Jenkins stopped fidgeting when a bottle of slivovitz was produced and passed round, together with slabs of smoked cheese which went down a lot slower. Col Zdravko, having made up his mind about things, suddenly seemed anxious to be rid of his visitors – "before it gets light," as he put it. "You won't be able to reach your friends today. It's too far – forty or more miles. You'll have to hide up during the day and continue tomorrow night – I'm sure you'll find your friends still waiting for you. I'll give you a guide so you don't lose yourself any further! Oh, and we have retrieved your missing canister – the one containing food."

As Beard and his men were about to depart, Col Zdravko approached Beard for a final handshake and, in a roughly emotional voice, said, "We are very grateful to England for giving sanctuary to our King – but we want him back when this war is done." Beard grinned and nodded. "We all want to go home, sir," he said, and turned to follow the guide who had been provided. He was a smallish man with a face almost entirely hidden behind a beard and moustache, and he looked quite elderly, though he moved as agilely as a goat. He led them at a cracking pace down the mountain-side, along a narrow gorge where the snow came up to their thighs, never pausing until they reached the foothills of the next mountain, and stopped for the night. God knows what the journey was in terms of miles, but it took them close on five hours, and when the guide finally called a halt they were all exhausted, even so they were grateful their canisters hadn't been appropriated by Zdravko and his men, and were agreeably surprised to find the contents of the food canister that had been recovered for them were untouched. They'd expected it to be a lot lighter.

They laid up among the trees during the day and slept as best they could, taking turns at keeping guard. It was bitterly cold with icy winds constantly showering them with snow. The conditions made it difficult to sleep and mostly they could only doze fitfully, and hope things turned out better when they resumed their trek. Beard simply hoped that their contact, Major Borisav, hadn't abandoned them. Almost before it was properly dark, they resumed their march, if wading through thigh-deep drifts could be called marching. It was exhausting work even for men as fit as them, and time-consuming, but some twenty miles later and just as darkness was lifting, their guide, who had no English, pointed to a barely visible and almost sheer track and indicated that someone would meet them ... eventually ... perhaps ... if it was safe. This was all conveyed in a series of arm-waving gestures that were more alarming than helpful; then growling "*Do vidjenja*," which Beard assumed meant "Cheerio," or something less friendly, he turned and retraced his steps at an incredible lick.

It was evident the partisans had had Beard's party under surveillance for some considerable time, for the five men had scarcely begun the arduous ascent of the extremely steep slope, than a knotted rope snaked down and a voice told them to hold on tight. Beard did not understand a single word of the strange language, but their import was clear. It was only once they'd started clambering up that it occurred to Beard that they might be climbing into a trap. But fortunately it was the partisans and not the Germans waiting for them, and in no time they were all, including their considerable and cumbersome equipment, hauled safely aloft.

One of the partisans had a smattering of German, another had a few words of Italian, and between the two of them – nothing was said about him being a whole day late – Beard was given to understand he and his men must follow the partisans through the forests to their camp. First they were allowed a ten-minute rest, during which Simms made the mistake of producing a packet of cigarettes and was, necessarily, compelled to pass them round to the dozen-strong Yugoslavs. He never saw the packet again, although it did appear that the partisans shared, at best, only three cigarettes which were passed from man to man with only a couple of puffs apiece. Before they moved off every stub was carefully collected and stored in a little tin as though they were priceless gems. Perhaps, in their way, they were.

The march through the forest – Beard thought of it as one forest although, at this level, the trees varied from oak to beech to fir, just like in the Carpathians, so perhaps the forest was in reality a number of extensive woods – seemed interminable. They appeared to follow no track, but the partisans never hesitated even though it was almost dark among the great trees. After a couple of hours marching, they started climbing and presently entered a pine forest where the trees were taller, the snow deeper and it was even darker. After another hour of climbing and, sometimes, descending, in the course of which they were frequently challenged by men armed with an international assortment of weapons, and all wearing the blood red star of Communism, they came, very suddenly, upon the partisans' camp.

It was sudden, even though the sweet smell of wood fires permeating through the trees had been noticeable for some time, and as they had got nearer there had been the hum of voices and even of music, even so, they still seemed to step from impenetrable forest into the clearing quite unexpectedly. It wasn't much, a bare cleared circle with a huddle of accommodations all round, some canvas with logs stacked high all round, some makeshift timber shacks, a couple more substantial than others. The snow, which lay thinner here, had been trodden into the ground.

There looked to be close on a hundred partisans in residence;

certainly it felt like a hundred pairs of eyes, at least, were turned on them when Beard and his weary party stumbled from the darkness of the forest into the fire-lit amphitheatre that was the camp. The eyes were dark, suspicious and, perhaps, hostile – in the way all strangers are greeted.

Beard's party was led directly across the clearing to what looked like an original forester's cabin. Before they reached it, the door opened and, finally, they were face to face with Major Borisav.

He turned out to be a woman.

When he'd recovered from this surprise, Beard stepped forward and offered her his hand, but this was ignored, and they continued staring at one another. The woman stood, her short, fat legs planted firmly apart, one hand on her ample hip, the other resting on one of two Lugers in her belt, and eyed him at first with suspicion, then curiosity, as though she were viewing some unexpected object, and in neither case in a very friendly manner. Beard stepped back, offered her a hopeful smile, and finally tried a salute. She acknowledged this with a nod, and turned to speak with the leader of the men who had brought him. Their talking went on for some time and Beard took the opportunity of examining his hostess further.

Except for her uniform and the red star peeping out of her fur hat, and, of course, the many weapons adorning her person, Major Borisav looked like any other housewife – though he had no idea if she had a husband lurking in the background. She was a dumpy sort of a woman: short and wholesomely plump, as he liked to imagine a motherly woman should be, with grey hair (what he could see of it) tied in a tight knot at her nape; she had a squarish face with very high cheek bones, and china blue eyes that stared so penetratingly they seemed to bore right through him; she had a wide, thin mouth with such a layer of downy hair on the upper lip that, if you were unkind, you might have called it a moustache. Beard thought she was about forty, but allowed that he might be outrageously off target, in either direction. She wore a rather smart donkey jacket that looked as if it might be made of bear skin (were there bears in these forests, Beard asked himself with some concern), men's trousers beneath a full black skirt, and calf-length brown boots. And in spite of it all, and the bulging pockets, she still looked very feminine. Beard thought so, anyway. He liked the look of her and hoped, even if she had refused his hand, she would prove friendly.

According to Major Pitt, Major Borisav spoke "adequate English": if she did, she chose not to practice it with him; he was told she spoke Serbo-Croat, which was the official language almost everywhere in the country, Slovene and Macedonian, but if she spoke anything else, English included, she resolutely refused to do so. The same air of mystery surrounded her name. Beard was only ever given that of Borisav, which was clearly a *nom de guerre*, though once he heard the name Iva used in association with her. Every now and then, she would turn to stare hard at him – or through him, and he smiled back at her as cheerfully as he felt able without looking imbecilic. It didn't seem to have any effect on her: no warmth lit her cold blue eyes. They were always sad, cold and uninviting.

Eventually, a youth of about Beard's age called Mika, who spoke quite good German, came forward and told Beard he would be his interpreter in all discussions with Major Borisav and see to any other needs. The youth wasn't much bigger than the woman and had the same high cheek bones, but his hair was black and wild and his eyes a chestnut brown, and, like Beard, he had no serious use for a razor. After introducing himself severally to them all, Mika led the way to a draughty shack and told them to make themselves comfortable. "This is where you will live during your stay with us," he said to Beard. "Anything you want, you ask – but please don't stray from here without an escort. It might be … dangerous. Our guards tend to shoot first, and then see who, or what, they've killed." Beard wasn't too sure if this was meant as a joke, or a warning to stay put at night, and decided he had his answer when he discovered a sentry on duty outside their quarters.

"I wouldn't have thought they had anything to hide from us, but I suppose they're reluctant to have us wandering around poking our noses into their affairs," said Beard, adding somewhat generously, "We all have our little secrets." Jenkins gave a non-committal grunt, and began unloading himself. "We'd best watch our own things," Beard continued, in a low, more urgent tone. "One man must always remain in this hut. Whatever else happens, we must make sure our equipment remains intact. Without our radio transmitter we've no way of getting out of here … and without our explosives, we're wasting our time here."

He wondered if they were anyway, for in the course of a long and laborious conference with Major Borisav through the medium of Mika (who seemed extraordinarily polite to them, and almost affectionately deferential to the major), it seemed improbable that they stood an earthly chance of succeeding in their mission. By all accounts they would be fortunate if they even got a glimpse of the bridge, let alone managed to destroy it. The entrances at both ends of the tunnel were guarded day and night by machine-gun posts, the tunnels themselves, on either side, were constantly patrolled by dog-handlers, maintenance men were watched every moment that they worked, and the mountain tops on either side of the bridge had their own network of guard posts and large areas were known to be mined. Additionally, the SS and Gestapo were very active in the neighbourhood.

"You might say," said Major Borisav, "that anybody caught even looking at those mountains is liable to be arrested … and once that happens, they're seldom seen again. We have tried and failed many times ourselves. Although we have asked your people to have yet another go, I don't believe, sir, that you will have any greater success – though we will support your efforts in whatever way we can. But, I think it is impossible."

"Still, I must see Romeo and Juliet for myself," declared Beard, who was pretty certain this last part had been Mika's personal view rather than any interpretation of the major's, "if only to convince myself it can't be done. There has to be a way, somehow. I presume someone can take me to spots from where I can examine the possibilities?"

"It will not be easy. It can only be seen in daylight and the Germans are always on the watch. They have eyes everywhere," replied the major, her own eyes studying Beard so intently she must have been assessing his ability to do what no one else had been able to achieve. She could not have been very optimistic for she shook her head and uttered a grim sigh. "But," she added after a prolonged pause, "we have to keep trying – or they will kill us, anyway. I shall accompany you myself … but, I promise you, it is impossible."

"Then I'm sure you're hoping for a miracle, otherwise you wouldn't have sent for us," declared Beard blithely, but there was no answering twinkle in those blue eyes.

"We stopped believing in such things the day the Germans came," she observed stonily, "but if you believe in miracles, I hope you find one."

Beard smiled, and hoped so too. They were seated on logs around a fire with the thick trees acting as a canopy through which the smoke filtered and dissipated in the atmosphere. Major Borisav sat with her hands clasped round her legs which she pulled up so that she could rest her chin on her knees; her eyes were fixed on Beard's face throughout the lengthy translations, and more intently so when he spoke. In fact, her lips seemed to follow his words as closely as her eyes: it was as though she was repeating the words. Beard was pretty certain, from occasional raisings of her brows and sudden narrowing of her eyes, that German wasn't quite as foreign to her as she made out. This was particularly noticeable when he'd mentioned the local nicknames for the two mountains, Romeo and Juliet, for it told her that he had discussed his mission with someone else: the Cetniks. He supposed the pretence gave her more time to think, and study him. Quite clever of her, really – if tiresome. He wondered if she also understood English as "adequately" as he'd been given to understand, and made a mental note to be extra careful what he said in her presence and to warn his men to do the same – just in case.

Beard enquired about train passengers and the nearest train stations, and was informed that only certain workers were allowed to travel on the trains; they had to have special passes, occupy specific carriages where they were constantly watched, were liable to frequent searches and were not permitted to travel during the hours of darkness – when there was a curfew anyway. The only exceptions were for collaborators and women who went with the German soldiers. Beard sensed the loathing that burned out of those blue eyes at the mention of these women. But usually the only traffic at night, went on Major Borisav, was freight. So far as the district was concerned this meant agricultural produce which, at this time of year, was virtually non-existent. What there was was restricted to two days a week – except in the case of milk, which was transported daily.

"The Germans love their milk," she said, with a distaste that was so virulent that she gave a little shudder.

Beard smiled; he assumed her revulsion was for the Germans, and not the milk, but perhaps both were abhorrent to her. "So where's the local station?" he asked.

"Zrmojice – it's about two miles from the southern end of the Subway, that's the Romeo side. It's not a proper station, of course, more of a halt, but it's the only station of any sort for twenty miles in either direction."

"Towns? Villages?" pressed Beard with patient doggedness; he was trying to form a map of the area in his mind. "Where do the people live? And the Germans ... where are they billeted?"

"Mostly in Hèvic, that's about halfway between the station and the mountain. It's not much, it's a very small town. But it's ours, and I was born there." Major Borisav's voice seemed to catch in her throat at this point, and her eyes became softer, but only for a moment; and when she resumed speaking, the cold returned to her eyes and the bitterness took over her voice. "There's not much there ... a few shops, an inn, a few score little houses, a tiny church and the local council office, where a doctor tends our needs once a fortnight – or oftener if need be." She ticked off the landmarks wistfully, as Mika related them, and then her tone took on an even harsher note. "Not much ... but the Germans found it necessary to destroy even the little we had on the first day they arrived. They razed the church, commandeered most of the best houses, occupied the council office and rounded up dozens of people there and then and sent them off to concentration camps – we don't know where, or if they're still alive. And still the Germans weren't satisfied ... they wanted to make a public example of someone."

Major Borisav suddenly stood up and began stomping to and fro, her small fists clenching and unclenching at her sides, her chin resting on her chest and her eyes tightly closed. Presently, she came to a standstill and, remaining on her feet, resumed speaking, though in a different tone: her voice was now hoarse with an emotion she still could scarcely control, and there were tears hiding in her eyes. "We didn't have a mayor, of course, just a sort of leading citizen, Nikola Zivkovic. He was my ... " She had to pause a moment as her voice choked. She quickly recovered and when she resumed speaking there was a new steel in her voice. "The Germans called him a burgomaster ... and they burned him alive in the middle of the square and made everyone watch. His blackened skeleton still hangs in an iron cage from a sort of gibbet as a warning to the people to conform. The pigs won't let us remove his poor bones so that we can give him a proper burial. Several people have been shot trying."

Tears she was unable to check rushed down Major Borisav's cheeks and she turned to hurry away, but not before Mika had moved to her side and squeezed her hand in both of his and raised it to his lips. Beard was astonished at such a demonstration of the young man's compassion, and he was further amazed when he saw great tears welling in the boy's own eyes. Perhaps, he pondered, the two were related in some way, as he knew many people were who lived in rural areas. Everyone was a cousin to his neighbour in the country – if not something closer. It might be that they were both related to this poor wretch in Hèvic. Hadn't she begun to say he was her something-or-other? Husband, possibly?

Beard had to wait until the evening meal before he had the opportunity of pursuing his discussion with the major, who by then seemed to have fully recovered. She greeted Beard and his men with her familiar coolness – a severe nod, as they all gathered round a trestle table of freshly-sawn planks. In the middle sat a vast, round-bellied pot, its sides blackened by smoke, in which was a steaming stew from which a disturbingly unidentifiable aroma assailed the diners. In the course of swallowing mouthfuls of the stew, the major's downy lip became so markedly darker it did indeed look like a moustache, but it vanished the instant she licked her lips or wiped her mouth with the back of her hand. The system appeared to be for each person to dip whatever utensil he possessed in the pot, and return for more – while it lasted, and they had the stomach for it.

"What do you suppose this muck is?" asked Jenkins with a grimace, leaning forward to take a second brimming helping.

"Probably mule," suggested Simms seriously, chewing hard.

"Or dog," put in Sgt Stubbs, speaking with his mouth full and his lips dribbling.

"Could be almost anything," said Felbridge, his mug clanging against Simms's as they both dipped into the pot together.

"It's hot – which is what counts," declared Beard, whose memories of childhood hunger were too recent for him to be finicky over what he ate. Besides, he was hungry – and it tasted all right to him.

Much the same comments were passed round when a bottle of some fiery wine was produced.

"Looks like piss," said Simms solemnly, peering at the liquid in his mug.

"Tastes like it too," was Sgt Stubbs's verdict, opening and shutting his mouth.

"It probably is piss," agreed Jenkins, draining his mug indifferently.

Beard grinned, gulped down a mouthful of the burning spirit which brought tears to his eyes, and glanced hurriedly across at the major. He was agreeably surprised to see a gleam of amusement warming her cold blue eyes. He was even more convinced that she understood English, as well as German. Nevertheless, Mika continued to act as her interpreter, laboriously passing on her words.

"It's a raki, we make it ourselves – but you're better off not knowing what from," smiled Mika, and once again Beard wondered if this was the major's view or his own.

He then got down to business. He'd already lost a day by landing on the wrong mountain, and couldn't afford to lose any more time. He was surprised no comments had been made about his lateness, and guessed the partisans had been aware that he'd parachuted on to the wrong mountain – they'd probably watched him land. Well, that was something he had to put behind him. If they weren't concerned, there was no reason why he should bother. He told Major Borisav that he wanted to have a look at the bridge and explore the tunnel approaches first thing in the morning; he would accompany her with Jenkins, while Simms and Sgt Stubbs went with someone else to see what could be seen at the station and, perhaps, Hèvic. Major Borisav and Mika put their heads together and talked away for some moments, before the major nodded her head and Mika turned to address Beard on the results of their deliberations.

"That will be OK, major," he said politely. "The major and I will accompany you and your corporal and show you what we are able, and Janez – he's my younger brother, will escort the other two, though the major says going into Hèvic itself is out of the question. Certainly in daylight. We will leave camp at four o'clock, if that's agreeable."

Beard nodded. The sooner they got cracking, the sooner the job could be tackled – or abandoned, and they could head for home. He hadn't been given any specific deadline by which to complete the mission, but he'd been told a submarine would be waiting to pick them up from about Tuesday, November 2 – less than a week away, and he knew it wouldn't hang around for too many days. Still, that was something they could fix over the radio. "We might have to make several trips," he said, "it rather depends on what we learn tomorrow – and what ideas we come up with."

Mika said that was understood and, as the major whispered in his ear, smiled and added: "The major says you've very young to be a major."

Beard stared at Major Borisav and was pleased to see the smile still in her eyes, but he wasn't about to tell her that it was only an acting rank, nor that he'd held it for less than a week. "How old should a major be?" he asked, his eyes remaining on hers. Then he turned to Mika, and commented: "I think we are both much the same age, but war has matured us beyond our years. We're as old as we have to be ... sometimes, I feel bloody old."

Mika nodded understandingly, but when he looked back at the major, Beard saw that the smile had gone and been replaced by pain, but they softened somewhat when she saw him regarding her. Thinking she might be on the verge of weeping again, he turned to Mika and they discussed their programme for the next day.

Chapter Twenty-seven

Romeo and Juliet, Oct-Nov, 1943

It was bitterly cold on the mountain next morning. There had been quite a fall of fresh snow in the night and its wetness penetrated their various layers of clothing as they pressed themselves down into a grave they scooped out among a number of stunted pines almost at the point where Juliet began her steep drop. It was an exposed position but the only one from which they might expect an unobstructed view of the bridge. It was quite misty early on and Major Borisav said they had to take advantage of this if they were to get really close: they were unlikely to get another opportunity. The only trouble was that once daylight came their position would be in full view of the enemy and they'd probably have to stay put for hours before being able to crawl away unobserved. Bearing this in mind, Beard and the major made themselves as comfortable as possible, while Jenkins and Mika found a similar hole on the opposite slope, the idea being that this would enable them to get a more comprehensive picture of the problems they faced.

It didn't quite work out like that for the nearest either team could get to the bridge was some 200 yards, and in the course of the next five hours that's all they did see: the bridge, with Romeo and Juliet perched protectively above it like a pair of lovers' wings, and, for the space of about twenty seconds, two trains – and even then they didn't really see them for they were hidden by their own belching smoke. Gone in a puff of smoke, mused Beard with a sigh. The bridge itself was spectacularly unimpressive. It comprised a continuous steel span of some 90 feet and was supported at either end by massive concrete buttresses in addition to suspension cables. It was ugly, but functional. It carried a single set of tracks with a walkway on each side. There were military huts and pillboxes at either end and guards marched with monotonous regularity across the bridge itself. What a God-awful way to spend a war, he thought.

At the end of five hours, Beard felt that if he didn't move soon he never would. He was frozen stiff and wasn't certain he hadn't got frostbite as well as paralyzing cramp. It was a good job he'd made his sketch of the bridge right at the outset because his fingers were now stiff with cold, even with two pairs of gloves. He had instinctively pushed himself hard up against the major in their little grave and, far from moving away, she had pressed back against him: it seemed they were both determined to share as much of the other's bodily warmth as possible. Twice she rummaged in her rucksack and gave him a slice of black bread and an inch or so of German sausage; he nodded his thanks and ate gratefully, washing the food down with a couple of mouthfuls of snow. Later on it began to snow heavily and they were soon buried, though they kept their heads clear so that they could continue their observations. But when the binoculars started freezing to his eyes, Beard decided he'd had enough. Besides, the snow virtually obliterated the bridge so where was the point in watching?

Under cover of the driving snow and early darkness, they moved back with extreme caution to the comparative shelter of the pine forest, where they were soon joined by Jenkins and Mika. They all stood stamping their feet and slapping their arms in a bid to restore warmth and circulation to their limbs. The steam from their bursting lungs was almost like another train. Beard was moved to see Mika massaging Major Borisva's arms and back and, even, gently rubbing her cheeks; he was pleased to see that the major accepted these ministrations with very real pleasure. She actually gave a few little laughs and patted Mika's face almost affectionately, which Beard thought was most surprising behaviour between an officer and – and whatever rank Mika held. But his thoughts on the matter vanished in the icy wind as the major produced a thermos flask from her sack and started pouring steaming hot drinks. He had no idea what it was, he only knew that it burned his insides deliciously; he later learned that it was a concoction made from chestnuts – a sort of ersatz coffee.

After a bit the snow stopped and before the light went altogether, they went to have a look at one of the tunnel entrances from the other side: the southern side. It did not offer any fresh encouragement. Apart from a string of pill boxes and what looked to be barracks, there was a battery of AA guns and barbed wire to keep civilians at least a quarter of a mile from the tunnel entrance. Armoured cars regularly patrolled the railway line itself. Beard looked glum. Perhaps they were right after all. Perhaps it was impossible. And with this depressing thought growing in strength within him, they trudged back to camp half frozen and wholly depressed. Nor were spirits raised when Simms and Sgt Stubbs reported on their day spent watching the station at Zrmojice. There was a German presence at the station, of course, but apart from a couple of trains the highlight of their vigil had been the arrival of a load of milk churns drawn by a German army half-track.

Sgt Stubbs, drawing Beard aside, whispered confidentially that he had climbed a tree and examined Hèvic through a pair of binoculars. "I saw this skeleton thing the major spoke of swinging in the wind," he said, making a grimace. "The gallows stands in a sort of square ... and there was a guard close by, though he didn't seem to be paying much attention to anything."

Beard nodded absently. About the only good news was supplied by Felbridge, who said he had contacted HQ to report their safe, if late, arrival and been told that their sub would rendezvous with them as arranged.

The following day, Saturday, October 30, Beard and Jenkins went to have a look at the station. They spent another boring day getting colder and colder and, as with the others, the only moment of interest came with the arrival of the milk churns. A *Feldwebel* appeared from wherever he had been keeping himself warm and personally checked the seals on every churn, and then remained with them until a train screeched to a halt alongside. An officer descended from the train, examined the seals himself and then watched as each churn was loaded aboard. Finally, he locked the door of the carriage and returned to his own snug compartment, from which he could observe the entire length of the train in comfort. It all looked very efficient, and foolproof. But was it?

Up to this moment, Beard hadn't really had any serious thoughts about the station, one way or the other: nor of the milk; he'd simply wanted to see what happened at the station. But now a slow, almost imperceptible, smile formed at the corners of his mouth and the light in his eyes grew definitely brighter. An idea was forming somewhere deep in his brain. He wasn't sure of all the details, but it was a definite plan. This mission might not be so impossible after all. He called to Janez, who was their guide today, and questioned him at length about the distances between certain points and the times of trains, and whether or not they ever varied. He emphasised the importance of both times and distances. In the end, Janez sent a man, together with Beard's watch, off to double-check the details as far as was possible.

Back at the forest camp, Beard's new enthusiasm was soon picked up by Major Borisav and, after she'd questioned Janez over the activities of the day, she determined to quiz Beard over the fresh animation in his appearance, and called Mika over to join in the discussions – or interpreting, which ever she chose to call it.

"It's good that you're looking cheerful today, major, but you mustn't get your hopes up too much," she said earnestly, and with evident regret. "We have often thought of these milk churns ourselves, but there is no way we can make use of them in the way you have in mind ... packing them with explosives, I suppose. The Germans control the churns from start to finish. They collect them at the chosen farms and physically check that there is only milk inside, and the moment this is done the churns are sealed. Even then they are never out of the Germans' sight. They are loaded on to a wagon which is towed by one of their own half-tracks and escorted by another vehicle all the way to Zrmojice – where the seals are again checked before the churns are put on a train. So, you see, there's absolutely no opportunity to tamper with the milk either before it is collected at the depots, while it is in transit, or before it leaves the station – and certainly not once it has left."

Still Beard smiled. "I'm not in the least interested in the milk, major," he cried dismissively. "The Germans can have it all. What I have in mind is to line the insides of the churns with explosives, and then seal these with a thin coating of metal, and after that they can pour in as much milk as they like. The more the better."

Mika had to repeat this to the major before she comprehended the significance of the inner seal. When she did understand, a glint of excitement lit up her blue eyes and a smile, an eager smile, touched her mouth. It was gone almost immediately to be replaced by a puzzled frown. "Is it really possible?" she asked, incredulously, but plainly wanting to believe. "How can you make this metal thing? Your plan depends upon this, doesn't it?"

Beard nodded. "Yes, without the metal seal it won't work," he said, suddenly serious. He looked hard at the major, whose eyes were now clouded with doubts, and then turned thoughtfully to Mika. "Is there a blacksmith in the district? Someone who we can trust absolutely?"

Without even bothering to translate, Mika himself answered. "Petar Spiljak. He's the best – and a partisan, even if the Germans make him work for them. You can depend on him for anything you require."

"Good," said Beard with enthusiasm. "We must meet with him tomorrow and discuss how we can make these tin skins. I'm certain with his knowledge of metals, he'll provide us with some sort of solution. Do you think we could see him tomorrow?"

"It's Sunday, the very best day. I'll fix it with him today," exclaimed Mika, borrowing some of Beard's ebullience.

Major Borisav, whose face had seemed to brighten somewhat as Mika spoke to her, now looked grave again as another difficulty occurred to her. "But what ... how will these things help?" she asked, in an agony of perplexity. "How will your explosives go off without someone there to trigger it – at the exact second?"

"Oh, that's the easy part," declared Beard with a confident smile. "I'll use a timer device which will detonate the charge at a pre-set time. That's why it's so important we get the times and distances right. Otherwise, even if everything works as it should, all we'll achieve is a bloody great hole inside the mountain, and leave the bridge intact. So, first thing tomorrow I must see your blacksmith, and everyone else must concentrate on checking the times of the trains, the time it takes for them to get from Zrmojice to the tunnel mouth and – and this is the crucial part, the time it takes from the moment it enters the tunnel till it emerges on the bridge. So, yes, it's all a matter of split-second timing. And let's hope the engine driver doesn't cock everything up by being in a hurry to get home for his wife's birthday!"

Beard's enthusiasm spread to the rest. Mika beamed and clapped his hands as he realised the possibilities. The major was smiling again: very tentatively at first, and then more wholeheartedly; and when Janez returned from some errands Beard had sent him on, she gave him a huge hug and they strolled off together hand in hand. Extraordinary bunch of soldiers these, thought Beard staring after them with a knowing smile.

Over the next couple of days everyone worked on some aspect of Beard's plan. Relays of partisans maintained a constant watch on every inch of the railway line: every inch that was visible to the eye, that is. Everything was timed and measured, repeatedly. There were generally no trains on a Sunday: it depended on the needs of the Germans. So, starting on the Monday, the times of every train were checked at every stage from the moment it entered the tunnel at one end, traversed the bridge, and emerged at the other. The length of time the train actually spent on the bridge was especially important since this was where the explosion had to take place to be effective, so not by a hair's breadth could the timings be wrong.

After the first day, it was simply a matter of checking the previous day's timings; not by more than a couple of seconds did anything vary, and Beard knew, to within those two seconds, exactly how long he should set the timers for. The train would take 12 minutes 40 seconds to travel from Zrmojice, reach the tunnel entrance, where a special track key needed to enable it to continue was collected, pass through the tunnel and come out on the bridge. That was the moment at which the charge had to be detonated and, providing the pre-set timing device did what it was supposed to do, that's exactly what would happen. The bridge, the train and anything in the immediate vicinity would be blown to smithereens.

Beard's time was almost wholly taken up with Petar Spiljak. He could not recall ever having seen a blacksmith before, but his impression of them had been that they were always giants, with limbs and shoulders comparable to such creatures. Spiljak in no way matched this image, except perhaps in the arms and shoulders which were certainly powerful. For the rest he was of very ordinary height, pale and skinny, but he had strength in his face and a fire in his dark eyes that bespoke great energy. He was full of enthusiasm for Beard's plan and they spent the first day discussing details of how to implement it. There was no problem over the metal lining, he said; once the explosives had been put into place, he could add the layer of molten metal by way of a mould, something like a jelly. This metal skin, which would be very thin and light, but tough, would start four inches below the surface of the milk and taper very gradually so that any probe the Germans might insert, looking for foreign bodies, would simply slide over the smooth surface right down to the bottom.

"What happens if one of the pigs wants to guzzle a couple of pints of milk?" asked Spiljak thoughtfully, as they circled a churn and weighed up outstanding problems.

"We'll have a pitcher of milk handy for him," retorted Beard easily, "or, better still, a bottle of wine – make sure you piss in it first!"

It was decided that the whole operation would be put into effect at the last farm from which churns were collected. Five churns out of a usual total of thirteen would be used. Beard and his men would press the explosives – a mixture of plastic explosive, thermite, slabs of TNT and, for good measure, a quantity of gun-cotton; it was everything they had – round the insides, and then Spiljak would add the metal coating. The timers would not be inserted until it was known the Germans had left the previous collecting point, a distance of exactly two miles and forty yards, and once this was done Spiljak would complete the tin coat seal and the churn could be topped up with milk.

Everything proceeded according to plan. In fact, everything went so smoothly Beard became anxious. Something had to go wrong soon, it always did. But this time, it didn't. The explosives were transferred to the farm and were soon in place inside the churns. Simms, who had once worked in a foundry in Sussex, assisted Spiljak in the makeshift forge, and Felbridge helped Beard with the preparation of the timers. Sgt Stubbs and Jenkins were given the task of ensuring that there was no surprise visit to the farm by the Germans; they watched every road and track for miles around in company with the partisans. The station, too, was under constant observation, but the routine there never changed. Trains ran to schedule with variations never more than an odd second or two.

By the end of the week, on Friday, November 5, all was ready, but it was decided to postpone the implementation of the plan until the next day, in the expectation that while the milk would be in demand as usual, there would be fewer Germans on duty over the weekend. There were, anyway, a number of things that cropped up at the last minute which meant delaying the big moment. Another problem arose with an alarming radio message stating that the submarine that was supposed to pick them up had been torpedoed, and, instead, an MTB was being diverted to collect them but wouldn't be able to reach the selected area before the 10th of November. A sudden blizzard didn't help matters, either.

"Won't this freezing weather stop the cows giving milk?" asked Beard, with some unease, even though the cattle were housed in barns for the winter. "It must affect the yield."

"We give the ladies an extra feed to make sure it doesn't," laughed the farmer, after Mika related the concern. "It's a bit like when babies are born: they come what may when it's their time. With cows, they need milking every day – else they'd explode! Anyway, the Germans demand so many gallons, and that's what the cows have to give."

In the early hours of Saturday morning, Beard, Jenkins and Simms slipped into Hèvic accompanied by Spiljak. Their object was to acquire a suitable German vehicle, for Beard had no intention of tramping through the snow all the way to the coast when his job here was done. However, their mission was twofold. In addition to acquiring an eminently suitable half-track, ensuring it contained ample petrol and extra cans, and sabotaging a score of other vehicles as a matter of course, they also recovered, with the help of Spiljak's bolt cutters, the skeletal remains of Nikola Zivkovic, Jenkins and Simms efficiently dealing with several guards in the vicinity. The gruesome bundle of bones were tipped out of their iron frame and into a blanket which was hurriedly placed aboard the half-track. Beard gave a moment's thought to hanging up one of the Germans in the place of the skeleton, but decided against it, not for any squeamishness or because he thought such action unbecoming for a British officer, but because he didn't want to linger there in the heart of Hèvic a second longer than necessary. He felt they were too exposed and, having achieved their purpose, it seemed silly to risk discovery at this stage – and he'd thought of something else he needed to do.

Leaving Simms and Spiljak to take the half-track out of the town, he and Jenkins, following directions given to them by Spiljak, and dodging patrolling soldiers, found the building they were looking for – a place bristling with aerials – hidden behind a hedge of firs. The place was guarded front and back but such obstacles presented little difficulty to experienced men like Beard and Jenkins, though Beard, who had no wish to advertise their visit to the building, had to pull Jenkins after him when the latter showed an inclination to despatch the sentries. They were soon on the roof, and having made sure they were unobserved, they scooped a hole in the snow beside a sort of pylon and Jenkins gratefully placed the Teller mine he'd been humping (it had been taken from their newly-acquired vehicle) in the hollow space. A moment later Beard had fixed a timing device to a ball of plastic explosive which he attached to the mine, and replaced the snow. All being well the mine should blow the building apart about the same time that the milk churns were exploding, and the lack of communications would add to the Germans' confusion. He and Jenkins descended from the roof and crept silently away.

Three hours later they were back in the partisan camp with their macabre bundle, having hidden their newly acquired vehicle in a convenient place discovered by Spiljak; the snow, which was still falling steadily, would soon obliterate all tracks. The partisans were respectfully delighted when Spiljak revealed the contents of the blanket, which was hastily pulled aside. One after the other they came up to stare down at the pathetic collection of bones, muttering prayers, some silent, some whispered audibly; they could not have acted more reverently had they been paying homage beside a catafalque in some great cathedral.

Beard noted that when Major Borisav came to pay homage the remainder drew back leaving her standing there alone: alone with Mika on one side of her and Janez on the other; the two boys supported the woman, and tears that had been held back for two years rolled unchecked down the faces of all three. Beard was left in no doubt but that a very close relationship existed between the three – and the skeleton. He was quite unprepared, however, for what happened next. When she had finished grieving over the remains, the major walked firmly up to him, pulled his head down and kissed him hard, and wetly, on both cheeks. She then stepped back, whispered "*Hvala*," which he assumed meant "thank you" or some such thing, and hurried off supported by the two brothers.

The end, later that same day, as in so many things, was something of an anti-climax. Everything went like clockwork, as it should but often doesn't. Beard was waiting at the farm when word came that the Germans had left the last collecting point; he set the timers and Spiljak sealed them inside the liners, and Simms topped the churns up to their normal level. The Germans arrived, rude and aggressive as ever, plunged their probing rods into each churn without discovering anything untoward, sealed them, watched as two farm-hands loaded the churns on to the wagon with the rest, and left – taking the bottle of wine put out for them. So far so good.

At the station things continued to go according to plan. The churns were re-examined and loaded, and the train went on its way: it was bang on time. There was a moment of alarm when the engine driver spotted a dog on the line and increased his speed, putting him ahead of schedule, but he lost this gossiping when he collected the key before entering the tunnel. He was back on time. Each minute seemed to take an hour as the train disappeared inside the tunnel, taking an age as it travelled noisily along, but finally it emerged puffing on to the bridge ... and nothing happened!

Enveloped in its own steam, and virtually invisible, it puffed across the bridge and disappeared into the opposite tunnel. There was no explosion. Beard gaped, disbelieving his eyes, and ears. What had gone wrong? It had to be the timers – they must be faulty.

But, in that same moment, back in Hèvic, there was an almighty blast as the mined radio building blew up ... and, almost simultaneously, there was a muffled roar from inside the tunnel and the whole mountain seemed to tremble, and go on trembling for minutes on end. It was like an earthquake. Everything shook. Huge cracks appeared all over the surface of the mountain, trees toppled over, avalanches were set off and rocks were hurled far and wide, some landing in Hèvic itself.

But the bridge remained intact.

It still straddled the gorge beneath the protection of Romeo and Juliet. Beard refused to believe the report when he was told, and rushed to a fresh vantage point, to see for himself. True, Juliet did appear to be leaning slightly further forward, but yes, the bridge was still there : standing proud. It was as though it was mocking him. He swore with a savage, bitter fury. He'd been defeated by one second : at most, two. He'd failed, like all the others before him. It was his personal failure. It had been his plan : the fault was all his. The plan had depended on timing, and this hadn't worked.

It was only when Jenkins pointed out, rather obviously, that it would take the Germans for ever to clear and rebuild tunnel, that Beard realised that perhaps they had succeeded after all. True, the bridge was still standing, but it was isolated, wasn't it? The railway line itself was blocked – buried under a mountain. For a few moments he was too overcome at this about turn in their fortunes to speak, then he and Jenkins punched the air with their fists, danced a little jig and joined in the cheers of scores of others, and modestly accepted the congratulations of everyone.

Still, it would have been nice if the bridge had gone, and left a void.

Beard and his men wasted no time lingering in the vicinity. Once the cheering was done, and the realisation that even if they hadn't destroyed the bridge it now served no useful purpose, they were on their way, after minimal farewells, in their hi-jacked transport with Mika at the wheel.

Mika knew every inch of the countryside all the way to the coast and, although the journey took them two days, they were able to avoid every single road block – largely by using forest fire-breaks and secret tracks known only to animals and a few others, like Mika. It was not hard to envisage the furious searching that was going on, the sounds were all about them – and in the sky above, but they bore a charmed life all the way to the coast, with the bitter cold seemingly their only enemy. At a point near Rogoznica, well to the north of Split, Mika concealed their vehicle and contacted some friends who led them on foot several miles to a place where they had a hidden boat. It was another day before Felbridge was able to raise their MTB contact – only to be told that it would be another two days before it could reach them. There was nothing to do but wait.

While they were waiting, Beard and Mika discussed the events of the last few days. Beard was concerned that while he was able to escape now that the job was done, those who were left behind would probably have to pay dearly for their success, but Mika assured him he would never be blamed.

"The Germans often kill our people for nothing," he declared soberly, "at least this time it will be for something – in addition to the skeleton business. Of course, all those who helped us – Spiljak, the farmers and the rest, will have to go into hiding for the remainder of the war."

"Take care of your mother, Mika," said Beard quietly. "She needs her sons about her."

Mika grinned. "How long have you known? We tried so hard to keep it a secret – it wasn't easy, and it seems we didn't even fool you. We thought the fewer people who knew her identity and about our family ties the better, for security reasons."

Beard gave a little shrug. "An orphan can spot such ties a mile off," he said with a small smile. Actually, the realisation of the relationship had come very slowly..

"Mother would've have wanted to adopt you if she'd known," said Mika seriously.

"I'd have liked that," returned Beard quietly.

Mika stared in silence for several moments. "Thank you so much for bringing my father back home to us," he said, with a catch in his voice. "Mother can begin to be happy again now."

Beard nodded at the remembrance of the skeleton he'd brought home for the family to bury. There didn't seem much need for further words, and for some hours they hardly talked at all, and when they did it was never of personal matters but only about their recent adventure concerning the bridge.

It was only when Beard and his men boarded the boat to rendezvous with the MTB two days later, that Mika leaned forward and whispered rather shyly, "Mother told me to give you her love and to say that she will never, ever forget you. She thanks you so much for giving her back her husband." Beard was too embarrassed to make any response, and he stayed silent and simply pressed the other's hands. It was enough, and all there was time for.

Beard turned and gave one final wave as the small craft moved out to sea. It seemed like hours later, but was probably less than one, when a light flashed in the distance and recognition signals were exchanged. Presently Beard's tiny craft drew up along-side the MTB and he and his men clambered aboard and were on their way with hardly a moment to thank their Yugoslav friends who, themselves, were already heading back home.

□ *Gibbs paused in his narrative to tell his audience that, in the event, the effects of the terrible explosions within the mountain, coupled with the early efforts of winter, completed Beard's mission two months later, when the bridge finally collapsed. Its buttress at one end had been so mortally weakened it simply teetered forward, bringing Juliet down with it, and everything – including the bridge – crashed far below into the gorge.*

Inevitably, Romeo had followed Juliet.

And just as inevitably, Queenie took up the story as Beard moved closer to home.

Chapter Twenty-eight

Home leave, January, 1944

The MTB deposited Beard and his team at Limassol, Cyprus, where, to their surprise, they were met by Major Yeo, who had flown up from Beirut at the behest of Brigadier Charington. His orders were to allow the team one night's R&R and then fly them directly to Cairo, where they would be debriefed.

It was not much of a welcome, but then they hadn't expected too much. Major Yeo was magnanimous in his personal congratulations at their achievements as he shook each man's hand, but once he'd said his piece, that was it; and all the men wanted, after a good meal and many beers, was a long soak in a hot bath, and a much longer sleep in a real bed. They achieved all their needs except, perhaps, the lie in, which was cut short by the demands of their plane and its need to keep to a schedule.

They arrived Cairo, on November 15, and were met by Gibbs, all smiles and bonhomie, and the moment the congratulations were done they were whisked off to an underground complex where, after a very good meal, the debriefings began. These filled the remainder of that first day and continued the following day. Beard, who had known what to expect, had started on his detailed report before leaving Cyprus, continued it during the flight, and completed it ahead of his interrogations. But after an initial de-briefing by the Intelligence people, Beard and his men were released (on the 18th) long enough to be presented to Charington and some other top brass.

"So, Mr Beard, you succeeded where all the others failed, eh? You did a very good job. Very well done indeed, all of you," declared Charington, smiling expansively, his green eyes positively shining.

"Thank you, sir. We were indebted to the local partisans," said Beard evenly.

"So I read in your report," said the brigadier. "But you were the inspiration and leader of it all. Excellent piece of writing, that report of yours. Read like an adventure story, what? Yes, quite a remarkable feat this mission of yours. Excellent work." He gave what might be described as a chuckle, or even a chortle, and went on, "I know you chaps thrive on escapades like this, and I suppose the first thing you want to ask for is more of the same, eh?"

"A spot of home leave first would be appreciated," suggested Beard rather daringly.

Charington wiped his suntanned bald head and first nodded, and then shook his head. "Leave, eh? You'll have to see Gibbs about that. Lot more de-briefing ahead of you yet, I'm afraid, though before we can let you go. But you've certainly earned something for your achievements. Leave certainly, and we might be able to dig up a medal for you."

And with this indeterminate suggestion, he wandered off and it was some time later that Gibbs himself settled the leave matter. "Don't unpack, Robert, we're all here till at least the middle of January. The Intelligence blokes want you and your lot back for some more of their searching questions, and then we have to help with the planning of things in Italy – *our* sort of things. So, for the moment your leave will have to be out here, and we'll miss both Christmas and the New Year back home. But, we'll get there eventually."

And, of course, they did. On January 12, Gibbs summoned Beard and announced, "We're headed back to Blighty tomorrow at 0740 hrs, and that's thanks to Charington who's laid on a special plane." He added with a wink, "There's talk of a Second Front, which will probably occupy some of our time. You really need to get back into training, but first, you all get three weeks' home leave the moment we land – and, aren't we lucky, we'll be arriving just in time for the weekend. Oh, and for some reason, their excellencies have seen fit to award you a Military Cross for your activities in Poland. Congratulations."

"Am I still an acting major, sir?" Beard enquired bluntly.

"Of course, Robert, keep your crowns," responded Gibbs cheerily. "Your promotion was on the recommendation of Charington. He felt you needed a more senior rank for that bridge job, and on your successful return he told me you were to keep the rank. He was quite insistent – so it's been gazetted."

Beard was headed to The Dials on Saturday, January 15.

Queenie was in her kitchen, warming herself at her Aga, which she kept giving unnecessary wipes with a cloth that she kept permanently handy for that purpose in her apron pocket, when she looked round and saw Beard (whom she only ever thought of as Jarvis) standing by the door smiling at her. She felt an immediate tightness in her breast, which was both wonderful and painful in the same breath, and a mist formed in her eyes as she gazed at his image while her mind wrestled with the possibility that he might actually be real. This indecision lasted only seconds, and then they were in each other's arms – and there was no doubting the solidity of the other.

She uttered the single word "Jarvis!" and held him tightly to her and then let him go in order to have another look at him, and then clutched him to her again, and kept repeating the procedure until she'd had her fill; finally, she held him at arm's length and examined him at her leisure, like a mother, lovingly and anxiously. She saw the faint shadow of the scar above his right eye straight away, and wondered if there were other scars hidden from view. Again and again she searched his face, and finally she knew what it was that gave her heart an extra tug. He was no longer a boy: he was a man. There was a hardness in his face and a steeliness in his eye that she had not seen, nor ever hoped to see, before; his soldiering had left its mark on him in a way his bitter childhood had not. And he'd started shaving for real!

Beard regarded her in his turn. He saw the shadow that crept across her face like a sun cloud as it reached her eyes, and he guessed the reason. He knew he wasn't the same as when he'd gone away from here two years ago – God! was that all it was?; he felt different inside, and he supposed it showed on the outside as well. Well, people did change as they grew up, and when they'd had the sort of experiences he'd had the process was bound to be quicker, too quick, perhaps, and the changes inside would be even deeper than those visible to the naked eye. Or were they? Queenie evidently saw something that disturbed her. Well, mothers did, didn't they!

"Hello, Mum," he said, and much of the anxiety vanished from her eyes at his greeting. He saw a light rekindle there, a warm glow of sheer pleasure that spread over her face, suffusing her cheeks. In all other respects, apart from the inevitable tiredness the war inflicted on them all, she looked as well as he'd ever seen her, and that in spite of Sam's death. She had lost weight, and he doubted if it had anything to do with the rationing, which had never seemed to involve her, anyway. He remembered that in the past whenever she'd lost weight, however little, she had invariably looked more attractive – and sometimes even younger. Well, she didn't look all that young now, but she looked very lovely. All right, her frame was still substantial, but she looked quite beautiful in her matronly way, and there were other improvements. Her yellow teeth were definitely a lot whiter, and more even. He supposed she'd been to a dentist, and if so what emergency had compelled her to do so. Her hair seemed different, too; not quite so tawny, perhaps: a lighter colour, a touch more grey and thinner, but it was also less of a hedge gone wild, being now secured in tidy waves with only a few wisps showing their independence.

Their examination of one another completed, and really it took hardly any time at all, Queenie recovered herself sufficiently to push Beard into a seat at the table, on which she cleared a space with a single sweep of a massive forearm, and began plying him with all manner of food – deaf to his protests that he'd had enough, that he was bursting and that he was beginning to feel sick. She smiled tolerantly back at him, and told him a mother knew best – and to eat his food up! They talked incessantly all the while that he was eating, and the only moment of despondency came – inevitably – when Sam's death was mentioned. A sadness stole into Queenie's eyes, and lingered an unconscionable length of time.

"'E was good an' kind, was Sam," she said in a strangely gruff voice. "We wasn't ever married – you knew that, of course – but I loved 'im better'n a 'usband. He was my friend, my very best friend. The most wunn'erful man I ever knowed. I miss 'im terribly."

Beard nodded and passed a comforting arm round her shoulders. "I know, Mum," he said gently. "I loved him, too … like a father. He was the only one I had. Now, there's just the two of us and we … "

"An' Ruth," interjected Queenie, in a shocked voice.

"And her," agreed Beard, with a smile. "How is the little pest?"

"Oh, don't ever call 'er that, Jarvis – she loves you so much," admonished Queenie in quick protest, but smiling at the same time. "She never stops thinkin' and talkin' about you, and prayin' for you, too. You 'ave no idea how frightened she's been not knowin' where you was an' whevver you was 'live or dead. You ain't much of a letter writer, is yer, lovey? Gawd knows wot'd 'appen to 'er if anyfink ever did 'appen to yer, Jarvis. Die 'erself, I wouldn't be in the least surprised, straight up, I wouldn't."

"Well, I'm here live an' well, so she won't need to go that far, will she? She knows I love both of you," declared Beard, more amused than alarmed at the idea of Ruth turning up her toes. "As for letters, a soldier doesn't have the time for such things – he's too busy keeping himself and his men alive for you lot back home. She can't have it both ways, can she? It's me ... or a blasted letter!"

Queenie smiled. Letters were unimportant *now*. Now that *he* was home, she was too happy to think anything but lovely thoughts. She didn't want to know anything about his part in the war: she only wanted to hear his voice and, occasionally, to be able to touch him, and feed him, of course.

Beard pressed Queenie about their few mutual acquaintances. Mrs B., she told him, was well and living for the day her boys returned from the war; she was a frequent visitor at The Dials, in the hope of hearing news about Jarvis, and they often went shopping together – "so she don't never go short, lovey!" Mrs Molly, who had had the veins removed from her other leg, dropped in almost daily for a lunch-time cheese and pickle sandwich and a bottle or two of stout in the evening; she had become a favourite with the Americans and did such a roaring trade with them that she had permitted their Stars and Stripes to stand beside the Union Jack at her flower pitch; "they don't know wot money is, nor flowers neither, bless 'em," she'd cackle. "Most don't know one flower from t'other – just summat big an' colourful is all they wants ... to show off to their gals. An' wot makes them 'appy, makes me rich!" Mrs Gunning, the Mafeking Widow, was still looking for a husband – but her eyesight wasn't what it was, especially once she'd settled into her second glass of port! "Once she come in when there was an engagement party on, an' she asked, particular like, if you was still in the running wiv Ruth," Queenie recalled with a teasing smile, stretching out a hand to capture one of his, and give it a bit of a squeeze.

"Little Ruth!" he exclaimed, pretending amazed indifference. "What on earth put that idea into her head? Bet it was the port."

"Ruth ain't so little no more," declared Queenie. "Like you, she's growed. She's a young woman, almost."

"Don't be daft, Mum," laughed Beard, "she's still at school, I bet."

"Yes," Queenie allowed, "but she's in 'er last year, an' very growed up. She's almost sixteen."

"How nearly?"

"Very," insisted Queenie. "And it's high time you two got yerselves engaged, 'an married, an' all, m'lad."

"Now what chance do I get for such nonsense, Mum?" he cried defensively. "Let's get the war over first, then I'll start looking around."

Queenie's eyes widened. "Look arahnd!" she echoed him. "You don't 'ave to look arahnd, Jarvis, Ruth's already 'ere waitin' to be arsked, ain't she? Bin waiting blinkin' years, she 'as."

Beard coloured as he stared back at her. "People change as the years roll by, Mum," he told her in a quiet, steady voice, and fixing his eyes on the table top. "Anyway, Ruth's still a child. Let her grow up first."

Queenie smiled, and reached out simply to touch him, any part of him; she gave his elbow an affectionate squeeze. In her heart she told herself that they were both children still, but the war had changed Jarvis in a way it had not touched Ruth. He had seen the raw face of the war, perhaps even killed someone himself, and it had left its mark on him. She could see it in his eyes, his face, his voice and the way he carried himself; she could almost feel the responsibilities he bore. Look at him! A major, and him not even eighteen yet, officially. He was her Jarvis still, yet when she looked into his face, especially his eyes, it was almost like staring at a stranger. The thought of what experiences he'd had frightened her. She smiled, a little sadly, and murmured, "An' you, lovey, you're an ol' man, I s'pose!"

Their exchanges were constantly interrupted by first one and then another of the pub's staff. Fred Akers, the potman, his teeth safely hidden away, greeted Beard with an unfamiliar friendliness and respect – doubtless in deference to his uniform. He was followed by Queenie's under-manager, Mavis, whose red face took on an even deeper shade as she folded Beard in her powerful arms and planted kisses on both his cheeks. Then came the barmaids, Millie and Hannah, who both added their kisses. Millie was still as small and dumpy as ever, but she had more colour in her face, there was a happy sparkle in her blue eyes and her blonde hair, released from its confining knot, danced loosely and attractively at her shoulders as she stood on tip toes to give Beard a welcome home kiss. "She's goin' steady wiv a sergeant in the Tank

Corps," confided Queenie. "Changed 'er completely. Be a blessing for all them kids of hers! I 'ope she's told 'er sergeant abaht 'em!" Hannah had grown into a very pretty girl since Beard had last seen her. She'd shed much of her girlish awkwardness, and shyness, and even acquired a pleasing figure. Her coppery curls flopped over Beard's face as she, almost coquettishly, kissed him full on his lips. "Saucy gel!" snapped Queenie, but there was a fondness in her smile as she playfully smacked the girl's behind. "She 'as 'er 'art set on some GI corporal named Toni Spaghetti – or sumfink like that. Says 'e 'as 'is own business back 'ome, as a cook –   so 'e's probably got one of them 'ot dawg stands. " Beard grinned. It was plain Americans weren't Queenie's favourite people, but then, he didn't know that they were anybody's.

It was Hannah (nowadays she preferred to be called Honey, which was what her Toni called her) who alerted Ruth to the fact that Beard was home. She was scrubbing the outside steps when she saw Ruth's navy blue-coated figure approaching snail-like along the pavement. Ruth seemed to be navy blue all over – or, if not navy, then black. Apart from her coat, which was more a raincoat than an overcoat, she wore black woollen stockings and black shoes, a dark scarf that looked navy, and a navy beret pulled down over one ear. Navy gloves completed her uniform ensemble. The scarf was wound a couple of times round her neck and the ends trailed far down her back, along with her twin braids – tied with rubber bands. The only portion of Ruth herself that was visible was her shiny pink face, with its neat little mouth, half hidden by the scarf, short, straight nose and dark eyes that were never quite still. She had grown two or three inches over the past two years, and looked to be possessed with the confidence of a young lady. She was, of course, just fifteen, though by her way of reckoning such things, she was practically sixteen – at the very least.

"Ruth!" shrieked Hannah at the very top of her lungs, which was very high indeed, frantically waving her scrubbing brush in the air to attract the other's attention. Half the world was startled into turning to gape at her; Ruth merely came to a standstill and stared, and, after a moment or two, waved her school satchel by way of response. She resumed her progression, but with no great hurry, and Hannah impatiently rushed to meet her though only a score or so yards separated them.

"He's 'ere, Ruth! He's 'ere!" she screeched excitedly, her voice only slightly lower than her previous scream, pushing her hand inside Ruth's arm and fairly tugging her along the pavement towards the pub's entrance. "Jarvis! He's come back from the war," Hannah exclaimed, hardly able to contain her enthusiasm. "Oh, Ruth! He looks absolutely gorgeous in his uniform ... so growed up and 'andsome," she gushed, "and his chest full of medal ribbons."

"Jarvis! Home!" gasped Ruth weakly. She thought for a

moment that she was going to faint, and clung on to Hannah, almost afraid to let go. She wasn't prone to fainting fits, or any other fits that she knew about, but she felt decidedly light-headed. A million words stuck in her throat: as many thoughts filled her spinning head. She found herself quite unable to speak – for the first time in her life. This, she was convinced, must be an indication of some serious mental disorder. Would he remember her? Would he still love her ... like he'd promised to do for ever? But had he ever, really? Had he found someone else? The questions ... the doubts … tore at her heart. Everything seemed to swim before her eyes, but through it all she could see Hannah's nodding, reassuring and beaming face.

"Yes, yes, yes Ruth!" cried Hannah, "he's come back to us. He's wiv yer Mum."

Ruth heard the words as through a long, long tunnel; but they were clear and as the words translated their meaning to her spinning brain, everything else became clear. The world stopped see-sawing on the edge of oblivion. She tore herself from Hannah's supporting arm, flew up the steps of The Dials and raced through the building shedding her outdoor clothes on the way, with the result that by the time she reached the kitchen, and stood panting in the doorway, she presented herself to him very much as a schoolgirl. If only she'd been wearing a pretty frock – the one he'd bought her, instead of her detested shapeless navy school tunic and blouse which not only made her look as ugly as it did, concealing what feminine allure she possessed, but labelled her a child into the bargain. It was so humiliating! But she had no time to wallow in her regrets, not with Jarvis standing only feet away.

Her eyes devoured his face with such an adoring intensity that she was blind, in that first rapturous moment, to the fact that his gaze was considerably less passionate and, perhaps, even verged on amused puzzlement. The moment she'd seen him her heart had first missed a beat, stood stock-still, and then pounded like a battery of war drums. Her feet, so light, so fleet, a moment before, were now like anchor weights; she was unable to move. But she was unaware of this. For the moment, it was enough that he was here in front of her, and entirely undamaged. He looked taller and years older. Well, he would do, wouldn't he, it had been years since she'd seen him; she imagined she looked older to him, as well – perhaps as old as seventeen! She enjoyed an inner giggle at the thought.

Finally, they flew at each other and met in mid-flight, he laughing and she crying; and Queenie looked on and did both. Beard swept Ruth up off the floor and swung her round and round, and then he put her down and kissed her, not passionately, but firmly. There was no touching of tongues this time, just hard smacking kisses in the region of her mouth and other parts of her face that got in the way of his lips. Ruth returned each of his kisses at least a hundredfold, showering every part of his face with quick, hot and wet kisses. She would have liked the kisses to be more intimate, more leisurely and much longer, but accepted that now was not the right moment – though deep in her heart she was sure it would be all right. When she had had enough (for the moment) of bruising and washing his face with her kisses, she turned her attention to his uniform and pressed her lips to each of his four ribbons.

"I know what they're for," she sang out. "The first is an MC, the next is the war one, the sandy one is for North Africa, and the pretty one is the Italy Star and the bronze oak leaves are for some outstanding act of heroism. You must be terribly brave, Jarvis."

"Everybody gets them – just for being there," Beard told her with a dismissive laugh.

"And they've made you a major," she exclaimed, fingering one of the crowns on his shoulders. "How is that possible at your age?"

Beard gave a shrug. "It goes with the job," he explained simply.

"Well, they're very nice," insisted Ruth. "The crowns and the pretty ribbons."

After this initial exchange, Ruth and Beard found their voices together, and for more than an hour they sat opposite each other at the kitchen table and shouted questions and answers, and very few of either made much sense having regard to the occasion. But, then, an absence of a month is like a year to the young; one that endured beyond a year was as a lifetime to them. But the months and years dissipated as the words were hurled backwards and forwards, and very soon it was as though they had never been parted. Gradually their war of words became less a contest to see who could shout the loudest and get the most words in, and settled into a quieter more normal conversation, in which questions were actually heard and answered. In time there were moments of silence between them, and their gossiping became more prosaic. Ruth even found she could think of other things than love – or, at least, other things at the same time.

"I see you have parachute wings on your sleeve, Jarvis," Ruth said, fingering the badge in question. "You never told us about them. What terribly dangerous things did you have to do, and where?"

Beard looked uncomfortable. "I'm not allowed to talk about such things, Ruth," he said, rather lamely.

"Well, if it's a military secret you'd better not tell me any more ... I'm only interested in having you home safe again."

"Good," said Beard simply.

Ruth, deciding to shelve the question of secrets for the moment, but only for the moment, gave him one of her sweetest smiles which should have immediately put him on his guard. "May I call you Jarvis again – please?" she asked innocently.

"No! You mayn't," he replied, quite sternly. "Do you want to get me shot as a spy?"

"Good heavens no, Jarvis. Oh, I'm sorry, there I go again ... but it's very hard for me to call you by someone else's name."

"You must keep trying, Ruth. You simply must," insisted Beard. "I've got away with it so far, I suppose because I've been abroad where nobody knows me by any other name, and I'll most likely be stuck with being Robert Beard till the end of the war."

Ruth stuck her tongue out at him. "Now that you're home – Jarvis, where will you be stationed?" she asked.

"We're in Chelmsford, Essex. Place called Apple Tree Camp. Haven't seen it yet."

"Essex!" she cried, shocked. "How will I ever be able to visit over there?"

"You won't," he told her firmly. "No visitors permitted."

"You might just as well be back in India, Jarvis!"

"I've never been there ... " he observed blandly.

"Oh, shut up!" she exclaimed, with a giggle. "It's where you were supposed to go, anyway."

"If I had gone there, I wouldn't be back here now, would I?" Beard argued. "And I'd probably be a prisoner of the Japanese – or worse!"

Queenie burst out laughing. "Stop it, the pair of you! Two years apart – an' already squabblin' like you was still children! You must be in love!"

"Oooh, yes!" sang out Ruth happily, clapping her hands as she turned her sparkling eyes to Beard for his confirmation. "We are, aren't we, Jarvis?"

"I expect so," he replied, in a voice that was noncommittal and unenthusiastic. He looked at her fondly enough, though, perhaps even lovingly, but when he spoke his words didn't echo hers. "You're all grown up, aren't you!" he declared, and somehow managed to sound surprised at the discovery.

"Oh, yes, awfully," she cried, pleased that he'd noticed the fact. It wasn't what she'd hoped he was going to say, but it was a start. Why wouldn't he say that he loved her? Men were so slow to declare themselves. It was so infuriating. She knew she'd have to be patient.

Queenie, sensing a temporary truce between them, shooed them both away while she got on with the dinner preparations. Beard took the opportunity to re-familiarize himself with the much loved building, with Ruth dogging his footsteps, and reacquainting himself with old friends as he met them. Then, he decided on a long soak in a bath full of perfumed water and bubbles, having taken the precaution of locking the door so that he could enjoy his bath without interference.

Ruth, against whom this precaution was chiefly aimed, busied herself in the time-consuming ordeal of preparing herself for the evening meal. The result was that Beard emerged looking as pink as a boiled shrimp but smelling divinely, and Ruth descended the stairs dressed up to the nines – in a green woollen dress, laddered stockings (a gift from Hannah's GI, Toni) and her pink bunny-rabbit slippers. She was also wearing all her jewellery: Beard's St Christopher medal and the coral necklace and silver bracelet he'd given her. Beard gallantly told her she looked very nice. Ruth, who could have wished for a more generous compliment, responded by saying he smelt rather gorgeous – for once.

The dinner was a feast: leek soup, roast lamb and baked apples with brown sugar and cloves. Beard savoured everything in its turn, and every mouthful was a song in Queenie's heart. But Ruth had no appetite; she was too excited to eat, and only picked at her food or pushed it round the plate. It wasn't until the meal was done and they were all in the parlour that she perked up. This was when Beard produced his spoils from the Augusta safe he'd blown open.

First, he pinned the brooch and cameo to Queenie's heaving chest and gave her a kiss with each, and then he produced the ring he'd instinctively made up his mind was for Ruth. The moment she saw it, her eyes lit up, her mouth opened, and she thrust out her left hand and wiggled her third finger with impatient eagerness. She would have closed her eyes in the sheer bliss of the moment, but she couldn't take her eyes off the ring, or him, as he pushed it none too gently on to her finger. Her hand wasn't all that small, but the finger was of such proportions that the ring was a very loose fit. Naturally, Ruth wasn't going to admit that for a moment. She clenched her hand, which she had never thought of as being anything but enormous before, and assured herself that it would become so and that, anyway, the ring would fit better the more she wore it. She determined never to take it off.

It was plain the ring was too large, so Beard produced the pearl necklace he'd acquired from the same source, and said, "You can have this necklace if you'd prefer."

Ruth clutched the ring to her breast, alarmed at the very idea. "Oh, no!" she said quickly, pausing a second to put her lips to the square blue diamond. "You keep the necklace, and I'll keep the ring. It's all I've ever wanted – *your* ring, Jarvis, and it'll soon fit perfectly as I grow into it. Besides, I've got a necklace, haven't I? My coral beads."

Beard nodded, not having expected her to surrender the ring – and wondering whether he shouldn't have given her the necklace instead in the first place. He knew it was too late now, as he underwent a suffocating assault from Ruth, who threw herself at him and smothered him with kisses. It was all very pleasant, even if it did leave him gasping for breath. He assumed girls didn't need to breath at such moments! It wasn't until much later that he noticed she'd scratched his neck with the ring.

"Does this mean we're officially engaged, Jarvis?" cried Ruth, turning to him in excited wonder as if the thought had just struck her.

She'd been showing her mother the ring – Queenie's first reaction had been to shake her head as the ring hung loosely on the tiny finger – and now the two of them were staring at Beard.

Beard gaped back. Now he was sure he should have given her the necklace. He'd given no thought to anything so drastic; not really – not so that an answer was expected, there and then. But clearly Ruth was waiting for one, and he didn't know what to say. He was pretty sure he wanted to say Yes, his heart told him he wanted to, but his brain sounded a caution. Alarm bells sounded. Perhaps, this was not the right moment to make such a bold decision. He hesitated still. "What?" he cried, discomfited by the question. He looked desperately from one eager face to the other ... and almost wished he was on any other battlefront.

"Engaged ... engaged to be married!" Ruth exclaimed exasperatedly, the tiniest of frowns touching her brow. She could not comprehend his apparent lack of enthusiasm.

Beard's jaw sagged a little further. "I hadn't really thought about it," he said weakly, staring at Ruth rather helplessly. He wasn't sure, but Queenie seemed to be trying to hide a smile. He sighed, and frowned his confusion, and indecision.

"I've been thinking of nothing else all my life," declared Ruth, staring at him in some astonishment, and disappointment. "Don't you love me, Jarvis?" she asked bluntly.

"Of course I do," he assured her hastily. "You know I do."

"There you are then," declared Ruth triumphantly; "we must be engaged!"

Beard felt a sigh coursing through him, and when this had completed its course he took a very deep breath. He felt very uncomfortable; he felt trapped; he felt vulnerable. "I really can't be thinking of such things at this time, Ruth," he said, speaking with infinite care, weighing each word before releasing it. "I'm a soldier. I'm not properly free to make such a commitment. The Army pushes me this way and that, and I go where I'm sent. I'm often in the midst of great danger." – Oh dear, I shouldn't have said that, he thought. – "It would be distracting to have such matters on my mind when it should be concentrating on keeping myself alive." Was she really such a distraction? he asked himself

Ruth looked neither convinced nor satisfied; neither did she care to be thought of as a distraction; even so, she seemed, however reluctantly, to accept what he said as being the only answer she was going to get – for the moment. At any rate, he'd given her a ring and she wasn't ever going to give that back – not once it fitted properly. "But when the war's over, then we will be engaged?" she pressed.

"Oh yes, almost certainly. I expect so," he answered vaguely, and not really seeing any end to the war. "I'm sure it'll be all right to make decisions like that then," he added, feeling safe enough to offer her such futuristic reassurance.

"And then we'll be married ... and live happily ever after?" cried Ruth, who managed to conjure up a feeling of excitement from his seeming optimism. She already felt betrothed, war or no war.

"Of course – in a castle!" answered Beard airily, forcing a smile, before hurriedly returning to earth. "But you've quite a bit of growing up to do first, haven't you, Ruth?" he told her, and immediately felt he'd stepped into a minefield. Ruth made to wag her ringed-finger at him, but at the last moment was afraid the ring might fall off; so, instead, she poked her tongue out at him.

"You both have," thought Queenie, feeling things had gone as far as it was safe for the moment.

Ruth, in the tiresome, pleading, wheedling way of a child, finally won over her mother and was given permission to stay off school for at least the first week of Beard's leave. In fact, Queenie decided to award herself a holiday so that she could enjoy Beard's company as well. And as there were the two of them – and the two he loved best in all the world – Beard was quite agreeable to have their constant company.

Their first visit, at Queenie's insistence, was to a jeweller's where Ruth's ring was left to be sized to fit her. Ruth, who had gasped unbelievingly when the jeweller remarked (with a curious glance at Beard) that the ring was probably worth close to £200, left her "engagement ring" behind with the utmost unwillingness. Beard himself had been agreeably surprised at its value, and wondered what the rest of his loot was worth. Perhaps he was a rich man! Or had been before giving away his plunder.

Mrs Molly's red beak drew them straight to her, and the moment she saw the trio she let out a scream that scattered both pigeons and potential customers. She had hardly changed since Beard had last seen her. A khaki scarf seemed the only difference; it was wound over her head, under her chin and wrapped a couple of times round her neck before the ends disappeared somewhere within the shapeless black coat that was her uniform in war and peace. Her face was as old, and ageless, as ever: wrinkled and yellowish grey; the lines about her eyes might be deeper and the bristles on her chin whiter, but there was a bright enough sparkle in her blue eyes as she threw up her mittened hands to welcome her friends.

"Jarvis!" she cried, in a voice as deep as a frog's. "You're back 'ome from the war an' lookin' so smart an' 'ansome. Back to see yer sweet'art, eh!" She turned her eyes towards Ruth and gave her a knowing smile. "Ruthie, darling, 'as 'e popped the question yet?" she croaked, her stained teeth adding nothing to the smile. Ruth blushed, but not unhappily. "Not exactly, Mrs Molly," she whispered back, loud enough for all to hear, "but he's given me a ring – only it doesn't fit ... and he's promised to marry me – when the war's over." Beard wasn't quite certain that he'd gone that far, but Mrs Molly congratulated him with a rough, bony kiss and then proceeded to do the same to Queenie and Ruth, both of whom she presented with bouquets which she produced from her Aladdin's basket like a veritable Father Christmas: snowdrops for Ruth, and anemones for Queenie. Then she shooed them away, with promises to see them later back at The Dials, as a huge black GI approached waving a fistful of notes.

The gasometer looked to be on the rise when Beard, Queenie and Ruth turned into Grafton Road. Mrs B., who had been sipping tea beside her range when they called, very quickly had a fresh pot drawing on the hob for them. While the tea was infusing, and after the hugs and kisses and exclamations of surprise and delight had run their course, Beard plonked the parcel he'd been carrying around all day on the kitchen table and declared "This is for you, Mrs B." It contained ten pounds of assorted teas, mainly Ceylonese and Indian, but also some from China and Kenya; there were also little packets of herbal teas like jasmine and camomile. Beard had been adding to the collection on free moments in Cairo and the lot had been flown home separately with the rest of his personal gear – and had arrived home before him. Mrs B. could not have been more pleased and grateful had Beard given her the Crown Jewels; she was like an excited child with a new, special toy – and in the course of repeatedly thanking Beard, she succeeded in spilling so much tea from the cosy-covered pot that Ruth had to take over.

Mrs B., having virtually no news to impart, took a long time telling the little she had; her two sons were still in North Africa or Italy, she wasn't sure which, and she had no knowledge of Scruffy's activities – not that any was expected from that quarter. She hadn't even any gossip to pass on about St Boniface's which was only round the corner, though she supposed Father Neame was still the Rector. Some of the children were back in residence at the Home – she knew this because she sometimes saw them being marched to the local baths, and often thought they didn't look a lot cleaner on the march back, just a little thinner.

Beard reflected that the routine went on much the same whether he was there or not, and possibly because of this, his thoughts turned to Sam. Sam had been the nearest thing to a father he'd had, and Beard determined to pay his respects to Sam in some way and, as there was no grave, he made arrangements for a Requiem Mass to be said by Father Daly at St Clare's. He explained to Ruth, who pointed out that there'd already been several and that it must be wrong to keep pestering God when so many others were dying every day, that he hadn't attended these Requiems and assured her that the more prayers offered the better. Ruth said that although her mother hadn't exactly become a Catholic, she had started going to Mass with her on Sundays just to keep her company, but she thought it was really because "it makes her feel closer to Daddy."

Beard asked her if they ever heard anything about Lily, but Ruth simply shook her head. "Don't ever mention that woman's name, Jarvis," she whispered. "Mummy goes a little crazy at the very thought of her. To be honest, we both hope she has found her reward in the next world."

And so they all attended the service at St Clare's on a dismal Friday morning. Ruth knelt silently weeping on one side of Beard, and Queenie sat doing the same on the other, her hand holding tight to his arm. Beard knelt in the middle stone-faced and dry-eyed. He hadn't cried since he was a child, when he'd sworn never to do so again; and now that he was a man, he found that he couldn't – and even that gave him relief. He felt an inner peace within him as he thought of Sam whittling away at bits of wood, fashioning angels for the Angels.

When they returned home, Queenie led Beard to her bedroom and showed him Sam's George Medal. It had been presented to her by an anonymous assistant commissioner of the Metropolitan Police, and had lain in its case in a drawer ever since. Beard stared at the medal and, while knowing that it was a tribute to Sam's bravery, he couldn't help but think it a poor exchange for the man. Ruth told him, when they were alone, that Queenie had little interest in the medal; a not-very-good photo of her and Sam taken by poor Mr Liebenberg meant far more to her. They all went to church again on the Sunday, Beard being tucked between Queenie and Ruth, and neither releasing some hold on him though they juggled with prayer book and rosary when the dictates of the service necessitated movement.

Ruth made the most of the day. Her holiday ended the following morning. Try as she might, she was unable to win Queenie round to allowing her a second week off school. No amount of wheedling had any effect, though she begged and cried and stamped her foot, and generally went into a regular tantrum. "I'm almost a married woman!" she protested, waving her ringless hand. But it was all to no avail. Off she was packed to school with dire warnings if she should stray on the way. Never did a pupil crawl more unwillingly to school.

Queenie, too, returned to her duties of running The Dials, and so Beard, liberated from the clinging Ruth, found himself free to do as he pleased. He took the opportunity to take the packet of old coins he'd acquired in Augusta to a dealer acquaintance in Holborn, Charlie Tanney, who had been introduced to him by Nelson. Beard knew he'd get an honest deal with Charlie who, he was not surprised to learn, knew Queenie. Charlie said he'd have to shop around to find the right buyer, and Beard told him to do the best he could and gave him his bank details so that he could send him a cheque. "It's a nest-egg for Queenie in case I don't come back from this war," he told him.

Having disposed of this matter, quite suddenly Beard

remembered that seemingly distant day in December, 1941, when he'd called at an address in Brewer Street to collect Bertie at the end of their embarkation leave. Bertie, as befitted a god, had been in the arms of a girl. Beard had not seen her face, only her dark head buried in Bertie's gold one. Today, when he rang her doorbell hoping for news of Bertie, and saw her face, well, he thought she was pretty enough to be a goddess herself. She was tall, with dark brown hair that hung loosely in wavy curls and was very slim. He saw, too, the alarm in her hazel eyes when she saw his uniform, and his heart sank as he feared the worst. They knew of each other but had never met, so when Beard introduced himself tears bubbled behind Maud's eyes, but she clenched them back, and even gave him a wan smile as she invited him in.

Beard had heard Bertie had been badly wounded about the time he was hitch-hiking back from Poland. Bertie had been nosing around some islands in the South Aegean Sea when his MTB was bombed from the air and then shelled by a passing E-boat. Bertie had managed to escape behind a smoke screen but he had been severely wounded; he'd been hit in the leg by a large piece of shrapnel, another piece had smashed several ribs and several other shards had torn into other parts of his body. His crew had steered the boat home under his direction as he lay on the deck. His leg had been amputated below the knee and he'd undergone two other operations in Italy before being flown home for more, and was currently convalescing in a hospital at Horley, on the Surrey border, just off the Brighton road.

"You haven't come with bad news have you, Mr Beard?" she asked anxiously.

"It's Robert – or Bobbie as Bertie calls me." And just then, he remembered her name: Maud Hussey. "Not at all, Maud, I have no news of any sort. I'm just back from the Middle East and know nothing," Beard told her in a quick, reassuring voice. "I heard Bertie was convalescing down at Horley in Surrey, but I was hoping I might find someone at home here to give me an up-date on his condition. And I find you – and," he exclaimed in a brightening tone, "all sparkling with diamonds. Congratulations!"

Maud raised her hand to examine her engagement ring, gave a small smile and pinked a bit. Then, as she put the kettle on to make them a coffee, she said softly, "Thank you. He gave it to me the first opportunity he had – between operations."

"Very romantic," declared Beard, with a grin.

"I couldn't stop crying when he produced the ring from among his bandages: happiness for me, but I was so afraid I might yet lose him because of his wounds. Of course, there's no fear of that now, though he looks so … awfully damaged, I sometimes have doubts about him being able to lead a normal life with only one leg."

"Bertie's a fighter. He'll come through this business all right, you'll see," Beard told her cheerfully. "By the Spring, we'll all be waltzing down the aisle at your wedding."

"Oh, do you really think so," she exclaimed, hope brightening her eyes.

Beard nodded positively. "Of course."

"I go to see him as often as I can, but I have to work …"

"Do you have to work today?" interposed Beard.

"No."

"Then let's go and see the blighter together, shall we?"

And so the coffee was forgotten.

An hour later they were on a Green Line coach that put them down just outside the hospital, which was carved out of acres of farmland and comprised fifty or more brick-built Nissen hut-type buildings and miles of concrete paths. Beard and Maud reported at the administration building and were escorted to Hut K-5. In the ward itself beds were lined up on either side, some curtained off, all draped in the traditional red blankets. Wheelchairs figured predominantly. Most of the patients were seated alongside their beds either reading or staring boredly around them; there were little groups talking together and some were playing cards or chess; a few of the patients had visitors. One of these was Bertie and his visitor was his sister Poppy, looking very fetching in her Red Cross uniform; her golden hair lit up the ward..

Bertie was sitting in a wheelchair, his right arm in a sling and the remains of his left leg encased in bandages on some sort of platform extension. He was wearing blue silk pyjamas and a very colourful and floral dressing gown of the same material. He saw Maud at once and a smile spread across his face as he waved, and she ran towards him and embraced him with both arms and her lips. For a few moments they were oblivious to the world, and when they parted, blissful, unabashed and breathless, everyone broke out laughing and talking. Bertie, still holding Maud's hand, saw Beard and in a another moment he had reclaimed his hand and he and Beard were shaking hands and exchanging the sort of coarse badinage in the way of soldiers who had faced death, and couldn't believe their good fortune at being still alive. Their greeting might have been a little more boisterous, only Bertie's scarred chest was swathed in a fresh bandage and Beard hesitated about being too exuberant. Maud and Poppy embraced and started to chatter, which gave the two men a chance to catch up on each other.

"Where have you sprung from, Bobbie?" demanded Bertie.

"Here and there," replied Beard vaguely, adding a grin. "Mostly the Middle East."

"I see you're now a major and you have a Military Cross to go with the bronze oak leaves on your chest, Bobbie, so you must have helped two old ladies across the road from a pub after pinching their purses."

"Nothing as dangerous as that," returned Beard. "And you, Bertie, I hear you have a DSO, or something pretty. Does that mean you got up early one morning?"

"Something incredible like that," agreed Bertie, and then they were asking after various colleagues, and when and where the invasion was likely to take place.

After a few minutes, Beard relinquished Bertie to Maud and turned to Poppy, who looked as stunningly beautiful as ever, and with what he felt was great daring kissed her firmly on her mouth; he was delighted, and surprised, that she not only failed to pull away but even responded to his embrace, in a ladylike way. The fact that it felt a lot safer kissing her than Ruth, his supposed fiancée, amused him sufficiently to raise a grin.

"I thought your good works were confined to Dorset," Beard teased, with a twinkle in his eyes as he stepped back to look at her. "I never expected to see you here."

"Why shouldn't a sister visit her wounded hero brother?" she countered. "Come to that, I'm surprised to see you here. I understood you were still sunning yourself in the Middle East."

"We're just this moment back," he told her. "We're all enjoying a spot of leave. We're stationed near Chelmsford, but I've hardly seen the place so far, only long enough to dump my gear and grab a leave pass."

"You're looking very fit, Bobbie, but a lot older than your years," Poppy said, as she studied him openly. "Responsibility has aged you. Oh, don't be alarmed, you're as handsome as ever."

They both laughed.

"I see you are now a major – Bertie always said you'd end up a general. And you have an MC, Bobbie. Congratulations," she exclaimed. "Isn't it an adorable colour." They both smiled. "What terrible feat of daring earned you that?"

"They never tell you these things, Poppy. I expect it was a spare one they had, and my name came out of the bucket,"

She made a face at him. "Well, can you at least say where you won it?"

"The Middle East," he answered, giving her a steady smile.

Poppy knew he wouldn't say anything about his heroic deeds. Men never did, not the ones who'd faced death, and won. Bertie was the same : he told her nothing. Said he was one of the lucky ones; he'd survived. And that was it. She sighed, almost lost in her thoughts.

"How long have you known Maud?" Beard asked, breaking the spell.

"Almost since you two silly boys went running off to war," Polly replied. "Bertie had fallen in love with Maud during those few mysterious days the two of you were in London, and he wanted everyone to know it. Naturally, he told his family first, and she and I have been exchanging letters ever since. They did all their courting by letter. And since the news of Bertie's wounding, and especially since he's been back in England, we've seen quite a bit of each other. He's not allowed up for very long yet, just a couple of hours or so. Sometimes, when I've got enough petrol, I drive her down here, and then take her home with me to Highways for a break. Why don't the two of you come back with me tonight?"

"That's very kind of you, Poppy. I'd like that fine. Thanks awfully," nodded Beard, and added mischievously, "Will it be safe with Georgina around? I suppose she's still teasing half the West Country!"

"Georgina? Not a bit of it, you're quite safe, my hero," laughed Poppy musically. "She's Mrs Harvey Middleton now and has a baby daughter called Jemima, and there's another one on the way."

"I'm very pleased for her," said Beard sincerely, and added drily, "and I'm sure her marriage has made a lot of other wives very happy, too."

"I expect quite a few husbands are relieved as well," smiled Poppy.

"And I'm sure you must have many suitors queuing up in the wings yourself?" he declared inquisitively.

"Hundreds," she laughed, "but only one that matters, and he's somewhere at sea. He's Lieutenant-Commander Ben Mayhew and he's beautiful. Tall, dark and handsome, and with the loveliest smile you ever saw." She blushed and, as Beard's dark eyes looked askance, she went on, "I was already in his arms when we fell in love. We were dancing." Another blush and a smile: both exquisite. "It happens that way sometimes. One look, one touch, one word, and you know. It's sublime magic," she added, picking her words out of heaven. "His family have a huge property by the New Forest. They're farmers in a big way, mostly in Dorset and Hampshire. Ben read law at Oxford, but he's more interested in being associated with something agricultural. Auctioneering, perhaps."

"And?" pressed Beard.

"Yes, we're engaged," she admitted happily. "I have his ring, and it's beautiful too, but I don't wear it often now, when he's at sea. It makes me feel sad, and frightened, that he's not with me, but far away and in danger. I'll wear it for you one day, but not now. We plan to get married the moment the Navy lets him go."

"I imagine there'll be lots of weddings around that time. Make sure I get an invite to yours," said Beard, grinning.

"Of course."

"And in view of your kind invitation to stay, I'd better ring home – you know, The Dials, and tell Queenie." said Beard.

"Of course," nodded Poppy approvingly. "Do it now."

When he'd finished phoning Queenie, who told him to relax and enjoy himself, Beard returned to Bertie and remarked, trying to appear casual, "Apart from this self-inflicted wound of love, how are you, really?"

"Fine," declared Bertie, deciding this was a serious question. "Practically recovered."

"What he really means, Bobbie, is that when he's finally discharged from here, he'll be invalided out of the Army and we'll get married, and start from there," announced Maud, her tone in keeping with the seriousness of the discussion.

Beard had not expected otherwise, still the confirmation came hard. He wondered what on earth he'd do if placed in the same situation. The Army was all he'd ever known. All he knew was how to kill, and to keep his head down.

"So, what'll you do?" he asked Bertie.

"Don't worry about us, Bobbie," Bertie replied with a cheery grin. "I may not be of any more use to the Army, but I'm not going to sit on my backside for the rest of my life. I shall turn my attentions to the family's estates, and if Maud is happy there, we'll settle in the area. It was always my intention to turn my hand to farming when the time came. It's simply come rather sooner than I'd expected."

"Before he does anything, once the Army releases him, you're both coming home to Highways with me for a long, long rest," declared Poppy. "Maud can play nurse, while she waits to become your wife."

"Can you see her letting me rest!" cried Bertie, regarding Maud with a great deal of affection. "She'll have me grooming the horses all day and making love to her all night!"

"Who could ask for more!" laughed Maud happily, standing up and walking behind him so that she could put her arms round his neck and lay her own cheek against his. "Right now, darling, you couldn't even get your leg over a horse!"

Bertie turned his head and gave her a lengthy kiss and then, taking hold of her hands so that she stayed bending over his shoulder, he asked Beard: "Enough about my prospects, how about yours, Bobbie? What's the situation with that girl of yours? The one that was always writing to you, and sending you ridiculous presents. Only a girl in love does that sort of thing. What was her name?"

Beard coloured slightly. "Ruth," he said, after a moment's pause, as if he'd had to dig into his memory, when really, nothing was farther from the truth. He was savouring the name within himself, before imparting it to his friends. Sometimes in the past, it had irritated him to have her referred to as *his* girl because he was never sure if *he* thought she was and, if she was, whether it truly pleased him. Today, at this moment, it did. Oh, yes, it meant something now. He felt the need to have someone of his very own, someone he could open his mind and heart to, someone who would always be there understanding, comforting, encouraging and, yes, loving him – in the same way that Bertie had his Maud and Poppy had her Ben. He supposed it was being in the company of these happy people that brought these thoughts circulating so freely in his head. If only these needs didn't desert him when he was with Ruth. Why was he only having these feelings when she was out of reach? He decided it was most likely because they were both so young still. He sighed. It was a poor, unsatisfactory excuse. It didn't occur to him that he might be scared to make the move. "She's still at school," he said aloud after a long pause.

Bertie raised a quizzical eyebrow, but there was only gentle laughter in his eyes. "She's still your sweetheart, isn't she?" he said. "You engaged yet?"

Beard blushed deeper. "I think there's some sort of understanding along those lines – provided I survive the war," he answered, his voice barely more than a confused whisper, his eyes staring back with uncertainty. "I gave her a ring, at least. She regards it as a wedding ring as well as an engagement ring, so I'm not too sure of our status." He meant it seriously, and wondered if life mightn't be easier, perhaps even safer, back in the war

Maud shushed Bertie's outburst of laughter first with her lips and then by telling him, "Stop teasing Bobbie, darling."

"Just make sure you hurry back when it's all over … don't let her slip away, old man," Bertie said, when he'd finished kissing Maud and brought his amusement under control.

Beard spent four days at Highways, which had been largely taken over by Americans. Poppy's parents retained a wing which was sufficient for their current needs, and there were still rooms to accommodate Maud and Beard. On the fifth day, Beard felt an urge to be back where he belonged, in London with Queenie and Ruth, so he returned to The Dials. There was still the weekend and another whole week of his leave left.

On the Saturday, an official-looking letter arrived at The Dials addressed to Major Robert Beard, and they all sat round the kitchen table staring at the rather large envelope, postponing its opening, fearful of its contents. Beard was sure it was the usual cancellation of his leave and, with an uneasy smile all round, he finally tore open the envelope and withdrew a sheaf of papers. He studied them with great concentration, his expression changing rapidly from frowns to wonder and ending in a wide smile, and perhaps a slight blush.

"It seems I've been awarded an immediate DSO," he told the anxious faces beside him, happy surprise taking possession of his entire face. He raised a particularly officious-looking document and swished it about in the air for all the world as though he were Neville Chamberlain just returned from Munich, and grinning all over his face

"No—oo!" exclaimed Queenie in wonder.

Ruth clapped her hands. "Let's see," she cried excitedly.

Beard passed the document to her with the exhortation to treat it carefully because it was an official document.

"What's it for, Jarvis?" ventured Queenie, as Ruth read extracts from the citation, sometimes softly to herself, but mainly out loud to them all.

"Mostly for staying alive, Mum," he replied with a grin, regaining his composure.

Beard examined some of the other documents, and he grinned all over again.

"And," he announced, "my appointment as a brevet major has been approved."

"So you're a major now instead of a captain? What's the brevet mean?" queried Ruth.

"It means it's a temporary rank without extra pay," said Beard, making a wry face.

"That's not fair," Queenie declared.

"It's the Army way. The cheap way. Give the man the rank and responsibility, but not the pay."

"Congratulations anyway, Jarvis," said Queenie. "I like crowns."

Beard stared back, and grinned; it was a day for grinning.

"So, you now have two special medals – one for something you did in Poland, and the other for services in Yugoslavia. What on earth were you doing in those places, Jarvis?" gasped Ruth, still straining over the War Office document. Beard retrieved the document from her as it dipped into a saucer of marmalade.

"It's really a fuss about nothing. In Poland, I merely escorted an old man and his family home after they'd got lost, and in Yugoslavia, I was supposed to blow up a bridge, and blew up a bloody mountain instead."

"Stop swearing, lovey," smiled Queenie.

"So what happens now, Jarvis?" pressed Ruth.

"I imagine there'll be an investiture sometime, somewhere," Beard said impassively. "I'll be ordered to parade before some general who'll stab me in the chest as he pins the medal on and I'll die of lead poisoning, or," he broke into a boyish grin, "the investiture may be at Buckingham Palace, and the King will do the honours."

Queenie gasped, and touched the tips of her fingers to her mouth. *Her* Jarvis, up before the King! The wonder of it, and her fingers, kept her silent for a whole minute. Then, all she could say was, "Wouldn't that be summat!" Ruth, having clapped her hands till they hurt, simply gazed pridefully at Beard and contented herself with a long "Oo-oh" of joy.

"Of course," added Beard, straight-faced, "they may simply arrive in the post."

During the last days of his leave, Beard and Ruth were mostly alone together. They went for walks along the Embankment, and when they'd had their fill of watching the boats on the Thames, they went window-shopping in Oxford Street, visited the swimming baths where Sam had taught them both to swim, and when they had exercised enough, Ruth held his hand in a cinema, and when they remembered to eat, they did so at some very odd dockside cafés, at one of which they shared most of a yard-long eel. Though what Beard remembered most, and enjoyed most, were the frequent long kisses they exchanged; he was growing accustomed to accepting and giving kisses, and found it a pleasing occupation; he was getting better at it, too. He wondered if this meant he was truly in love, as Ruth repeatedly assured him. He was becoming more sure of it himself.

On the very last day of his leave, Queenie joined them at a posh restaurant where they danced between courses, and afterwards went to a theatre and saw a whodunit thriller –   only Ruth fell asleep towards the end and never did discover who did what to whom, for Beard and Queenie gave her differing versions and refused to budge, so infuriating her that she accused them of falling asleep too.

These last few days had been among the happiest in Beard's life. At times, Time had stood still, at others it had raced by; but now, all the days had been used up. His leave was over, and it was time for him to go and be a soldier again.

Beard had to be off before dawn the next morning, so he said his good-byes the night before, and Ruth had sobbed through every kiss, refusing to let him go, and when at last Queenie tucked her into bed she continued to weep until exhaustion laid her to rest.

Queenie, as he'd known she would be, was up to see him safely off with a flask of tea and a parcel of sandwiches big enough to feed his entire unit. It seemed that half the uniformed world was headed his way and Beard was thankful his new rank entitled him to a first-class seat and a modicum of comfort.

Chapter Twenty-nine

Investiture and Invasion, May, 1944

As Beard settled in at his new camp in Chelmsford, there were further congratulations from colleagues, several of whom were also recipients of awards. "What's the form? Do I have to book a room at the Palace, or what?" he asked Major Yeo, who was receiving a bar to his DSO; Gibbs was receiving a similar decoration.

"They'll let you know when they want you, Robert. Apart from your gongs, the only thing you're likely to get out of the occasion is two days' leave – that's the going rate for medals. As for a room at the palace, you blighter – it's in one door, straight out through another and no loitering in between ... best bib and tucker, your bloody smartest salute to anyone who gives you a glance, and it's 'Yes-sir, no-sir, three bags full, sir' – and not another word, or you'll end up in the Tower. So, no telling HM any lascivious stories – he's heard them all before. But for the moment, the form is that you present yourself in the mess forthwith and buy all your brother heroes a drink!"

"Will I sober up in time for the investiture?" asked Beard, pretending anxiety.

"Who cares!"

Beard gave a pretended shudder at the thought, but his face couldn't conceal the pleasure which still welled within him. He'd felt ten foot tall when Queenie had stitched the new red and blue ribbon on his tunics.

Gibbs had been promoted to brigadier and Major Yeo was now a colonel, and the group had been considerably enlarged and reorganised. It now comprised three squadrons, each with four to five troops of up to twenty men, and each commanded by a major. Beard was given Squadron C, with a Capt Louis Clapton as his second in command, and two other officers: Lts Giles Summerbee and Colin Pardoe. Beard led the 1st Troop, Clapton the 2nd and Pardoe, newly promoted to captain, the 3rd.

Summerbee, tall, slim and darkly handsome with a formidable moustache, quite the equal of Gibbs's, came highly recommended direct from the Brigade of Guards. Pardoe, who was shorter, rounder and with a mop of black hair, had previously served in the Parachute Regiment and taken part in the Torch landings in Algeria, but his main recommendation was being fluent in French which someone "up there" thought might be useful "over there."

Beard guessed that he had someone else "up there" – probably Gibbs himself – to thank for the inclusion of many of his old companions, notably Sgt-major Trumpett, Sgt Stubbs, Cpls Jenkins, Felbridge and Simms, all of whom he assigned to his troop. Most of the newcomers had seen action somewhere, those who hadn't had skills that made them equally important. A newcomer was Pte Tony Blossom, who was in the Jenkins mould. Fair-haired and with a round, cheeky face, his last address had been Colchester glasshouse, though he had excelled himself previously for he had been a corporal and wore a DCM ribbon. Beard grabbed him for his Troop.

Capt Clapton proved to be an excellent organiser and his cheerful energy and enthusiasm ensured that he got what he wanted, which was the very best out of the men. He and Summerbee were largely responsible for the training programme, which left Beard free to give lectures and demonstrations when required as well as joining in planning issues presided over by Brigadier Gibbs. The training, which Beard joined in when he was free to do so, went on relentlessly, day and night, and included realistic battle courses which had a way of knocking the cockiness out of those who thought they knew it all.

Early in April, Beard rang The Dials. "Mum?" he shouted in the way of people on the phone when speaking over long distances. "I shall be coming to London for a couple of days on the 18th – that's a Tuesday. Can you make sure you and Ruth are free?"

Queenie, who had been busy in her kitchen and whose arms were flaked in flour and hands sticky with dough, bawled back: "Is that you, Jarvis?"

Beard grinned. "No, it isn't, Mum – it's Robert Beard!"

Queenie chuckled. "What's the matter, darling? Are you in trouble, lovey?" she asked, immediately concerned.

"No, Mum," Beard assured her. "We're going to a party and you and Ruth must be on your best behaviour and put on your best frocks. I'll be calling for you at 11ack emma. We have to go somewhere first, and then we're having a big celebration. Now, write the date and time down carefully, and tell Ruth or you'll go and forget it."

Queenie stared at the mouthpiece. She'd never liked telephones; it seemed an unnatural way of conversing; she liked to see to whom she was talking, not have the words floating disconnected through the air. "What's it all abaht, Jarvis?" she asked anxiously, trying to recognise his face in the horrid mouthpiece. "You're not doin' a bunk from the Army, is yer?"

Beard laughed gaily. "No, darling, nothing like that. Nothing's wrong at all. It's a happy day – and they've given me two days' leave to get over it!" He could almost hear Queenie's brain ticking over.

"Can't yer give me a 'int at wot it's all abaht, Jarvis?" she cried, peering desperately into the mouthpiece.

"We're off to keep an appointment you should have kept with

Sam, Mum," he told her teasingly, after a moment deciding how to tell her.

She knew straight away. "It's the Palace! Oh, Jarvis! You're goin' to get yer medals! We'll see the King! We will see 'im, won't we? Really an' truly? Oh, Jarvis, Ruth'll be so excited!" She was close to strangling the mouthpiece in her own excitement.

"Now, Mum, it's supposed to be secret ... so don't tell Ruth or Lord Haw-Haw will be spouting about it on the wireless."

Queenie giggled, and decided the telephone wasn't really so awful after all – sometimes; she renewed her wary inspection of the dark hole from which his voice came crackling through. "I'll 'ave to tell 'er summat, Jarvis. She'll want to know what's so special about the date," she insisted.

"Well, be careful, Mum ... tell her that if she goes blabbing all over London, I'll be court-martialled, cashiered and the King'll have me hung, drawn and quartered!"

Queenie stared at the mouthpiece which was suddenly hateful to her again; she didn't believe what it said, but you never knew – not these days. "Oh!" was all she could manage.

"And, Mum, you simply must remember to call me Robert Beard – or the same thing will happen!" Beard warned her.

"Oh!" said Queenie again, but this time she smiled.

"And you must impress upon Ruth to do the same," he told her.

"Yes, Jarvis," she whispered back.

The day of the investiture arrived. It was dull, wet, windy and cold, but Beard hardly noticed such trivialities. He was scarcely aware of anything that day, and remembered very little more after. It was a magical day: a day when the world stood still and dreams came true. All those receiving decorations and many others besides were gathering for the party that was to follow. Beard had hoped that Bertie would be present, but Maud told him over the phone that he was still confined to hospital and would have to await his turn.

Beard arrived at The Dials promptly at 11 o'clock to find Queenie in a dressing-gown and her hair in a confusion of paper curlers, and screaming at Ruth, who was flitting about in a slip and very little else, to "get yer skates on an' make yerself decent ... or I'll wallop yer be'ind – an' leave yer be'ind!" Ruth was ready long before Queenie, but eventually both presented themselves to Beard in a manner that suggested he had kept them waiting. He didn't mind a bit; he had said 11 o'clock knowing that neither would be ready on time, and their taxi arrived, as arranged, at 12.15 – still with two hours before they were due at the Palace.

If they were proud of him, Beard was equally proud of his two ladies. He thought Ruth looked absolutely gorgeous in the green dress she had told him about so often and which was now to have its first public airing – and before the King! Her dark hair hung in neat waves and curls around her shining face and an absurd little white hat, a cousin of a skullcap, sat on her head with a filmy net hanging from it and covering her forehead. Her velvet brown eyes shone with a radiance that intensified the longer she gazed at Beard, as though he were the king. For the rest, she wore a sort of shawl, or perhaps it was a stole, across her shoulders, her coral necklace and the bracelet he'd bought and, of course, her "engagement" ring which now fitted snugly on the appropriate finger of her left hand. Indeed, her appearance took his breath away, so much so that he simply stared and it was not until a frown appeared in her eyes that he realised he was expected to say something approving.

"You look lovely," he said with quick simplicity, his eyes continuing to shine with admiration. It was enough: all she wanted to hear. With a joyous cry, she bounded forward and flung her arms round his neck, kissing him with eager energy – and only withdrew when Queenie told her to take care not to crease her dress or muss her hair, and then only withdrew so that she could admire him in her turn. Beard was dressed in Bertie's dress uniform with creases so sharp they looked almost painful; and what with a positively shiny Sam Browne belt and shoes that gleamed like glass, he really was a breath-taking figure.

"You look lovely too, Jarvis!" she exclaimed breathlessly, clapping her hands.

Beard, who was inclined to agree with her, gave her a small bow and a rather boyish grin – as he smoothed out imaginary creases she'd created in his uniform.

Queenie, who thought they both looked gorgeous, had thought when she'd first seen herself in her bedroom mirror that she looked rather like a red barrage balloon; but that had only been her first impression. Now, she thought perhaps she didn't look too bad after all, not so much like a huge blood-red sun, more ... more like a proud mother who was off to see the King in his Palace with her children. No, she'd do, she told herself. The sense of the occasion made her feel beautiful, and knowing that was all that mattered. Her face glowed with happiness and was reflected in her eyes. Unusually, she had spent a long time over her appearance, and Mavis had done wonders with her unruly hair. Well, at least it was safely out of sight beneath her enormous cherry-coloured hat, which had a brim so wide she'd be dry in the heaviest cloudburst – which was quite on the cards. It had been quite impossible to find a pair of elbow-length gloves to cover her navvy-like arms and she'd had to settle for a pair of satiny gloves – and already there was a split in one of them. But none of this mattered, she felt like a queen as Beard told them both it was time to go.

He presented each of them with an orchid he'd obtained from

Mrs Molly, and led the way to the waiting taxi to the cheers of most of the street who were gathered on the pavement to add their voices so as to share in the royal appointment. Jarvis was one of their own.

If the taxi ride seemed to be over before it had started, the business at the Palace seemed to take for ever, and yet it was hard to remember anything about it afterwards. Beard remembered the pompous officials, Queenie and Ruth being whisked away to be seated at a designated place from which they could watch the proceedings, and the tedious queuing as he climbed the stairway to the first floor reception room where the presentations were to be made; identities and the decorations to be received were double-checked, places in the line-up changed, and then he was ushered into the room itself with a batch of five other men, his name was checked one last time, and slowly he moved further inside the ornate room, standing still every few moments and moving forward again a pace or two when directed, and finally he was at the front ... the next time he moved it would be to stand before his King.

When the moment arrived, Beard moved like an automaton. He stood to attention, straight as a ramrod, and stared straight in front without really seeing anything; he was conscious when the medals were placed on the tiny hooks attached to his uniform and remembered to shove his hand forward for the ritual handshake, and assumed the limpness of the touch was due to the King having had to do the same thing a hundred times already. Thank God he hadn't given the hand a right royal squeeze as he might have done ordinarily.

"Congratulations, Mr Beard," said a voice: it was the King's! "Two decorations ... very well done indeed." Beard blinked. "Sir!" he responded dutifully, and a whisper at his elbow sent him marching smartly away.

The celebrations began with a lavish dinner at a West End restaurant, and continued with an orchestra for dancing, and a bar that was unlikely to run dry in a week. Once the heroes of the day had tired of inventing stories concerning their deeds, which was pretty soon because nobody was in the mood to listen, Beard introduced Queenie and Ruth to as many of his particular friends as he was able. Most had wives, sweethearts, girlfriends or parents present, and those who had none of these things had brought their mistresses – even if they had only been acquired that day. Sgt Stubbs, who was rumoured to be the most married man in the British Army, although of course only one of them was a legal affair, brought two of his "wives" – and they both seemed to get on extraordinarily well together.

Ruth was quickly claimed by Beard's friends for dances, and though she would far sooner have danced every dance with Beard, she enjoyed the novelty of being the centre of attraction and happily moved into the arms of successive partners – just so long as she didn't entirely lose sight of him. Queenie, too, was frequently asked to dance – once she'd removed her hat which otherwise would have created acres of space around her – but she quickly tired and was quite happy to sit and chat with other parents and watch the young ones enjoying themselves.

At the height of the party, Ruth overheard one of Beard's men telling the others "watch out, lads, that's the Boss's girl," and her heart sang with pride at the realisation that they were talking of her. She rushed to tell Beard, flying at him with such force that they both finished sitting on the floor, which didn't greatly please her, though she burst out laughing at first, for he showed little inclination to get up again. "Of course you're my girl, Ruth," Beard told her in a flood of kisses, "you've got my ring, haven't you?" She nodded, her eyes gleaming with sheer happiness, and whispered, "Yes, darling, and it's mine for ever, and so are you."

They were both hoisted back to their feet by a forest of willing hands, and Beard seemed perfectly sober again once he was standing upright. Ruth took no chances after that and tried her hardest to retain him for her exclusive use, whether for dancing, singing, talking or simply sitting holding hands. But he must have succeeded in eluding her fairly frequently for when the party broke up and everyone dispersed, he had to be carried shoulder high to the waiting taxi – and his jacket was bedizened with Iron Crosses!

He was still first up in the morning, unaware that he'd slept through the last blitz on London, and not too sure where he was – until Queenie placed his breakfast before him: bacon, eggs, sausages, tomatoes, mushrooms, kidneys, black pudding, fried bread – the lot! What she called a breakfast fit for a hero. However he felt, Beard left the plate spotless. By tradition, orphans didn't leave food on their plates, not even when they were grown up and hungover, and had stood before the King..

And suddenly, his two days' leave was over. Next morning, he returned to the war.

The training gathered in momentum; when they weren't on realistic battle exercises, they were jumping out of aircraft, marching across moors, climbing over frozen mountains or clambering up cliff faces – generally in the pitch black of night and in the teeth of biting winds and driving rain. Rest periods were taken up with lectures ranging from the use of explosives to communications by wireless, or any other means that might be available; and for good measure, Beard and Capt Pardoe tried teaching the men a few basic phrases in German and French. The results were more comical than promising.

Early in May there were frequent disappearances of senior

officers, and though no explanation of these absences was given it was obvious that they were concerned with the impending invasion: the long-awaited Second Front. Then, around the middle of the month, Beard and a number of other middle-rank officers were summoned to a SHAEF briefing at Windlesham, near Virginia Water in Surrey, where, in an underground room the size of a football pitch, they were told the precise nature of their job in occupied France, but still they were given no idea as to the location of where they would operate, nor, of course, when they might expect to be off – except that it would be soon, probably.

Their task, wherever and whenever it might be, would be to set up secret camps, liaise with the Résistance groups and try to co-ordinate their activities to coincide with D-Day, and, of course, to be ready to create havoc themselves with the enemy's supply lines; they had also to work in close harmony with other Special Forces units, like the SAS and SOE. The collection of information, so accurate as to provide the RAF with pin-point targets, and the speedy communication of it to GHQ, was regarded as paramount : the vital element of their work. There was almost too much for the brain to absorb, but somehow it was; it had to be; their lives, and those of their men, depended on it.

Finally, Gibbs's men vacated their Apple Tree camp overnight and dispersed to a number of airfields where, as the senior officers had been told the date of D-Day, they were sealed in. Beard and half his squadron, who were locked in at Keevil aerodrome in Wiltshire, were scheduled to spearhead the start of things on the night of Thursday, May 25; Capt Clapton and Lt Summerbee, with the remainder of C Squadron were to follow on the Saturday, while Gibbs and the other two squadrons would follow on Sunday, mainly from Fairford airfield in Gloucestershire. For all, the war games were over, and the battle was about to commence.

Beard and his officers were shown detailed maps of the areas in which they would be operating. The details on the maps were quite extraordinary; as one beaming colonel informed them, "Ignore that haystack, gentlemen, it's not there any more. The farmer started using it yesterday and it was mostly gone this morning." This may well have been part of his morale-boosting spiel, but the maps were incredibly detailed and even as they examined them fresh information was being added all the time. Someone "over there" was working overtime tapping out messages.

They all spent their final hours in England memorizing freshly-issued maps of their landing area, especially where they were to rendezvous with the reception committee, who might be Maquis or the SOE. Then they studied the detailed maps of the areas in which they would be operating : they studying went on till they almost knew every back door into Paris. When they tired of this, which was when they were nearly blind, they checked their equipment and mountains of supplies, the bulkiest of which was ammo, and tucked into a very substantial dinner of steak and chips. Afterwards, they checked their parachutes, and the officers attended a final briefing. There was time for a short sleep, though some, like Beard, wrote letters ... and then, after giving their parachutes a final inspection, they were on their way out to the Stirling bomber that was to fly them to their destination. Rain slapped them in their faces as they walked. At this stage only Beard knew the date of D-Day. He planned to tell his officers once they landed in France.

It was 23.17 hrs on Thursday, May 25; they were due to jump at 02.00 next day.

"Where we going, boss?" joked Jenkins, as the plane gathered speed for the take-off.

"Paris!" shouted back Beard, with a grin to the rest of the men.

For them the invasion of France was under way.   Operation Overlord had started.

□   *"It were a loverly day when 'e got 'is medals," sighed Queenie, and having had one big sigh she indulged in another pleasurable one, and then smiled. "We 'ad a King then, now we got 'is daughter fer a Queen, an' now we got our Jarvis back wiv us – pity is, 'e don't know none of this. We talk away, an' 'e don't know nuffink abaht wot we're talkin' abaht. It's such a awful shame."*

"I'm sorry about that, Queenie," said Beard sincerely, raising his head fractionally to see her better. "It's terrible for you, I know, and I suppose if that's true, it must be terrible for me, too. The difference being you know it, and I don't. But I hope we haven't come to the end of your story, because I'm finding it quite fascinating. I can't fathom how I can be this Jarvis of yours, but he seems to bear a charmed life. In view of my presence and condition here, I almost wish I were him."

"Well, you are, lovey," said Queenie, heaving another sigh. "I've just about done wiv the story for now. D-Day is upon us, and someone else will 'ave to tell yer abaht that 'cos I know nuffink abaht military affairs or wot you done in 'em."

"Well, I expect that part is down to me, too," declared Gibbs, who had already been contributing much of these details. He gave himself a stretch and added, "But we'll have to break it off for a couple of days, because Matron insists that Major Beard has a complete rest from us all, and as you know, she is the general here."

There was a small titter among the visitors and the Matron, Miss Ivy Flinn, explained in an authoritative voice, "As you will be aware, the needs of a patient take precedence over all else. There are treatments that require continuation, and other things."

"No more operations, please?" cried Queenie anxiously.

"That's for the surgeons to decide, but I don't believe so,"

answered the Matron, giving Queenie a comforting pat on the hand.

"The break will be good for all of us," declared Mr Fennell firmly. "It'll give me the chance to hunt up Ruth. The latest information I have is that she is no longer in America, but tootling around in Canada – which is no great help, of course."

"It'll also give me the opportunity to study Ruth's letters to Beard about this time," said Gibbs. "When we reconvene, I'll continue with Mr Beard's subsequent career, starting with his role in the Invasion of France."

But it didn't quite work out that way because on the second day of their break, Mr Fennell finally made contact with Ruth, and for the moment D-Day was put on hold, and Ruth herself took centre stage.

Chapter Thirty

Ontario, Canada, August 11, 1959

Ruth was driving north along Route 10 out of Westport, Ontario, Canada, heading nowhere in particular, in the back were Damien and Edna Hatch, his nanny, when the car phone buzzed. It was a brilliantly sunny day, the top was down and her dark hair was flying in the breeze; and she had to drive a mile or two until she saw a suitable place to pull-in off the road and she could call back on the phone.

"Hello," she cried into the mouthpiece, her voice louder than usual because she was speaking to someone three thousand miles away. It was the first time they'd spoken that year and it was a minor miracle that he'd been able to get her number, which was new, since she had been touring for several months and hadn't had much cause to call home in Vermont. "Hello, John. How are things? Mother keeping well?"

It was a poor connection and some words seemed to somehow get garbled in transmission, but she picked up the name Jarvis and was immediately all ears and doubly attentive. "I didn't catch that, John … what was that about Jarvis? Is he home? Is he on leave? What's that, John? Oh." There was a tightness in her throat as a feeling of unease touched her. "Is he all right?"

John Fennell gripped the phone tighter and had another go. "No, darling, I'm afraid he's not. Jarvis was badly injured in Oman – that's near Saudi Arabia, in January, but he's now in a military hospital here in London."

"Is he all right?" Ruth asked again. "Is he recovering?" she pressed, amazed at the calmness of her voice, when inside she was in a turmoil of anxiety. She'd never heard of Oman but gathered it was in Persia, which she knew vaguely about.

"He's recovering, but it's a slow business," shouted John, unsure if his words were getting through, there was so much interference on the line. He wondered how much to tell her, not wanting to frighten her. Queenie had told him Ruth had to be told, but he had to be gentle. How was that possible with the news he had to impart? "Jarvis was unconscious for a couple of months, but now seems to be mending." Mr Fennell paused to consider how to continue. "But, there is a problem," he added simply, and paused again.

Ruth waited for him to continue: a second seemed interminable; and after two of these endless aeons, she jumped in and demanded, "What's the problem, John? Tell me, at once." Her last words came in a half-shriek of fear. Her mind ran wild as she imagined every possible injury: a leg, an arm … ; she daren't imagine further.

"It's a form of amnesia," John told her in a rush of words. "He has absolutely no memory of either events or people prior to the explosion." He knew at once he shouldn't have used that word, but it was out now, and perhaps it was for the best. She'd have found out soon enough. "He didn't know his own name when he regained consciousness, nor even that he was in the Army. Nor does he know anyone, not even people closely associated with him …like General Gibbs. Not even Queenie herself. She's beside herself, though she tries hard not to show it. She's got it all bottled up inside her. One of these days she's going to have an explosion of her own. I'm afraid for both of them." And he knew straightaway he should never have said that, either.

"I'm coming straight home, John," Ruth told him without further consideration. It was something she had no control over. If Jarvis was hurting, she simply had to be with him. She was quite convinced in her mind and heart that Jarvis would know her the instant he saw her; she refused to think otherwise. She dare not. "Just tell me what hospital he's at and tell Mum not to worry. Everything's going to be OK. I'll probably see you tomorrow." She wrote down the name, Millbank Military Hospital, Embankment, Room 601.

"How'd you like to go to England, Edna?" she asked the dark-haired, red-lipped young girl sitting beside Damien.

"Oh, yes!" exclaimed Edna quickly, her brown eyes sparkling with excitement. "When?"

"Today!"

"Oh!" Edna's loose hair bobbled as she nodded her head furiously.

Ruth spent an hour on the phone at the restaurant in Perth where they stopped to eat. She fixed overnight flights for the three of them from Ottawa to London Heathrow, arranged for her car to be suitably garaged until her return, phoned her bank so that she could collect travellers' cheques in Ottawa and in London, picked out a suitable hotel for their stay and rang the family back in Vermont to explain things, and did the same for lawyer Tyrell. And when she'd finished phoning, she gave an audible sigh of satisfaction. She hadn't been a personal secretary to the boss for nothing!

Returning her attention to Damien and Edna, she exclaimed, "What's good to eat? I'm starving!"

Ruth arrived, a little breathless, at Millbank Hospital late in the afternoon next day with armfuls of flowers, fruit and chocolates – and a large smile that contained equal measures of love, hope and anxiety, and all the courage she could muster.

When she was shown into his ward – it was really a large private room – and saw Jarvis lying prone on his bed, his body so still it was as though he were lying on a bier, she dropped everything, gave a strangled cry and ran to his bedside. All that courage she had relied on dissipated in that first sight of him. She did not know what she had expected, but the sight of the tubes and other gadgets into which he appeared to be plugged unnerved her; they scared her half to death.

Before Ruth could reach the bedside, Queenie rose from her chair hidden behind a screen, and caught hold of her daughter, and held her fast. "Leave him be, dearie," she cried, "he's only sleeping. It's not a natural sleep, though. It's call an induced sleep. They 'ad ter do sumfink to 'im this morning, so there's nuffink yer can do to wake 'im up. He'll come out of it presently, an' I'm sure the moment 'e sees yer, he'll remember ev'ryfink. You'll see."

Nurse Willoughby, having collected the flowers, chocolates and most of the fruit – another nurse was pursuing some apples and an orange that were rolling determinedly across the floor – that Ruth had dropped, had put the flowers in a vase close to Jarvis, and now approached mother and daughter and returned the other things to Ruth. "Don't be frightened, darling," she told Ruth, "he'll be awake again in time for tea." The nurse looked at her fob watch, and added, "About half-an-hour. I'll get you a cuppa to keep you going till then. Nothing we can do till he wakes, can we, ducks?"

The moment the nurse had gone, Ruth handed the chocolates and fruit to Queenie and tip-toed towards the bed. She stared down at his face, and was relieved to see that it was quite undamaged, and as beautiful as ever. Well, there were a couple of fading scars and, now that she looked closer, his nose looked slightly different – like it had been broken and repaired, which it had; and looked better for it, she thought. He seemed to be breathing normally; she watched the rising and falling of his chest beneath his blanket. She dreaded to think what horrors lay hidden under the blanket. She was wondering if she dared kiss him – she needed to touch him, to feel the warmth of him – when Nurse Willoughby appeared at her elbow with a cup of tea. Ruth sipped at it gratefully. The drink gave her the moment she needed to summon up the courage to ask, "Is he … all there?" She was almost as fearful of the answer as she had been to ask the question. A smile, accompanied by several nods, were almost assurances enough, but Nurse Willoughby confirmed them with words. "As good as new," she said positively.

Ruth smiled gratefully, and thankfully, and the pain of fear she'd felt in her breast subsided. She took several deep breaths and, after another sip at her tea, asked if it would be all right to kiss him.

"Gently, dear," Nurse Willoughby told her, taking back the cup and saucer.

Ruth bent over Beard's sleeping form. She didn't dare use her hands in case she disturbed something under his covers. Her face hovered above his : she could feel the warmth of him now, and the little puffs of his steady breathing. She looked at his eyes, but they were shut tight, as they would be since he was sleeping. Her lips now closed over his mouth, and she bestowed a gentle kiss, as instructed. She kept her lips on his for as long as she dared. It lasted only a moment or two. There was no response, of course. She felt a disappointment, almost as if she'd expected her kiss to waken him from his slumber, like in the fairytales.

She straightened up, retrieved her tea, and took a sip to hide her despondency. The nurse brought her a chair, and she sat down automatically.

"You're Ruth, aren't you?" said Nurse Willoughby. "From America?"

Ruth nodded listlessly, her eyes fixed on Jarvis; she ignored his other name.

"I'm Susan," said the nurse. "I was here when he first opened his eyes and spoke. He just looked at me and said the one word, 'Ruth?' He was asking me if I was you, because he didn't know. It was then we realised he had amnesia. Yours is the only name he remembers."

Ruth turned to smile at the nurse. "That's nice. It's a small comfort. Thank you, Susan." She turned back to face Jarvis.

"We've all been waiting to see you, Ruth, hoping that when he saw you something would snap, and his memory would return," said Nurse Willoughby.

"Oh, I do so hope so," exclaimed Ruth desperately. "Surely he will? He must."

"We'll just have to wait and see, won't we. Just be patient, Ruth." She must be patient and let him rest, and not excite him, said Nurse Willoughby.

What impossible strictures!

Ruth nodded acquiescingly. "I'll sit here with him, if that's all right?" she said. "I'd like it if I'm the first person he sees when he wakes up. He's bound to recognise me. We're to be married. God, I hope he remembers that … it's been so long."

Nurse Willoughby patted her shoulder. "Sit as long as you like, dear," she said, and padded off.

Ruth was still sat looking into his face when Jarvis's eyes suddenly opened. They both blinked at each other simultaneously. He stared back at her, and in a coming-awake-croaking sort of voice said, "Hello."

"Hello, my darling," Ruth whispered back, hope soaring within her as she half-smiled.

Beard, his vision improving with every blink, liked what he saw. She was beautiful, and he liked what she called him. But why had she? Was she another of these people who claimed to have played a part in this other life of his? Oh, he hoped so. But she was a newcomer to the scene. He hadn't seen her before. "Who are you?" he asked quietly.

Inside, Ruth gave a silent sob. He didn't know her: he hadn't remembered her! She wanted to scream her disappointment, and let her tears flow freely, but told herself she mustn't; and somehow, she didn't. She kept all her frustration and hurt bottled up within her. Only, she thought, this was so unfair after all the years of missing each other. They'd promised themselves to each other following their latest reconciliation; both had been desperate to take their love to its highest level: marriage. They'd repeated this to each other in their latest exchange of letters which seemed like only yesterday, but might have been months or even years ago. Too many years? Oh God, she breathed, give us a break!

"I'm Ruth," she replied, almost defiantly. It seemed absurd he didn't recognise her.

"Ah, Ruth. The girl in the story," he said, easing himself up slightly, the better to see her. He examined her closely, taking in her very American clothing: the neat, beige suit and cream blouse, and her lovely free-hanging brown hair; and he noticed the coral necklace about which he'd heard mentioned several times. "You look very beautiful, Ruth. A bit like one of those film stars. But, I'm sorry, I don't know you."

"Oh, Jarvis! How can you not know me?" exclaimed Ruth wildly, "We've known each since we were children. We've loved each other all the while. We've been engaged for almost half my life. I've been waiting for ever for you to come back from your wars."

Beard had a feeling of embarrassment, which seemed unnatural since he didn't know the girl. He gave her as much of a shrug as he could manage in his prone position. "Why do you keep calling me Jarvis? The name keeps cropping up in the story they're telling. But I'm told, and my documents bear this out, that my name is Beard. Major Robert Beard," he told her, almost apologetically.

"Your name is Jarvis Brook," Ruth insisted impatiently, and if she hadn't been sitting down she would have stamped her foot in frustration. "You only took on the name of Beard to get into the Army. I've always called you Jarvis – and always shall, because that's who you are. Surely you read it in my letters?"

Beard stared blankly back at her. As with the others, he had no remembrance of her. He did not know her. "I'm most awfully sorry – Ruth," he murmured. "I know nothing of these letters of yours, I only know what's been told me."

"Darling, how can you possibly not remember me … we made love, for Christ's sake!" exclaimed Ruth, challenging him to forget that single exquisite night. "It was wonderful."

"I wish I could remember that, at least, but I can't. I'm sorry ;

very sorry," Beard said slowly, and very quietly. "I'd love to," he added, and there was sincerity, perhaps pain, in his eyes.

The tears she had striven so hard to control burst out in a flood, and Ruth felt an arm circle her shoulders and lead her away. Queenie whispered in her ear that everything would be all right, in the end. "It's his first sight of you, lovey," she said, as if this meant anything to her in that moment, "let's get you back to your hotel. A hot bath, a good meal and a sound sleep is what you need. Start afresh tomorrow. Besides, I'm dying to see Damien." She'd never seen her grandson in the flesh, only in photos, and they'd never been very good – blurry.

The hotel, quaintly called The Sweetings, occupied a corner site in one of those quiet side streets near St James's Park. It looked very posh, and expensive. Ruth had a first-floor suite, and an extra room for Damien. Queenie had never known such luxury, but felt immediately at home as she hugged Damien.

□ *Back in the hospital two days later, Ruth was introduced to the small clique of people who had been listening and contributing to Beard's history, and expressed approval for the story to continue. "I think I have to let the name Beard stand for the time being, or we'll be in a terrible muddle. Only in my heart will he remain Jarvis Brook," she told them with a smile. Robert Beard, today seated in a wheelchair, supported by many pillows, fixed his eyes on Ruth, as the others settled down to listen as his history was continued. Gibbs, taxing his own memory and depending heavily on those of many others, resumed with Beard's landing in France a few days ahead of D-Day.*

Chapter Thirty-one

Somewhere in France, Friday, 26 May, 1944

Beard followed the last of the supply canisters out of the plane, and the rest of the men followed behind. After falling like a diving tern for what seemed an eternity, he was jerked in the opposite direction as his parachute opened up, and he started breathing again. Ignoring the freezing wind, he felt the rain driving stingingly into his face, and looking about him all he could see were black clouds. It was even blacker beneath him. There was no sign of the three beacons they'd spotted from the aircraft only moments before. Instinctively, he grabbed at the quick-release and began paying out the rope attached to his kitbag until it was dangling some twenty feet below him. It seemed he had been falling for hours, but he knew it was closer to seconds ... and then he saw a light flashing off to the left, a series of flashes, and he endeavoured to guide the parachute in that direction. Well, at least a reception committee was there. He hoped it was a friendly one.

It had been a virtually uneventful flight – the only excitement being when the pilot took evasive action to avoid some determined flak, and Pardoe had spilt his mug of tea all over himself. It had been dismally dark inside the blacked-out plane; a blue-coloured bulb which provided the only light wasn't enough to enable the men to do anything useful, and so occasionally one or other of them would doze off before a sudden plummeting of the plane jerked them awake again. It was a relief when the RAF dispatcher took up his position by the door, even if the signs of strain and tension on their faces increased.

Beard made a good landing, even if it was a bit on the heavy side; he rolled expertly, and almost immediately was on his feet and gathering in his parachute. He glanced about him, hoping to see his men, but all he could make out were some vague figures in the distance gathering up some of the supply containers and scuttling off with them. He hoped they were part of the reception committee and that the supplies were being moved as rapidly as possible to a place of safety, and not being nicked. He was to learn that the French indulged in such wholesale pilferings with far greater expertise and energy than ever they showed in combating the enemy. It was not an encouraging introduction to his new allies, though he did find some Frenchmen he came to trust – just a very few.

He whirled round at the sound of voices and running feet and saw three figures approaching out of the rain. All were armed, and their weapons were pointing straight at him. The nearest, a shortish man with a dark round face and a beret pulled down over his eyes, pulled up when he was about twenty yards away, approached a few more paces, and came to a stop. His various odours advanced alone to assail Beard's nostrils. The ungodly mixture included *vin ordinaire*, whatever the French were using to make *ersatz* cigarettes these days, garlic – and other smells that were best left unspecified. Beard wondered how on earth the fool expected to evade the enemy, let alone ambush them, when they could smell him half a mile away. The man advanced a couple more paces, peered somewhat disparagingly at Beard, seemed about to smile and, instead, fingered the huge pistol at his waist and asked:

"*Jean-Luc?*"

It was the code-name Beard had been given. "*Si; c'est moi,*" he replied in what he hoped was adequate French. It seemed to be for the Frenchman broke into a smile and, stepping forward the last two paces, shook Beard's hand with Gallic enthusiasm, and then embraced him on both cheeks; he was unshaven and to Beard the greeting was like having his face scraped with sandpaper. He was glad to extricate himself from the man, who introduced himself as Rémy.

Rémy was anxious to get away from the landing site before the Germans got a fix on the place, and pulled urgently on Beard's arm. But Beard, while just as eager to be off, held back and shook his arm free. He wasn't going anywhere without his men. Jenkins and Felbridge were the first to come looming out of the darkness, the rain dripping off them. Both were breathing hard for, apart from their kitbags and the various items festooned about their bodies, they were carrying one of the supply canisters between them.

"Thought we'd better grab this one, sir," muttered Jenkins, eyeing Rémy with ill-concealed distrust, "the Frogs is disappearin' in all directions wiv the rest. You sure they're on our side?"

Capt Pardoe, the linguist, was the next to come loping up, and Beard at once took him aside and asked him to find out what was happening to the supplies that had landed with them, and also where was the British agent who was supposed to meet them here. Rémy must have caught the gist of their conversation for, the moment Pardoe began his translating, he launched into a torrent of indignant and excitable verbiage, each word of which was accompanied by a belligerent gesture of his arms and hands. The flow seemed never ending but, as his face grew darker and more offended, Rémy came to an abrupt halt and just as suddenly his face calmed down and he gave them all a quite pleasant smile.

"I think you've hurt M. Rémy's feelings, Robert," declared Pardoe, turning and giving Beard a wink. "He assures me that our supplies are safe and insists that it is routine for the reception committee to disperse such items the instant they're landed. They will be housed in various safe places against our need for them. Mind you, he does admit it's usual for 'a small proportion' of the supplies to go missing in transit.

As for our missing agent, whose name appears to be Mireille and not Mariel as we were told, I gather that he'll be waiting for us when we reach M. Rémy's camp. Right now – and I'd say the fellow's right, it's imperative we get the hell away from here. Rémy has transport waiting for us."

At that moment, Trumpett came lumbering up with one of the Maquis; between them they carried another of the canisters. Beard was wondering what dire threats from the sergeant-major had induced this co-operation, when he saw Trumpett's expression and all thoughts froze in his head.

"It's Hughie Kendal, sir. He's dead," said Trumpett gravely, his rain-streaked face quite grey in its anguish, his eyes deep pools of misery.

Beard stared disbelievingly. "Dead? How?" he cried incredulously. There'd been no firing, and Kendal was too experienced a parachutist to make a faulty landing.

"Came down in a tree – the only bleedin' one around," said Trumpett bitterly. "Head got caught in a fork ... almost got torn from his body."

"Where is he now?" asked Beard wretchedly.

"We buried him, sir – Frenchie here and me. He's called Gaspar," Trumpett indicated the Maquis who had helped him with the canister. "Shallow grave. I've taken note of its position – an' I've got Kendal's kit and personal effects, sir."

Beard nodded. "Thank you, Jack. Share the extra load among the chaps," he said flatly, then exclaimed: "We'd better shoot off, like the Frog says. Mr Pardoe is checking the men in and directing them to the transport that's waiting for us." There was still a delay of some moments as Gaspar stepped forward and insisted, solemnly, on shaking Beard's hand over and over again, and then the others in the landing party.

Beard, Pardoe and Jenkins squeezed into a Citroen which already held Rémy, the driver and three others – and with all eight of them brandishing weapons conditions inside were fraught with danger, discomfort and sometimes real pain. The car lurched forward, spraying water everywhere, with what seemed an alarming level of noise and exuding evil-smelling smoke from its rusty exhaust. The remainder of Beard's men, plus swarms of swarthy Maquis resembling pirates rather than freedom fighters, piled into a lopsided, tarpaulin-covered, bone-shaking lorry that appeared to be made up of bits and pieces of all manner of vehicles, and, from its acrid smell, ran on charcoal or some such fuel. Whatever their ancestry and other deficiencies, both vehicles sped away with creditable, if alarming, speed, hurtling along a sort of unmade-up track for more than an hour, and might have gone on for ever had not a man with a bicycle standing in a puddle in the middle of their path compelled them to stop. The man had a quick, urgent conversation with Rémy and their driver concerning (so Pardoe whispered to Beard and Jenkins) a German armoured car patrolling the main road about two miles ahead. The driver immediately swung off the track, ignoring the agonized squealing of the gears, crashed through some undergrowth and proceeded with scarcely any let up in speed along something that was barely more than a path, and no wider; the lorry constantly clipped off branches as it chased its leader.

"I suppose this bugger knows where 'e's goin'?" enquired Jenkins doubtfully, pushing the muzzle of someone's weapon out of his face. He felt uncomfortable, not because he was squeezed like a sardine, but because being so he couldn't reach for his knives; he felt distinctly disadvantaged, and vulnerable.

"He should do, it's his country. Still, I was under the impression we were going to ground in a forest just north of Orleans – which should've been a damned sight closer than this, always assuming we landed in the right place to begin with," retorted Beard bleakly, as the dreadful thought struck him. He turned to Pardoe. "Colin, see if you can find out where the hell we are – or at least where we're going. It'll be getting light soon."

Pardoe, in his perfect French, addressed the necessary enquiries to Rémy, and there followed heated arguments among all the Frenchmen in the car in the course of which it sounded as though every town and village in France was mentioned, and at the tops of their voices. Pardoe, ignoring the squabbling, which continued, shouted to Beard: "The general consensus appears to be that we're halfway between Orleans and the Forêt de Fontainebleau, which is where it seems we're headed ... "

"You're not trying to tell me we're lost!" cried Beard, now more angry than alarmed. That would come presently when he realised their position. Stranded in France, surrounded by Germans – and he was supposed to be finding suitable bases from which the rest of the squadrons could operate! All by tomorrow.

"No, Robert – nothing like that," laughed Pardoe, though with very little humour in his voice. "It seems that the Germans overran the area we were supposed to occupy late yesterday and some of those who would have looked after us were either killed or captured, or are now lying low themselves. From what I can make out, between the lines, the trouble stems from there being too many factions among the Résistance fighters. Too many groups ... too many leaders ... too many political differences ... and selfish ambitions in which fighting the Germans takes second place. I gather treachery is blamed for yesterday's raids. Good thing we didn't come a day early!"

Beard frowned. "So who are these people?" He indicated the Frenchmen in the car with a movement of his head, and instinctively lowered his voice to a whisper as though they understood every word. "And what's this place they're taking us to?"

"I really think they're doing the best they can for us in the circumstances, Robert. That raid last night must have knocked the wind out of them, but they didn't abandon us, did they? Rémy had to find us an alternative area in a matter of hours, and decided his own base in the Forêt de Fontainebleau was as good a place as anywhere for us to get started. They reckon it'll be somewhat safer, or at least easier, for us to settle in there – and we'll be able to do there what we would have been doing in the original place. It's simply a matter of a change of location. We'll still be able to harass the enemy communications in the Orleans Gap when we're organised."

Beard considered this, and while their new destination sounded a long way off from where they should have been – and wasn't it awfully close to Paris? – decided things were not so black as he had first supposed. Or at least, if they were, they might have been a lot blacker. But why hadn't that SOE bloke been there at the DZ to meet them?

"Colin, ask our friend about this Mireille chap," he said, a fresh frown clouding his eyes. "I'd've thought he'd have made an extra special effort to be around in view of yesterday's treachery. After all, we're supposed to liaise with him about our future activities so that we don't get in each other's way."

Pardoe had another conversation with Rémy, whose response was immediate and lengthy, accompanied by wreathes of smiles and winks, and a great many magnificent shrugs in spite of the confines of the packed vehicle. "I gather," Pardoe reported, darting in during a momentary pause in the other's rambling, "that our Mireille was involved in an act of sabotage involving a railway line, and was somewhat delayed. I'm assured he'll be at the camp we're heading for, either today or tomorrow. He may even be waiting for us. Don't know what the Frog finds so funny about the bloke."

"He's probably drunk," grunted Beard, before adding with a grin, "or thinks you and M. Mireille are lovers who can't wait to jump into the sack with each other!"

"Good God!" exclaimed Pardoe, appalled, until he realised Beard was joking.

Jenkins merely chuckled and, tapping Rémy's arm, gave a thumbs up, which sent the Frenchman into a paroxysm of laughter. Jenkins would have been more energetic in his own amusement were it not that with each movement he was in real danger of stabbing himself.

It was almost light when the two vehicles finally screeched to a halt; no sooner had everybody disembarked and the canisters had been lifted out, than they were driven off at furious speed. Carts, which Pardoe said were bullock carts for all that they were drawn by something akin to mules, materialised and were quickly loaded with the supplies and many of the men ; others were elected to walk ahead and behind the little convoy so as to give warning of any nasty surprises ; there were none. For close on an hour they travelled along sodden, deeply rutted tracks that were almost hidden by the trees on either side. In almost no time at all they were inside a real forest, yet there were ancient twisting tracks thankfully known to the mules for they appeared to be given no lead and left to make their own way at their own pace. And so they progressed through this arboreal world leading to heaven knew where. Certainly Beard had no idea, being content – well, perhaps resigned more accurately described his feeling, to allow Rémy to take them to his lair. Meanwhile, the forest grew thicker and darker, and the mules rumbled on.

Finally, covered in a million insect bites, they emerged in a cleared circle where an old woodsman's hut stood beside a tiny stream – it was more a woodland rill, really. The hut appeared to have been abandoned although there were signs of recent visits. The Maquis camp was a mile or so farther away, and it was so well camouflaged by Nature that they stumbled into it almost before they realised it was there – or they would have done had it not been for the guards and the smells of cooking. And almost as soon as they had sorted themselves out and had something to eat, Rémy, smiling hugely, appeared and announced to Beard that their Mireille had arrived.

Mireille – like Major Borisav – turned out to be a woman. Not again, thought Beard disbelievingly, though in this instance the woman was more a handsome young girl. It is impossible to say who stared the longer. It was Mireille who surfaced first.

"Jean-Luc, I presume," she said in perfect English.

"Yes, and you're Mireille, I presume," he responded with a smile, and taking his time as he continued looking at her.

Mireille, who was probably in her middle twenties, was beautiful, there was no denying that. Not at all Beard's vision of what a spy, or agent as they preferred to be known – if at all, should look like. Not with those deep brown eyes, with just the hint of sunshine around the edges: not with those delicious blonde curls peeping from beneath her tight navy beret: not with that exquisite little face in which everything was perfection, from the rounded chin to the delightful dimpled rosy cheeks. Beard had thoughts of being head over heels in love with her on the instant, but in the next, he remembered Ruth; his long-suffering, loyal and loving Ruth, and cringed with shame at his perfidy. But still he stared at the vision before him: the English spy! God, he thought, if she asked me for secrets I'd tell her everything I knew! Of course, he knew this was all nonsense.

Instead, when he found a voice, all he said, apart from "Hallo," was "You were lucky not to be at our original RV last night, or I might not have this pleasure now." It was gallant enough, but he wondered if perhaps he shouldn't be a little suspicious at her absence as she might have had forewarning of the ambush. Oh, surely not; not this gorgeous creature.

"Yes, much better blowing up a train," she returned, and if she saw the clouds of doubt in his eyes, she ignored them. "We lost some men there, too."

Beard, having had his fill, for the moment, of her mesmerising eyes, tore his own from hers to examine the rest of her, and the rest of her was in keeping with her role as a resistance fighter, and spy. She was tall and slim, yet sturdily built. Beneath her dripping oil-skin cape, she wore dark clothing: navy top and black trousers that disappeared into the tops of her boots. She had a pistol at her side and a Sten-gun over her shoulder, and he was sure there would be other weapons not on view. Oh yes, a formidable figure indeed.

"You'll be needing a place of your own for you and your men," Mireille suggested quietly.

"Yes, it's urgent," declared Beard, returned to earthly concerns at the sound of her voice. God, it was a voice to captivate mankind: especially him.

"How many are you?"

"Ten – no, nine. We lost a man in the landing. The rest of my section arrive tonight, so we'll be twenty-five in total," answered Beard, desperately trying to concentrate on the job, and not her. "And tomorrow, another three squadrons are due, plus an HQ section, and the Boss. That'll be about seventy-five more men. I'm to find at least three other sites for them."

"They don't give us much time, do they?" Beard shook his head, and gave a wry smile which gave him a rather boyish look, and prompted her to say, "Are you really the leader of your gang of cutthroats, Jean-Luc? Pardon me for saying so, but you do look young – very young to be a major."

Beard laughed. "There are moments when I feel very old indeed," he declared.

Mireille gave a small laugh in turn, as her laughing eyes examined his face afresh. So young, and yet there was a maturity in it that had nothing to do with years, only the war. She recognised the scars. She'd seen the same tell-tale signs in other men who had been close to the war: close to death. And he was just a boy – except that there were no boys in wars. They were all soldiers, alive or dead. The scar above his right eye had faded to a thin white line and was almost covered by new hairs, but she saw it instantly and wondered if there were other scars hidden beneath his uniform. Her smile deepened, as she mused over whether he shaved yet. "Come on, old chap," she said, the sunshine of her eyes laughing at him, "let's see what we can find for you first," she said quietly, and led the way to a battered Citroen.

"So, how did the train business go last night?" Beard asked, conversationally.

She didn't reply immediately, and for a moment he thought she wasn't going to, but then she said in a quiet, piqued voice, "Not very well. I was only there to make sure they didn't use the explosives for some private purpose. I was more an observer, really. And they didn't do all that well, either. They blew the line up all right but the only train that came along was able to pull up in time, and I suppose the damage will be repaired sometime today." She shook her head with annoyance at the futility of it all. "And some innocent French hostages will be shot in reprisal."

"Isn't this an unnatural occupation for … you?" he queried, thoughtfully.

Mireille offered him a dry smile, which had the effect of deepening her dimples rather enchantingly. "It's what I'm trained to do, the same as you," she replied evenly. "The war has made a nonsense of the different sexes. We're all the same now. We're all soldiers. The generals have discovered, rather belatedly, that women can kill just as easily as men. Others, of course, have known this for thousands of years! It's nothing I'm proud about. I'll be glad to be a woman again, and have babies in time. But, in the meantime, I am a soldier and have to do my duty, the same as you." Sitting behind the wheel of the car, she paused to consider how to proceed, then looked over at Beard and remarked casually, "There's been several men like you dropping into France recently. Of course, you're all over here in connection with the invasion …?"

The question was left dangling in the air, and Beard nodded, and left it there, only volunteering, "I suppose."

"When is it? Do you know? Where?" cried Mireille, disappointed that he hadn't told her anything; perhaps he didn't know, she mused; too young to be burdened with such secrets. "Judging by the torrent of wireless messages flowing into France every day and the armadas of bombers that come over day and night, it must be imminent."

"I'm sure you're right, Mireille. I guess we'll all know at the same moment … when it happens," Beard replied. "But certainly, it's got to be very soon now." It was as far as he was prepared to go on the subject. He wondered whether, with the weather as it was, if it might yet be postponed. "Right now," he continued, "I'm only concerned about establishing camps for the rest of my unit so that we can harass the Germans from the rear once it starts."

"Well, Jean-Luc, don't try and win the war single-handedly." Mireille indicated the decorations on his chest as he unzipped his camouflage jacket to give himself a scratch. "I see you've already got some medals, you don't need any more, so don't go doing anything brave."

"I don't take any unnecessary risks, Mireille. I've no intention of being a dead hero! That's why they gave me these," he grinned as he tapped his chest, "it was simply for being alive at the end of the day."

"Liar!" she smiled back. "Just take care."

"And you," he told her."

The landings over the next two nights were completed without incident, and with the new arrivals came Gibbs, who at once selected his camp from among those Mireille had suggested to Beard. Gibbs had then directed where the other squadrons should hang their hats, stressing that the communications camp was the most vital of all. He took command of everything the moment he landed, and spoke at length with Mireille in fluent French. Col Yeo was to liaise between the various squadrons, leaving the brigadier free to oversee the general planning of things, and indulge in forays of his own when necessary.

It continued raining for much of the following week, but for Beard and his men they were busy days. Mireille had proved invaluable introducing them to different Résistance leaders, and whispering advice on which were to be trusted – and some of them she trusted not at all, but still had to work with them. And it was thanks to Mireille's tireless assistance that Beard had a chance to reconnoitre the area. This he did, usually in a different vehicle each time, in company with Rémy, Mireille, Jenkins and anyone else who felt like a ride and was not otherwise engaged. On different occasions they crossed both the Seine and the Loire and examined villages from a safe distance through binoculars, learning which were occupied by the Germans and which were not but were still regarded as unsafe.

"Almost every village has an informer," whispered Mireille, out of earshot of their Maquis companions. "And the police, the Milice, who are under German control, are the worst of the lot ... they must be terrified of the coming invasion – the Maquis have lots of scores to settle." Beard was particularly keen to see any railway lines and bridges in the area, and noted that the larger bridges in particular were all well guarded.

On their fourth night in France, in company with Pardoe and Jenkins, and a carload of Maquis, who included Gaspar, Beard travelled some seventy miles to "have a look" at the railway line between Chartres and Rambouillet. For a long time that's all he did : look. The line, silvery-white in the wet darkness, was constantly patrolled; but there seemed to be a pattern to these patrols whereby some stretches were unguarded for twenty minutes or more at a time. Having made up his mind to leave his mark, Beard chose Jenkins and Gaspar to accompany him and, turning to Pardoe, said: "Get these fellows back to the cars, Colin. We won't be long." He grinned into Pardoe's disappointed face and added, "Make sure the buggers don't leave without us!"

An hour later, Beard and Gaspar were busy beside the track,

while Jenkins kept watch, pointing one of the new Stens fitted with a silencer in one direction and peering hopefully in the other. He was disappointed for Beard and Gaspar completed their business undisturbed and with the detonator due to do its work in about eight minutes, they all moved away rapidly and silently. They watched the explosion in the early dawn from half a mile away – just as a bored sentry came into sight.

"We should have done both sets of lines," frowned Beard, studying the extent of the damage once the smoke had cleared. It was not terribly impressive; just a buckled line and a modest hole. "And we should have done it on a bend – and in more than one place. Next time we'll go for the bloody points – that'll do some real mischief."

The return to camp was without incident, although Beard was concerned about the French waving their weapons as they sped through villages. "Don't they know better than to draw attention to themselves," he grated at Rémy through Pardoe. But Rémy, still unshaven, gave his beret a tug and smiled good-humouredly. "Don't scold them, M'sieu," he said, "they're excited. Life's been hard for all of them during the occupation. Today, they feel they've done something; not much, perhaps, but anything that inconveniences the Germans is an achievement. You can have no idea how we Frenchmen long for the invasion." Jenkins echoed Beard's sentiments when he muttered, "Well, tell the sods not to get us killed before it 'appens!" Pardoe didn't translate this but the way Rémy burst into laughter and launched into yards of verbosity made them all think he got the message.

Mireille took Beard aside next morning to thank him for the equipment brought over with the rest of his men, notably the MCR 1 receiver and Jedburg transmitter. She told him she had a million messages which she simply must carry to various other groups; that she needed to speak personally to various Résistance leaders, if only to stop them squabbling among themselves and keep their minds concentrated on the real enemy until the balloon went up; and, of course, that she needed to arrange air drops of supplies – if it wasn't for these, she doubted if they would pay her any heed at all.

It was *au revoir*, and as she moved towards one of Remy's fleet of every-ready Citroens, Mireille warned Beard against the French. "There are some very wonderful and brave Frenchmen, but there's so many others who are only interested in their own selfish dreams, and they're determined to achieve them at anybody's expense. We have to arm them ... but they're just as likely to turn the guns we give them on us as on the Germans. So watch your back, *mon ami*. The lot I'm leaving you with are perfectly reliable. I've had considerable dealings with them. They're a far safer proposition than that bunch around Orléans where you came down. Remember that."

"Jenkins looks after my back," he told her.

"And who looks after his back?" she countered drily.

"I do, of course."

Mireille gave a magnificently Gallic shrug, and smiled. "God bless you both," she said, kissing him on both cheeks, which Beard thought much more civilised than simply shaking hands, which was often more like a test of strength. Of course, a kiss on the lips would have been much more delightful.

She climb into the snarling vehicle, allowing a cloud of cigarette smoke to pour out, to the consternation of the driver who immediately started spluttering, and told Beard, "I'm heading towards the Morvans to begin with, but after that heaven knows where I'll be. I'll keep in touch, if I can, but I don't think we'll meet again till it's all over, Jean-Luc."

"Then, we'll meet for coffee in Paris," Beard declared boldly.

"I'd like that," she replied, with a last smile.

And she was gone in a puff of smoke as the exhaust joined in the farewells with an obnoxious blast of its own. The car quickly disappeared from sight, and Beard suddenly felt very alone, and after a while he found himself thinking of Ruth and, though he felt himself blushing with guilt inside, he didn't think she'd mind him doing a bit of flirting when he got the chance. Not really. It was little interludes like this that kept him sane. Well, that was his excuse.

"She's not another fiancée is she, Robert?" The voice, a yard or two behind him, brought Beard back to earth, and there was Gibbs staring in the same direction.

"No, not at all, sir," insisted Beard, now blushing on the outside, as he struggled out of his reverie. "She's been very helpful."

"I knew she would be," said the brigadier smoothly.

Beard stared, frowning, and then grinned. So Gibbs had been over in France while he and the rest were training furiously in safety back home. And not a word.

Mireille left on the last day of May, and though she took a sizeable portion of Beard's sanity with her, he was almost too busy to give her another thought. The various camps maintained a strict independence of each other, and operated with a freedom approved by the HQ staff who dealt with their flood of reports which were passed on to London.

Beard's problems were intensified by the ever-growing numbers of Résistance men who had to be discouraged from pre-empting the invasion. He quickly decided that there was no French equivalent of co-ordination, nor, come to that, of discipline The French were incapable of being disciplined, unwilling to take orders, but they were hungry for freedom and power and so, with ill-concealed resentment, they submitted to just as much training as was necessary to enable them to use the British weapons they so coveted.

While Beard and Clapton discussed tactics and strove to instil the absolute need for cooperation into the minds of the mostly disinterested and very uncooperative leaders, Pardoe and Summerbee, together with Sgt-major Trumpett and Sgt Stubbs, gave instructions in every weapon available. It was an uphill task since only Pardoe and Summerbee had any worthwhile French, but the Maquis must have been pretty desperate to learn, for learn they did. It was a different story when it came to field-craft: it was a skill requiring patience, and they had none of this. There were continuous fights among the various Résistance groups, some of which refused point blank to take orders from anybody – even their own leaders, and went home. It did not augur well for the coming conflict.

The thunder of bombers flying permanently about their destructive business, and the eruption of their cargoes on ever-closer targets, made many of those on the ground wonder if the real thing had happened – and someone had forgotten to tell them. On June 3, in the uncomfortably close village of Ste-Anne-la-Petite, to the north of Montereau, dozens of young Frenchmen, whose only allegiance was patriotism, took it upon themselves to launch D-Day on their own. Perhaps they thought the real thing had actually happened and simply could not contain themselves from taking up arms as a way of welcoming the Allies and getting them off to a good start. It was rather wonderful as they took to the streets waving tricolour flags and brandishing a handful of weapons they barely knew how to use; it was wonderful, and courageous, but only for a few moments; and then the stupidity and futility of their action became a reality. At least fifteen were killed on the spot, and many more died later in the day. The great tragedy of their magnificent foolishness was that it made already jittery Germans more alert.

In spite of this little uprising, Gibbs and his several units continued to collect information far and wide, and began leaving explosives with timers set to go off several days ahead at various suitable places. Summerbee and Pte Blossom, for instance, were able to penetrate a large ammo dump, while Trumpett and Simms did the same at a fuel depot. But London was more interested in information at this time. Locations and particulars of German garrisons and airfields, tank staging areas, ammunition, fuel dumps: no scrap of information was considered too insignificant to be of interest. And so Beard, plus scores of similar Maquis groups, worked round the clock seeking out hidden German units, asking questions and following up reports of suspicious movements. All the information was taken by runners back to the forest HQ where it was collated and transmitted by Phantom teams who had landed with the squadron.

Then, as the bombing reached saturation point, and the rain continued to teem down, the long-awaited coded message came over the wireless that D-Day was finally under way. Within seconds hundreds of telegraph poles were being blow up, railway lines that had escaped the air onslaught were sabotaged in a dozen places, roads were mined and isolated German garrisons were attacked.

"Wouldn't you think that on a day like this the bloody sun would come out – and rejoice with us!" cried Beard, and wondered where Mireille was and hoped she was safe. He looked up at the grey sky and the rain slapped him in the face. It had hardly stopped raining since he'd landed nearly a fortnight ago. To the north, and not too far away, was Melun, but he couldn't see a sign of it through the rain and cloud and mist. "Come on, lads," he shouted to his men, "we now have the green light to do terrible things to the enemy."

The proclamation of D-Day was as a call to arms to the waiting French, and no power on earth could hold its young sons, and thousands of their fathers and grandfathers, in check. They threw themselves at local enemy forces and, at first, enjoyed a limited success; but the Germans quickly recovered, regrouped and exacted a savage revenge. Beard, racing through a tiny burning village a few miles north of Puiseaux in a captured German scout car, now flying a tricolour bearing the Cross of Lorraine, saw the bodies of men, women and children hanging from gable-ends and garden trees. He heard later that a following lorry-load of Maquis, who had stopped to cut down the bodies, discovered four SS soldiers hiding in a shed and burned them alive in the pyre that had once been a village. It became an accepted fact that the Résistance did not seek to take prisoners, and those they did usually died slowly.

One day, Beard's heavily-armoured scout car was roaming along the Route Nationale between Sens and Villeneuve l'Archevêque looking for the turn off to Cerisiers, in which area they planned to do some scouting, when, on rounding a bend, they found themselves face to face with a German convoy. It had stopped alongside *une auberge* where, doubtless, the officers were robbing the *patron* blind, and scores of men were standing idly beside their vehicles. There was no time to reverse and Jenkins, who was driving, put his foot down and the vehicle raced forward while Beard, beside him, blazed away with the twin Vickers Ks machine-guns fixed in front of him. In the back, the giant Simms opened up with a Browning machine-gun, while Trooper Alan Moore alternately fired a Sten and tossed out grenades. However, this was no time for heroics and, even as Beard yelled "Get off the road," Jenkins was turning the wheel and they were crashing through the wood just as the Germans were recovering from their shock and firing back. But though mortar shells, bullets and other missiles followed them far into the woods, they did not receive a single hit, and the Germans were disinclined to follow on foot. Today everyone was being wise.

Emerging from the wood some hours later, Jenkins came to a

sudden halt and pointed. There, barely a quarter of a mile away, a camouflaged train packed with soldiers presumably heading for the Normandy front, stood puffing away at a halt taking on water. It stood all alone and unprotected, apart from the usual ack-ack guns and machine-guns that were part and parcel of all German military trains, and they were all pointing skywards. It really did appear a prime target. Beard looked at Jenkins and raised a quizzical eye; Jenkins nodded, and condescended a rare grin. "OK, Boss," he muttered. Beard turned to the men behind him and told them to check their weapons: this was going to be no time to run out of ammo, he told them. "We're going to catch a train, boys!"

The scout car rolled up alongside the rail track without any alarm being sounded and, as it neared the train itself and several uniformed figures waved at them, Beard, not for the first time, was glad he was riding in a German vehicle, and that they looked so disreputable as to pass for Germans! He waved cheerfully back and shouted abuse which was greeted with roars of approval. They passed only two carriages before Beard gave the order and every gun on the vehicle opened fire, pouring thousands of rounds of mixed lead, armour-piercing, tracer and incendiary bullets into the train. There were twelve coaches and several goods wagons apart from the open gun platforms. The noise of the machine-guns was deafening, and didn't seem any less so when they paused for breath, except that they must have been for it was then that they heard the screams of the injured and heard the shouts of those inside struggling to escape. Bodies hung out of shattered windows like bundles of bloody clothing, and several carriages were already belching smoke, for Moore, having emptied his Sten, had tossed phosphorous grenades into the train wherever he saw an opening. Even as the car raced alongside the train raking it with gunfire, heads poked out of windows to see what was happening and were spattered by bullets for their stupidity.

It took almost no time to reach the other end of the train; all four of them lobbed grenades into the engine driver's cockpit, and without pausing to see the effect busied themselves reloading their weapons. Jenkins then surged forward with the intention of getting them out of there as fast as possible but Beard shouted in his ear, "Let's go down the other side, Harry." And Jenkins, his scar livid with excitement, swung the car across the tracks and went down the other side of the train, where dozens of German soldiers were clambering out of blazing carriages in a desperate attempt to escape. They were the first to die, and then the machine-guns were raking the train again, taking their toll among the unseen enemy. By the time the car reached the far end, the train was well and truly alight; at least five of the carriages were blazing out of control, and from the explosions within the inferno it was evident the train was carrying a considerable range of ammunition.

"Once more, Harry, and then take us home!" yelled Beard, whose blood was boiling over with excitement. And down they went again, and as they did so, shells aboard the train began exploding and soaring in all directions. Deciding that it was becoming a bit dangerous, Beard tapped Jenkins's arm and pointed towards the distant woods. It was time to take cover; and fast. Jenkins was already bouncing over the uneven ground.

They were better than halfway back to the safety of the woods when one of the myriad shells shrieking randomly over the landscape, threatening everybody and everything in its path, struck the scout car a glancing blow with such force that the vehicle was sent flying and its occupants catapulted through the air; the shell continued on a new trajectory and came down God knows where. The car was the only real casualty: it was a write-off. Beard and his colleagues picked themselves up, dismissed their cuts and bruises, retrieved what they could from the wreckage, and continued on foot. There was no sign of any pursuit from the train, and it was just sheer bad luck about that shell finding them. Beard reflected that it was an instance of being hoisted on one's own petard. Well, it could have been worse.

They faced a seventy-mile march, which did not greatly bother them, but in the event they were able to clamber aboard a goods train as it puffed slowly up a very steep gradient. They remained undetected and the train took them to within a dozen or so miles of where they needed to be. It seemed almost ungrateful to do so, but Beard couldn't resist the opportunity of leaving his calling card, in the shape of a delayed explosive charge, before quitting the train. He would like to have seen the results of the explosion, but, not wishing to draw attention to what he regarded as his own back yard, he made sure that the detonation didn't take place anywhere near; in fact, he never even heard it in the distance. Perhaps his message was discovered in time.

Within two weeks of the invasion, Gibbs's three active squadrons, each splintered into smaller units, were spread far and wide and Beard's section, now occupying its third camp since landing, was split into three units of twelve men each operating independently. Beard, together with Summerbee, led one: Capt Clapton, the second: and Lt Pardoe, the third. The officers met up as circumstances permitted, and they'd report on their successes and failures, casualties and needs, and make plans for the next phase in their activities. Gibbs, who alone knew the whole picture, was everywhere, giving advice, giving orders, and generally giving of himself. Wherever danger was most threatened, there he would be, in the lead.

Although Beard and his men continued to live relatively charmed lives, there were moments of great danger when it looked as though all was lost. The Germans were well aware of their presence in the area, and roughly where they were hiding. But the forests covered a vast area and what with the heavily wooded hills all round, the Germans, in spite of informers, found it extremely difficult to find either them or their camps. Beard's camps were never discovered, though once when one was surrounded by several hundred Germans only fifty yards or so away, they extricated themselves, without firing a shot, by crawling several hundred yards on their stomachs along a shallow stream half buried by undergrowth.

The pattern of things changed to some extent once the invasion force became established. There were many branches of the Allied forces engaged on harassing operations behind enemy lines, attacking convoys of troops and armour with impudent bravery by day and night. For Beard and his men, the railways were still the favourite target. The local knowledge provided by Rémy and Gaspar played an important part in the success of these operations. Gaspar was cheeky enough to saunter up to workers engaged on repairing earlier sabotaged lines, and discuss with them the best places to lay charges. During a nine-day period, Beard's squadron sabotaged a 35-mile stretch of line between Paris and Dijon in 18 different places: five of the explosions took place on one night. Three trains were derailed.

Turning their attention to the Lyon line, Beard – accompanied by Jenkins, Simms, Rémy and Gaspar – found a machine-gun post and several other guards blocking the way to some key points. Beard remembered thinking of Rémy's assorted smells and feeling certain they would give them away as they crept forward to deal with the guards, but the two sentries in the machine-gun pit were immune to these distractions, and were despatched soundlessly. Beard, Simms and Gaspar then calmly laid the charges between the points, while Jenkins and Rémy manned the machine-gun ready for any trouble. There was none; the points were blown and for two precious days not a train could pass. As soon as the trains started running again, Beard and his men severed the line on either side of the points – again and again. The Germans retaliated by shooting hostages, but there was nothing Beard could do about that: it was the price of war. The three squadrons became such a menace that the Germans withdrew an entire SS Division from the front line to deal with them, but though their savage methods had a limited success and casualties inevitably mounted, Gibbs's men continued to wage their own brand of warfare.

Inevitably, as their actions became more audacious and Germans more desperate, there were growing casualties. Towards the end of July, Capt Clapton's unit was all but wiped out in an ambush that had the sting of treachery. There were three survivors, one so badly wounded he later died. Gibbs was on the scene immediately, and almost on his heels came a Capt Nigel Griffin and a dozen men to replace the unit. There was no time for mourning, that would come later; meantime, they got on with the war. Beard had so far lost one man killed and two wounded, and Pardoe had lost three men killed.

Early in August, Beard and Griffin combined to attack an oil refinery that the Germans had been operating secretly in the vicinity of the Forêt d'Orient to the east of Troyes and some 20 miles south of Piney. The Résistance had very little information on the place, other than the number of tankers continually toing and froing, and the fact that the area was exceptionally well guarded. This Beard's men discovered for themselves as they approached the forest, which in part was something like a heavily-wooded park. The whole area was bristling with gun emplacements, barbed wire and soldiers patrolling with dogs; there were even some tanks parked among the trees. The plan was to infiltrate the security ring, locate the factory, find out its function, destroy it with explosives and cover their withdrawal by mortar fire. Things didn't quite work out that way.

It was the dogs that did the damage. Felbridge, the marksman, his rifle fitted with a silencer, accounted for the dogs all right, but for some strange reason very few were killed instantly, and though they died quickly they did so very noisily. The alarm was raised. Lights came on and German soldiers were running everywhere, firing at every shadow. Beard's mobile covering force opened up from the outer road with mortars, both explosives and smoke shells, as he closed to within 100 yards of what was evidently the heart of the refinery. No wonder it had been difficult to locate. There were only two large buildings and a dozen or so lesser places, and from the air they would all looked more a part of the forest than anything to do with the war. But at ground level this air of innocence was at once subject to suspicion for then a marvellously-camouflaged concrete road could be clearly seen; it led right up to a giant subterranean parking area which could only be seen at ground level, and close up.

Covered by their own machine-guns, Beard and his party approached the buildings cautiously on foot. Jenkins and Simms cleared the flanks, evidently accounting for several Germans who had only wished to remain undiscovered. Beard, Griffin, Trumpett, Sgt Stubbs and Felbridge entered the underground parking area with a view to finding an entrance to the refinery itself, leaving Summerbee, Blossom, Thompson and Hill to organise defences outside and to search the other buildings. Jenkins and Simms told Beard they'd found a number of air vents. "We dropped an assortment of grenades down them," reported Jenkins. "After that, since there was plenty of petrol about, we poured a few gallons down the holes and set fire to them, but we didn't hear no screams or anyfink," he added disappointedly.

There was a huge steel door at the far end of the parking cellar and, since there was no key hole or any other obvious means of opening it, Beard assumed it was operated electrically from inside. There was a phone on the wall outside, but he ignored this, expecting that a password would be demanded. He chose, instead, to blow the door off its hinges. It took a powerful charge to do so but, after the devastating blast, it lay like a great steel blanket on the ground after its thunderous crash. Beard and his men were inside while the dust was still rising, and found themselves in a vast room that had the appearance of being a laboratory. There was only a handful of people in sight and they were eliminated before Beard reflected that it might have been sensible to take a prisoner or two for questioning. It seemed that the entire workforce had taken shelter even further below ground the moment the alarm was raised. Beard, forgetting all thoughts of prisoners, told Simms to make sure they all stayed below and out of the way. Simms did so by blowing up the entrances, knowing it would take a month of Sundays for the men to dig themselves out.

It was Felbridge who discovered the shaft that housed the heart of the complex machinery that kept the refinery ticking over. It was an awkward place to work in, and he, Jenkins and Beard spent some 15 minutes setting the charges while Pardoe and some others placed other charges above, organised the joining of all the wires into a single strand which would be attached to a remote control detonator once they were all safely outside. The moment came when all was ready, and Beard, after a quick look round, pushed the plunger down and then threw himself flat on the ground just inside a belt of trees. For a fraction of a second nothing happened, and then came a muffled roar, the ground shook beneath him like an earthquake, there followed a series of tremendous explosions and an endless cascade of debris which mostly missed him. When he raised his head every vestige of the complex had been flattened and the laboratory where they'd placed the charges was a huge ball of fire, with smoke and flames stretching high into the sky. He was wondering how the trapped workmen had fared, when Blossom came running up with a message from Summerbee that suggested it might be a good moment to leave. "You must have scared the shit out of those Jerries, sir," Blossom added, "they came pouring out of holes in the ground well before your big bang." Beard grinned; he should have guessed there would be other emergency exits.

Summerbee had rescued five German scout cars – destroying the rest, and in these Beard and his men scattered in as many different directions as the Germans arrived in force. Beard's vehicle, driven as usual by Jenkins, plunged straight into the forest, crossed an open area of fields and finally crossed the main road to Chaumont a few miles south of Vendeuvre. Finding nobody following them, Beard thought it might be a "good wheeze" to double back northwards instead of rushing southwards as they might be expected to do. All went well until they tried to cross the main road at Méry, where a Spandau concealed there for the purpose, succeeded in sending them crashing off the road. Unhurt, the four men dived for the inadequate cover of a vineyard and, on hearing their vehicle explode behind them, kept going with bullets searching the rows of vines for them.

They ran for close on an hour in single file, leaving the vineyard via a ditch that might well have been a dyke, it was half full of water anyway, crossing several fields and a minor road, and finally pausing when they reached a friendly belt of trees about a mile from some farm buildings. There had been no sign of pursuit, but Beard didn't doubt for a moment that there was a hue and cry going on for them. It would not take the Germans long to link them with the raid on the refinery. They'd be wanting their pound of flesh.

"Looks like we've thrown 'em off, Boss," said Blossom. "Perhaps," commented Beard, wondering if they had any right to think so when they were surrounded by Germans. "We are going in the right direction, aren't we, sir?" queried Simms, staring up at the sky as the clouds burst their banks and the rain came down in bucketfuls. "Oh yes, I expect so," Beard assured him, and again wondered if it mattered which direction they ran in. One thing was certain, he wasn't going to sit here and drown when there were farm buildings in sight. He sent Jenkins on ahead to check the buildings out, and when he waved them in they came at the double. The farmer must live elsewhere in the vicinity for there was no indication of any habitation in the buildings, but there were a few animals: two decrepit, sad-looking horses, half a dozen sheep that looked sick and frightened, and four huge pigs snorting away and having a simply wonderful time in a foot of putrid mud – all of which meant that the place wasn't abandoned. Someone would be along sooner or later to feed the animals. Still, Beard mused, they could shelter here for a little while. As soon as they moved into one of the huts, there was a rustle beneath some straw and a snake slithered into view. Jenkins had its head off in a flash and slung its four-foot carcass into the pig pen, where it was received with rapturous grunts and much squelching as the recipients fought like ... well, like pigs, for their share.

Less than an hour later, Simms, who was on guard, came running in to say that he could hear something in the vicinity. "Sounds like a half-track to me – and mighty close, too," he said, with quiet calmness. Beard rushed to the entrance, and he could hear the vehicle as well; in fact, it sounded like several vehicles – and they seemed to be headed straight at them. It was already too late to make a dash for it, and this was no place to stand and fight. They wouldn't stand a chance. The Germans, especially if they were SS, would simply burn the place down, and them with it. Where to hide? The rain was still teeming down.

"Into the pigs' shed, boys," he cried urgently, "perhaps the Jerries won't be keen to search it too thoroughly." He led the way and threw himself down in the filth and mud behind a great sow that displayed no inclination to budge, and only gave Beard a brief snort by way of greeting. Simms and Felbridge opted to scrape a space for themselves in what was virtually dung, grabbing up handfuls of dirty straw to cover their faces. Jenkins dived straight between two pigs that were idly rooting about as they lay sprawled in the filth. One of them fixed an amorous pink eye on him, and Jenkins rewarded her with a dig in one of her chops; the sow then manoeuvred herself so that her front paws and a considerable amount of her weight covered the disenchanted corporal. "I hope this bitch remembers I just fed 'er!" he gasped. From behind his pig, Beard whispered "I think she's in love with you, Harry!" And he gave a very creditable snort that was echoed all round.

Beard had been right in his thinking: the Germans weren't at all keen about exploring the interior of the pigs' shed; the stench and the oozing mud, coupled with vague rustlings that suggested rats, was sufficient to deter the most thorough of them. However, the pigs did interest them, particularly the luckless one that was on her own outside in the sty. She was shot dead, and the Germans spent most of the day carving up and cooking the carcass, having first singed off the hairs by throwing it bodily on the fire they built in the stable – after turning the two horses out into the storm.

The smell of roasting pork and boiling hams drowned even the stink of the pig house; it was enough to make the four men hiding there almost sick with hunger; and they had to go on laying in the filth, dreaming of the mouth-watering food that was only yards away, for hour after hour. Beard remembered wondering what the surviving pigs thought about the murder of their relative; he wondered if they realised the appetizing aroma that engulfed them all was, in fact, one of them; he believed they did, for not one of them had moved since the sound of the shot. Jenkins was only too well aware of this, for he had been unable to move a muscle in all that time, and he felt squashed flat. The four men continued to lay still and silent, alert for any sound that might mean they were about to be discovered, and all the while drooling over the smells and thoughts of what was cooking.

The Germans left, if not during the night, very early in the morning. It was already getting light when their vehicles roared away, and before they were out of earshot Beard, stiff as he was, had sprung to his feet and stared after them over the half-door of the piggery until they were out of sight. Behind him, Simms and Felbridge lifted the protesting sow off Jenkins who, as soon as the circulation returned to his limbs, gave his erstwhile sleeping partner a most unfriendly kick. They all cleaned themselves as best they could, but none of them felt nor looked any the cleaner no matter how much water they doused over themselves, nor did any of them smell any the better. So far as the pigs were concerned, they probably regarded their visitors as one of them!

Beard sent Simms to check that the Germans hadn't left anybody behind, and he returned a few minutes later to confirm that the place was quite deserted, that the Germans had burnt down the stable where they'd butchered and cooked their pig and that they'd either taken every scrap of meat with them or burnt what they couldn't, and that the two horses had returned and were walking round and round the ashes of their former home looking more lost than ever. The only other thing he had to report was that it had stopped raining, which of course they knew.

Beard said they'd better go while the going was good, ignoring Felbridge's appeal that they do as the Germans had done, and cook a meal first. "I'm starved, sir," he complained, searching in vain for a scrap of something edible among the ashes. "We'll eat on the move. I don't want to have to spend another night here with the pigs," declared Beard bluntly. "Couldn't we kill one an' take it wiv us?" asked Jenkins, selecting one of his knives. "Do you want to carry it, Harry?" grinned Beard. Jenkins hurriedly put away the knife as the other two men laughed. "We'll have to make do with our emergency rations – and let our imaginations pretend it's roast pork!"

Two days later, having had to continually dodge enemy patrols, they arrived back at their base in the forests of Fontainebleau to learn that one of their cars had been lost in the flight from the refinery raid. "I believe it was a burst radiator, but I'm not sure of the details – only that the vehicle was stuck on the road when it was suddenly surrounded," said Summerbee; "but we do know that all four men aboard were killed. They included Sgt Stubbs, Norman Webb, Billie Bellings and – one of our Frenchmen, M. Rémy. I'm very sorry, Robert." It was a cruel and disappointing conclusion to what had been an otherwise mostly satisfactory action, but there was no time for mourning.

August saw the beginning of the end for the Germans in France, as the invasion forces broke loose from the confines of Normandy, swept beyond Falaise and spearheaded armies in all directions. Operations Anvil and Dragoon on August 15 saw the landing of the 7th Army along the Riviera, and on the following day the Résistance took the opportunity of taking control of large parts of central and southern France. A week later, the French 2nd Armoured Division entered Paris. Beard fleetingly thought of Mireille, but there was no chance of their meeting for coffee as they'd planned. He hoped she was safe in someone's bed.

The race to chase the Germans clear out of France was reaching a climax. Beard found himself having to move farther east to accommodate the rapidly advancing Allies, notably the Americans who, by the 27th, had reached the Marne and did not look as if they intended stopping before they reached Moscow – well, Berlin, officially.

Beard, having repeatedly had to move his base as the Germans, with the Americans hard on their heels, retreated homewards through the Forêt de Fontainebleau, and now found himself in unfamiliar country north of Reims and looking towards the Ardennes. But, he was still engaged in the same business of harassing the Germans in their retreat, and he was still sending signals to London regarding suitable targets. Then, suddenly, it was September and there was a strong rumour that Gibbs's group was to be rested. The rumour turned out to be true, but before it happened ... there was a little matter of a few prisoners.

Beard and Jenkins were returning from shooting up some barges on the Aisne near Attigny, when Trumpett came roaring over the radio to say he and Simms had come upon a German colonel, who was accompanied by a sergeant carrying a white flag. "I'm not sure, sir, but I think the sod wants to surrender. Either that, or he wants *us* to surrender! It might be best if you had a word with him, sir ... or shall I just shoot the pair of them?" Beard told him to hang on, and an hour or so later found him sharing a bottle of wine with the two Germans beside a wood about ten miles from Le Chesne. It transpired that the colonel, who was under no illusion regarding the outcome of the war and did not wish to continue fighting a lost cause, wanted to surrender not only himself but his entire regiment. "How many men?" asked Beard. "Seven hundred and eighty-three, including sixty-two wounded," answered the colonel promptly, after holding his breath a moment or two.

Beard stared, completely taken aback. He'd been expecting the man to offer a dozen or so, perhaps a score. This was ridiculous. What was he expected to do with a whole battalion of prisoners? How could he guard so many? Or feed them? It was out of the question. Couldn't they simply sit tight and wait for the Americans to arrive? The colonel shrugged, understanding the other's dilemma. If they stayed put, he said, their own side would find them first, and that would be that. The SS, or some group like them, would have no qualms about killing a few hundred Germans who had lost their will to fight.

"Do you have doctors for your wounded?" asked Beard, after taking a deep breath. He knew this was the right thing to say, the responsible thing.

"Not enough," replied the other promptly.

"Where are these men of yours?" demanded Beard, looking round and wondering, rather belatedly, how many guns were aimed in his direction. The colonel indicated the woods behind them, and watched with alarm as Beard swung his Vickers in that direction. But it was only a reflex action.

Beard had no intention of opening fire; he only needed to be prepared. He explained the position to his own men and smiled when Trumpett growled, "I knew I should've shot 'em!" But Beard wasn't listening, he was speaking on the radio to Gibbs, who readily approved his plan. Beard would take charge of the Germans and move them quietly south, avoiding any contact with the enemy, if possible, and hand them over to the first Allied troops he met – they would probably be Americans.

"Since we're packing up here and going on home leave almost immediately, I suggest you ask the Yanks to provide you with transport back to Blighty, Robert," said Gibbs, in a voice that suggested he thought Beard's predicament rather amusing. "I'll get word to the Americans asking them to look out for you, and see you get home. Good luck, old man."

"What's the word, sir?" asked Jenkins suspiciously.

"We're going on leave, boys," answered Beard with casual cheerfulness, "but on the way, we'll deliver these Germans Mr Trumpett's lumbered us with to the first friendly soldiers we meet – most likely the Americans. The sooner we get cracking, the sooner we start our leaves."

"How on earth are the four of us going to move 800 prisoners, sir?" Trumpett demanded, more curious than resentful.

"Easy, Jack. I'll lead, and you bring up the rear," replied Beard smoothly.

"But we'll have to pass right through the German front lines, sir!" exclaimed Trumpett, incredulously. "We four could do it, but not with this shower."

"Oh, the Germans'll be looking the other way, Jack," smiled Beard. "You'll see."

A week to the day after the Allies launched their invasion of France, the Germans let loose their first V-1 flying bomb against London from the Pas de Calais. It was a rude awakening for a people who, having suffered and survived the terrors of the Blitz for years, had dared to believe that for them D-Day meant the end of the war. But on June 13, along came the V-1s to shatter their prayers of thanksgiving. There were only ten of them on this first day, and of these only four reached the fringe of the target area, including one at Gravesend and another in Bethnal Green, where at least six people were killed and nearly a dozen injured; but it was only the beginning of their new nightmare. Two days later, this new terror resumed in earnest: hundreds of the flying bombs were launched. On June 18, more than two hundred people were killed or wounded by a single V-1 which hit the Guards Chapel, Wellington Barracks.

It was officially announced that these flying bombs – instantly nicknamed buzz-bombs and doodlebugs because of their peculiar sound and erratic behaviour – were just "primitive" missiles that were incapable of being directed accurately; they were merely pointed in the right direction – and the rest was down to the vagaries of Chance. The trouble with the buzz-bombs was that, unlike the conventional bombers which came largely at night, they came at any hour – with only a few minutes' notice of them being overhead, and then only a few seconds' warning of their explosion when the engine cut-out.

This was the extent of Queenie's alert when a V-1 dived down and tore The Dials apart; the building seemed to half leap in the air, hover, give itself a terrible shaking, and crash face down in the middle of the road. But Queenie had no knowledge of even this brief warning for it was early evening and the bars were packed with customers who were either shouting – at one another or to barmaids – or singing lustily when the bomb called Time.

Beard arrived back in England on Friday, September 8, the same day that the Germans' latest secret weapon, the V-2, struck at London for the first time. The V-2 was something entirely different. This was a long-range guided missile that gave no warning of its approach. Its speed was so great that the first and only indication of its existence was its explosion. It was a terrifying weapon: and there was no defence against it. The first one landed in Chiswick: it killed only three people, but struck a new sort of fear in the hearts and minds of millions, for, it seemed, people liked to have some warning of their deaths, not to learn of it after the event. The supersonic boom was heard all over London, and left not only the capital but the entire nation stunned.

Landing at a distant airfield in Essex, Beard and his three companions did not hear the explosion, and though they were to hear soon enough about the new bomb they were not immediately concerned about either it, or its predecessor. They were too busy congratulating themselves on beating the rest of the squadrons home. They had been tremendously fortunate during their last two days in France, negotiating no man's land without any hostile incident and falling straight into the arms of a most obliging group of Americans, who had been told to look out for them.

Once they understood that the hundreds of Germans weren't after their blood and that Beard was handing them over as prisoners, they moved heaven and earth to accommodate him – that is, send him on his way. A brigadier appeared by magic, fêted the four men (with steaks and apple pie, enough chocolate to open up a sweet shop and a Bronze Star apiece – dismissing Beard's protests that they wouldn't be permitted to wear them) and then raced them back to a forward air strip from where they were flown home, with what Jenkins called "indecent haste." Trumpett nodded and added with a worldly grin, "Want us out of the way so's they can claim all the glory. That brigadier chappie'll probably be a full-blown general by tonight, and they'll all be giving themselves medals galore ... but what the hell, they done us a good turn, didn't they? Good luck to the bastards!" Simms agreed, observing that they'd be getting an early start to their leave. Beard said nothing, but agreed with everything. They were all asleep when the plane banked to land conveniently close to Chelmsford.

Beard had first to report at the Apple Tree camp where, after completing a most comprehensive report, he and his men were free to start their leaves. Rank had its privileges. As Beard had returned with two Jeeps, he was allowed to keep one for the duration of his leave as he had to visit the Airborne Corps HQ at Moor Park and, possibly might have to travel to Fairford to reunite with his squadron. He was not unduly concerned when told that there was no post for him: there had been some, he was informed, but it was probably still chasing after him: it would catch up with him eventually, or not.

Beard grinned; he hadn't had an opportunity of writing to anyone since going to France, and this would make a good excuse. Trumpett, Jenkins and Simms accompanied him to Moor Park, and from there they all continued into London. Beard had invited his men to join him in a welcome home binge at The Dials, and they had readily accepted.

It was then that Beard learned for the first time about the V-1 devastation. The Jeep pulled up where The Dials had stood for over a century, and it wasn't there. The four men remained seated, staring at the empty space. Empty was not the proper word; the space was occupied by a mountain of rubble, from which clouds of dust rose with every breath of wind. Some clever Dick had planted a sign on top of the bricks and mortar reading "Closed for the duration!" Some pathetic weeds, mostly willow-herb, had already taken root between the cracks: there were splashes of yellows and reds, looking rather dusty, like wreathes on a grave. A cat was sleeping in a small flat hollow, and a dog paused to piss on the broken remnants of the step: the very step on which Robert Beard (alias Jarvis Brook) had been found almost nineteen years ago. Now, everything was gone.

Trumpett turned his head to look at Beard. "Was this it, sir?" he asked, in a low voice that contained real concern.

Beard nodded silently. It was several moments before he added, "I'm afraid so, Jack." He tried not to think of Queenie and Ruth, but, of course, he knew he could not put off asking the question he dreaded. Had he lost both the only home and family he'd ever known? In the absence of any known parents, they had been his only family: his pretend family, and yet more real to him than anybody else could be. Were they alive, or dead? Well, he wouldn't find out sitting there.

"You chaps had better be on your way and start enjoying your leaves, and I'll see you all in three weeks' time back at the Apple in Chelmsford," he said, suddenly decisive. "I'm sorry about this, but I've got to find out what's happened here. We'll have to have our drink another time." But they wouldn't have any of it and refused to leave him, and they all walked round and over the debris though what precisely they were looking for none knew, for it was plain that whatever had occurred here had been some time ago and there wasn't going to be anything worth finding. In fact, there was. Beard yanked at a splintered portion of a door and there below, in a sort of deep hollow, he saw what he recognised as part of the huge Aga range: just a corner of it: it was lying at some absurd angle but still displaying its cream colour beneath the grime. The sight of the Aga – Queenie's pride and joy – somehow gave him hope. He could not conceive of Queenie abandoning it – live or dead.

The sight of four burly soldiers in airborne Dennison smocks, unfamiliar berets and rubber-soled boots, clambering over the bomb-site, soon attracted attention; and, indeed, some alarm, for they looked a rough lot, armed as they were with pistols and knives in their belts. In the end, Beard stopped a likely-looking passer-by and asked what had happened to the pub. "Got bombed, didn't it! Just after the invasion it were," said the man, astonished this wasn't known. "You been away, chum?" he asked, with a sort of amused curiosity and indifference. "It were one of them buzz-bombs, weren't it?" Beard nodded impatiently. "Was anyone killed?" he demanded desperately. The man stared. "Lor lumme yes, mate, a whole lot of people. It were packed at the time. I'd've been there m'self only the missus dragged me off to the flicks. Bloody good job, too! Bless her!" Beard seethed. "What about the people who lived here?" he cried. "The landlady and her daughter?" The man shook his head; he didn't know, and neither did any one else Beard asked; they were all strangers to the district, they claimed: passing by on their way home, to work or to the shops. They continued on their way shaking their heads, and muttering under their breaths at being questioned.

Finally, a postman happened along and put Beard out of his misery. Yes, declared the man as he dropped his bag at Beard's feet, both Queenie and the little girl were alive. No! he cried, as Beard grabbed hold of his collar, he didn't know where they were. No! he screamed, as Beard tightened his hold, he didn't know if either one was injured. Trumpett had to pull them apart when it looked very much as though Beard was intent on throttling the man. The postman disappeared faster than a buzz-bomb. Beard soon calmed down. For the moment it was enough to know that they were alive. But where? And was either one hurt? The thought of that halfwit postman calling Ruth "a little girl" brought a grim smile to his lips. Trumpett suggested that the local ARP or police should know what had happened to the survivors, but Beard suddenly realised someone else who'd know where Ruth was likely to be living. He turned to his three companions and shouted, "The school! They'll know where she's at!"

The Jeep roared down the road, for all the world as though a squadron of Tiger tanks was in pursuit, and certainly scattering any dawdler in its path, pedestrian or motorised.   Beard, now far more cheerful in the knowledge that his family was at least alive, eyed the streets along which he and Ruth had played and run wild to the vociferous annoyance of those they inconvenienced – just a few short years ago. But his eyes soon began to notice the many scars of the bombings as he shouted directions at Jenkins; they were so numerous it came as almost no surprise to find that Ruth's school had also been destroyed. Actually, it was the adjoining church of St Clare's that had taken the direct hit; the blast had flattened the school buildings, and a plane tree had crashed down on top of the debris. Beard learned from neighbours that several of the nuns had been killed, but there were no casualties among the children. The school was closed until further notice. Beard, puzzling over where to look next, was staring vacantly at a jam-jar of dead flowers left by the pupils, when he had another idea. Flowers! He turned to his men and cried, "Let's find Mrs Molly! She'll know!"

"You an' your wimmin, sir!" said Jenkins, with probably more good-humour than he intended for there was precious little in his eyes and his jaw was set just as stonily as ever. "Anovver fiancée, is it, sir? You seem to 'ave ladies wherever we go!"

Mrs Molly saw the Jeep approaching over the top of her floral fortress outside the ABC teashop, and when she recognised Beard her shrill cry of delight let the entire street know that he was come. She jumped up with such violent enthusiasm that her huge wicker basket toppled over scattering flowers across the pavement, but she paid them no heed as passers-by set the basket upright again and many hands returned the flowers to their rightful place; she had eyes only for Beard. "Jarvis!" she cried, her cackle emerging something like a screech, flinging her arms about him and never even noticing as her helmet – she had resumed wearing one, adorned with red-white-and-blue ribbons and flowers, with the advent of the doodle-bugs – fell to the ground with a metallic clatter and rolled away into the gutter, where it was retrieved by a grinning Jenkins.

"You'll be lookin' for your Ruthie, I s'pose?" grinned Mrs Molly, when she'd done hugging Beard and regained her breath. She looked very small in the midst of the four soldier giants; small and old, but certainly not frail. Financially, the war had been generous to her: it seemed that the war had instilled a hunger for flowers and trade had blossomed; she was far from being rich, but for the first time in her life she had sufficient money to enable her to look after herself in a degree of comfort. Her face was still wrinkled, but there was a healthier colour in her cheeks and her eyes were a brighter, clearer blue; however, her nose was just as red, her chin as bristly-white as ever, and she wore the same black frock-coat he remembered her always wearing. He didn't doubt that her wardrobe was as sparse as her frame. Even so, she was a determined, busy-looking woman and nobody's fool.

"Where are they, Mrs Molly? Are they all right … not injured, or anything?" cried Beard urgently, holding her gently by the shoulders as he stared intently into her eyes, seeking to read the answers there ahead of her reply.

"They're safe, Jarvis," she assured him almost at once. "Not 'urt nor nuffink like that ... though so many ovver poor souls was when the ol' Dials was 'it," she paused to reflect on what she'd said and Beard, frantic to know where they were, was beginning to squeeze her bony shoulders in his anxiety, when she continued: "That Mrs Bromley – 'er wot you used to lodge wiv ... she's took 'em in, dearie."

They all piled into the Jeep, Mrs Molly included. She paused only long enough to grab at Maisie, her sometimes helper, yelling at her to take over her flower pitch "for a tick" and to plonk her tin hat on the startled woman's head. As Trumpett and Simms lifted her bodily into the Jeep, Mrs Molly shouted only one instruction to her still-gaping deputy, "Mai–sie! Don't you go givin' nuffink away, d'you 'ear!" The Jeep darted away before Maisie could think of a reply or even wave goodbye, and very soon afterwards screeched to a halt in Grafton Road.

Beard had thought, indeed, had expected, Queenie and Ruth to show more amazement at his appearance than they did; certainly they were delighted, and in Ruth's case ecstatic, at seeing him, but neither seemed excessively surprised. They explained, when the trauma of the moment had passed and they could think of such mundane things again, that they had written several urgent letters to him telling him of their frightening experience and where they had moved to, and had supposed he had come in response to their appeals. Of course, they added laughingly, they hadn't expected him to bring half the British Army along with him! Not that they weren't welcome, they added.

Beard hardly liked to shatter their illusion, but he did; he told them he had received no letters and had come home purely as a result of an unexpected leave. Really, it was Mrs B. who was the most overcome with surprise. She greeted them with floods of tears and only recovered after several cups of tea, which Trumpett and Simms prepared without mishap despite the conflicting instructions of Queenie and Mrs Molly, who seemed equally at home in the establishment. Over gallons of tea (and stronger beverages), the tragedy of The Dials emerged ... and ended with all the womenfolk blinking back tears.

The bomb fell on Saturday, June 17. The pub was close to bursting at the seams, which meant that many of the customers were standing, and the noise was such that only the more recent arrivals were aware that the Alert was on. The roar of the explosion and the crashing of the ceilings and walls was the first and last thing many of the carousers knew of anything. Ruth, who had been helping out in her mother's bar, was in the process of returning from one of the cellars with four bottles of brown ale when everything upstairs appeared to fall down and she was trapped in the cellar – in the pitch dark. She was unhurt, though scared out of her wits, and wasn't rescued till the following day when a fireman burrowed his way through to her via a delivery hatch. "I was still holding one of the bottles," put in Ruth smugly. "An' still screamin' yer 'ead orf!" added Queenie, with a grim smile as she placed a great arm about her daughter's shoulders and gave her a squeeze.

The potman, Fred Akers, had been in another of the cellars changing a barrel. It was assumed that he had decided to have a snack, for sandwiches and pickled onions were later found spread out as though for a picnic, and must have chosen the very moment of the explosion to nip upstairs to retrieve his teeth. He was found beneath tons of masonry with every bone in his body broken and his head severed. Barely twenty feet away, Queenie had been blown into a space beneath a bar – wedged between cases of light ale and milk stouts – and emerged some hours later without a scratch. "Cheeky young copper said I were drunk!" exclaimed Queenie in pretended high dudgeon. Some other members of the staff were not so fortunate. Millie, the barmaid with all the children and high hopes of having just found a father for them, suffered a severed major artery in her leg and bled to death inside a minute. A coping-stone had crushed Mavis's right arm and a surgeon had to complete the amputation on the spot before she could be moved. "She's still in hospital, and likely to remain there for some time," said Ruth softly, her eyes wincing as she spoke. "She had a lot of other injuries, poor thing." The only other member of the staff, little Hannah with the GI boyfriend, had escaped relatively lightly, though she would be scarred for life; a piece of glass, or whatever, had ripped open her left arm from shoulder to wrist and the injury had required forty-seven stitches. Altogether, seventeen people had been killed and forty-two injured, many very severely. The dead – in the main they were mostly local residents and workers – included a Service wedding party: a Flight Sergeant and a Waaf corporal; the best man was the only survivor in a group of six, and he was hideously wounded. "I didn't even know their names," cried Queenie, with a catch in her voice that suggested she thought this the greatest tragedy of the lot. Mrs Gunning, the Mafeking widow, was another of the victims. "They say she was almost a hundred," said Mrs Molly, with a reverence the really old always inspire. "An' still lookin' for a 'usband!" observed Queenie, fondly.

"Well, she'll have her pick now!" muttered Beard, and immediately wondered if the remark was in poor taste. "Do you have any plans for the future, Mum?" he asked hurriedly.

But Ruth broke in before her mother could answer. "Isn't it marvellous about my school being bombed, Jarvis," she cried, adding in almost the same breath, "of course, I'm awfully sorry about the poor sisters who died – but, they're in heaven anyway, aren't they? Of course, it doesn't really affect me, not now. I'd already finished with that sort of school at the end of the summer term. I'm due to start business training, shorthand and typing and things like that. No more horrid school uniforms. Super, isn't it!"

"For heaven's sake, Ruth, you're only fifteen," exclaimed Beard, genuinely astonished.

"Sixteen, you beast, no wonder you never remember my birthdays, Jarvis," she retorted fiercely, but quickly smiled up at him. She might just as well have said seventeen, for the moment she'd become sixteen that's what she regarded herself as being – and she knew that he knew it, too. "Mummy says that when the war's over – any day now, she says – jobs will be hard to get with all the soldiers coming back home, and I need to be trained and already working before that time comes. And you don't learn in school the sort of things you need to know in an office, do you?"

"'Course you do, soppy," declared Beard instantly, though he had a feeling that there was some sense in what she said. "You learn how to use your brains – if you've got any."

"'Course I have!" she snapped back. "And don't forget, clever clogs, you were only fifteen when you ran away to join the Army – and you've not done so bad!"

Beard looked daggers at her, not only because she kept calling him Jarvis in front of his men, but because she was telling them his real age; she should know better. He turned quickly to look at his three men, and blushed as he saw their grinning faces. Masquerading as Robert Beard he was an adequate twenty-one-year-old: as Jarvis Brook, his real almost forgotten self, he was a wholly inadequate nineteen. This dissemination of his terrible secret so childishly might have serious repercussions for him in the future. He gave a shrug and a smile to his three cohorts. He'd trust these men with his life, but that did not mean he had to trust them with his secrets.

"Anyway," declared Ruth, taking advantage of the quiet moment, "it's not so awfully important for me, is it? I shan't be either a pupil or a worker for long, will I? We'll be getting married almost directly, won't we, Jarvis-darling? And I'll be a wife for ever!"

Beard stared at her in startled wonder, and hoped he didn't look too appalled at her words. But they did shock him. They left him bewildered and, momentarily, speechless. He had not given the matter of their betrothal any serious thought over the last few months, and to have it suddenly thrown at him in this bland, positive way ... well, he wasn't prepared for such a public declaration. His notion of marriage, if he gave it any thought at all, was that it was something a long way off in the future; something to be preceded by an extremely long engagement. Certainly, much longer than they'd endured so far. He even wondered if they were in fact properly, and officially, engaged. He'd have to think on that. It wasn't that he didn't love her. He was sure that he did, but the thought of marriage was something different. Surely, you only did it –

got married, only when you were really old – thirty, at least. Forty sounded better. It had the ring of maturity about it. It was all right for a girl to be married when she should still be at school, but a man had to make his place in the world before he could close the door on it, as it were. He didn't mind the engagement bit, he was sure, but ... his eyes suddenly frowned.

"You're not wearing the ring I gave you," he accused her, as his eyes settled on her hand. "Does this mean we're not engaged any more?"

"Silly boy!" Ruth teased him, but there was a look of alarm – or perhaps it was anger, deep in her eyes. "I lost the ring in the bombing ... along with everything else."

Beard remained silent. He'd been so relieved finding his family all safe and sound, he'd forgotten for the moment about the terrible destruction of The Dials.

"We lost everything," declared Ruth, taking advantage of his silence, "including Daddy's George Medal."

Queenie, feeling that things had probably already progressed too far and too rapidly along the stony road of young love, jumped in to save the pair of them any further confusion and hurt.

"The brewery's said they probably won't never rebuild The Dials, which ain't all that surprisin', I s'pose," she declared, and her sorrow was evident in her voice for all that she strove to put on a brave face, "but they've offered me a place ... a 'ouse, not anovver pub. I 'spect it's a place they got saddled wiv when some blackguard of a director skedaddled wiv more'n his share of the takings." She had absolutely no justification in saying any such thing, but she thought it sounded more interesting than simply saying it was all they'd offered her after her years of toil on their behalf; the fact that there was no legal obligation on the part of the brewery to do anything for her, was beside the point. "It looks all right – on paper. Lots of trees rahnd abaht, an' it's got a garden – too bleedin' big, Ruth says, but she would, wouldn't she!" – Ruth intervened to exclaim, "It's really beautiful, Jarvis." – "There's even a bit of a stream ... an' yer can see fields all rahnd for miles and miles, an' animals an' fings. 'Course," she added, with a long sigh and a little shake of her head, "it ain't in London – it's way out in Essex somewhere; place called Mayhill, what we can't even find on the map. It's supposed to be near a place called Tiptree, an' we can't find that neither."

"Essex? Why, Mum, that's right next door to London – we landed there from France this morning," declared Beard light-heartedly, though he had never heard of either Mayhill or Tiptree, either. "You'll be able to pop into London any time you want. Just a bus ride."

"Tiptree's on the road to Colchester," put in Trumpett. "That's a big Army garrison town. They got a glasshouse there. Probably busy these days!"

"They make jam there – at Tiptree," declared Jenkins, stroking the scar on his cheek thoughtfully as he tried to remember exactly where it was. "Used to before the war, anyway. Probably make gas masks now – or simply grow vegetables."

"It don't really matter, lads, we ain't goin'," declared Queenie, folding her arms and giving them all a frown of disappointment. "We can't. We've been offered the place ... but we've got to buy it. They won't rent it to us – even if we could afford the rent. An' if I don't buy it straight away, they plan to sell it off. The man said summat abaht it costin' them money just 'avin' it stand empty."

"How much do they want for the place?" asked Beard.

"Four hundred'n seventy-fifty quid," announced Queenie, as helplessly as though she were announcing the National Debt.

The sum meant much the same to Beard. It was an impossible amount. "How much you got, Mum?" he asked her bluntly, as his own feelings sank; all he had was his Army pay, which was paid directly into his bank. He hadn't had any opportunity of using much of it lately, even so he was sure there wouldn't be anything like four hundred quid in his account.

"Not even a 'undred pahnds, lovey. I could mebbe scrape up abaht forty quid. I fink. I'd 'ave ter sell fings to raise even that. We ain't never 'ad no money – 'ardly 'nuff to notice. The Dials were all we 'ad. Didn't pay much, but it were our 'ome. Ruth was borned there. It was all we 'ad. An' now we lost everyfing in the bombing, see." She gave a weary sigh.

"They might drop the price, Queen," suggested Mrs B., but her expression didn't look very optimistic.

"Not 'nuff to make any difference. Them that's got it tend to tighten their fists when the likes of me come near wiv an empty purse," said Queenie with a bleak smile.

"Well, it won't cost anything to have a look at this house of theirs," cried Beard, moving over to her and giving her an affectionate kiss – which took the bleakness out of her smile. "We'll go on Monday, all of us," he added decisively. "We'll make a day of it."

The idea of a day out in the country greatly appealed to the women, and after discussing it at some length they, too, gave the plan their approval, for all the world as though the decision had not already been made on their behalf. The women then shooed the men out of the house so that they could get down to the important business of preparing dinner, and warned them against coming back drunk, or late.

Beard led the way round the corner – past the patched-up wreck of St Boniface's where, he confessed, he had been an inmate; they all looked, shuddered and hurried past – to the Rising Sun. As soon as they all had pints before them, Beard looked hard from one face to the other and growled, "Let's get one thing straight, boys, whatever you heard back there about me – forget you ever heard it. I'm Major Robert Beard, and I'm your officer – and that's all you need to know." He studied their faces again. They might have been made of stone for all the expression they showed, save for a certain brightness in the eyes. "And, I'm very old!" he added, with a smile. "Of course, sir," agreed Trumpett gravely. "That's right, sir," Jenkins muttered blankly. "It's the war, sir, it puts years on you," contributed Simms in his turn.

After this understanding, Beard had little difficulty in persuading his friends to stick around for a couple more days, for he knew none of them had homes or womenfolk they particularly wanted to hurry back to. He fixed up beds for the trio at the Rising Sun, taking it for granted there'd be a bed for him at Mrs B.'s, and on the Monday, by which time the germ of an idea was taking shape somewhere in his head, all three readily agreed to "stick around for a few more days" to see what transpired.

Nobody was quite sure what he had in mind, including Beard himself. But he spent a long time on the phone at the Rising Sun. First he made a very brief call to his bank to discover the extent of his credit, then he spent a long time trying to locate Bertie – eventually discovering that his convalescence was now transferred to Highways or, more exactly, to Poppy's loving care; they had a longish chat together before an officious operator cut them off for official reasons. Next he told Jenkins to see if he could get hold of a builder's lorry, complete with tools, but not to get into any trouble. Beard knew that Jenkins had a wide range of useful, if villainous, contacts, and from the smirk on Jenkins's face he didn't doubt a vehicle of sorts would materialise. He, Trumpett and Simms then returned to The Dials' graveyard on a reconnaissance mission.

They were all back in time for the house-viewing trip; the women, dressed in their best and armed with picnic goodies, travelling in the Jeep with Jenkins, and the others riding in a battered-looking lorry with a tarpaulin top which Jenkins assured Queenie he'd borrowed from a "mate in the trade." Queenie decided against enquiring as to the nature of the mate's trade, but had a secret smile at the thought of Sam frowning from afar.

□   *"Oh, I remember this day," sang out Ruth, " It was a wonderful day. Jarvis, you simply have to remember this. You gave us back our lives with a new home. Please, remind him – indeed, us all, of this joyous time you came to share with us, John."*

And John Fennell, having cleared his throat in legal fashion, proffered Beard his best summing-up smile, and relived that happy time, when he also knew Beard as Jarvis Brook, and became privy to some secrets unknown to the rest.

Chapter Thirty-two

Somewhere in Essex, September, 1944

Mayhill was not so much a place as a locale, and took its name from the first house to be built there. It comprised a track variously composed of bricks, cobbles and a lot of mud that led up a gentle slope and disappeared into a huddle of trees. There were a dozen houses, six on each side, staggered so as not to stare at one another; and where they might have glimpsed each other, dense hedges made sure they did not. Privacy, it would appear, was the prime requisite for the occupants, but perhaps that belonged to the past.

With the exception of that first house, which was called Maytree Cottage, each house was named after a fruit tree, though you had to look very hard to find any name sign, most having fallen victim to the elements. In some instances, too, you had to look (and you did so in vain) for the tree that identified a particular cottage. One of the happy exceptions was Peartree Cottage: this was the object of Queenie's excursion.

Beard and his party were met here by the brewery's agent, Mr George Woolven, who was also the local undertaker, and Miss Nora Hatchet, a village woman he had engaged to come in to give the place a bit of a "doing." There was quite an orchard at the front, if five trees can be said to constitute an orchard, for in addition to the peartree, there were two appletrees and one each of plum and quince, and they all stood peaceful and green with laden boughs knee deep in grass, buttercups and all manner of colourful weeds. Nearer the house, which stood some eighty yards from the pathway, were jungles of other plants that gave hints of a once orderly garden, and leading up to the front door was an ash path over which a wide variety of creeping plants had crept so as to create a carpet. The house itself was built of stone and brick, with red tiles on the roof and upper storey and a hooded front door that formed a small open-air porch. There was a row of four mullioned windows on the ground-floor and another row of tiny casement ones above, and wisteria, ivy and wild roses fought each other for a foothold anywhere they could. The building had clearly had additions to the original to accommodate either a growth in the population of the household or its prosperity, or both. This was immediately apparent within from the floor surfaces which were variously of stone, timber or tiles; the maze-like long, narrow passages, the size and quality of the rooms, some were very small indeed, others had fine panelled walls, and parts of the house had gas and others electricity – and some parts had neither one nor the other.

Queenie, who had rushed straight into the house after the door had been opened for her by Mr Woolven, continued her tour in company with Mrs B. and Miss Hatchet and then promptly flopped down on the only chair in the stone-floored kitchen. "I do like it, Edna," she whispered to Mrs B., though at a pitch Miss Hatchet was well able to hear. The room gave the appearance of being low-ceilinged until you realised you had to step down into it. The kitchen contained both gas and electricity and there was a double sink by the long window, which looked out on to the back garden where gooseberry and currant bushes could be identified in spite of its overgrown state. The stream about which they had been told was barely visible; it emerged as a trickle from a drainage pipe sticking out of the hillside where the little wood of mainly oak and silver birch watched over the houses. The trickle continued, mostly unseen, to Maytree Cottage.

Miss Hatchet, who was a small, dark, ugly thing with a heart of gold, was a little disconcerted by the number in the touring party but, by means of repeated washing-ups, she managed to provide endless cups of tea which she handed round as people appeared from various quarters of the house and garden; she would like to have given them a couple of biscuits each, but she had not anticipated such an army and there were only seven of her favourite petits fours in the tin she'd brought – and so, feeling that such dainty things would be lost in the mouths of the four hulking great soldiers (she had a feeling they would probably have swallowed the tin and all without noticing), she shared them out among the ladies, giving Ruth two because she looked hungry and two to Mr Woolven because – well, he looked hungry, too.

Mrs B., returning from a quick look outside, claimed that she could smell the sea from the doorstep; Queenie smiled but didn't say anything for, knowing that the sea was what united her with her lost sailor sweetheart, she knew that this was simply Mrs B.'s way of saying she felt at peace here. "It's the North Sea, missus," remarked Jenkins, who had followed her in. "Ain't so very far from 'ere, I s'pose. They collect oysters 'long that bit of coast." Mrs Molly, who was not one to miss an opportunity for making an extra bob or two when it cost her nothing, came puffing into the kitchen with her arms brimming with wild flowers and declared to everyone, but especially Miss Hatchet, that Mr Woolven had given her permission to pick as many as she liked. "Ain't 'e a pet!" she cooed.

Beard could see that Queenie had already fallen in love with the place, but he wondered if she could possibly bury herself in such an isolated place after a lifetime spent in the hurly-burly of a London public house. He smiled as the women took it in turns to occupy the solitary chair, and Miss Hatchet kept apologising that there weren't more. "I was only told to expect you, Mrs Hoggins," she said.

"Do you really think you'd be happy here, Mum?" Beard asked, gazing at her with concern in his eyes. Queenie nodded her big head, and he saw tears glistening not too deeply in her eyes. "You don't think you'd be lonely ... or find it too quiet – once the novelty of it all had worn off?" he pressed gently.

"Oh, no, Jarvis, I love it. It's what I really want," Queenie cried, the tears rising to the surface. "Peace an' quiet is what I want now. London don't mean a whole lot to me no more. It ain't meant very much since Sam was killed. An' now," – she gave a massive shrug, and a single tear escaped her clenched lids – "wiv The Dials gorn an' Ruth's school bombed an' 'er abaht to ..."

Beard came to her rescue and turned to Mr Woolven – who had come in from the garden and was hovering in the doorway –, anything to give her a chance to compose herself. "I presume there's a school of some sort locally, Mr Woolven?" he enquired casually, ignoring Ruth's smothered gasp but conscious of her eyes burning into his back like bullets.

"Yes, indeed, sir," answered Mr Woolven, readily, "there's a fine primary school here in the village – that's Stonecross, of course: it's just the other side of the hill – five minutes' walk is all; there's a little lane you cut through. Classes are held in the church hall – they're run by Mrs Elliot, the vicar's wife, and her helpers. The older children go over to Tiptree." He turned to inspect Ruth with a smile, but frowned instead as he met her glaring eyes and blazing cheeks.

"Don't you dare think I'm going to any rotten village church school," she snapped, aiming her anger directly at Beard's grinning face. "I've left school, in case you've forgotten. I'm starting training for business next term – in London."

Beard laughed, and blew her a kiss. "Of course you are, darling," he said easily, ignoring the inch of infantile tongue she poked at him.

Beard looked towards Queenie and saw that she was as composed as she was going to be for the present and, turning to Miss Hatchet, who was still thrusting cups of tea at people at every opportunity, said: "Miss Hatchet, why don't you show these ladies over your village, while Mr Woolven and I have a chat?"

He beamed at her so amiably that there was almost nothing Miss Hatchet wouldn't have done for him; she wasn't used to smiles from men. Very soon the womenfolk had disappeared down the lane between Plum and Greengage cottages on their way to the village and, leaving his men to their own devices but with strict warnings against doing any permanent damage, Beard strode up the slope towards the woods with Mr Woolven, who sweated alongside him. Beard was keen to haggle over the asking price of Peartree Cottage as he was accustomed to doing over anything he bought, but this procedure did not appear to be the way things were done when it came to property, and Mr Woolven proved an adept businessman despite his puffing, and conceded very little; he was not, he insisted, mopping his funereal face, empowered to reduce the brewery's asking price.

"If we were discussing my own business – I am a funeral director," – he produced a card from a suitably black wallet and handed it to Beard, as they stopped and began retracing their steps – "as I say, if we were discussing an interment, I might see my way clear to offering you a modest discount."

"Let her move in before you start burying her, Mr Woolven," exclaimed Beard with pretended alarm, which set the undertaker off in a flood of embarrassed apologies.

In the end, Mr Woolven, with or without authority, dropped the price by £25 and, feeling that he had won a major victory, Beard, deciding against asking Simms to work him over, accepted before the man decided that he might have overstepped his mandate. Beard explained that his leave was short and he needed to have everything sorted out straight away; in short, when was the earliest moment that Queenie and Ruth could move in?

"Why, major, the moment the money's paid and the papers are signed," said Mr Woolven, his respect for the young officer growing as he savoured a successful conclusion to their discussion. It was all a question of money: everything in life depended on money, the more so if you didn't have any. That was the trouble these days, nobody had any money – and if they had, they weren't spending it on houses, not with the war and all. He wondered if this lad – for that was all he was, hero or no – had the necessary money, or any money, come to that – and the thought started him off sweating again even though they were strolling along. "'Course, you'll have to see a solicitor first," he said, warningly. The sooner something was signed, the better he'd be pleased; the funeral business was so much easier – and so much more rewarding. The dead – and there were so many of them these days – never quibbled over fees.

Beard had never had dealings with a solicitor before; he regarded them, as he did most people in any sort of authority, with suspicion. But he didn't have any option, and neither did he have time to be choosy. The nearest firm of solicitors was in Tiptree, and it was there that he met Mr John Fennell, of Haddock, Grayling and Sprag, whose offices were conveniently above a teashop. He'd frowned darkly at the shiny name-plate outside, thinking they sounded a fishy lot, but once inside and finding none of these gentlemen existed and that the man he sat opposite didn't have two heads that looked in opposite directions, he was greatly encouraged; indeed, he was gratified to find that Mr Fennell not only had just one head, but a handsome and cheerful one at that. He liked the man immediately. Mr Fennell seemed of indeterminate age, but was probably in his middle forties or early fifties; he was a slight but well-rounded man, with thin grey hair and grey eyes that were both steady and benign and gave him an air of trustworthiness; he also had a club-foot, which explained the silver-topped stick standing beside him in a corner. He greeted Beard with a smile, a handshake and sent his clerk, who must have been at least seventy, downstairs for a pot of tea and some cakes. Beard smiled, supposing it would all go on his bill, and tucked in.

He never knew what prompted him to do so, but he told Mr Fennell everything. He unloaded his orphanage history, explained why he had taken on someone else's identity to get into the Army, told all about his association with Queenie and Ruth and how they had been bombed out, and that he was here to see about buying them a house. It was like making a confession, and he felt a lot better for it; it was as if he had been relieved of an enormous weight – like a suit of armour. Almost at once he wondered if he had made a great mistake but, looking quickly into the solicitor's kindly, understanding eyes, he didn't believe so. He looked as honest a man as Beard had ever met : and he'd learned to read men.

"You seem to have been at war – fighting, at any rate, all your life, Major Beard," smiled Mr Fennell, pouring fresh cups of tea.

Beard fell short of telling him where his money had come from (Charlie Tanney had sold the looted coins for some £850 and the money had been sitting in Beard's bank account for about a month), only that he had raised the money to pay for Peartree Cottage and everything that needed to be done had to be completed before his leave ran out.

"No problem there, major," Mr Fennell assured him, "I can handle everything for you – while you're off winning the war for us," he gave Beard a shy sort of smile. "It'll take some time for the paper work to be completed, but if you are prepared to give me your cheque for the purchase, I'll be happy to see this business through on your behalf. Once the cheque has been cleared, which will take only a day or two, I doubt if there will be any objection to your – Mrs Hoggins moving in. The brewery's only interested in the financial side. Once they have their money that'll be the end of them so far as Peartree Cottage is concerned. I'll arrange about a surveyor's report for you this very day."

"I want the deeds made out to her – Queenie Hoggins," said Beard quietly; "it's to be her home. Hers, and her daughter's"

"She'll have to sign some papers too, then," said Mr Fennell, with a tiny worried frown. "Are you quite certain about this Major Beard? You must realise that you'll be left with very little, a few hundred is all – plus, of course, your monthly pay cheque, which I see you don't appear to dip into very often."

"I don't get much opportunity where I am these days. Mess bills are about the only things I sign cheques for, and on active service I don't have to pay for those, so, it's just when I need a bit of pocket money," said Beard soberly. "Don't be concerned about me. I've never had anything in my life, so I'll not be missing it now. My two ladies are all I want in this world, Mr Fennell," he added. "Pretend or otherwise, they're my only family."

Mr Fennell nodded again, and smiled understandingly. "As you wish then, major," he said simply. "I'll get things moving at once. He made a steeple of his long fingers as he paused to consider how best to continue. "I can guess how you acquired the single large deposit in your bank account, major, and I can imagine the tax people will take an interest in it eventually. Of course, you can always claim to have won it gambling, but they'll still want their share. So, be warned. If there are further 'winnings' ahead, I suggest you bear this in mind. If you acquire what we shall term trophies in the course of your travels, I have a wide range of reliable contacts who will give you an honest price for them, under the counter, of course, and I would be happy to advise you how best to circumvent the tax thieves!"

"That's very generous of you, Mr Fennell, I had overlooked these people," grinned Beard. "I don't want you landing yourself in any trouble, but if I should acquire further trophies, be sure I'll remember your offer."

"My pleasure, major," returned Mr Fennell, with a thoroughly villainous smile that sat oddly in his honest face. "Meanwhile, I'll see if I can't persuade the brewery to lower their asking price."

"I didn't think solicitors believed in miracles," laughed Beard. "I've already got their agent, Mr Woolven, to knock £25 off the asking price, but if you can get them to drop any more off, so much the better. I leave it all in your hands."

Beard took the opportunity to make a will leaving everything to Queenie and Ruth, then spent several minutes signing documents – and the all-important cheque. He explained that Queenie had been known as Mrs Trotter as a matter of convenience, but since Sam's death she had reverted to her own name of Hoggins because, since there had been no marriage, Ruth was officially Ruth Hoggins. It was the name on her Identity Card and other necessary documents, though when she lived at The Dials she had always been known as Ruth Trotter. The change, once again, was a matter of convenience. Mr Fennell seemed in no way shocked, nor even surprised, at this explanation; indeed, he thought it very sensible with Ruth about to enter the world on her own. Beard also discussed changing his own name back to Jarvis Brook, but Mr Fennell advised against it, and suggested he see out the war first. Beard said that he would arrange with Bertie to act for him while he was overseas – if anything needed signing or further funds were required, but Mr Fennell said he doubted if he'd need to trouble that gentleman; they could complete the paperwork while Beard was still on leave, and he also promised to keep an eye on Queenie once she was installed, and to act on her behalf should any financial difficulties arise until such a time as Beard returned.

Finally it was all over and, much to his surprise, Beard found that the business had taken little more than two hours. He felt he had been talking for weeks. The shedding, or rather sharing, of his secrets in this way had somehow purged him of what had become an increasing burden. He felt quite light-headed, but was quickly brought down to earth again when, on arriving back at Peartree Cottage, he found Queenie on the verge of tears and Ruth fussing helplessly around her.

"What on earth's the matter, Mum?" he cried, going straight to her and taking her hands and kissing each in turn.

"Oh, Jarvis, it's this place ... I do love it so," she told him in a desperate sort of voice that was entirely foreign to her, as her face struggled for self-control. "It already feels like 'ome. I don't want to leave. But, I suppose we must, 'cos we'll never be able to afford it."

Beard gave a happy, carefree laugh. "Mum, you don't have to leave – not ever, unless you choose." She stared, his words seemingly incomprehensible to her as she tightened her grip on his hands. "I've just bought it for you, darling," he told her proudly.

Ruth gave a shriek and flung her arms around his neck, and he was uncertain whether she was laughing or crying. Queenie simply continued to gape, and blinked repeatedly, but no tears emerged. After several moments, she managed to ask in a hoarse whisper, "How?" In contrast, Ruth stopped strangling him long enough to yell accusingly, "Where did you steal the money, Jarvis?" When they let him be long enough, Beard briefly explained the purpose of his mission to Tiptree and what he had arranged with Mr Fennell. As his story unfolded, and he related only those parts he chose, and certainly not how he had come by the money, their interruptions became fewer until, towards the end, they listened in complete silence. And the silence continued for some moments after.

"Jarvis-love," said Queenie at length, "how can I let you spend all your money on me in this way? You've your own future to think about ... "

"How can you refuse me, Mum," he said quietly, touching her cheek as softly as if it had been a baby's. "You who've given me the only love I've ever known."

She didn't cry, nor did she speak; the three of them simply hugged one another in silence. Words seemed wholly superfluous: they could never have found the right ones. In the end, it was Queenie who broke the spell.

"I've already chose me bedroom," she grinned at them.

Beard thoroughly enjoyed the hectic couple of days that followed – the planning, the arranging, the scheming; he never seemed to be still or to have a moment for other things. He marshalled his forces like a general, with few of them knowing what the other was about; what they did know was that they all did as they were ordered, even Ruth. On that first day, he'd enlisted the services of Miss Hatchet: she would accommodate Queenie and Ruth in her home until Peartree Cottage was ready for them, and find beds for Mrs B. and Mrs Molly until they returned to London. Miss Hatchet, who had willingly acquiesced, had been both startled and delighted at the suggestion, and they had all trooped down to her home in Stonecross where she made her guests so welcome Queenie was sure they were her first visitors in a very long while.

Even Mr Woolven's services were secured before he could vanish to pursue his less demanding, but far more rewarding, life burying the dead. Beard persuaded him – pointing out that only paperwork hindered legal right to occupation – to let Queenie have a key to the cottage so that she could measure up for curtains and carpets and such like; and instructed a now more willing Mr Woolven (who saw a profit to be made here) to arrange for workmen to carry out such redecorations as Queenie directed. Mr Woolven, who had in mind his underworked gravedigger, also agreed to find a man to clear the garden. A price was agreed, and Beard emphasised that the money would be paid – through Mr Fennell – only when the work was satisfactorily completed. Mr Woolven had winced at the thought of having dealings with a solicitor, even one who was known to him, but, money was money, no matter who gave it to him, and he had agreed.

Stonecross boasted a pub called the Fallen Oak: the name apparently referred to a tree which fell on and demolished a former inn on the spot at the turn of the century; the locals simply called it the Oak. It was here that Beard and his men stayed for a couple of nights, and where they discussed their plans. Beard was keen to leave someone behind in case Queenie needed a pair of strong arms in the course of moving in, and also to ensure that Mr Woolven carried out his duties; as Trumpett professed to know something about plumbing and electricity, and also voiced a liking for the local ale, he got the job.

Beard, after giving Queenie some money with which to buy the bare essentials in the way of furniture and the like, returned to London on the Wednesday with Jenkins and Simms, and Mrs B. and Mrs Molly; no, he told Queenie secretively, he couldn't tell her what he'd be doing. "It's Army business," he said significantly, placing a finger on his lips. "Very secret. We'll see you in a few days," he added. "After we've done all the scrubbing!" cried Ruth sulkily. "It's what grown-up women do best," Beard called back, and fled.

In London, they reunited Mrs Molly and her flowers with an anxious Maisie, promising to see her again soon, and then retired to Mrs B.'s place in Grafton Road, which would be their base of operations for the duration of their stay in town. The first thing Beard discovered was that Ruth had slipped a package into his kit; it was the usual two handkerchiefs which signified his birthday. "Happy birthday, darling," said the card, "take special care of yourself and come home to us soon. Lots of love, your own, for ever, Ruth." Her name was followed by a kiss for every year of his life. He counted them carefully: there were nineteen, which was his (Jarvis's) proper age. His birthday was tomorrow.

Mrs B. was in seventh heaven at the prospect of having a houseful of young men to look after again. In the event, she saw precious little of them. They went out early in the morning, taking the lorry with them, and returned to the house in the early evening so covered in dust they looked as though they'd been working in a quarry. They were hungry and dog-tired, but they wouldn't tell her what they'd been doing; she didn't need to be a mind-reader, however, to know that whatever they were up to they were not having much success at it – she could see that in their tired faces and by their cheerless manner; they just ate, talked very little and went to bed early, and she continued washing whatever clothes they weren't wearing. It wasn't until the fourth day, when they returned home much earlier than usual, that she saw smiles on their faces and knew everything was all right again – that they'd achieved whatever it was they were after; and, infuriatingly, they still wouldn't tell her anything. But the gloominess had vanished, and that night they all celebrated at the Rising Sun.

They all slept in the following morning, which just happened to be Saturday; all except Mrs B. who, good housekeeper that she was, was up as usual and had breakfast all ready – and nobody there to eat it, save herself. She did wonder, though not very strongly, if perhaps the three men had gone out as usual without her knowing; she tip-toed upstairs to investigate, and found them all in bed. All three opened an eye as she opened the bedroom door to have a peek, but none stirred and as the eyes closed again she retreated as silently as she was able; she felt that they were entitled to their rest, and in no way blamed their inertia on the previous night's merrymaking – well, not wholly.

Towards ten, the three men surfaced, and their first thoughts were of breakfast. This was eaten at an unusually leisurely pace ... and at midday the previous night's celebrations resumed at the Rising Sun and, though she still did not know what it was all about, Mrs B. was pleased to join in. The only thing that struck her as being out of the ordinary was that Beard seemed to spend a prodigious amount of time on the telephone. Even Charlie Brooks, the landlord, was moved to comment on the fact, but perhaps he was more concerned about people wasting time talking in this way when they should be drinking. "Your young major's havin' a 'ell of job finding a gel, Mrs B.!" he said, with very little effort to conceal his irritation. Mrs B. ignored the remark, but Jenkins ordered another round of drinks and Brooks dug up a smile from his till.

No one kept track of the number of calls that Beard made, but when he rejoined his friends after an hour glued to the phone, Simms asked: "All fixed up then, Boss?" Beard nodded, without making any explanation, and shouted another round. "From the barrel this time, Charlie, not your slops!" he add mischievously. Brooks was sufficiently taken aback to respond by thumping the counter with the flat of his hand, and then bursting out laughing. "You cheeky young sir," he said between chuckles. "Just for that, the drinks is on me!" The remark was greeted by a deathly silence throughout the bar, and the unhappy Brooks felt obliged to do the same for his other customers; however grudgingly he did so, he saw the humour of it all for he gave Beard a wink as the empty glasses were thrust at him from all directions. Later, they collected Mrs Molly and Beard treated them all to dinner at a posh (frightfully expensive, anyway) restaurant in the West End, and in the evening they to a musical extravaganza at a theatre in St Martin's Lane.

First thing next morning, Trumpett turned up in the Jeep with Queenie and Ruth, and Mrs B. understood at least one of his phone calls. Ruth's face had lit up the instant she spotted Beard, but except for a few quick kisses and almost without a word, he exchanged places with Trumpett and, with a wave and a "See you on the 22nd, boys," was driving off leaving the sergeant-major, Jenkins, Simms and a very bewildered Mrs B. staring after him.

The four days they spent at Highways were very enjoyable – the weather was fine, and the Americans had decamped to France. Beard was delighted to be reunited with Bertie, who appeared to be recovering well and walking on both legs, the real and the false, though admittedly only for a few paces ; and both Poppy and her mother welcomed Queenie and Ruth so warmly it was like a family reunion all round. Lady Pamella and Queenie got along extraordinarily well – in the way that mothers invariably do when neither has designs on the other's children; and despite the difference in their ages, Ruth and Poppy had their heads together like a pair of sisters – and Beard conceitedly supposed that they were talking about him all the time. He was only half right.

Ruth, certainly, spoke of very little else but him; however, Poppy's words almost exclusively concerned Ben, his ship and their whereabouts. When the two girls could tear their thoughts away from their loves, they turned their attention to horse riding. Ruth, who had only seen draught-horses pulling drays close up before, was introduced to a giant mare called Black Pudding. The animal was certainly very black and very fat, and Ruth was a long time mastering the technique of climbing aboard her – and staying put; nor did it end there, for it was as long again before she dared loosen her grip on Blackie's mane or to let go of the saddle. But, at length, she did both and sat up straight – and to her huge delight, and perhaps surprise too, she didn't fall off – though this may well have been more due to her shrieks which rendered the horse incapable of movement than to any undreamed of equestrian ability.

Beard spent a very large proportion of his time with Bertie, who said that he and Maud were planning on being married as soon as ever he was properly recovered. He pressed Beard about making it a double wedding, but Beard said he had to see the war out before he could go that far. "And by then you and Maud will be married with children," he laughed. "Are you sure Ruth will wait that long, Bobbie? Women don't like being kept waiting," said Bertie in a quite serious voice. "Oh, yes," answered Beard assuredly. "She'll wait for me, I'm as sure of that as I am of her. We've loved each since for ever." He waved in Ruth's direction, but her attention was elsewhere, though on the same theme. Love. It didn't help when Poppy kept flashing her brand-new engagement ring, describing each sparkling stone as though it was a favourite child, nor when she went into huddles with her mother and Ruth to discuss wedding dresses and honeymoons. Ruth kept touching her naked finger, and then trying to hide her hand and at the same time glancing sadly up at him. Beard promised her it would be replaced – but told her she had to be patient. She stared, not comprehending his words: didn't he know that where love existed patience could never be? He smiled so irritatingly back at her, almost teasingly, she could have cried.

There was little opportunity for any of them to be alone, though one evening Queenie did manage to thank Beard for lending her his Mr Trumpett. "I never seen a man wot could do so much an' make so little fuss abaht it," she declared. "He rewired the whole blinkin' 'ouse, dug out the stream proper so's there's a little pond, 'e also replaced one of the winders – an' that was after washin' them all, an' lor' knows wot 'e's bin up to in the kitchen – 'e's 'ad all the gas pipes up. 'Ope 'e knows 'ow to put 'em togevver agin. An' 'e still found time to take me an' Ruth shoppin' for furniture in Chelmsford and ovver places. Do you think I could keep 'im, lovey?" Beard laughed and gave her a big kiss. "You'll have to ask the Army, Mum, he belongs to them for the present. Perhaps he'll be open to offers after the war!" Ruth, too, found moments to be alone with him ... and amused herself by running her fingers all over his face, especially his chin, and exclaiming how rough his skin felt now that he had to shave for real. Beard wasn't too sure if she was being saucy or not.

Lord Thierry liked to walk around his estate with Beard: they did so daily, sometimes briefly accompanied by Lady Pamella. The talk was invariably about when their sons would return home, but rarely touching on the war itself, although Lord Thierry proudly showed off the magnificent and extensive repairs and alterations carried out in both the house and grounds by his American visitors. He looked aghast when Beard joked that they'd probably send him the bill when they were safely home. Stafford probably missed the Americans more than anybody: he now had to rely solely on his lordship's cellars for his needs! He evidently had a very real fondness for his "cousins across the Atlantic," for on a visit to the Laughing Pig, Beard discovered that Bunty had presented him with another son – and that the poor child had been christened Eisenhower! On reflection, Beard wondered if perhaps this was not an indication on Bunty's part as to the nationality of the true father!

It wasn't until they were about to leave that Beard could snatch a few moments alone with Poppy; Ruth had generally made sure of that. "I won't ask you who this Jarvis person is, Bobbie – it's *you* she loves," said Poppy, slipping her hand inside his arm. Beard smiled affectionately at her and tightened his arm. "How is Bertie, really?" he asked her.

"He's mending, Bobbie – but he'll be a long time mending, and that's what he hates the most. He's impatient to stop being a patient, and especially, he wants to be able to walk normally, and not just a few paces," Poppy said, and looked hastily round to make sure she hadn't been overheard. "He can't get used to the fact that he'll never be as active as he was again. He puts on a brave face for everyone, but sometimes when we're alone the hurt shows – and I could cry."

Beard looked at her with concern. "Was I wrong to ask him to look after my affairs? There was no one else to ask. I don't have many friends, and very few that I trust absolutely. But if you think it's too much for him ... "

Poppy shook her head vigorously and gripped his arm. "Oh, no, Bobbie, it's wonderful for him and he's delighted to do what little he can. He needs something to occupy his mind."

Beard gave a little smile and stooped to touch the hand on his arm with his lips. "He'll be all right once he's able to walk properly and gets the green light to go ahead with his farming career, marries Maud and they set up home together. I'm sure you're largely responsible that Bertie's recovered as well as he has. I wish you and Ben a very happy married life – and that you have lots of babies so as to make old Stafford jealous!"

Poppy laughed and blushed very prettily, and laid a warm kiss on his cheek. "What about you, Bobbie?" she asked softly. "Ruth loves you so very, very much – but she needs reassuring. Don't frown so! I know that you love her, too. Tell her so ... again and again and again. That's all a girl ever wants to hear from her lover – all she listens to, anyway. And she's so desperately unhappy about losing the ring you gave her."

Beard, who had begun to look rather uncomfortable, cleared his throat and suddenly looked quite cheerful. "That's all in hand," he declared, his eyes twinkling. Poppy looked askance, but he'd said all he intended to.

When Beard, Queenie and Ruth arrived back in London, Mrs B.

was waiting there for them at Grafton Road. In fact, several people were waiting: Trumpett, Jenkins, Simms and Mr Fennell, the solicitor. Trumpett came forward, gave Beard a thumbs up and said, "Everything's in order, sir. Went very smooth, sir." Beard nodded, and shook hands with the solicitor. He had arranged that Mr Fennell should meet them here so that he could drive Queenie and Ruth down to Peartree Cottage – or to Miss Hatchet's place if need be. It had been a slow journey from Highways because they had seemed to hit one convoy after the other, as a result of which – thankfully – there was little time available for farewells. Beard and his men, their leaves almost at an end, had to report at Chelmsford almost directly, and they were on their way without even stopping for one of Mrs B.'s cups of tea. It was all so sudden they were gone before Queenie and Ruth realised. A few quick words, a torrent of hurried kisses, a final hug ... and they were gone.

"There's a letter waiting for you in the cottage," Beard shouted as they roared away. His words were still ringing in Ruth's ears when the first of her tears began to tumble.

Ruth had felt hurt and bitterly disappointed at the suddenness of his departure, but all was forgotten and forgiven when they arrived at Peartree Cottage. It was like a new building from without, and within it was completely transformed. Queenie very nearly fainted when she entered the kitchen, for there, all polished like new for all its dents and scars, was her beloved Aga. In a note on the kitchen table, and even that was her own, Beard explained that he and his men had systematically sieved through The Dials debris in an effort to retrieve what was possible. The Aga had been their main target and it had taken them several days to extricate since they'd had to shift tons of masonry by hand. There had not been a great deal more that wasn't smashed to pieces, but they had managed to retrieve a few items that would help them to feel more at home – the kitchen table, some pots and pans, a few chairs, a chest of drawers, a cupboard and even her own bed – though it had needed a new mattress, and a number of personal bits and pieces. There was also a small cardboard box on the kitchen table. Inside was Sam's George Medal, a number of important documents and every item of jewellery that Queenie and Ruth had owned, including Ruth's engagement ring.

Ruth had her engagement ring back on the moment she saw it, and at once started to cry. Queenie raced through the house identifying little treasures recovered from The Dials, and then she shed a few tears of happiness, but being a very sensible and practical woman, she was very quickly polishing the Aga.

"What a blessed boy!" she murmured to Ruth, who still sat at the kitchen table admiring her hand – or rather the ring restored to it. "Those boys must've worked like navvies right through their leave. God bless them all."

"Oh, yes," sighed Ruth blissfully.

At Keevil aerodrome in Wiltshire two nights later, as they climbed aboard a Stirling, Beard turned to his men and said: "Come on, lads, you've had your leave, now let's get back to the war and get our share of the loot before it's all gone. I'm skint."

"That was one of the happiest times of my life," declared Queenie, "and the start of a new one that has been equally happy." Amen to that, Ruth added dreamily.
"How's that, Queenie?" asked the Matron, who was now known to them as Miss Ivy Flinn.
"Oh, you'll 'ave to wait an' see, Ivy," Queenie replied, and added with a smile, "I am so enjoying this story. If only Jarvis would wake hisself up and remember."

Chapter Thirty-three

Somewhere in Germany, October, 1944

Beard returned to France to find that the whole pattern of the war, his role in it at any rate, had changed. As the German forces in France were being pushed remorselessly back, Gibbs's new orders were to operate well behind the front line in Germany itself, gathering intelligence of army movements, hitting constantly at the enemy's supply lines and chasing down the top war criminals. The French may not have been wholly trustworthy, but at least there had been a modicum of safety among them. Now, Beard and his men faced operating in the midst of an entirely hostile population, and relying solely on air drops for supplies.

Beard's plane put them down on an airstrip close to the forest of Raismes, near Valenciennes in north-eastern France. Here they were reunited with the remainder of their squadron, and moved almost at once to an isolated holding camp some forty miles north-east of Brussels. But before heading for the Führer's Fatherland, there was a surprise ceremony.

The French were so delighted to have been almost liberated and so eager to see the back of their liberators, that they distributed decorations left and right like confetti at a wedding. Beard, along with several of his colleagues, found himself the recipient of a Croix de Guerre in this display of largesse. He wasn't sure its bestowal was worth the ordeal of having some smarmy Frog general standing on tiptoe to kiss him on both cheeks, but as Gibbs growled, they might as well accept the things with as good grace as possible. "I don't suppose they love us any more than we do them, so don't start getting excited over their kisses, Robert! It's all in the line of duty, as they say."

A week later, Beard's squadron was assigned a role in that part of Germany lying between the Maas and the Rhine. Their principle task was to locate rocket launching sites and gather intelligence.

Although dropping in something of a gale, the men landed without any major mishap, regrouped and quickly set off to seek out targets. Two of the six Jeeps dropped with them had been smashed beyond repair, but Beard was confident of quickly replacing them with German vehicles. The squadron split into its several Troops, with Capt Nigel Griffin, the new leader of the 2nd Troop, heading north towards Holland; Capt Pardoe and his new aide, Lt Ian Harris, a fresh-faced, freshly commissioned Guards officer and fresh, too, to active service, went south expecting to link up with the Americans; and Beard, plus a new 4th Troop, under a Capt Clive Pitman, headed east, in the direction of the Rhine. The main aim of them all was to locate missile launching sites, which Intelligence reported as being "somewhere in the area." They were to radio back the positions so that the RAF could destroy them; and if they couldn't find any, they were free to indulge in a manner likely to cause maximum inconvenience to the enemy.

Beard, having quickly assessed Pitman as being a more than competent officer, sent him off on his own with instructions to keep in touch. Three days later, he sent off Summerbee and Trumpett with half his Troop, arranging a rendezvous a week hence so that they could compare notes. Beard, leaving the remainder of his Troop to establish a base, set off in their one available Jeep to see what he could find. Jenkins drove them through what appeared to be a vast well-wooded park. Clinging on in the rear of the vehicle were Felbridge, Trooper Blossom and Sgt Sidney Curtis, a recent transfer from the Green Howards who had seen action at Cassino.

After a couple of hours, Beard called a halt. His sixth sense gave him warning of habitations, humanity at least, nearby. They concealed the Jeep and proceeded on foot. "Remember, men," he warned softly as his men fanned out into the drizzly darkness, "the natives round here are Germans, so don't start getting too friendly."

"Does that go for the women, too, sir?" asked Blossom with an enquiring grin.

"Especially them," grinned back Beard. He looked round knowing, even if he couldn't see him, that Jenkins would have him in his sights. He was safe there. To Beard's left would be the dependable Trooper Felbridge with his deadly rifle and the radio on which they all depended, while Sgt Curtis was somewhere far ahead. Beard couldn't see any of them, but he knew they were there and that they'd respond at once to any signal from him, just as he would to any alarm from one of them. The only sound he could hear was that of the rain plopping against those leaves waiting to fall. It was a sign of a long, hard winter ahead. He was thinking of this when he became aware of the sound of a fast-flowing river. He assumed this would be the Maas, or something running into it.

Beard had lost none of his ability to move soundlessly through woods, which was just as well. As the trees thinned out, he paused behind a substantial birch to acclimatize his eyes to the lightening density of the darkness. He was thinking that dawn could not be all that far off when a sound, as of a person clearing his throat, shattered the stillness; for a moment, he could not place the sound and it was only when his straining ears caught the rhythmic breathing of the other that he realised someone was standing the other side of the tree. *His tree*! Beard felt himself almost stop breathing as he reached for his knife and, with infinite care, edged snake-like round the bole. He saw the outline of the man, who was leaning against the tree, and for a fraction of a second their eyes stared expressionlessly into the other's. The German's eyes did not have time to express either alarm or wonder; he was dead. Beard's knife flashed and buried itself in the man's heart; he gave the weapon an extra twist knowing that another blow was unnecessary. He was more concerned with catching the man's body and pushing its face into the ground to muffle the throes of death. It stopped twitching only after what seemed an extraordinary length of time, but was probably little more than a minute. Using a torch with great care to examine the man's *Soldbuch*, Beard discovered that he was an artilleryman. After dragging the body back inside the tree line, Beard helped himself to the man's Schmeisser and pistol, checking that both were loaded, pocketed some spare magazines, and continued on his way.

After a few moments, Beard paused to reflect. He deduced that the man he had just killed was a sentry, that being so someone would be along sooner or later to check up on him; another thing was that sentries tended to be guarding something. What? Beard peered about him, but the dark had come quickly and he could see nothing but shadows and the outline of trees and bushes, certainly no other guards nor any buildings. He moved carefully back into the protection of trees, and presently found – well, he nearly decapitated himself making the discovery – a telephone cable strung through the trees beside what appeared to be a track leading somewhere. The track was plainly in constant use and, having examined the ruts and decided that some very heavily-laden vehicles had made them, Beard whistled to his unseen companions, withdrew some forty yards back into the forest, and together they followed the track on a parallel course. After about two miles, the terrain dipped and the trees came to a sudden finish. The ground ahead of them had been cleared and the large open space was filled, in an orderly manner, with wooden and canvas accommodations, and the entire area was surrounded by mountains of barbed wire and overhung with camouflage netting. Soldiers were very much in evidence, as were the guards and checkpoints.

Beard was busy making a sketch of the camp, and it was so sprawling he couldn't see it all, when he caught a faint sound; he froze, save for one hand that that already held his pistol with its silencer attachment; a single finger switched off the safety catch. He was unsure what had alerted him, it might have been a damp twig being carelessly trodden on, or a tiny pebble being kicked; he held his breath as he turned round, trying to place the sound. And then he saw Blossom moving wraith-like towards him out of the gloom. Even though his young face looked as if it had survived several wars, it still managed to look a cheeky face, especially when he grinned, like now. "Sorry about the racket, sir," he whispered, rather loudly. "I didn't want to startle you, sir," added Blossom easily, giving his fair hair a good scratching as he surveyed the camp below. "Next time give me a whistle, I might have shot you – by mistake," said Beard, putting the safety catch back on.

Blossom grinned. "What do you reckon this place is, then, sir?" Beard shook his head. "Some place they want to keep pretty secret," he said. "Doesn't look to have the sort of buildings that you'd expect if it was some sort of factory – unless everything's underground; Jerry seems to like digging." Blossom's grin widened. "Perhaps they're digging their graves!" They both chuckled.

It was Sgt Curtis who provided the explanation. Tall, lean, immensely strong and generally taciturn, he arrived about an hour later, moving expertly from cover to cover and dropping down beside Beard and Blossom with barely a whisper of sound. "Heard you all from yards away, sir," he declared softly, with a grin. "It's a storage depot for them missiles of theirs – the V-1s and 2s, sir," he explained, his voice flat and unexcited. "I got right up close to the wire – it's electrified by the way, sir – and watched some blokes lifting some crates about. I was able to make out the word *Vergeltungswaffe Ein* on the side of one box. I remembered it was what they called their retaliation weapon." Beard gave a hurried nod.

"I'm afraid our presence may very quickly be known, sir," Curtis added, with a rather bleak expression. "One of the sentries spotted me ... actually, we met face to face – and I had to kill him." The sergeant looked so apologetic about it that Beard couldn't help but smile. "Don't worry, sergeant, I left another one back there somewhere," he said. "Me, too – two of the buggers," declared Blossom cheerily. Beard shuddered, and wondered what Jenkins's tally would be, but it was an hour or so be fore the corporal materialised beside the others.

"You know that road over there," he jerked a thumb in the direction of the track Beard had stumbled across, "it leads to a narrow gauge railway line. Just the one track. Don't know where it goes to, but it starts at the end of this 'ere road – about seven miles away. There's some points there and quite a few wagons parked. There's also some well camouflaged sheds, and about half a company of troops. The ones I saw were SS. I wanted to have a go at the points, but there were too many Jerries around to be able to do anything without being seen. Could 'ave a go tonight, if yer like?"

Beard shook his head. "I think we'll get out of here pretty damned quick, boys, and let the RAF have some target practice. Where's Felbridge?" And right on cue, they all heard the radioman approaching. "Having a party?" he drawled, squatting beside them.

It was some three hours before Felbridge was able to raise Gibbs, who had a Phantom radio section with him, and pass on the information; it was another two hours after that before Gibbs called them back to say that London had been informed. He advised Beard and his men to get out of the area as quickly as possible, although there was no knowing when a strike could be made. It was moments like this that made Beard wish they had more Jeeps with them: he missed their mobility and their fire-power. Beard gave himself a mental shrug, and told Felbridge to warn Trumpett of the impending air strike and to fix a different RV somewhere farther north, and deeper into Germany. Even as Felbridge was contacting Trumpett, Beard gave the order to move out. "We'll have to find some wheels if we're going to keep hopping about like this," he told the men. The remark was greeted with low murmurs of agreement, and Beard was not blind to the fact that both Sgt Curtis and Blossom instantly lengthened their stride and disappeared ahead. He turned to give a wink to Jenkins, who nodded approvingly.

Eight miles farther on they were all riding in a German three-ton lorry. Jenkins, wearing a coal-scuttle helmet complete with swastika and SS runes, occupied the driving seat and alongside him sat Beard, looking rather grand with his much-braided peaked cap with its death's head symbol. The headgear was the only addition to their normal attire: the rest of them was regarded as being sufficiently nondescript and, anyway, screened by the vehicle – with the fluttering swastika on the bonnet the ultimate deterrent. In the back, crowded round a mounted heavy machine-gun, the remainder sat looking as indifferently German as they could with only one helmet between them. This was worn by Felbridge who claimed to have the only head big enough to wear it. The others agreed about the size of his head! Sgt Curtis, who took up position behind the gun, wore a German forage cap which he carried around for just such occasions. Blossom's only gesture in this direction was to remove his beret and stare bare-headed over the sides of the lorry, waving at an occasional passer-by, civilian or otherwise, with one hand, while the other held the Sten gun, which was fitted with a silencer, just in case. Following, at a discreet distance, came their Jeep, driven by Cpl Cole, who had been with Beard in Tunisia, with Pte Tom Hill, his "postman" in Cairo, to keep him company.

Beard didn't enquire too deeply into how the lorry had been acquired. He gathered it had stopped to enable the four occupants to have a "piss and a smoke," as Blossom put it. Curtis and Blossom had simply pounced while the Jerries were thus occupied. "Took no more'n ten seconds, sir," said Curtis coldly. "We just rolled the bodies in a ditch – an' was out of there even quicker in case there were more of 'em followin' behind. But there weren't an' we just got off the road an' waited for you to come along."

Beard listened to the blunt explanation with an absent nod, and only wondered if the pair might have missed the opportunity of searching for useful papers among the bodies in their haste to be away. But the immediate priority was to remove themselves as far as possible from the vicinity, and Jenkins was never one to dawdle. It often surprised Beard – even though they kept to side-roads and often tracks that were in no way roads at all – that they were able to drive for hours through Germany itself, and in a stolen German Army lorry, without any real hindrance. They never came across a roadblock that compelled them to stop; and even at the occasional crossroads where a military policeman directed the traffic, they were impatiently waved on, and sometimes even received a salute, to which Beard responded. He imagined the SS insignia on the lorry was a sort of passport – nobody wanted to fall foul of the SS! He'd immediately put on what he hoped was a fearsome scowl, but this didn't have much effect at the very next junction.

It was manned by two genuine SS troopers, one of whom fondled a machine-gun attached to a motorcycle combination that stood at the road edge, while his partner stood in the middle of the road and flagged them down. Beard shot the man in the side-car, and Jenkins put his foot down and ran over the other. At a word from Beard, the lorry screeched to a halt and Beard, shouting to the three men in the back to follow him, dashed back to drag the bodies out of sight. " Strip them – their uniforms might come in handy," he decided on impulse, and in almost no time the bodies were stripped. "Take a big-headed bastard to fit into these," declared Blossom, his arms full of boots and clothes, staring straight at Curtis. But Curtis only grinned back. "You're right, chum," he said evenly as he and Felbridge were busy manhandling the motor cycle aboard the lorry.

They hid the lorry deep in some woods about 15 miles inside Germany from Kaldenkirchen, on the Dutch border, and then left, using the motor cycle and the Jeep as beasts of burden, for another densely wooded area some twenty miles further inland where Beard had decided to set up a temporary camp. He really needed to get much deeper into Germany if he was to become effective. They'd been in Germany almost a fortnight now, and Beard thought they hadn't done too badly. The squadron was strung out as far south as the Ardennes, where Capt Griffin was operating, and his own Troop was adequately dispersed and, hopefully, functioning well. He was pleased his own section had enjoyed an immediate success by stumbling across the rocket depot: it would give them all a fillip.

They'd had to duck off the road and hide in the undergrowth as a long convoy of military vehicles clattered by, but eventually found a suitable place and quickly established themselves and took stock of their situation. Beard kept in touch with the dispersed sections of his Squadron without interfering with their activities : it seemed sensible to leave them to their own devices. He decided to split his own Troop into three camps of no more than half a dozen men within a reasonable distance so that they could cover a wider area, coordinate their raids and pool their information; if the worst happened and one camp was discovered, he did not want them all to be caught. He put Lt Harris in charge of one of these camps and Lt Jack Middlebrook, another newcomer, the other. This left Summerbee and himself free to coordinate their actions and at the same time indulge in forays of their own. However, Beard decided to include Trumpett in his camp and to this end he sent word to the sergeant-major and his men to join him.

Beard hadn't expected to be so pleased to see Trumpett but, after all, it was rather like meeting a close relative – a three-year friendship was a long while in wartime. The two men shook hands, each gripping the other very firmly and neither displaying any wish to be the first to let go. In the end they did so simultaneously, as by mutual agreement, and they spent the next several seconds unconsciously flexing their hands and grinning at one another. "Good to see you, Jack," said Beard warmly. "Any problems?"

Trumpett shook his head as they squatted down inside a decidedly small tent – it was small for men of his stature, anyway. "We was glad you warned us to keep clear of that bomb depot place. The RAF blew it to blazes, an' pretty well most of the country-side around it."

"Good – it was one of those V-1s that destroyed The Dials!" cried Beard, his face glowing with satisfaction.

Summerbee joined the two men and they talked at length about the state of the war, or rather the part they were playing in it, poring over maps and discussing routes to possible targets and agreeing that the first priority was to organise supply drops at a suitably distant spot. "What we really need is some more Jeeps," declared Beard emphatically. "Our prime role is the gathering of intelligence, and we won't learn much if we're restricted to humping all our worldly goods on foot, or thieving. I don't mind the thieving, but it draws attention to us. Besides, we need the firepower the Jeeps provide, as much for defence as attack."

He asked Trumpett if anything interesting had turned up during his recent travels, and the sergeant-major told him, "We spotted some V-1 launching ramps, sir, marvellously well camouflaged they were, too. We radioed their position to Mr Yeo, an' bless me if the air force didn't come over a bare two hours later an' blow 'em all to kingdom come. Trouble was, we hadn't got far enough away an' in the hue an' cry that followed we found ourselves surrounded by Jerry. We had a bit of a fire-fight, but we managed to give 'em the slip. Trooper Sanderson got hit. Lost most of his left hand. The first I knew of it was when I saw him stoop down to pick up one of his fingers!"

"Where's he now?" asked Beard expressionlessly, although he felt a shiver within him.

"Major Yorke of B Squadron happened to have a doctor with him, and he paid us a visit an' took him away. He's probably safely back in Blighty – and happy to be home for Christmas."

At the mention of Christmas, Beard felt an irresistible urge to be home himself. He wondered if it was an odd sensation for an orphan who had spent his life in institutions, especially since Christmas had never meant all that much to him – but, then, the only ones that had meant anything to him were the ones he'd spent at The Dials. Now, of course, it would be Peartree Cottage, and just the thought made him homesick – and he'd never even slept there. But he knew it was his home too, and he wanted to be there with Queenie and Ruth. They were his family; they represented the only semblance of a home he'd ever known – his only joy and happiness; they'd shared their home with him when they were able, and given him their love unreservedly. If he loved anybody in this world, and he believed he did, it was them. The thought of Ruth kindled a smile in his heart: it was reflected in his eyes and touched his lips. He always felt happy when he thought of her. At moments like this, he had no doubts whatever that he would marry her – and was eager to. Wouldn't it be simply marvellous if they could all be together this Christmas! There was a lot of talk about Christmas among the men, even talk of peace by Christmas ... there was always talk.

The talk, of course, came to nothing, and Beard continued to wage his own brand of warfare, determined to be as big a thorn as possible in the backside of the enemy. His attempts had only limited success, and were achieved at a heavy cost. Lt Harris and half his section were lost. Harris had gone south expecting to link up with the 1st US Army at any moment, but only succeeded in losing touch with half his men when they split up; in his effort to find them, Harris and the remainder of his section had apparently been captured after mistaking a German patrol for Americans. This was only learned when the Americans, who had already met up with the other half of the section, found the sole survivor; critically wounded, he lived only long enough to whisper the barest details of what had happened.

[*Nothing was ever discovered about the fate of Lt Harris and the remainder of the section, but in view of what was subsequently to come to light about such events, there is no doubt that all five missing men were murdered. The War Office showed very little interest in such matters after the war, being content with the year-long show-piece trials at Nuremberg.*]

Griffin's Troop came through unscathed despite ten days of continuous activity. He and his men had achieved nothing spectacular but had nevertheless continuously harassed the enemy whenever they met. He had strafed two convoys, setting several lorries ablaze, ambushed a small patrol, sabotaged a bridge in the course of repair, mined several roads –   and even sunk a barge on the Maas. "Unfortunately, it was empty," he grinned as he related his adventures to Beard over mugs of rum-tea. "Still, I should think we gave Jerry a few sleepless nights. The men performed very well."

"You all did," Beard told him warmly.

Gibbs, who seemed to be everywhere and all at the same time, dropped in on Beard for a two-hour visit, and though Beard pressed the need for more Jeeps in the next supply drop, he had no opportunity to raise the possibilities of leave at Christmas. Gibbs was gone, and the winter intensified. It was becoming desperately cold living in fragile tents even with the help of sleeping bags, and two pairs of everything. Already there had been heavy snowfalls, and when it wasn't snowing it was raining bullets of sleet, and the bitter winds seemed to be with them always. No matter how they protected themselves, the winds icy fingers found a way through their clothing and wrapped themselves round their bodies until they were well nigh frozen. Beard kept a constant check on the health of his men, making sure they were as dry and warm as possible and that they all had at least one hot meal a day – however uninteresting it might be. Beard shivered as he sat with his hands gripped round his knees.

If it hadn't been for the need to keep the men fit, Beard gave serious thought of closing down operations for the winter, but knowing the decision was not his to make, he had them out whenever the weather permitted. Often there was very little they could do, but at least they could keep active and watch the enemy.

The highlight of this dreary period was the visit of a newly-appointed padre, Captain Adam St George Parsons, though whether he would have been greeted quite so enthusiastically if he hadn't brought a sackful of mail with him is debatable. Beard's share was quite formidable for in addition to an early Christmas set of handkerchiefs from Ruth (whose shirt-tail was she carving up now, he wondered) and a new letter, there were also her three missing letters telling him about the bombing of The Dials and of their move to Mrs B.'s – and, of course, begging him for a letter *"although I expect they'll give you compassionate leave if you explain about us being bombed out and losing every blessed thing except our lives."* Beard abandoned his visitor to the others while he pored through the letters, and the padre moved understandingly away to give solace to those who did not have the comfort of a letter, giving them cigarettes and sweets in their place.

"My Darling," wrote Ruth in her latest letter, *"The Peartree is a dream that could only be improved if you were here to share it – then it would be heaven. Mummy loves it, I love it, and we both love you for it. Thank you, thank you, thank you for our lovely home – and for the treasures you rescued from The Dials, especially my beautiful ring which I never dare take off now – and do, please, try and be with us for Christmas. Oh, wouldn't that be simply too wonderful after what's happened to poor Daddy and The Dials! I know I mustn't ask for too much, but an awful lot of homes have heard that their loved ones will probably be getting Christmas leave – all the way from France, or wherever they are. Couldn't you be one of those, darling? We haven't had a Christmas together for years and years. It's not fair of the Army always keeping you from us, and you tell your general I said so – and*

Mummy, too! I know I'm being silly, but we miss you so much. I know there's nothing you can do about it, my darling, but I shall be praying that you get leave – and if you don't, I shall simply pray for you, as always. Pray that you're safe, and that you'll come home to us soon."

The letter went on to describe Ruth's business career course in Bloomsbury, which meant she stayed up in London with Mrs B. during the week and went home on Friday evening. Ruth thought she was doing quite well, although she found the work hard and hated the hours she spent learning Pitman's shorthand. *"It's just like Chinese – and horrid,"* she wrote, *"but apparently it's essential."* Friday was the best day of the week because it was the end of the week, and she could run away to The Pears and think of him. *"So please, my darling, send me a letter soon and tell us you'll be home for Christmas!"* She went on to say that his room was always ready for him, but that so far only Rosie and George had slept in his bed. Queenie, it seemed, had settled down instantly in her new surroundings and quickly made friends both among her neighbours and in the village. Mrs Tyler (above, at the Cherries) and Mrs Baylis (below, at the Damsons) were always in and out or gossiping through the hedges and exchanging recipes. *"I do believe they're all in the black market because you never saw so much food in your life – even at The Dials!"* Beard was astonished that the censor had let that through, but supposed that individual was involved in black market deals as well. And why not? People had to look out for themselves as best they could in these times: some laws were meant to be tiptoed over.

Ruth said that Mr Fennell, the solicitor, came over from Tiptree quite often to see for himself that all was well and to enquire if they needed anything, and seemed in no way deterred from continuing his visits when told they needed for nothing. *"I think he finds Mummy 'interesting.' I don't think he's met anyone like her before! He always has tea with us when he comes over and the two of them jaw for ever! It's rather sweet in a way. He's very partial to Mummy's cakes – I don't suppose he gets proper cake anywhere else. He always has two huge slices."* I bet you do, too, smiled Beard. *"I think his gammy foot puts him off travelling very far and making new friends,"* added Ruth. Mr Woolven, the undertaker, was frequently to be seen, but Ruth was of the opinion that he was only on the look out in case anyone might be in need (or about to be) of his professional services. *"I hate him,"* confided Ruth, *"he always seems to be measuring people with his fish eyes!"* Mr Crabtree – *"we call him Mr Crab, of course!"* – the gravedigger sent by Mr Woolven as a gardener, seemed to forget where he was – and dug exceedingly deeply! Miss Hatchet was another frequent visitor and she and Queenie were very "thick" in the kitchen. *"They're making home-made gin and things. Perhaps Mummy's going into the bootlegging business!"* suggested Ruth.

She added that Ben, who presumably was home from the sea,

and Poppy planned to visit them in the new year, and concluded by saying: "*Mummy sends her love to you and all your men, especially that sergeant of yours – Mr Trumpett? I think Mummy was so impressed by all the work he did that she wants to adopt him! My love goes only to you, my darling. God bless, and come home safely to us – for Christmas if you can.*" There were two postscripts; one accused him of forgetting her birthday – her seventeenth! – again, and the other told him that Mavis, who had received such terrible injuries in The Dials bombing, had died in hospital.

When he looked up, still clutching his letters, from his mammoth read, Beard saw that Capt Parsons had returned and was standing just outside the tent patiently waiting. "Come in, Padre, you'll freeze out there," he called and, waving the letters, said "Thank you for these. They mean more than all the world to us." The padre smiled and replied quietly that he was merely the postman. "Ah, but I like to think God sent you," grinned Beard. The priest produced a flask from his haversack that very definitely did not contain communion wine. They were both quite merry and the flask empty when Jenkins poked his head in to say "Grub's up, sirs!"

While Capt Parsons was still with them, Beard's troop received its promised delivery of Jeeps: three of them; there were five, but one of them crashed through the ice in the middle of a lake and, after bobbing about rather conspicuously, sank; and the other simply smashed into a thousand pieces when two of the chutes candled and it crashed to the ground. As Trumpett observed, at least the timber in which the vehicles had been so zealously crated would provide them with a ready supply of fuel for Christmas fires.

"Well, what a godsend you've been, padre," cried Beard enthusiastically. "First letters, and now Jeeps. It must be a good omen for Christmas leave!"

But there was to be no such miraculous Christmas stocking for any of them, for this year, Father Christmas wore a steel helmet and a swastika on his breast, and he came early so you couldn't slip away on leave; he came in a blizzard in his hundreds of thousands through the Ardennes with his sights set on the Channel coast, the aim being to split the Allied armies.

Gibbs sent word ordering all three squadrons to join him, and his voice sounded urgent. "The Krauts are on the bloody offensive!" he said.

It was Saturday, December 16. The Battle of the Bulge had begun. Beard and as many of his men he could contact, reached the Ardennes that same night, and were in action within an hour of arrival.

Chapter Thirty-four

Battle of the Bulge, 16 December, 1944

And fight they did. Always on the move. The Germans, who called their offensive Autumn Fog, came steamrolling through behind an hour-long barrage by mortars, rockets and the notorious 88s along an 85-mile front.

They came through the Losheim Gap, the same route the German blitzkrieg had taken in 1940 – and it was as lightly defended today as it had been then. It was through this seven-mile corridor that the tanks, armoured cars and heavy guns poured almost unopposed: men of the 5th Panzer Army, the 6th SS Panzer Army and the 7th Army with its twenty divisions. A quarter of a million men, with thousands of tanks, armoured cars and assault guns.

There was only one way to meet such an onslaught, and that was to sidestep it. Beard did this skilfully, and as speedily as it was possible in the atrocious conditions. The heavy snow and bitter cold, and more particularly the continuous bombardment, made worse and more terrifying by the hollow boom of the train-mounted guns far to the rear of the Germans hurling their fourteen-inch shells at targets miles behind the American lines, and shaking the ground like an earthquake – these all combined to dictate the movements of Beard's four Troops, who numbered a touch over a hundred men..

Mostly it was a case of keeping their heads down, and moving only as opportunities presented themselves. These were very few, but risks were sometimes imposed upon them, and casualties ensued. Two men were killed and four wounded in the first hour. Beard saw that the injured were made as comfortable as possible, and continued seeking to get round the massive German force and tackle it from the rear. But this proved an impossible ambition for the invading force had a depth and breadth beyond their capabilities; the seven-mile-wide corridor through which the Germans were steamrollering was heavily protected on both sides to a depth of scores of miles. And it was these forces that Beard had to infiltrate to achieve anything. A lot of men died in the attempt, but the rest succeeded, slowly.

Beard was on the northern edge of the flank, and surrounded by the enemy, and movement was the only way to survive. Even so, it seemed almost impossible to disengage himself and press forward. It was a case of one evasive action after the other: evasive because there were so many of them, and so few of him; he'd never seen the Germans in such numbers, and with so much heavy equipment. It was three days before he was able to break away to keep his rendezvous with Gibbs and the other squadrons south of Losheimergraben, which was several miles north of the gap. He'd repeatedly had to take diversionary routes to avoid ever-increasing enemy presence, and on two occasions they had had to battle their way past roadblocks manned by Germans in American uniforms. He'd lost four more men and had two others wounded, neither too seriously; and one of the Jeeps was damaged and had to be towed.

Gibbs, looking remarkably cheerful and unruffled, greeted them like it was a gathering of the clans. They met in a narrow opening of a forest where the firs stood like white ghosts and an icy wind howled through slapping their faces with snow that wasn't at all soft. Yorke and his B Squadron had been the first to arrive, and had already been assigned their area of operations and sent on their way. Other men of Beard's own squadron and from the others converged at the rendezvous in dribs and drabs throughout the day, and for many of them it was the first time they'd seen each other since pre-invasion days at Chelmsford.

Beard acknowledged shouted greetings from men he hadn't seen in a long while, and waved to his Troop commanders as they arrived. Nigel Griffin's B Troop was followed some hours later by Colin Pardoe, C Troop. There was no sign that day of Clive Pitman's D Troop, nor could Felbridge raise them by radio, and Beard feared the worst. But there was little time to dwell on such matters or to renew acquaintances; a quick handshake or a slap on the back, a few quick questions and answers about where they'd been and with what success, a hurriedly eaten bowl of hot soup and a shared drink was all they had time for. The sounds of battles were loud and ferocious, and dangerously close, and Gibbs had no intention of them being caught in the open.

"Gentlemen," he told them, "there are reportedly three German armies on the move, and heading our way." He stood very tall in his Jeep, his fair hair waving in the bitter cold wind, his moustache frozen white, and grinned at the circle of attentive faces. "It would seem a good idea to move out of their way." The ring of serious faces broke into chuckles. "So, the plan is for the various Troops to infiltrate their lines in groups of five or six and do terrible things in their rear. I imagine supplies, especially petrol, will be their main concern – so concentrate on them. I'll attach my HQ section to Mr Appleton's squadron and operate with them. Communication is vital. Keep in touch, if you can, and," he paused and gave a wave all round in a manner that was not dissimilar to a Nazi salute, "if we don't meet up before, happy Christmas to everyone!"

There was a hasty, though careful, study of maps as the different groups were assigned areas in which to operate, but finally Beard's group moved off. They had been resupplied with food, ammunition and petrol thanks to a convoy of lorries Col Yeo had somehow managed to wriggle through the German lines. Beard had acquired a replacement officer for Lt Harris: a Lt Tim Morrison, dark-haired and built like a rugby player. With Morrison came the four survivors of Lt Harris's ill-fated section, so now the 3rd Troop's strength stood at 32 men, which worked out just right with the transport they had, which was more German than Allied.

Beard had hoped to rest the night at Gibbs's base, but the area was already coming under fire, so it made sense to move on. They pushed forward thirty odd miles before Beard called a halt so that they could eat and catch up with some sleep, which they hadn't had for three nights. He gave Trumpett the task of arranging sentries up to five miles deep and gave the newcomer, Lt Morrison, the job of organising hot food – and a truly excellent job he did; he later revealed that his family had a string of hotels and restaurants back in England and that he'd attended a top culinary course as part of his education. On this occasion, he achieved miracles with a stray something-or-other one of the men found tied to a tree near an abandoned forester's cabin that had been blown up. Someone said that it was a particular breed of sheep: someone else, probably nearer the truth, suggested it was a wolf. Of course, Jenkins swore that it was nothing but a mangy dog, a German one, but that didn't stop him from adding, as he ate voraciously, "pity it were such a small critter."

The following day, Wednesday, December 20, as the panzers were knocking on the door of Bastogne, Beard split his 1st Troop into four sections, each with two Jeeps, and sent them forth to do battle as opportunity presented itself; Summerbee commanded one section and Jack Middleton another. As usual, Beard gave Trumpett a section of his own, knowing that the sergeant-major was probably more experienced than any of the officers – himself included. They were to rendezvous in four days, but maintain radio contact daily.

Trumpett's Jeeps disappeared in one direction while Beard moved off in another: none of the vehicles made all that much noise, though this may have been due, in part, to the explosions that roared all around them – even if at a relatively safe distance. It was hilly, heavily-forested country and the only open areas were covered in deep snow; when it wasn't snowing, there was drizzle, and fog and haze, and there seemed to be always an aggressive wind, bitter cold and stinging. All around them battles could be heard: large or small they all sounded ferocious – and too damned close for comfort. Beard hunched over the Vickers machine-gun in the front of his Jeep and occasionally blew on his frozen finger tips, and wished he had a nice thick beard to keep his face warm – instead of the smooth, pink skin he seemed destined to have all his life. Beside him Jenkins, well-bearded (blast him!), blew clouds of warm air into the freezing atmosphere and picked his way with infinite care so that he scarcely disturbed a twig. In the rear, his eyes and ears searching for the least hint of danger, Felbridge crouched with the radio and his trusty rifle. In the second Jeep, some fifty yards behind, were Sgt Curtis, Tom Hill and Blossom, who were equally alert for anything out of the ordinary. With so many eyes watching it seemed unlikely that they would be taken by surprise come what may – but one never knew.

There were Germans everywhere, hundreds of them, and not all of them were in uniform; that is, they were in uniform, but American ones. Lieut-Col Otto Skorzeny, Hitler's favourite commando, had been ordered to train his men to masquerade as Americans and operate behind the American lines creating as much confusion and panic as possible. In the event very few of Skorzeny's men penetrated the lines, though those who did achieved successes beyond their most optimistic hopes. Apart from changing signposts and cutting telephone wires, genuine American forces were personally directed down wrong roads by very realistic gum-chewing, baseball-talking bogus GIs. One of their greatest successes was the cutting of the main telephone cables linking General Omar Bradley's 12th Army Group with General Courtney Hodges, his commander in the north. Militarily Skorzeny's main role was to secure bridges over the Meuse to make possible Hitler's goal of a drive to Antwerp, but an abortive parachute drop north of Malmédy put paid to such ambitions, though perhaps the key to everything was, in spite of the cruel weather, the speed with which the Americans responded to the situation with both men and armour; and once the skies cleared, and the Allied air forces could get to work, defeat for the Germans was inevitable.

Beard once again became aware of Skorzeny and his operations when Jenkins brought their Jeep to a sudden, but silent, halt and pointed through the trees. There, about 150 yards ahead, was a group of Americans engaged in manhandling signposts at a crossroads in a high valley that cut through the hills. They were so obviously Americans; they wore GI combat uniforms for a start, and their transport was American – a lorry with the distinctive white star of liberation. Yet something, he couldn't quite put his finger on it, made Beard hesitate. "Are they phonies, Boss?" enquired Jenkins, turning to raise a quizzical eyebrow.

Beard shook his head uncertainly. "I don't know, Harry. Something seems wrong down there," he said. Sgt Curtis, who had joined them to find out what was up, intervened to observe, "Didn't think the Yanks would be this far advanced, sir – not with Jerry bull-dozing everything in the opposite direction. And what the hell are they doing? Normally the first thing the Yanks think about is establishing their PX, and here they are farting about with bleeding signposts. It don't make sense." Beard nodded. "I think that's what bothered me, sergeant. Why should Americans be messing about with signposts? The only people who'll benefit from them are themselves." He paused as he stepped out of the Jeep. "You stay here, sergeant, and cover us with the Browning. I think we'll take a closer look at these fellows. You stand by your radio, Felbridge, and all of you be on your guard. Jenkins and Blossom, you're with me – and I don't want to hear a sound from either of you."

The breaking of a twig would have sounded like a shot, but the three – Beard, Jenkins and Blossom – moved forward flat on their stomachs without making a sound. They spread out and were very quickly within 25 yards of the Americans, and still unseen; a few trees, heavy with snow, some rocks and an occasional skeletal bush all helped to conceal them. Finally they were within earshot of the Americans, and to a man they were all talking in German. Beard listened to the conversations and it was all the usual chit-chat of soldiers about their homes and the girls they'd left behind, only their homes were Hamburg or Oberhausen, and their sweethearts were called Renate and Etta. A man reading a copy of *Der Panzerbär* – he was also munching at a foot-long German sausage – was the real clincher. Beard turned and signalled to Curtis, and the sergeant opened up with the Browning. Two short bursts and seven bodies lay in bloody heaps in the snow.

Beard waited for any sign of movement, but there was none. A gurgling sound off to the left made him swivel round in that direction with his Schmeisser ready for instant action. He relaxed almost at once for there, some twenty feet away and partly hidden by a jutting rock, lay the body of another "American"; his trousers were down by his ankles and his throat had been cut; he held a Luger in his right hand. Standing over him and wiping his knife with meticulous care was Jenkins, the scar dark against his cheek. "I think he had in mind to shoot you, sir," Jenkins said casually. "He was having a crap at the time." Beard grimaced. "When aren't they?" he muttered.

Blossom, who had already checked inside the lorry to see if anybody else was hiding there and was now emptying the pockets of the dead – and the contents clearly showed they were Germans, looked up with a grin and shouted, "Well, at least he died happy, Harry!" Jenkins picked up the sausage which had fallen to the ground, wiped some blood off it, and took a hearty bite before passing it round. There were other tasty rations in the lorry as well as useful weaponry and ammo, and Beard decided the lorry would be a useful acquisition and Hill took the wheel as they proceeded on their way.

Two days later, Beard was wounded; not very seriously, but enough to incapacitate him for nearly three weeks. He and Trumpett had just been reunited and were alone watching up to a thousand German paratroopers advancing in skirmish order over open ground: they were heading straight towards them. "Do you think they want to surrender to us, Mr Beard?" asked Trumpett, his voice a mixture of curiosity and amusement. "I should think they more likely want to kill us, Mr Trumpett," replied Beard, grinning. "But, I doubt if they know we're here – they certainly can't see us." In a more serious mood, Trumpett suggested that perhaps they should move while they were able. Beard readily agreed, but it seemed that if the oncoming troops couldn't see them, and they were marching uphill, the crew of a hidden mortar section possibly could.

As soon as Beard and Trumpett began their stealthy withdrawal mortar shells rained down all round them. Several times they threw themselves face down in the snow as shells exploded uncomfortably close. It was the trees that bore the brunt of the assaults and the two of them were just congratulating themselves on having escaped unscathed when Beard was hit. Jagged shards of shrapnel tore into both his legs, just above the knees, and he fell to the ground quite unable to move. Blood poured from the twin wounds like beer from a barrel with its bung removed; at least the sight of his own blood rushing away to soak into the ground momentarily took his mind off the excruciating pain he felt. Trumpett, who was as experienced as many a doctor when it came to treating fresh wounds out in the open, was at his side in a moment, ripping at his trousers with a knife and then tightly bandaging both mangled legs. "You're not moving on these, sir ... though it probably looks worse than it is," said Trumpett conversationally, as he tied the two legs together. "They say it's a good sign when a wound bleeds freely." Beard wanted to show his unconcern with a smile, but the pain was such that all he could manage was an inarticulate "Up yours, Jack!"

Trumpett gave a sort of mirthless grin and grunted as he hoisted Beard over his shoulder and moved off through the trees, ignoring the sounds of the paratroopers who were now less than 200 yards off, but veering away. The mortars, probably sensing that they had achieved their purpose, were now silent. Trumpett, with never a thought about what might be behind him, continued carrying Beard for over a mile, only putting him down a few of times to examine and re-bandage the wounds, and to rest his own aching body. He seemed tireless, although the sweat poured out of him and his breathing became noticeably laboured towards the end; but never a word of complaint escaped his lips during the journey. They barely exchanged a word all this time, though on the occasions when Trumpett did stop, he would mutter soothingly to Beard: words like "You're doing fine, sir," and "Hang on, sir, we're almost there!"

Beard had drifted in and out of consciousness during the march, but he was wide awake when the doctor called in by Felbridge arrived on the scene. Trumpett, with that special sense of direction that men like him possessed, had marched almost in a straight line to where they had left the Jeep and panted out, "The Boss has been wounded. Get a Doc quickly." That had been a bare half-an-hour earlier. The radio call had been picked up by Captain Douglas March who had been with another unit only a few miles away looking for casualties, on either side, to

practise on. Now, having examined and treated Beard, he declared:
"You're really rather lucky, Mr Beard. Two nasty, very deep cuts – but
no metal needing to be cut out. I've cleaned the wound' and done the
necessary repairs, but really, the shrapnel ... it might even have been just
the one piece ... appears to have simply sliced through both legs and
gone on its merry way. No damage to bones; just a nice clean wound."

Beard grimaced and would probably have said something
abusive, only he was so relieved it wasn't too serious – even if he did
feel like hell.

"I've given you the necessary injections and stitched up the
wounds, and that's really all that needs to be done," continued Capt
March. "You won't be able to move for a couple of weeks or so, of
course, not till the stitches come out, so I suppose I'd better see about
evacuating you to some proper place to convalesce. How does that
sound, eh?"

Beard didn't like the sound of it at all, and said so. "Certainly
not, Doc," he declared determinedly, "I'll mend here where I am – with
my men. They'll do whatever has to be done. Perhaps, if you're still
around, you could look us up in a fortnight to take the stitches out?"

Capt March nodded; it wasn't a serious wound, though he didn't
doubt but that it was bloody painful; so long as the man kept off his feet,
it didn't really matter where he rested up. He looked again at Beard, and
decided against arguing the matter. "Just let me know where you are,
and I'll try and find you," he said. "The stitches, as I said, will need to
come out in about two weeks. Until then keep the wounds clean and see
that someone changes the dressings every day until the wounds close.
I've left you bandages and some pain killers – you'll need 'em once the
injections I've given you wear off. If you need anything else, anything at
all, give us a ring. Like the Windmill, the surgery never closes!"

Beard nodded his thanks and, feeling decidedly drowsy,
wondered if the sod had already given him something to make him sleep.
Doctors loved playing God!

"Meantime," said Capt March, moving towards his own Jeep,
"you and your men want to give serious thought about getting a proper
roof over your heads. Blizzards are forecast – and it's Christmas Eve
tomorrow."

"Thanks, Doc. Happy Christmas!" said Beard, in a dozy sort of
voice. He was sound asleep before the doctor drove off.

Summerbee, who heard of Beard's injuries via Felbridge, arrived
on the scene later that night, and the following day he took them to a
most desirable residence on the eastern slopes of the Schneifel, roughly
south-east of Hallschlag. He'd discovered the place a week or so earlier
when dodging an armoured squadron and, though he'd ignored it at the
time, he'd stored it away in his memory box as being a suitable hiding

place for the future – like now.

Tucked away among towering pine trees in an isolated fold in the hills, it could probably be described as a castle, but whatever it was, it served the needs of Beard and his men to perfection. Apart from being almost completely hidden until you were right on top of it, there was a stone wall all round and a heavy wooden gate leading to a large courtyard. The house itself looked solid enough, and gave the appearance of having been there for a couple of hundred years, at least. There were two storeys with dark wooden storm shutters at the windows, and a sort of turret on the roof. Ominously, a swastika flag fluttered from a pole there, but then most probably every house in Germany was expected to display at least one. Apart from dark smoke puffing out of squat, cowled chimneys – it was filtered by the surrounding trees before being lost in the atmosphere – there was no sign of life, but no one doubted that a score of eyes watched as the outer gate was forced.

Troopers raced through the opening and fanned out to surround the house and search the many outhouses and stables; two men took up stations at the front door, and a machine-gun guard was posted at the outer wall where the enormous wooden gates now hung disconsolately. Summerbee drove straight up to the front door which was opened almost before he had a chance to hammer on its panelled frame with the butt of his revolver. In the doorway stood a slender, grey-haired, thin-faced woman who straightened her back and lifted her negligible chin a fraction as a modest sign of her resentment of the intrusion. Troopers poured through the doorway pushing past a small collection of people, nearly all female and looking old and terrified, and sped through the house floor by floor. Summerbee, with a mixture of barbarous German and French, told the woman who had opened the door that they were English, that he was commandeering the place temporarily and that she and everyone else there would do as they were ordered, or be shot. It is doubtful if the woman understood a fraction of what he shouted at her, although the purport of his words were obvious; she answered him in far better English.

She was, she told him, and not without a certain pride in her voice, Baroness Ilse von Schopenhuber, that there were eight others in the household, all women except for two elderly family servants, that there were no weapons – apart from a couple of hunting rifles – in the house so far as she knew, and that, since she had no option in the matter, they were welcome guests, though, she hoped, they would not outstay their welcome. Her last remark was accompanied by an embarrassed, almost apologetic, little smile.

Summerbee, who had listened with some astonishment to her excellent English, gave her a brusque nod and ordered all the inmates into a single room and placed a guard to watch over them. He then personally searched the entire house, including the roof, and took possession of the hunting guns; he searched the surrounding district from the battlements and was pleased that, while it afforded a scenic view, there was nothing menacing to be seen. He left the swastika flag as it was, deciding that its absence might attract attention, but ordered a machine-gun to be set up in the tower.

It was only after these precautions had been taken that he allowed Beard's stretcher to be carried into the house, and ordered the baroness to show the way to a suitable bedroom on the first-floor. She took one look at Beard's sweaty, pain-filled young face – he doesn't even shave! she observed – and any lingering hostility in her face vanished. She led the way to her own son's room. Helmut's room. He wouldn't be needing it ever again. He'd been killed in the terrible tank battle at Medjez-el-Bab in Tunisia almost exactly two years ago. He'd been little older than this boy.

The baroness had a mother's knowledge of nursing and she practically took over the care of Beard, allowing only Trumpett to share in the tasks – and then only because she couldn't lift Beard by herself. Between them they bathed him, fed him and fussed over him like a pair of anxious parents. Beard had a fever during the first couple of days – probably due to shock and loss of blood – and spent most of the time sleeping; when he was awake, he heard their voices as if in a dream in which he was a distant eavesdropper, and his eyes followed them everywhere without really seeing anything, their shapes being only vague outlines; he didn't speak, so far as he knew, and seemed only to open his mouth when he was fed. On the third morning, which was Boxing Day, his temperature was back to normal and he felt more like his old self – except that his legs ached like the devil, and he wondered where the hell he was. He felt hungry, so he knew he must be alive! He opened his eyes, and now he could see clearly: and there, lounging in an armchair, was Trumpett – resplendent in the top half of a Father Christmas costume, with the whiskers lying in his lap. The latter's face beamed as their eyes met.

"Is it Christmas Day already, Jack?" Beard asked, and his voice seemed to creak from lack of use, like it needed oiling; at least, that's what it sounded like to him, and he was also surprised at the effort even those few words took.

"You've missed it, sir," smiled Trumpett. "It was yesterday. You woke up a couple of times, but I don't think you knew it – 'cept when we fed you. Sleep was the best Christmas present you could have had, sir. Done you a power of good."

"Where the hell are we, Jack?" asked Beard, struggling to a sitting posture. He looked about him, taking in the well-furnished room, the lofty ceiling and the curtained windows. "That doctor fellow – Captain March, he hasn't got me in his bloody hospital after all, has he? I seem to have been asleep ever since I last saw him."

Trumpett explained what had happened and where they were. "Considering we're surrounded by Germans we couldn't have picked a better spot – and that's down to Mr Summerbee. He found it. We're utterly isolated in the middle of some mountain forest. We haven't seen a sign of Jerry. Plenty of planes flying overhead, mostly ours, and sometimes you can hear guns far off to the west on the other side of the mountains. The lads have been enjoying the break, though Mr Summerbee has patrols out keeping an eye on things."

"So, Santa, what sort of Christmas did you have? Corned beef, I suppose?"

"Not on your life, sir," cried Trumpett, grinning hugely. "As soon as we'd tucked you up in bed, Mr Morrison, who, as you know, has a flair for cookery, looked over the kitchens straight away. The only thing was there weren't much in the way of festive delights, nor anything else, come to that: the larders were bare. And that's where our lads came in. Your Jenkins an' that new boy, Blossom." Trumpett paused to spread his arms to express his wonderment. "Don't ask me where those two got it all, but after an absence of some eight hours – we were sure they'd been captured! – back they came on Christmas morning with a couple of geese, a whole pig, a cured ham that must have been lifted off someone's table, sacks of flour, sugar and potatoes, plus a couple of score eggs, several crates of wine – and a deer which Jenkins swears was standing in the middle of the road when he hit it."

"Aren't we lucky to have such well trained men, Jack!" grinned Beard. He was sure the two men were too experienced to have left any sort of a trail. Still, he hoped there wouldn't be any repercussions, after all, someone must be missing the food. He dismissed his misgivings – there were always looters around near a battlefront: none better than the Germans themselves. They sat in silence for some moments, each with his own thoughts and memories, before Beard looked up and added, rather shyly "Thanks for everything, Jack."

"Thanks? Whatever for?" frowned Trumpett. His cheeks darkened, and he looked decidedly uncomfortable.

"For saving my life, for one thing, you idiot," said Beard levelly.

"It was nothing," said Trumpett, looking more uncomfortable.

Beard's eyes fluttered as he nodded, and promptly dozed off – and didn't even dream of the Christmas he'd missed. When he woke again, which was probably no more than an hour later, the baroness was there talking softly with Trumpett.

"You mean, this boy ... this young man is the leader of all you men? He really is a major? He seems so awfully young."

"Well, he may be young in years, but he's old in experience, as they say."

At this moment, Beard opened his eyes and saw her properly for the first time. He'd been aware of her presence before without really seeing her – even if she had bathed and fed him, and combed his hair, and kissed his cheek. In fact, it seemed to him that two people had kissed him. Or had he dreamed them both? He looked at the woman, or at least her profile for she was half turned away from him and he saw more of her back than her front. She looked a very ordinary little body: not very tall, rather skinny-looking and with long grey hair hanging loose down her back even though it was fastened with a jewelled comb at her nape; she was dressed entirely in black, and he wondered if she was a widow. He supposed so. A lot of women seemed destined to end this war being widowed, or dead; perhaps even both.

She seemed to sense that he was watching her for she suddenly turned, and he saw her face for the first time. She smiled at him, and he liked the smile; it was, he thought instinctively, a mother's smile. At least, it was how he dreamed a mother would smile. He remembered Queenie smiling something like that at him when he was young – and that was probably the last time he saw her! He warmed towards this new mother-figure, but wondered how it was that the lovely smile didn't reach her eyes. It was a thin face, neither beautiful nor ugly, blank really, long and very pale, in fact with no complexion at all, and the deep forehead was even whiter. But it was the unsmiling, pain-filled eyes that made all the difference to her face, and made it interesting. They were, he was almost sure, a very pale blue, but they might equally have been a soft grey; the colour seemed to change the longer he stared, first one and then another. It must be some trick of the light. Whatever colour they were, he thought them loving and beautiful. They were also round and sad, and gave the impression of being well washed; Beard suspected they cried a lot. Perhaps that explained her black dress. Her lips looked soft and cool, and he felt a tingle go through him at the thought that they might have kissed him. Oh, he did hope so! He had lately come to like kisses, and he didn't get the chance very often. He wondered if she might kiss him again, and again he hoped so. The longer he stared at her, the more he liked the look of her, and in the way of these things, he wondered if she was anything like his own mother. His real one. The one who hadn't wanted him. No! she couldn't be anything like this lovely lady.

"You look very much better today, major," the woman said with a cheerfulness that didn't match her melancholic countenance, but as she moved towards him, Beard thought her voice even more lovely than her eyes.

"My name's Beard, Robert Beard," he told her, trying to match her tone and failing miserably. His words emerged in a sort of squeaky lump, all jumbled up together and rushing out too fast. Of course, he didn't notice this; he was aware only that his lips stayed ever so slightly parted, as though in expectation of another kiss – if indeed there had been a previous one. He almost closed his eyes waiting for the caress.

But it never came, though her deliciously cool hand did briefly touch his brow. He thought it must be scalding to the touch, but apparently it wasn't for she showed no sign of injury. Indeed, she gave him a fresh smile, and for the space of several moments he wasn't sure but that it wasn't almost as beautiful as a kiss might have been. It seemed to him that the woman's smile finally lit up her lovely eyes and, momentarily at least, banished the sadness from them.

"Sleep is a great healer, Major Beard," she told him softly.

"It takes away the pain for a little while," he acknowledged, struggling to show her a smile. "I think in the circumstances, and certainly while I'm confined to this sickbed, we might dispense with formalities, ma'am – please feel free to call me Robert, if you wish."

She beamed down at him. "Robert – I like the name. It's strong," she said, and in the same breath, as she saw him wince, she asked anxiously, "Are you in pain now – Robert?" She leaned forward to touch his cheek.

"Not bad pain, ma'am," he assured her, staring at her retreating hand. It was a lady's hand: so long, so elegant, so heavenly cool. "It's more like pins and needles, only more so. I want to move my legs, but I can't ... "

"And you mustn't, sir," interposed Trumpett, moving forward as though to physically prevent Beard from moving, though he had made no effort to do so. "Just another fraction – the least part of a fraction, an' the shrapnel would've been sawing through bone! As it is, you have two enormous gashes above your knees an' the word is you'll simply have to wait for them to mend before you move. The Doc said you wasn't to get up for at least a week, and even then only if the wounds was healing – new skin closing up is what he said. An' you should use crutches at first."

"They're only cuts, for heaven's sake!" expostulated Beard.

"Yes, sir, right down to the bone," retorted Trumpett. "Bloody lucky no arteries were severed, if you ask me."

"You must do as he says, Robert," said the baroness seriously, absently lapsing into German.

"Yes, ma'am," replied Beard dutifully. "I generally do, and this time I don't really have much option, do I?"

Beard, without realising it, answered in German, and she, at once realising *her* mistake but recognising his German to be better than her best English, clapped her hands with delight and from that moment spoke only in German to him – and Trumpett, finding his services no longer so much in demand, took himself off to see what the rest were up to.

In the course of the week during which he was compelled to remain in bed, Beard and the baroness – Ilse, as she told him he might call her – became quite friendly, and he learned her history. She was only just a German, she told him with an almost girlish giggle, having been born in Mittenwald, right on the Austrian border; a few yards farther south and she would have been an Austrian by right, instead of by marriage. She had married an Austrian nobleman, Wolfgang Gerhard von Schopenhuber, in Salzburg Cathedral just before the first World War and her first home had been in Mozart's lovely city, and all three of her children had been born there, though they hadn't started arriving till after the war because her husband was away fighting. "That first war destroyed the Austrian empire, and sowed the seeds for the destruction of Germany, if not the whole of Europe, in this one," she said in a sad voice, and pain filled her eyes. The family had moved to their present home in 1932, the year before Hitler became chancellor.

"It was the beginning of the end," Ilse sighed. "My husband, who was an engineer and owned a factory in Schleiden, just to the north of here, was killed early on in the war in Poland – and not even in the fighting. A bridge he was working on blew up and collapsed, and he died. I understand that he drowned rather than was killed by the explosion, though I suppose it was a combination of both. Poor darling. He lived for his family. We were his pride and joy, as he was ours." She paused briefly and a faraway smile touched her lips, as though in secret communication with her dead husband. "Helmut, our elder son – this used to be his room – was killed in North Africa two years ago. He was just twenty-one. Kurt, our younger son, was reported missing at Stalingrad in February last year. No one is very hopeful that there'll be any survivors from that place, even among the prisoners. He was two years younger than Helmut. That leaves just me – and Katja, our baby."

Ilse had come to a sudden stop, her words seeming to catch in her throat with a tiny sob. She turned her head and looked round the room, nodded, and finally her eyes settled on Beard again. "You mustn't mind Katja, Robert," she said, speaking quite calmly, although her eyes looked brimful of tears, "she ... she is not well in the head, though it's her heart that's broken. She doesn't understand things properly ... she just hasn't been able to adjust mentally to our succession of tragedies. She knows that her father is dead, but she hasn't been able to grasp that she's probably lost both her brothers as well. I think she's simply closed her mind to such a possibility. She's taken refuge in a little world of her own to escape reality. I'm horribly afraid that if she did understand everything that's happened she'd go out of her mind completely." She paused again to gather up and control her emotions, and Beard waited patiently for her to recover and continue. "I mention all this, Robert, because Katja in some way associates you with being her brother Helmut, simply because you're in his room. I've seen her coming in here to put fresh flowers on the table – I don't suppose you've even noticed them. Boys never do! And I've watched her kiss you while you were still asleep because that's what she did in the old days."

"Am I like him – Helmut?" asked Beard in the sudden silence, seeing the vase of pine sprigs and holly for the first time. So, he hadn't imagined it: he had been kissed by someone else – Katja. Poor mad Katja! And she imagined he was her brother!

"Not a bit, Robert!" she laughed, almost with relief to be talking of something else. "We're all fair-haired and blue-eyed, just like all good Germans are expected to be. And you're dark all over – just like a gypsy! Lovely black wavy hair and the most gorgeous velvet brown eyes. You're certainly as handsome as my boys, Robert."

"Thank you, ma'am," said Beard politely, his blushes causing her to laugh again, very softly. "I've not been accused of that before! I'm happy to go along pretending to be a brother for Katja while I'm here, if it helps her. But don't you think it'll upset her even more when I leave – which has to be as soon as I'm able to move normally?"

Ilse nodded, all traces of the laughter of a moment ago gone. "You're right, of course," she agreed, her voice sad and meditative. "But, for a little while she will be happy again. She may not have another chance, poor darling."

"All right," Beard nodded, not without some hesitancy, "if you're sure."

Before he could say more or Ilse could thank him, the door opened and Katja's appearance silenced them both. She carried a fresh posy of twigs to the vase, changed the water, and came and sat on the bed. "How's Helmut today, *Mutti?*" she asked, kissing first her mother and then Beard.

She was taller than her mother but with the extra flesh of a teenager, and her blonde hair was short and straight, though an odd curl fought for survival in inaccessible places. Her eyes were startlingly blue, and they stared at Beard in a disturbing manner: they were very bright and intense. Something about them made him want to shiver, and he tore his own eyes from hers and explored the rest of her face. It was rounder than her mother's but seemed just as small, with a tiny rounded chin and a well-shaped nose, and a small pale mouth in between. Beard decided she was quite pretty for all her pallidness. He gave her a brotherly smile which her own lips barely answered; instead, she captured one of his hands, holding it quite tightly, and bestowed little kisses all over it. He remembered Ruth doing similar things.

But Katja was a restless soul and was soon promenading round the room, talking all the while – of things he knew nothing about. It did not seem to matter for she prattled on at such a pace, darting incongruously from one subject to another, that he was given almost no opportunity to make a contribution, which was probably just as well. It puzzled him that she believed him to be her brother. He'd have thought that if she'd had a mental blackout, it would have blotted out all memory of Helmut and not substituted a stranger in his place. He supposed a psychiatrist would have an explanation for it. He just thought it terribly sad … and a bit frightening.

Katja was a gifted pianist, and it seemed the one accomplishment unaffected by her mental unbalance. She played exquisitely, and she played endlessly, hour after hour – that is when she wasn't being a sister to Beard.

But towards the end of the first week into the New Year, his legs felt, and looked, sufficiently healed, to warrant sending for someone to remove the stitches, and Beard had Felbridge contact Summerbee about finding Captain March, or some other medical person, to put him back on his feet. It took nearly a week to locate Capt March, and the rest of the week to bring him through enemy lines and finally to install him secretly into the castle. The doctor cheerfully removed the stitches as Beard winced with every snip, and then told his patient that he must take it easy for another ten days or so, and use his legs sparingly. The doctor stayed long enough to share in a deer hunt, and then left to answer a call to tend a wounded man in Jack Middlebrook's Troop. As soon as he'd gone, Beard was out of bed and clattering round the house on crutches.

Katja would escort him everywhere, ready to catch him should he fall – well, ready to help pick him up if he did. She had him join her in the music room where the only furnishings were the piano and a few chairs; she had an elegant couch brought in for him and for several hours each day he was obliged to recline on it and be an audience of one at her concerts. He quite liked the classical music she played, even if he didn't understand it, but deep down he wondered if he didn't enjoy playing the favourite big brother better. She was always chattering at him, holding his hand, stroking his face, giving him big sisterly kisses, pressing little gifts on him, and generally fussing round him, fetching him things and running errands for him. Beard was mindful that Ruth, whom he had once thought of as a pretend sister, had never been this attentive to his needs. Perhaps after they were married, if they ever were, she'd become more like Katja.

As Beard's legs became stronger, he grew more restless and after a few days of the musical entertainment, he found more and more excuses to be elsewhere, explaining that he was under orders to exercise as much as possible. Katja seemed to understand – at least, she reluctantly excused him from the couch – but this did not mean she relinquished him from her presence entirely; she would follow him tirelessly on his explorations of the house and did not seem to notice that he frequently got lost in passageways and cellars where she and the real Helmut had played hide-and-seek not so very long ago, nor think it odd that he didn't remember his own relations who were sitting out the war in the house. Stranger still was the fact that few of these relations appeared to notice either: only one or two seemed to remember anybody called Helmut and none recognised him as not being Helmut; perhaps they were all slightly mad. Or simply tired of what had happened to their world and, probably, impatient to be out of it altogether.

There was a moment of panic when great aunt Katharina greeted him with the words "I was told you were dead!" – but being ninety-seven herself, she'd got him mixed up with a nephew who'd been dead forty years. The relations were mainly ancient aunts and distant cousins who, without exception, were twisted up with rheumatism, just like so many corkscrews, and were mostly deaf and near-blind as well. Even so, Beard thought some, and at least the servants, must have had some recollection of him (as Helmut), so he assumed they had been told to behave accordingly. As for the only two men of the household, Willi and Erich, they were well into their eighties and not too sure of anything: one had been a valet, the other a gardener, but their only interests now seemed to comprise sitting in front of the fire and recalling tales of old Austria.

With his legs now almost completely mended, Beard was impatient to get back to the war, or at least to be back among his men. He felt trapped and vulnerable behind the solid walls of the house. It was all very pleasant living like a king in his castle, but he was a soldier and not a king; and nor could he go on pretending to be a mad girl's dead brother indefinitely; it was all very wearying, and unnatural. His men were being sent out on a rotation basis: three or four days at a time, and then back they'd come for a warm to be replaced by the next batch. Beard had a feeling they were enduring these hardships simply to protect him, and it gave him a nasty feeling of inadequacy. Besides, it was unfair. Of course, Summerbee or one of the other officers assured him that the men were doing routine patrols and acquiring intelligence concerning the enemy, but they both knew this was only partly true. Now that he was fit again – he'd practised running through the long corridors, Beard was eager to be on the move; he dared not imagine they could remain undiscovered for very much longer; it seemed quite incredible, even in these lonely mountains, that their presence had passed unnoticed for so long – and with one of the great battles of the war going on all around them. It was tempting providence to stay put longer than was absolutely necessary – even with Summerbee and the rest guarding the approaches to their hideaway for miles around.

And so, as the second week of his convalescence drew to a close, Beard made a point of being with those of his men who were in residence as much as possible – but even then he could not shake Katja off. She continued to accompany him everywhere, hovering patiently in the background while he spoke with his men. She did not seem to notice that he spoke to them in English, nor that both he and they wore strange uniforms; she was only aware that he was her brother, and that he'd have to go away again soon – and she wasn't going to miss a moment of his leave. This had been the explanation given by Ilse for his presence; she hadn't said anything about the other men and, Katja, if she thought about them at all, probably thought they were there to protect him, as was their duty.

Beard and the remainder of his troop left their haven soon after two o'clock on the morning of Sunday, January 14. They left secretly and silently at four-minute intervals, and only Ilse was aware of their departure; she watched each vehicle leave from a darkened window and, as the very last disappeared through the restored gateway, she cried softly to herself. Beard had said his goodbyes a bare two hours before, leaving it until the last possible moment. They'd both known the moment had to come and when it came they had very few words to say to one another: he'd asked her to explain things as best she could to Katja, saying that he didn't trust himself to say an adequate goodbye to his new pretend sister; and Ilse had told him to take care and said that she'd pray for his safety and happiness all the days of her life. Now, as he drove off into the darkness without a backward glance, she knew she was saying goodbye to the last of her sons, pretend or otherwise.

"God bless you, dear Robert," she sighed, and she was still crying when Katja found her and complained that she couldn't find her brother. Presently, the pair of them were crying in unison.

□ *The household remained undisturbed almost to the end of the war, when it was briefly discovered by a group of Russian deserters. They remained in occupation for three days during which Katja was repeatedly raped. When they left, Ilse shot her daughter and then herself. The Luger she used was one Beard left with her for her protection.*

Chapter Thirty-five

The Ardennes, January 15, 1945

Before first light, Beard and his Troop were sixty miles to the
east, out of the mountains but still in hilly woods within sight of the river
Kyll. Their instructions were to sit tight until Gibbs could join them,
probably in a day or two.

"We need to arrange a supply drop," Beard told Summerbee as
they shivered in a makeshift shelter just inside a forest of firs. At least
the trees afforded a break from the icy wind, but the bitter cold wriggled
through and found them out. They daren't light a fire, however, and had
to rely on small primus stoves to heat up food.

"Pity we couldn't stay in that nice snug house till it was all
over," Summerbee said, remembering how warm the kitchen had been,
though he had spent the least time of all sharing the comforts of that
establishment, being constantly out with patrols.

Beard grinned. "It was amazing finding that refuge practically in
the middle of a battlefield," he said, staring absently back towards their
recent mountain retreat. He thought of them as a household belonging
more to the past than the present: caught up in a war which had hurt
them beyond endurance; and dreading what the future held for them. Ilse
was the single flame that still flickered, but he feared that this flame was
about to be snuffed out.

Around midday, Felbridge was able to contact Col Yeo about a
supply drop, and Yeo, having enquired after Beard's wounds and been
told that all was fine now, was able to give the co-ordinates for a drop
two nights later. Before that happened, Gibbs turned up looking as
cheerful as if he were on a skiing holiday – although he arrived in a
German half-track armed to the teeth. After shaking hands all round and
distributing cigarettes and bars of chocolate like a veritable Father
Christmas, he plonked himself beside Beard and those officers who were
not on duty, and explained that the Allies were now on the offensive, and
chasing the Germans back across their own lands.

"But there's a lot of fight left in them," continued Gibbs, now
producing a flask of rum from which he splashed generous quantities
into the mugs thrust at him "and they're not going quietly." There was a
brief pause as the men sipped at their revitalised drinks before he went
on. "Now listen, Robert, at present I'm operating around Houffalize –
that's to the north of Bastogne. For the moment, I want you to move your
men south to the Prüm region, but give the St Vith area a wide berth.
The Yanks are charging through there, and I don't think they intend
stopping till they reach the Rhine. In any case, our role is now changing
somewhat. Up till now, you've been used very much as shock troops on

both sides of the fighting lines, and I assure you your efforts have been much appreciated by our masters. I understand medals or food parcels are in the offing, but don't get too excited, we all know what these promises are worth," he gave a sardonic grin, and passed the flask round again.

"Anyway, before these goodies can find us, we're ordered to move unobtrusively farther into Germany, gathering intelligence and indulging in acts of sabotage as the opportunities arise, but our prime target now is to block the escape of top Nazi officials and Gestapo and SS leaders. They'll all be trying to disappear back into the Fatherland, or some neutral country like Sweden or Switzerland – there are reports even of an escape route via the Vatican." He gave a bitter smile at the thought of these butchers escaping under the mantle of holy orders, and felt that the Vatican would have a lot of explaining to do if it proved true. He strode over to his vehicle and returned with a satchel stuffed with photos and details of the top wanted men. There were hundreds, possibly thousands of names. "Here you are, Robert, cast your eyes over this lot when you've got a free moment – and let your chaps see them, too. I'll give you the word when we're to disappear into the heart of Germany."

Gibbs saw that his audience was showing signs of falling asleep: yawning, at least. He knew that it was the raw cold that sapped their energies ; that, and the lack of sleep and the need for hot food. Only Beard seemed to be really paying attention, though even here it was waning. Gibbs could understand this. The small print of war, the everyday skirmishes and battles were boring to those not involved; and for those doing the fighting, especially those like Beard who operated behind the lines and were physically in touch with the enemy on a daily basis, the survivors simply moved on to the next battle. Now, they were being pushed further into the firing line, and greater dangers.

And so the war continued, Gibbs went on. After continuous fighting, Beard's squadron had found itself, on Sunday, April 15, in the vicinity of Bergen-Belsen extermination camp where 13,000 rotting corpses were piled high on a pyre, and 50,000 emaciated, starving and sick people very near to joining them. The stench of these bodies was as overpowering as the sight was sickening. Beard, who had detected the tell-tale smell of burning flesh while still miles away, halted close to the miles of barbed wire that surrounded the camp; he had felt himself reeling, but he was quite incapable of turning his head away from the obscene spectacle. He recovered as a voice called out to him, "Get your men away from here, Robert."

It was Capt March who had tended him when he'd been wounded in the Ardennes, and who now shouted the warning as he saw Beard's column of armoured Jeeps approaching. "There's typhus here, and Christ knows what else. It's unbelievable inside. Bodies dead in cots and being eaten by the other inmates, others lying about with rats gnawing at their bellies as they watch helplessly." Horror crept into his voice as he continued, "This is an evil place, Robert. Get away from here quickly, and make sure you and your men are properly inoculated." And Beard had nodded, waved and turned away feeling sick, but it was another 20 miles or more before he could get the stench of the place out of his nostrils.

And so it went on. The squadron pressed eastwards, pausing only to fight a series of vicious little actions against isolated units and to tackle a more formidable obstacle of Spandaus and panzerfausts in the area of Amelinghausen, until it reached Lüneburg. Here, Gibbs authorised a pause, and Beard commandeered a small hotel and a row of houses as billets for his men. The buildings had all been knocked about by either shells or bombs but they were habitable and, having lived in the open since leaving Ilse's castle, Beard regarded the accommodations as luxurious. He occupied what was described as the "royal suite" and slept the clock round in a regally huge four-poster bed. When he surfaced, he spent another hour or so soaking in an enormous tub, drinking bottles of beer that Jenkins had acquired from somewhere and screaming at the staff to keep the hot water flowing – or else.

The squadron remained in the town for two days and, discovering a British medical unit on hand, Beard insisted that all his men be checked over in view of their recent proximity to Bergen-Belsen. Apart from that the men rested, which meant that they went on a series of binges, collected all manner of booty and, in spite of Monty's "no fraternization" order, enjoyed the favours of many a well-built *Fräulein* – and in some cases her mother, too! Beard, himself enjoying the pleasures of Klara, the buxom blonde maid who was constantly in and out of his hotel room, hoped they hadn't escaped the diseases of the death camp only to succumb to the oldest one in the world! He took another bath to be on the safe side so far as he himself was concerned, but as he was joined in the tub by Klara – and her sister Gretl – it is doubtful that the bath served any but a pleasurable purpose.

While the squadron was still resting and refitting in Lüneberg, Beard, whose unit had already detained or shot any number of the names on his lists of wanted Nazi war criminals, was approached by the Field Security people in the town with a request that he and his men help search the town for prominent Nazis known to be in hiding in the area. But Beard, who had been able to tick off some of the names on the ever-lengthening list, had to decline. He would dearly have liked to remain in Lüneburg, if only to enjoy the services of Klara and Gretl, but the war continued to demand his participation, and he had just received orders to continue his travels.

The squadron left Lüneburg that same day, Tuesday, April 24, and crossed the Elbe at Lauenburg three days later. Almost as soon as they had done so orders came through that under no circumstances were British forces to cross the Elbe: the eastern side, he was warned, was earmarked as Russian territory; and so Beard, muttering nasty things about the Russians, re-crossed the river the next day and headed north into Schleswig-Holstein.

Almost at once, Lieut Kendal, who had been seconded to 2nd Troop, came racing up to Beard shouting, "I've got a general who wants to surrender!" Beard raised a brow and asked with only mild interest: "Is he on the wanted list, Hughie?" Kendal gaped back, astonished at this reaction to his news. "You don't understand, sir," he cried, "he wants to surrender his whole damned division – some ten thousand men!" It was Beard's turn to gape, but when he spoke he did so calmly and quietly ; he'd been down this road before. "Where exactly are they?" he asked wearily.

Kendal waved back into the distance. "Miles away from here, sir. The other side of Schwarzenbek. Strewn out almost as far as ... " – he consulted his heavily-creased map, and stabbed at it with a finger – " ... here it is, an area called Sachsenwald."

Beard found the place on his own map. "Are they armed?"

"Good heavens, no. Most of them don't seem even to have any uniform – certainly not a complete one.   They really do look disorganised, sir. A real rabble."

"Well, I expect they've had a hard war, Hughie," said Beard, with unexpected sympathy. "I suppose you'd better head them back to the Elbe – keeping our side of it, of course – and hand them over to the MPs there. They're sure to have a cage for prisoners there by now."

Kendal looked startled. "I can't control ten thousand prisoners with a handful of men, sir," he protested.

"They won't give you any trouble," Beard grinned reassuringly at Kendal. "All they want is to get away from the battlefields. The routine is, one Jeep in the front to lead the way and another at the back to shoo them along – that's all you need, Hughie. Four-man job."

"But they'll be stretched out for miles!" cried Kendal, not quite certain if Beard was being serious.

"So?" queried Beard archly. "They're not going to run away, are they? And it's a lovely day for a walk!"

"How am I supposed to feed them?" cried Kendal bewilderingly. "We've only our own rations, nothing much to spare."

"Well, they'll either have to feed themselves or go hungry, as we've had to do many times in the past," replied Beard soberly. "We haven't the ability of God to feed an army with a few loaves and fishes." He gave a sardonic grin and added, "Tell your prisoners to pray for another miracle!"

Kendal still looked doubtful, and Beard told him: "There's

nothing more we can do, Hugh. It's either that or shoot the bastards!"

Kendal managed a grin at that then, as it struck him that perhaps Beard wasn't joking, hurried away to implement his suggestion – the march to the Elbe, that is.

Two days later, that miracle Beard had so glibly suggested to Kendal, manifested itself as they were all gathered round Felbridge's radio … and they heard the first report of Hitler's suicide. It was April 30 : a day they would never forget.

"Does that mean the war's over?" asked Jenkins flatly, staring round at the circle of stunned faces; the general view was it was a great pity he hadn't done so six years earlier.

"I don't think so – not for us," said Beard after a moment. "I suppose someone will tell us when it's over … when to stop. But this new man Dönitz says Germany will go on fighting, so it looks like it isn't over, quite yet."

But it was. It took a few more days, that's all. As the negotiations were under way, Beard's squadron pressed ahead intent on preventing top Nazis fleeing to Sweden, passing through Lübeck almost without stopping, and finally halted at Kiel on Friday, May 4 – as the word came that all German forces in North West Germany, Holland and Denmark would be surrendering at 8am the following day. Montgomery had accepted their surrender on Lüneberg Heath that same day.

And so, it was finally all over. The end had come gradually for Beard before coming to this sudden stop. It was clear from the willingness of the enemy to surrender that the end was close, but there were still pockets of fierce resistance. The last days had been painful ones with many of his men being killed with the peace hovering almost within sight: over the next hill: a breath away.

Now, the end came as something of an anti-climax. The war was too recent, too fresh, it was still all around them … there were too many corpses lying about that needed burying. Casualties had become heavier in the closing days of the war, among both officers and men, and Beard's squadron seemed to have borne the brunt of the losses. Bitterest blows had been the deaths of long-time companions Jack Trumpett, Harry Jenkins, Jimmy Simms and Aidan Felbridge – all killed within a fortnight, all within sight of the end. No, Beard was not in the mood to rejoice at victory, not just yet, but he let the squadron loose to celebrate the occasion as it chose; he himself drove out of Kiel, northwards to a place on the coast called Schönberger Strand, and celebrated the peace with a swim in the sea. He was not in the least surprised to see Blossom, who had assumed Jenkins' role of watching his back, doing just that from the beach: old habits died hard.

On Monday, May 7, as the Americans were signing what they regarded as the real unconditional surrender of Germany at Rheims, Beard was ordered to pack up and bring the squadron back to Belgium:

to a place called Poperinghe; the squadron, he was told, was going home. Well, they'd heard that one before. There'd been rumours of a diversion to Norway where 300,000 Germans appeared unwilling to surrender. But first there would be leave, surely.

The squadron was scattered over a wide area, and Beard fixed a rendezvous at Lüneburg from where they could all gather for the journey home. But first, Beard had a rendezvous with Klara and Gretl at his former hotel where he spent his last two nights in Germany.

Two days later, the squadron was in Poperinghe, and on Friday, May 11, they sailed for Tilbury aboard tank-landing ships; ahead of them was one last little skirmish. Waiting on the quayside as the ships tied up was an army of Customs officers, determined to relieve the returning heroes of any illegal spoils. But, as the great bow doors swung open, Beard roared out to his men: "Go, go, go, lads! Stop for nobody! RV in two days!" It had all been planned back in Belgium: their rendezvous was to be the Apple Tree Camp at Chelmsford. Beard led the way, his Jeep screaming off the ship, scattering the startled Customsmen, racing through the dock area ... and within two hours his men were scattered all over Essex, and beyond, placing their trophies in, hopefully, safe places.

Beard headed directly for Stonecross – or rather the Fallen Oak, where the landlord readily agreed to store his loot with no questions asked. Actually, Beard had very little in the way of spoils : apart from a few Lugers and such like, there were a few carpets, some bolts of cloth, a crate of china, one or two questionable paintings, some rather nice wine glasses (three now broken) and a box of silverware, mainly cutlery; there had been other things, of more value, but they had been lost in the way that things tended to get lost on battlefields, and apart from two gold cigarette cases and an armful of watches, a ruby necklace apiece for Ruth and Queenie which both turned out to be made of glass, and two promisingly large diamonds he'd kept in his pocket wrapped in a handkerchief for months, that's all there was.

After a couple of drinks in the snug, Beard drove round to Peartree Cottage – only to find the house empty. Mrs Tyler from the Cherries next door rushed in to tell him that Queenie and Ruth were up in London for a few days with Mrs B. for the victory celebrations – and why hadn't he let them know he was coming home? Mrs Baylis, the neighbour from the Damsons, wanted him to share her dinner, but he excused himself saying that the only thing he wanted was some sleep. He determined to seek Ruth and Queenie out in London the following morning, but he was still sleeping at midday when a persistent hammering on the front door brought him back to life. He could hear Mrs Baylis (or Mrs Tyler) assuring someone that "the young officer is definitely at home – probably enjoying a lie-in, sir."

Beard, instantly wide awake and alert, flung open a window –

and there below was Colonel Kemp, wearing a big smile – which was never a good sign.

"We've got orders, Robert," he said without preamble, once they'd got rid of Mrs Tyler and they were seated in the kitchen.

"I'm on leave," Beard pointed out, rather aggressively.

"Cancelled," declared Kemp amiably. "We're off to the Far East on Sunday."

"That's tomorrow, isn't it?" Beard cried, after some rapid calculations.

"That's right."

"But I thought we were destined for Norway."

"Not us. Not now. You and I, and a few other lucky chaps, are off to Ceylon to prepare quarters and arrange jungle training for the rest of the men," said Kemp, now showing a sort of apologetic smile. "There's still the other war, Robert. The Japanese. We've still got to beat those yellow devils. We'll be needed for the invasion of Malaya soon."

Beard stared dumbly at Kemp. Some home-coming! Family away celebrating the peace, and here he was about to be sent off to war again ... on the other side of the bloody world. He'd never really paid much attention to the Japanese thing, but, of course, it was a war as well. And he was needed for this one, too. Well, why not? he thought with a shrug ; a war was a war, and that's what soldiers were for, wasn't it? Still, he would have enjoyed a breather in between; a chance to kiss his ladies, at least, and perhaps even discuss a wedding.

He left a brief note for the women to weep over, jokingly telling them that he'd probably end up in the Indian Army after all, and an hour later was off to a new war.

□ *"Oh, we was so disappointed to have missed you, Jarvis, even if it would only have been to say Goodbye," cried Queenie.*

"Oh, Jarvis, if only we'd discussed weddings then, we'd probably have a score or more grandchildren by now," cried Ruth, smiling at the thought, and raising her eyes to meet those of Beard. She refused to think of the children he'd probably left throughout the world.

Beard stared back, frowning and wondering at her appetite; and then he smiled. He enjoyed smiling at her.

Queenie, having given Beard a wistful stare, took up the story from the general.

Chapter Thirty-six

Peartree Cottage, Essex, May 13, 1945

Queenie, Ruth and Mr Fennell returned from London on the Monday. Mr Fennell was in the party because he enjoyed being in Queenie's company, because there was the promise of cakes to be eaten, and because the victory celebrations provided him with a perfect excuse to indulge himself in both pleasures; and apart from that, he and his car were needed for the excursion. He parked Tired Bill – the affectionate name for the gleaming black Ford Anglia he'd had for simply donkey's years, and which had its origin in the registration letters, TB – at the bottom of Steep Road.

They walked up the hill, after sharing out the parcels, the women in the lead and Mr Fennell limping in the rear, their hearts and faces still full of the joy and excitement engendered by the hectic activities of the past few days – and themselves still festooned with the streamers and flags of many nations (several unknown) which they had acquired from countless street parties. Ruth waved to various neighbours who came out to see what the commotion was all about, and the trio continued up the hill, Ruth dancing in circles, Queenie rolling somewhat in her efforts to do the same, and Mr Fennell – well, puffing, though very happily. Every few yards Queenie and Ruth indulged in a bout of exuberant singing, not always the same song and not always the same verse, but making a very patriotic din; Mr Fennell, looking as pleased as Mr Punch, who used the pauses to catch up with his companions, was too engaged in his puffing to contribute to the singing, though he did contrive an occasional throaty "ho-hum-hum" as he recognised (or thought he did) a familiar chorus.

In spite of being the last to enter The Pears – Queenie and Ruth, having laid down their packages, had flopped directly on to a sofa, it was Mr Fennell who discovered Beard's letter lying on the kitchen table. He had gone straight through there to relieve himself of his parcels and to ensure that one in particular – the one containing Mrs B.'s sponge cake with icing and cherries on top, was safely laid to rest. In fact, there were two envelopes: a very thin one addressed to Queenie and Ruth, and a much fatter one addressed to himself. He opened his own and out tumbled a thick wad of American dollars, and a brief note in which Beard explained his whereabouts and asked Mr Fennell to look after the money, invest it if he thought this best, telling him about some other loot he'd left at The Oak, and asking him to continue to "watch over the ladies" until he got back. Mr Fennell smiled absently at Beard's request, which was already a duty he would not have shirked for all the world, and tucked both the money and the letter safely away in his pocket. The smile vanished the moment he picked up the other letter: *their* letter. No need to guess its contents: he knew. He bore it solemnly through to the sitting-room and presented it almost apologetically to the women.

Ruth, instantly recognising Beard's hand, gave a squeal of delight and, snatching at the envelope and kissing it all in the same movement, tore it open, extracted the single sheet of paper, and commenced reading. In an instant, her happy, eager face was transformed. It seemed to crumble even as the others looked on. Astonishment, disappointment, anger and heartbreak all took their turn in her youthful countenance before her features settled in a more or less permanent look of misery. First the pink flush of her cheeks gave way to a wanness that was almost colourless, then her rounded chin stiffened even though her pouting lips trembled as if she were on the very brink of tears ; indeed, her soft brown eyes were already glistening wetly. She slumped dejectedly back on the sofa, her shoulders drooped and her head sagged so that her chin rested on her breast – and still she clutched the letter tightly in her lap.

Queenie, receiving no replies to her anxious questions but guessing the reason for her daughter's apparent despair, gently prised the crumpled letter from Ruth's fist, smoothed it out and read it. It didn't take her long, it wasn't a very long letter, and when she'd done she nodded her great head understandingly, as if to say "I knew it," and turned to comfort Ruth, letting the letter drop to the floor. Mr Fennell took the opportunity to stoop and retrieve the letter, and read through it quickly before returning it to its torn envelope and laying it on a dresser ledge.

"My Dear Dears," Beard had written in a very hurried scrawl, *"I'm so sorry to have missed you. I only crossed over from Belgium this morning and came straight here, but I gather from Mrs Tyler next door that you're all whooping it up in London Town – something to do with the victory in Europe! Unfortunately, I'd hardly arrived home – actually, I was having a kip – when my colonel arrived and said we were off to the Far East. There's another war out there, you know – and another victory to be won. I'd forgotten all about the Japs! Anyway, I'm to go to Ceylon first ... and then I expect it'll be Burma, unless we decide to invade Malaya straightaway, which seems unlikely. I've no idea how long this business will go on : years, I expect. Don't worry, I'll be all right. I always am! Just don't forget me – and don't forget to write, Ruth – and remember I shan't be needing any scarves out there either! I've left a few things with Mr Bentick at The Oak which you might find useful – but don't touch any of the guns! There's some carpets and bolts of cloth and lace and things ... including some porcelain plates from Meissen which are supposed to be priceless, so don't play with them – and some rubies for your birthday, Ruth ... so don't accuse me of forgetting ever again! If there's anything you need, Mr Fennell will look after you. Must dash now before Gibbs shoots me! See you when I get back. Love."*

And the signature was Robert Beard!

"I hate you, Jarvis Brook!" cried Ruth, with such vehemence she thought that perhaps she did. But surely, she told herself immediately, that couldn't be so. She loved him. She knew that – and he should know it. She'd told him so often enough. But Ruth did not know what to think at the moment. It was as though – like her heart – she had no control over her thoughts. She was not at all sure what she had expected; she only knew that the wholehearted way in which she had joined in the victory celebrations up in London for days on end had been solely on the premise that now, at long last, he would be coming home for good. She had taken it for granted that with the end of the war, he would be returning, like the rest of the soldiers – some of whom were already being demobbed, and marry her – and that they would then live happily ever after, raising a family of beautiful babies and falling deeper and deeper in love.

"I hate you, Jarvis Brook!" she said again, softer this time, a little more sadly, and again she knew she didn't mean it – even if he had broken her heart. She had waited so long for him to come home: it seemed longer than all her life. She had waited, especially, to hear him properly proclaim his love; she had waited, with a barely controllable impatience, to be married in white with apple blossom falling about her and the angels singing their hallelujahs as a crocodile of bridesmaids danced behind her. She had dreamed so long of him becoming her husband – and making love to her for ever and ever.

"I hate you, Jarvis Brook!" she said yet again, this time in the merest whisper. In an even softer voice, so that only her crushed heart could hear, she added "I do love you really, Jarvis!" She resolutely refused to call him by any other name – and certainly never by that hateful Robert Beard name. Let him give it back to its owner. He was Jarvis Brook: *her* Jarvis Brook – and she wanted him, now. Only, he was never there.

"I hate you, Jarvis Brook!" this time the words rang out sharp and clear, even without conviction.

"No you don't, darling," cooed Queenie, giving her a comforting squeeze. "You love him. You always have, and you always will."

"He's hateful," insisted Ruth, sniffing against her mother's shoulder. "I'm always writing to him, telling him how much I love him and generally pouring my heart out to him – and he never writes back to say anything kind or give me any hope. And now, when at last he does write, it's to say he's off again – and he's cruel enough to mention the word love, which of course he doesn't know the meaning of, and adds insult to injury by signing himself with that horrid name Beard when he knows how we hate it." She paused just long enough to wipe her brimming eyes before adding, "Oh, Jarvis, you're hateful!"

At this point, as the two women seemed more intent on clutching hold of one another and were otherwise quiet, Mr Fennell dared to think that the moment was right for him to speak up for the absent warrior. How could he, a mere man, know that in matters concerning the heart, which to a woman's way of thinking could only mean love, men's views were neither encouraged nor accepted? Indeed, protocol, which as a solicitor he should have been aware of, unwritten though it might be, demanded that men remain silent in such matters, leaving the decisions to those who knew about such things – women. But he did not know, and besides, wasn't he in love himself? Perhaps it was this that gave him the courage to speak.

"I don't think Major Beard can be accused of any wrongdoing, my dear," he said in his grave courtroom voice. "He is a professional soldier – and a very gallant young officer, if I may say so – whose first duty is to obey orders. He has been ordered to the Far East, where we are still prosecuting a war against the Japanese, and that is where he has gone. It is his duty. And you have a duty too, my dear, and that is to support and love him." Gosh, he didn't know how he'd dare add that last bit.

The women, who had forgotten his very presence, broke away from each other and turned, in unison, to give him a withering glare. How dare he! Men were not supposed to have opinions on such matters, or if they had, they weren't supposed to express them out loud. Mr Fennell, looking rather like a small boy caught doing something he ought not to be, fidgeted and fixed his gaze on a point an inch above Queenie's head – a ploy he habitually adopted with success in court. When he lowered his eyes, Queenie gave him a frown of a smile and sent him on his way with an inclination of her head. "See you tomorrow, John," she told him, in a friendly voice, "and thank you for looking after us in London." Mr Fennell offered her a smile, wondering if this was allowed, and, with a single hungry glance towards the kitchen and the realisation that there was to be no cake today, he tiptoed away feeling that the lot of a suitor was not always a happy one. But he was already forgotten.

Ruth cried and cried, and went early to bed. Sleep didn't come easily, and she read and reread his letter until her tears almost washed away his words, and the flimsy paper disintegrated. The longed-for peace had come, and instead of coming home Jarvis had already found himself another war. He was already on his way to the other side of the world, and he'd be farther away from her than ever he'd been before. It wasn't fair. It was like being left a war widow. Finally, she sobbed herself to sleep crying, "I hate you, Jarvis Brook!" repeatedly; but even in her tormented sleep, her lips said "I love you, Jarvis!" In the morning she would light a candle and say a prayer to keep him safe and bring him back to her.

  □ *Gibbs took over the story-telling from Queenie at this stage.*
Beard, blissfully unaware of the turmoil he'd left behind him,

slept most of the journey to Kandy Airport in Ceylon, waking up only to change planes and refuel, first at Gibraltar and then at Salalah in the Dhofar region of the Oman – where they also picked up a sheikh and several of his wives. It felt good to be back in the warmer belts, though by the time he landed in Ceylon he found the temperature and humidity such that he doubted he'd be able to do much in the way of training. However, after two days spent attending lectures and seeing the sights in Colombo, he found that when the need arose his energy was quite equal to the occasion; he made this discovery while drinking iced beers with some fellow officers beneath a giant banyan tree in a tropical paradise of a garden, when a cobra dropped out of the tree with a plop (and a hiss) and landed just a few yards away. Beard was up on his feet and fifty feet away almost before the snake could stretch itself out of its disturbed sleep, and, while he might have been shaking, he hadn't even raised a sweat.

It all changed during the next few weeks as the jungle training got under way in earnest. Beard never stopped sweating, and by the time he emerged at the end of the course he'd lost nearly a stone in weight (and, he was sure, several inches in height), and he'd always thought he never had a surplus ounce of fat on his body; he felt sure that he must look like a stick insect. It had been hell, and he thanked God he hadn't been with the 14th Army in Burma for the last three years. The training had been rugged and realistic: perhaps too realistic.

Col Yeo had had to be evacuated to a base hospital after sitting on a nest of scorpions, and Summerbee retired for treatment after discovering – too late – that the tickling inside his shirt was caused by an extremely large and poisonous spider; both men made satisfactory recoveries, but circumstances did not require them to repeat their jungle ordeals. Beard was neither bitten nor stung – well, not exactly; almost inevitably, he was tortured by mosquitoes and developed a mild form of malaria – so much for the mepacrine tablets! though perhaps if he hadn't been taking them regularly he might have been a lot worse off, as it was he had a temperature above 104 for several days; and then there were the leeches, the blood-sucking leeches, which clung to all parts of his body as he waded across the Sittang.

The reason Beard was wading through this wide and treacherous river was because the war out there had come to a sudden end, and he was on his way to liberate some of the prisoner of war camps – just in case the Japanese decided to massacre the captives before surrendering. The war had ended with an almighty bang: in fact, two bangs. A new and fearsome bomb – the atomic bomb – had been created, and delivered to the Japanese mainland. The first was dropped on Hiroshima on August 6, and virtually obliterated the city. Three days later, during the course of which Russia, with an eye on Manchuria and North Korea, took the opportunity of declaring war on Japan, Nagasaki was destroyed by a second bomb. The writing was on the wall for the Japanese, and the Russians hurriedly invaded first Manchuria and then Korea as Japan sought desperately for terms; but there were to be no terms. The surrender was to be unconditional, with the threat of more bombs if the Japanese dithered.

On Tuesday, August 14, the Japanese accepted the Allied demand for unconditional surrender, though it was to take several weeks to implement among the scattered Japanese forces, and meanwhile, the Russians were gobbling up territories as fast as ever they could – the latest being the Kurile Islands. It seemed the Allies were too preoccupied with the suddenness of peace to pay any heed at the moment; by the time they realised what was happening, it was too late. On August 20, Mountbatten, the supreme commander in South-East Asia, broadcast surrender instructions to the Japanese forces, and on September 2, MacArthur accepted the overall surrender aboard the battleship Missouri in Tokyo Bay; the actual treaty terminating the state of war was still years away.

With the end of the war, Beard found his thoughts turning away from martial matters and focusing on the likelihood that he'd be heading home; and thoughts of home reminded him of Ruth, and the inevitability of marriage. He could see no obstacle to returning home now and, as he meditated on this marital prospect, he somewhat crudely reflected that it was best to get it over and done with, finally. If that sounded rather like callous indifference, he didn't mean it that way. He loved Ruth. He was sure of that, but reflecting on the matter of marriage, he wondered at the need to go rushing into anything quite so final. Plenty of time to discuss that when he got home. Yes, they'd get married, eventually. He was sure there had to be a period of courtship first; and he'd read somewhere, he was sure, that girls loved long courting days. Well, that was all right. He wanted to please her in every way. He really did love her; he always had. Meantime, he'd send her a nice long letter: a loving letter. That was the safest thing, and best done at this safe distance.

But he was saved from even this inconvenience by Yeo who called him into his office one morning (it was September 13, the day that the Japanese forces surrendered in Rangoon) and told him, cool as you please, that he'd be jumping into Burma the following day to open up as many PoW camps as he could find, disarm the guards and hold tight until other forces could get through in strength. Oh yes, and while he was waiting perhaps he could put his Japanese prisoners to work building an airstrip to facilitate the evacuation of the British PoWs, who would probably all be in need of medical treatment.

"It looks like being our only contribution to sorting out the mess out here," Yeo added, somewhat wearily. "The rest of the lads won't be coming out to join us, Robert. In fact, I expect we'll all get the call to come back home shortly."

"Well when the call comes, don't forget me out in the jungles with the Japanese," said Beard with sudden concern.

"You'd best get your airstrip built pretty quickly, then, Robert," smiled Yeo, his almond eyes twinkling. "You won't be entirely alone. Dougie March will head the medical team, and he'll have his own chaps. That'll leave you free to see that your Jap workforce keep at it."

"Who else will I have with me ?"

"Giles Summerbee will go as your second in command. He seems to have got over his affair with the black widow, as he insists it was, and he might come in useful for cooking the lads a decent meal. We'll drop suitable supplies as soon as you give us a location. There'll be six other men. Sgt Barry Harper, your old friend Cpl Blossom – sorry, he's been made up to sergeant, and then there's four other troopers needing some exercise." The colonel shuffled some papers and looked up at Beard. "You'll also be taking Captain Parsons. I'm sure there'll be a use for the padre, even if it's only to convince the survivors that all their troubles are over – and when he's not lying to them, I expect there'll be plenty of other poor devils needing to be buried, and others needing prayers said over their graves."

Beard nodded. "I'd better study some maps ... see where we're going, have a word with the men and see about supplies."

The party jumped into Burma from a single Dakota the following morning, which just happened to be: September 14, Beard's birthday – and he was either 20 or 22, depending on who he considered himself to be. He was the first to jump and, although the pilot (already hurrying home to his breakfast) assured him that they were dropping over a bend in the Sittang where the jungle was unlikely to encroach too densely, looking around as he rushed earthwards, Beard couldn't even see the river; the lowering mists that swirled everywhere were like an impenetrable canopy that hid even the dark green of the jungle – until he was almost on top of it. Then, in the space of a few seconds, through sheets of rain, he saw everything at once: the silvery ribbon of the river, which was wider than he'd expected, and the multitudinous greens of the jungle, which stretched as far as the eye could see in every direction; and then he hit the ground with a squelch – and found he was on the wrong side of the river. This was the reason he had to cross the river, and how he came to be covered in leeches.

Beard instinctively looked round for Jenkins, but of course his place had been filled by Blossom. The man had slipped quietly into Jenkins's shoes as Beard's unofficial bodyguard, and approached now with his cheeky grin. They were already well used to one another. "Feel like a swim, Blossom?" Beard asked the sergeant. "You want me to take a rope across, Boss?" said Blossom, eyeing the far bank which seemed to grow farther away the longer he looked. "We'll take it together," replied

Beard, looking at the water with no great relish, "after I've checked we're all here safe and sound – and not lost too much equipment."

The only casualty was Capt March, the doctor, who had landed in a thicket of bamboo and ripped his left arm open from elbow to wrist, and had to be stitched up by one of his own team, Sgt Ted Palmer, who in peacetime was a vet. There were six medicine-men in March's team: half, including Palmer, were genuine RAMC men, and the remainder "volunteers." There were also two native soldiers of the Frontier Force Regiment, Cpls Wok and Sok (these were not their real names – they were altogether too impossible to pronounce!), who were both trackers and interpreters, speaking Burmese and Japanese rather better than they did English. Beard had to speak to them via Sgt Harper who spoke Urdu, the common language.

The first task, after checking that everyone had arrived more or less safe and sound, was to gather up the supply canisters. These contained mostly food and medicines for the soon-to-be-liberated captives, and none was damaged in the drop – although one had to be retrieved from the river. Beard and Blossom soon had a rope across the river, and remained standing in the water until the last of the men and supplies were across. It was only then, when they emerged from the muddy, discoloured water, that they discovered the leeches attached to their bodies. March, producing a bag of salt from his bulging medical bag, made them strip off everything and then supervised proceedings as one of his men dabbed the parasites off. Finally, they were ready, and with Wok and Sok leading the way, they plunged into the jungle. It was like stepping into hell. A hell in which they were virtually blind for it was impossible to see more than a dozen or so yards ahead in the dense undergrowth.

The monsoons were not yet over and the rains fell incessantly, and heavily. There was never a moment of the day or night when the men weren't dripping wet, and it would have been the same had the monsoon season been over, for the oppressive humidity that was a permanent feature of the jungle would ensure that their clothing was constantly saturated by perspiration. How they all envied Wok and Sok who wore dhoties and very little else, but Sgt Harper, with the experience of several years' service in India, told the men that while natives were inured to insects and leeches and needed little or no clothing for protection, Europeans would be stung, bitten and scratched all over if they wore such minimal clothing. Even the jungle vegetation, which seemed all thorns and spikes, appeared to give Wok and Sok the miss; not so Beard and his men, who were constantly clawed at by both the vegetation and all manner of animal life. They tried rubbing mud over bare skin to repel mosquitoes, but as fast as they put it on the rain washed it off.

Beard came to hate his new beard – even though it was still not much of one – as whole families of insects set up home in the damp, unattended soft bristles and caused him endless irritation. The only thing to do was to keep moving, and hope that Wok and Sok knew where they were going. They seemed to: at any rate, they never seemed to hesitate. Tirelessly they hacked a path through the mountainous undergrowth with machetes, though Beard insisted they all shared the arduous task as the rain fell relentlessly and stoked up the temperature inside the jungle. The heat sapped everyone's strength and, of necessity, there were frequent rests during which they listened for any sound that might give warning of danger. There was none, certainly none that could be associated with Japanese treachery. Even so, the jungle seemed to have sounds of its own which, occasionally, Wok and Sok disappeared to investigate. Mostly the sounds were of animals: a distant roar, a closer growl, the incessant chattering of monkeys, the unnerving shriek of birds and the eternal rustlings all about them that kept them constantly thinking of snakes and other horrors.

Towards the end of each day – tropical days and nights are of equal length, so darkness comes as suddenly as daybreak – Wok and Sok would vanish mysteriously and an hour or so later a very pleasing aroma of cooking would permeate above the stench of the jungle. It was advisable not to enquire too closely what it was they cooked, nor to linger over the eating – and this had nothing to do with the millions of insects that sought to share the meal. The men had their suspicions, but they were hungry and they knew they had to eat to keep up their strength, and besides, it didn't taste all that bad; in fact, it often tasted bloody good. So good, that the restaurateur in Summerbee insisted on knowing what each delicacy was and writing down its recipe. There were delicious python steaks, boiled monkeys, roasted lizards and something found in the river which could have been some kind of eel.

They emerged from the jungle quite suddenly after four days to find themselves up to their knees in monsoon flood-waters. There was a lot more marching and wading, but finally ahead them loomed their last obstacle, Wok assuring Beard they'd see their destination at the top of the hill. It was really a hill, but to the sweating, gasping men laden like Sherpas it was like climbing Everest: a sheer jungle-clad mountain, at least. But they made it. As the party paused for breath near the crest of the mountain, Wok pointed to a shiny strip of metal just visible through the trees in the valley far below. It was the railway line built through the jungle by the Japanese with slave labour, Sgt Harper translated. "Our chaps were the bloody slaves, of course," he added. The PoW camp was somewhere on the other side of the track, possibly four or five miles from where they were.

The Japanese flag was still flying over the camp when Beard and his team of interpreters approached some two hours later; he knew that

Blossom was behind him, and the knowledge gave him a sense of added confidence. The Japanese must have been aware of their presence for some time for they were lined up in parade fashion by the main gate, their commanding officer, a major, standing in front in his immaculate uniform with its highly polished leather belts and straps, and clutching his sword in a gloved hand. Beard gave him a curt appraisal, noticed that the Japanese soldiers were unarmed, and looked around for signs of prisoners.

At first, all he could see were a few thin, yellow faces peering out of ramshackle bamboo huts, but very soon skeletal, emaciated figures emerged and stared back ... and then, ever so slowly at first but gradually picking up if not in volume then in numbers, cheers rang out all over the camp and more and more men tottered into view, and some collapsed to the ground after only a few steps, but still managed to raise a cheer and wave feebly as they lay in the dirt. The cheers were as thin as the men who mouthed them: they did not have the strength to shout louder, and their sunken eyes, unashamedly streaming tears, still gazed disbelievingly at their deliverers; and there were some who simply stared incomprehensibly.

The Japanese major, who was introduced as Major Hioto, bowed formally to Beard and murmured "*Konnichiwa!*" Beard, who had offered the very minimal of salutes, turned to Sgt Harper and growled, "Is he swearing at me, sergeant?" Sgt Harper grinned broadly and said, "No, sir, it's a sort of Japanese greeting. Very respectful. Mind you, he's probably cursing you under his breath!" Beard muttered something evil under his breath in his turn, then snapped, "Tell him to get on with it." Hioto then proceeded to give a verbose report concerning the camp and its inmates; he added that the men were enjoying a rest day today.

Beard finally got fed up with the ordeal of protracted translations through the three languages, and told Sgt Harper to tell Hioto to "Shut up!" and surrender his sword and pistol. For the first time, Hioto's face lost its calm suavity. The chubby round bronzed face turned grey and seemed to sag; he even looked as if he might cry. It appeared that he did not mind surrendering his pistol, one of the Nambu breed, but the sword was a very different matter. It had been presented (touched, at any rate) by the Emperor himself and was a symbol of his own authority. He demurred, he argued, he begged, he gripped the scabbard in both his hands and appeared determined never to let it go. It was only when Beard muttered an impatient order to Sgt Harper and Wok unsheathed his machete and took a step towards him, that Hioto, grim-faced though he was, somewhat hurriedly relinquished his sword. Beard at once snatched at it, determined to have it as a souvenir. He then allowed Hioto to return to his quarters to collect his personal belongings, and forgot all about him for the moment. He pointed to the fluttering Japanese flag and told Blossom to "take that thing down" and to put a proper flag up; but no Union Jack could immediately be found and so, for the present, a white sheet with a red cross painted on it was hoisted – to more cheers from the prisoners.

Capt March and his team were soon busy attending to the sick and dying men, and Summerbee at once set about organising meals, having discussed with March the sort of fare that the starved prisoners could stomach, making use not only of the stores they'd brought with them but also the ample supplies of the Japanese. Capt Parsons asked Beard if he had any specific orders for him, but Beard very solemnly said he wouldn't dream of telling a man of God what to do. "You just do whatever you think God expects you to do, Mr Parsons," he said. "I'll only ever give you orders in a real emergency." The padre smiled his gratitude and said briskly, "Then I'll help Mr March with the sick, Robert." Beard was pleased when he discovered that most of the padre's supplies comprised, not Bibles, but thousands of cigarettes and about twenty pounds of barley sugars; far more use in the circumstances.

Beard made a quick tour of the camp area, with Blossom always at his heels, shaking bony hands and talking with the men. There were dead men lying in odd corners where they had died, if not unnoticed, forgotten in the general struggle to survive. Perhaps they were the lucky ones, Beard thought, covering one face that was already being devoured by great fat flies. There was no proper cemetery outside, but almost everywhere there were shallow graves with only broken crosses to mark their position at the edge of the jungle; in some instances, the graves were so superficial that skeletal bones protruded. Beard counted some thirty graves, but didn't doubt there were many more scattered about.

"Where's that Nip major, sergeant?" Beard asked Sgt Harper, who was still guarding the Japanese soldiers near the main gate.

"Still packing, I think, sir," replied Harper vaguely; he'd been too busy searching the soldiers to give much thought to the man.

"Get the bugger out here," said Beard, angry at the thought that the fellow was probably stuffing half a dozen suitcases. "Tell him he's going nowhere for the moment and that he and his men have work to do. Mr March will be needing all the orderlies he can get, and there's graves to be dug. And tell him one will be his if he puts a foot wrong."

Harper darted off grinning, and returned almost at once looking quite serious. "He's dead, sir," he exclaimed.

Beard stared. "How?" he asked, more in curiosity than concern; he'd heard no shot.

"He done himself in, sir. Hara-kiri, I think it's called," replied Harper, with a grimace. "He slit his belly right open with a bloody big knife, sir. Not a pretty sight at all."

"I'd have done it for him, Barry," said Blossom, exchanging grins with the sergeant.

"I wonder if that's what he wanted his sword for," said Beard thoughtfully.

It was well into October before Beard and his men left the camp. There were, in fact, three such camps within a radius of 30 miles and Beard collected all the personnel in the largest, which happened to be the first one they reached. The total number of prisoners, who included British, Indians, Burmese and Australians, was 2,070: more than 30 of these died before they could be evacuated: there were also more than 400 known graves. The number of Japanese who surrendered totalled 216: the figure would have been considerably greater had not some die-hards made a last-ditch stand shouting "Banzai!" and died to a man, others had fled into the jungle – and were probably still there, and two more officers committed hara-kiri and another was found dead in somewhat suspicious circumstances – which Beard felt justified in ignoring.

Beard had the surviving Japanese working day and night, and the first task he set them to was the digging of a grave for Hioto – that was after Blossom had acquired the knife used in the ritual death, and Beard had taken possession of a little bag of rubies that was found secreted in the region of the major's groin. Beard discarded the bag with distaste and placed the rubies – there were nine of them, all shapes and sizes, and varying in colour from deep crimson to pale rose, plus some other stones – in one of Ruth's handkerchiefs, which he then pushed into one of his safer pockets. Another trophy was an ivory Buddha, nine inches high, decorated with minute gemstones: Hioto had been found dead at the feet of the idol. Beard wrapped it carefully in the Japanese flag that had so recently been fluttering over the camp, and stored it carefully in the rucksack that he carried everywhere – but in spite of these precautions, it "went missing" before he left India.

The airstrip was completed in ten days. Beard had the Japanese, officers included, working in shifts sixteen hours a day. It was a tremendous feat bearing in mind the tools to hand. Obstructing trees were blown up and hauled aside by two luckless elephants that happened to be passing by with their mahouts, then the roots had to be dug out and dragged away, and finally the whole length of the runway had to be levelled and rolled by whatever means could be devised. Beard belatedly thought they should have held on to the elephants for this purpose, but they had proceeded on their pilgrimage, and so the work was mainly achieved by marching the Japanese backwards and forwards hour after hour until the loose, moist soil looked firm enough to risk a landing on.

Fortunately, among the released prisoners was a Royal Engineer officer who, despite his pathetic condition, was able to give advice on the best site for the airstrip – bearing in mind the nature of the ground and the proximity of mountains, jungles and rivers all around; unfortunately, as soon as the airstrip was completed and pronounced suitable, the monsoons returned and virtually washed it away. For four days the rains fell and, though supplies were dropped by parachute, there was nothing that could be done but to sit it out. Wok and Sok did little to raise spirits by pointing out that the monsoons were not due to end for another month, and observing that the brief respite they had enjoyed in which to build the runway had been a little gift of the gods. Beard, and doubtless many of the others, wondered which band of mocking gods they meant. However, on the fifth morning the rains ceased as suddenly as they had started, the sun came and started drying things out, and Beard had his Japanese work force repairing the damage as soon as it was practical.

The first plane landed safely – ignoring a couple of alarming bumps and a lengthy slide before coming to a standstill – about the middle of October. It was quickly followed by others bringing in doctors, nurses, medical equipment, proper beds, and engineers and materials to make the airstrip more durable. In the course of the next three weeks, a shuttle of planes evacuated the prisoners in never-ending streams. But it was a slow business: many of the men were simply too sick to be moved straight away: some required immediate surgery, and needed convalescence before they could be flown out; and some were too far gone to be saved, and died without ever knowing they had been freed from their hell.

Beard continued to run the camp as a military hospital, but, having no proper medical qualifications, he felt somewhat surplus. He busied himself keeping the Japanese working, but the airstrip was now in the hands of British engineers and ground staff and there was not a great deal left for Beard and his men to do, apart from keep an eye on their Japanese workforce who were never idle – but they weren't very popular in the wards. Beard helped out as best he could: he wrote letters for the patients, fetched and carried for them, listened to their dreams of getting home, and read to them.

There was one man in particular he used to read to: L/Cpl Billy Wootton of the West Kents, who was 23 and came from Tunbridge Wells, and who was suffering from everything that was going, from malnutrition to dysentery, malaria to beriberi – and on top of all that his eyes had been burned out by the sun, and he was quite blind. Throughout his captivity his constant companion, his only treasure, had been a paperback edition of *David Copperfield,* which his sister Jane had given him at the end of his embarkation leave saying "it's a big, fat book that'll keep you going till you get back home."

Billy had read it through twice, and had a yearning to hear the story "one last time"; he asked Beard to read it to him if he could spare the time. Beard looked first at the man, who was clearly never going home, and then at the book: it was in nearly as bad a condition as its owner, with several pages missing and a hundred dog-ears; and he knew straight away that he would make the time to read it. He picked it up, wondering how far he would get into the story before Billy died, and commenced reading. He returned each day, to continue the story; Billy seemed always to hear him coming and had the book ready for him in his hands by the time he reached his bedside. Eleven days after the readings began, they ended. Just as David Copperfield was arriving at Salem House, Billy was arriving in the next world. Even though Beard had been expecting it, the end still came as a shock.

Capt March had come into Beard's quarters one afternoon and said quietly, "Billy died during the night, Robert." Beard looked pained, and March added: "You did more for that boy with your reading than I could with my medicine. You took his mind off his pains for a little while with the adventures of Mr Dickens." Beard shook his head and said, "I wish I could have finished the book for him." After a moment's silence, March said with a grim smile, "We buried the book with him first thing this morning." Beard nodded and, though his mouth felt suddenly very dry, he managed to murmur hoarsely, "That was very thoughtful of you, Doug. I expect Billy's reading it himself now." He wondered if he should write to the sister, but decided against it; he'd already written too many such letters. March would see to it that she heard the right sort of lies, which was all you could write. People back home didn't understand what it was like to die in places like this: bodies torn apart and in constant pain that prayed only for a quick death. The less Jane knew about Billy's end the better.

Finally, towards the end of November, the last of the PoWs was evacuated: the last, that is, of those who would be going home; the remainder would remain in their jungle graves until those responsible for such matters decided where their final resting place should be. Beard and his small command flew out, first to Rangoon and then on to Colombo in Ceylon where Kemp told him they were all flying home almost immediately.

Unfortunately, Beard suffered another bout of malaria and had to be hospitalised. By the time he was released from convalescence, it was 1946 and he found himself all alone, his men having returned to England in time for Christmas. It was the middle of February before he was allocated a berth on a plane and he could follow them. It was then that he discovered his ivory Buddha was missing from his kit: he supposed it had been pinched while he was in hospital. Miraculously, he still had his rubies, and his other trophies were also intact.

As he leaned back in the plane, Beard pondered about his future. If, indeed, he had one. He knew that with the end of the war units were being disbanded wholesale, and he really couldn't see how, or why, a secretive outfit like his could escape the general run down of its Services by the War Office. He fell asleep just as it struck him that he wasn't with the War Office, but with the Foreign Office – unless they too decided they didn't need him any more. Kemp had confided that he was leaving the Service anyway and would probably go into farming, or write a book. Well, he'd soon learn his fate.

Finally asleep, Beard forgot everything, and dreamed of Ruth, and of a wedding..

Chapter Thirty-seven

Norfolk, England, February, 1946

Beard did not have long to learn his fate. Before he was able to begin his leave, before he could even phone Queenie and Ruth to let them know he was home, the first of the hammer blows was delivered when he attended, as ordered, at the Duke of York's Barracks. Here, in Room 312, he stood uneasily before a comfortable-looking general, who waved him to an uncomfortable-looking chair while continuing to peruse some papers in front of him. Beard sat rigidly at attention on the very edge of his seat looking straight at the general, whose nameplate identified him as Lieutenant-general Lord Godfrey Friston Green.

"Major Beard?" enquired the elderly officer, removing a monocle as he glanced towards his visitor.

"Sir," responded Beard, in a polite, attentive manner.

"You have been away from these shores so long, out of reach, so to speak, that your award of a bar to your DSO for distinguished leadership and courage under fire over a prolonged period in north-west Europe and Germany during 1944-45 has fallen into my hands, and I have pleasure in passing this honour into yours, major."

It was plainly a prepared speech. Beard had been aware of the award for some time, Gibbs had told him it was somewhere in the pipeline and would catch up with him in due course, and now that he held it in his hands he was unmoved; such honours belonged to the past. "Thank you, sir," he said flatly.

If the general had expected any other response, he did not allow it to hold up the rest of his business with this impassive officer. He asked directly: "Is it your wish to remain in the Army now that the hostilities are over, sir?"

"Yes, sir," answered Beard hastily. It was not a question that he had anticipated, and he had no ready answer for it. "Of course, sir."

"Then you must understand, Mr Beard, that you will not do so in your present rank. These wartime promotions, I'm sure you will be aware, are very rarely substantive." Beard had not been aware of this, and he had a sick feeling in the pit of his stomach, as though he had been kicked there. "A lieutenancy is the best you can expect in peacetime," declared Sir Godfrey, and his voice now sounded rather solemn: perhaps he was embarrassed at having to make such an announcement. He concealed his discomfort by occupying himself polishing his monocle, which he breathed on and rubbed with a blue silk handkerchief, repeatedly lifting it up to see how it sparkled. "Of course, being attached to the Foreign Office rather than the Army, you may stand better opportunities for advancement. But my feeling is that you may have to remain a lieutenant for quite a number of years – unless, of course, there's another war, but we can't be too optimistic about that, can we? Once in a lifetime is the rule, if you're lucky."

Beard felt stunned. He'd half expected to drop down to captain – after all, he was still being paid as such even if he did wear a pair of crowns on his shoulders with the blessing of the Army, but not all the way down to a lieutenant. No! Never in his most pessimistic moments had he thought they'd do that to him. He felt himself blush, not with embarrassment, but with fury. It was as though he had been stabbed in the back. He felt sick and bruised all over. It was unjust, unfair, and downright insulting. And to think this kick in the balls had been preceded by a further decoration. He stared hard at the man on the other side of the desk. If anyone should lose his rank it should be this old fart! In fact, he should be retired to make way for young men like himself.

The old fart, having exhausted his preoccupation with his monocle, now busied himself reading through Beard's dossier again. Finally, he turned to look out of the window in the direction of the Thames and then on towards the Royal Chelsea Hospital, at the same time congratulating Beard on having had a really excellent war.

"It doesn't seem to have stood me in much stead, does it, sir?" declared Beard bluntly. In his view, anyone who had survived the war had had a good war. He gave a long, silent sigh. Perhaps he was being unfair in his turn; but he couldn't bear the thought of being reduced almost to the ranks, not after all he'd gone through to get where he was. It would be like being sent back to school. It really was too much. It wasn't right: not fair.

"It's a matter of common sense, Mr Beard," said the brigadier impatiently; he had had to deal with scores of such cases recently. It was never pleasant; it was an ordeal for both of them, especially for the man being demoted, or dismissed.

"In wartime we need all the men we can get: in peacetime the needs are obviously not the same. It's a matter of logistics, common sense ... call it what you will."

"Yes, sir," responded Beard, his voice a mixture of resentment and anger, his face – his dark eyes, anyway, full of hurt and misery.

"So, you still wish to remain in the Army – in the rank of lieutenant?" pursued the other, returning his attention to his papers.

Beard, fidgeting on his seat, gave a grim smile. He felt like chucking it all in, but where was the point? At least it was a job; he might not get one in the unknown civilian world. "I don't seem to have any real option, sir," he replied. "It's the only profession I know."

"Right. I've already been in touch with your former Brigadier Gibbs, who is now Major-general Sir Osbert Harden Gibbs, and who still heads his department at the FO. He doesn't want to lose you, but for the moment you're to be attached to the Parachute Regiment as an independent Intelligence officer. In other words doing much the same as you've been doing ever since the Foreign Office took you on. It's the very best we can do for you, major – sorry, lieutenant. Is that acceptable?"

Beard gave a dejected shrug, and nodded. He mouthed a "Yes, sir," not trusting himself to speak out loud.

"Good, that's it, then, Mr Beard. There's just a couple of papers I need you to sign," declared the general, almost amiable now that the business was done. He watched as Beard signed in the places shown, and went on: "The battalion you'll be joining is in training up in Norfolk – place called Little Harling, near Thetford, to be precise. They're scheduled to go to Palestine shortly, which is why I suspect you've been chosen for this particular assignment. I believe Gibbs wants your eyes and ears in the Middle East, and presume he'll contact you out there when he's ready. But, first things first: you're entitled to a month's return home leave. So you'll report at Little Harling at 23.59 hrs on ... oh, let's be generous and give you an extra few days ... make it the seventeenth of March – and as a lieutenant, Mr Beard. You may wear your crowns until then." He paused as he studied the ribbons on Beard's chest. "Don't see many lieutenants with your decorations, Mr Beard."

"Am I to be deprived of them as well, sir?" asked Beard bitterly.

"Good God, no," cried Sir Godfrey, shocked at the suggestion. "I'm sure you earned them, my boy."

"I earned my rank, too, sir," retorted Beard coldly.

The general, embarrassed again, lowered his eyes, staring down at the papers before him without seeing them. "I'm sure you did. I'm sorry," he said, giving a tiny shrug of helplessness. "Good day to you, sir."

Beard had had in mind raising the matter about changing his name back to his rightful one, but he felt too depressed to care one way or the other. All he could think of was getting out of the building as fast as possible. He wasn't capable at that moment of thinking clearly about such things as names, and, besides, shouldn't he have a word with Scruffy about the matter first? He saluted the general and almost stumbled from the room, and somehow managed to complete his documentation without displaying the bitterness he felt. Once outside, he found himself trembling as waves of self-pity swept over him, but as he hurried away, anywhere he could lose himself, these feelings turned again to anger; then, having had his fill of this, he suddenly found himself smiling, albeit joylessly. Well, he told himself, the sods might have used him as a major, but as they'd never paid him as such he wasn't really all that much worse off, was he? He knew it didn't sound very convincing, and he certainly didn't fool himself, but he did feel just a little better for having had the thought, so much so that he had another one – he'd find a quiet pub and work out what to do, if he didn't drink himself into oblivion first, in which case nothing would matter.

The Three Jugs in New Peel Street, off the Pimlico Road, wasn't all that quiet, but as things turned out Beard did not get drunk, nor any distance at all along that road. He was toying with only his second beer when his attention was drawn to a rather superior type of voice, which vaguely touched a chord in his memory. It wasn't difficult to locate the voice, for it was the sort that could be heard in every distant nook and cranny, and even round corners, and besides the man was sat like a king on his throne surrounded by an admiring circle of – strangely, mostly men. Beard would have thought that such an elegant figure, coupled with its mellifluous voice, would have attracted more ladies – but perhaps they were all at home now that their husbands were returned from the war.

Having located the man through the medium of the huge mirror behind the bar, Beard studied the man at his leisure, more curious than anything else. He was in the uniform of a major in The Royal Horse Guards (The Blues), and the uniform looked as immaculate as its wearer looked dashing. There were three rows of medal ribbons on his breast, including the DSO and MC and a couple Beard didn't recognise, and two wound stripes. The major – it rankled with Beard that this pretty fellow was actually a major, while he was now a mere lieutenant – really did look a magnificent sight, and as he examined the face Beard felt that he had seen it before, but where? The face and the voice, he knew them both, but could place neither.

The man was recounting casually, and with seeming modesty, but in a voice that was determined to be heard even above the traffic outside, a tale of extraordinary daring in some unheard-of region of Normandy that had his audience gasping. Beard frowned, but he was really concentrating more on studying the hero himself rather than on listening to his story. He really was a gorgeous sight; tall and slim, with beautifully coiffured blond hair and the face of a film star below. Not a young face, perhaps forty or more, but devilishly handsome; it was smooth and well tanned with very blue eyes, and a wide sensual mouth. Good God! even the fellow's lips seemed to ring a bell, which surprised Beard exceedingly, for, while he took pleasure in remembering a girl's lips, he wasn't aware of ever having even noticed a man's mouth before – except, maybe, when about to punch it! But, he definitely knew this man from somewhere. Where? He was becoming irritated over not remembering.

In the end, it was the man's own audience who provided the elusive clue. The major, who had evidently just been asked which of his medals had been awarded for the deed of valour he'd been regaling them with, tapped one of the ribbons on his breast. Beard noticed straight away that the hand was missing most of one finger, but what startled him and held his attention were the positive squeals of ecstasy from among the adoring throng that sounded so effeminate and out of place. Nor were they content with their cries of "Ooohs" and "Ahs" and "What a pretty one, ducky!" They crowded in on the major, their hands stretching out to touch and stroke him; one of them even captured a hand and pressed it to his lips, and several others fondled him in a most intimate manner. The major, who had an arm draped round the neck of his nearest companion, evidently revelled in the attentions being shown. He fondled nearby faces, blew kisses at those he couldn't reach and tittered like a ... He's a bloody poofter! They all are!

The realisation, at long last, that he was in a Queers' House, set Beard's mind whirling. So how on earth could he have known the major – if that's the sort of thing he got up to? He'd detested anything like that all his life. He'd experienced it only once when he was running away from one of the Homes – St Hilda's, it was. It had nauseated him at the time, and for years after the memory of the ordeal had haunted him. Even now, he couldn't quite place the major – not until he saw him rise, and limp off to the Gents with his arm still round his plump little friend. And then the truth struck him with a suddenness that was painful in its clarity, but even then he couldn't remember the despised man's name, so effectively had he erased it from his memory. He leaned over the counter and asked the barman in a low, earnest, urgent voice :

"Who is he? The major? What's his name?"

"The major, sir – why, he's our own darlin' hero, sir," gushed the barman proudly. "Should 'ave had the bleedin' Victoria Cross after all he's done. Been everywhere, done everything, he has, sir – North Africa, Italy, Greece an' places in between. I heard he done a lot of hush-hush work behind the lines ... he was even dropped into Germany to get top secret plans to help in the invasion. He was terribly wounded in Normandy, but they only give him a bar to his DSO!"

"The name, man! The name!" snapped Beard, grabbing at the man's tie and pulling him forward half across the bar counter so that their faces were only inches apart. "What's his bloody name?"

The barman, his eyes almost popping out of his pink, sweaty face, gasped out: "He's an Honourable, sir ... Major the Honourable Oliver Roland."

"The bastard!" snarled Beard, and shoved the barman backwards with such force that he finished up on the floor behind the bar.

"Sir!" exclaimed the barman, terrified that Beard was going to follow him over the counter, but when he dared to raise his head above the bar there was no sign of his assailant – only a swinging door that suggested his exit. The barman gave a deep breath of relief, and searched round the bar to make certain. There was no sign of the horrid stranger – he obviously had a screw loose, somewhere! – and here was the major coming back to tell another of his marvellous stories. The barman made himself a pink lady to soothe his nerves: he'd have a tale to tell himself tonight!

But Beard hadn't gone far: only to a phone kiosk outside. He waited there the few minutes it took the Military Police to arrive, accompanied them back inside the pub and, ignoring the petrified barman who dived out of sight, pointed to the bogus major who, many years ago had been described to him by Sam as a "dishonourable honourable."

Oliver Roland looked up in startled amazement at the intrusion, then his face paled and his shoulders seemed to sag in resignation. He took one look at the two huge MPs – their hard, unsmiling faces, their guns, their truncheons, their handcuffs, and offered no resistance, nor made any further pretence of being a military person, but as he was escorted past Beard, who was standing stony-faced alongside an MP sergeant, he asked with an air of pained curiosity,

"Who are you, darling?"

Beard remained silent, not trusting himself to speak or act calmly.

"Do I know you?" persisted Roland, wincing as one of the MPs tugged at his handcuffs.

"I should hope not," growled Beard emphatically.

Roland stared back in perplexity, plainly wanting to learn more from his denouncer; he was intrigued by the hostility in the face, and by the naked hatred in the dark velvety eyes – such beautiful eyes! The officer was so young, a boy almost ... could they, was it possible they had been lovers? If so, it must have been long, long ago for the face – and even if it did look cruel now, it had a certain appeal – held no recognition for him.

It was the MP sergeant who inadvertently brought a glimmer of enlightenment to the business. Turning towards Beard, whose eyes were fixed on Roland, he said: "We're very grateful to you, sir. We've known about this gent for some time, but could never nail him. He was always moving around, changing pubs and that sort of thing. How did you happen to know about him being a phoney?"

"A man – perhaps I should say a little boy complained about him ... said the swine had assaulted him years before the war and that he had a busted leg, a damaged finger and a bit of his tongue missing – so it was pretty plain he couldn't have been in the Army."

"Who was this boy? Where is he?" demanded Roland, eyeing Beard with suspicion.

"I think he said his name was Jarvis ... but it was probably something else entirely," replied Beard, staring the Honourable straight in the eye without the slightest sign of recognition. "I expect you know what boys are like," he added contemptuously.

Roland stared back, now more puzzled than suspicious. He

remembered the incident all right. He wasn't likely ever to forget it, was he? He'd had a wonky knee ever since, and lost his sense of taste over the injury to his tongue, and even his broken finger had gone gangrenous and had to be amputated. No, he wasn't likely to forget that night, not ever. But he didn't remember the name Jarvis. A thought suddenly struck him: could this fellow have been that boy? The thought was still struggling for comprehension in his brain when there was a tug on his handcuffs, and he was marched out of the building.

Beard watched his childhood seducer until he was out of sight and then, after signing a statement for the sergeant, he left himself.

Beard found another pub which really was quiet. It was in his mind to drink the place dry, but attracted by culinary smells that pervaded the bar, he had steak and kidney pie and an apple crumble instead. It was in the course of devouring the pudding that he made up his mind about how he was going to spend his leave. He would get married, and use it as his honeymoon! He felt he'd kept Ruth waiting long enough, though it had been the war that was the real culprit. He felt a need for Ruth. He'd loved her as long as he could remember. Now was the time to declare it to her in terms of marriage. He'd been afraid of that commitment long enough : perhaps it was just the word itself that had scared him. He was fearless now.

The decision came as much a surprise to him as the suddenness with which it was made. He had thought that when the time came for him to take the plunge, it would occupy weeks, if not months, of protracted mental argument. And here he was arriving at this momentous decision in no more time than it had taken him to swallow a single pint. He ignored the fact that he'd had years and years to reflect on the matter, and that, anyway, Ruth had really made the decision for him when he'd given her the ring; besides, he must have realised what he was doing, proposing, when he gave it to her. Now that he had finally acknowledged the fact to himself, he knew what he must do. He recovered his gear from the left luggage department at the station, and, regretting the fact that he no longer enjoyed the use of his own personal Jeep, took a train to Tiptree where he intended to call on Mr Fennell and beg a lift to Mayhill, and Ruth ; and he'd plight her his troth once and for all on the spot.

But Mr Fennell wasn't in his office: he was over at Mayhill visiting Queenie – at least, that's what his ancient clerk said, only he called her Mrs Hoggins. Beard found that he'd just missed (by a good hour) the twice-a-day bus (subject to cancellation at the whim of the driver, who also owned the bus and would far sooner go fishing than drive it) to Mayhill, which was why it was late afternoon and already dark before he reached The Pears.

Mr Fennell was indeed there, still eating cake with Queenie, but

Ruth was nowhere to be seen. It was only now that Beard remembered that she lodged in London with Mrs B. during the week while she was at work; but today was Friday, so she would be coming home – probably quite soon. Beard sighed and blamed himself for not remembering earlier. He should have gone to see Mrs B. while he was still in London, waited for Ruth, and then they could have travelled home together.

Meanwhile …

Queenie hurled herself at Beard and greeted him thunderously between quite savage kisses, while her arms hugged him bear-like to her. He felt crushed, but loved it. She ruffled her fingers through his short but obstinately wavy hair, stroked his face and generally poked at him as though looking for hollow spaces, all the while declaring how wonderfully surprised she was to see him. When the opportunity briefly presented itself, Mr Fennell thrust out a hand at Beard, who shook it warmly and mouthed a grinning "How are you, sir?" at the beaming solicitor. Then Queenie, with a second wind, felt the need to welcome him all over again, very physically, and when she had done she plonked down on to a settee and puffed noisily away like a pair of old bellows, before starting to sob with great enthusiasm. Beard smiled as he sat beside her and placed an arm round her heaving shoulders; he knew that her tears were only an expression of her great joy at seeing him again.

As soon as she had done crying, for the moment, Queenie started bustling around in the kitchen and presently they were all seated round a table having tea and more cake, Mr Fennell on one side of her and Beard on the other. Mr Fennell, at that moment, had eyes only for the sliced cake; Beard, who couldn't remember ever seeing her looking so well (it must be the country air), had eyes only for Queenie. She saw him watching her and, after a quick loving smile, the questions flowed. "You look pale, Jarvis – are you well?" "Why are you so yeller?" "Are you wounded anywhere?" "Where've you sprung from?" "Are you finished wiv the Army?" "Why don't you never write to us?" "Where are you chasin' off to next?" "How long can you stay?"

The questions, and many others, flowed from her tongue with the speed and regularity of bullets fired from a machine-gun. Beard fended off the barrage as best he could, parrying some, slipping past some others, but assuring her that he was well, just a touch of malaria, nothing serious, and all gone now; and, yes, he was still in the Army, but he was now only a lieutenant because it was peacetime, and his next posting looked like being to Palestine – but first he had a month's leave. He paused for breath and told her, because he knew she would be asking after him presently, that Mr Trumpett and all the others who had helped in the recovery of her treasures from The Dials rubble and to the renovation of The Pears had been killed in the last few months of the war; she seemed to have had a premonition for she didn't say anything, just nodded her head slowly a few times, and quietly cried again for a little while.

The talking went on for hours, with only a break for a five-course supper which only Beard seemed to tackle seriously, for both Queenie and Mr Fennell only wanted to hear of his adventures against "them 'orrible little yeller devils," and to see the sparkling rubies that he'd managed to bring safely home; they somehow looked a lot smaller here than they had in steaming Burma. Beard had begun to wonder when Mr Fennell was going home – it had even crossed his mind that perhaps he was already home, that he lived here now! – when he suddenly rose and said it was time he went. He and Beard exchanged vigorous handshakes and promised to see one another again very soon, and Beard noticed that Queenie and Mr Fennell kissed goodnight at some length when she saw him to the door. It pleased him immensely, filling him with a warm feeling, for he thought Queenie was the sort of woman who wouldn't be happy living on her own, which she would be once Ruth and he were married. It would be better if she had a husband of her own, too.

After Mr Fennell had gone, they sat together on the settee, Queenie's arm tucked comfortably inside his, far into the night talking about this and that, and sometimes sitting for long spells without speaking, just enjoying the other's nearness. As far as Queenie was concerned her son had come home, and she was perfectly contented.

"You an' Mr Fennell seem very cosy together," said Beard, breaking one of their silent spells.

Queenie smiled, quite prettily, and lowered her eyes, and came as close to blushing as ever she had in her life. She didn't say anything for a moment, contenting herself with giving his arm an extra squeeze. "He loves me," she murmured after a while.

"I could see that. And you?"

"I think so, Jarvis. Yes, I'm sure. He's a very good man. Kind an' gentle. We – we're comfortable together. A body needs company, specially as it gets older."

Beard turned and leaned over to kiss her cheek. He'd noticed straight away how much better she spoke and guessed that this had been unconsciously influenced by her association with Mr Fennell. He smiled fondly down at her and gave her an extra kiss. He remembered when he'd had elocution lessons at St Hilda's; talking proper, they'd called it. "Then be comfortable, Mum," he whispered to her. "It's called being in love, darling! And, as you say, love needs a partner. Don't let yours escape ... be happy with him. He'll keep you warm!'"

Queenie's very ample face seemed to grow even fuller as her very evident happiness took complete possession of her features. Her cheeks filled out and positively glowed, her eyes shone, her lips purred – or they might have done had she made a sound. As it was, they parted like a young girl's eager for a kiss – and *she* a matron with a grown-up daughter! "Yes, Jarvis," she said, but the words remained secret to her heart. A tiny sigh of contentment was the only sound that emerged from her. They went on sitting silently together, both happy with their thoughts.

Then had come the second hammer blow.

"It looks as if Ruth won't be home before tomorrow now," he said, looking at his watch, after another long interval of silence. He'd been so engrossed with Queenie's romance, his own had all but slipped by unnoticed. Well, almost. And hadn't he been excited all day at prospect of proposing to Ruth this evening? How dare she not be here to welcome him home, and be proposed to! He'd a jolly good mind not to do so when she did finally condescend to turn up – or at least, to make her wait a day longer, only he couldn't afford to lose any more days. Then he became aware that Queenie was staring at him in an odd way, almost as if he were some peculiar stranger. He raised his brows questioningly.

"She's not here, lovey," she answered, frowning.

"What do you mean, not here? She's late is all, probably missed her train and decided to stay in town with Mrs B, in which case we won't see her till tomorrow." He saw a shadow cloud her slate grey eyes. "She's not gone off and joined the ATS, has she, Mum?" Beard said with a forced laugh, though he was becoming concerned as to where exactly Ruth was.

"No – I don't think they take girls any more," exclaimed Queenie, fidgeting with her hands. "No, Jarvis, she's in America! She must've told you. She wrote you often enough."

"America!" cried Beard in utter stupefaction. If she'd said the moon, he could not have been more dumbfounded. What the devil was she doing over there? "No!" he said in a shocked voice. "She never told me. If she did, I never received her letter. In fact, I didn't receive any letters from anyone while I was in Burma." It wasn't surprising, he reflected, with the chaos out there at the time, with everything about-turning to come home and India rushing into independence. "What on earth is she doing over there? When's she coming home, Mum?"

"Oh, Jarvis, I thought you knew all about it," cried Queenie, startled that he didn't. "You remember Hannah, our washing-up girl at The Dials? Well, she got married to her GI – Toni Spagicci. I'm still not sure of his name – it's something like that. I always have to think of spaghetti to get me tongue round it. Anyway, Ruth was one of Hannah's bridesmaids an' when Toni fixed up a plane home, Hannah insisted on Ruth going over for a holiday."

"I'd have thought newly-weds would want to be alone," observed Beard with heavy sarcasm. He knew *he* wouldn't want anyone else along.

Queenie gave a very small smile. "Well, Jarvis, they weren't exactly on their honeymoon. Hannah's expecting sometime in May or

June. She'll be glad of a friendly face from home when the time comes. Ruth's been with her for nearly six months."

"What! However long does Ruth plan to stay?" cried Beard, his astonishment now complete and turning to exasperation. "When's she coming home, for heaven's sake?"

"Well, I think her visa allows her to stay for up to twelve months, but she's working for a big American law firm who think very highly of her, so she might not be coming home, not if she can get a residential visa, or whatever they call them things. Anyway, she's hardly likely to return before Hannah and the new baby are comfortably settled. It's a shame, Jarvis, you keep missing one another."

"But that means she won't be home much before the end of the year," declared Beard, quite appalled. "I've only got a month's leave, God knows where I'll be by the year's end."

"You mustn't be cross with her, darling," insisted Queenie, taking hold of his arm and holding him tightly. "It's her very first holiday abroad – her first holiday anywhere, really, an' she was so excited about going, specially to America. Remember, Jarvis – and I know you couldn't help it, 'cos you had yer orders, but she was terribly upset when you didn't come home like the rest of the soldiers when the war finished – the one in Europe, I mean."

"But I did," protested Beard. "You were all celebrating in London when I arrived. I was going to join you up in London the next day, but I got hauled away to Burma. I only had time to leave you a note to explain."

"Your not being 'ome for Christmas neither, well, that was the last straw," continued Queenie, scarce noticing his interruption. "It was awful us all missing one another when the war ended. But you was only 'ome fer that one day when we was celebrating VE-Day in Town. It was terrible finding yer note to say you'd been 'ere, and was already on yer way to Burma. The trouble is you never ever write to let us know what's goin' on, do you? If she'd known you was coming 'ome, she'd have been here waiting for you – like she's always been. America had simply been an escape from the waiting. A girl can wait for only so long, Jarvis: not for ever."

"I didn't know myself until the day I landed," cried Beard, exasperated. "Anyway Ruth knew I'd come home eventually," he excused himself weakly, wondering if perhaps he had taken Ruth too much for granted, but quite sure that if he had it very definitely wasn't his fault. She'd known he was a soldier, and had to go where he was ordered. "We're engaged, for heaven's sake! She knows that I love her – just as she knows that I can't come running home to her every time she feels lonely. I expected her to wait, like any other girl."

"If only you'd written an' told 'er her these fings, lovey," said Queenie gently. "A girl needs to be told very often that she's loved. And she needs to see her betrothed oftener than every few years. You couldn't 'spect Ruth to go on sitting at home twiddlin' her thumbs for ever wivvout a word of love or encouragement from you. It wasn't fair of you, Jarvis. At least you could have sent her a letter, it would've made all the diff'rence, dear."

Beard knew he was being reproached : knew, too, that he deserved every word of the censure; he knew she was right, but he didn't feel entirely to blame. Why should he? "You can't write letters to sweethearts when you're stuck in the middle of a jungle surrounded by Japs and snakes an' things," muttered Beard defensively.

"I know, darling, even so ... " Queenie began wretchedly, before stopping with a shrug of her enormous shoulders. There really was no excuse for such lack of effort

Beard sighed. "You know, Mum, I actually hurried home today with the idea of asking Ruth to marry me straight away so we could have the whole of my leave as our honeymoon," he whispered to her dejectedly. "Now it seems I won't even see her – and God alone knows when we'll get another opportunity." He gave a rueful grin as he added, "And it's not every day that a fellow gets the nerve up to propose and actually wants to get married."

Queenie started to weep again, and her sobs were loud and painful to Beard's sensitive ears. In between her great shudderings, she kept crying "Oh, Jarvis ...Oh, Jarvis," but nothing seemed to relieve the ache she felt in her breast, and eventually they both fell asleep in each other's arm ... and wakened in the early hours feeling stiff, cold, tired – and still wretched. And then they went upstairs to their respective beds, and for a long time neither could sleep, and when he did drop off, Beard dreamed he and Ruth were children again and playing at weddings: he thought it a nightmare.

By the time he'd eaten one of Queenie's enormous breakfasts, Beard, as is the way with the young, especially young men, had put the previous night's disappointment and his dream behind him, and as the day progressed it got farther and farther behind him until it was in danger of being lost from sight altogether. Well, after a fashion. He wouldn't, couldn't, ever forget about Ruth completely, not for long. After all, he addressed his freshly lathered face, they were both very young still, and he'd returned to the thought that there was all the time in the world for them get round to this marriage business, absolutely no need to go rushing at it. They'd marry ... when the moment was opportune. They'd know when this was … when the time came. First, they'd have to be reunited.

Once again he cut himself while shaving, and once again swore, and because she was on his mind, he blamed Ruth! He hoped he'd master the art of shaving before he bled to death. Meantime, there was his leave to get on with. Since, for no fault of his, there could be no wedding or honeymoon, he'd have to think of some other way to occupy the time. And it was *her* fault this time, not his.

Queenie, too, put the agonies of the night behind her, occupying the day, a cold but sunny Saturday, with showing off Beard to all the neighbours and anyone else they chanced to meet. Beard was on his best behaviour and everyone regarded him as being a credit, and a comfort, to Queenie – whatever their relationship might be. Mr Fennell arrived on cue with Tired Bill after lunch, and took them on a grand tour of the countryside, which didn't look all that appealing at that time of the year, although he proudly pointed out land-marks which he thought interesting: like the old county lunatic asylum which had been used as a barracks during the war, the village fire station that had gone up in flames one night in suspicious circumstance, the vicarage which had been the home not only of the minister but his *three* wives, two of whom were discovered buried within a walled rose garden, and a tumble-down boarding house which he said had been the home of a famous music hall artiste whose name meant nothing to either Queenie or Beard. It came as no surprise when the car finally pulled up at The Farthingales Tea Rooms, between Great and Little Tothams, which just happened to specialise in home-made cakes and shortbreads – and where Mr Fennell was received with that special deference reserved for very special (that is, regular) customers.

Next day, as the newly-liberated voices of countless church bells vied with each other in the unlikely hope of attracting the godless to services, Queenie, who would normally comment that "it'd take more than a bloomin' bell to get her out of her bed on a Sunday morning" if she had a mind to lie there, observed from the warm comfort of her Aga, "Isn't it wonderful to hear the bells again, Jarvis."

Beard, recovering from another huge breakfast, secretly thought that the silence imposed on the bells by wartime regulations had been a marvellous idea, and thought the restrictions on their use ought never to have been lifted; he observed bleakly that they gave him a headache. But he added with a quick smile as he saw her eyes cloud: "I don't really mean that, Mum, it's just that bells have been ruling my life for as long as I can remember. At the homes we had to rise to the command of a bell, and go to bed at the order of another ... and in between these two bells were dozens more telling us when to pray, when to eat, when to talk, when to change classes, when to play ... oh yes, Mum, I can do without bells for the rest of my life, and especially on Sundays."

Queenie crossed over to him and patted his hand. "Them 'orrible days is behind yer, Jarvis," she said earnestly. "Today the bells is simply God's music, and is simply for our enjoyment an' pleasure."

Bells, as far as Beard was concerned, only tolled: they did not make music. He thought of saying that if she loved them so much she should answer their summonses and go to church, but he didn't want to say anything that might aggravate her, so he answered, "They are rather lovely, aren't they!"

Beard and Queenie went by train up to London the following morning, for since he could not be with Ruth, Beard felt an urge to look up Mrs B. and any survivors of The Dials blitz that were around, and of course he wanted to see Maud who would be able to give him news of Bertie's progress.

In the event, it was Bertie himself who opened the door of the flat in Brewer Street when he and Queenie called – and from somewhere behind him Maud's voice sang out, "Who is it, darling ?"

Bertie, with an instant smile, flung out his hand without a word and pumped away at Beard's hand as energetically as if he was using a real pump. Bertie, who was leaning on a stick, would most likely have carried on with this silent greeting for some while longer, had he not suddenly espied Queenie hovering in the background. He dropped Beard's throbbing hand immediately and turned to take Queenie's which he shook with great gentleness before, with old-world charm, he stooped and touched the work-worn limb with his lips. Maud then appeared in the doorway, instantly recognised them both and flung her arms first round Beard and then as far as she could round Queenie, before ushering them into the flat.

It was Queenie who noticed the gold band behind Maud's engagement ring first and held on to the hand as she exclaimed, "Congratulations, dear." Beard spun round and saw the hand, or rather the rings – the extra one, that was being admired. "You two," he cried, staring from Maud to Bertie with smiles of amazement and congratulations. "You're married!" The two accused moved to stand beside each other and hold hands, though not the ringed one which Maud waved at her visitors, and displayed their happiness with wide sheepish grins – well, Bertie's was decidedly sheepish, decided Beard. Congratulations, further handshakes, hugs and kisses occupied several moments and ended with Queenie having what she later called a "lovely cry," though at the time it was excessively loud and off-putting. When they had all recovered their emotions, Beard, saying nothing of his own marital status, asked: "When did all this happen?" And, with an exquisite blush, Maud, with a quick peek at Bertie as though seeking confirmation, replied, "Oh, ten days ago!"

"What! You mean you're on your honeymoon!" cried Beard, mortified at the thought that he might be intruding, and not be entirely welcome.

"I'm not sure that we've actually started it yet," declared Bertie, giving Maud a squeeze to cover his confusion at the thought of what he had just said. "We were married last Saturday – last Saturday week, that is, down at Upbridge. Maud and I arrived together in an ambulance from Horley. The hospital only released me for that one day, and then only after a lot of arm twisting. I spent my wedding night back at the hospital!"

"I was there, too," emphasised Maud with a happy grin, "if not in the same bed. It was lonely in that side ward, and there was you with all those nurses fussing round you."

Bertie exhibited the look of one who had suffered from the ordeal. "The whole family, including my two brothers, Poppy and Ben, was there … and I expect Mother's still crying! We would have invited you but nobody seemed to know where you went after The Dials was bombed, and I did hear that you were still playing soldiers somewhere. Stafford was there, surrounded by his squalling children, and had to be taken home in a cart. He loves a wedding – other people's, that is! You'd think with all his progeny he'd get the message ... I bet Bunty's asked him enough times! Still, he's a lovable old rascal, most of the time," said Bertie.

"Poppy and Ben interrupted their honeymoon in Ireland to come," Maud put in.

"Honeymoon!" cried Beard, raising an incredulous brow. "They've been married for more than a year."

"Just goes to show how much in love they are, doesn't it! Our honeymoon is going to last for ever!" announced Maud, with another adoring look at Bertie, who pretended to be shocked by the remark. "By the way," she added, wheeling round to Beard again, "Poppy's expecting – sometime in July! Isn't it wonderful! I'm going to have lots and lots of babies – all boys, and all as beautiful as Bertie!"

Beard laughed out loud and gave her a big smacker of a kiss on the lips, and then raised his eyes in mock sympathy at Bertie. "Marriage seems to agree with you, Maud," said Beard, grinning at the domestic bliss all around, "you're looking very lovely."

"She always has done, old boy," declared Bertie proudly.

"Oh Jarvis, if you continue saying sweet things like that, Ruth'll never let you out of her sight," cried Maud, her dark eyes flashing mischievously.

"Well, she's taken herself off to America – so she'll need pretty powerful eye-sight," retorted Beard drily. "Gone for a year, if you please. Probably never see one another again. And, believe it or not, I was going to propose, marry and honeymoon her during this leave of mine."

"Oh Jarvis," cried Maud again, but this time there was distress in her voice. "How terrible for you – and Ruth. She'll be heart-broken at having missed you. If only she'd known you were coming home. You must write to her immediately and explain things to her."

"That's the trouble, he never writes to nobody an' so nobody never knows where he is – or when he's coming 'ome," cried Queenie in a vexed voice, although she tucked her arm in his as she shook her head and gave him a wistful little smile. "Just turns up out of the blue after years of silence. It don't give folk any chance to make plans. If Ruth 'ad known you was coming home, Jarvis – especially with marriage on yer mind, why, she'd have been waitin' on the church steps for yer. You 'ave to write an' tell folk what's 'appening, Jarvis."

Beard certainly wasn't going to admit that he hadn't known he was coming home to marry Ruth, and that he'd only made this decision to cheer himself up after learning that he was to be demoted and loaned out to a strange regiment. He shrugged. He didn't feel like writing to anyone at the moment. "It won't help things this leave, Mum. I'll write to her, but it won't bring her home any faster, will it? I'll be gone again before she can possibly be here. And anyway, you said she wanted to stay with her friend after she'd had her baby and wasn't expected home until much later in the year – and I expect to be in Palestine by then. It's a great pity we've missed each other because I'd really decided we'd get married. She's been on at me long enough about it – ever since we were kids. Ironically this is the longest leave I've ever had – and heaven knows if I'll ever be in the same frame of mind again. We'll just have to see what happens on my next home leave. Perhaps she won't come home at all. Perhaps she's already forgotten about me."

"She'll never ever do that, Jarvis, not as long as she draws breath," declared Queenie emphatically. "You're her whole life. Nothing will ever stop her loving you."

"She loves you, Jarvis! She always has," insisted Maud warmly.

"Of course," agreed Bertie, equally confidently.

Beard knew that they were right. It was only his bitter disappointment, the frustration of it all that made him feel so dispirited. If only he'd come home a few weeks earlier, if only he hadn't been delayed by that wretched malaria bug ... then, he was sure, Ruth would never have gone off to America. If, if, if ... no use being depressed, was it? Not about anything. She was over there, and he was over here, and that's all there was about it. He'd have to wait, and in the meantime there were other things to be getting on with – like his leave.

"Well, my dears, I'm sure you don't want me taking up your honeymoon time," he grinned at Maud and Bertie, "so Mum and I will take you out to lunch at Simpson's and then leave you to get on with your lovemaking! We'll take a run down to Highways – and keep Poppy and Ben awake instead!"

"You won't, old son," chuckled Bertie, "they went back to Ireland almost as soon as the wedding was over."

"Good God! Deserted all round! How much longer do they want?" exclaimed Beard, marvelling at such stamina. "And you two, I suppose you've given up eating since you got married?"

"Almost," admitted Bertie.

"Of course not, Jarvis. We'd love to come and eat with you," declared Maud, her eyes pretending to scold Bertie even as her lips nuzzled his cheek, "and then, we'll be glad to see the back of you for a month or two – or more. We might try to beat Poppy's record!"

"You'll never survive, none of you!" laughed Beard. "Here's everyone either having babies or wallowing on honeymoon, and my girl runs away. It's simply not fair!"

It was meant as a joke and treated as one, and over the meal it was forgotten entirely. Bertie was already out of the Army and did not appear to have any intention of ever working again – not in the foreseeable future, at any rate; he did not appear at all surprised that Beard intended to remain in the Army, and wished him well in Palestine.

"I expect it will be another of your hush-hush assignments, and you'll come back a general with loads more medals," Bertie suggested, raising a questioning eye. "Possibly," replied Beard non-committally, deciding not to mention that he'd already been demoted; it would be too humiliating. But he did tell them he would be attached to the Parachute Regiment in Palestine, as an independent Intelligence officer. First, however, he had to join them in Norfolk, where they were training. Maud told him to be sure to look up her parents who lived in happy seclusion behind a wall of plum-coloured bricks in a quaint little cottage they had christened Little Humming Bees – after the myriad bees that thrived on the lavender fields that surrounded them at Babingley. The cottage, she added, was the size of a beehive. Beard promised he would do so, and made a mental note not to – in case the bees decided to make friends with him.

Before they all parted for the night – Beard and Queenie to Mrs B.'s and Bertie and Maud back to their matrimonial nest – Beard promised to visit them again before he went up to Norfolk. Somehow, they all knew he wouldn't keep his promise. The following day, Beard decided that since everybody else had deserted him or was otherwise engaged, he'd go and look up Scruffy. To his surprise, Queenie declined to accompany him, saying she'd prefer to keep Mrs B. company; she said that Scruffy was really his friend and that she hardly knew him; and she added, rather mysteriously, that she had her reasons for not going. He thought she'd probably reveal her secret reasons on his return; perhaps.

Beard took a train to Sheffield and a bus from there to Hathersage and, as Sam had done a few years before, found Aunt Dolly in the garden of her cottage. She was not gardening, of course, for this was February and the ground was rock hard and buried under layers of snow and winter debris. There was a cold wind blowing down off the

Peaks and she was well wrapped up in a long-skirted coat and had a blue-woollen beret on her head and several yards of multi-coloured scarf round her neck. She had evidently been walking up and down the path near her gate, for it was the only part where the snow had been trodden flat, and must have seen Beard approaching for she was waiting for him at the gate.

"Aunt Dolly?" asked Beard, giving her a smile and a little playful salute.

She stared into his face, examining it all over as if she were looking for some landmark. Whether or not she found it, Beard never knew, but after she'd had her fill of looking him over, she nodded her head. "You're Scruffy's friend Biffer, aren't you?" she said quietly, a thin smile lighting up her watery-blue eyes.

Beard nodded, and immediately wondered how much she knew. He was pretty sure Scruffy would have told her everything, which made his position, his identity at any rate, rather insecure. But, did it matter any more? They were both of age, and though they had assumed names of others, if it was still a crime it had been committed with the very best of motives. "Yes, ma'am, Major Robert Beard at your service," he said out loud. "I'm just back from overseas and thought it'd be nice to look up my old chum Scruff."

"You'd better come in, Mr ... Major Beard," she said, with a sort of hesitant catch in her voice, as she lifted the latch on the gate.

Beard followed the tall, stooping figure up the path and into the stone cottage, which was like a doll's house: pretty, with leaded windows, a sturdy green-painted door and pine-wood smoke pouring out of a hooded chimney. Inside, on the ground-floor, there were only two rooms, a sort of parlour which was also where meals were eaten and a kitchen which was all cupboards and corners and had very little space, with a bit of a hall in between leading to some dark stairs that disappeared steeply aloft. She showed him into the parlour while she went into the other to make some tea, declining his offer of assistance saying if he was anything like Scruffy in the kitchen she could manage better on her own.

In a very short while she joined him in the parlour: between them on a table stood a brown teapot wearing a floral woollen cosy, brown bread and butter with a dish of what looked like plum jam, a plate of scones and a jam-sandwich cake with a dusting of flour. She watched him dive into the feast with evident pleasure, though she seemed to have a mouse's appetite herself, only nibbling at things as she talked. And how she talked! About all the things she and Scruffy had done together, about what wonderful company they were for each other, and about the great love and affection that had grown between them. If he noticed how all her remarks seemed to be in the past tense, Beard assumed it was because Scruffy wasn't there, and guessed he must be at his work. But

Beard, being busy with the business of eating, mostly only listened.

Now that she had removed her outdoor clothing, he saw that she had no figure at all, being thinner than the meanest rake; her face, too, was thin and parchment white with the eyes, such a wistful-looking blue, like a mist, set in pronounced hollows. He wondered how old she was: she looked nigh on ninety with her almost white hair, but he calculated she was nearer sixty, if that; he wondered if she was ill, and decided she probably was: most old people seemed to get ill. One thing was certain, she enjoyed a good chin-wag, hardly pausing as Beard continued tucking in. She seemed to come to an abrupt halt, however, as he finished eating. Her face became even greyer, her eyes dimmer and she fussed nervously with a tiny hanky in her lap. For several moments there was complete silence during which he watched the muscles in her lined face twitching spasmodically, but finally, in a voice far removed from that which she had used while chatting, she whispered haltingly:

"Scruffy's dead, Mr Beard ... he was in an accident ... just over a year ago."

Beard, who liked to think that nothing ever surprised him, was shaken rigid. Now he realised the significance of her constantly speaking as if in the past. When he had recovered himself sufficiently, he moved to her side and placed a comforting arm round her frail shoulders, and said gently "tell me about it, Dolly," and slowly the story was told, the woman's spirits growing as she related it.

Scruffy and his aunt had loved one another from the start and were perfectly happy together: they were as near mother and son as it was possible to be without it being so; indeed, they probably loved one another more than the real ones did. They didn't want much more than each other; Dolly had her widow's pension and sold a few cakes in the village, and Scruffy earned a couple of pounds a week as a forestry worker and did odd jobs where he could, and caught rabbits; they didn't have a lot of money, but they had enough, and they were as near perfectly happy as it was possible to be. Their happiness was shattered one day when bureaucracy came knocking at their door. Robert Parkin, Scruffy's alias, was required by the Army. He had evaded call-up in his own name, only to be caught up in someone else's – someone who was dead, anyway. As it happened, he was rejected for military service on account of his flat feet – so he would never have been accepted for the Indian Army, and all the scheming between him and Beard had been quite unnecessary. But, though the Army didn't want him, Scruffy had been directed under the Bevin Boy scheme to train at a local colliery as a miner, where apparently flat feet were acceptable.

Scruffy had hated every moment he spent in the mines, said Dolly, but there was nothing he could do about it. "He used to say that it was like being buried alive, and that he only came alive again when he was home again with me," she added, with a deep sigh. The accident had occurred on Tuesday, November, 14, 1944. A lift, or cage as the men called it, had plummeted hundreds of feet – and Scruffy had been one of 32 miners killed. "It was the worst day of my life when I was called to identify him," said Dolly, her eyes wincing at the memory. "His poor body was smashed to pieces." He was buried at Hathersage, beneath a Scots pine and facing the Peak country that he had come to love. The colliery had paid for a gravestone and, she hoped Beard wouldn't mind, but he would be remembered forever as Robert Parkin and not by his real name, Robert Beard.

"He'll always be remembered as Scruffy to us," said Beard, a trifle huskily. It seemed ironic that he had gone off to war and returned almost unscathed, while poor Scruff had stayed at home and got killed digging for coal. It didn't make sense. It was so unfair.

Beard stayed with Dolly for nearly a week. Apart from the fact that he felt it his duty to stay awhile, they got along very well. They talked a lot, she did at any rate, and went for walks when the weather permitted through the nearby woods at the edge of the Peak District, and they visited Scruffy's grave. There wasn't a lot to see for the grave was under several inches of snow and Beard had to wipe the headstone to make out some of the words. There wasn't much to see there, either. Just the name: Robert Parkin; and something about a tragic accident ... and being sadly missed by his Aunt Dolly. There didn't seem to be much need for anything else. Those few engraved words said it all: they told of a life that was no more, and the fact that he was missed. Beard found himself wondering who the devil Robert Parkin had really been, and couldn't even remember him. He was pleased to see that Dolly wasn't as lonely as he'd thought, for even during his brief stay she had several visitors from the village: mostly ladies swapping recipes or exchanging home-made goodies (one brought a piping hot rabbit pie and stayed to share it), or simply dropping in for a chat – or perhaps just to check that she was well, for like all good neighbours, they were caring.

On the morning that he left, with snow shoaling down in great feathery lumps, Dolly asked Beard if he intended to keep Scruffy's name for always, and after a moment's thought, he said: "I don't know about for ever. It begins to look like I will as long as I'm in the Army – and that could be for ever!"

"Doesn't it ever upset you, carrying someone else's name? Living their lives, sort of," pressed Dolly, a strange intensity lighting her eyes.

"Not really," replied Beard easily. "What's in a name, as someone once wrote. I don't know what my true name is – and probably never will. I got given one 'cos I had to be called something. It was Sam Trotter – him that found you for Scruffy – who christened me Jarvis Brook. Then I took Scruffy's name for reasons you know – and I've kept it ever since. 'Course, certain people still call me Jarvis. People like

Ruth."

"She your girl?" smiled Dolly.

Beard nodded quickly, as if to get the acknowledgement over with. He hoped she was still ... even if he was cross about her not being where he wanted her.

"Is Mr Trotter keeping well? Please remember me to him," said Dolly, as he pushed out a hand to bid her farewell.

Beard stared at her, somewhat uncomfortably. It had never occurred to him that she wouldn't know, but, of course, how could she? "Sam's dead, too, Dolly," he told her gently. "He was killed in the Blitz nearly three years ago." He paused a moment and then added, "He'd been promoted sergeant and been awarded the George Medal."

He didn't know what sort of reaction he'd expected from her, perhaps tears, perhaps some trite emotional remark; but she only stood there, perfectly still, staring back at him with a drawn face and sad, dry eyes. "He was a very good man. The best I've known," was all she said.

Beard took her hand and kissed her rough cheek. "I hardly knew him myself, but I loved him like he was my own father. He was the best man in the world."

When Beard got back to Grafton Road and told Queenie – and Mrs B., for she knew and kept all their secrets – of Scruffy's tragic death and of Dolly's sentiments regarding Sam when she heard of his, Queenie declared : "She's a very good woman herself."

After a few moments of intense thought – evident from the contortions her face went through – Queenie added : "I think it's all right to tell yer now, Jarvis, that Dolly weren't really Scruffy's aunt." Beard gasped his utter surprise, but she silenced him with a motion of her hand. "Fact is, she ain't even Dolly, but a woman called Martha Longley." Beard gave another gasp, and again was silenced.

"It were all something concocted between 'er an' Sam ... an' I'm sure with God's blessing, if not man's. It certainly had my fullest approval. Sam told me all about it – there was never no secrets between us." Queenie paused to indulge in a few happy memories of Sam, and then went on to relate, as best she could remember, how Martha had nursed the dying Dolly in Thurcroft, in West Yorkshire, and how she had swapped identities when Dolly had died simply so that her pittance of a pension would continue to be paid.

"Times was cruel in them days, Jarvis," explained Queenie grimly. "It was a struggle to survive even if you had a job, it were impossible without, an' she – Martha, who became Dolly, had no job an' no money. Sam said Martha had been as an angel the way she looked after Dolly, an' didn't deserve no punishing over a few-bob-pension."

"How did Sam find out that Dolly weren't Dolly ?" asked Beard thoughtfully.

"It was her hair, weren't it," grinned Queenie. "When he first started lookin' for her, he traced her to Grays where she was one of two Burton sisters. The other one was called Violet – she were Scruffy's mother and got drowned on a ferry in the Thames. The thing was both sisters were remembered as having coal-black hair – an' when Sam found a solicitor what Dolly dealt with, he said she had hair the colour of gold. So she couldn't be Dolly."

"She could have dyed her hair – most girls seem to," Beard pointed out.

"The roots'd give 'er away, dear. Women – workin' women, that is, weren't so thorough abaht such things in them days," snorted Queenie. "Sam was no fool. He knew about things like that – even if 'er hair was turnin' grey when he found her."

"Well, it's white now – though, come to think of it, there were a few strands of faintly yellow in it," said Beard, searching his memory. He smiled as he remembered Dolly asking him what it was like living under someone else's name! In the next breath, he added: "She was right about Sam. He was a very good man. I loved him"

"So did I," said Queenie fervently, and patted his hand. "Me, too," said Mrs B.

On the eve of the end of his leave and his departure for Norfolk, Queenie, now safely back at The Pears, asked Beard if he'd written to Ruth.

"I'm not writing to America," he replied huffily.

"It's 'er you'd be writin' to, not the bleedin' country," she snapped back.

"I'll write when she's back home – where she belongs."

"An' where'll you be then? Probably the other side of the world again. An' how'll you know she's home then, heh?"

Beard remained silent and it was left to Mr Fennell, who was driving Beard to the station in the morning and was staying the night, to tell them to "stop squabbling like children" and to make the most of their last evening together; and for the remainder of the evening and much of the night, they did exactly that. It was a time for reminiscing, for singing old songs, telling risqué stories, drinking too much, eating too much cake and making promises that were forgotten as soon as they were made. Like writing letters. The last thing Beard remembered before going to bed was thinking that Queenie and Mr Fennell would most likely be married long before Ruth and himself! Perhaps he would write to her one day.

He did, but it wasn't the letter he wanted to write.

Norfolk was cold, wet, windy, flat and uninviting when Beard arrived, but he did not greatly care. It did not seem to matter either –

because there was nothing he could do about it, neither did the fact that he had to present himself as a lieutenant. He was genially greeted by his new CO, Lieut-Colonel Harry Spiers, who cheerfully told him to make the most of his spell in Norfolk as they were scheduled for the sandy wastes of Palestine in the very near future. "Not your regular kind of work, Mr Beard," he smiled, "more a policing job. Keeping the peace between the Jews and the Arabs ... with no thanks from either side. They've been at it for thousands of years, but once again the world's politicians, namely the United Nations, are interfering where they're not wanted. But I suppose you know all about this independence for the Jews, what?"

Beard nodded; he knew how to behave in his subordinate rank. "As you say, sir, they've been at it for a long time, and we made things worse for them when we drew up boundaries in their vast desert world after the First World War and imposed laws on them. We let the Arabs down then, and it looks like we're intent on interfering again today. We may have done a lot of good throughout the world, under the guise of empire-building, but the British are guilty of doing immense harm too, especially in the Middle East."

"Isn't it just as well we're soldiers, and merely have to follow orders, Mr Beard," observed Col Spiers. "This Palestine mission, may well be our last opportunity to put our training to some use in the deserts, heh?"

Beard settled in quickly. His fellow officers were friendly and the men of the platoon he was given were keen. It seemed strange, unnatural and embarrassing to be a junior officer after his years of being in charge, but he put his best face forward and carried on. There was a lot of parachuting when the weather was right, and when it wasn't there were exercises on the ground, where it didn't much matter what the weather conditions were like. When the snow was too deep or the rain too heavy, there were always lectures and other methods of occupying the men's time indoors. Never a moment was wasted: even when the training was done, there were always sporting activities – football, rugby, boxing and cross-country running. Beard felt very much at home. In between all these activities, there were parties in the mess and invitations to various functions around the county from those who felt it their duty to be seen to entertain, if not all the King's men, at least his officers. It was at the very first such ball that Beard met Cynthia Bunney. She told him he should call her Cyn: it sounded like Sin.

Beard woke up in bed with her the following morning in an establishment calling itself the Black Cat: it was hidden away down a country lane on the outskirts of Feltwell. The place was neither an hotel nor a brothel, but a place run by a respectable middle-aged widow called Sarah Lynch as a place of relaxation for officers and their ladies; it is assumed it was financed by those availing themselves of its facilities by means of donations, generally a fiver a time. When Beard wakened and saw the large white shape alongside him, he recognised it as Cyn – although all he could see of her as he blinked his eyes were her two firm breasts which were pointing straight at him, the nipples thrusting forward, his first thoughts were that he'd been in this situation before, perhaps too many times; still, he was loath to stir.

He was not too sure where he was, he had a vague recollection of having been at some posh party, of leaving there in company with another officer and a couple of girls, of arriving at some house in the middle of nowhere, of meeting some jolly woman (Sarah) who greeted him like an old friend, and of tumbling into bed almost immediately with Cyn. He knew that they had made love during the night, but he wasn't sure how many times, he was only aware now of a stirring in his loins that signalled an urge to do so again. He extricated his face from between her warm, pulsating breasts, delighting in the soft squelching noise he made as he did so, and wondered how he hadn't suffocated in there. What a way to go! he thought, his need for her growing.

His movement, slight as it had been, stirred Cyn and her wide, full lips parted as she blew gin-scented breath into his face; her mouth remained slightly open, and her breathing continued at a regular pace, sounding almost as though she were purring. Beard was conscious that her breath was warm: he was conscious, too, of his hardness against the soft, warmth of her body. After a moment, she opened first one eye and then the other, and blinked the sticky sleep away so that she could examine him; he did the same. He saw that the eyes staring, with growing recognition, at him were green, speckled with yellow or grey, perhaps both, it seemed to depend how intently he looked into them. The eyes stared out through long lashes: above them the brows looked so perfect they might have been drawn; for the rest, the face was a healthy round pink, with a high forehead, a pointed nose, a chin that only just avoided being pointed and on her upper lip there was a fine down, which showed dark even against her olive skin; her hair was dark, almost black, and the long tresses were strewn everywhere – over the pillow, and over both of them. She was lovely, Beard told himself.

"Good morning, general!" she greeted him, and her voice was also like a purr.

"Hello," replied Beard, his voice thick and rather intense.

Cyn, feeling his hardness poking at her, turned slowly on her back and parted her legs wide. "Come on in, darling. You're always welcome," she whispered with an eagerness that matched his own.

It was another two hours before they got up, compelled by pangs of hunger and the need for a different kind of rest. There were two pools of clothing on the floor beside the bed: hers and his. After they'd dressed they went downstairs where they found Mrs Lynch chattering to a row of caged canaries – which became mute the moment Beard and Cyn entered the room. Mrs Lynch, her eyes twinkling, told them that she had not expected them down for breakfast, but she was impressed that they had almost missed their lunch as well. They all laughed – and sat down to lunch, although it would not have been awfully early to have had afternoon tea! Beard ate voraciously, Cyn hardly at all; she said she was too tired to eat.

During the meal, Beard discovered that Cyn, who at 20 was the eldest of three daughters of a local landowner and magistrate, lived at nearby Hockwold Hall on the edge of the fens; she rode at point-to-points, played the piano "not at all well," went to concerts, watched cricket and rugby matches "because that's where the boys are," and generally speaking did very little else of any consequence. Beard, who doubted if this was really so, also learned that they had been driven to the Black Cat by Delicia Stanfield, who had been Capt Radvers (always called Radders) Westwood's partner for the night. Westwood was the adjutant of Beard's company. The Westwoods had apparently had lunch at a more normal hour and were at present out walking. "Walking!" cried Cyn, her face evincing shock but her eyes full of laughter – and lust, "all I want to do is get back to bed. That's the only healthy exercise for a girl! Aren't you done eating yet, Bobbie?" Beard murmured "nearly", but he wasn't going to hurry his pudding – stuffed baked apples, no less. Besides, he needed to restore his energy. But Cyn's suggestions in these circumstances were tantamount to being demands, and Beard, while reluctant to leave a solitary apple on the table, followed her upstairs with eager excitement.

The trouble was he followed her – and always eagerly – up the stairs too often over the next couple of months. Whenever he was at liberty, and he seemed to have an exorbitant amount of free time, he and Cyn were at it. Every weekend, and sometimes during the week, they would find their way, either to the Black Cat and Sarah's excellent cooking, or to some distant out of the way pub where food was of secondary interest (to Cyn anyway) and they were left in peace to get on with their lovemaking. They became regular visitors at inns all over Norfolk ... and suddenly June arrived; and with it came the bitterest of all the hammer blows.

They were in the Hangman's Noose near Methwold when the blow fell.

Cyn, who for an inordinate time had been examining her naked figure in the full-length mirror in their room, turned to find Beard also regarding her shapely form – and evidently enjoying what he saw. She sat down on the bed, covered her unusually anxious face with both her hands, and presently announced in a tearful, tragic voice, "I'm pregnant, Bobbie!" And then she proceeded to sob in earnest.

Beard stared, uncomprehending at first, and then, as the meaning of what she said sank in, in astonished disbelief. It wasn't possible, was it? He'd always used a condom, hadn't he? Well, no, not on that first occasion ... when they'd gone at it almost non-stop for two whole days. He studied her figure with renewed, and very different, interest and couldn't discern any difference in her shape.

"Are you sure?" he asked, the words emerging almost painfully from his suddenly dry throat as he tried to keep the misgivings from his voice.

"Of course I'm bloody sure," she snapped, moving her hands from her face and laying them over her belly, as though supporting a baby. She had stopped crying now, but her face, still glistening from her tears, looked woebegone and frightened.

"You don't look any different, Cyn," he insisted, his eyes continuing to search her body for some sign. He moved a hand towards her, but she shrank out of his reach, and new tears began to roll down her cheeks and splash on to her hands.

"Well, I am," she cried, quite fiercely. "I must be two months gone – I've missed two periods. The first time, I didn't think too much about it ... it sometimes happens. But not twice. Oh, Bobbie, what are we going to do?" The question emerged as a wail.

"Have you seen a doctor, Cyn?" Beard asked gently, finally capturing one of her hands – and being almost surprised at not finding a baby underneath.

"I don't need to see a doctor – not yet. A girl knows – feels these things in her body. Oh Bobbie! there's a life inside me! I'm carrying your child!" She began to bawl, but stopped almost at once as a thought seemed to hit her between the eyes. She flinched from the pain of it and cried: "Mummy ... Daddy – he'll kill me! You too, Bobbie!"

"Perhaps he'll only spank you," he suggested light-heartedly.

"Don't be disgusting!" she cried, and resumed her bawling for a moment longer and then, leaning forward, she fell awkwardly into his arms and cried: "We'll have to marry, darling – and quickly."

Her words screamed through Beard's head. They stunned him. He felt pole-axed. The simplicity of her solution appalled and terrified him. And yet, when he had his thoughts under control again, he could think not of Cyn and her baby – *his* baby! – but only of Ruth. Oh, Ruth, what have I done! The cry seemed to come from his very soul.

"You've cut it a bit fine, Mr Beard," declared Col Spiers, looking up from Beard's application to marry. "You wish to marry by special licence on Tuesday – and we're off to Palestine on Friday morning – at the crack of dawn. You'll have to be on base on the Thursday evening. Not much of a honeymoon for either of you. Won't she wait till you get back?"

"It's not that simple, sir. We can't wait," said Beard simply and stone-faced.

"I see," said the colonel with understanding. "I'm sorry it's – like that, Robert. We'd have liked to give you a proper regimental wedding ... but, if this is the way it has to be, so be it. Of course you have my permission – and I hope congratulations are in order."

Beard couldn't bring himself to smile, even sadly. "Thank you, sir," he said, accepting the other's hand and then stepping back and saluting.

The wedding took place at Brandon Register Office. Apart from the principals and officials, the only people in attendance were Capt Westwood, his best man, Cyn's two sisters and her parents, all of whom glared daggers at Beard throughout ; apart from Cyn, who was as happy as a June bride should be, everybody looked as though he or she would sooner be anywhere else on earth. The registrar seemed to take an age as he scrawled down the meagre details with an old-fashioned pen that seemed incapable of holding any ink and had to be repeatedly dipped in an ink-well, but it was all over within thirty-five minutes and as he stepped outside in the rain with his bride, Beard hardly felt married at all. Cyn's parents gave her hugs and kisses, but continued to glare at Beard ; in fact, her father looked as though he would as soon horsewhip his son-in-law as shake his hand. The two sisters kissed the bride with considerable affection and enthusiasm, but when it was Beard's turn they could manage no more than a shy peck apiece before scuttling obediently back to their parents. Beard had a sensation of being unclean, as well as unmarried. Westwood alone joined them for a fish and chip wedding breakfast, and scooted off as soon as he decently could.

The two-night honeymoon was spent at a seafront hotel at Hunstanton, and though the groom might have felt unmarried, his bride demonstrated the very opposite, and was most demanding. Beard behaved dutifully, he felt he should, and besides, he enjoyed making love to her. It was simply that he hadn't wanted her as a wife: only a ... well, a mistress, perhaps. If only he hadn't been so hungry for his oats that first time! But he knew it had been the anticlimax due to Ruth's absence in America. If only she had been at home!

It was not until the second day of his honeymoon that it suddenly struck him that as he'd been married in the name of Beard rather than Jarvis Brook, he might not be married after all! For a few moments, his hopes rose, but not for long; whatever the name, he knew the Law would consider that he had used her as a wife, and that would be that. The Law was always on the side of women. They should never have been given the vote, he thought angrily. Then his attention was called by Cyn, who wanted some more loving while she still had a husband.

He gave her a sort of smile as he looked down at her, and he wondered when the baby would start to make itself visibly apparent. Try as he might, he could see no sign of its development in Cyn's belly which, while substantial, did not seem a great deal different to when he met her, though she assured him she had put on pounds and pounds and chided him over his blindness. He had been told, by those who claimed to know about these things, that there would be no real sign until the start of the fourth month, so it looked as if he was just going to miss seeing the "bulge." He was going to miss everything – being a husband and a father. In a way, he felt sorry for Cyn. She was going to have to cope entirely on her own, but then she must know that separation was part of being a soldier's wife. He hoped her parents would stand by her. He thought they probably would, since he wouldn't be around. He felt more and more unmarried as he stretched out beside his wife.

On the Thursday night, back in camp at Little Harling, while the bustle of their departure the next day was going on all around him, when he should have been thinking only of his wife, Beard finally stole a few minutes in which to write to Ruth. He couldn't put it off any longer, but what to say? He addressed the envelope first simply to give him more time to think: he would send it to The Pears. The very thought of the cottage made him think of Queenie, and he knew he would have to write to her as well. He wrote that letter first; it was very brief, and said very little more than that he was married – and that a baby was on the way. He gave no explanation, nor offered any apology. There didn't seem to be anything he could say, nothing satisfactory: the deed was done and that was the be-all and end-all of it. He did admit to feeling desolate at the thought of the hurt he had done Ruth.

And then came the *real* letter: the one to Ruth. It would be the hardest he'd ever written in his life. How to tell her without breaking her heart, when his own was already shattered? It was impossible. It seemed he could only add to her hurt no matter what he wrote. In a way, he still didn't understand what had happened to him. He'd come home with the intention of getting married, but everything had gone horribly wrong. He had married all right, but not the girl he loved. He had only affection for his wife, a sense of doing right by her, but it was still Ruth he loved. How could he explain this to her? How to begin? After an agony of indecision and heartache, he began as she had done so often to him in the past.

"*My Darling*," he wrote, and the words simply flowed.

Ruth didn't receive her letter for many months: not until she returned home from America towards the end of November. She had hoped to be in time for her mother's marriage to John Fennell in late October, but had been delayed by successive obstacles: a hurricane or typhoon called Gwendoline, a dock strike and a scare concerning Hannah's baby, a girl called Petunia, which turned out to be nothing more than a touch of colic but caused Ruth to miss her sailing. When she eventually arrived at The Pears, there waiting for her were her mother, a stepfather ... and Jarvis's letter, now nearly six months old. He had not sent any other.

When the letters – both envelopes contained in a larger one – had arrived, Queenie had read hers very slowly with growing astonishment and sadness; she'd read it over and over again before the full import had sunk in. It wasn't much of a letter: it was blunt and cold, brief – and seemed unbearably cruel; it had torn at her heart and set her off weeping. Her crying had been spread over several days: the tears came every time she thought of Ruth and Jarvis, and they were always in her mind. In her more rational moments she reflected that she'd done quite a bit of crying since being bombed out of The Dials, but in those days she'd had to be tough; nowadays, she had more time to think as a woman – a wife and a mother, and more time for tears. In the end the tears had dried up, and she wondered what she should do with Ruth's letter. It lay in her bag for nearly a week, and might have stayed there indefinitely, had not her new husband advised her either to post the thing or place it on the mantelpiece to await Ruth's return; and this is what she did – placed it on the mantel, and got on with her life. She never mentioned it in the two letters she sent to Ruth, but it stood there on the mantel as a daily reminder of heartbreaks ahead.

Ruth saw the letter almost the moment she swept into the cottage parlour laden with parcels and looking very grown up and American in her smart, colourful clothes, but there was no early opportunity for her to sit down and read it. First there were the greetings, over and over again, and congratulations on the wedding, the viewing of the wedding photos and the opening and exclamations over the presents, and, of course, the tasting of the wedding cake. "Ev'ry scrap of cake he has now, John calls weddin' cake!" laughed Queenie fondly. "We has it ev'ry day." Ruth declared that she would call Mr Fennell 'John' in future; she could never call him Daddy – that could only ever be Sam's title, even if he was now her stepfather, but she loved him like he was a second father. This arrangement seemed to satisfy everybody and they settled down to exchanging all their bits of news, which included the fact that Poppy had had a son "who is so like a little angel in that he sleeps and eats and does damned all else that we're after calling him Paddy after the saint of this land where he was born, Ireland."

Inevitably, Jarvis's [in this household he was never Beard] name was mentioned, and just as inevitably Ruth saw the shadow leap into her mother's eyes, and felt a chill of fear in her breast. "He's all right, isn't he, Mummy? Not wounded or anything, is he?" she cried anxiously.

Queenie shook her head quickly, tried to smile, but the cloud stayed in her eyes. "No, darling," she assured her, "not that I know of. Last I heard, he was in Palestine where all that trouble with the Jews is goin' on. But he don't never write, do he? Don't never get hurt, either!"

Ruth could sense an undercurrent in the room and, feeling a fresh ache in her breast, she glanced quickly from Queenie to John and back to Queenie. "Something's up, isn't it?" she cried, with growing alarm. "Something's happened to Jarvis, hasn't it?"

But neither would admit to anything. Queenie's eyes were bursting with a gathering of tears. Ruth leapt to her feet, beginning to tremble as a dread fear took hold of her heart.

"He's dead! Jarvis is dead, that's it, isn't!" she cried in a low pain-filled voice, scarce believing her own words, but feeling them squeezing the life out of her heart.

"No, darling, he's alive and well so far as we know. The Army would've let us know if he weren't, and they haven't," Queenie assured Ruth quickly, but still unable to say the dread words she'd read in his letter. "He sent yer a letter, lovey," was all she could say.

It wasn't until she escaped to her room that Ruth had a chance to look at her letter. She sat on the bed holding the creased envelope in her hand. Usually – well, usually there hadn't been any letter, but on the rare occasion that he scribbled her a few lines, she'd have excitedly torn open the envelope to gobble them up, but not today. After the reluctance downstairs by both Queenie and John to talk of Jarvis, and especially the way Queenie had withdrawn into herself when the subject of her letter from him came up, Ruth had a premonition that they knew its contents and wished that she wouldn't. That was suspicious in itself among three people who had no real secrets from each other. Ruth's unease grew as she flattened out the envelope and stared at his writing. He'd only written her name and a c/o The Pears. There was no stamp, so it had most likely been contained in another envelope, possibly to Queenie herself. Why hadn't Jarvis posted it? Why hadn't Queenie forwarded it?

Finally, with a growing trepidation, Ruth tore open the envelope and pulled out the letter, and the very first words she read brought happiness back to her face and filled her heart with joy.

"*My darling*," Ruth read, and she repeated the words back to him wherever he was, "*I have loved you all my life. I love you especially at this moment, and I'll love you for always.*" Ruth sighed blissfully and whispered to herself "I know, my darling, and I'll never stop loving you." She kissed his words and hugged the letter to her before, her face radiant with happiness, returning to devour the remainder of his letter. The rapture disappeared from her face almost at once and was replaced by a look of utter disbelief, incredulity, horror and pain. The colour drained from her face, her eyes filled with tears, her whole body trembled. She wanted to scream that it wasn't true, that the words weren't there. But they were. She forced herself to read them repeatedly to be sure. She felt that she was dying, and certainly her heart seemed to stop beating for several moments, but then it resumed its pounding and each beat added to her agony. Finally, the tears escaped and flooded down her cheeks, splashing on to his letter and making puddles on the words until they became blurred, but they were already burned for ever in her mind and heart, and in her very soul.

"I wouldn't ever willingly hurt you, you know that, I hope – but I'm afraid I probably have. You see, I have married someone else," he'd written. He'd made an attempt to delete the word "probably," but it was still legible. *"Her name is Cynthia Bunney. You won't know her : I hardly know her myself. And yet, that cannot be true, for I made her pregnant. That is why I have married her – not for love, for love never had any part in our association, only lust. I'm afraid men are lustful, Ruth, but please believe me when I say there was never anything more in it. I don't suppose that justifies anything, or makes you feel any better towards me. But when she told me she was pregnant and that I was the father, there was nothing else I could do – only do the right thing, and marry her. I won't call it an honourable act on my part, for my part in the whole affair has been nothing short of dishonourable. In fact, my decision was not even made with her in mind – not really; my concern was almost entirely for the baby. I could not bear to think of it starting out in life as I did – without a name, without either parents, home or love. No child should endure that sort of misery. I could not abandon this child of mine to become an orphan like me. I so desperately wanted it to have a better beginning than I did. And it was because of my feelings concerning this that I have done what I have. At least no one will be able to call it a bastard. I am sorry to have hurt those I truly love, and ask them, especially you, Ruth, not to forgive me, for my actions do not deserve such generosity, but to understand my reasons.*

I am writing this on the eve of flying back to the Middle East – Palestine, this time. I don't know when I shall be home again, or what sort of a future I shall have with my new family. Certainly I shall have no welcome from my wife's family: I thought her father was going to shoot me at the wedding – that was after the wedding. What a wretched business that ceremony was. It seemed longer and more dreadful than even our honeymoon, mercifully cut short by the regiment being rushed abroad. I've made arrangements for Cyn – that's my wife – to move into married quarters, but she says that since I'm not there she'd sooner make peace with her family and move back home, which may well be the best thing with the baby coming. I feel I should be with her at such a time, but I must confess I have little genuine desire to be so. We'll have to see what happens. Tonight, I simply feel too depressed to think that far ahead. I only wanted to say I'm sorry, and to hope that in time you can find it in your heart to forgive me. God bless you and Mum." He'd signed it *"Yours sorrowfully."*

Ruth had wanted to die, and for some little while she was almost convinced she was getting her wish, but time passed and she was still there prostrate on her bed, sobbing fitfully, moaning with misery, and, every so often, crying his name out loud – Jarvis! And then she became quiet and forgot about dying, and instead found herself thinking not only about what had happened, what she had lost, but what was likely to happen in the future. Her thoughts were jumbled and lot a lot of them made very little sense, but at least she was in control of herself again. She'd stopped shaking and crying and calling out incoherently. She felt herself growing calmer: her breathing became more regular and even her heart, which she was still sure lay bleeding and shattered somewhere in her breast, seemed to pound with renewed appetite. Probably an hour had passed since she'd opened the fateful letter.

Presently, she felt sufficiently recovered to resume her life, or at least to take the first steps in that direction. She sat up on the bed, picked up the scattered pages of his letter with only a slight trembling of her lips, folded them very carefully back into their torn envelope and pushed it out of sight – but not out of reach – under her pillow. With what seemed an extraordinary effort (she discovered she had pins and needles and almost crumpled to the floor), she limped to the bathroom to wash her face – hoping to wash away some of her misery, but feeling that she wasn't very successful. She dabbed at her eyes with a cold flannel, but they remained resolutely red and swollen from weeping. She shrugged, straightened her hair and went downstairs.

Queenie took one look at her daughter's unhappy face and, although she could see that Ruth was over the worst of her distress, she gave John, who looked quite as concerned as herself, an urgent sign to make himself scarce, feeling that the presence of a man at that moment might be unwelcome to Ruth; he disappeared with speed, silence and discretion. Ruth, hardly noticing him, fell straight into her mother's arms and for some while they sat there simply holding one another, occasionally groaning, sometimes allowing a sob to escape them, but not speaking. For the present the need was only for the nearness and warmth of a loved one: words would come presently, there was no hurry.

It was Queenie who eventually broke the silence. "You all right, lovey?"

Ruth nodded, but couldn't conceal the woebegone look that haunted her face. "Yes, Mummy," she said, in a whisper that was equally full of woe. "It was an awful shock, but I'll be all right ... in time. I still can't believe it, even though I accept that it's true. But it just doesn't seem possible. I've loved him almost all my life, and I was so sure we'd marry and love one another for the rest of our lives." She paused, because her lips trembled so that she couldn't form any words, nor could she control a sudden gush of burning tears. "Oh, Mum," she cried, when the moment was over, "I feel so utterly lost, so empty! I never minded the waiting, not really, because I always thought it would come out all right in the end. But now, it can't, not ever, can it?"

Queenie sighed hugely. No words of comfort or hope came to her, so she kept silent and simply rocked gently to an fro with her arms round Ruth. She certainly wasn't going to tell her that Jarvis had come home to marry *her*! She couldn't. Not yet: not for a long time – maybe, never. Oh, if only Ruth had been here instead of in America.

"Poor Jarvis. It must have been a terrible time for him. I hope he'll be happy," cried Ruth after a lengthy pause, and she seemed a little brighter herself as the words escaped her lips.

"He doesn't deserve to be," retorted Queenie severely. She marvelled at her daughter's generosity although, deep down, she echoed the sentiments.

"It's not his fault, Mummy," Ruth exclaimed instantly, extricating herself from her mother and sitting bolt upright, "I'm not a little innocent. I know that men play around when they're away from home. Especially the young ones, like Jarvis. I always had a secret suspicion that he ... that he was sowing his oats, as they say. I hoped he wasn't, but I was sure he was – and I don't believe I really minded. I was sure it was really nothing more than an anticlimax after some battle and that they wouldn't mean anything ... I didn't mind so terribly, because I only wanted him to be safe, and because I knew he would come home to me when it was all over. But, he didn't, and he's not going to, is he? Not now. It's all over. That's the part that hurts most. Never to see him again, or hear his voice, or touch him."

Again Queenie remained silent. She knew, far better than Ruth, the ways of men – and women, too! Boys or girls, they all had to have their flings, and none ever thought of the consequences until it was too late. Oh Jarvis! she sighed.

"Of course, he doesn't love her – this girl he's married," declared Ruth, and her voice, emphatic now, contained the faintest hint of triumph, as though this exonerated Jarvis from any wrongdoing. "He's simply being honourable. He's just doing the right thing by this girl in her time of trouble."

"It's his trouble, too. That hardly makes his action all that bloody noble," Queenie felt obliged to point out.

"But he doesn't love her, Mummy," insisted Ruth, with growing warmth. "He's made a mistake and he's sacrificing himself because of it. I call that noble. If he loved her, I couldn't bear it, but he doesn't."

Queenie couldn't see that this was much consolation, but she bit back the words that wanted to rush out.

"I shan't stop loving Jarvis, not ever," declared Ruth decisively, and as if this declaration solved everything, she kissed her mother and announced that she was going to bed – and that she'd remember him in her prayers as usual.

Ruth did more than pray for Jarvis, she wrote to him. The very next morning, after a somewhat turbulent sleep that left her exhausted but nevertheless resolved to carry on with her life, she penned the briefest of letters; she thanked him for his own letter, expressing no comment on its contents, wished him every happiness for the future, and said that she would remember him always with the deepest affection. And that was all, except that she whispered to herself as she posted it, "I'll love you for always, my Jarvis!" And she lingered by the red pillar box as though expecting him to reply.

Back home, Queenie told her she should go for a long cycle ride to take her mind off her grief and John Fennell offered her a slice of cake saying it would build up her strength, but Ruth shook her head to both and fled to her room. She had made up her mind about what she was going to do. First she removed Jarvis's engagement ring from her hand, where she had placed it as a matter of course, without even thinking, when she'd dressed, and, after staring wistfully at the tiny square blue diamond with its attendant brilliants for several minutes, she finally touched it with her lips and placed it in a little box along with the bracelet and the coral necklace and all the other things he'd given her – including the glass necklace he'd told her was supposed to be made of rubies, adding that the lousy Germans had cheated him … and her, and shut the lid down quickly. She wouldn't ever wear them again. The next thing Ruth did was to tell Queenie that she was returning to London the following week to resume the office career she had started. And she did exactly that. At the end of the week she was back with Mrs B., and it was as though nothing had changed – except that she felt empty inside, and her heart never did mend.

Queenie, not knowing that Ruth had written to him, also wrote to Beard. She felt she should scold him for letting Ruth down so, but she couldn't and, instead, wished him happiness in the future, just as Ruth had done. After all, he was her boy, and she loved him, too. She couldn't find the words to speak of his marriage, so she told him about her own and added hurriedly that he would always be welcome in her home.

John Fennell, in his capacity as the new man of the house, as well as friend, solicitor and unofficial stepfather to Jarvis, also wrote. He was afraid the womenfolk might not feel disposed to extend any words of kindness to Jarvis, and he felt someone should. He congratulated Jarvis on his marriage and said he fully understood his decision – "his very courageous and selfless decision" – in the matter, and expressed the wish that future events went smoothly; and in telling of his own happy tidings, extended a welcome to Jarvis and his family on his return to England. In the meantime, he added, he would continue to look after

Jarvis's affairs as before.

□ *"That was the worst time in all my life, Jarvis," cried Ruth as the session came to a close. "I never thought I'd recover from the hurt you caused me."*

"It wasn't me. I'm sure I could never behave in such a way," stated Beard adamantly from the wheelchair to which he had progressed. "I am not this man of yours, Ruth."

"Do not be alarmed, Jarvis, when you are yourself again you will remember that I long ago forgave you, and that we love each other," Ruth answered him firmly, adding, "Just hurry up and remember, darling."

Beard fidgeted in his chair. "Believe me, I'm beginning to want this whole business resolved as soon as possible. I'm getting tired of being 'the other man' in this affair. I'd love it if you could love me as myself, Ruth."

"I do, darling," cried Ruth, frustration creeping into her voice. "I do. I do. Wake up, my darling."

Beard stared hard at her. But it was no good. He did not know her ; did not remember her, and he wanted to so much.

In the silence that followed, Gibbs took up the story-telling once again.

Chapter Thirty-eight

Jaffa, Palestine, July, 1946

Beard did not like Palestine, but he did not mind that, he didn't suppose he would like anywhere during those days. He was kept constantly busy, and he didn't mind that either. He was glad of it, it was what he needed – it meant he did not have time to torment himself with thoughts of the disasters he'd left behind him in England.

He arrived there a fortnight before the King David Hotel in Jerusalem, was blown up. There was danger all around in this blood-thirsty Holy Land. "The unholiest place on earth," as Col Spiers observed when, within a week of their arrival, his armoured car had been blown up, three men had been killed by sniper fire and, inevitably, two men reported sick with VD, and were promptly put on a charge

The British, exhausted and bankrupted by the recent war, were as eager to be rid of their Palestine mandate obligations as its peoples, both Jewish and Arab, were to see the back of them. The Jewish community, the *Yishuv*, were determined to have their Israel, and the Arabs were just as determined to crucify every Jew in the land, before or after independence. The British were charged with keeping the peace. It was an impossible and thankless task, and many men bled and died in the attempt.

Beard's battalion was based in Jaffa on the coast, and his company was continuously patrolling along the Plain of Sharon as far north as Acre. But, as the Intelligence officer, Beard had an almost free hand to operate where he thought best. He was allocated a Jeep and four men as his escort: a corporal and three privates. He very soon decided that life in Palestine was more dangerous than anything he'd experienced during the war; here there were no friends. Both Jew and Arab was a potential enemy who wanted to kill or maim them – but would settle for seeing the British go so that they could concentrate on the more important fight against each other. There was no respite: treachery and murder stalked them in every street in every town, and followed them in the desert wastes. As Capt Westwood quoted, "A policeman's lot is not a happy one!"

Within the first two months of his arrival in Palestine, Beard twice had drivers shot dead beside him, but that was almost the nearest he came to personal injury. Others in the battalion were not so fortunate. An officer and two NCOs were kidnapped while arranging billets at Hadera and held hostage against the lives of three members of the Jewish terrorist group which blew up the King David Hotel and who were due to be executed for various acts of murder and sabotage. When the three terrorists were duly hanged, so too were the three hostages.

Their bodies were found hanging from beams in an otherwise empty banana warehouse.

Retribution was savage and threatened to get out of hand before the authorities, who had turned a blind eye as troops exacted punitory revenge for their late comrades, almost reluctantly heeding anxious orders from Whitehall, decided that enough was enough and ordered a halt to the orgy. There were, inevitably, isolated acts of revenge by British troops, but they remained isolated.

It was the middle of October before Beard received any mail from home. Then, it was a solitary one from Ruth. He stared at the envelope for simply ages, noticing that she still addressed him as Major ("Thanks for memory, anyway," he smiled grimly), but hardly dared to touch it. Finally, he snatched it up and tore it open, and out fell her little letter. It *was* a little letter, too, so unlike her past ones: only the one sheet of paper. His heart fell at her very first words. He was no longer "my darling"; he had been downgraded to a lowly common or garden "my dear." Even so, it was a kindly letter; she called him Jarvis and, while expressing surprise at his marriage, she congratulated him and his wife, and hoped everything would go well with the baby's birth. She concluded with a prayer for his continued safety in the Army, and a wish for his happiness in the future. Its brevity and good wishes tore at his heart; he could feel the pain that went into penning those few words; he ached for her in the way of a husband. He longed for another letter from her, one opening the door to invite him back into her life: her heart. But, none came. Nor did any other letters arrive for him.

He had been expecting some sort of billet-doux from Cyn (he still hesitated to call her or even think of her as his wife), even if with little eagerness, and was more surprised than disappointed when nothing came. He obstinately refused to write to her before she did. He'd imagined a new bride, especially a pregnant one, would be bombarding her absent partner with letters proclaiming her everlasting love, and demanding confirmation of his. But the weeks and months passed and no letter arrived, and he felt relieved rather than disillusioned. Wait a minute, though, it was already November and the baby, according to Queenie's reckoning, was due at the latest sometime in December. He might already be a father! But no, surely, she would have written to say so, wouldn't she? There would be the matter of extra maintenance. But, she hadn't written him a line since he'd been in Palestine. Perhaps there was some medical problem. He knew difficulties occurred with births. Why didn't she write and tell him something? Like, he had a son!

And finally, only weeks before the baby was due, her letter arrived. It was brief, and it contained a bombshell.

"*My Dearest Bobbie,*" she had scribbled in pencil, "*you'll hardly believe this, I scarcely do myself, but I'm not having a baby after all! It was a false alarm, it seems. What they call it – a phantom pregnancy? Isn't it simply marvellous news!"* Beard stared at her words and, as she had written, hardly believed them. *"I don't know what went wrong. I definitely missed one period and thought I had the next, but apparently I hadn't. Mum says it's not all that uncommon to miss the odd curse. I could hardly believe my ears when the doctor gave me the all clear. Isn't it fabulous news, darling. My family is over the moon. Hope you're enjoying yourself out there, Bobbie. I'm having a lovely time now this nightmare is over. Lots of parties. A bunch of us are going to Le Touquet this weekend. Wish you could be with us. Love."*

He was still sitting dazedly on his bed, Cyn's letter clutched in his hand, when Westwood found him.

"What's up, Robert? You look like death. Bad news?" he asked, eyeing the letter.

Beard looked up without really seeing his friend – the man who had stood at his side at his wedding, and, because he didn't know how to answer him, passed the letter to him. Westwood frowned, doubtfully, but after another look at Beard proceeded to read it.

"What do you think, Radders? Do you reckon she took me for a ride?" Beard asked as the other returned the letter.

"Her family's wealthy, she had no reason for such a deception," replied Westwood carefully. "No, Robert, I prefer to think she genuinely thought she was pregnant, and simply panicked." He paused before adding, "It was a phantom baby, Robert."

"The baby may be a phantom, but she isn't !" retorted Beard. "She's ruined my life for ever. I'm bloody well married to her, aren't I!"

"Pah!" snorted Westwood. "She'll probably be as glad to be rid of you as you are her. She's had her scare over the baby, now that's over she may well be as keen to be rid of this sham marriage of yours as you."

"You may be right, Radders," Beard conceded, "but I can't do much out here."

"Don't leave it too long, Robert," Westwood cautioned. "She could begin to feel comfy in her role. Get some reliable solicitor to sort it out."

Beard gave Westwood's advice much thought without reaching a decision. He knew he had to do something. But not sure what, nor how. He wasn't able to devote very much time to the problem, for he was kept pretty busy staying alive as the Arabs and Jews continued their efforts at exterminating each other, and murdering as many British peacekeepers as they could on the side. In the end, it was Cyn herself who suggested the way out. She presented her solution in her second letter which reached Beard, most appropriately, during Holy Week in 1947.

"Dearest Bobbie," she wrote, or rather typed, *"this marriage of ours seems a very strange and unsatisfactory business. It isn't anything*

like what I dreamed married life would be like. In fact, with you out there and me back here, it's hardly a marriage at all. It's a pretty hollow thing, whatever it is. I wonder if you feel the same? You must do! But you never write, so I can't be sure. But, now that there's no baby to consider ... " It was a longish letter, and towards the end, she suggested that an annulment of their sham marriage looked the easiest way out. *"Please, darling, write to me and tell me what you think – and what we should do,"* she wrote. That was the part of the letter that set Beard's heart surging with hope.

He felt exquisitely, even dangerously, light-headed as he came to the end of the letter. If the first reading had amazed him, the second thrilled him, while the third spurred him into action. An annulment: that was the key. It didn't sound nearly so awful as a divorce. She'd pointed out the course they should follow, and he hurried along its path. But, he wrote, not to Cyn, for an inner voice advised him that this was not the way these things were done, but to John Fennell; and he wrote to him not in the capacity of his stepfather, but as his solicitor. He enclosed both Cyn's letters and asked Mr Fennell to represent him in the matter, and secure an end to the marriage by whatever means possible, but hopefully by annulment. Beard posted the letter the moment it was finished, just in case he was called away and missed the opportunity of setting things in motion.

Almost a year passed before Beard received a scrap of paper informing him that he was no longer married. The badly-typed and stamped document was sent by Mr Fennell, who also enclosed a congratulatory and chatty letter, and added that all the financial aspects of the divorce, including his own, appeared to have been settled by Cyn's family. Apparently, they were that eager to sever all ties him. Beard smiled, and felt suddenly quite drained. He was free! And for days he didn't dare think of what this unexpected freedom might mean. Only in his heart did Ruth continue to exist in spirit form; he'd tried not to think of her – well, not too often – for he could see no purpose, no chance of anything coming of it. But, now ... now that he was free again, he dared to dream that perhaps he'd been offered a second chance; at any rate, he was free to hope. He decided against writing, certainly so soon after being liberated – it seemed a little indelicate; and besides, he felt that words on a piece of paper would be insufficient. He needed to speak to her when he opened his heart. Would she listen? Would she even see him? Did he have any right to hope she would do either? He wanted so much simply to hold her. If he was able to do that, then their hearts would beat together, and their lips would follow suit. If. It wasn't easy, but he'd have to be patient a while longer – at least his heart was no longer such a dead weight.

In 1948, Beard's battalion was withdrawn to Cyprus, though Beard himself remained in Palestine, watching and listening, sharing the tense excitement of all around as the day of partitioning neared. Britain had already relinquished her mandate in Palestine to the UN, and all she was interested in now was getting out and staying out with as good a face as she was able to muster. The UN, acting with a rare urgency, had adopted a plan on November 29, 1947, by which Palestine was to be partitioned into Jewish and Arab states, with the British mandate officially terminating on August 1, 1948, to coincide with the planned partition date. But with mounting deaths the British had already had more than enough. With violence all around them and unable to intervene, they jumped the gun and announced their decision to quit Palestine once and for all no later than May 15, 1948. This in turn prompted the *Yishuv* to implement that part of the partition plan as it affected them: and they duly proclaimed the state of Israel on the 14th, the eve of the British departure. The Arabs invaded the following day, but were repeatedly repelled and defeated with the UN standing impotently aside ... but the British, including Beard, were already gone, leaving the Arabs and Jews free to murder one another to their heart's content, just like in the old days.

Beard, having spent six months billeted on Cyprus, was now parted from his regiment. His extraction had been engineered by Gibbs, whom he'd met in the dying days of the British presence in Palestine. Beard had been under no illusion that their reunion was accidental. The general, in mufti, claimed to be "simply having a last look round" the area, taking stock of things as the British retreated everywhere as never before. Jordan had led the rush for independence in 1946, India followed impatiently the following year, and now Israel had seized its independence. Even Cyprus, which had a history of occupation going back to 1450 BC when the Egyptians had invaded, wanted to shake itself free from British "protection" – though only to replace one occupier with another. The trouble was there were two suitors, the Greeks and the Turks; and so once again, the British were caught in the middle of two warring factions. But Gibbs's parting words to Beard in Palestine had been, "I'll look you up again on Cyprus, Robert. Wait there. Listen to the whispers in the street and in the air. Watch out for the Archbishop there. Makarios. He's too involved in politics."

And today, as the year drew to an end, they met at Green Bay to discuss the future. "It's time we extricated ourselves from policing jobs, Robert," Gibbs told Beard, and then confided that having him demoted to lieutenant and transferred to an active regiment had been the only way possible of preventing his being retired from the Services altogether. "Our old Department was being mothballed in the name of economy," he explained, with a sigh of sheer incomprehension. "Short-sighted lunacy, of course," he added contemptuously.

"Now, they want us back and I'm hunting up likely men. You, of course, have never been out of sight; you and a few others. But there'll be a lot of new faces, in a lot of new countries. Incidentally," he added casually, "I'm able to restore your captaincy, Robert, now that you've left your Para friends, but you'll have to wait a bit longer for anything more."

"Is the pay retrospective, sir?" Beard asked instantly.

"No, it isn't, you blighter!" laughed Gibbs

"Well, it's a step in the right direction," said Beard equably; he then added thoughtfully, "I'm delighted to be back with the Department, but I wouldn't have thought there was much for us to do with the Empire crumbling, if not gone completely."

"Oh, you won't have idle hands, Robert," smiled Gibbs, toying with his once fierce moustache, now a greyer, thinner, but neater affair. "There'll always be some distant conflict where our energies, and expertise, will be required behind the scenes. How have you enjoyed your holiday on Cyprus, by the by?"

Beard was immediately on the alert. He'd been energetically training for the past six months in the heat of the island's summer, as well as gathering intelligence and reporting it, and was sure Gibbs knew it, since these snippets of news ended on his desk. So, something must be up. "It was all right, sir. I shall have fond memories of the sandy beaches, the Troödos Mountains, the cedar forests and especially the bars and cheap but potent wines …"

"Stop it, Robert, you sound like a tourist guide," interposed Gibbs, chuckling. "I note you don't mention the troubles brewing among the natives, some wanting union with Greece, others with Turkey and, as usual, some priest, Bishop Makarios, stirring the pot. Believe me, there's going to be trouble here."

Beard gave an expansive shrug. "It was ever thus," he murmured laconically.

"Well, it won't concern us – not in the foreseeable future," declared Gibbs with a nonchalant air. "We're done here, Robert. We're off home to England."

Beard sat up straight and stared at Gibbs with excited surprise. His mouth formed the word "When?" but before it could be uttered, Gibbs announced, "Tomorrow afternoon. We fly out at 1205. So pay your bills and get packed."

Home! The word had only one meaning for Beard: Ruth. The opportunity of seeing *her* again, and perhaps … oh, he mustn't anticipate. He must win her back. Woo her. He had no real experience of this, but he'd learn ; and quickly. He daren't lose her again. He might not have much time.

Chapter Thirty-nine

Peartree Cottage, November 17, 1948

It was cold, wet and windy when Beard and Gibbs landed at Brize Norton, the exact opposite of what they'd left behind on Cyprus. But Beard didn't care, he wouldn't have minded had there been six feet of snow; every mile they travelled drew him that much closer to Ruth. His only worry was whether or not she'd be home this time; and, also, whether his honourable attentions would be acceptable.

Gibbs told Beard to take two weeks' leave and then report at their old Apple Tree Camp at Chelmsford. "I expect you can amuse yourself during that time," he said, knowing full well the state of affairs in Beard's turbulent private life. He added dryly, "Beware of any strange ladies who cross your path, Robert. A fortnight is all that I can allow you. Then, I think, the Far East beckons. If it's not the Russians, it'll be the Chinese. Be convenient if they could destroy each other, and leave the rest of us in peace. But, I think Communism still has a role to play in world affairs."

But Beard wasn't listening. He headed straight for Essex, and Mayhill. He did not know what sort of reception he would receive. Well, he did really; he knew that Queenie would smother him with maternal embraces that would come close to either crippling or suffocating him, and that it would be lovely; he knew that John Fennell would greet him with equal warmth, though he expected it would be far less bruising; but he could not anticipate Ruth's greeting – and wondered if it would be anything more than subdued and polite. Then again, perhaps she wouldn't be home. It was a Tuesday, the 17th: perhaps she'd be away in London, at work; of course, she would. He'd have at least another three days to wait before he could see her. All these thoughts, and a million others, recurred through his head as he approached The Pears.

He was right in almost every respect. Queenie engulfed him in her powerful arms and almost swamped him with her tears of happiness, Mr Fennell shook his hand and slapped his back for several minutes before relaxing and offering him a slice of cake, and Ruth, as he'd expected, was missing. But neither was she in London; she was not even in the country, but in Germany. It was hours later and well into the night, as they sat together on the familiar settee, before Queenie got round to explaining that Ruth had gone to Freiburg in the Black Forest to attend a friend's wedding. Bertie and Maud and Ben and Poppy had broken off their respective honeymoons to attend, too.

"Honeymoons!" cried Beard, with a rather scornful laugh, "Ben and Poppy are an old married couple – with a grown up kid!"

"Not quite, lovey," chuckled Queenie, slipping her arm inside his and giving them both a squeeze. "Paddy's more'n two now – an' a real charmer. I seed 'im when Ben and Poppy flew over on their way to the wedding. Paddy stayed with his gran'parents at Highways while his parents was in Germany."

Beard frowned. It suddenly struck him that if Ruth was still over in Germany, the wedding must have been fairly recent and so she'd be heading home imminently. "When was the wedding, Mum?" he asked, feeling a sudden surge of hope.

"Towards the end of July," replied Queenie, dreamily. She'd have loved to have been there, but she'd had an unseasonal heavy chest cold at the time and couldn't go. She and John had had to make do with two huge slices of cake brought back by Ben and Poppy.

Another, deeper frown as the thought struck Beard that he and Ruth might miss each other once again. Where the devil had she got to? "Well, that was four months ago, isn't she back yet?" he demanded irritably, a cold fear taking possession of his pounding heart.

"No, darling. She stayed on with Bertie an' Maud for a tour through Switzerland, Italy, Spain an' all them other for'in places. I've 'ad sev'ral cards so I keeps track on 'er. She sent me a card from Venice a coupla weeks ago. Looked a posh place in the picture, but she said it were perishin' cold an' that they was headin' down to Rome – you know, where your Pope lives – next." Queenie paused for breath, and then tried to remember where she'd got to in her story. She couldn't, so she went on, "Don't know when they plan to come 'ome, Jarvis, but I don't s'pose they'll be in too much of a hurry as Maudie was abaht four months on in July – pr'aps a bit more. Anyway, she's due late next month."

"I'd have thought Ruth would have felt in the way in the circumstances," Beard suggested ruminatively. His inner thoughts revolved around the fact that everybody seemed to be getting married and raising families except him. He hadn't even been able to sire a son, phantom or otherwise. All he'd achieved in life was an arranged divorce.

"Oh, a woman likes to have a female friend arahnd when she's expectin', lovey. They likes to gossip abaht fings wot men doesn't un'erstand. Men 'as their uses, but there's times when they's plain useless – they just gets in the road of women's ways of thinking."

Beard smiled at Queenie's occasional lapses into Cockney vernacular. He seriously wondered if Queenie knew what she was talking about, because he had no idea. Perhaps she was right : perhaps women did talk a different language. "I wonder if I shouldn't try and catch up with her out there," he suggested thoughtfully, almost as if he was thinking out loud.

Queenie's arm seemed to stiffen in his and there was one of those things that people call a pregnant pause before, after taking a prodigiously deep breath, she said: "I wouldn't, lovey." Beard stared at her, his dark eyes questioning her. There was another pregnant pause: a bit longer. "Ruth isn't just tagging along. She's not on her own. She has a friend with her."

The way Queenie squeezed the words out, each one an enormous and painful effort, Beard knew it had to be a man – and he hated him, whoever he was. Her words shocked Beard. It was something Beard hadn't even thought about, or, if he had, dreaded and hid away; and now, hearing the words out loud, albeit in a hoarse whisper, the realisation of it scared him. The chill he'd felt at his heart earlier now seemed like a lump of ice: a huge, painful iceberg that all but stilled his breath. And this puzzled him too. How could numbness and pain exist together? However it was possible, he was conscious of both, and there was nothing exquisite in their twin pains: they hurt him almost to the point of screaming. But all he said was, "Who is he, Mum?"

"Philip. Philip Goodwood. He's an American she met at one of her evening classes. He's an accountant – something like that, anyways," cried Queenie, her voice hoarse with emotion. "He's a nice boy, Jarvis – handsome, too."

Beard hated him even more. "Couldn't she wait for me to get home?" he muttered bitterly.

"You couldn't, lovey. You went and got yourself wed just 'cos she weren't arahnd when you needed her," Queenie said evenly, taking and patting his hand. "A girl has to look out for herself. Opportunities don't come ev'ry day, do they?"

"Is it serious?"

Queenie's shoulders gave a massive shrug. "Who knows? There's talk of him returning to America where he has a big job lined up, and her going wiv 'im."

"They're not engaged, or anything like that, though?" he demanded desperately, grabbing at any straw like a drowning man.

"He give her a ring." Queenie felt him tense beside her and heard him give a sigh that seemed endless.

Beard gave a grim smile: the sort a man might give before being shot. "So did I," he said, with a tired resignation. "That's it, then. I've lost her for good."

"I don't hardly ever see her wearing it," Queenie added quickly. "Only when they're togevver. Pr'aps it don't mean all that much to 'er – not like the one you give her."

"Well, she's not wearing that one now either, is she?" said Beard, a trifle bitterly.

"You can't blame Ruth, lovey," replied Queenie defensively. "You didn't exactly treat her all that well, did yer? Never wrote to her or remembered her birthday, nor nuffink like that. I'll allow you was generous enough when you was with her, but out of sight she was out of yer mind, an' you was always away someplace with yer soldiering. An' even after you give her yer lov-erly ring an' swore undying love to her, wot 'appened? You ups an' marries some ovver gel wot yer didn't even know after lettin' her pull the wool over yer eyes about havin' a baby. Oh, I know you thought you was doin' right by her, lovey, but you had no business sniffin' round her in the first place – even if you are a bleedin' man! You should've done right by Ruth first, m'lad. She's loved you all her life. An' even when you went an' married this other gel, she forgave you – like she done always. She's wrote yer lots of lovin' letters since then wot yer never answered."

"I only received one – a lovely one, wishing me and Cyn well," interposed Beard. "I didn't reply to it. It was the sort of letter that didn't need an answer. It was a very short letter, Mum. I half expected – hoped, anyway, that she'd send another letter, but she didn't."

"Of course not! You was married, Jarvis," Queenie cried heatedly. "You 'ad no right to expect anyfink more from Ruth – not arter you got yerself wedded, and 'er having spent all 'er life lovin' you. No, Jarvis, you didn't deserve no more letters or consideration from her, an' you 'ave no right ter 'spect 'er to sit around twiddlin' her fingers. You was out of 'er life for ever, so far as she knew. She's a beautiful young woman – with a young woman's needs. An' once you was married, what was she expected to do? It weren't her fault yer marriage didn't work out, an' weren't even necessary. Mind you, lovey, I'm glad in a way that you're free again, even if you have lost Ruth through your stupidity."

"Thank you, Mum," whispered Beard, giving her a dry peck on the cheek. "I'm glad to be out of that wretched marriage, as well – and sorry, too, to have lost Ruth in the process. Bitterly sorry. I hope ... I hope she'll be happy with this Philip of hers. But it won't stop me from always loving her."

Perhaps because he accepted that he had now irrevocably lost Ruth for ever, Beard came perilously close to repeating his earlier folly when Gibbs sent him up to Yorkshire to take part in a huge exercise on the moors there in late January, saying the exercise would do him good. Beard had had to extricate himself from the war-games to go in search of a dentist; he arrived on the outskirts of Sheffield in the middle of the night aboard a Centurion tank with his frightfully swollen face peering left and right out of the turret in search of assistance, and eventually spotted a constable cowering in a doorway. The officer, having recovered from finding the tank's 20-pounder gun pointing straight at him and deducing the problem from Beard's tortured face and incoherent mumblings, clambered up on the tank and directed the driver to the nearest hospital. Inside of an hour, Beard had had all four wisdom teeth extracted – and, as his tank had returned to its role in the war games, he was given a bed for the remainder of the night in which to recuperate.

It was the bed that did it. It introduced him to Nurse Roberta Tomlin. His bed was her responsibility, and she took her work very seriously. Her beds were the tidiest in the ward, and their occupants the neatest and cleanest and the most fussed over in the hospital. The fact that Beard's bed stood all by itself in a room adjoining the main ward made no difference. Nor did the fact that he was a soldier and not really ill at all, but only suffering from a sore jaw. He was in her charge and as such qualified for her full attention. Not a sigh or a groan, or even a gentle clearing of his throat, went unnoticed; he was expertly nursed whether he needed it or not, and as for bed pans and bottles, they seemed to arrive in anticipation of his needs. Because he was a serving soldier and his unit was camped out in the open, where snow lay deep and winds howled, the rules governing his admission were relaxed and, instead of being sent on his way in the morning, he was allowed to remain until he was considered well enough to go and convalesce back with the Army.

Beard, apart from feeling somewhat sore in the region of his jaw, felt as right as rain and by the second day was beginning to take a healthy young man's interest in his nurse, Roberta. She was well worth looking at, even in her uniform frock and the ridiculous cap-thing she wore that looked like a collapsed seagull; but it was the black stockings disappearing mysteriously up her legs beneath the dress that really stirred his juices. He strained his neck trying to follow them up her thighs, but seldom got more than an inch or two above her knees. He was perfectly aware that she knew very well where his eyes were straying, but it did not seem to bother her. Indeed, she seemed to appreciate his ogling, and, being well aware that he was not a proper patient and finding him as handsome a specimen as she was likely to find on either side of the Pennines, she told him that he could call her Bobbie provided he behaved; she did not press this point – about his behaving, that is, and when he begged a good night kiss (which she gave him) and followed this up with a similar request in the morning, she invited him home for supper before he returned to camp.

Home was a flat opposite a park in Hallam: it was more a bed-sitter, really – one and a half rooms to be precise. The half-room comprised a curtained-off hole containing a sink, three gas rings and a larder with a mesh screen to keep out resident mice. The central feature of the main accommodation was the bed, which was large and unmade. There was also a chest of drawers, another tiny curtained recess that served for a cupboard, a small table littered with books, papers and two empty beer bottles, one chair with a suspect leg and a sort of ottoman covered with faded blue velvet propped up against a wall.

The bed really seemed the safest place to sit, and while he sat on it and Bobbie busied herself in her "kitchen," Beard discovered a number of canvases and drawings which suggested a secret artistic talent. Her works were mostly of scenic views and flowers, with an occasional face or a well-muscled figure, both male and female; he thought they were jolly good, even if they weren't. He also discovered that when she removed her headgear and let down her hair, it stretched right down her back; it was more ginger than anything else, though she insisted it was actually Titian, and when that was all that covered her body – as now – she looked ravishingly beautiful. They never did eat supper that night. She jumped straight on to the bed with him, and they didn't leave it until he had to leave the following afternoon.

Beard returned to his soldiering, and returned to Bobbie at every opportunity. There was no doubt about it, they clicked together: their bodies did, anyway. For close on two months they were seldom apart. Whenever their free times coincided, they were together. They rarely did much else but go to bed, but occasionally they went for short walks in the country, or went to a pub for a breather, on Saturdays they invariably went to see a repertory show, sometimes the cinema, and for several days when the light was right she had him posing while she sketched or painted. While she was painting, she wore a smock-frock that was completely open at the back and very little else; he was sure this was entirely for his delectation. He loved to watch her, especially her mouth which was full and pinky-red and almost always half open and laughing. She was a short, chubby girl, with rounded almond-coloured cheeks, a comfortable-looking nose, and had greenish eyes that sometimes looked far away but were always clear and bright, and laughing, too. It seemed the most natural thing in the world that as their relationship developed, their thoughts, as they came up for air from their love-making, should start to revolve around, and finally settle on, union of another sort.

And on an occasion verging on April 1, when they came up for air, a wedding was arranged, as the saying goes. Beard approached a fellow officer, Peter Bartlett, and asked him to be his best man. "What, again!" cried the startled officer, who was well aware of Beard's previous march down that road, and of his escape. "You're not serious!" But Beard was serious, and adamant. He knew that he had now lost Ruth for ever: she might even be married herself by now; and he felt comfortable with Bobbie. They got on so well together: he already felt married to her, so why not tie the knot officially.

And so the marriage was arranged ... but it got no further than the stag party which, somewhat contrary to tradition, Bobbie also attended. It was a very alcoholic night, with at least a hundred toasts, and when they came to on the morning of what was supposed to be their wedding day, neither could see any good reason why they should get up and go through with it – even if it did leave the luckless Bartlett standing at the door of the register office with an armful of pink carnations! "We've already got all we want without all that palaver, haven't we, darling?" exclaimed Bobbie, and promptly resumed snoring in Beard's arms.

As things happened, the decision was wise, and opportune. Less than a fortnight after what was supposed to have been their wedding day, Gibbs sent Beard a signal telling him, in effect, to get himself back to Chelmsford by the next train.

Bobbie seemed to take his departure in her stride, at least on the surface. It was almost as if she had been expecting his news. There were no tears or accusations: no scenes at all. "It's been lovely, Bob," she exclaimed, as they hugged each other in the familiar bed for the last time. "I'll never forget you, my darling. You mustn't worry yourself about me. There are no strings attached to either of us. You concentrate on keeping yourself safe, and when you do come home ... well, we'll see. Perhaps both our lives will be changed by then."

Beard nodded to Bobbie. He hadn't looked forward to telling her his news, and was relieved at her very undemanding and practical attitude. He didn't expect that they'd ever meet again and, while he was sure he wouldn't forget her, he was conscious that this didn't actually cause him any pain. He gave a tight little smile as he looked down at her. It had been a very close run thing – he'd so nearly been a husband again; he considered his score as being one and a half marriages!

He told himself sternly that there'd be no others.

Arrived at Apple Tree Camp, Beard was greeted by Gibbs who said simply, "Get weaving, Robert. We're off to India!" Beard blinked back and asked, "What's up? Has war broken out there?" Gibbs shook his head and grinned. "Not yet," he said, "you're going out as a military attaché so make sure you have a smart trousseau – dress uniforms and stuff like that. We fly out in mufti, and when you get there make sure you watch your manners, and leave the ladies alone." Beard nodded: he wondered if he was acquiring a reputation, and wasn't sure it was one he wanted; not now. "And what will my job be, when I'm not annoying the ladies, sir?" he asked, politely. "I'll tell you on the way, Robert," Gibbs retorted, and Beard was almost sure the other chuckled.

Gibbs probably did explain to Beard precisely what his job as an attaché entailed, but whether or not the latter took it all in is debatable. Beard appeared to sleep all through the flight to India: sleeping, and dreaming of his lost Ruth ... and she seemed to be dressed for a wedding! Whose? He woke with a start as the plane hit an air pocket, and wiped the sweat from his brow. It was probably just her suttee garb, he decided facetiously, overlooking the fact that this would mean – if he was her husband, he'd already be dead, and burning in hell!

As the plane circled to land at Bangalore, he suddenly smiled. He didn't believe in miracles, but sometimes they happened, didn't they? And he was still thinking of Ruth.

Now, what was it Gibbs had been telling him about his job?

□   *"Really, Jarvis, just how many wives have you got scattered round the world?" Ruth protested, though there was amusement in her dark eyes, and a smile on her rouged lips.*

"I'm a bachelor to the best of my knowledge and belief," declared Beard, which didn't really answer her question.

"Well, all this philandering will have to stop once we're married," insisted Ruth.

"Is this a proposal, Ruth?" he asked her, grinning hugely.

"I'm already spoken for, darling," smiled Ruth coyly.

"Someone's a lucky man."

"Yes, you are, Jarvis," agreed Ruth, "so make sure you behave."

"Stop it you two," laughed Queenie, "you're acting just like when you was kids. Stop yer nonsense, an' let the general carry on wiv 'is story."

And the general did, but it was a couple of days later.

Chapter Forty

India, April 7, 1949

They touched down at Bangalore on April 7, and Beard loved the place from the start, and thought how different his life might have been had he come to India in 1941, instead of falling in with Gibbs. Possibly the weather had a lot to do with it, and the fact that it was the first country he'd been to where he hadn't been greeted by gunfire. But Beard was suspicious. They were there for some specific reason, and he wasn't fooled by this attaché business.

"So why did we really come to India in such a rush, sir?" he quizzed Gibbs as they stretched their legs in the city's Cubbon Park the following morning.

"I did right when I picked you up in Egypt, Robert. You've always been a shrewd and perceptive chap," observed Gibbs.

"It's what's kept me alive," said Beard bluntly.

"What happened to that chum of yours? The one who transferred to the Special Boat Squadron. I heard he was badly wounded and lost a leg."

"Bertie, you mean. Bertie Hartwell," said Beard. "They gave him a tin one and he copes very well – he runs a farm and is raising a family of his own on the side."

"Do you still have ambitions of your own in that directions?" asked Gibbs casually.

"All the time. I've just had a narrow escape up in Yorkshire – though this one was by mutual agreement. All most amicable. I'm hoping it'll be a case of third time lucky. I keep making a fool of myself and getting tied up with the wrong girl. I'm horribly afraid I may have missed my opportunity with the right one now."

"I'm sorry to hear that, Robert," said Gibbs softly. "But I'm sure you won't give up."

"Never! Even if she is married," declared Beard emphatically. "But, you still haven't answered my question as to the real reason for this trip, sir."

"Nothing specific. We just need to be in position in case something erupts," answered Gibbs, resuming their slow perambulation. "There's the tension of war in the air involving all the big countries like China, Russia and America. The Communists are spreading, gobbling up all in their path like a red lava and the United Nations haven't really a loud enough voice yet to be effective. The unfortunate Koreans look to be the next victims. The great threat is of atomic warfare. That would end the world."

"I thought that was God's prerogative."

"Like the good book says, God works in mysterious ways," smiled Gibbs. Then, coming to another halt, he told Beard, "Enjoy India while you can, Robert, it's a wonderful country. I'll come for you when I need you. But I warn you, I won't leave you long."

And that's what Beard did: enjoyed India like a tourist. He sent Queenie a postcard with an elephant scene, and another to Maud and Bertie (same elephant picture) remembering to ask after their new baby – he'd forgotten what kind it was. He wanted to send one to Ruth, too, but he didn't know where to send it and, anyway, he imagined she might be married to her Philip by now and any words from him would be regarded as an intrusion.

During his first few weeks, Beard found the Indians very friendly, generous, courteous and generally well educated, and supposed that all these things had surfaced with the departure of the British! He imagined it must be hard to be proud when one's country was occupied. He was often amused, and sometimes embarrassed when, in talks with Buddhist monks and other learned men, it emerged that civilisation in India could be traced back to 3500 BC, whereas there was no trace of anything significant in Britain before the first century AD – when the Romans came, and dragged them along the stony road to civilisation.

Beard found his life in India really something like a summer holiday. And one of the Buddhist monks gave him a beautiful ruby for Ruth. He treasured it, as he did the thought of the opportunity of presenting it to her. There was work to be done, certainly, but he still found of time for elephant rides, tiger hunts (without ever seeing a tiger), and visiting all the shrines and temples he came upon; he saw the Red Fort at Delhi, cast a patriotic eye at the Victoria Memorial in Calcutta's Maidan Park, spent an exceedingly lazy weekend on a houseboat on Dal Lake in the Kashmir with the Karakorums in the background for company, and, right at the end, marvelled at the magnificence of the Taj Mahal in Agra.

"It's almost worth dying to have a tomb like that," Beard declared enthusiastically to Gibbs, who had suddenly appeared at his quarters that morning following a trip to China. Beard continued feasting his eyes on the white marble mausoleum's reflection in the ornamental pool.

"I wouldn't be in too much of a hurry, old man," said Gibbs drily, "your opportunity may be closer than you think."

The tourist in Beard died first, and as he turned his gaze from the shimmering water, he was instantly a soldier again. He raised his brows questioningly, knowing his "lovely holiday" in India was over: it had lasted less than a year.

Gibbs, fanning himself with a panama hat, muttered that a new war in Korea was beckoning them. He went on to explain that at the end of the war, Korea had been divided at the 38th Parallel, with Soviet

Russia "policing" the north, and the US the south. But, of course, this hadn't satisfied the Communists: they wanted it all. "And they've come damned close to achieving their ambition," said Gibbs grimly.

The invasion came on June 25, 1950, and two days later, the UN Security Council, at the behest of the Americans, called for military sanctions against North Korea. Three days later, President Truman ordered in American combat troops from Japan to help the South Koreans. The war went disastrously for the South, before the North's advances ground to a halt in August.

"By then they had captured Seoul, the southern capital, and pushed the US and South Korean forces back to a small perimeter around the southern port of Pusan – and there they are standing fast, holding on grimly," said Gibbs, and his voice was grim too.

"And what do you want us to do, sir?" asked Beard airily.

"You and I – and, I suppose, a lot of others, are ordered to get ourselves to Tokyo with all possible speed," replied Gibbs. "There, we are to place ourselves at the disposal of the Americans, and join General Douglas MacArthur's Eighth Army for service in Korea."

Beard had followed the conflict over the wireless, but had never supposed his involvement would be any closer than this. It came as a nasty shock to be ordered into the fray – and leave his Indian paradise.

"Isn't all this beyond the remit of an attaché, sir?" enquired Beard, unimpressed – in the best tradition of soldiers.

"Nonsense," declared Gibbs, almost breezily. "Excellent opportunity of meeting the Chinese in the field. We must bag a few of their top men, and get them to talk."

Beard studied a map for some moments and declared straight-faced, "It's one of the United States, isn't it?"

"It probably will be before we're done," growled Gibbs, scowling at their orders, which were stamped Urgent in red ink.

They arrived in Japan on August 28, 1950, and found themselves, to all intents and purposes, more *in* than merely attached to the American Army. They were escorted by US military policemen to another aircraft and flown down to Osaka from where, still with their escort, they were driven to a vast military camp.

Here, Gibbs and his party, which now included scores of assorted British soldiers who had been in transit elsewhere and simply been hijacked, were handed over to Colonel Hugh Colley who, despite his American uniform was a Scots Guards officer – and wore the British crown and pips to prove it. He explained the British presence by saying they were to form a Reconnaissance Strike Battalion.

The colonel, rangy, dark and very professional in his manner, gave a shrug and a smile and added that it wasn't even a proper battalion: it numbered barely three hundred men, enough for three companies.

This had been all the men with parachute qualifications he'd been able to round up in the area at short notice, and with most of them that was the only qualification they had for being there.

"I was delighted when Lord Charington cabled and mentioned you chaps holidaying in India, and said I could make use of you – if you were agreeable. I hadn't expected he'd send me a general, though." Gibbs gave a low growl and said their orders had probably come from the same club in St James's. Col Colley chuckled, and, turning to Beard, continued: "His lordship mentioned you, sir, without giving much away, beyond saying you should be a general, too. I can't manage that, captain, but you'll find you've been promoted to major. It's been gazetted. I need an experienced officer to take over one of the three companies. You'll take over A Company. And you, general, I'll be happy to have you working alongside me in HQ Company and help with planning." He paused, grinned at the two men, and said, "We could do with lots more like you chaps."

Beard acknowledged his promotion with a small bow and a big smile, though inside he did wonder if it was a rank he would hold just for the duration of this present job, or whether it would be a permanent one – and also whether he would be paid as a major. "Let's have a look at the chaps we do have, sir," he suggested with a show of enthusiasm."

"They're a ragtag bunch of men, I'm afraid, the real flotsam and jetsam of soldiery," said Col Colley, grinning as he raised his brows skywards. "We've had the deuce of a job just rounding up these fellows. There's all sorts from half a dozen Commonwealth countries. And I dare say a few of them aren't all that keen about going to war on the end of a parachute – many aren't paratroopers as you understand the word. Just wanted the badge, really. And never seen action."

"Well, I gather they'll be getting the chance now," commented Beard.

"Are you able to be more specific about the role of this battalion in whatever lies ahead, colonel?" Gibbs enquired, looking up from a large map.

"The plan is to drop the battalion about twenty miles behind enemy lines when MacArthur invades Korea," replied Col Colley. "I can't tell you where the landing will be, of course, nor when – but you don't have a lot of time. Your main task will be to provide the invading force with intelligence of enemy positions, strength and all that sort of thing. So good communications are essential. You will not go out of your way to engage the enemy – though, of course, you will defend yourselves as the situation demands. Your priority is to keep the Americans advised of what is ahead of them. That is why they've set up this outfit."

"The Americans always seem to have so much of everything, are they unable to provide their own airborne units?" queried Gibbs with uncompromising bluntness.

"Apparently not, sir," answered Col Colley succinctly.

"I notice that all the men – including yourself, sir, – are wearing American uniforms. Why is this?" asked Beard, more curiously than belligerently.

"Because it's better than our stuff, Mr Beard," said the colonel agreeably. "Most of us – as indeed you still are – were in KDs when we arrived here. It's going to be pretty chilly in Korea come winter. Minus 30-plus or thereabouts. So you'll be glad of GI clothing."

"And we have to take orders from the Yanks, sir?" persisted Beard.

"You take your orders from me, major," said the colonel sharply, but his face softened into a smile as he added, "*I* have to take my orders from the Americans. And my advice from them is that we've very little time to get into shape – so train them like mad, sir!"

His advice was right. Two weeks was all the time available to hone the men into an adequate fighting unit. At least at the end of this time they were fit: fit to drop, as the saying goes! Beard took them on endless cross-country runs that seemed to be mostly up mountains, the NCOs saw to things like PT and weapon-firing, there were other sessions of unarmed combat and, of course, when they were all fit to drop, that's what they did next ... out of aeroplanes on the end of parachutes! Each man made at least three or four jumps during the fortnight, mostly at night, some at 2,000-ft and some very much less.

As Col Colley remarked when there was no more time for training, "They may not be entirely keen about going, but at least they're fit to go."

They moved out of the camp to an airfield on September 14, and Beard didn't even notice that it was his birthday. He was twenty-five.

Chapter Forty-one

Korea, September 14, 1950

As invasions went, it was quite a brilliant affair. Anything that succeeds is brilliant, according to the Army manual! And the invasion was certainly successful. The amphibious landing took place far behind the enemy's lines, at Inchon on South Korea's west coast, about 25 miles west of Seoul. In a co-ordinated move, UN forces broke out of the Pusan perimeter and struck northwards. Beard's "battalion" preceded the sea landings by some hours, their nine planes going in with a massive aerial armada that maintained a non-stop bombardment that went on for days.

Beard's was the last of the planes to disgorge its passengers, which meant that they were the farthest behind the lines. The only casualty was to one of the two South Korean interpreters who jumped with them: he got caught up in his lines immediately on exiting, and was, in effect, hanged. Major Perceval Dunlop, who led B Company, landed virtually on top of a small armoured column hidden on the edge of a large wood and had quite a little scrap before extricating himself and radioing the details to MacArthur's flagship from where the war was currently being run: twenty minutes later US fighter-bombers plastered the area, and Dunlop and his men were glad to be out of the strike zone. Col Colley, who went in with C Company, landed some dozen miles farther on, found nothing in the vicinity and went to explore a ridge to the north which seemed an obvious defence line: this, too, he found deserted and after checking that two small bridges had not been mined, he radioed back that all was quiet and that he was holding the line and protecting the bridges.

Beard's men found themselves strewn across a farm that the North Koreans had evidently commandeered; they were greeted with a furious burst of light machine-gun fire and then by mortar shells and Beard, whose men suffered five killed and four wounded, quickly withdrew and radioed the particulars back to HQ. Again, US fighter-bombers were over the spot within minutes and razed everything to the ground – and had a bit more fun machine-gunning terrified farm stock that stampeded in every direction. Beard, having called for his casualties to be evacuated, searched the farm buildings but found only bodies and debris, but his men did capture a few chickens and collected a bucketful of eggs to take along with them to augment the detested K-rations their American allies had showered on them.

The North Koreans, who had believed their invasion of the south would lead to a welcoming uprising and weren't equipped for any lengthy conflict, least of all against the might of the United States, under the UN banner, were quickly routed and pushed back across the 38th parallel. It had been thought, by the men on the ground, that this would mean the war was ended, but it seemed the plan now was to liberate the whole of Korea, reunite the two halves, and destroy the Communists for good.

Accordingly, UN forces swept into North Korea on October 7, captured Pyongyang, the capital, and chased the enemy northwards. They continued to withdraw with such speed and enthusiasm it was more like a cross-country race than a military campaign. The trouble was Beard and his men, who were now equipped with Jeeps, were caught between the two forces, the retreating North Koreans and a continually advancing UN line that left them less and less space in which to manoeuvre. Beard did his best to harass the retreating enemy, but found his main difficulty was in keeping up with them. There were frequent breakdowns involving the Jeeps, and Sgt Eddie Goulden, of The Royal Engineers, was killed by a mortar shell. He was their only casualty in the dash north. There was very little opportunity for any prolonged fighting, the most that had to be contended with were some long-range exchanges of machine-gun and sniper fire which was more a nuisance than any real danger. As for radioing back intelligence about the enemy's activities, this was largely a waste of time since the information was out of date almost as soon as it had been relayed. Mostly Beard was reminding the Americans that his battalion was on their side, and would they please stop shelling them.

But that was before they reached the Yalu River, which separated North Korea from China, just as the bitter winter was beginning to make itself more of a problem than the enemy. The latter had largely taken refuge across the border, but the UN forces were forbidden to enter China.

The Chinese had already warned the Americans that they might enter the war if the UN forces came near the Yalu. On October 25, Beard found himself looking down on the river – he also found himself engaged in close fighting with several hundred Chinese "volunteers" who were extremely well equipped; after tasting each other's blood both sides beat a hasty retreat to see what the generals (American) would decide to do. Their decision, almost at once, was to press on with their offensive. The Chinese retaliated in massive numbers and the UN forces, over-extended, heavily outnumbered and ill-equipped to take on a fresh enemy in the arctic conditions, were soon in full retreat. It was a complete reversal of fortunes, and worse was to come.

Beard and others of the extravagantly-named Reconnaissance Strike Battalion were particularly affected by the reverse. One moment they had been the vanguard of a triumphant army and able to whistle up assistance at the drop of a hat, the next their role had changed to that of a rearguard, and it was every man for himself in the pell-mell retreat. The Chinese, in their hundreds of thousands, harried the fleeing UN forces with savage disregard   for life –   their own included. Col Colley's company was trapped in a long, winding valley and almost annihilated: out of 100 men only 27 escaped, including the colonel, who led the survivors to safety weeks later. Beard, who had lost contact with both Colley and Dunlop almost as soon as the Chinese appeared on the scene, received orders to hold a frozen ridge designated as Hill 127 for as long as possible – and then retire as best he could.

He had less than 60 men at this stage, but they held that hill, which commanded a view of two roads that disappeared like white snakes towards the tree-lined mountains rising behind them, for close on two days as wave after wave of yelling, bugle-blowing Chinese hurled themselves forward with complete disregard for their lives. They died in their hundreds, some within yards of Beard's men, but there were always thousands more following behind. A few got behind Beard's wriggly line, and were gunned down there. The hilltop was mercilessly bombarded by artillery and mortars and continuously raked by machine-gun fire. Casualties mounted with alarming rapidity: more than 40 per cent by the second day, including two officers killed. The only surviving officer was a doctor, Captain Matthew Hawley, who crawled along a furrow in the deep snow to tell Beard, who was firing one of the company's two heavy machine-guns, that more of his patients were freezing to death than were dying from their wounds.

"There's nothing I can do for them, major," he said plaintively. "The wounded really have to be evacuated ... otherwise we'll lose them all."

There wasn't much of the doctor's face that Beard could see. Like his own, it was encased in a balaclava and had a scarf wound round and round, and there were icicles forming in the vicinity of his nose. Only the eyes were visible, and they were red-rimmed and swollen. His breath escaped through its protective layers in white bursts of condensation.

"We must *all* get off this hill, Doc," said Beard, blinking his eyes against the bitter, stinging cold. "We can't hold it – each time they attack, I expect them to overrun our positions. We've been very lucky – but it can't last. The men need rest and hot food in their bellies ... and besides that our ammo is getting too low."

He paused to wipe his eyes of the stinging snow and to slap his freezing hands together. It didn't seem to warm him up at all, but there was a tingle of pain in his fingers – so perhaps the movement was doing some good; he repeated it again and again. He felt his teeth chattering, or rather felt them wanting to: his jaw felt frozen, and he slapped his face several times to stir some vestige of circulation. The cold was so intense each word was painful to articulate, each one seemed to emerge like something frozen in the air, and he closed his chapped lips quickly with each word. The pain increased with each extra word he squeezed out between his set teeth. It was hard to think when your head was frozen, or felt like it was.

"I've twenty-two men left capable of firing a weapon – at least, I did at the last count two hours ago. It's probably less now." Beard paused after this long speech of frozen words. He had to wait while his jaw thawed sufficiently to enable him to continue. The pain was excruciating. He buried his head in his gloved hands and tried to think; and that, too, was painful. He wanted to simply close his eyes and fall asleep, and block out the cold. But he knew that would be fatal – so that part of his brain was functioning. He knew he wanted to live. He lifted his head and shook Hawley, who had started to snore.

"Wake up, Doc. We need you," Beard gasped out. "It's time to go. Start moving your wounded out now." He paused, clapped his hands together, and tried to think. "Take them all, and as many men as you need, and head through the mountains. If you aim south-west you should reach our lines, eventually. Just keep going."

"What about you?" asked Hawley, shaking himself awake, his greeny eyes widening in concern.

"Leave me half the men to cover your departure," replied Beard, "We'll catch up with you in a day or two."

"There's three men at least who won't make it. They're dying now – moving them would simply hasten their deaths."

"Leave them here, Doc," said Beard without any hesitation. He did not even ask who they were: he did not dare, in case they were close friends. "We'll have to rely on the humanity of the Chinese."

Hawley gave a little shiver of apprehension. "Poor bastards. It would be kinder to shoot them now," he muttered, more to himself than to Beard. "I think I should stay behind with them, major," he said with some determination.

"No, Doc," declared Beard quickly and firmly. "I need you to take charge of the evacuation. You'll save a damned sight more lives that way than by staying here. Just make those who can't be moved are as comfortable as possible – and shoot off! We haven't got much time. Johnny Chinaman won't be frustrated much longer. I'll radio our situation and let them know we're forced to evacuate. And that'll be it."

He was right. As Capt Hawley disappeared into what was left of the night with twelve able-bodied men, the Chinese, ignoring the worsening blizzard conditions, launched yet another assault under an umbrella of flares. Shells from their big guns pounded the summit of the hill as, with automatic guns blazing and bugles blaring, their troops emerged from their hiding places and charged up the slopes that were already littered with their comrades' bodies. Beard, who had been left with nine men, lost three of them in the first bombardment. The three wounded men left behind by Doc were all unconscious, and Beard thought it the best thing for them; he winced at the thought of abandoning them, but there was really nothing he could do for them. The assaults continued relentlessly for six hours.

It was quickly evident that this time the Chinese would not be repelled long, and after three more hours of emptying magazine after magazine into the advancing hoards with very little effect, and with their last machine-gun knocked out, Beard gave the order to scatter. He was surprised his limbs responded so readily; he'd expected them to be frozen useless, and he almost wished they had been for the pain, as his activity awakened the circulatory system, was agonizing. He floundered in the snow from man to man, tapping each of the six survivors on the shoulder and tapping his helmet. The first man he touched was already dead, shot in the head. It was Cpl Fred Peterson, R.A., whom he barely had a chance to get to know well. A cheerful, competent man was all Beard knew of him.

"We're going … RV in forest to east … Make your own way … Go now!" he yelled at each of the others as he reached them, surprised his words didn't die in the freezing atmosphere. But they must have penetrated the men's ears for they all moved at a rate of knots.

Beard waited only long enough to see the last man disappear before, having rolled a couple of grenades down the hill, racing after them and the distant trees as fast as he could. If he didn't hurt so much from the pain of his restoring circulation, Beard might have laughed at the thought that he was racing. Each step was a fresh agony as, with each step, it was a case of having to lift a leg out of snow drifts that were feet deep and following where it fell. It was a very slow business and he was thankful for the continuing snow which hid him from view and covered his tracks. He reached the trees safely, and found that whatever the distance, it had taken him close on two hours.

Almost at once he was joined by two of his men, L/Cpl Ian Hackett and Pte Paul Fielding, so he reckoned they must have been watching for him. It was essential to keep on the move, to fight the cold and to escape any pursuers, and they were soon pushing on through the forest, being joined soon after by two others, Ptes Mike Milton and Jack Cookson ; it seemed that the fifth man didn't make it. Behind them they heard a sudden burst of gunfire from the hilltop, and Beard guessed that the three wounded men left behind had been despatched. So much for Chinese humaneness. He looked around for any sign of Mr Hawley and his column, but there was none; the snow, which was falling heavily, had obliterated everything. "Good luck, mate," he whispered.

After several days of playing hide-and-seek with enemy patrols, Beard came to the conclusion that the Chinese had cut the escape route to the south, and decided there was no option but to continue east since all other directions were barred. The cold had now become so intense it was painful to breathe let alone move, but again they had no option – they either carried on as best they could, or died. Two of his men,

Fielding and Milton, were suffering from frostbite, and Beard wasn't certain his own fingers were all that they should be. They felt numb, but when he clapped his hands very hard an exquisitely painful shock returned to them, so he knew they were all right – and kept slapping his arms against his sides to keep the circulation going. He thanked whatever god was responsible that they were all wearing American issue clothing suitable to the conditions; he was sure that had they been kitted out in British gear they'd have all been frozen solid by now. In addition to their GI issues, they had also acquired bits and pieces of the padded uniforms worn by the Chinese – and in spite of all these layers, which gave them the appearance of pregnant walruses, they were still bitterly, even dangerously, cold.

Each night, having gratefully guzzled down the despised K-rations and swallowed scalding hot mugs of black tea, they huddled together beneath a tarpaulin sheet and slept fitfully; each morning their makeshift tent resembled an igloo – and when they forced their way out it was like the young emerging from some giant egg. And every morning, Beard reminded the men against touching anything metal with their naked hands "or it'll stick to you for ever – or till something's amputated!" He always added the last bit as a joke, but nobody laughed: it was too cold for that. Besides, laughter used up energy, and they needed all theirs to survive the day. One of the men with frost-bite to his hand was in a bad way

The Chinese guns sounded uncomfortably close behind them, and all around, but they weren't being fired at them. Beard was becoming increasingly concerned that they might be completely surrounded, and that it didn't really matter in which direction they travelled. It would not be easy – probably be next to impossible – to slip through the Chinese cordon, but he'd have a damned good try if it came to that. He sometimes wondered how Mr Hawley and his lot were faring, and hoped, but with little optimism, that they had got through; he thought that their Jeeps had most likely been frozen into immobility or drowned in some snowdrift, and that their only hope lay in being found by some patrol – though if this was a Chinese one, they would most likely meet the same fate as the wounded back on Hill 127.

It served no purpose brooding on such things and he tried not to dwell on them, but it was difficult. If his thoughts didn't touch on Hawley, they came upon Colley and Dunlop: there was no comfort in any of his thoughts. Nor was there any in his own predicament. He knew they couldn't go on much longer like this: they were almost out of everything – food and ammo, though they'd had little use for the latter as they'd seen nothing they needed to shoot at – yet it seemed likely the cold would kill them before the enemy got the chance.

Actually, Beard had been correct: the Chinese had cut off the escape route to the south – on November 26. Their main forces continued southwards, reoccupying Pyongyang on December 5, but a substantial army kept squeezing the trapped UN forces in the Chosin area, pushing them ever closer towards the sea. There were up to 40,000 men in the pocket – mostly US marines and infantry, but including men of the 41st Royal Marine Commando and odds and sods like Beard – fighting their way towards the bridgehead at Hungnam, from where it was hoped to effect a Dunkirk-style evacuation. Beard, of course, had no way of knowing any of this at the time. The first intimation he had that he was in this fast shrinking pocket came when he was challenged by a very English voice.

They had been chased into a narrow valley by a couple of MIG fighters some hours earlier and had spent most of the intervening time floundering about in waist-deep drifts. When they had finally stumbled out of the white wilderness on to what appeared to be a highway of solid ice and had been challenged at a roadblock – there was a gun position on either side of the road, across which was strewn a barrier of tree-trunks and barbed wire – it had been like a miracle: the first day of summer and Christmas all rolled into one; it reduced them almost to tears of relief.

"Halt!" repeated the voice. "Identify yourselves." It took only a minute to convince the voice that they were neither Chinese nor North Korean, nor even Americans, but British soldiers, and then a Commando corporal showed his face and eyed them suspiciously. It wasn't surprising. They looked like fat bundles of clothing, anything but British with their mixture of American and Chinese uniforms. Only after Beard had produced his personal documents was the corporal satisfied. He gave Beard a respectful salute and waved him through the barrier. "Corporal Coombe, sir," he grinned amiably. "Good thing you didn't come along the road, sir, it's been heavily mined."

Beard nodded, and grinned back. The "road" was merely a white ribbon where countless feet and wheels had trodden the snow into hard-packed ice. It was littered with abandoned vehicles and weapons. "I can't tell you how good it is to see you, corporal. I didn't even know there was a road. Where the hell does it lead to, anyway?"

"Hungnam, sir," replied Coombe, stamping his feet on the ice. "That's where we're being evacuated from. It's the other side of a place called Hamhung, which you should be able to see a few miles down this road." The corporal paused and looked rather wistfully in that direction. "You'd best not delay getting to Hungnam, sir. Our officer, Mr Cotton, says the beachhead is shrinking every day. We're pulling back ourselves to new positions at 1500 hours – if we're not overrun before then!"

Beard and his men stayed only long enough to share a stew of corned beef and various other ingredients he had difficulty in identifying. It tasted all right, and at least it was hot. So, too, was the tea – heavily laced with some fiery spirit, which again it was probably better not to identify. Beard considered examining Fielding's frost-bitten hand, but decided against it; there was nothing he could do for the man and in view of the ominous smell from the swollen limb, he felt it would be kinder to leave its treatment to someone better qualified. Fielding would probably lose his fingers – at least. He turned to the corporal. "Right, we'll be pressing on, corporal," he said, feeling rather uncomfortable, as though he were deserting the man in his moment of greatest need, and extending his hand, "Good luck to you and your men."

"And you, sir," echoed Coombe, cheerfully enough, shaking the proffered hand vigorously. "You'll probably catch a ride before nightfall, sir – and we'll be chasing close behind."

Beard grimly wondered if they would, and hastily pushed the thought out of his mind. It didn't help. The corporal was right, however; they did find space in some transport. Even so, it was a slow and cruel journey in which they inched along in company with hundreds of other vehicles. The ice-road that wound precariously through gaps in the hills was shelled at frequent intervals, and several times fighters swooped down to strafe the snail-like column. Miraculously very few of the trucks were destroyed; occasionally, however, one would be blown up or be set ablaze by incendiary shells from the planes, and that would lead to long delays as the wrecks were manhandled aside. The cold, which seemed to intensify, caused far greater suffering. Beard could not remember feeling so utterly miserable for so long. There was not a part of his body that was not affected. The cold actually hurt, and there was no relief from the pain; it was as though one's actual bones, even one's very soul, was frozen.

The journey to Hungnam took four days: a lot of men died on the way; but, at length, they reached the port, and there in the bay were scores of ships – and seemingly hundreds of smaller craft ferrying to and fro between them and the shore. So, it was another Dunkirk. It was three more days, during which both the port and the ships were continuously shelled, before Beard and what was left of his command – L/Cpl Hackett and Cookson – were able to ferry out to one of the evacuation boats. He had had to leave the other two men Fielding and Milton with a field hospital unit – the doctor there said Fielding had gangrene and would definitely lose his hand, if not his whole arm; Milton, with two bullets in his chest, had been a victim of the strafing as they approached the port. Beard was advised that the man was unlikely to survive. While they were waiting to be evacuated, Beard could only watch as shells bombarded the motionless ships, and his heart gave a jerk each time one was hit, for each one lessened their chances of escape. He had been unable to discover whether or not Colley or Hawley had passed through the port, but did ascertain that Dunlop had been evacuated nearly a week earlier – on a hospital ship. Finally, on December 15, after being machine-gunned by MIGs and almost sunk by Chinese artillery on the mainland, his ship weighed anchor and ploughed away at her best speed

– which seemed awfully slow.

Beard found himself back in Japan, and sincerely hoped he had seen the last of Korea – North or South, but his hopes were soon to be dashed. The Chinese offensive southwards swept on back across the 38th parallel, recapturing Seoul on January 4,1951, and sweeping on till January 15, when a shortage of supplies and firepower finally brought it to a standstill far south of Seoul. At this point, Truman, fearful of becoming embroiled in a war that might include the Russians, abandoned any plan for the military reunification of the two Koreas and returned to his original goal of halting Communist aggression in the south. Accordingly, the US Eighth Army took the offensive once again on January 25, followed on February 21 by the entire UN command in a powerful attack labelled Operation Killer. The Communists fought stubbornly, but they were pushed relentlessly back

Beard, who had been sent off on leave to thaw out – "get pissed and get laid", as his American commander told him – was thrown back into the fray in time for the initial US offensive. However, before that happened, he had been able to track down Col Colley and Dunlop. The latter had borne a charmed life while fleeing the Chinese in North Korea, and though he received a bullet wound in the leg had managed to bring most of his men through to Hungnam and safety. Even his wound turned out to be the proverbial million-dollar one: it earned him a ticket home. In the magnanimous way that they did these things, the Americans gave him a Purple Heart and a Silver Star and were preparing to fly him home when Beard traced him – living like royalty in a convalescent camp on the outskirts of Tokyo.

"Why not come with me, Robert?" cried Dunlop in a conspiratorial voice. "The Yanks'll probably give you another decoration for going AWOL!" Beard, who had been handed both a Silver and Bronze Star in much the same way as if they had been a couple of doughnuts, shook his head laughingly. "They'd more likely shoot me! It's bad enough being shot at by the enemy, but I'd just as soon not give my friends the opportunity – they might not always miss!"

It was Col Colley himself who told Beard the news about Hawley. "I don't know how he did it, Robert," Colley gushed, as they stretched out in the bar of a Tokyo hotel taken over by the military for the "rest and relaxation" of officers in transit, "but Hawley waltzed right through the Chinese lines without once being fired upon. I can only assume that for once the enemy chose to recognize the inviolability of the Red Cross – more likely there were better targets in the vicinity. Hawley's luck held out right up to the moment he reached the safety of an American sector. Then he stepped on one of our own bloody mines!" Beard swore. "Was he badly hurt?" he asked. "Lost his left leg, just below the knee," replied Colley in a clear but strained voice, signalling for more drinks. "Hawley told us of your heroic last stand on Hill 127, facing the might of China almost alone. I'm sure he'd be happily surprised to know that you escaped unscathed with some of your men. Damned good show, old man. Hawley and all the wounded men he brought through – the remnants of your company, Robert – were flown down to Hong Kong after initial treatment, and are probably on their way home by now."

Colley made light of his own experiences. He and the 27 survivors of C Company had avoided being caught in the Chosin trap – "we were just lucky, like Hawley" – and had made their way south, passing through the Chinese ring with only a minor scare or two, and reached the UN lines after only one really hairy set-to about twenty miles from home. "Lost two men and had three wounded," he said quietly. "Fortunately, the Chinese didn't seem interested in chasing after us, or we'd all have been goners."

The first thing Beard noticed when he returned to Korea via Pusan was that the South was tropical compared with the North: it wasn't, of course, but it was definitely very much warmer, and seemed to get more so every day. Once the invasion was fully achieved, Beard's original reconnaissance outfit no longer existed, but he and Colley found themselves doing much the same job as before, this time spearheading the advance of the US Seventh Division. The unit, which was called Small's Scouts after its American commander, Brigadier Earl Harvey Small, numbered some one thousand men: a mixed bag of many nationalities, but mainly Americans.

The Scouts did more than merely reconnoitre the enemy, they attacked him savagely in quick sorties at every opportunity. In this sort of warfare casualties inevitably mounted with every success, and among these was Colley, who was killed by sniper fire during the recapture of Seoul on March 14. Beard had already by-passed the capital and the first he knew of Colley's death was a signal from Brigadier Small which informed him of the "regrettable loss" in one sentence, and expressed "great pleasure" in promoting him to lieutenant-colonel in his place in the next.

It was to be a short-lived promotion: the fighting was almost done. The UN forces reached the 38th parallel by April 22, and this time there was no crossing into the north again. Beard became a major again and they stayed put along the line ... and awaited developments. Truce negotiations opened at Kaesong, North Korea, on July 10, 1951, but it was another two years before an agreement was signed at Panmunjom.

Long before that, however, Gibbs extricated Beard from Korea and in the comparative safety of Hong Kong confirmed his promotion to major; but best of all, late in November, he arranged a month-long home leave for Beard. "I'll look for you at the Apple Camp early in the new year, Robert. So, Happy Christmas," Gibbs said cheerily.

☐   *"Korea sounds awful, and such a waste of life," said Ruth, giving a shiver at the thought of Jarvis almost freezing to death. "I think, if you're all agreeable, that I should relate the next part of this story. It is very personal, lovely too, and I think I will be rather less embarrassed telling it, than listening to it. Anyway, only Jarvis and I know it all."*

Everyone readily agreed. "If you're sure, lovey," murmured Queenie, giving her a squeeze of encouragement.

Beard looked on, wondering. What was this personal thing? He couldn't understand his sudden feeling of excitement for her to continue.

Chapter Forty-two

Peartree Cottage, Mayhill, December 2, 1951

As usual, it was cold, wet and windy when Beard landed back in England, but he didn't mind a bit. He was home, and he was smiling as he squelched up Steep Road towards Peartree Cottage with the rain spitting off his waterproof cape like hailstones. He didn't have his key to hand, so hammered on the front door impatient to fall into Queenie's arms.

But it was Ruth who flung open the door to discover who was making such a din. And her first sight of him seemed to create a spark of alarm, perhaps a flash of pain, but these images were followed so instantly by expressions of joy that Beard was sure it must have been his imagination, influenced by a splash of rain.

For a full minute they simply stood staring at one another in utter astonishment, Ruth with a tea towel in her hand and her mouth agape, Beard still dripping on the doorstep and his eyes large with wonder. He had not expected – hoped to find her here.

"You!" exclaimed Ruth, still in a daze: again, a moment of alarm pain seemed to dim her eyes, but it passed as she stared at him transfixed.

"Me!" confirmed Beard, shaking the rain off his face.

"Jarvis," cried Ruth, recovered from her moment of panic, reaching out to pull him in out of the rain, "where on earth have you come from?"

"India, Korea, Japan, Hong Kong … take your pick," he replied lightly, shedding his cape and backpack and dropping a largish military holdall, and then standing erect before her in his best uniform.

They remained standing there in the hall, not speaking, simply devouring one another with their eyes, and still marvelling at what they saw. Beard wasn't sure when he'd last seen Ruth, only that it seemed an age ago. So far as he was concerned, she had scarcely changed, except that she was now a woman, and no longer a girl. What was she now? Twenty-three? Her face was the same, only it looked more defined: fuller and smoother, perhaps pinker. It was the same face, simply more grown-up and, to him, more beautiful. And yet, for an instant, she had looked frightened to see him. It had passed now, but it had worried him. Her pansy-brown eyes looked brighter, and her hair looked different – a lighter shade of brown, and hanging in waves down to her shoulders. He smiled at the memory of her braids. He didn't really notice what she was wearing beyond the fact that it was something brightly colourful.

Ruth remembered exactly when she'd last seen Beard. It was when he'd recovered her engagement ring from the debris of The Dials and set her mother up in The Pears, and that was way back in the war. Ever since then they had agonizingly missed each other as he'd chased one war after the other round the world, and she herself had been visiting abroad. But, she had followed his career as best she could, mainly from Queenie, for he rarely answered any of her loving letters – the beast! His last one, she'd remember for ever. It had told her of his marriage, and though he'd said it was a matter of honour, it had hurt her like nothing before. Of course, she'd heard that it had been annulled almost straight away, but the heartache had lingered. He looked much the same as ever. There seemed to be more of him, but he still had that lean, hard look of a man who lived with danger, and thrived on it. But his dark eyes were still keen and bright and when he smiled, as he was doing now, they were beautiful – and, dare she say it? – had a come-to-bed appeal. Her heart gave a little leap, and she swallowed hard. She saw that the bullet scar above his eye had almost faded away. As ever, he looked gorgeous in uniform. He seemed to have collected more medals, but they didn't greatly interest her. She was only concerned for his safety.

"I seem to have forgotten your birthday, again," Beard said suddenly, having had his fill of feasting his eyes on her for the moment.

Ruth gave a little laugh which was as music to his ears. "Well, you've managed to arrive just in time for yours, Jarvis," she said joyfully enough, though that cloud was back to momentarily darken her eyes. And what was that frown for? Beard wondered if perhaps he was missing something.

At this moment, a cry came from the kitchen. "Who've you got there, Ruthie?" and with the question scarcely out of her mouth, Queenie discovered the pair of them standing in the hall, and Beard lost any opportunity of asking intimate questions of Ruth; indeed, the pair had not even had the chance to touch, let alone kiss, and Beard so wanted to smother Ruth in kisses and hold her tight. But his chance was gone for the moment. Queenie gave a shrill cry of delirium and flung herself at Beard, pulling his head down to kiss those parts she couldn't reach, and shooting out breathless brief questions in between which, of course, he was given no opportunity to answer. Finally, exhausted, she dragged him into the sitting room where they all, Ruth included, collapsed on to the sofa, with Beard trapped in the middle, though he was permitted to stand long enough to exchange handshakes and hugs with John Fennell, who had been quietly sitting there reading his paper, waiting for the ladies to complete their energetic and voluble welcoming.

"Are you here for Christmas, Jarvis?" gasped Queenie.

"Yes, and possibly New Year, too," answered Beard.

After the Hurrahs, Beard had to tell them all his adventures since they'd last seen him, and he told them as much as he felt he was permitted, making it sound like a holiday tour. For the most part he concentrated on India, which he had so enjoyed, and skimmed over the

Korea War by simply saying it was perishing cold, minus 32, and made them laugh about the "igloos" they'd had to sleep in, but caused a few frowns when he told of being bathed and massaged by geisha girls in Tokyo. "Disgraceful hussies!" cried Queenie, but she was laughing as she spoke. In her next breath, she told Beard he must be starving and sent both him and John Fennell off to the Fallen Oak across the way in Stonecross, with a warning not to drink too much and to be back on the dot – without mentioning the actual time in her excitement, while she and Ruth prepared a feast befitting the return of a hero from the wars. "But first," she told him, "take yer bags 'n' stuff up to yer room or yer won't be able to get aht of the 'ouse."

Safely ensconced with their pints in the snuggery at The Oak, Mr Fennell revealed a secret that Beard would have been desperately keen to have asked Ruth, but might have thought too indelicate, or perhaps impertinently intrusive, to do so. He explained that he had put it all in a letter he'd written to Beard, but had then decided it might be interpreted as being interfering, and he'd destroyed it. However, now, with Beard here, sitting beside him, he wasn't so sure. Anyway, he felt he had to say something on the matter.

"The top and the bottom of it all, Jarvis, is that although Ruth is continuing to work for a law firm in New York, when she came back from America she came home alone," he declared, like a barrister in court, only much softer. "She told us that she had broken with her Philip and returned his ring." Mr Fennell, continuing in a gentler voice, added that she'd apparently told Mr Goodwood that she didn't think it would ever fit properly.

Beard's heart seemed to leap from his breast at these words. He could hardly bear the pain, it was so wonderful: exquisite and agonizing.

But there was more. Much more. Mr Fennell was not a lawyer for nothing. Once given the floor, so to speak, he orated for all he was worth, even though he introduced his words with the prelude that perhaps he had no right speak, and perhaps his words were better left unsaid. He hurried on before Beard could either agree or disagree.

"I believe, even though she never speaks of you, Jarvis, that you are very frequently in Ruth's thoughts these days. I suspect that you have never been out of her heart," Mr Fennell declared, and those few words scorched through Beard's own pounding heart, which somehow seemed to have returned to his body. "She burst into such a bout of weeping when we told her of your divorce, that we became quite alarmed. It seemed she would never stop, but of course, she did, after a while," said Mr Fennell, very seriously. "And a few days later, she was wearing a coral necklace you'd given her as a child and which Queenie said she hadn't worn for ages.

"Jarvis, dear boy, I do believe that if you were to speak with her about the true feelings of your own heart, Ruth, far from being upset, would be extremely happy. One of you has to open a door, and I believe it's up to you, Jarvis."

Beard nodded, already formulating words to win Ruth's heart again. His own kept repeating that *what he thought he'd lost for ever, might still be his.* But, what was that John Fennell was saying?

"You have no time to waste, Jarvis," the other said evenly, "Ruth is returning to America on Tuesday afternoon, so there's only today and tomorrow for you to act."

"Christ!" ejaculated Beard, "Not again." He was thinking of another month's leave being wasted, with her flying away the moment he was finally here. He'd had a momentary dream of them having a whole month together in which to plan their lives.

"And there's another thing you should know, Jarvis; she may have another suitor," Mr Fennell revealed tonelessly. "Ruth has mentioned, in a casual sort of way, but often enough, a man she calls simply O K. I presume this is some sort of nickname and that he has a proper name, but you know how anomalous Americans can be about such things." He let the name sink in, then resumed, "He's a very wealthy lawyer, and Ruth has said they are very close friends. They are always together in New York. She has hinted about talk of marriage, and she wears his ring – occasionally."

"But she has *my* ring," protested Beard, already hating this new rival.

"And you've been married, and divorced, since giving it to her, Jarvis," Mr Fennell said calmly, "and, your work keeps you away for years on end, and it's unfortunate that your leaves have rarely coincided with Ruth being at home. If you were only able to maintain contact by writing, Jarvis." Mr Fennell concluded by spreading his hands in an empty gesture.

Well, it was simply impossible, thought Beard. He had all the time in the world – a whole month, in which to win, wed and love Ruth, only she wouldn't be here, would she? She'd be over in America giving this new bloke a free field. It simply wasn't fair. Every time he came home, she was missing – or about to be. There was only tomorrow, and then she'd be gone again. What could he hope to achieve in one day? Well, he'd simply have to make time, find a moment to remind her that he'd loved her all his life and that he wanted to marry her. He'd remind her she already had his ring, and now he wanted to give her another : a gold ring. They belonged together. But, she was flying away to be with this new man in her life. Mr OK! What a ridiculous name! The decision had to be hers. They simply must talk before it was too late. If she flew away without them having some sort of understanding, he felt he'd lose her for ever. He'd never have another chance. The fervour of his feelings as these urgent, passionate thoughts raced though him, made it difficult for him to breathe, he became so breathless. When he'd calmed down a bit, he resolved to speak such words to Ruth that, for all his sins, she would forgive him – and, perhaps, even learn to love him again, though in his heart he believed she'd never stopped loving him, not really. All he needed was to have her alone to convince her.

But there was no time: no opportunity. Queenie, unwittingly perhaps, monopolised virtually his whole time; or made a third in all his doings; or had Ruth helping her in the kitchen ; and when they were all free, they all sat together, talking together, and watching the ceaseless rain streaming down the windows. It was a terrible year for rain, they opined. Beard kept glancing at Ruth, and occasionally their eyes would meet and hover together, and it was like being endlessly kissed, or making love. But these moments of ecstasy were rare and brief, almost the blink of any eye, and the talking went on.

Monday passed, and it was all over. There had been no opportunity for Beard to press his love. Ruth had packed and sorted her travel documents. She had to leave early in the morning, Mr Fennell would be driving her to the airport, so they all went to bed early, giving final kisses to each other on the landing as they disappeared into their respective bedrooms; Ruth first, then John and Queenie, and Beard last.

Beard knew he would never sleep. He lay on his back, his head full of unhappy thoughts, and listened to the sounds of the house creaking as it settled down for the night. It might sleep, but he wouldn't. Once the house was still, he listened to the sounds outside. The rain had stopped: it, too, was sleeping. Nearby, a cat gave a shriek, prompting a dog to bark, and up near the copse came the deeper bark of a fox. All the animals were awake, keeping him company. The hours passed : at least, they seemed like hours : perhaps it was only one.

Suddenly, there was a new sound – inside the house. Beard's ears pricked up like one of his friends outside. He was wide awake and fully alert. He identified the sound at once. It was the sound of a door opening; he knew that by the distinctive squeak. Whose door? He knew that, too. It was hers. He had stopped breathing, the better to listen. He heard her first footstep, and continued counting them. They paused for some seconds outside Queenie's room, and then proceeded towards his. Beard took a deep gulp of air, and listened with even greater intensity. The footsteps halted at his door, remained still for a moment, and then he heard his door open and the rustle of her clothing as she entered his room and closed the door again with almost no sound. The swish of her clothing drowned the sound of her feet as she crossed the room, and then she was at his bedside.

"Are you awake, Jarvis?" Ruth whispered.

"Of course," he whispered back, and now he was breathing fast trying to keep pace with the pounding of his heart, and he was sweating, and there was a stirring in his loins.

"May I come in with you, darling?" she asked, her lips almost at his ear.

Jarvis tried to say "Of course" again, but the words stayed in his mouth, so for answer he pulled back the bedclothes to accommodate her, hoping she could see. Plainly she could see enough, for he heard her shuck off what he assumed was a dressing gown, followed by a different rustling, shimmering sound as something flimsy fell to the floor, and then she was sliding into his bed as naked as on her natal day. She had his shorts off almost as quickly as she'd shed her clothing, and at once their arms and legs entwined, and their mouths merged and their tongues were in communion in feverish darts.

Beard felt such an urgent need to enter her there and then and let loose the juices that were like an inferno bursting to erupt, but somehow he delayed, pleasuring himself exploring every inch of her body with his lips, savouring especially the firm mounds of her breasts and the nipples which were standing rigidly to attention as though waiting for his lips. It was an invitation to which he eagerly responded. But then he could wait no longer. His hands were stroking the insides of her thighs, which she kept parting wider, and then he was inside her. And the volcano erupted, and went on and on with every thrust. She moaned deliriously with every movement, pulling him further into her as her legs circled his sweaty body. And it was the same each time they made love. He did not know how many times it happened, he seemed to have endless energy, but sometime later, sated by their efforts, they lay peacefully in each other's arms, whispering the words of love that each had longed to say for so long, and that was almost as wonderful as their love-making had been. Almost.

In the end, they fell asleep, their hot, sticky bodies pressed hard against each other. Beard had anticipated dreams of heavenly magnitude, but he had none; he didn't need any, really; hadn't he visited heaven itself that night? Besides, wasn't she here beside him?

He woke suddenly to find Ruth already up and wearing her nightdress and dressing gown. She sat on the bed and bent over him as he opened his eyes. She smiled and kissed his lips gently. Then, she placed a finger on her lips to silence him, and said,

"I have to get back to my room now, Jarvis. Thank you for the loveliest night of my life, darling. You'll be in my soul for ever. Don't think badly of me."

"Never!" cried Beard, startled at the suggestion that he might; he was now wide awake. How could he ever think badly of her, especially now that they had mutually demonstrated their love so sublimely.

"Love me, always, darling," Ruth whispered, stroking his face with the back of her fingers, ever so softly, like a feather's touch.

"Always," he echoed, his hands reaching upwards to pull her head down. The smell of her perfume, which he hadn't noticed before, seemed to draw him like a magnet. He was stirring beneath the blankets: he wanted her again; he needed her.

She seemed to sense his desire; her eyes, had he been able to see them, showed that she shared the same need. But Ruth forced herself to be strong; she took a long, deep breath to steady herself and, feeling nearly in control of herself, murmured, with a catch in her voice, "I wanted you to know, darling, that I love you more than anybody in the world," and added in a softer whisper, "and always will, come what may."

She leaned forward and gently kissed his mouth, the tips of their tongues touched briefly, and then she was gone. Beard counted her steps as she returned silently to her own room. Fifteen.

He looked at his bedside clock: it said 4.30. He knew he wouldn't sleep. But he did, and he slept late. And when he entered the kitchen only Queenie was there. Ruth was gone: gone to be with this OK chap; and he hadn't even thought to ask about him and her. Well, he'd been more pleasurably engrossed, hadn't he?

"You've missed saying Goodbye to Ruth. She's gone, lovey," said Queenie, and he could tell from her eyes and the tone of her voice that she knew his secret, and guessed that, like him, she had listened to the patter of feet on the landing during the night.

□ *Ruth gave a sigh as she finished her story, but it was a sigh of pure pleasure, for she sat there with her eyes and the happiest smile imaginable suffusing her entire face. "That was the most beautiful night of my entire life," she murmured dreamily. And then she added, "And if you don't hurry up and wake up, Jarvis, it'll have to last me my whole life."*

The others smiled, also happily, and then Gibbs took over the story-telling.

Chapter Forty-three

Johor, Malaya, February, 1952

Christmas and New Year's Day at home had been marvellous, but on January 2, Beard reported at the Apple Tree Camp at Chelmsford, and about a month later was ordered to proceed to India. He spent nearly four months in Pune, which he found thoroughly delightful, but in late February, 1952, Gibbs took him away from this paradise, sending him a signal to present himself at the Malayan Scout base at Johor at his earliest convenience, which he interpreted as meaning without delay.

Gibbs intercepted him in Singapore where, in the course of a sumptuous dinner and much wine, Beard was encouraged to eat and drink well as it was likely to be his last decent meal in a very long while. This in no way diminished Beard's appetite and he continued to eat and quaff his thirst as he listened to Gibb's brief but colourful history of the British presence there, from the days of the East India Company, that became the Straits Settlements, until it was declared a British Crown Colony, though like many British possessions since the war both Singapore and mainland Malaya wanted complete independence. "And they'll achieve it pretty soon now, I should think," concluded Gibbs.

It wasn't until they'd retired to a quiet verandah area outside, where palms rustled in a light breeze that also wafted floral scents from nearby gardens over them, for their coffees, that Gibbs told Beard what he was doing in Malaya. It was really an extension of his history of the country.

The Communists, largely Chinese immigrant workers for the flourishing rubber and tin industries, had existed in Malaya – still affectionately regarded in those days as the Straits Settlements – since the early 1930s. But their voices, while always complaining, were low; they had no muscle. This they acquired, courtesy of the British who were too intent on saving their own necks to think of the future, when the Japanese invaded Malaya in 1941 – and conquered the entire peninsula in barely three months. The British armed the Communists to fight against the Japanese in the jungles: they were then called guerrillas; at the end of the war, these guerrillas not only kept and hid their British arms, but acquired a formidable proportion of the vast Japanese arsenal surrendered by General Itagaki, and they hid these too, ready for use in their fight for a voice in the coming independence talks: they then became known as terrorists – the CTs.

Gibbs paused to signal for more coffee, and to make sure Beard was still awake and listening, and then continued to explain the state of play in Malaya. Encouraged by the success of their brothers in the new Communist China, and still further emboldened by the humiliating departure of the British from India and Burma, and the belief that the once mighty *Tuan* was a spent force in Malaya, where a new Federation was already ruling, the terrorists were ready to be bold themselves. They dug up their hidden caches of weapons and launched their offensive of murder and sabotage between April and June 1948. At first, the victims were prominent natives employed on the rubber plantations, with public executions and lengthy declamations to horrified spectators on the justice of their war against imperialism; on June 16, the first European was murdered: the Malayan Emergency was declared on the same day. A succession of Army forces were trained to take the war to the terrorists, but the CTs simply melted back into the jungles after their attacks – and ambushed any pursuer at their leisure; the jungles really were a terrorists' paradise. The Malayan Scouts (SAS) aimed to change that.

And this was where Beard came in. He was to join these Scouts in their jungle forays, rigorously question any prisoners taken, especially the leaders, and most particularly he was to pursue the most prominent of the terrorists, known as Ah-Soh, or that's what it sounded like. "The soldiers call him Arse-Hole," growled Gibbs.

Beard grinned, and hoped he'd never meet the fellow.

"But as I say, your primary task, Robert, will be Intelligence gathering and reporting," continued Gibbs, drying his moustache which had dipped into his coffee, "though you will obviously act as the situation dictates. Accurate intelligence is what you're there for to provide – leave the fighting and stuff to the soldiers; they're mostly SAS, so you'll be in good hands, and you've done your share. We need to know who the CTs are, where they are, how many they are and what they're planning. Their leaders need to be eliminated." He paused to make sure he had Beard's attention. "Ah-Soh is their top man so far as we know. If he's found and captured and won't talk, kill him. He's behind so many of the murders and kidnaps and rapes. Make sure he's dead."

The general's words were blunt, cold and firm. Beard nodded his head, and again hoped their paths never crossed, though if he did, he knew he would have no qualms about killing the man, prisoner or otherwise.

If Beard had thought his wartime training would be sufficient to excuse any jungle training course, his expectations were quickly disillusioned. His arrival at Johor was followed by a two-month stint at the Kota Tinggi jungle warfare school, which he felt far exceeded anything in the manual pertaining to any observer. But, as he had done throughout his career, Beard excelled in the training; he proved himself relentlessly efficient, and his talent for leading men and adapting to every situation the jungle tormented him with, made him a natural for any eventuality that might arise.

At the end of the training, Beard was posted to Ipoh where further acclimatisation continued and he took a crash course in Malay. During this period he was told to select four men to act as his team and, running his finger down the list of names available, he found two men whom he knew very well: Sgt Jack Piper and Trooper Tony Blossom. He selected both at once and, since he needed an officer, picked out a Lt Edwin Tyson for no better reason than that he was born in Battersea. Tyson, of the Norfolk Regiment, had been in Malaya for a couple of years and considered himself very much an authority on things; at least he would be able to advise Beard on where and what to drink. Beard also selected two specialists, Cpl Ian Jones as his R/T man and Trooper Karl Blake, an accredited marksman.

Blossom was marched before Beard under close arrest accused of being involved in an affray. Beard, eyeing his one-time corporal, only just managed to hide his smile. "Affray?" he frowned at the seriousness of the word, and looked towards the sergeant-major for an explanation. It seemed that Trooper Blossom had created something of a disturbance in a bar. "He threw another soldier through a window and when two Malay policemen tried to arrest him, he knocked them both down, and then proceeded to hit out at everyone within reach," declared the sergeant-major sonorously, adding with extra emphasis, "When our own MPs arrived, there were seven men on the ground, sir, and the accused Blossom was making immoral advances to a native girl."

"So it was really just a fight, a punch-up – hardly an affray," commented Beard.

"If you say so, sir," replied the sergeant-major with stony correctness.

"These Malayan policemen, have they lodged any complaint ?"

"No, sir, they're content for Blossom to be dealt with by you."

"And what's all this about immoral advances?"

"Blossom had his hand inside her blouse – he was playing with her tits, sir."

"Has she complained?" asked Beard blandly.

"No, sir."

I should think not, thought Beard; probably annoyed that Blossom's advances had been brought to a premature end! Aloud, as he knew he was expected to, he gave a stern lecture to Blossom and warned him regarding his future conduct – and then dismissed the charges. He could sense the sergeant-major's outrage, but he ignored the silence that greeted his decision and ordered the room cleared – except for the prisoner, who remained at attention. He looked very much as he had when Beard had first met him: fair hair a little lighter and thinner, perhaps, but the same slight, yet immensely strong build, and even his face had the same trampled-over appearance – being heavily bruised, but still cheeky.

"So what happened to your stripes, Blossom?" Beard asked when they were alone, motioning the other to a chair. "The last time we served together was in Burma. You were a corporal then – and a bloody good one."

"I've been in a few scrapes, sir. Fights mostly. Been busted twice – and done a spell in the brig. I put my name forward for this lot in Hong Kong. I was with the RAs there."

"Well, we were a good team once, Blossom, and I'm sure we will be again," said Beard, returning the other's grin. "We'll have to see if we can't get your stripes back."

"Blimey! that'd be a turn-up. The sarn't-major'd shit hisself!"

Blossom did get his stripes back, but not immediately. It was not until he and Beard had returned from their first big jungle operation, lasting more than three months. He didn't really have much chance of getting into trouble, Beard saw to that – and, anyway, he was too good a soldier to put a foot wrong in the field. Although they had been part of a large force that included Gurkha Rifles, Royal Marine Commandos, African and Fijian troops, plus Malayan police, Dyak trackers imported from Borneo and two SAS squadrons, Beard's own little team operated on their own, but very sensibly. Beard's force was attached to a smaller unit that had been parachuted far ahead of the main attacking force to cut off the CTs' escape routes. The main force had advanced into the jungle from a line of fortified villages which had been established to isolate the CTs, forcing them ever deeper into the jungles and denying them access to food supplies.

Major Gordon Temple, the commander of the force which included Beard and his team of four, quickly dispersed the men into four roughly equal groups, and Beard moved off with one knowing that it would take them at least four days to reach their allotted position even though it was little more than 30 miles away. There was no hurrying in the jungle: a mile an hour was regarded as quite an achievement; any faster and they might miss vital clues to the presence, recent or otherwise, of the enemy, and that would make the difference between living and dying for in a shoot-out there would only be a split second between killing and being killed: the first man to shoot was the winner, it was as simple as that. So, progress was painstakingly slow and cautious, the men constantly pausing to listen for any extraneous sound and examining every inch of ground around them.

In the jungle trees soared up more than 200 ft, bursting into a mushroom of leaves at the top; their branches interlaced and effectively blotted out the sunlight, and what with smaller trees below stretching blindly for whatever light penetrated and thus producing a thick canopy of their own, there was perpetual gloom below: visibility was rarely more than 20 yards on the jungle floor. This and the dense undergrowth combined to make progress slow in any case. And then there was the animal life. In spite of the high temperatures and severe humidity which meant that they were never dry, the men had to keep their arms and heads covered for protection against bites, scratches and stings – and there were all manner of creatures determined to make their presence felt. There were scorpions and poisonous spiders, leeches and centipedes, hornets and armies of mosquitoes and myriad insects intent on making their lives a misery. The larger animals, and they included the very dangerous seladang (a type of water buffalo), an occasional elephant and even a tiger, tended to take evasive action when they met – but they couldn't rely on this. The worst, so far as the men were concerned, were the snakes, and in parts, particularly in the swamps, they seemed to be everywhere ("knee-deep," as Blossom was moved to complain on occasion); and the worst of all these were the venomous black and white, sometimes black and yellow, kraits which, while they might scuttle away, were just as likely to rear up at a soldier.

Time had no meaning in the jungle. It was the jungle that dictated everything, especially progress. It was ten days before Beard's men gained their first intelligence that there *might* be some CTs heading their way. The news was brought by the Iban tracker who had been assigned to their group; he was a small, lithe man who wore a sort of skirt and had an unpronounceable name, but was called Paw-Paw for convenience – it bore some slight resemblance to part of his real name, and he seemed to like it.

Paw-Paw emerged soundlessly from the jungle a few yards from Beard, a rifle in one hand, his blowpipe in the other, and said there were seven terrorists approaching. Beard, who had acquired sufficient Malay to hold a conversation of sorts, understood that there had been eight. Paw-Paw patted his blowpipe and gripped his blood-soaked parang significantly, and flashed a triumphant grin. Beard guessed the man had despatched No 8 with a poisoned dart and most likely cut off his head for a trophy – he wondered where it was, and knew he didn't want to know, but was concerned as to what their evening meal might be. He was glad the Dyak didn't do their cooking, though they did sometimes provide its ingredients.

They settled down to wait for the terrorists; it was a long wait, and more than once Beard thought either Paw-Paw had made a mistake, which was most unlikely, or that the terrorists had taken another route, in which case they would probably never find them. But, after two days scouts positioned deep in the forest returned to report hearing the sound of approaching men, and an hour or so later the first of the CTs showed himself: at least, he showed a tiny portion of his face, very briefly. Beard would never have seen him had it not been for a movement in a clump of towering bamboo: two of the canes were pulled apart and the face stared out for a few seconds before disappearing. So, they'd finally arrived!

Well, he wanted at least one of them alive so that he could question him, Beard thought, remembering the real purpose for his presence. But he was not too optimistic.

During the long wait, the soldiers had prepared the ambush, remaining constantly vigilant, scarcely moving, always listening; no fires were permitted, so they ate their emergency rations cold. The tireless Paw-Paw continuously disappeared into the seemingly impenetrable forest, returning after several hours to repeat the word "seven" and, pointing vaguely behind him, sometimes adding "near" or "come soon." He was not a great talker, but his mouth seemed to be always chewing; nobody wanted to know what: they had their suspicions, and that was enough. Paw-Paw was missing now, and Beard grimly supposed he was somewhere behind the CTs with his blowpipe, probably picking out his choice of heads.

Beard was positioned, and he hoped adequately hidden, almost in the middle of some evil-smelling, thickly-leafed bush and almost completely surrounded by a forest of grass that stretched 12 ft high. He felt reasonably safe, although he didn't doubt that the grass was rich with snakes and such like. Well, he couldn't expect everything, and he did have a good view of what passed for a junction in the jungle track. It was about 15 yards in front of him. His team was spread on either side of him, and they were protected by other soldiers. They were as ready as they could be: all that was needed was the enemy.

After that first glimpse, an hour passed before anything happened. Apart from the eternal rain that dripped through the branches high above, there was not a sound. Even the animals had stopped their eternal chattering, which was probably suspicious in itself. Wonder if they have siestas, Beard wondered, but, watching an army of huge black ants on the march just in front of him, he decided not. Beard was wearing an olive-green sweatband around his head to keep the sweat out of his eyes, and another around his neck; he supposed they served their purpose, but he had to keep wringing them out and, anyway, they seemed to rot very quickly. He cursed the beard that he had once thought would never come; it was thick enough now and permanently wet, and was home to a thousand insects whose combined itchings made his life a hell. A faint sound tore his eyes away from the marching ants, and his hands tightened on the pump-action shotgun, loaded with 12-bore SG shot, that he favoured these days.

Paw-Paw, it seemed, couldn't count! At any rate, numbers did not have the same meaning for him as Beard; seven was the limit of his understanding of numeracy – he knew there were other numbers above this, but they meant nothing to him; for him, a lot of men, whether they numbered seven, seventy or seven hundred, meant seven. It was as simple as that. Which was why the expected seven CTs numbered more than thirty!

They emerged slowly, cautiously, suspiciously, examining the trees above them, the jungle all around and the ground at their feet. Beard automatically counted them off as they appeared in a long crocodile. It was very obvious that there were more than seven, and when he'd counted up to twenty, he began to be concerned. He knew his group would hold their fire as long as possible, waiting until as many as possible presented a target, but they could wait only so long without risking discovery. That moment came as one of the CTs stopped in his tracks and swung his Soviet submachine-gun, a PPSh-41, in the direction of Sgt Piper and was shot dead in the same instant by a single shot from the latter's M1 Carbine.

Before the terrorist's body had reached the ground, Beard and the others opened up on the following CTs and for close on a minute the sounds of gunfire and the screams as men were hit filled the air. In the enclosed space beneath the canopy of trees the sounds seemed excessively loud, and so did the silence that followed. It took a while for the cordite to disperse in the normal steamy atmosphere of the jungle, and the soldiers remained hidden and still until visibility was adequately restored.

On the ground lay sixteen bodies, not all dead; some attempted to crawl way, others cried out in pain, a few twitched convulsively. Beard had momentary thoughts that someone among them might be encouraged to speak, but the soldiers had no such sentiments. They had been on too many of these patrols. The rule had always been: no prisoners – especially wounded ones. Beard listened as single shots despatched these wounded men and then the silence was complete: there was no more moaning, no more movement; and no opportunity of gaining any information from them. The soldiers remained motionless, and alert; they waited, silently and patiently, to see if any more of the terrorists would break cover. Several CTs had been seen to dart back into the cover of the jungle when the shooting began. Somewhere farther back in the jungle a terrible human scream shattered the utter quiet, and was followed almost immediately by another similar cry. Beard assumed that Paw-Paw was busy collecting "snacks," and was thankful the Dyak was on his side, not that he'd risk turning his back on the fellow for long!

After what seemed an eternity but was probably no more than ten minutes, there was the faintest of rustles in the towering grass beside him. Beard, motionless though he was, froze still further. A snake! That was his instinctive thought. He shivered even as the sweat raced down his body. The last thing he wanted just now (or any other time) was to have a bloody snake crawling over him. There was another rustle, more prolonged this time. With infinite slowness, Beard inched his head towards the sound, dreading to see a forked tongue spitting out at him. There wasn't, but he gripped the parang at his side as the sound was repeated. He held his breath, his eyes and ears straining for sight or sound of whatever the danger was. Almost imperceptibly two blades of bamboo grass parted, and a pair of black eyes met his. They were a man's eyes, even if they were as immobile and staring as a snake's, and they were set in a darkly yellow face that was topped by a tangle of black hair. Before they had time even to blink, Beard's arm swung savagely and the blade of the parang struck cleanly across the man's eyes and went on to take off the top of his head. Dead the man undoubtedly was on the instant, but his body seemed to take an awful time settling down.

The momentum caused by this decapitating swipe probably saved Beard's life. As the top of the man's skull disappeared into the grass, another terrorist who had been just behind him fired. The bullet smacked into the ground where Beard had been lying a fraction of a second previously: it struck less than two inches from where he lay now. Beard, whose parang was firmly embedded in the dead man's head, already had his hands on his shotgun and as he rolled to one side he fired at the second man who had unwisely adopted a crouching position and so presented more of a target. Actually, Beard had barely seen him and had fired largely by instinct at where he supposed the man to be. There were five rounds in the internal magazine and another in the chamber, and Beard managed to fire off two shots without the terrorist firing a second round. At a distance of less than five metres, the effect of Beard's two shots was devastating. The man's body was torn to pieces. Beard pumped another three rounds blindly into the grass on the off-chance that there were more of them behind, and had the satisfaction of hearing a brief scream. It was a brief satisfaction, however, for there was a fresh sound behind him, and he rolled over pushing fresh rounds into the magazine as his eyes searched the opposite clump of grass for a sign of the new threat. He saw nothing, but heard a choking, retching sound followed by a brief sort of threshing noise, like someone desperately trying to live. It didn't last long, and almost immediately there followed a familiar whistle.

Beard let loose his long-held breath and relaxed his grip on the shotgun, as Blossom whispered, "It's me, Boss. I got this one. You OK?" Blossom, continuing to wipe the blade of his knife on his victim's shirt and to press the man's face into the ground, looked up and gave a wicked grin as Beard's head came into view a few feet away. Beard saw that the dead man, whose body still gave convulsive jerks, had had his throat cut. There was blood sprayed all round him and Blossom, having finished cleaning his knife, was now wiping his blood-soaked hand on the man's shirt.

"Thanks, Blossom, I didn't know about this one," said Beard with a calmness that was more forced than casual. "I got three more on the other side – but only just!" Blossom nodded and finally took his hand away from the back of the corpse's head, but only so that he could more easily rifle the man's pockets and strip the body of its weapons and other equipment; this included a soggy bag of cooked rice which he commenced eating by the handful; he offered to share the meal, but Beard declined – with thanks. "I see you got most of their brains spattered over you, sir," continued Blossom in as matter-of-fact voice as he could manage with a full mouth. Beard, who hadn't noticed, gave a grimace of distaste and began flicking the bits of human detritus off himself, but before he'd finished he was grinning back at Blossom, who declared: "We done well, sir."

Yes, they had done well. A high body count, but no survivors to question. In the heat of such battles, it was kill or be killed. It always was. And you didn't take chances when it was over. A wounded enemy was still dangerous: probably more so : he knew he was going to die, and might have pulled the pin out of a grenade as he lay on it. Many a soldier had been killed when he turned the "still form" over.

There would be other successes, but never on such a scale. The final tally that day was at least twenty-seven, which meant that several had managed to escape – and they disappeared so effectively even Paw-Paw couldn't pick up their trail. In addition to the sixteen killed in the main ambush and the extra six accounted for by Beard and Blossom, five others had been cut down trying to flee by Lt Francis and his party who appeared on the scene at exactly the right moment – and it was anybody's guess as to Paw-Paw's tally. Two further heads, or what was left of them, were found hanging by their hair from tree branches above the victims. It was pretty obvious that Paw-Paw ate a portion of his victims; he always gave the appearance of having just eaten – something. Beard wondered if he should put a stop to such goings on, but decided it was more than his life was worth: he wanted to keep his own head!

Beard's only concern was that the success of the ambush had not resulted in any men being taken alive whom he could question, though he did wonder, if the Geneva Convention rules were to be observed, if they would have been forthcoming. But then, these rules had a way of being misinterpreted, or ignored altogether ; it depended on the circumstances. So, Beard had to work hard to gain any intelligence. Mostly he relied on native villages for vague scraps of information.

It had been their first contact with the enemy. It was also to be their last during this particular operation. For the next two months they saw nothing more threatening than a seladang, which they gave a wide berth to, and a lot of snakes, which they also did their best to avoid. Paw-Paw, who looked as well-fed as ever despite his lack of "trophy fare," was often seen to chase after a snake and he was suspected of supplanting his preferred delicacy with one of them. At any rate, when the unit emerged from jungle and returned to civilisation after some four months, Beard found he had lost close to a stone, while Paw-Paw had actually gained weight!

Beard spent almost four years in Malaya, and if it hadn't been for the Suez affair in 1956, he might well have served a further four years there. As it was, operations such as his first very successful one in the jungle, were repeated with monotonous regularity, though never with the same degree of success. But, Beard did have the opportunity of questioning several captured CTs during that time; mostly they were wounded men, but they still gave very little worthwhile information to Beard, who bent those rules many a time. But they were an elusive lot in the jungle. In fact, he returned to base on one occasion without sighting a single CT, even though his unit pursued a particular band for close on three weeks – they always remained just beyond reach and, finally, disappeared altogether. However, the constant probing patrols through the jungle had the effect of keeping the CTs on the move and creating a feeling of insecurity among them,

The long leaves between operations – they seemed long, even if they weren't – were times of sheer bliss for Beard and his men: almost like waking up to find themselves back home. There were no words he could envisage to adequately describe the delirious joy of that first real bath after four months in the jungle: simply lying there in the warm, soapy, perfumed water that contained nothing more menacing than a huge ball of sponge or a yard of loofah; the pleasure of that first shave that rid him of both whiskers and animal life, and presented him with a rare view of a tanned, naked face – which he sometimes thought was quite handsome, and other times seemed to be unnaturally aged; the delicious feel of clean, fresh, cool linen on his body – after months of wearing the same filthy, damp uniform that was only taken off so that the leeches, or some other horror, could be scraped off; the absolute wonder of that first meal, eaten off real china plates set on dazzlingly white table linen – the fresh fruit, the green vegetables, the rarest of roast beef, the coldest of ice creams, the choicest of cheeses that simply melted in his mouth, and, of course, that succession of the coolest of beers; and finally, there was the exquisite, almost sensual, thrill of sliding between cool, soft, white sheets and being able to sleep with both eyes shut – and if it took him a few days to become accustomed to the softness of the bed, he never complained!

That first leave had been marred by a letter from home awaiting him. It was from John Fennell and contained the news that Beard had dreaded, but half expected. Mr Fennell kept it very short and to the point. *Ruth had married her Mr OK.* She was now Mrs Harold O. K. Marchant, having married within a couple of months of returning to America, and gone honeymooning "somewhere in the Bahamas." There was a PS to the letter, which turned the screw for Beard, to the effect that Ruth was pregnant when she and her husband finally returned home.

God! they hadn't wasted any time, he thought, though he had no idea how long the honeymoon had lasted. His head was overwhelmed with memories of the night he and Ruth had finally made love at The Pears, and he felt sick at the thought of this OK chap enjoying the same joy. He trembled all over at the thought, and simply could not think of a life without her. He'd said it before, but life just wasn't fair. And now, she was having someone else's child. It was more than he could be expected to endure.

He did not reply to John, nor did he communicate with Ruth, to congratulate her on her marriage. He didn't trust himself. He could not properly explain this to himself; he made excuses, telling himself he didn't have the time, that he was too weary, that they'd understand back home. It was something he could put off till he thought the moment was right; and that moment never seemed to quite arrive, and so it was put off again and again ... and gradually became less urgent in his mind. Meantime, he had been on two more jungle tours, and emerged desperate for the delights of intervening leaves.

As soon as he felt sufficiently restored to the civilised way of life, and he was always surprised how speedily he adjusted, Beard became a regular tourist. He visited all the main towns and places of interest in Malaya, courtesy of the RAF at Kuala Lumpur; they were tickled when he told them he didn't mind jumping if there was no place to land! But he never had to go to such extremes. It was fitting that his first visit should be to the island of Penang, where Francis Light of the East India Company established the first British presence in the peninsula in 1786; subsequently he toured places like Singapore, where every bed he slept in boasted that Sir Thomas Stamford Raffles, another Company man who established a trading station there in 1819, had similarly been an occupant – which made Beard think, if it was true, he must have been a bone idle sod! And then there was Malacca from where, in 1826, the British East India Company united its various acquisitions into a colony called the Straits Settlements.

But it was back in Ipoh that Beard, playing in his only representative cricket match for England – he'd been happily drinking in a palatial hostelry when he'd been recruited for a Combined Services team against some local dignitary's eleven – scored 76 not out ... before a monsoon washed the stumps away and ended the proceedings. Beard always maintained that if it had not been for the rain, he'd have scored a century on his debut for England, but it must be said that the consensus had it that if he had not been outrageously pissed, he'd have probably been out for a duck!

On the very same day, Beard met Bluebell and his interest in cricket waned – other than to achieve his missed century in the number of times he made love to her. He never achieved this, either, but it wasn't for want of trying. Her name wasn't Bluebell, of course. She had one of those names that began with an A and then ran interminably right through the alphabet and back again: it was excruciating to pronounce, and so he settled on Bluebell – not because her eyes were blue, they were as black and mysterious as an ebony night, but because she was wearing a blue sari. It was her night for blue. She was an Indian, though there was something of the Chinese about her shining eyes, and her mother was, in fact, of Chinese descent.

Bluebell was petite, her skin more tawny than brown, and her face was small and round, and quite lovely. Her uncle was a dealer in gemstones, and when Beard mentioned, in a pause between making love to her, that she was his birthday present – it wasn't his birthday, of course: it was only just September and the year was 1953, and he was either nearly twenty-eight as Jarvis, or two years older as Beard – and the very next time he saw her she presented him with a beautiful blue sapphire, saying very solemnly that it was his birthstone. Beard was amazed and delighted, and didn't dare ask if she'd helped herself to it from her uncle's shop. She was obviously pleased to see his pleasure, and over the next year or so she found all sorts of excuses for giving him further stones until he had a collection that included amethysts, emeralds, rubies, opals, a diamond which, with a bit of imagination, looked to be shaped like a heart, and two very large pearls which she said he should give to his sister Ruth. He hadn't even noticed that he'd mentioned her, either as a lover or a sister, and now that he was reminded of her he felt embarrassed and guilty, but that didn't stop him from accepting the pearls – and thanking Bluebell in a way they both found equally beautiful, satisfying and thoroughly exhausting.

It was after his fourth jungle tour that Beard, freshly bathed and smelling human again, suddenly realised he hadn't seen Bluebell since his return to civilisation. She hadn't been in any of the usual places that they met – and she was normally the one who found him; he'd always joked that she had better intelligence than the Army. He had been thinking of breaking things off with her, not wanting to become too attached. The trouble was, he couldn't find her. She seemed to have vanished into thin air. He thought, very briefly, of calling at her uncle's shop, but decided it might prove embarrassing if the uncle pressed him about his relationship with his niece. He was aware that Orientals had strict views on such matters. In the end, he had enlisted the assistance of Blossom in the search, and it was Blossom who discovered her whereabouts.

She was in jail!

It transpired that Bluebell, far from being the niece of the gems dealer, was his employee. Her duties were largely concerned with keeping the records of purchases and sales, but she had been dipping into the stocks for some considerable time. Another sideline had been to extract whatever information she could from soldiers she met, mainly in bars, and passing it on to contacts in the Min Yuen, who were the CTs' contacts outside of the jungles and who provided them with food, money and information. She had been unmasked by an undercover member of the Army's Special Investigation Branch when she contacted a suspected Min Yuen member and passed on information, and a sizeable bag of gemstones. It seemed she had been under observation for several weeks. Unlike her associates, who were subsequently hanged, Bluebell had made a clean breast of her activities and was sentenced to eight years imprisonment in a military stockade.

Christ! A bloody spy! Beard could scarcely believe it: he didn't want to. He wondered if the SIB had had him under observation, and watched him perform! He grinned, and blushed, and hoped Gibbs never caught wind of his activities. He was sure he hadn't spilled any secrets – not to her, or anyone else, he was too well trained. But, suddenly his thoughts turned elsewhere, and his face brightened. If the SIB didn't know about his association with her, they wouldn't know about the gemstones she'd given him either, would they? Well, they very definitely weren't going to find out about them ; not them, nor anyone else. One thing was certain, however, he had to separate himself from them, get them away somewhere safe.

There was really only the one course of action open to him: he had to get them safely delivered in England ; and the only person he could think of sending them to was Mr Fennell, whom he trusted implicitly. He wrote to Mr Fennell, asking him to safeguard the enclosed package against his return – and to share the proceeds from the contents with the family if he didn't. He'd added a second note for Queenie assuring her that all was well and expressing a vague hope of coming home "one day" because he needed her to fatten him up again, and that meantime he was keeping his head well and truly down. He found a suitable postman for his package in a friend who was returning to England almost immediately; he promised to deliver the package personally at Pear Cottage.

Long before he might expect any response from John Fennell, Beard was sent off on another operation., at the beginning of which he took the opportunity to restore Blossom's stripes, which he did with a dire warning of what would happen should it ever be necessary to remove them again. Cpl Blossom beamed, almost impudently.

The operation, in Selangor on the Malacca Strait coast, covered a large part of the great Telok Anson swamp, which was only about 30 miles north-west of Kuala Lumpur but was as far removed from that centre of civilisation as it was possible to be. The CTs were known to be hiding in the swamps and emerging, with ever-increasing arrogance, or perhaps it was only desperation, for they were being severely squeezed by the Army, to steal food and carry out various acts of murder, kidnap or arson before disappearing back into the swamps. The difficulty continued to be to find them.

The swamp, which measured some 10 by 18 miles, was largely composed of iron-brown water, which varied in depth from shin to neck high. Sometimes it was necessary to fashion canoes of a sort to make progress, and at night the men slept in hammocks slung between the trees that soared out of the water. Tree roots and fallen trunks, with their sharp points, made progress through the water painfully slow, but they were not the only hazard: the waters were alive with snakes and other unpleasant creatures, and there were always the leeches. The leeches preyed on those parts of the body that were submerged: anything above the water-line was targeted by mosquitoes and a thousand other insects.

Visibility was rarely more than thirty yards, and the mists that rose like steam from a bath and swirled about above the waters and hovered overhead reduced it still further. It was a nightmare of a place to travel through, and sheer hell to live in – no wonder the terrorists had enjoyed its privacy undisturbed for so long. But it was not all water: in parts it was only sticky mud in which boots sank to a depth of several inches and could only be extracted slowly and with a loud squelching sound, which Beard was sure could be heard for miles around; sometimes the feet emerged minus the boots, and the men had to grope blindly to retrieve them.

Beard asked himself what on earth he and his team were expected to achieve tagging along with the soldiers on this mission. There was little, or no, chance of obtaining anything in the way of Intelligence here. But, of course, a soldier went where he was ordered, and Gibbs had intimated that it might be worth while. The swamps, which had their share and more of jungle, were surrounded by the jungle proper, and it was among these trees that Beard and the rest were parachuted from Beverleys. The noise of this machine undoubtedly gave the CTs adequate warning of intruders, which was why for three weeks they ploughed through the swamps without finding a trace of their quarry. The soldiers had been split into four teams, each approaching the centre of the swamp from a different angle, and each evening they would contact a HQ section to report progress and success. Well, there was never any success to report.

Then, at long last, as a prolonged spell of monsoonal rains threatened to drown them all, one of the teams reported finding a sign. It was only a piece of dislodged bark, but it was sufficient; it led to other finds and, eventually, a naked footprint – a very recent one.

Ten days later a figure was spotted and pursued, and killed. It turned out to be a woman. She was little more than four foot six, as scrawny as only a body that size could be, and she was armed with a knife, a hand-grenade and an extremely ancient Chinese pistol that was in serious need of repair though, as she did not appear to have any ammunition for it, neither she nor anybody else was in any real danger from it. Her only other possession was a small bag of rice with a lump of turtle meat – which the finders devoured. All four teams now converged on the area in which the woman had been shot, and after another week or so another figure, this time a man, was sighted – but he made good his escape, leaving behind not so much as a twisted leaf to help his trackers.

Beard had been given command of one of the four teams, and when he reported this latest setback to Gibbs's HQ, he was told that Ah-Soh, the CT leader he had been seeking for so long, had been reported in his area recently. It was not known exactly where he was but it seemed that Ah-Soh had been continuously raiding just beyond the swamp area even though it was now virtually ringed by troops and police. "It may be that he's looking to set himself up as a sort legendary hero figure with a sort of grandstand battle," said Gibbs drily, "but God knows where he'll pick for it. Take care, Robert."

A plume of smoke some three days later provided evidence that Ah-Soh was indeed able to move about almost at will, regardless of the forces pitted against him. Beard moved cautiously alongside other soldiers towards the black pall of smoke and, just beyond the outer fringes of the swamp, was met by a grim-faced Malay Police captain, who told them Ah-Soh had razed a Catholic missionary hospital and school to the ground and murdered everybody associated with it. "It's a terrible sight. I've never seen butchery on such a scale," the policeman said. "Women and tiny children – and they carried off the Mother Superior."

Beard frowned, and stared towards the burning complex which was still about four miles away. He'd been able to smell the burning for some while, and now there was that other smell, too; one that he hadn't smelt since approaching Belsen all those years ago: the smell of burning flesh – human flesh. "Why'd they take her?" he asked curiously. "Surely, she'd only slow them down – and I imagine the bastards'd be hell-bent on getting as far away from here as possible."

The captain, who identified himself as Jack McIntyre, originally from Oxshott in Surrey but for 25 years a policeman in Malaya, gave a weary shrug. "Just to torture her some more, I suppose. Perhaps they wanted some more fun with her, poor soul."

"Are sure it was Ah-Soh?" demanded Beard aggressively. It always made him angry when innocent bystanders, especially helpless people like nuns and small children, were slaughtered in this way.

"Oh yes. He makes no attempt to conceal his identity – almost enjoys boasting of his achievements," said McIntyre, wiping the sweat from his fat, round face with the back of a very hairy hand. "One of his victims wasn't quite dead when my men got here – even though she'd been repeatedly bayoneted through the belly. She was able to whisper his name before she died .. and to say that they'd taken Sister Kate with them."

"Sister Kate?" queried Beard, surprised that a nun should be known quite so familiarly. All the ones he'd known – admittedly a long time ago – had been so prim and proper over such things, but perhaps he was out of touch.

"The Mother Superior, Sister Catherine – but she was always called Kate," the other explained. "She's been out here longer than I have. A wonderful woman who did marvellous work throughout the country, nursing and teaching as well as converting. She's greatly loved and respected by all. Many think of her as a saint."

"She may well be one already if Ah-Soh's got hold of her," said Beard, hoping he didn't sound too callous.

McIntyre nodded. "Ah-Soh's left quite a trail back into the swamp, so you might be able to catch up with him."

"I gather we have him pretty well ringed already, he won't escape this time," said Beard with a quiet determination. He didn't doubt that Sister Kate had already been martyred. "We're resting here a while before going in after him. I'll take a look at his handiwork at the mission first."

There wasn't much left of the mission, just a collection of burned out shells of buildings, whose blackened walls leaned at grotesque angles waiting to collapse. Those buildings that had been built of timber or bamboo had already disappeared: they were no more than mounds of smouldering ashes. The police had already collected up the bodies that had been strewn all around; there were forty-seven of them, and they now lay in two rows, the adults separated in death from the smaller bodies of the children who had been their charges in life. There had been no time to cover the dead and the children's bodies looked pathetically tiny alongside those of the nuns and lay teachers. The savage wounds of all of them gaped sickeningly as Beard stared down. Nearly all of the corpses showed signs of horrific mutilation. In some instances limbs had been hacked off – a child's leg, a woman's arm. Efforts had been made to disfigure faces as much as possible; noses had been sliced off, mouths slit and cheeks skewered, apparently with burning sticks. Almost without exception the bodies were naked, and in several instances it was plain that the clothes had been burned off by the simple expedient of being thrown on top of a fire or into a blazing building. A policeman who was noting down details of the victims, said that all the women had been raped; no, he didn't know if this had been before or after they were murdered.

"Were there no survivors at all?" asked Beard, sickened by this appalling massacre of innocents, especially of the little babies.

"No, sir," said the officer, looking up from his notes and shaking his head with infinite sadness. "Only Sister Kate is unaccounted for – and she'd be better dead than in the hands of that butcher. Poor sweet lady. She deserves to be in that heaven of hers, if ever a soul did."

Beard's men, and the rest of the soldiers, pulled out at first light. During the night, he had been in contact with the three other teams none of which had any news of CTs in their vicinity, and he had reported the massacre to Gibbs. "Make sure the bastard doesn't slip through the net, Robert," came Gibb's bleak voice over the radio.

The trail was fairly easy to follow. The terrorists had been over-confident, or in too much of a hurry, to cover their withdrawal properly, or perhaps they were indifferent. Perhaps they were being lured into a trap. Ah-Soh's last stand. Whatever, it was four days before Paw-Paw waded back through the swamp to report hearing sounds ahead. He looked puzzled and when Beard asked what was troubling him, Paw-Paw said: "They got a woman with 'em, Boss. I heard her first. Heard her scream ... not loud, but long and drawn out. It was a very chilling sound. Later it became more a series of groans. I think she's hurt pretty bad, Boss."

Beard didn't doubt that and, like the policeman back at the mission, thought it would have been better for her had she been killed with the rest. Paw-Paw was able to give him a rough fix on the terrorists' position and this was passed to the other teams by radio. Beard told them no one was to be allowed to escape, but of course they knew that. The nun would doubtless present a difficulty. He didn't suppose there was any chance of rescuing her alive, but you never knew.

The following day, they approached to within sight of where Paw-Paw had heard the scream, and the next day they could detect a faint smell of cooking among the foul stenches of the swamp. They crept forward, inch by inch, gradually encircling what appeared to be the area of the camp, penetrating so close they were able to distinguish the body odours of the terrorists. Even as the lookouts were pin-pointed, Beard caught a soft moaning sound. It was a sound to chill the hearts of those who heard it: it was an inhuman sound, more that of a snared, wounded animal suffering some unbearable pain. It could have been made by almost any of God's creatures. He supposed it was the nun.

By nightfall, Beard's group had eliminated the outer guards and they moved in on the camp. There were several bashas visible and several figures moving silently about.

In a slight clearing, a little apart from the bashas, Sister Kate looked to have been crucified. She lay naked on the wet earth, her legs spread-eagled and fastened to stakes in the ground, her arms were stretched wide along a fallen tree and her hands had been pinned to the log with knives hammered through the palms, and her head – Beard winced at its sight – rested against this log. One eye had been gouged out and a cloud of flies was feasting on the blood that oozed from the dark hole. There did not seem to be an inch of her body that had not been abused; she had plainly been continuously and methodically whipped, there were ugly black weals everywhere; her breasts had been slashed and all but severed and there were other knife cuts and burns on her stomach.

Beard felt sick and angry as he stared at the tiny tortured body: a living corpse was how he saw it. Even as he watched, taking in the entire camp area, a man appeared and gave Sister Kate's emaciated body a savage kick to make sure she was still alive. He grinned as she gave an involuntary little shriek that was little more than a whimper, and kicked her again. As she made another piteous sound, the man knelt between her bruised and bleeding thighs, scattering a swarm of fat flies, and unbuttoned his fly. At this moment, as the man grabbed at her hips and moved his body closer to hers, Beard shot the man dead with a single bullet through the back of his head.

The shot made no sound for there was a silencer fitted to Beard's pistol, but the terrorist toppled forward on top of Sister Kate and it was her agonised shriek that gave the alarm. It wasn't really a battle, nor even much of a fire-fight: it was more like target practice. Very few shots were fired at the soldiers, and when the shooting stopped after a few minutes and silence returned, nineteen terrorists lay dead or dying, and three had the indignity of being captured relatively alive.   Ah-Soh was not among them. Beard quickly identified his body by the two scars on his forehead, and gave him kick to speed him on his way to hell. He then turned to Sgt Piper and told him to make sure the rest were properly dead, and to hang the three that had been captured if they were slow in being helpful; he then hurried over to where Sister Kate lay.

Blossom had already tossed the dead CT off her body and while he released her feet, Beard pulled the knives out of her hands. Her single blue eye stared up at him, but he didn't know if she could see him. The eye was swollen and blood and pus was leaking from it. Her lips, which were also torn and bleeding, seemed to be moving, and he wondered if she was trying to say something or merely instinctively praying. There was an ominous sound to her breathing and Beard now saw that the left side of her frail chest had caved in, probably as a result of a blow from a rifle butt, and he suspected all her ribs were smashed and most likely her lungs had been pierced. He covered her emaciated frame with a blanket, but even this kindly act only caused her fresh agonies. She gave another pathetic shriek, and her mouth trembled. Beard turned helplessly to Blossom, who said he believed her spine was broken. Beard nodded and told Blossom to leave them alone.

Beard had seen death too many times to have any doubts that she was not only dying, but very close to death itself. She should already be dead, but she refused to die easily. He thought she probably had only an hour or two left, though he knew that sometimes death came very slowly to those determined to fight on, the victim lingering on for an extra day or more, each moment extending the body's excruciating agony. There was nothing he could do to ease her pains. She was beyond the help of any drugs. A sudden hollow sort of a sob escaped from somewhere within her, and this made up his mind.

Beard drew his pistol from his belt, released the safety and, without any hesitation, placed the muzzle at her temple and squeezed the trigger. There was the plop as the silenced weapon fired, her head jerked, there was a last gasp of breath, and then she was dead. In death her face seemed to relax, it almost seemed as though a smile touched her broken lips. She was already at peace. Beard closed her one remaining eye, the robin's-egg blue eye, that seemed to stare gratefully up at him. "Forgive me, Sister Kate," he said quietly, and covered her over.

"We'll take her back to the mission," he told Lt Francis, "She'd probably like to be buried among her friends. They're probably her only family."

Beard could not know that once he had been a member of that family; that she had been instrumental in securing his birth certificate in the name of Jarvis Brook; that she had made sure of his future safety, first in a crèche and then at an infants' home in Hayes; and that she gave him one of his very earliest kisses. And now he had killed her, and he was glad to have done so; and he sensed that she had blessed him with her dying breath.

A number of letters had accumulated at Ipoh by the time Beard returned there. There were official ones, family ones and two from Ruth, who was now called Mrs Marchant and had an address in the Green Mountain State of Vermont, USA. It was a long time before he dared open either of her letters. First he showered and had a long hot soak in a bath, then he found clean clothes and sought out the best restaurant in town and ate to repletion and drank ice-cold beers until he felt he'd had enough, and then went for a slow stroll beside the Kinta River and through the Old Town, before heading back to his quarters.

It was time to read his letters.

As of old, he collected his letters before him and sorted them out date-wise; he would save Ruth's letters to the very last, because he didn't want to hurry over them, knowing that he would want to read every word many times over, and to immerse his mind amidst them for a long, long time. He raced through the official ones first: mess bills, invitations to various functions and one stating he had been had been recommended for a decoration for his services in Korea, a country he had hoped never to hear mentioned again.

There were three from Queenie and John, which of course were written by John, probably at her dictation, certainly with her promptings. He was about to open the first of these, but at the last moment couldn't resist an urgent need to read *her* words first, and he snatched up the first of Ruth's envelopes which had an old look about it though bearing a fairly recent date stamp.

Withdrawing the letter, he saw it had been dated originally March 3, 1952 ; this had been crossed out and replaced by August 17, 1954. It was short, and read as follows:

"*Dear Jarvis,*" – he noted at once that he was no longer "My Darling," and it gave him an empty feeling in his stomach – "*I am now married to OK, and called Mrs Marchant. You may already have heard this from Queenie and John, but you move about so frequently and get involved in so many wars, that I'm never sure if you receive letters – and of course you never write any! But I wanted you to know for sure that I was married. In fact, I now have a son, Damien, whom I worship. He is now four and is adorable. When I look at him, I think of you. Is that wrong? Jarvis, my dearest, I want you to know that this marriage of mine can never come near to equalling the love that we have shared all our lives, and which reached its pinnacle in our one night of love-making. The memory of it will be my comfort all the days of my life. I shall always be a dutiful wife to OK, but I cannot share the depth of love I have for you with him. It is all yours, darling. I have only respect left for my husband, but I love our child completely. I hope this is making sense to you. Please, keep safe.*"

The second letter was dated February 11, 1955.

"*My Darling,*" she wrote, and just those two words thrilled him. "*I have to tell you, I feel you are entitled to know, my husband has died – the day after Thanksgiving Day last November, and I am consequently a widow, but with the joy of a wonderful son. OK was unwell for over a year. We knew he would not recover, even so, his death when it finally happened was a dreadful shock. His family, with whom I have never been able to get close, were heart-broken. More so, I must confess, than me. I mourned, of course, but not as deeply as I feel a wife should. There were personal reasons. My comfort now is Damien. He is my joy, my everything. OK was one of those multi-millionaires, so I guess I'm now a rich lady! But there is legal hassling going on over his estate, so I suppose it'll be a year or so before it's all sorted out. I'm pretty weary over the long illness and death and things, and am thinking of getting away from it all (leaving my own lawyer to keep his eye on my inheritance) with Damien and Edna, his nanny, who has become one of my best friends out here. I am now an American – US passport, and all that. Actually, I have dual nationality. Well, Jarvis, that's all my news for now. Please, if you get the opportunity, drop me a line so that I know you're safe. The address on this envelope will always find me.*"

Beard was staggered, shattered, overwhelmed, astonished, stupefied … all of these things, and many more; most of all, he had a feeling of freedom, as if some impenetrable wall or barrier had been lifted from his heart and he was able to breathe again. Ruth, his little

Ruth, had been married; she'd had a child; and now she was a widow. She was a free woman, and she loved him. He hadn't lost her! Oh, he should be with her now, to comfort her in her loss, if she was grieving, but most of all to press his cause. Well, there was little chance of that in the immediate future, with him out here in the Malayan jungles, and doubtless Gibbs would have other assignments lined up that would prevent him holding Ruth in his arms where she belonged. Well, he simply must write a letter to convince her of his undying love, remind her that they were still engaged, and ask for the rest of her hand.

"*My Darling*!" he began; it never occurred to him to address her any other way: it had been their practice ever since her very first letter. He wrote a lot of words, but not too many, just enough to reach out and touch her heart, and concluding, "*If I am being presumptuous, please forgive me – it is only because I love you so, and I need your love, my Ruth.*" And no sooner were his thoughts written, than they were posted. And only when all that was safely done, did he mutter with a grin, "Fancy me, hitched to a Yankee bird!"

Beard had only one more jungle operation, which was relatively uneventful, before he left Malaya for good. There was trouble brewing in Egypt which threatened the Suez Canal, and Gibbs decided Beard and his team might be more usefully employed in that area. Almost overnight they were transported via Singapore to Nicosia in Cyprus, where they joined thousands of paratroopers and other military forces, all waiting for the word to "Go."

In the event, Suez was something of a disaster – thanks largely to the interference of the United States and Soviet Russia through the medium of the United Nations; neither of the great powers wanted to see Britain's prestige in the Middle East grow at the expense of their own influence.

Early in November 1956, Beard and his men joined an airborne team that dropped at dawn on Gamel airfield, outside Port Said, and just had time to consolidate key points south of the port and almost the entire length of the canal, when a cease-fire was ordered – and they were all hastily returned to Cyprus.

It was there, in Nicosia, that Beard received a letter from Ruth some two months later. It was all that he could have ever wished for – even if it was terribly short by her standards, more a note, or even a telegram, really; or was he simply delirious! She promised that a much longer one would soon be on its way, and this was merely to stop him worrying in the meantime.

"*My Darling*," she wrote, "*I have loved you all my life and will do so for the rest of my life. Your letter has made me the happiest woman in the world. The first thing I did after reading it was to put your beautiful ring back on my finger. I won't take it off again until I see you*

– so, please, hurry home to me, my darling – either here in America, or in England. I will be wherever you wish. I had been so afraid we had lost one another for ever – I had feared we were grown irrevocably apart, that you might even have remarried – I was afraid that you didn't love me any more, and I felt my life was ended. Your letter has changed all that – you have revived my heart which had been too frightened to dare to hope...that you do really and truly love me   ... and so I know, my dearest, that instead of ending, my life is only just beginning." There was more, but they were simply enormous kisses.

Beard thought his joy was almost too great to endure; his happiness was such that he thought he would explode. He felt dazed and light-headed, he wanted so desperately to be with Ruth. But, for the moment, he had to make do with writing to her. He poured his heart out to her, told her she would never know another moment's sorrow, said it was quite beyond his powers to describe the depths of his love for her, showered her with a million or two kisses, and said he expected to be posted home very soon.

But he wasn't. He received orders to transfer his team to Aden, where he joined other units in preventing the Radfan guerrillas stirring up trouble in the Protectorate, until, towards the close of 1958, when he received a signal to report to Col Eugene Oldroyds at the SAS HQ at Bahlah, west of Nazwa, in the Oman.

□   *And that, declared Gibbs, concluded Major Beard's history. "It's where our story began, and now it continues in real time. It's time to wake up, Robert," he said, smiling.*

Chapter Forty-four

Millbrook Hospital, London, August 11, 1959

The silence in the ward seemed strange to Beard: strange, uncomfortable, unsettling; and he did not like it. Where were they all, these strangers who claimed to know and love him? He missed them, especially the girl called Ruth. God, she was a beauty! And she said that they were engaged, and had already made love! He'd been embarrassed when she'd proclaimed it to the world so blatantly. Was it truly possible for him to forget such moments of sheer magic? It hurt just imagining the possibility. But try as he did, and how he tried, he was still unable to recall anything. Either they were all mad, or he was. It had to be them.

He'd read and listened to the letters that supposedly had passed between them. There was no mistaking his handwriting, so how was it possible that he had no recollection of writing them? And some, particularly hers, were lovely to read, as she herself was beautiful to look at, though he thought her lovely dark eyes were too often misty with sadness. And if she imagined him to be this Jarvis Brook of hers, he could well understand her feelings. He had listened to the story of his life, in which the name of Jarvis Brook appeared intertwined, and, while it was entertaining up to a point, being full of adventurous incidents, he was unable to associate himself in any of them.

Beard was seated in his wheeled-chair, which for the moment had replaced his legs; he spent a lot of his time in the chair nowadays, getting used to being out of his bed, and soon now, he'd been told, he'd start learning to walk again. The thought of putting pressure on his "new" leg sent shivers through his body, keen as he was to experiment. In preparation for these exercises, Mrs Mussels, the physiotherapist, was now torturing his limbs on a daily basis and seeming to discover new pressure points of pain each day. If only he didn't feel so wonderful when she'd done! He was expecting another visit to hell any moment, and found himself idly ogling Nurse Olive Beckett's long and shapely legs as she stripped his bed and put on fresh sheets, squaring the corners in the regulatory manner; he followed the black stockings from ground level up as far as he could, and was hugely disappointed that his view ended midway up her plump thighs.

"I think you're about ready for a cold blanket bath, major!" declared a laughing voice at his side, and tearing his eyes from the legs, he found Nurse Willoughby smiling down at him. He blushed and smiled back. "You can't stop a chap looking, Susan," he whispered back.

"I have good news and bad news for you," declared Nurse Willoughby, tucking a blonde curl out of sight. "You're not having physio today because Mrs Mussels has the toothache."

Beard grinned, and said : "And the bad news?"

Nurse Willoughby giggled. "No, it's the other way round, you bad man. I've brought you a visitor."

"Who?" asked Beard, knowing he wouldn't know the person. "The Queen lady?"

"No, it's the Ruth lady!"

Beard visibly brightened.

And there she stood, appearing on cue, right beside his chair. "Hello, Jarvis," she greeted him, smiling down into his surprised face until Nurse Willoughby pushed a chair under her, and then she was looking up at him. She was happy to see a smile of pleasure on his face, and her own widened, and hope crept into her breast.

Beard was pleased to see her. Well, why shouldn't he be? She was pretty, and all the other strangers who had been his audience in the past weeks were elderly. Not that that was their fault, that's what people did: grew old; but, given the choice, he preferred her smooth face to their wrinkly ones. She was wearing a shortish, browny, tweedy skirt and a lighter coloured jacket with a sort of lilac-green blouse underneath. That was the extent of his interest in her attire at the moment; he was preoccupied with exploring her face. Her dark brown hair hung in tidy waves down to her neck and there was the beginnings of a fringe above her deep forehead. He took in the coral necklace at her throat and the faintly blue diamond ring on what he knew to be the appropriate finger, but it was her shining brown eyes that held his attention: they were mesmeric. He was drawn, hypnotised into staring deeply into them, and saw his reflection in them. He saw, too, a deep longing, and wondered at why.

"I don't mind being *your Jarvis*, if that pleases you," he told her in an easy friendly tone, wheeling his chair round so that they faced one another. But, of course, he didn't feel like this Jarvis; he felt only like himself: Robert Beard. Oh God, he thought as he stared at her.

"Of course it pleases me, Jarvis, because that's who you are," answered Ruth, with a toss of her hair, her voice low and earnest.

"This is a strange situation we find ourselves in, Ruth," he said, almost shyly, wanting to hold her hand, but uncertain how he should behave, not really knowing her. "I suppose one of these days, I'll come out of this amnesia thing and find that we're brother and sister, or an old married couple."

Ruth managed a small smile. She didn't care for the "old" part, but she did like the suggestion of marriage. "Let it be soon, Jarvis, please," she murmured.

"Dr C." – he hastily explained his Drs A., B. and C. labelling system – "says that it'll probably be some sudden shock that'll do the trick – trigger my memory back to normal. Not quite sure what sort of a shock he has in mind. Perhaps another blow to the head."

"Oh, I hope not, " said Ruth quickly. "You've been knocked about enough already."

Beard nodded agreement, appreciating her concern. "I understand from what's been said that you live in America?"

"Yes, but I was born here in England. Queenie is my mother," Ruth explained, adding in her next quick breath, "I'm a widow." She realised at once, of course, that he'd heard all this before, but he was showing interest which was a promising sign.

"I heard something about a child?"

"I have a son, Damien." He'll lose interest now, she thought.

"He must be a great comfort to you." He'd wondered if he should make some remark about the boy's father, but decided against it; he was only interested in the boy's mother.

"He is," said Ruth firmly, her eyes blinking as her thoughts turned to the child.

"How old is he?" Beard asked; it seemed a most natural question.

"Nine," she replied, holding his gaze.

"Who does he take after, you or his father?" There, that would do about him.

"His father, definitely," said Ruth, with an earnest little smile that might have been described as desperate.

Beard saw it, and the forlorn look that dulled her beautiful eyes, and wondered. What was she holding back? What was it she didn't want to tell him? She'd already claimed him as a fiancé and that they'd made love – presumably a pre-marriage affair, and a hell of a long time ago. Surely there could be nothing she need keep secret from him. What? "You must be very proud of him," he said, meaning the boy.

"I am proud of them both, father and son," declared Ruth firmly, thinking that he wasn't giving her much help. She'd hoped that by talking together, something would jar his memory, if it was only the timbre of her voice. But it wasn't happening.

"Of course."

"Perhaps you'd like to see Damien?" she cried, almost in desperation, and immediately thought how ridiculous her suggestion was. If he didn't know her, how on earth could he be expected to recognise her son? Well, he couldn't have her without the boy! She knew the idea was unreasonable and foolish, but people in her low state of morale had to be excused for lacking good sense. "At least he'd be a change of scenery for you. Someone young."

"If you like," Beard replied simply. "But, they're talking about another operation. One of my wounds was to the head, and there's a suggestion that they might be able to tinker about up there and wake up my memory-box. Perhaps, afterwards, you could bring the boy in – if you still want to." He gave a wry smile. "Be strange if I do remember you after the op."

"I'd like to bring him in before any operation, Jarvis," said Ruth urgently. "Just to show him off. I'd like you to see him first."

Beard knew – his body knew it – it was time he was back in bed, and there right on cue was Nurse Willoughby with a cup of tea for Ruth. As the nurse was pushing him towards his bed, Beard called back over his shoulder to Ruth, "You'll have to have a word with Dr C. about that, but make it soon. They don't hang about here."

Ruth was anxious about still further operations, and she didn't hang about either. She saw Dr C. there and then, and any proposed operation was postponed indefinitely. "It would have been only a probing operation, my dear," he told her. "Best avoided, anyway, if possible." And Ruth had kissed him, and, after quite a lengthy chat, she'd gone back to her hotel feeling almost happy.

Two mornings later, it was the 13th, she gave Edna the day off and picked clothing for Damien: a Vermont T-shirt depicting the Green Mountain, blue-jeans, soft white boots and a chequered jacket that zipped up the middle. She watched him dress with pride and love and, after a hearty breakfast, off they went together.

"Where we going today, Mom?" he asked in an educated American accent. "We're going to see a man in hospital, darling," she told him. "Who is he?" he pursued. "He's a wounded soldier," she replied briefly. Damien showed signs of interest. "Was he in a battle?" Ruth shrugged. "I expect so, honey." Damien gave the matter some more thought, then asked with no great interest, "Do we know him?" Ah, thought Ruth, this was the crunch question. "We'll have to see, won't we?"

Beard, having survived the attentions of Mrs Mussels, was stretched out rather inertly in his wheelchair, when Ruth entered and she wasn't quite sure if he was awake, and she asked tentatively, "Jarvis?"

His body still tingling from the ministrations of the physiotherapist, and just beginning to feel the exquisite benefits of her work, Beard was immediately alert. He opened an eye, and when he saw who it was, he opened the other; of course, he'd known straight away who it was; her voice was already like his best friend. Whoever she was, he had become attached to her in some odd way. It must be something in her voice. He found his own and murmured, "I'm Beard, will I do? You can call me Jarvis if you wish. I'm becoming accustomed to it, as I am with you."

Ruth gave a little laugh, which was quite unintentional for she was not in a laughing mood, being come on serious business. However, laugh she did as she exclaimed, "That's good because it's your name, and the only one I'll ever call you."

Beard pulled himself up as far as he was able, and examined her. He always enjoyed looking at her, and he thought he detected a new light in those pansy eyes today, and perhaps a new determination in her face. Something was afoot. "Are the others with you?" he enquired. "I thought we'd done with the story-telling."

"No, I'm all alone, Jarvis," she answered, then, after a deep breath, she added, "But I have brought you a visitor."

"Who?"

"My son," she replied softly, and, at a signal, Damien appeared at her side. Ruth fixed her eyes on Beard, looking to examine every facet of his reaction.

For a whole minute, the boy stared into the face of the man in the wheelchair. The calmness of his initial peek was followed by one of bewildered astonishment, then he took a step forward to make sure his eyes weren't deceiving him, and frowned. Then he looked round at his mother, and saw that she was nodding to him and smiling in an odd manner, and he turned back to continue examining the man. And suddenly, he realised what it was.

"You look just like me" he cried, his voice pitched high in amazement. "At least, if I was old like you."

Ruth gave a small chuckle, and returned her gaze to Beard, wondering breathlessly what his reaction to her son's observation might be, and to the boy himself. She thought Damien might say something further, but he remained staring at the man in the chair, neither of them uttering a word.

Damien stepped closer, and stopped.

The moment the boy had appeared at his mother's side, Beard's eyes had been transfixed with the same astonishment. His eyes roamed over the child's face, back and forth, ticking off every feature, and hardly believing his own eyes. The examination mirrored that of the boy's, and as they both continued to stare at one another, Beard realised that he was looking at his own reflection – had he been a boy again.

This could only be his son!

In the moment of the realisation, something clicked in Beard's head. It wasn't physical, it just happened: like passing from the blackness of night into the brilliance of daylight, only all in a trice. There was no pain, but it seemed a very heavy veil had been lifted enabling him to see everything much clearer, and in the same instant he knew his memory was tumbling back, filling the gaps his head. Where had it been, he wondered. This memory of his. He felt quite light-headed, and hoped he wasn't about to faint; he didn't. He supposed it was the sudden shock of discovering he had a son that had restored his memory. God! don't ever let me lose it again, he whispered.

Beard finally dragged his gaze from the boy and lifted them to his mother, staring at her in bewilderment, and a new recognition. Their eyes locked, understanding seeped into his head, and he raised his brows in wonder, almost incredible disbelief.

"Ruth?" he asked hesitantly, knowing it was she; the question came with a wry smile and a slow shake of the head. How in the world could he have not known her immediately?

She nodded, her face engulfed in happiness as she laughed and moved towards him. In a moment she was at his side and in his arms, and their lips touched, lightly at first, then with an urgency that might have been called savage. When they parted, breathing heavily, Ruth was shedding happy tears as her hands roamed over his face and the front of his pyjamas, just touching him. It was an insistent tugging at her skirt, that brought her down to earth, and she found Damien gazing up at her with a puzzled expression. Blushing as befitted the occasion, she stooped to give him a wet kiss, which he shrank away from.

"Is this my Daddy?" he asked her boldly.

"You'd better ask him, dear," she replied, turning her eyes back to Beard.

"I think I am, Damien," he said and, feeling a pinch from Ruth, added, "Yes I am," and he smiled down at Damien, who grinned back. For a moment or two they continued to stare at one another, then father and son shook hands: solemnly at first, then furiously.

"I knew you were the moment I saw you," cried Damien excitedly, "you look exactly like me."

"Well, I knew you too – and I was so happy to see you it had the effect of restoring my memory," said Beard.

"Did you lose it?" demanded Damien.

"I did."

"How?"

"I'm not exactly sure," Beard admitted seriously. "I think there must have been a bang, and it simply disappeared."

Ruth, in a bid to stem the inevitable flood of questions for now, lifted Damien up on to his father's lap so that they could have a hug, and she could get a word in. But Damien got in before her.

"If you're my Dad, who was the other guy? The one that died – Mr OK? I called him Dad, too."

Beard was equal to the occasion. "Mummy thought she'd lost me when I went off to war, and she needed someone to help looking after you, and so she turned to OK."

"You're not going to die too, are you?" asked Damien anxiously.

Ruth and Beard burst into laughter and hugged him before Beard declared that he was immortal, and hurriedly explained he planned to live a very long time.

And a long time later, after Drs A., B. and C. had examined Beard and expressed their amazement at the suddenness of the recovery of his memory in every aspect, "a real miracle" they'd called it, and Queenie had taken charge of Damien, Ruth and Beard were finally able to discuss their happiness. "So, darling," said Beard, his eyes twinkling as they hadn't done for years, "we can certainly name the day and almost the hour our son was conceived. What a shame we couldn't have married at the same time." Ruth squeezed herself into him, and whispered back, "Mum said she'd heard me trotting to an' fro to your bedroom, and listened to ev'ry sound of the bed. As she put it, 'it were a wonder the bleedin' springs didn't snap, lovey!'" They both chuckled, and Ruth went on, "The pity was we were both going in opposite directions at the time. You were flying out to India almost directly, and I was headed for the States that very same day."

She paused to give him a long kiss. "I hadn't imagined that one night of love-making would do it, but it did. I was having a sort of affair at the time with Henry O. K. Marchant, who was a multi-millionaire. He was always asking me to marry him, and when I found myself pregnant, I accepted him. I had no idea where you were, nor how to contact you in your secret army life, and I needed security for my baby. OK was an opportune alliance. It's very sad that you've missed knowing your son's growing up. It's been sad for both of us, too – Damien and me."

"You never had any more children," said Beard quizzically.

Ruth smiled ruefully. "No. It turned out OK was infertile. He could make millions with ease, but he hadn't a worthwhile seed in his body."

"Didn't he know? Did he think Damien was his?"

"No, not for a moment, but he never accused me of anything. He was happy to accept Damien as his own, and was always generous towards him," said Ruth, and her gratefulness showed in her eyes. "He was ill for about a year before dying of an aneurysm in his brain. That was nearly four years ago. His estate has been occupying most of my time since. I think Damien and I are worth something over a hundred million dollars, plus shares and property in Vermont and Florida."

"Cor!" exclaimed Beard, his mouth wide open for several moments. "Weren't 'is family upset? Did they give you any trouble?"

"No, not at all. There was plenty to go round and they got their share. I think they knew about OK not being Damien's father, probably through the family doctor. But they never said a word and were generally kind, but kept aloof."

"The bastards," cried Beard.

"Well, that can't be said of Damien. At least he was born in wedlock – but not to his father!"

Beard chuckled as he figured that one out. He looked at Ruth and then their son, and thought : Like mother, father and son: we're all bastards! Especially me! And we don't give a damn because we're exceedingly happy with our lot. He didn't give voice to his thoughts, not ever.

Chapter Forty-five

Millbrook Hospital, August, 1959

For Beard it was like being born again. His body felt different, certainly his heart did; it felt stronger, beating with renewed purpose. And it was so nice to know who he was again, and who other people were and now, of course, the story of his life that he'd been listening to for weeks had real meaning, including why he had two identities. He'd have to do something about that; he couldn't go around answering to both Jarvis Brook and Robert Beard for ever, especially now that his Army days were coming to an end.

Most of all, it was just too lovely to comprehend having Ruth all to himself, and being able to fall in love all over again. Though it seemed that there'd never been a time when they weren't in love, even when they'd had separate spouses, and that in itself was perplexing. Of course, he would still be stuck here in the hospital for some months before they could be properly together; he yearned to have her in his bed making love to her as they had once so long ago. Nine years ago. And he had a wonderful son as a memory of that exquisite night: the night of memories that had been his sole companion all these years. He had so much to catch up with, and couldn't wait to be a real father for Damien, and give him lots of brothers and, perhaps, an odd sister or two.

Ruth was already making plans for their wedding which, she told him firmly, would take place "just as soon as you get up out of your bed, Jarvis." The discussions went on daily around Beard's wheelchair when Ruth brought in a succession of girl friends to examine him. He, of course, took no part in the talks : it was more than his life was worth. He might be the oblique subject of these incoherent chatterings, but his only role was to be on show looking handsome and smiling, and very silent. It was as well because he could make very little sense of the excited jabbering. He simply smiled a lot, especially when Ruth caught his eye, and when she flaunted her engagement ring under his nose and said it was high time he gave her another one to keep it company. "A gold companion" was what she'd actually said.

He was allowed to say, loud and clear, that he loved her when required to do so, but anything else he had to hold back until her female companions had departed; and then it was his turn, briefly. Ruth would almost suffocate him with two or three hundred kisses before jumping up and running off herself, crying, "There's so much to see to about the wedding, it's not fair, you men do nothing, and take all the credit." And Beard simply shook his head: the wedding was at least a year away.

There were many visitors he was very pleased to see. Special among them was Mrs B., who now lived on the Channel Island of

Jersey where her two sons had opened an hotel with their gratuities. She had given her house in Grafton Road to Queenie as a sort of *pied-à-terre* and it was here that many of Beard's other visitors stayed. She had been one of his earliest visitors and, having expected to find him closer to death, was encouraged at finding him much nearer in the opposite direction; so much so that she had stayed on, and now that a wedding was in the air, she determined to remain in Grafton Road indefinitely, comforting Ruth and keeping Queenie company.

Other visitors included Maud and Bertie, together with their four children, who had put up at the Brewer Street flat, which they now owned jointly with Ben. And as Ben and Poppy arrived from Ireland, where they were settled, around the same time with their brood – young Paddy now had twin brothers, Sean and Brendan – , the flat threatened to overflow, but they managed to sort themselves out – with the help of kindly neighbours, who probably came to regret their impulsive generosity!

Ben and Bertie visited Beard daily during their stay, and were rewarded by being present when Beard's memory returned. "It's time you got married and settled down," declared Ben jovially. "Yes, you can't loaf in bed for ever," added Bertie. Beard managed an aggrieved smile and retorted, "I'm only waiting to be unchained from this chair."

One morning, when Beard and Ruth were whispering words of love to one another, a nurse came to announce a most unexpected visitor. "He's a Catholic priest," she confided in an awed voice. "Father Neame – says he used to be your rector."

Beard looked at her blankly. It was a long time since he'd had dealings with priests of any kind, but his newly-restored memory served him well: he recalled the man from his Battersea days. "Oh dear," he murmured. "You behave yourself, Jarvis!" hissed Ruth, rising automatically to her feet beside Beard's chair as the priest, who was quite the tiniest man she'd ever seen, approached on the other side.

"Sit down, child," Father Neame said with a wave of his hand. He sank into a chair the hovering nurse pushed forward, and he turned to thank her.

Father Neame adjusted the thick lenses on his nose, fidgeted with the chain that connected the glasses to an ear, and leaned forward to peer at Beard – and immediately frowned. One thing a teacher prided himself on was remembering his pupils' faces. "I think there must be some mistake ... I was told Robert Beard was here. But you're not him." Father Neame blinked his bright green eyes, and studied Beard's face with a renewed intensity. "But, I do know you, don't I?" he exclaimed, searching his memory. "I just don't remember your name ... I'm terribly sorry."

So, it was all over; he was undone! After all these years, his bluff had been called and his true identity was about to be revealed – by a priest he hadn't seen in more than twenty years. Well, almost. It was only his name that eluded the good father.

"It's Jarvis Brook, Father," Beard admitted, lowering his voice in case there should be any eavesdroppers, not that it really mattered any more. "Scruffy – that's Robert Beard, and I swapped identities – he wanted to go and live with an aunt he'd discovered, so I took his place in the Army, and I've borne his name ever since."

"You young rascals! The things you boys get up to!" chuckled Father Neame, staring from Beard to Ruth and back to Beard, shaking his head in wonderment. "So, where is the real Robert Beard?"

"He's dead, Father," said Beard quickly. "He was killed in a pit accident during the war under another name. He had a happy life up to then."

"The War Office had me down as his next of kin, which I why I'm here," said the priest. "I presume that means you since you appear to have dual identities."

Beard shrugged. "As an orphan, I didn't have any next of kin, Father. I had to put a name down, and I picked you. I'm sorry if you've been inconvenienced."

"Not at all. It's afforded me an unexpected day out," said Father Neame, smiling. He went on to say that St Boniface's had long been razed to the ground, and that he was now retired to a retreat in Chertsey. "Do you plan to be Robert Beard for always?" he asked.

"Certainly not!" intervened Ruth abruptly.

"No, Father," grinned Beard, taking hold of Ruth's hand and raising it to his lips. "Ruth would never stand for it! She's known me all her life as Jarvis Brook, and she won't accept any other for herself. We'll be getting married as soon as I get out of this place, and when we do it'll be in my own name. We'll be Mr and Mrs Jarvis Brook!"

"Darling!" cried Ruth ecstatically, leaning across the wheelchair to kiss him several times, and then blinking wet eyes of happiness at the priest. "Do hurry up and get well," she whispered, turning back to Beard, "there's so many babies needing to be born!"

Beard grinned at her, and then took a quick look round to see if any one was listening, but there was only the priest, and he was smiling.

"I hope you'll all be very happy," said Father Neame, "and, I hope you'll invite me to the wedding."

Beard, in one of their private moments, had told Ruth he was worried that his injuries might prevent him from being a proper husband; he might be physically incapable of giving her children, and he so wanted his marriage to be a real one in every way. He knew babies were important to her: they were to him, too. Ruth rushed off to seek an interview with Dr C – who turned out to be Mr Archibald Ernest Wolferton – and discuss the problem. Right from the start he put her at her ease, first by congratulating her on the forthcoming wedding, and then by telling her that there was absolutely no reason why they shouldn't have children: a dozen, if they wished. "Your soldier needs the exercise," he joked.

Ruth felt as though she were floating on air. Her heart sang joyously, her eyes shone and her cheeks glowed. "I think half a dozen will be enough, thank you," she replied with a demure little smile.

Mr Wolferton leaned forward on his elbows and regarded her seriously. "You'll have to be patient with him, Ruth," he told her. "Your major has been dodging death for most of his life. The injuries he sustained should have killed your young man, the fact that they didn't is something of a miracle. But, since I don't believe in miracles, I can only put it down to his general physical condition, which was really quite extraordinary, and, of course, the excellent work of several renowned surgeons and the untiring and devoted skill of the nursing staffs." He smiled playfully at Ruth, who was too excited to respond. "Your soldier is going to be all right, my dear, in every sense. But it is going to take time. He's going to be with us – or convalescing somewhere else, for some time yet. Perhaps another year, perhaps more. His body has had a tremendous shock. It's had to be patched up: rebuilt, almost, in parts. He'll feel awkward at first, something like the Tin Man in the Wizard of Oz ... it'll be like learning to walk again. But, I suppose you'll expect your young man to be standing upright beside you at the church, not sitting in a wheelchair!"

Ruth managed a very small smile, but she was anxious about what was coming next. "You must both accept that, physically, he'll never be the man he was. As I said, he'll recover and lead a perfectly normal life, but he'll probably have to put up with some degree of physical discomfort in later life. His back is going to be his worst enemy. We've achieved wonders with it, but in the years ahead it'll quite probably cause him problems, and some pain. And then there's that leg of his. It looks like it's going to be fine – but, and you must be prepared for this, my dear, it'll most likely give him gyp from time to time and make him irritable. A man, especially a man who's led such a physically active life as he has, hates to find he can't do the sort of things he's always taken for granted. It makes him feel inadequate, and he may become depressed. He's finished his career in the Army, and I expect they'll find him a suitable civilian job. He'll hate that, too! So you see, my dear, you'll be taking on quite a handful. It won't be easy. It'll mean tremendous patience and understanding on your part. There'll be some hard times ahead for you. Do you think you can manage?"

Ruth stared steadily across the desk at the doctor. "I love him, doctor," she said simply, and gave him a quick smile to show that she was ready for anything. But if she was calm on the outside, inside her heart was holding its breath. She prayed that God would be merciful to them. When she reached Beard's side, she kissed him quickly and said, "Don't scare me again, darling. We'll have a dozen children, six of each," and in case he saw something in her eyes that he shouldn't, she bent her head to kiss him again, and murmured in his ear "Everything's going to be fine, darling."

There was no point in trying to set a date for the wedding: that was out of their hands; they would have to wait until those medical people responsible for Beard's treatment were able to give some clue as to his release. The one thing that could be decided was to bury the name Robert Beard once and for all. Ruth was quite adamant ; she never had and never would call him anything other than his true name: Jarvis; and since she'd be changing her name to match his soon, she wanted that to be the right one, too; and she planned for Damien to adopt his father's name as well. Beard, who had used Scruffy's name for so long now that he found it hard to think of himself using any other, nevertheless readily agreed, and so delighted both Ruth and Queenie, and John Fennell was invited to set the wheels in motion to make it legal, militarily and otherwise – and especially pension-wise.

Three months later, the deed was done. The papers were signed, and Robert Beard became Jarvis Brook once more – although, as Mr Fennell sagely observed, he had never really been any other person: it was Robert Beard he had never been, not really, not legally. For the remainder of his stay in hospital, however, it was decided that it would be less complicated for all if Beard kept his illegal name as any change at this stage might cause horrendous difficulties, and even disasters.

Beard was giving his son Damien exciting rides through the hospital corridors, to the alarm of Miss Flinn, the Matron, and any others in his path, when Lieutenant Colonel Geoffrey Johnstone appeared on the scene and became the first "outsider" to use Beard's new official name.

Col Johnstone, who looked more venerable than martial, was a sort of regimental rehabilitation officer, who had visited Beard on several occasions; the first time to convince himself Beard was still alive, and subsequently to notify him that he'd been awarded a bar to his DSO for services in Korea and another to his MC for services in Malaya, and lately that he was in line for some Omani gong for – er, services in that country. Beard declared rather brusquely, "I don't need any of these things any more. Medals and all that stuff belong to the past, and don't really mean a thing in the present."

On today's visit, Col Johnstone called him "Major Brook," and went on to say that the change of name had caused consternation at both the Foreign and War Office Records Departments. "It'll take them years to untangle the mess, old man. God knows what name they'll put on your pension documents – probably something totally different!" He gave a deep chuckle for he had little respect for the clerks buried in those gaunt buildings but, seeing Beard's look of concern, added   "Only joking, major. They'll sort it out, in time. But you've certainly stirred 'em up – I don't suppose the blighters have worked so hard since the war!"

However, it transpired that the real purpose behind the colonel's visit on this occasion was to discuss what Mr Brook had in mind to do when he left the Army, for he assumed Beard would not wish to retire completely at the age of 34 – or whatever age he was when he was finally let loose into the world again, pointing out that governments tended to be niggardly when it came to pensions for their erstwhile heroes. The colonel was plainly ignorant of Ruth's inherited wealth, and as far as Beard was concerned he would remain so.

Beard had never given the matter of employment outside the Army much thought, and said so. "I only know about soldiering," he said. "It's the only thing I've ever done."

Johnstone nodded understandingly. "It's always the same with regulars," he observed thoughtfully, adding that there were various openings depending on competency and aptitude. After lengthy, sometimes argumentative but mostly humorous discussion, the colonel came up with a possible solution.

"There seems to be only one course open to you, my friend. You're not really qualified for anything in the civilian world, but you've had a decent education and you're accustomed to writing detailed reports of your operations – the ones about your exploits in the field, I mean," he paused to give Beard an apologetic smile. "Yes, old man, there's only the one job left open to you: journalism!"

Beard looked startled. "Journalism!" he cried, "but I've hardly read a paper in my life."

The colonel grinned. "Better start doing so now then, Mr Brook," he said, but seeing the other's look of uncertainty, he went on, "journalism is ninety per cent common sense – and you've plenty of that. When the time comes, I'll give you a letter of introduction to someone in Fleet Street. We've got friends in practically every walk of life."

And so Beard started reading newspapers every day, and finding many of them exceedingly boring. Sometimes, he would get Ruth to read them to him – especially the lengthy articles in papers like *The Times* and *The Daily Telegraph*. "I never realised there were so many different words in the English language, especially so many meaning the same thing, and we owe most of them to our foreign invaders," Beard declared one morning. Ruth, raising her eyes from a Letter to the Editor, commented with a perplexed frown, "Punctuation is a mysterious business." Beard grinned. "And spelling." he retorted.

He gave them both a rest on Sundays – when papers were banned. These were the best days, so far as Ruth was concerned. They indulged in long gossips about everything and nothing, their future together and Beard's enthronement as Editor of some great publication. It was all lovely nonsense. Best of all, because Damien had to be a part of these sessions, was the story-telling times, when Beard revealed a latent ability to invent endless exciting or scary tales that had his audiences holding their breaths or shrieking with laughter, and even asking if some of them were true.

"You should think about writing books, Jarvis," cried Ruth, clapping her hands as he ended a romantic tale.

Beard gave her a look of pretend horror.

They made plans that repeatedly had to be postponed. Beard's convalescence proved a lengthy business. The whole of 1960 passed, and still no date could be set for the wedding.   But, after some minor setbacks, Beard was temporarily transferred to Roehampton Hospital near Richmond where, with the help of various apparatus of torture, he learned to stand on his own two feet again – and walk. A further tidying-up operation – spinal fusion, they'd called it – had also been necessary on his spine: one of the new metal discs had moved fractionally and had had to be readjusted. It was all rather exhausting, and it all took time. Damien, who had been found a place in a private school in Earls Court, kept asking Ruth if his new daddy was going to die. She reassured him each time he asked her if she was sure. She was as anxious as her son as her wedding seemed to be an ever distant event. She often cried in Queenie's arms, and when she was alone.

Beard experienced good and bad days. The really bad days were when he first tried his crutches – and found he couldn't move his left leg. He'd been expecting to walk without them after a day or two, and he couldn't even walk *with* them! He knew moments of panic, but they were quickly over. He very soon mastered the technique with the crutches – and then found that he was able to cope with just a pair of walking sticks; and then only one; and finally none – though one was always to hand. He was back on his own two feet some two years after being blown off them. The left leg still hurt, it was often quite sore, and sometimes the rebuilt foot ached abominably. But regular exercising enabled him to bend the new knee, and he persevered every day with his walking, and every day he extended the distance he covered until he was walking fifty to a hundred yards at times – on level surfaces – with almost no limp at all. Slopes presented something of a challenge, and Beard was instructed to exercise more with weights and to practice on steps and raised planks in the gym. It was agony to begin with, but it grew easier. Shorter strides seemed to be the answer.

"Be patient, major," said Mr Wolferton. "You may think you're strong again, but your not: not yet; your body needs time to adjust. It's a tough time for your muscles, too. Remember, they haven't been used for nearly two years. If it hadn't been for Mrs Mussels, you'd still be on your back in bed. You mustn't expect to run before you can walk."

Beard's convalescence was spent at Virginia Water in a place euphemistically called The Royal Lodge. Apparently, it had once been the love-nest of a prince who was also his country's ambassador to the Court of St James's; however, after a revolution had deposed his family, the property was acquired by the British government who, with a rare generosity, presented it to the Services for its present purpose. It wasn't exactly a palace, but it was palatial alongside similar such establishments, and the grounds were really magnificent and extensive. As far as Beard was concerned his quarters were royal indeed, though it was some months before he was able to explore the many secret corners of the gardens and the paths through the woods. At the outset he was restricted to the large flagstone area over-looking an enormous sweep of lawn, but by degrees he and Ruth were able to extend their walks to little secluded spots where a considerate gardener had placed seats in almost hidden niches. It was on such benches that they pursued their courtship and continued their wedding plans.

There was accommodation at the house for weekend visitors, and Ruth never missed an opportunity to stay, though it never occurred to her to invite Beard to her room. Well, possibly it did, but she didn't take advantage of the opportunity. Neither did Beard, though he too thought about it often enough. He was defeated by the mountain of stairs between their rooms, by patrolling staff armed with pills and syringes and by the thought that even if he could manage the obstacle course discreetly, he'd be worn out by the time he arrived.

Then, quite suddenly, the waiting was almost done. The years and months had passed: the date was fixed: Saturday, April 8, 1961, at the newly-built St Clare's Church. It was a utility version of the original, but it provided the same services. The wedding could have been the previous week, but Ruth absolutely refused to be married on April Fool's Day!

Now, the final week had arrived; there were six days to the wedding. The guests were beginning to converge on London and urgent discussions went on morning, noon and night as Ruth hovered between the various groups. The women were in their element: they were out of their minds, and loving it. Weddings were their big chance – probably their only chance, Beard dared to imagine – to dictate things and speak their minds, and they made the most of the opportunity. Every minute detail of the event was discussed, criticised and generally condemned before being accepted – though they really meant "it'll have to do." Nothing escaped those tongues, not even the cake.

Ruth spared Beard, who kept out of the way at his Virginia Water quarters, just one afternoon from her preparations, but her thoughts never strayed far from the wedding plans. It was as she was pouring tea for them, and laughingly remarked that this was the longest time she'd been out of her wedding dress in a week, that she suddenly looked up at Beard and asked anxiously: "What about you, Jarvis – what'll you be wearing?"

"Pyjamas!" he rejoined, adding without a pause, "the blue silk ones you think so becoming. I hardly wear anything else these days!"

Ruth shrieked with laughter and splashed tea everywhere. "Silly boy!" she cried gaily. "Be sensible. What have you got? You'll have to hire a morning suit. Or," she clapped her hands with delight as a thought struck her, "you're still Army, so you could wear a scarlet dress uniform like Ben did – and wear all your medals."

Beard looked doubtful. "I'd never be able to walk down the nave lugging all that tin around. There's seventeen of the little devils!" he pointed out, but seeing the disappointment in her eyes, he said "Oh, all right, just this once – and only the pretty ones. Mind you, I'll have to scrounge a suit from somewhere first."

"Bertie can fix that," said Ruth instantly, and with that decided she told him, "and warn him to tell your soldier friends that there'll be nuns and other ladies around so they must behave themselves and watch their language."

"You sound just like a wife," he teased her.

She leaned forward and gave him a long kiss. "You won't be disappointed, my darling," she whispered, as her fingers stroked his cheek. "Just a little longer, my love. If we're married half as long as we've been engaged, it'll be worth it. You'll see."

And really, Beard had very little to do. Between them, Bertie, who was to be his best man, and Ben arranged everything. Bertie duly delivered the scarlet dress uniform to Beard as the day approached. "And don't bleed all over it if you feel faint!" he cried, after critically examining Beard's much repaired body. "Fine pair, aren't we, with only one sound leg apiece between us, and ready for the Wedding March!"

A whole crowd of recuperating patients joined Beard, Bertie and Ben in an unofficial stag party at an hotel on the Bath road, and such wild goings on ensued – two revellers were found singing among the tombstones of a nearby church and said they were waiting for a train – the police good-humouredly arranged for everyone to be returned to The Royal Lodge in a couple of police vans in the early hours.

That was two nights before the wedding. On the eve of the day itself, Beard moved into an hotel near the Aldwych as a convenient launch pad for his wedding the following morning.

     □ *And now, we return the name Beard to its owner, buried under another name at Hathersage, in the Peak District, and follow Jarvis Brook to the altar.*

Chapter Forty-six

St Clare's, London, April 8, 1961

There were those who said Ruth fairly raced down the nave in her eagerness to marry Jarvis – and they meant it lovingly, and not in criticism. In truth, the speed of her progress was dictated by the ability of Mr John Fennell, her stepfather, to keep up with her. It was his big day, too, and he had no wish for it to be over before he'd had his full share of it. He marched – in so far as a man with a club-foot is able to march – at a pace in keeping with the stirring beat of the Wedding March, his heart almost bursting with happiness and his face positively beaming with pride at the feel of her hand tucked inside his arm. He fixed his eyes on the distant altar – and secretly hoped he wouldn't arrive there too soon, for then his brief duty would be done, and she would be holding another's arm.

Ruth felt she was walking on air: she was quite sure that if she hadn't been holding on to John Fennell's arm she would have floated up to the rafters; she tightened her grip and he gave her hand a reassuring squeeze. Far from racing down the nave, she thought she was crawling along its length – which seemed at least twenty miles long; it had seemed no distance at all at the rehearsal. She could barely see the altar or the priest, but she put this down to her veil and the fact that her eyes were misty with tears of joy; if it hadn't been for their bright scarlet tunics, she didn't think she would even have seen Jarvis and his best man. Oh, I am sure I would, she told herself immediately; I see him in my dreams, so I must be able to see him when I'm awake. Indeed, she wasn't really conscious of anyone else. He'd given her a necklace incorporating the blood-red ruby the Buddhist monk had given him in India as a wedding present, and she wore it now in place of the usual coral.

She was aware of crowds on either side, craning and whispering their Ohs and Ahs and uttering exclamations of admiration and good wishes – but she didn't see them; she was hardly conscious even of the colourful retinue of little attendants clinging with noisy whispers to her train and happily oblivious to the deafening shushes of their parents. The altar, ablaze with flowers, was looking a lot nearer now and she could see Jarvis quite clearly. He looked beautiful, as always.

At a signal from the priest, Jarvis and Bertie stepped forward to await the bride. Jarvis stared calmly at the priest, who offered him a smile of encouragement. He was not Father Daly, who had been exiled in retirement to somewhere called Furness in the shadow of the louring mass of Black Combe in far off Cumberland, but a new man called Father Lucius Whittell. Jarvis would have preferred the priest of his youth, but it didn't really matter – just as long as there was someone to say the magic words. His own role in the ceremony seemed to consist of nothing more than two little words: I do; and he had been rehearsing them all morning, and was pretty sure he had them off pat. He was suddenly conscious of a dull ache the length of his left leg, and drew in a sharp breath. "You OK, Bobbie?" whispered Bertie with a frown of concern. "Sure, Bertie," returned Jarvis, "just a touch of pins and needles. I'm told all bridegrooms suffer from it!"

He turned for a first glimpse of his bride.

Their eyes met when she was about ten paces from him and, veil or no veil, his heart gave a little leap in his breast: painful and exquisite. He had never seen her looking more beautiful. He wondered if he had ever looked at her properly before. Of course he had. Millions of times. But he was sure he'd never seen her looking so radiant; well, of course, she'd never been this close to being married before, and every bride looked beautiful on her wedding day – or desperate! Jarvis momentarily wondered if *he* was looking any different, and decided that men always looked themselves: manly and magnificent!

Ruth was wearing what he'd been told was a gown of pale ivory: it looked plain white to him – white, and posh. God, she looked gorgeous in it! Her large, fawn-like eyes never left his; they lit up her entire face, as they always did when she was ecstatically happy. She was quite tall for a girl – her head would rest very comfortably against his shoulder and she had barely to raise her heels to touch his lips with hers – and her dark brown hair hung in neat dark bunches of waves and curls on either side of her face.

He'd known her – off and on – practically all his life, but it did seem to him that he was looking at her for the very first time. Perhaps it was the first time he'd really looked at her and thought of her as a woman, instead of a schoolgirl. And now that *she* was all grown up, he wondered if *he* was. Somehow, he felt like a very small boy who was about to be presented with a very special present. *Her!* He gave her a shy, boyish smile, which she returned with such undisguised love it was all he could do to stop himself sweeping her up in his arms there and then and smothering her with kisses.

In the last seconds before she joined him, Jarvis tore his eyes from her to take a quick peek at those who had come to witness their betrothal and to share in their rejoicing. There seemed to be an unholy lot of them, but he allowed that this was probably because it was a very small church. The first people he saw – because they were the nearest – were Queenie, her neighbour Nora Hatchet, Mrs Molly and her friend Maisie and Mrs B. They were all sat in the front row, decked out in their Sunday best frocks like a collection of gaudy butterflies, conspicuous beneath a rainbow of hats that would have kept a monsoon at bay and all hugging veritable armfuls of flowers – and some were proudly sporting the jewellery that Jarvis had looted for them in past campaigns. Behind them, resplendent in their uniforms bedizened with clinking medals, he spotted an impressive, rigid Gibbs, alongside Maud and Bertie and Ben and Poppy alternately casting scolding glances at their respective broods and grinning encouragement at him. Seated unobtrusively farther back, Father Neame looked absorbed in his breviary, though doubtless he would emerge from his prayers once the liturgy of the wedding began.

Jarvis recognised several officers and men he had served with, particularly those who were to form his guard of honour. Blossom looked extremely smart and appeared to have been made up to sergeant, unless he'd just stuck the stripes on himself for the occasion. There were others whose faces he recognised but for whom he could give no name – he felt rather guilty about this. He frowned at the sight of Doctors A., B, and C. who looked guiltily up from their discussions to give him a professional appraisal, and equally professional smiles. Were they expecting some calamity to happen? No, he decided; they looked too pleased with themselves: they were simply here for the show! Nearby sat a whole gaggle of nurses, many of whom he recognised – and most of whom knew more about his body than ever Ruth would do! He caught the eye of Matron, who gave him a little smile of approval at the same moment as a tear rolled down her pale, bony cheek to splash into the lip of the orchid provided by Mrs Molly; he gave her a broad wink. He was sure that there were among the congregation several who had no deckle-edged invitation card: women who wouldn't have missed a wedding for the world, and men who hoped there might be a drink or two at the end of it; and, as far as he was concerned, they were all welcome.

Ah, here she was!

Ruth joined him at the foot of the altar, and for now no one else existed. Their arms briefly brushed against each other and their eyes met excitedly before the priest called them to order. It had been arranged that they would stand throughout the ceremony, for although Jarvis knew he could kneel down all right, he wasn't so sure that he would be able to rise again with the same ease – and he didn't want his marriage to start by embarrassing (or frightening, which it was more likely to do) his wife. At least he was able to stand on his own two feet. He straightened his back as far as he was able, and concentrated on the words of the service. Even as he did so, he suddenly recalled the prophecies of Granny Zilla. She'd told him that he would become a leader of men, experience great pain and know a great love – and everything she'd forecast was about to be fulfilled.

"I do," he replied in a loud clear voice when Father Whittell asked the question that completed the gypsy woman's predictions.

"I do," echoed Ruth, extremely promptly, her voice small in comparison but the words spoken with equal fervour.

Behind them, the front row burst into a flood of happy tears.

After the wedding feast and bawdy toasts, and having mingled long enough among their guests, Ruth and Jarvis were able to slip away and revive themselves with a kiss and a cuddle, and a few marital words.

"Don't you dare get drunk, Jarvis," insisted Ruth, smiling, "I've waited a lifetime for tonight."

"Aren't you forgetting Damien?" he grinned, nibbling at her ear.

"Never!" she cried vehemently. "You know what I mean. Every day without you has been a lifetime, and every night a torment."

"We've a lot of catching up to do then," he said, his hands pulling her even closer.

"We should get to bed early, Jarvis," Ruth suggested archly. "You look tired."

"Minx! We've not had dinner yet, and I'll need all my strength," he laughed softly.

She giggled. "Pig! We'll claim headaches as soon as you've scoffed your pudding."

"I might want seconds ..."

"Don't you dare! You have your headache, or I'll give you one."

"I look forward to our honeymoon, darling," said Jarvis, and he lifted one of her hands to his lips, and gave the palm a very long kiss.

At this moment, they were discovered and obliged to join in the celebrations with the rest and, much later, there was a sumptuous dinner for family and special guests, and then the dancing went on through the night, and by the time the bride and groom retired they just fell asleep with barely a kiss between them. But, early in the morning, they made up for it severally, and before a late breakfast it is to be expected Damien had a sibling on the way.

Later, leaving Damien in the joyous care of Gran Queenie and others, as they were headed off on their secret honeymoon in Tunisia's sunshine, Ruth informed Jarvis he would have to wait until their return to see her wedding gift to him.

"I have you, darling," he declared, after a protracted exchange of kisses, "I don't need anything more."

"Silly boy," she said, after recovering her breath, "we have to live somewhere, and I've bought you a lovely house in a tiny Sussex village."

Jarvis, overwhelmed, in a pleased way, gasped, "How big?"

"Enormous," she responded, with an enormous smile.

"Are you expecting a large family?" he asked, mischievously.

"Huge, darling," she said, sweetly.

Wondering if the place would be big enough to absorb this population explosion, he asked out of mild curiosity the name of this favoured village.

"Jarvis Brook!" Ruth sang out laughing, and she laughed again when they all moved in some three months later and she announced that she was pregnant.

The Epilogue

Ten years later, Ruth and Jarvis, and their seven children, moved for good to their other family home in Vermont in the United States. Damien, now nineteen, was accepted for Harvard where he was to read American History, and later became a university lecturer.

His four brothers and two sisters easily adapted to the American way of life and are currently graduating through the school system towards high school and, perhaps, college. For the moment though, they are simply growing up and having fun; loving life.

Ruth and Jarvis are now settled in the ways of proud parents, and looking forward to grandchildren – Damien is courting! Ruth is very much a part of local life, belonging to any number of charitable groups and activities throughout the State. Jarvis, reluctantly deciding golf was too arduous, has taken up fishing; he says he enjoys the peace and that it helps him forget his lifetime of wars. The fish seem to have taken to him, too! Between bites, he thinks about that book he plans to write.

Every year, the family vacations in a different State, planning to take in all fifty before they're through. They've done Hawaii and Alaska and are now concentrating on mainland America, working west to east.

Once a year, or oftener, Queenie comes over to count her grandchildren, and to tell them stories about their father who, she assures them, arrived on her doorstep in a carrier-bag. They don't believe her, but they love her stories of his subsequent adventures. Mrs B., now very ancient, came over once, armed with packets of tea, and memorably visited Boston, where they know all about tea!

Ruth and Jarvis, who both knew hard times in their younger days, consider themselves blessed in each other and their children, and are grateful to America for enabling them all to live out peaceful and rewarding lives within its boundaries, and are proud to say out loud, God bless America!

THE END

Made in the USA
Charleston, SC
18 June 2013